Harry Potter
AND THE DEATHLY HALLOWS

J.K. ROWLING

7

英汉对照版

Harry Potter

哈利·波特与死亡圣器 [下]

〔英〕J.K. 罗琳 / 著

马爱农 马爱新 / 译

WIZARDING WORLD

人民文学出版社
PEOPLE'S LITERATURE PUBLISHING HOUSE

WIZARDING WORLD

CHAPTER TWENTY

Xenophilius Lovegood

Harry had not expected Hermione's anger to abate overnight, and was therefore unsurprised that she communicated mainly by dirty looks and pointed silences next morning. Ron responded by maintaining an unnaturally sombre demeanour in her presence as an outward sign of continuing remorse. In fact, when all three of them were together Harry felt like the only non-mourner at a poorly attended funeral. During those few moments he spent alone with Harry (collecting water and searching the undergrowth for mushrooms), however, Ron became shamelessly cheery.

'Someone helped us,' he kept saying. 'Someone sent that doe. Someone's on our side. One Horcrux down, mate!'

Bolstered by the destruction of the locket, they set to debating the possible locations of the other Horcruxes, and even though they had discussed the matter so often before, Harry felt optimistic, certain that more breakthroughs would succeed the first. Hermione's sulkiness could not mar his buoyant spirits: the sudden upswing in their fortunes, the appearance of the mysterious doe, the recovery of Gryffindor's sword, and above all, Ron's return, made Harry so happy that it was quite difficult to maintain a straight face.

Late in the afternoon he and Ron escaped Hermione's baleful presence again, and under the pretence of scouring the bare hedges for non-existent blackberries, they continued their on-going exchange of news. Harry had finally managed to tell Ron the whole story of his and Hermione's various wanderings, right up to the full story of what had happened at Godric's Hollow; Ron was now filling Harry in on everything he had discovered about the wider wizarding world during his weeks away.

'... and how did you find out about the Taboo?' he asked Harry, after explaining the many desperate attempts of Muggle-borns to evade the Ministry.

第 20 章

谢诺菲留斯·洛夫古德

哈利没指望赫敏的怒气一夜就会消掉,所以第二天早上见她基本上只用阴沉的脸色和尖锐的沉默交流,他并不意外。罗恩在赫敏面前保持着不自然的严肃态度,作为继续忏悔的表现。实际上,当三人在一起时,哈利觉得自己像人数寥寥的葬礼上唯一不在哀悼的人。但在与哈利单独相处的不多时间里(打水、在树丛下找蘑菇时),罗恩就会没皮没脸地快活起来。

"有人帮助我们,"他一直说,"有人派来了那头牝鹿,有人在支持我们。消灭一个魂器了,伙计!"

销毁挂坠盒让他们受到鼓舞,他们开始讨论其他魂器可能在哪儿,尽管以前已讨论过那么多次,但哈利还是感到很乐观,相信第一个胜利会带来更多的突破。赫敏的阴沉破坏不了他欢快的心情:运气的突然转好、神秘牝鹿的出现、格兰芬多宝剑的复得,最重要的还有罗恩的归来,使哈利开心得很难保持一副严肃的面孔。

临近黄昏时,他和罗恩又从凶巴巴的赫敏跟前逃开,一边假装在光秃秃的树篱下寻找不存在的黑莓,一边继续交换新闻。哈利终于给罗恩讲完了他和赫敏四处流浪的故事,包括戈德里克山谷遇险的全部经过;罗恩正在向哈利报告他这几个星期在巫师界了解到的各种消息。

"……你们怎么发现那个禁忌的?"讲完许多麻瓜出身的巫师仓皇躲避魔法部搜捕的故事后,罗恩问哈利。

CHAPTER TWENTY Xenophilius Lovegood

'The what?'

'You and Hermione have stopped saying You-Know-Who's name!'

'Oh, yeah. Well, it's just a bad habit we've slipped into,' said Harry. 'But I haven't got a problem calling him V–'

'NO!' roared Ron, causing Harry to jump into the hedge and Hermione (nose buried in a book at the tent entrance) to scowl over at them. 'Sorry,' said Ron, wrenching Harry back out of the brambles, 'but the name's been jinxed, Harry, that's how they track people! Using his name breaks protective enchantments, it causes some kind of magical disturbance – it's how they found us in Tottenham Court Road!'

'Because we used his *name*?'

'Exactly! You've got to give them credit, it makes sense. It was only people who were serious about standing up to him, like Dumbledore, who ever dared use it. Now they've put a Taboo on it, anyone who says it is trackable – quick and easy way to find Order members! They nearly got Kingsley –'

'You're kidding?'

'Yeah, a bunch of Death Eaters cornered him, Bill said, but he fought his way out. He's on the run now, just like us.' Ron scratched his chin thoughtfully with the end of his wand. 'You don't reckon Kingsley could have sent that doe?'

'His Patronus is a lynx, we saw it at the wedding, remember?'

'Oh yeah ...'

They moved further along the hedge, away from the tent and Hermione.

'Harry ... you don't reckon it could've been Dumbledore?'

'Dumbledore what?'

Ron looked a little embarrassed, but said in a low voice, 'Dumbledore ... the doe? I mean,' Ron was watching Harry out of the corners of his eyes, 'he had the real sword last, didn't he?'

Harry did not laugh at Ron, because he understood too well the longing behind the question. The idea that Dumbledore had managed to come back to them, that he was watching over them, would have been inexpressibly comforting. He shook his head.

'Dumbledore's dead,' he said. 'I saw it happen, I saw the body. He's definitely gone. Anyway, his Patronus was a phoenix, not a doe.'

"那个什么？"

"你和赫敏不说神秘人的名字了！"

"哦，是啊。那只是我们不知不觉养成的坏习惯，"哈利说，"但我还是不怕叫他伏——"

"**别说**！"罗恩大吼一声，吓得哈利跳到了树篱中，赫敏朝他们皱起眉头（她正在帐篷口埋头看书）。"抱歉，"罗恩把哈利从荆棘丛里拽出来，"可那个名字被施了恶咒，哈利，那是他们盯梢的办法！一说他的名字就会打破防护魔法，造成某种魔法干扰——我们在托腾汉宫路就是这样被发现的！"

"因为说了他的名字？"

"正是！你不得不承认他们这招够绝的，而且也有道理啊，只有真正想抵抗他的人，像邓布利多，才敢说他的名字。现在他们在这名字上设了个禁忌，说它的人都会暴露行踪——这样搜捕凤凰社的成员又快又方便！他们差点抓到了金斯莱——"

"不会吧？"

"真的，一帮食死徒堵住了他，比尔说的，但他奋力冲了出来，现在逃亡在外，像我们一样。"罗恩若有所思地用魔杖尖挠了挠下巴，"你觉得那头鹿会是金斯莱派来的吗？"

"他的守护神是猞猁，我们在婚礼上见过，记得吗？"

"哦，对了……"

他们沿树篱走了一段，离开了帐篷和赫敏。

"哈利……你觉得会是邓布利多吗？"

"邓布利多什么？"

罗恩似乎有些窘，低声说道："邓布利多……那头鹿？我是说，"罗恩用眼角瞟着哈利，"他是最后保管那把真宝剑的，是不是？"

哈利没有笑话罗恩，他太了解这问题背后的渴望：邓布利多找到办法回来了，邓布利多在照看他们，这幻想中有一种难以形容的安慰。他摇了摇头。

"邓布利多死了，"他说，"我亲眼看到的。我看到了尸体。他肯定是走了。再说，他的守护神是凤凰，不是鹿。"

CHAPTER TWENTY   Xenophilius Lovegood

'Patronuses can change, though, can't they?' said Ron. 'Tonks's changed, didn't it?'

'Yeah, but if Dumbledore was alive, why wouldn't he show himself? Why wouldn't he just hand us the sword?'

'Search me,' said Ron. 'Same reason he didn't give it to you while he was alive? Same reason he left you an old Snitch and Hermione a book of kids' stories?'

'Which is what?' asked Harry, turning to look Ron full in the face, desperate for the answer.

'I dunno,' said Ron. 'Sometimes I've thought, when I've been a bit hacked off, he was having a laugh or – or he just wanted to make it more difficult. But I don't think so, not any more. He knew what he was doing when he gave me the Deluminator, didn't he? He – well,' Ron's ears turned bright red and he became engrossed in a tuft of grass at his feet, which he prodded with his toe, 'he must've known I'd run out on you.'

'No,' Harry corrected him. 'He must've known you'd always want to come back.'

Ron looked grateful, but still awkward. Partly to change the subject, Harry said, 'Speaking of Dumbledore, have you heard what Skeeter wrote about him?'

'Oh, yeah,' said Ron at once, 'people are talking about it quite a lot. 'Course, if things were different, it'd be huge news, Dumbledore being pals with Grindelwald, but now it's just something to laugh about for people who didn't like Dumbledore, and a bit of a slap in the face for everyone who thought he was such a good bloke. I don't know that it's such a big deal, though. He was really young when they –'

'Our age,' said Harry, just as he had retorted to Hermione, and something in his face seemed to decide Ron against pursuing the subject.

A large spider sat in the middle of a frosted web in the brambles. Harry took aim at it with the wand Ron had given him the previous night, which Hermione had since condescended to examine, and had decided was made of blackthorn.

'*Engorgio.*'

The spider gave a little shiver, bouncing slightly in the web. Harry tried again. This time the spider grew slightly larger.

'Stop that,' said Ron sharply. 'I'm sorry I said Dumbledore was young, OK?'

Harry had forgotten Ron's hatred of spiders.

'Sorry – *reducio.*'

第20章 谢诺菲留斯·洛夫古德

"可守护神会变的,不是吗?"罗恩说,"唐克斯的就变了,不是吗?"

"是的,但如果邓布利多复活了,他为什么不现身呢?为什么不直接把宝剑交给我们呢?"

"我不知道,"罗恩说,"大概跟他为什么在世时没有交给你,为什么留给你旧飞贼,留给赫敏一本儿童故事书,是一样的道理吧?"

"什么道理呢?"哈利转身盯着罗恩的面孔,急于想听到答案。

"我不知道。"罗恩说,"有时候,有点坚持不住时,我就想他是在拿我们寻开心或——或只想给我们增加点困难。但我现在不这么想了。他给我熄灯器是有道理的,对不对?他——嗯,"罗恩耳朵通红,全神贯注地用脚尖踢着脚边的一簇青草,"他一定知道我会离开你们。"

"不,"哈利纠正他说,"他一定知道你一直都想回来。"

罗恩似乎心里很感激,但仍然有点窘。也是为了换个话题,哈利说道:"提到邓布利多,你有没有听到斯基特对他的描写?"

"哦,听到了,"罗恩马上说,"人们议论很多。当然,要是在别的形势下,这会是个特大新闻——邓布利多跟格林德沃曾是好朋友。可是现在,只不过是给了不喜欢邓布利多的人一个笑柄,给了所有认为他多么完美的人一记耳光。我倒觉得没有什么大不了,他那时还很年轻——"

"像我们这么大。"哈利说,就像反驳赫敏那样。他脸上的表情使罗恩决定不再谈论这个话题。

一只大蜘蛛挂在荆棘丛中一张结了霜的蛛网上,哈利用罗恩昨晚给他的魔杖对准了它。赫敏屈尊检查过这根魔杖,断定是黑刺李木的。

"速速变大。"

蜘蛛微微哆嗦了一下,在网上轻轻晃动。哈利又试了一次,这次蜘蛛变大了一点点。

"别这样,"罗恩急道,"我不该说邓布利多当时还年轻,我道歉,行了吧?"

哈利忘记了罗恩讨厌蜘蛛。

"对不起——速速缩小。"

CHAPTER TWENTY — Xenophilius Lovegood

The spider did not shrink. Harry looked down at the blackthorn wand. Every minor spell he had cast with it so far that day had seemed less powerful than those he had produced with his phoenix wand. The new one felt intrusively unfamiliar, like having somebody else's hand sewn to the end of his arm.

'You just need to practise,' said Hermione, who had approached them noiselessly from behind and had stood watching anxiously as Harry tried to enlarge and reduce the spider. 'It's all a matter of confidence, Harry.'

He knew why she wanted it to be all right: she still felt guilty about breaking his wand. He bit back the retort that sprang to his lips: that she could take the blackthorn wand if she thought it made no difference, and he would have hers instead. Keen for them all to be friends again, however, he agreed; but when Ron gave Hermione a tentative smile, she stalked off and vanished behind her book once more.

All three of them returned to the tent when darkness fell, and Harry took first watch. Sitting in the entrance, he tried to make the blackthorn wand levitate small stones at his feet: but his magic still seemed clumsier and less powerful than it had done before. Hermione was lying on her bunk reading, while Ron, after many nervous glances up at her, had taken a small wooden wireless out of his rucksack and started to try to tune it.

'There's this one programme,' he told Harry in a low voice, 'that tells the news like it really is. All the others are on You-Know-Who's side and are following the Ministry line, but this one ... you wait 'til you hear it, it's great. Only they can't do it every night, they have to keep changing locations in case they're raided, and you need a password to tune in ... trouble is, I missed the last one ...'

He drummed lightly on the top of the radio with his wand, muttering random words under his breath. He threw Hermione many covert glances, plainly fearing an angry outburst, but for all the notice she took of him he might not have been there. For ten minutes or so Ron tapped and muttered, Hermione turned the pages of her book, and Harry continued to practise with the blackthorn wand.

Finally Hermione climbed down from her bunk. Ron ceased his tapping at once.

'If it's annoying you, I'll stop!' he told Hermione nervously.

Hermione did not deign to respond, but approached Harry.

'We need to talk,' she said.

第20章 谢诺菲留斯·洛夫古德

蜘蛛没有缩小。哈利低头看着黑刺李木魔杖。他那天用它施过的每个小魔法似乎都不如用凤凰尾羽魔杖来得有力。新魔杖拿在手里陌生而别扭，就像把别人的手缝到了他的胳膊上。

"你只是需要练习。"赫敏说，她刚才悄悄从后面走过来，焦急地看着哈利努力让蜘蛛变大和缩小，"完全是信心问题，哈利。"

哈利知道赫敏为什么希望魔杖好用：她仍在为弄断了他的魔杖而内疚。哈利咽回已经到嘴边的反驳：她要是觉得没有区别，就会把黑刺李木魔杖拿去，把她自己的换给他。因为热切希望大家重归于好，哈利接受了赫敏的意见。但当罗恩试探地对赫敏笑笑时，赫敏又噔噔噔地走开了，消失在她的书后。

夜幕降临，三人一起回到帐篷里，哈利值第一班。他坐在帐篷口，试着用黑刺李木魔杖让脚边的小石头升起，但魔法好像还是不如以前流畅有力。赫敏躺在床上看书，罗恩不安地瞟了她好多眼之后，从背包里掏出一个小小的木壳收音机，开始调台。

"有一个节目，"他悄声告诉哈利，"播的是真实的新闻。其他电台都倒向神秘人一边，遵循魔法部的路线，但这一个……你听了就知道，精彩极了。只是他们不能每晚都播，怕受到突袭，不得不经常换地方，而且你得知道暗号才能收到……问题是，我上次没听着……"

他用魔杖轻轻敲着收音机顶部，小声念着胡乱想到的词，一边偷偷瞥着赫敏，显然害怕她发作，但赫敏却只当他根本不存在一样。有十分钟左右，罗恩边敲边念，赫敏翻着书页，哈利继续用黑刺李木魔杖练习魔法。

终于，赫敏从她的床上爬了下来，罗恩立刻不敲了。

"如果打搅了你，我就停止。"他紧张地说。

赫敏没有屈尊回答，而是走向了哈利。

"我们需要谈谈。"赫敏说。

CHAPTER TWENTY   Xenophilius Lovegood

He looked at the book still clutched in her hand. It was *The Life and Lies of Albus Dumbledore.*

'What?' he said apprehensively. It flew through his mind that there was a chapter on him in there; he was not sure he felt up to hearing Rita's version of his relationship with Dumbledore. Hermione's answer, however, was completely unexpected.

'I want to go and see Xenophilius Lovegood.'

He stared at her.

'Sorry?'

'Xenophilius Lovegood. Luna's father. I want to go and talk to him!'

'Er – why?'

She took a deep breath, as though bracing herself, and said, 'It's that mark, the mark in *Beedle the Bard.* Look at this!'

She thrust *The Life and Lies of Albus Dumbledore* under Harry's unwilling eyes and he saw a photograph of the original letter that Dumbledore had written Grindelwald, with Dumbledore's familiar thin, slanting writing. He hated seeing absolute proof that Dumbledore really had written those words, that they had not been Rita's invention.

'The signature,' said Hermione. 'Look at the signature, Harry!'

He obeyed. For a moment he had no idea what she was talking about, but, looking more closely with the aid of his lit wand, he saw that Dumbledore had replaced the 'A' of Albus with a tiny version of the same triangular mark inscribed upon *The Tales of Beedle the Bard.*

'Er – what are you –?' said Ron tentatively, but Hermione quelled him with a look and turned back to Harry.

'It keeps cropping up, doesn't it?' she said. 'I know Viktor said it was Grindelwald's mark, but it was definitely on that old grave in Godric's Hollow, and the dates on the headstone were long before Grindelwald came along! And now this! Well, we can't ask Dumbledore or Grindelwald what it means – I don't even know whether Grindelwald's still alive – but we can ask Mr Lovegood. He was wearing the symbol at the wedding. I'm sure this is important, Harry!'

Harry did not answer immediately. He looked into her intense, eager face and then out into the surrounding darkness, thinking. After a long pause, he said, 'Hermione, we don't need another Godric's Hollow. We talked ourselves

第20章 谢诺菲留斯·洛夫古德

哈利看看仍抓在她手里的书，是《阿不思·邓布利多的生平和谎言》。

"谈什么？"他担心地问，迅速想到书里有一章是写他的，不知道自己有没有勇气听听丽塔对他和邓布利多关系的描述。赫敏的回答却完全出乎意料。

"我想去见见谢诺菲留斯·洛夫古德。"

哈利瞪着她。

"什么？"

"谢诺菲留斯·洛夫古德，卢娜的父亲，我想去找他谈谈。"

"呃——为什么？"

赫敏深吸了一口气，像是鼓起勇气，说道，"是那个记号，《诗翁彼豆故事集》里的记号，看这儿！"

她把《阿不思·邓布利多的生平和谎言》塞到哈利不情愿的眼睛底下，哈利看到了邓布利多写给格林德沃那封信的照片，正是邓布利多那熟悉的细长斜体字。他真不愿意看到那些文字真的是邓布利多写的，而不是丽塔的杜撰。

"签名，"赫敏说，"看签名，哈利！"

哈利看了，一时不明白她在说什么，但借着魔杖的荧光细看时，他发现邓布利多签名中阿不思的第一个字母A是个小小的、像《诗翁彼豆故事集》中那样的三角形符号。

"呃——你们在——？"罗恩试探地问，但赫敏一眼就制止了他，又回头转向哈利。

"它不断出现，是不是？"她说，"我知道威克多尔说这是格林德沃的标志，可它又分明刻在戈德里克山谷那座古墓上，墓碑上的年代远在格林德沃之前。现在再加上这个！我想，我们没法问邓布利多或格林德沃它是什么意思——我甚至不知道格林德沃是否还活着，但可以去问洛夫古德先生啊，他在婚礼上戴了那个标志。我相信这很重要，哈利！"

哈利没有立即回答。他注视着赫敏那热切的面孔，然后凝视着外面的黑暗，沉思起来。过了许久，他说："赫敏，我们不要重蹈戈德里

CHAPTER TWENTY   Xenophilius Lovegood

into going there, and –'

'But it keeps appearing, Harry! Dumbledore left me *The Tales of Beedle the Bard*, how do you know we're not supposed to find out about the sign?'

'Here we go again!' Harry felt slightly exasperated. 'We keep trying to convince ourselves Dumbledore left us secret signs and clues –'

'The Deluminator turned out to be pretty useful,' piped up Ron. 'I think Hermione's right, I think we ought to go and see Lovegood.'

Harry threw him a dark look. He was quite sure that Ron's support of Hermione had little to do with a desire to know the meaning of the triangular rune.

'It won't be like Godric's Hollow,' Ron added, 'Lovegood's on your side, Harry, *The Quibbler*'s been for you all along, it keeps telling everyone they've got to help you!'

'I'm sure this is important!' said Hermione earnestly.

'But don't you think, if it was, Dumbledore would have told me about it before he died?'

'Maybe … maybe it's something you need to find out for yourself,' said Hermione, with a faint air of clutching at straws.

'Yeah,' said Ron sycophantically, 'that makes sense.'

'No, it doesn't,' snapped Hermione, 'but I still think we ought to talk to Mr Lovegood. A symbol that links Dumbledore, Grindelwald and Godric's Hollow? Harry, I'm sure we ought to know about this!'

'I think we should vote on it,' said Ron. 'Those in favour of going to see Lovegood –'

His hand flew into the air before Hermione's. Her lips quivered suspiciously as she raised her own.

'Outvoted, Harry, sorry,' said Ron, clapping him on the back.

'Fine,' said Harry, half amused, half irritated. 'Only, once we've seen Lovegood, let's try and look for some more Horcruxes, shall we? Where do the Lovegoods live, anyway? Do either of you know?'

'Yeah, they're not far from my place,' said Ron. 'I dunno exactly where, but Mum and Dad always point towards the hills whenever they mention them. Shouldn't be hard to find.'

When Hermione had returned to her bunk, Harry lowered his voice.

克山谷的覆辙了。我们说服自己去了那里，结果——"

"可是它不断出现啊，哈利！邓布利多把《诗翁彼豆故事集》留给了我，你怎么知道我们不应该去搞懂那个记号呢？"

"又来了！"哈利觉得有点烦躁，"我们总想让自己相信邓布利多留下了秘密的记号和线索——"

"熄灯器就挺有用的。"罗恩帮腔道，"我认为赫敏说得对，我们应该去见见洛夫古德。"

哈利瞪了他一眼，相信他支持赫敏与想知道三角形如尼文的含义无关。

"不会像戈德里克山谷那样的。"罗恩又说，"洛夫古德是站在你这一边的，哈利。《唱唱反调》一直都在支持你，总对大家说必须援助你！"

"我相信这很重要！"赫敏认真地说。

"可如果重要的话，你不觉得邓布利多临死前应该告诉我吗？"

"也许……也许这是需要你自己去弄清的东西。"赫敏有点像抓救命稻草似的说。

"是啊，"罗恩拍马屁地说，"有道理。"

"没道理，"赫敏没好气地说，"但我还是觉得应该去找洛夫古德先生谈谈。一个把邓布利多、格林德沃和戈德里克山谷联系在一起的符号是什么意思？哈利，我敢肯定我们应该把它弄明白！"

"我想还是投票表决吧，"罗恩说，"赞成去见洛夫古德的——"

他的手立刻举到了空中，比赫敏还快。赫敏狐疑地颤抖着嘴唇，也举起了手。

"二比一，哈利，对不起。"罗恩拍着他的后背说。

"好吧，"哈利又好气又好笑地说，"不过，见过洛夫古德之后，我们要想办法去找其他魂器，行吗？哎，洛夫古德住在哪儿呢？你们有谁知道？"

"离我家不远。"罗恩说，"我不知道确切的地点，但爸爸妈妈提到他们时总往山上指。应该不难找到。"

赫敏回到床上之后，哈利压低了嗓门。

CHAPTER TWENTY   Xenophilius Lovegood

'You only agreed to try and get back in her good books.'

'All's fair in love and war,' said Ron brightly, 'and this is a bit of both. Cheer up, it's the Christmas holidays, Luna'll be home!'

They had an excellent view of the village of Ottery St Catchpole from the breezy hillside to which they Disapparated next morning. From their high vantage point, the village looked like a collection of toy houses in the great, slanting shafts of sunlight stretching to earth in the breaks between clouds. They stood for a minute or two looking towards The Burrow, their hands shadowing their eyes, but all they could make out were the high hedges and trees of the orchard, which afforded the crooked little house protection from Muggle eyes.

'It's weird, being this near, but not going to visit,' said Ron.

'Well, it's not like you haven't just seen them. You were there for Christmas,' said Hermione coldly.

'I wasn't at The Burrow!' said Ron, with an incredulous laugh. 'Do you think I was going to go back there and tell them all I'd walked out on you? Yeah, Fred and George would've been great about it. And Ginny, she'd have been really understanding.'

'But where have you been, then?' asked Hermione, surprised.

'Bill and Fleur's new place. Shell Cottage. Bill's always been decent to me. He – he wasn't impressed when he heard what I'd done, but he didn't go on about it. He knew I was really sorry. None of the rest of the family know I was there. Bill told Mum he and Fleur weren't going home for Christmas because they wanted to spend it alone. You know, first holiday after they were married. I don't think Fleur minded. You know how much she hates Celestina Warbeck.'

Ron turned his back on The Burrow.

'Let's try up here,' he said, leading the way over the top of the hill.

They walked for a few hours, Harry, at Hermione's insistence, hidden beneath the Invisibility Cloak. The cluster of low hills appeared to be uninhabited apart from one small cottage, which seemed deserted.

'Do you think it's theirs, and they've gone away for Christmas?' said Hermione, peering through the window at a neat little kitchen with geraniums on the window sill. Ron snorted.

'Listen, I've got a feeling you'd be able to tell who lived there if you looked through the Lovegoods' window. Let's try the next lot of hills.'

第20章 谢诺菲留斯·洛夫古德

"你只是为了重新赢得她的好感。"

"在爱情和战争中一切都是合法的,"罗恩得意扬扬地说,"刚才嘛,两者都沾了一点儿。开心点吧,现在是圣诞节期间,卢娜在家!"

次日早晨,他们幻影移形到一个清风习习的山坡上,望见了奥特里·圣卡奇波尔村庄的美丽风光。凭高远眺,村庄像一片玩具小房子,散落在透过云层斜射地面的巨大光束中。他们站在那里手搭凉棚朝陋居望了一会儿,只看见高高的树篱和果园,遮住了那座歪歪扭扭的小房子,麻瓜不会发现。

"感觉真别扭,这么近,却不能回去。"罗恩说。

"哼,你最近又不是没见过他们。你在那儿过了圣诞节。"赫敏冷冷地说。

"我没回陋居!"罗恩惊讶地笑了,"你以为我会回去告诉大家我把你们给甩了?是啊,弗雷德和乔治听了准会很来劲的。还有金妮,她一定非常理解。"

"那你去哪儿了?"赫敏惊讶地问。

"比尔和芙蓉的新家,贝壳小屋。比尔对我一直不错,他——他听说我干的事之后也不以为然,但没有唠叨个没完。他知道我是真心后悔了。家里其他人都不知道我在那儿。比尔跟妈妈讲他和芙蓉不回去过圣诞节了,想两个人自己过。你知道,这是他们婚后的第一个节日。我想芙蓉也不在乎,你知道她多讨厌塞蒂娜·沃贝克。"

罗恩转身背对陋居。

"上去看看。"他带头翻过山顶。

他们走了几个小时,哈利在赫敏的坚持下穿着隐形衣。低矮的山峦间似乎只有一座小木屋,看上去也已无人居住。

"你觉得那会不会就是他家,他们出去过圣诞节了?"赫敏隔着窗户朝一间整洁的小厨房里窥视,窗台上摆着天竺葵。罗恩不以为然地哼了一声。

"听着,我有种感觉,从洛夫古德家窗口应该能看出里面住的是谁。还是到前边山里找找吧。"

CHAPTER TWENTY — Xenophilius Lovegood

So they Disapparated a few miles further north.

'Aha!' shouted Ron, as the wind whipped their hair and clothes. Ron was pointing upwards, towards the top of the hill on which they had appeared, where a most strange-looking house rose vertically against the sky, a great, black cylinder with a ghostly moon hanging behind it in the afternoon sky. 'That's got to be Luna's house, who else would live in a place like that? It looks like a giant rook!'

'It's nothing like a bird,' said Hermione, frowning at the tower.

'I was talking about a chess rook,' said Ron. 'A castle to you.'

Ron's legs were the longest and he reached the top of the hill first. When Harry and Hermione caught up with him, panting and clutching stitches in their sides, they found him grinning broadly.

'It's theirs,' said Ron. 'Look.'

Three hand-painted signs had been tacked to a broken-down gate. The first read

The Quibbler. Editor: X. Lovegood

the second,

Pick Your Own Mistletoe

the third,

Keep Off the Dirigible Plums

The gate creaked as they opened it. The zigzagging path leading to the front door was overgrown with a variety of odd plants, including a bush covered in the orange, radish-like fruit Luna sometimes wore as earrings. Harry thought he recognised a Snargaluff, and gave the wizened stump a wide berth. Two aged crab-apple trees, bent with the wind, stripped of leaves but still heavy with berry-sized red fruits and bushy crowns of white-beaded mistletoe, stood sentinel on either side of the front door. A little owl with a slightly flattened, hawk-like head peered down at them from one of the branches.

'You'd better take off the Invisibility Cloak, Harry,' said Hermione, 'it's

第20章 谢诺菲留斯·洛夫古德

他们又往北幻影移形了几英里。

"啊哈！"罗恩叫道，狂风拍打着他们的头发和衣服。罗恩指着上方，他们新到的这座山的山顶上，有一所古怪透顶的房子矗立在蓝天下，像巨大的黑色圆柱，后面有个幽灵般的月亮挂在下午的天空中。"那一定是卢娜的家，还有谁会住在那样的地方？看上去像个大车！"

"根本不像车。"赫敏皱眉望着那圆楼说。

"我说的是象棋里的车，"罗恩说，"用你的话说就是城堡。"

罗恩腿最长，先跑到了山顶。等哈利和赫敏气喘吁吁、捂着生疼的肋部追上之后，只见他眉开眼笑。

"是他们家，"罗恩说，"看。"

三块手绘的牌子钉在毁坏的院门上。

第一块：

《唱唱反调》主编：X. 洛夫古德

第二块：

请你自己挑一束槲寄生

第三块：

别碰飞艇李

院门吱吱嘎嘎地被他们推开了，曲曲折折的小径旁长满了各种奇异的植物，有一丛灌木上结满了卢娜有时当耳环戴的橘红色小萝卜形果实。哈利还仿佛看到了疙瘩藤，赶忙离那枯根远远的。两棵被风吹弯的老海棠树守卫在前门两侧，叶子已经掉光，但仍然挂满小红果和一蓬蓬缀有白珠的槲寄生花冠。一只脑袋略扁、有点像鹰头的小猫头鹰在一根树枝上朝他们窥视。

"你最好脱下隐形衣，哈利。"赫敏说，"洛夫古德先生想帮的是你，

CHAPTER TWENTY Xenophilius Lovegood

you Mr Lovegood wants to help, not us.'

He did as she suggested, handing her the Cloak to stow in the beaded bag. She then rapped three times on the thick, black door, which was studded with iron nails and bore a knocker shaped like an eagle.

Barely ten seconds passed, then the door was flung open and there stood Xenophilius Lovegood, barefooted and wearing what appeared to be a stained nightshirt. His long, white, candyfloss hair was dirty and unkempt. Xenophilius had been positively dapper at Bill and Fleur's wedding by comparison.

'What? What is it? Who are you? What do you want?' he cried, in a high-pitched, querulous voice, looking first at Hermione, then at Ron, and finally at Harry, upon which his mouth fell open in a perfect, comical 'O'.

'Hello, Mr Lovegood,' said Harry, holding out his hand. 'I'm Harry, Harry Potter.'

Xenophilius did not take Harry's hand, although the eye that was not pointing inwards at his nose slid straight to the scar on Harry's forehead.

'Would it be OK if we came in?' asked Harry. 'There's something we'd like to ask you.'

'I ... I'm not sure that's advisable,' whispered Xenophilius. He swallowed and cast a quick look around the garden. 'Rather a shock ... my word ... I ... I'm afraid I don't really think I ought to –'

'It won't take long,' said Harry, slightly disappointed by this less-than-warm welcome.

'I – oh, all right then. Come in, quickly. *Quickly!*'

They were barely over the threshold when Xenophilius slammed the door shut behind them. They were standing in the most peculiar kitchen Harry had ever seen. The room was perfectly circular, so that it felt like being inside a giant pepper pot. Everything was curved to fit the walls: the stove, the sink and the cupboards, and all of it had been painted with flowers, insects and birds in bright primary colours. Harry thought he recognised Luna's style: the effect, in such an enclosed space, was slightly overwhelming.

In the middle of the floor, a wrought-iron spiral staircase led to the upper levels. There was a great deal of clattering and banging coming from overhead: Harry wondered what Luna could be doing.

'You'd better come up,' said Xenophilius, still looking extremely uncomfortable, and he led the way.

第20章 谢诺菲留斯·洛夫古德

不是我们。"

哈利采纳了建议,把隐形衣交给她塞进串珠小包。赫敏在厚重的黑门上敲了三下,那门上嵌有铁质圆钉,还有一个鹰形门环。

不到十秒钟,门打开了,谢诺菲留斯·洛夫古德站在那儿,光着脚,穿的好像是一件污渍斑斑的长睡衣,长长的、棉花糖似的白发又脏又乱。相比之下,比尔和芙蓉婚礼上的谢诺菲留斯真算是整洁的了。

"什么?什么事?你们是谁?你们要干什么?"他用一种尖锐的、抱怨的声音说,先看看赫敏,又看看罗恩,最后看到了哈利,嘴巴张成了一个圆圆的、可笑的O形。

"您好,洛夫古德先生,"哈利伸出手说,"我是哈利,哈利·波特。"

谢诺菲留斯没有跟哈利握手,但没有贴近鼻梁的那只眼珠一下瞟向了哈利的额头。

"可以进去吗?"哈利问,"我们有点事想请教您。"

"我……我不知道是不是合适。"谢诺菲留斯小声说。他咽了口唾沫,迅速地往花园里扫了一眼。"非常意外……说实话……我……我觉得我恐怕不应该——"

"不需要多久的。"哈利说,对这不大热情的迎接有点失望。

"我——哦,那好吧。进来,快,快!"

三人刚跨进门槛,谢诺菲留斯就把门撞上了。他们站在哈利见过的最奇怪的厨房里。房间是标准的圆形,感觉就像待在一个巨大的胡椒瓶里。所有的东西都做成了弧形,与墙壁相吻合:包括炉子、水池和碗柜,并且都用鲜艳的三原色绘满了花卉、昆虫和鸟类。哈利觉得看到了卢娜的风格:在这样封闭的空间里,效果有点强烈得令人受不了。

在房间中央,一个铸铁的螺旋形楼梯通到楼上。楼上传来咔啦咔啦和乒乒乓乓的响声,哈利心想不知道卢娜在干什么。

"最好上楼吧。"谢诺菲留斯说,仍然显得非常不自在。他在前面带路。

CHAPTER TWENTY   Xenophilius Lovegood

The room above seemed to be a combination of living room and workplace, and as such, was even more cluttered than the kitchen. Though much smaller, and entirely round, the room somewhat resembled the Room of Requirement on the unforgettable occasion that it had transformed itself into a gigantic labyrinth comprised of centuries of hidden objects. There were piles upon piles of books and papers on every surface. Delicately made models of creatures Harry did not recognise, all flapping wings or snapping jaws, hung from the ceiling.

Luna was not there: the thing that was making such a racket was a wooden object covered in magically turning cogs and wheels. It looked like the bizarre offspring of a workbench and a set of old shelves, but after a moment Harry deduced that it was an old-fashioned printing press due to the fact that it was churning out *Quibblers*.

'Excuse me,' said Xenophilius, and he strode over to the machine, seized a grubby tablecloth from beneath an immense number of books and papers, which all tumbled on to the floor, and threw it over the press, somewhat muffling the loud bangs and clatters. He then faced Harry.

'Why have you come here?'

Before Harry could speak, however, Hermione let out a small cry of shock.

'Mr Lovegood – what's that?'

She was pointing at an enormous, grey spiral horn, not unlike that of a unicorn, which had been mounted on the wall, protruding several feet into the room.

'It is the horn of a Crumple-Horned Snorkack,' said Xenophilius.

'No it isn't!' said Hermione.

'Hermione,' muttered Harry, embarrassed, 'now's not the moment –'

'But Harry, it's an Erumpent horn! It's a Class B Tradeable Material and it's an extraordinarily dangerous thing to have in a house!'

'How d'you know it's an Erumpent horn?' asked Ron, edging away from the horn as fast as he could, given the extreme clutter of the room.

'There's a description in *Fantastic Beasts and Where to Find Them*! Mr Lovegood, you need to get rid of it straight away, don't you know it can explode at the slightest touch?'

'The Crumple-Horned Snorkack,' said Xenophilius very clearly, a mulish look upon his face, 'is a shy and highly magical creature, and its horn –'

第20章 谢诺菲留斯·洛夫古德

上面的房间似乎既是客厅又是工作间,所以比厨房还要乱。简直有点像有求必应屋那次变成的令人难忘的大迷宫,堆着许多个世纪以来藏进去的东西,只是这个房间小得多,而且是标准的圆形。每一处表面都有一堆堆的书和纸。天花板上吊着精致的动物模型,都是哈利不认识的,在拍着翅膀或动着嘴巴。

卢娜不在。发出那些响声的是一个木头家伙,有许多靠魔法转动的齿轮。看上去像工作台和一堆旧架子杂交出来的怪物,但过了一会儿哈利推测这是一台老式印刷机,因为它在吐出一份份《唱唱反调》。

"请原谅。"谢诺菲留斯大步走到机器跟前,从一大堆书和纸底下拽出一块污秽的桌布,书和纸一齐滚到地上。他把布蒙到印刷机上,盖住了一些乒乒乓乓和咔啦咔啦的响声,然后转向哈利。

"你为什么来这儿?"

哈利刚要说话,赫敏轻轻地惊叫了一声。

"洛夫古德先生——那是什么?"

她指着一只巨大的灰色螺旋形兽角,它与独角兽的有些相似,安在墙上,伸入房间几英尺。

"那是弯角犀兽的角。"谢诺菲留斯说。

"不是的!"赫敏说。

"赫敏,"哈利尴尬地小声说,"现在不是时候——"

"可是哈利,那是毒角兽的角!是B级交易物品,放在家里是极其危险的!"

"你怎么知道它是毒角兽的角?"罗恩问,在奇乱无比的房间中尽可能迅速地远离那只角。

"《神奇动物在哪里》上讲过!洛夫古德先生,您必须马上除掉它,您不知道它轻轻一碰就会爆炸吗?"

"弯角犀兽,"谢诺菲留斯非常清楚地说,脸上一副顽固的表情,"是一种害羞的、非常神奇的动物,它的角——"

CHAPTER TWENTY   Xenophilius Lovegood

'Mr Lovegood, I recognise the grooved markings around the base, that's an Erumpent horn and it's incredibly dangerous – I don't know where you got it –'

'I bought it,' said Xenophilius dogmatically, 'two weeks ago, from a delightful young wizard who knew of my interest in the exquisite Snorkack. A Christmas surprise for my Luna. Now,' he said, turning to Harry, 'why exactly have you come here, Mr Potter?'

'We need some help,' said Harry, before Hermione could start again.

'Ah,' said Xenophilius. 'Help. Hm.' His good eye moved again to Harry's scar. He seemed simultaneously terrified and mesmerised. 'Yes. The thing is ... helping Harry Potter ... rather dangerous ...'

'Aren't you the one who keeps telling everyone it's their first duty to help Harry?' said Ron. 'In that magazine of yours?'

Xenophilius glanced behind him at the concealed printing press, still banging and clattering beneath the tablecloth.

'Er – yes, I have expressed that view. However –'

'– that's for everyone else to do, not you personally?' said Ron.

Xenophilius did not answer. He kept swallowing, his eyes darting between the three of them. Harry had the impression that he was undergoing some painful internal struggle.

'Where's Luna?' asked Hermione. 'Let's see what she thinks.'

Xenophilius gulped. He seemed to be steeling himself. Finally he said, in a shaky voice difficult to hear over the noise of the printing press, 'Luna is down at the stream, fishing for Freshwater Plimpies. She ... she will like to see you. I'll go and call her and then – yes, very well. I shall try to help you.'

He disappeared down the spiral staircase and they heard the front door open and close. They looked at each other.

'Cowardly old wart,' said Ron. 'Luna's got ten times his guts.'

'He's probably worried about what'll happen to them if the Death Eaters find out I was here,' said Harry.

'Well, I agree with Ron,' said Hermione. 'Awful old hypocrite, telling everyone else to help you and trying to worm out of it himself. And for heaven's sake keep away from that horn.'

Harry crossed to the window on the far side of the room. He could see a stream, a thin, glittering ribbon lying far below them at the base of the

第20章 谢诺菲留斯·洛夫古德

"洛夫古德先生,我认出了根部的槽纹,它确实是毒角兽的角,太危险了——我不知道您是从哪儿弄来的——"

"买来的,"谢诺菲留斯执拗地说,"两星期前,从一个可爱的年轻男巫那儿买的,他知道我喜欢美妙的弯角鼾兽。我想给我的卢娜一个圣诞节的惊喜。好了,"他转向哈利,"你究竟为什么来这儿,波特先生?"

"我们需要一些帮助。"哈利抢在赫敏前面说。

"啊,"谢诺菲留斯说,"帮助,唔。"他那只好眼睛又瞟向哈利的伤疤,似乎既恐惧又着迷,"是啊。问题是……帮助哈利·波特……很危险……"

"您不是一直在告诉大家,首要任务就是帮助哈利吗?"罗恩说,"在您的那份杂志上?"

谢诺菲留斯回头看了一眼蒙着的印刷机,它仍在桌布下面乒乒乓乓、咔啦咔啦地响着。

"呃——是啊,我发表过那个观点。然而——"

"——那是叫别人做的,不包括您自己?"罗恩说。

谢诺菲留斯没有回答,不停地咽着唾沫,目光在三人之间扫来扫去。哈利觉得他内心在进行着某种痛苦的斗争。

"卢娜呢?"赫敏问,"我们看看她是怎么想的。"

谢诺菲留斯噎住了。他似乎在硬下心肠,最后,他用颤抖的、在印刷机的噪音中几乎听不见的声音说:"卢娜在下面小溪边捕淡水彩球鱼呢。她……她会高兴见到你们的。我去叫她,然后——嗯,好吧,我会尽量帮助你们。"

他从螺旋形楼梯下去了,接着传来前门开关的声音,三人对视了一下。

"懦弱的老家伙,"罗恩说,"卢娜的胆量是他的十倍。"

"他可能担心如果食死徒发现我来过这儿,他们会有麻烦。"哈利说。

"哼,我同意罗恩的看法。"赫敏说,"讨厌的老伪君子,要求别人去帮助你,自己却往后缩。天哪,千万别靠近那只角。"

哈利走到房间那头的窗口。他望见一条小溪,像一条闪闪发光的

CHAPTER TWENTY   Xenophilius Lovegood

hill. They were very high up; a bird fluttered past the window as he stared in the direction of The Burrow, now invisible beyond another line of hills. Ginny was over there somewhere. They were closer to each other today than they had been since Bill and Fleur's wedding, but she could have no idea he was gazing towards her now, thinking of her. He supposed he ought to be glad of it; anyone he came into contact with was in danger, Xenophilius's attitude proved that.

He turned away from the window and his gaze fell upon another peculiar object, standing upon the cluttered, curved sideboard: a stone bust of a beautiful but austere-looking witch wearing a most bizarre-looking headdress. Two objects that resembled golden ear-trumpets curved out from the sides. A tiny pair of glittering blue wings was stuck to a leather strap that ran over the top of her head, while one of the orange radishes had been stuck to a second strap around her forehead.

'Look at this,' said Harry.

'Fetching,' said Ron. 'Surprised he didn't wear that to the wedding.'

They heard the front door close and a moment later Xenophilius had climbed back up the spiral staircase into the room, his thin legs now encased in wellington boots, bearing a tray of ill-assorted teacups and a steaming teapot.

'Ah, you have spotted my pet invention,' he said, shoving the tray into Hermione's arms and joining Harry at the statue's side. 'Modelled, fittingly enough, upon the head of the beautiful Rowena Ravenclaw. *Wit beyond measure is man's greatest treasure!*'

He indicated the objects like ear-trumpets.

'These are the Wrackspurt siphons – to remove all sources of distraction from the thinker's immediate area. Here,' he pointed out the tiny wings, 'a Billywig propeller, to induce an elevated frame of mind. Finally,' he pointed to the orange radish, 'the Dirigible Plum, so as to enhance the ability to accept the extraordinary.'

Xenophilius strode back to the tea tray, which Hermione had managed to balance precariously on one of the cluttered side tables.

'May I offer you all an infusion of Gurdyroots?' said Xenophilius. 'We make it ourselves.' As he started to pour out the drink, which was as deeply purple as beetroot juice, he added, 'Luna is down beyond Bottom Bridge, she is most excited that you are here. She ought not to be too long, she has

第20章 谢诺菲留斯·洛夫古德

细带子躺在远远的山底。他们这里很高,他遥望陋居,可是被另一片青山挡住了看不见,只看见一只小鸟从窗前飞过。金妮在山的那边,自从比尔和芙蓉的婚礼之后,他和她之间的距离从来没有这么近过。但她不可能知道他正在遥望她、思念她。他想也许应该为此庆幸,因为凡是他接触的人都会有危险,谢诺菲留斯的态度证明了这一点。

他转身离开了窗口,目光落在另一件奇异的东西上:一座半身石像立在乱糟糟的弧形柜子上,是一个美丽但面容严厉的女巫。她戴的头饰古怪透顶,两边伸出一对弯弯的、金色助听筒似的东西,一双闪闪发光的蓝色小翅膀插在头顶箍的皮带上,而额头的另一道箍上插着个橘红色的小萝卜。

"看这个。"哈利说。

"真迷人,"罗恩说,"奇怪他怎么没戴到婚礼上去。"

他们听到了关门声,片刻之后,谢诺菲留斯从螺旋形楼梯爬了上来,他的细腿穿上了长统靴,手里用托盘端着几个不配套的茶杯和一只冒着热气的茶壶。

"啊,你们发现了我最可爱的发明。"说着,他把托盘塞进赫敏手里,走到雕像旁的哈利身边,"按照美丽的罗伊纳·拉文克劳的头型塑造的,十分相称。过人的聪明才智是人类最大的财富!"

他指着那助听筒状的东西。

"这是骚扰虻虹吸管——可将一切干扰从思想者的周围区域排除。这个,"他指着小翅膀,"是比利威格虫的翅膀,可导入高级思维状态,最后,"他指着橘红色的小萝卜,"是飞艇李,可提高接受异常事物的能力。"

谢诺菲留斯走到茶盘前,茶盘被赫敏好不容易搁在堆满东西的柜子上,看上去岌岌可危。

"可以请你们喝一点戈迪根茶吗?"谢诺菲留斯说,"我们自己做的。"他开始倒出一种甜菜汁般深紫色的液体,一边又说:"卢娜在谷底桥那边,知道你们来了非常高兴。她捕到了不少彩球鱼,差不多够

CHAPTER TWENTY   Xenophilius Lovegood

caught nearly enough Plimpies to make soup for all of us. Do sit down and help yourselves to sugar.

'Now,' he removed a tottering pile of papers from an armchair and sat down, his wellingtoned legs crossed, 'how may I help you, Mr Potter?'

'Well,' said Harry, glancing at Hermione, who nodded encouragingly, 'it's about that symbol you were wearing around your neck at Bill and Fleur's wedding, Mr Lovegood. We wondered what it meant.'

Xenophilius raised his eyebrows.

'Are you referring to the sign of the Deathly Hallows?'

第20章 谢诺菲留斯·洛夫古德

给大家熬汤了。她应该很快就会回来。请坐下来加点糖。"

"现在,"他搬掉扶手椅上那一堆高高欲倒的报纸,坐下来跷起穿着长统靴的双腿,"我能帮助你什么呢,波特先生?"

"嗯,"哈利望了一眼赫敏,她鼓励地点点头,"是关于您在比尔和芙蓉婚礼上戴的那个标志,洛夫古德先生。我们想知道它有什么意义。"

谢诺菲留斯扬起眉毛。

"你指的是死亡圣器的标志吗?"

CHAPTER TWENTY-ONE

The Tale of the Three Brothers

Harry turned to look at Ron and Hermione. Neither of them seemed to have understood what Xenophilius had said, either.

'The Deathly Hallows?'

'That's right,' said Xenophilius. 'You haven't heard of them? I'm not surprised. Very, very few wizards believe. Witness that knuckle-headed young man at your brother's wedding,' he nodded at Ron, 'who attacked me for sporting the symbol of a well-known Dark wizard! Such ignorance. There is nothing Dark about the Hallows – at least, not in that crude sense. One simply uses the symbol to reveal oneself to other believers, in the hope that they might help one with the Quest.'

He stirred several lumps of sugar into his Gurdyroot infusion and drank some.

'I'm sorry,' said Harry. 'I still don't really understand.'

To be polite, he took a sip from his cup too and almost gagged: the stuff was quite disgusting, as though someone had liquidised bogey-flavoured Every-Flavour Beans.

'Well, you see, believers seek the Deathly Hallows,' said Xenophilius, smacking his lips in apparent appreciation of the Gurdyroot infusion.

'But what *are* the Deathly Hallows?' asked Hermione.

Xenophilius set aside his empty teacup.

'I assume that you are all familiar with "The Tale of the Three Brothers"?'

Harry said, 'No,' but Ron and Hermione both said, 'Yes.'

Xenophilius nodded gravely.

'Well, well, Mr Potter, the whole thing starts with "The Tale of the Three Brothers" ... I have a copy somewhere ...'

第 21 章

三兄弟的传说

哈利转身看看罗恩和赫敏，他们俩似乎也听不懂谢诺菲留斯说的话。

"死亡圣器？"

"是的，"谢诺菲留斯说，"你从来没听说过？我不奇怪。只有很少很少的巫师相信这些。记得你哥哥婚礼上那个愣头小伙子，"他冲着罗恩点点头，"还抨击我戴着一位著名黑巫师的标志！真是愚昧。圣器一点也不'黑'——至少不是在那种低级的意义上。人们只是用这个标志向别的信徒展示自己，希望在探求途中得到帮助。"

他放了几块糖在戈迪根茶里，搅了搅，喝了一些。

"对不起，"哈利说，"我还是没有完全明白。"

出于礼貌，他也尝了一口杯子里的饮料，差点吐了出来：那东西很难喝，好像有人把干鼻屎味的比比多味豆榨成了汁。

"是这样，信徒们寻找死亡圣器。"谢诺菲留斯说着咂了咂嘴，显然是表明戈迪根茶的滋味妙不可言。

"但死亡圣器是什么呢？"赫敏问。

谢诺菲留斯把他的空茶杯搁到一边。

"我想你们都熟悉《三兄弟的传说》吧？"

哈利说："不熟悉。"但是罗恩和赫敏都说："熟悉。"

谢诺菲留斯严肃地点了点头。

"好的，好的，波特先生，这一切都始于《三兄弟的传说》……我有这本书……"

CHAPTER TWENTY-ONE The Tale of the Three Brothers

He glanced vaguely around the room, at the piles of parchment and books, but Hermione said, 'I've got a copy, Mr Lovegood, I've got it right here.'

And she pulled out *The Tales of Beedle the Bard* from the small beaded bag.

'The original?' enquired Xenophilius sharply, and when she nodded, he said, 'Well then, why don't you read it aloud? Much the best way to make sure we all understand.'

'Er ... all right,' said Hermione nervously. She opened the book and Harry saw that the symbol they were investigating headed the top of the page, as she gave a little cough and began to read.

'"*There were once three brothers who were travelling along a lonely, winding road at twilight –*"'

'Midnight, our mum always told us,' said Ron, who had stretched out, arms behind his head, to listen. Hermione shot him a look of annoyance.

'Sorry, I just think it's a bit spookier if it's midnight!' said Ron.

'Yeah, because we really need a bit more fear in our lives,' said Harry, before he could stop himself. Xenophilius did not seem to be paying much attention, but was staring out of the window at the sky. 'Go on, Hermione.'

'"*In time, the brothers reached a river too deep to wade through and too dangerous to swim across. However, these brothers were learned in the magical arts, and so they simply waved their wands and made a bridge appear across the treacherous water. They were halfway across it when they found their path blocked by a hooded figure.*

'"*And Death spoke to them –*"'

'Sorry,' interjected Harry, 'but *Death* spoke to them?'

'It's a fairy tale, Harry!'

'Right, sorry. Go on.'

'"*And Death spoke to them. He was angry that he had been cheated out of three new victims, for travellers usually drowned in the river. But Death was cunning. He pretended to congratulate the three brothers upon their magic, and said that each had earned a prize for having been clever enough to evade him.*

'"*So the oldest brother, who was a combative man, asked for a wand more powerful than any in existence: a wand that must always win duels for its owner, a wand worthy of a wizard who had conquered Death! So Death crossed to an elder tree on the banks of the*

第21章 三兄弟的传说

他漫不经心地扫视着屋里成堆的羊皮纸和书，但赫敏说："我有一本，洛夫古德先生，就在这里。"

她从串珠小包里掏出了《诗翁彼豆故事集》。

"原文？"谢诺菲留斯一针见血地问道，看到赫敏点头后，他说，"好的，那你为什么不把它读出来呢？这是让大家都弄明白的最好方法。"

"嗯……好的。"赫敏紧张地说道。她翻开书，轻咳了一声，开始读起来，哈利看到他们调查的标志就印在那页的上方。

从前，有三兄弟在一条僻静的羊肠小道上赶路。天色已近黄昏——

"是午夜，妈妈一直对我们这样说。"罗恩说道，他伸了个懒腰，双手抱在脑后听着。赫敏气恼地瞪了他一眼。

"对不起，我想如果是午夜会更让人害怕！"罗恩说。

"是啊，我们的生活里的确需要多一点恐惧。"哈利忍不住脱口而出。谢诺菲留斯似乎没太注意，而是一直盯着窗外的天空。"继续讲吧，赫敏。"

他们走着走着，来到了一条河边，水太深了，无法蹚过，游过去也太危险。然而，三兄弟精通魔法，一挥魔杖，危险莫测的水上就出现了一座桥。他们走到桥中央时，一个戴兜帽的身影挡住了他们的去路。

死神对他们说话——

"对不起，"哈利插嘴道，"怎么是死神对他们说话？"

"这是个传说，哈利！"

"哦，对不起。继续。"

死神对他们说话了。死神很生气，他失去了三个新的祭品——因为旅行者通常都会淹死在这条河里。但是死神很狡猾。他假装祝贺兄弟三人的魔法，说他们凭着聪明躲过了死神，每人可以获得一样奖励。

老大是一位好战的男子汉，他要的是一根世间最强大的魔杖：一根在决斗中永远能帮主人获胜的魔杖，一根征服了死神的巫师值得拥有的魔杖！死神就走到岸边一棵接骨木树前，用悬垂的树

CHAPTER TWENTY-ONE   The Tale of the Three Brothers

river, fashioned a wand from a branch that hung there, and gave it to the oldest brother.

"'Then the second brother, who was an arrogant man, decided that he wanted to humiliate Death still further, and asked for the power to recall others from Death. So Death picked up a stone from the riverbank and gave it to the second brother, and told him that the stone would have the power to bring back the dead.

"'And then Death asked the third and youngest brother what he would like. The youngest brother was the humblest and also the wisest of the brothers, and he did not trust Death. So he asked for something that would enable him to go forth from that place without being followed by Death. And Death, most unwillingly, handed over his own Cloak of Invisibility.'"

'Death's got an Invisibility Cloak?' Harry interrupted again.

'So he can sneak up on people,' said Ron. 'Sometimes he gets bored of running at them, flapping his arms and shrieking ... sorry, Hermione.'

"'Then Death stood aside and allowed the three brothers to continue on their way and they did so, talking with wonder of the adventure they had had, and admiring Death's gifts.

"'In due course the brothers separated, each for his own destination.

"'The first brother travelled on for a week or more, and reaching a distant village, sought out a fellow wizard with whom he had a quarrel. Naturally, with the Elder Wand as his weapon, he could not fail to win the duel that followed. Leaving his enemy dead upon the floor, the oldest brother proceeded to an inn, where he boasted loudly of the powerful wand he had snatched from Death himself, and of how it made him invincible.

"'That very night, another wizard crept upon the oldest brother as he lay, wine-sodden, upon his bed. The thief took the wand and, for good measure, slit the oldest brother's throat.

"'And so Death took the first brother for his own.

"'Meanwhile, the second brother journeyed to his own home, where he lived alone. Here he took out the stone that had the power to recall the dead, and turned it thrice in his hand. To his amazement and his delight, the figure of the girl he had once hoped to marry before her untimely death, appeared at once before him.

"'Yet she was sad and cold, separated from him as by a veil. Though she had returned to the mortal world, she did not truly belong there and suffered. Finally, the second brother, driven mad with hopeless longing, killed himself so as truly to join her.

"'And so Death took the second brother for his own.

"'But though Death searched for the third brother for many years, he was never able to find him. It was only when he had attained a great age that the youngest brother finally took

第21章 三兄弟的传说

枝做了一根魔杖,送给了老大。

老二是一位傲慢的男子汉,他决定继续羞辱死神,他想要的是能够让死人复活的能力。死神就从岸上捡起一块石头给了老二,告诉他这块石头有起死回生的能力。

然后死神问最年轻的老三要什么。老三是最谦虚也是最聪明的一个,而且他不相信死神。因此他提出要一件东西,可以让他离开那里而不被死神跟随。死神极不情愿地把自己的隐形衣给了他。

"死神有件隐形衣?"哈利再次打断道。

"这样他可以偷偷摸摸地朝人靠近,"罗恩说,"有时他厌烦了冲过去袭击人们,挥舞着胳膊大声尖叫……对不起,赫敏。"

然后死神站在一边让兄弟三人继续赶路,他们谈论着刚才的奇妙经历,赞赏着死神的礼物,往前走去。

后来兄弟三人分了手,朝着各自的目的地前进。

老大走了一个多星期,来到一个遥远的小山村,找到了一位曾经与他有过争吵的巫师。自然,他用那根接骨木做成的"老魔杖"作武器,无疑获取了决斗的胜利。对手倒地而亡后,他继续前行,走进了一个小酒馆,大声夸耀自己从死神手上得来的强大魔杖如何战无不胜。

就在那个晚上,老大喝得酩酊大醉后,另一个巫师蹑手蹑脚地来到他床边偷走了魔杖,并且割断了他的喉咙。

就这样,死神取走了老大的命。

与此同时,老二回到了他独自居住的家里,拿出可以起死回生的石头,在手里转了三次。让他惊喜交加的是,他想娶但不幸早逝的女孩立刻出现在他面前。

可是她悲伤而冷漠,他们之间似乎隔着一层纱幕。她尽管返回了人间,却并不真正属于这里,她很痛苦。最终,老二被没有希望的渴望折磨疯了,为了能真正和她在一起而自杀身亡。

就这样,死神取走了老二的命。

但是,死神找了老三好多年,始终没能找到他。老三一直活

CHAPTER TWENTY-ONE   The Tale of the Three Brothers

off the Cloak of Invisibility and gave it to his son. And then he greeted Death as an old friend, and went with him gladly, and, equals, they departed this life.'"

Hermione closed the book. It was a moment or two before Xenophilius seemed to realise that she had stopped reading, then he withdrew his gaze from the window and said, 'Well, there you are.'

'Sorry?' said Hermione, sounding confused.

'Those are the Deathly Hallows,' said Xenophilius.

He picked up a quill from a packed table at his elbow, and pulled a torn piece of parchment from between more books.

'The Elder Wand,' he said, and he drew a straight vertical line upon the parchment. 'The Resurrection Stone,' he said, and he added a circle on top of the line. 'The Cloak of Invisibility,' he finished, enclosing both line and circle in a triangle, to make the symbol that so intrigued Hermione. 'Together,' he said, 'the Deathly Hallows.'

'But there's no mention of the words "Deathly Hallows" in the story,' said Hermione.

'Well, of course not,' said Xenophilius, maddeningly smug. 'That is a children's tale, told to amuse rather than to instruct. Those of us who understand these matters, however, recognise that the ancient story refers to three objects, or Hallows, which, if united, will make the possessor master of Death.'

There was a short silence in which Xenophilius glanced out of the window. Already the sun was low in the sky.

'Luna ought to have enough Plimpies soon,' he said quietly.

'When you say "master of Death" –' said Ron.

'Master,' said Xenophilius, waving an airy hand. 'Conqueror. Vanquisher. Whichever term you prefer.'

'But then ... do you mean ...' said Hermione slowly, and Harry could tell that she was trying to keep any trace of scepticism out of her voice, 'that you believe these objects – these Hallows – actually exist?'

Xenophilius raised his eyebrows again.

'Well, of course.'

'But,' said Hermione, and Harry could hear her restraint starting to crack, 'Mr Lovegood, how can you *possibly* believe –?'

第21章 三兄弟的传说

到很老以后，才最终脱下隐形衣，交给了他的儿子，然后像老朋友见面一样迎接死神，并以平等的身份，高兴地同死神一道，离开了人间。

赫敏合上了书。过了一会儿，谢诺菲留斯似乎才反应过来她已经读完了。他把目光从窗外收回，说道："就是这样。"

"对不起？"赫敏有点困惑地问。

"那些就是死亡圣器。"谢诺菲留斯说。

他从肘边堆满东西的桌上捡起一根羽毛笔，又从书堆中抽出一张破羊皮纸。

"老魔杖。"他在羊皮纸上画了一条竖线。"复活石。"他在竖线上面添了个圆圈。"隐形衣。"他在竖线和圆圈外面画了个三角形，就成了令赫敏如此好奇的那个符号。"合在一起就是——死亡圣器。"

"但故事里没有提到'死亡圣器'这个词呀。"赫敏说。

"是的,当然没有，"谢诺菲留斯说，那自鸣得意的样子令人恼火，"那是个传说，是供人娱乐而不是给人教诲的。我们知道这些事的人，却会看出古老的传说里提到了三件东西，或圣器，它们合在一起，就会使拥有者成为死神的主人。"

片刻的沉默，谢诺菲留斯瞄了一眼窗外。太阳在天空中已经很低。

"卢娜应该很快就捕到足够的彩球鱼了。"他轻声说。

"您说到'死神的主人'——"罗恩说。

"主人，"谢诺菲留斯轻挥了一下手说，"征服者，胜利者，随你喜欢怎么说。"

"那么……您的意思是……"赫敏慢慢地说，哈利能感觉到她努力想使声音中不带有怀疑，"您相信这些东西——这些圣器——确实存在？"

谢诺菲留斯再次扬起了眉毛。

"当然。"

"但是，"赫敏说道，哈利能听得出来她的克制开始崩溃，"洛夫古德先生，您怎么可能相信——？"

CHAPTER TWENTY-ONE

The Tale of the Three Brothers

'Luna has told me all about you, young lady,' said Xenophilius, 'you are, I gather, not unintelligent, but painfully limited. Narrow. Close-minded.'

'Perhaps you ought to try on the hat, Hermione,' said Ron, nodding towards the ludicrous headdress. His voice shook with the strain of not laughing.

'Mr Lovegood,' Hermione began again. 'We all know that there are such things as Invisibility Cloaks. They are rare, but they exist. But –'

'Ah, but the Third Hallow is a *true* cloak of invisibility, Miss Granger! I mean to say, it is not a travelling cloak imbued with a Disillusionment Charm, or carrying a Bedazzling Hex, or else woven from Demiguise hair, which will hide one initially but fade with the years until it turns opaque. We are talking about a cloak that really and truly renders the wearer completely invisible, and endures eternally, giving constant and impenetrable concealment, no matter what spells are cast at it. How many cloaks have you ever seen like *that*, Miss Granger?'

Hermione opened her mouth to answer, then closed it again, looking more confused than ever. She, Harry and Ron glanced at one another, and Harry knew that they were all thinking the same thing. It so happened that a cloak exactly like the one Xenophilius had just described was in the room with them at that very moment.

'Exactly,' said Xenophilius, as if he had defeated them all in reasoned argument. 'None of you have ever seen such a thing. The possessor would be immeasurably rich, would he not?'

He glanced out of the window again. The sky was now tinged with the faintest trace of pink.

'All right,' said Hermione, disconcerted. 'Say the Cloak existed ... what about the stone, Mr Lovegood? The thing you call the Resurrection Stone?'

'What of it?'

'Well, how can that be real?'

'Prove that it is not,' said Xenophilius.

Hermione looked outraged.

'But that's – I'm sorry, but that's completely ridiculous! How can I *possibly* prove it doesn't exist? Do you expect me to get hold of – of all the pebbles in the world, and test them? I mean, you could claim that *anything's* real if the only basis for believing in it is that nobody's *proved* it doesn't exist!'

第21章 三兄弟的传说

"卢娜对我讲过你，姑娘。"谢诺菲留斯说，"我推断，你并不缺乏才智，但遗憾的是太狭隘，眼光短浅，思维封闭。"

"或许你应该试试那顶帽子，赫敏。"罗恩说道，一边朝那滑稽的头饰点点头。他的声音有点发颤，努力忍着笑。

"洛夫古德先生，"赫敏又开始说道，"我们都知道有隐形衣那样的东西。它们很罕见，但确实存在。然而——"

"啊，但第三个圣器是一件真正的隐形衣，格兰杰小姐！我是说，它不是一件施了幻身咒，或带有障眼法，或用隐形兽的毛织成的旅行斗篷，这些一开始能够隐形，但时间长了就会渐渐显出实体。我们说的是一件能让人真真正正、完完全全隐形的斗篷，永久有效，持续隐形，无论用什么咒语都不可破解。像那样的隐形衣你见过几件，格兰杰小姐？"

赫敏张嘴刚想应答，但又把嘴闭上了，看上去困惑无比。她、哈利和罗恩互相看了一眼，哈利知道他们都在想同一件事：就是这么巧，有一件完全符合谢诺菲留斯描述的隐形衣，此刻正在房间里，就在他们身边。

"正是这样，"谢诺菲留斯说，好像他已经在辩论中击败了他们三个，"你们都没见过那样的东西。拥有者将会无比的富有，难道不是吗？"

他再次瞥了一眼窗外，天空染上了一抹最淡的粉红色。

"那好吧，"赫敏说道，显得有点慌乱，"就算隐形衣是存在的……那石头呢，洛夫古德先生？那个您称为复活石的东西呢？"

"怎么啦？"

"嗯，它怎么可能是真的呢？"

"那你证明它不是呀。"谢诺菲留斯说。

赫敏看起来愤愤不平。

"可这——对不起，可这完全是荒唐的！我怎么可能证明它不存在呢？您要我去找到——世界上所有的石子，统统测试一遍？我想，您可以宣称任何东西都是真的，如果相信某个东西存在的基础只是没人能证明它不存在！"

CHAPTER TWENTY-ONE — The Tale of the Three Brothers

'Yes, you could,' said Xenophilius. 'I am glad to see that you are opening your mind a little.'

'So the Elder Wand,' said Harry quickly, before Hermione could retort, 'you think that exists too?'

'Oh, well, in that case there is endless evidence,' said Xenophilius. 'The Elder Wand is the Hallow that is most easily traced, because of the way in which it passes from hand to hand.'

'Which is what?' asked Harry.

'Which is that the possessor of the wand must capture it from its previous owner, if he is to be truly master of it,' said Xenophilius. 'Surely you have heard of the way the wand came to Egbert the Egregious, after his slaughter of Emeric the Evil? Of how Godelot died in his own cellar after his son, Hereward, took the wand from him? Of the dreadful Loxias, who took the wand from Barnabas Deverill, whom he had killed? The bloody trail of the Elder Wand is splattered across the pages of wizarding history.'

Harry glanced at Hermione. She was frowning at Xenophilius, but she did not contradict him.

'So where do you think the Elder Wand is now?' asked Ron.

'Alas, who knows?' said Xenophilius, as he gazed out of the window. 'Who knows where the Elder Wand lies hidden? The trail goes cold with Arcus and Livius. Who can say which of them really defeated Loxias, and which took the wand? And who can say who may have defeated them? History, alas, does not tell us.'

There was a pause. Finally Hermione asked stiffly, 'Mr Lovegood, does the Peverell family have anything to do with the Deathly Hallows?'

Xenophilius looked taken aback as something shifted in Harry's memory, but he could not locate it. Peverell ... he had heard that name before ...

'But you have been misleading me, young woman!' said Xenophilius, now sitting up much straighter in his chair and goggling at Hermione. 'I thought you were new to the Hallows Quest! Many of us Questers believe that the Peverells have everything – *everything!* – to do with the Hallows!'

'Who are the Peverells?' asked Ron.

'That was the name on the grave with the mark on it, in Godric's Hollow,' said Hermione, still watching Xenophilius. 'Ignotus Peverell.'

第21章 三兄弟的传说

"是的,可以。"谢诺菲留斯说,"我很高兴看到你有点开窍了。"

"那么老魔杖,"哈利在赫敏反驳之前赶快说,"您认为那也是存在的吗?"

"哦,那个就有无数的证据了,"谢诺菲留斯说,"老魔杖是最容易追溯的圣器,因为它传承的方式比较特殊。"

"是怎么回事呢?"哈利问。

"是这样,只有从前一任主人手上缴获这根魔杖,才能成为它真正的主人。"谢诺菲留斯说,"你们一定听说过,恶怪埃格伯特屠杀恶人默瑞克后,获得魔杖的事吧?也听说过,戈德洛特在儿子赫瑞沃德拿走魔杖后,死在了自家地窖里吧?还听说过恐怖的洛希亚斯杀死巴拿巴斯·德弗里尔,抢走了魔杖吧?老魔杖的血腥踪迹溅满了整部魔法史。"

哈利瞥了赫敏一眼。她朝谢诺菲留斯皱着眉头,但没有反驳。

"那么您认为老魔杖如今在哪儿呢?"罗恩问。

"唉,谁知道?"谢诺菲留斯说,眼睛盯着窗外,"谁知道老魔杖藏在哪儿呢?线索到阿库斯和利维亚斯那里就模糊了。谁说得清他们哪个真正地打败了洛希亚斯,又是哪个拿走了魔杖呢?谁说得清又是什么人打败了他们俩呢?历史,唉,没有告诉我们呀。"

一阵沉默。最终赫敏生硬地问道:"洛夫古德先生,佩弗利尔家族同死亡圣器有什么关系吗?"

谢诺菲留斯似乎大吃一惊,此时哈利的记忆深处动了一下,但他没能抓住。佩弗利尔……他听说过这个名字……

"原来你一直在误导我,姑娘!"谢诺菲留斯说,坐得端正多了,两眼瞪着赫敏,"我以为你们对于探求圣器还很陌生呢!我们大部分探求者都相信佩弗利尔家族与圣器大有关系——大有关系!"

"佩弗利尔家族是谁?"罗恩问。

"在戈德里克山谷,有那个标志的墓碑上的名字,"赫敏说,仍望着谢诺菲留斯,"伊格诺图斯·佩弗利尔。"

CHAPTER TWENTY-ONE

The Tale of the Three Brothers

'Exactly!' said Xenophilius, his forefinger raised pedantically. 'The sign of the Deathly Hallows on Ignotus's grave is conclusive proof!'

'Of what?' asked Ron.

'Why, that the three brothers in the story were actually the three Peverell brothers, Antioch, Cadmus and Ignotus! That they were the original owners of the Hallows!'

With another glance at the window he got to his feet, picked up the tray and headed for the spiral staircase.

'You will stay for dinner?' he called, as he vanished downstairs again. 'Everybody always requests our recipe for Freshwater Plimpy soup.'

'Probably to show the Poisoning Department at St Mungo's,' said Ron under his breath.

Harry waited until they could hear Xenophilius moving about in the kitchen downstairs before speaking.

'What do you think?' he asked Hermione.

'Oh, Harry,' she said wearily, 'it's a pile of utter rubbish. This can't be what the sign really means. This must just be his weird take on it. What a waste of time.'

'I s'pose this *is* the man who brought us Crumple-Horned Snorkacks,' said Ron.

'You don't believe it, either?' Harry asked him.

'Nah, that story's just one of those things you tell kids to teach them lessons, isn't it? "Don't go looking for trouble, don't pick fights, don't go messing around with stuff that's best left alone! Just keep your head down, mind your own business and you'll be OK." Come to think of it,' Ron added, 'maybe that story's why elder wands are supposed to be unlucky.'

'What are you talking about?'

'One of those superstitions, isn't it? "May-born witches will marry Muggles." "Jinx by twilight, undone by midnight." "Wand of elder, never prosper." You must've heard them. My mum's full of them.'

'Harry and I were raised by Muggles,' Hermione reminded him, 'we were taught different superstitions.' She sighed deeply as a rather pungent smell drifted up from the kitchen. The one good thing about her exasperation with Xenophilius was that it seemed to have made her forget that she was annoyed with Ron. 'I think you're right,' she told him. 'It's just a morality tale, it's

第21章 三兄弟的传说

"完全正确！"谢诺菲留斯说，学究气地扬了扬食指，"伊格诺图斯墓碑上死亡圣器的标志是有力的证据！"

"证明什么？"罗恩问。

"哎，故事里的三兄弟实际上就是佩弗利尔三兄弟，安提俄克、卡德摩斯、伊格诺图斯！他们就是圣器的最初拥有者！"

谢诺菲留斯再次瞥了一眼窗外后，站了起来，拿起托盘，朝螺旋形楼梯走了过去。

"你们留下来吃晚餐吗？"他喊道，又一次消失在楼梯下面，"每个人都问我们要淡水彩球鱼汤的菜谱。"

"可能是为了拿给圣芒戈医院中毒科看的。"罗恩小声地说。

等到能听见谢诺菲留斯在楼下厨房里走动后，哈利才开始说话。

"你怎么想？"他问赫敏。

"哦，哈利，"赫敏倦怠地说，"绝对是一堆胡言乱语，不可能是那个标志的真实含义。这肯定只是他的胡诌而已。真是浪费时间。"

"看来这果然就是带给我们弯角鼾兽的那个人。"罗恩说。

"你也不信？"哈利问他。

"咳，那个故事只是讲来教育小孩子的玩意儿，不是吗？'别惹麻烦，别跟人打架，别乱碰不该碰的东西！埋头干你自己的事就好啦！'细想起来，"罗恩添了一句，"可能这个故事也说明，为什么接骨木魔杖常被认为不吉利。"

"你说什么？"

"那些迷信说法之一，不是吗？'五月生的女巫嫁麻瓜。''恶咒在黄昏，破解在午夜。''接骨木魔杖，决不会兴旺。'你们一定听说过。我妈妈满肚子都是这些。"

"哈利和我都是麻瓜养大的，"赫敏提醒他说，"我们听到的是另一些迷信故事。"此时一股十分刺鼻的气味从厨房飘上来，她深深地叹了口气。对谢诺菲留斯的恼怒能带来一个好处：赫敏似乎忘记了她本来在生罗恩的气。"我认为你是对的，"她对罗恩说，"这只是一个说教故事，

CHAPTER TWENTY-ONE   The Tale of the Three Brothers

obvious which gift is best, which one you'd choose –'

The three of them spoke at the same time; Hermione said, 'the Cloak,' Ron said, 'the wand,' and Harry said, 'the stone.'

They looked at each other, half surprised, half amused.

'You're *supposed* to say the Cloak,' Ron told Hermione, 'but you wouldn't need to be invisible if you had the wand. *An unbeatable wand*, Hermione, come on!'.

'We've already got an Invisibility Cloak,' said Harry.

'And it's helped us rather a lot, in case you hadn't noticed!' said Hermione. 'Whereas the wand would be bound to attract trouble –'

'– only if you shouted about it,' argued Ron. 'Only if you were prat enough to go dancing around, waving it over your head and singing, "I've got an unbeatable wand, come and have a go if you think you're hard enough." As long as you kept your trap shut –'

'Yes, but *could* you keep your trap shut?' said Hermione, looking sceptical. 'You know, the only true thing he said to us was that there have been stories about extra-powerful wands for hundreds of years.'

'There have?' asked Harry.

Hermione looked exasperated: the expression was so endearingly familiar that Harry and Ron grinned at each other.

'The Deathstick, the Wand of Destiny, they crop up under different names through the centuries, usually in the possession of some Dark wizard who's boasting about them. Professor Binns mentioned some of them, but – oh, it's all nonsense. Wands are only as powerful as the wizards who use them. Some wizards just like to boast that theirs are bigger and better than other people's.'

'But how do you know,' said Harry, 'that those wands – the Deathstick and the Wand of Destiny – aren't the same wand, surfacing over the centuries under different names?'

'What, and they're all really the Elder Wand, made by Death?' said Ron.

Harry laughed: the strange idea that had occurred to him was, after all, ridiculous. His wand, he reminded himself, had been of holly, not elder, and it had been made by Ollivander, whatever it had done that night Voldemort had pursued him across the skies. And if it had been unbeatable, how could it have been broken?

第21章 三兄弟的传说

一眼就能看出哪一个礼物最好,你会选择哪一个——"

三人同时说出了答案。赫敏说"隐形衣",罗恩说"老魔杖",哈利说"复活石"。

他们互相望着,一半是惊讶,一半是好笑。

"本来是应该说隐形衣,"罗恩告诉赫敏,"但如果有了老魔杖的话,你就不必隐形了。一根永不会输的魔杖,赫敏,别傻了!"

"我们已经有隐形衣了。"哈利说。

"并且它帮了我们很多忙,大概你没有注意到吧!"赫敏说,"而那根魔杖注定会招来麻烦——"

"只有当你大声炫耀,"罗恩争辩道,"只有当你傻到拿着它跳来跳去,高高挥舞,还唱着'我拿到永不会输的魔杖啦,你要是有本事就来试试呀',才会有麻烦。你只要闷声不响——"

"是啊,可你能闷声不响吗?"赫敏一脸怀疑地问,"我看,他告诉我们的唯一一个真实情况就是,几百年来一直流传着超强魔杖的故事。"

"是吗?"哈利问。

赫敏看起来被激恼了,她的表情那么熟悉可爱,哈利和罗恩相视一笑。

"死亡棒,命运杖,许多个世纪以来,它们以不同的名称出现,通常被一些黑巫师所拥有,对外吹嘘。宾斯教授提到过一些,但——哦,全是谬论。魔杖再强也强不过巫师。一些巫师就是喜欢炫耀自己的魔杖比别人的更长更好。"

"但是你怎么知道,"哈利说,"那些魔杖——死亡棒和命运杖——不会是同一根魔杖,被冠以不同的名字流传了许多世纪呢?"

"什么,难道它们真的就是死神做的那根接骨木魔杖?"罗恩问。

哈利笑了,他脑子中突发的奇想毕竟太荒唐了。他提醒自己,他的魔杖是冬青木的,不是接骨木的,而且是由奥利凡德制作——不管那个晚上伏地魔在天上追来时这根魔杖做了什么。再说,如果它永不会输的话,怎么会断掉了呢?

CHAPTER TWENTY-ONE   The Tale of the Three Brothers

'So why would you take the stone?' Ron asked him.

'Well, if you could bring people back, we could have Sirius ... Mad-Eye ... Dumbledore ... my parents ...'

Neither Ron nor Hermione smiled.

'But according to Beedle the Bard, they wouldn't want to come back, would they?' said Harry, thinking about the tale they had just heard. 'I don't suppose there have been loads of other stories about a stone that can raise the dead, have there?' he asked Hermione.

'No,' she replied sadly. 'I don't think anyone except Mr Lovegood could kid themselves that's possible. Beedle probably took the idea from the Philosopher's Stone; you know, instead of a stone to make you immortal, a stone to reverse death.'

The smell from the kitchen was getting stronger: it was something like burning underpants. Harry wondered whether it would be possible to eat enough of whatever Xenophilius was cooking to spare his feelings.

'What about the Cloak, though?' said Ron slowly. 'Don't you realise, he's right? I've got so used to Harry's Cloak and how good it is, I never stopped to think. I've never heard of one like Harry's. It's infallible. We've never been spotted under it –'

'Of course not – we're invisible when we're under it, Ron!'

'But all the stuff he said about other cloaks – and they're not exactly ten a Knut – you know, is true! It's never occurred to me before, but I've heard stuff about charms wearing off cloaks when they get old, or them being ripped apart by spells so they've got holes in. Harry's was owned by his dad, so it's not exactly new, is it, but it's just ... perfect!'

'Yes, all right, but Ron, the *stone* ...'

As they argued in whispers, Harry moved around the room, only half listening. Reaching the spiral stair, he raised his eyes absently to the next level and was distracted at once. His own face was looking back at him from the ceiling of the room above.

After a moment's bewilderment, he realised that it was not a mirror, but a painting. Curious, he began to climb the stairs.

'Harry, what are you doing? I don't think you should look around when he's not here!'

第21章 三兄弟的传说

"那你又为什么选了石头呢?"罗恩问他。

"嗯,如果能让人复活,就可以让小天狼星……疯眼汉……邓布利多……我父母……"

罗恩和赫敏都没有笑。

"但是据诗翁彼豆说,他们并不想回来,对不对?"哈利说,想着刚刚听过的故事,"我想,关于起死回生的石头的故事不会太多,是吗?"他问赫敏。

"是啊,"赫敏沮丧地答道,"我认为除了洛夫古德先生外,不会有人欺骗自己说这种事真有可能存在。彼豆很可能取材于魔法石的故事,你知道,那是一块让人长生不老的石头,而这是一块起死回生的石头。"

厨房里传来的味道越发浓烈,有点像内裤燃烧的气味。哈利担心,那东西端上来后他能不能吃下几口,弄不好会伤害谢诺菲留斯的感情。

"那么,隐形衣呢?"罗恩慢慢地说,"难道你没有意识到他是对的?我太熟悉哈利的隐形衣了,都没有去想一想它有多好。我从没听说过还有哪件隐形衣像哈利的这样,绝对可靠,穿着它我们从没有被发现过——"

"当然不会——穿上它之后我们是无形的,罗恩!"

"但是他说的关于其他隐形衣的事都是真的,那些也不是一个铜板十件的便宜货,你知道!我以前从没有仔细想过,但是我听说,隐形衣穿久了效力会减弱,或者会被魔咒打穿留下破洞。哈利的隐形衣原先是他爸爸的,所以不算新了,对吧,但它却是……完美无瑕!"

"是的,不错,但是罗恩,复活石……"

他们俩低声争辩着,哈利在屋里走来走去,没有仔细听。走到螺旋形楼梯时,他心不在焉地抬眼朝楼上看了看,突然被吸引住了,他自己的面孔正从上层的天花板上朝他看。

短暂的迷惑之后,他意识到那不是镜子,而是一幅画。出于好奇,他登上了楼梯。

"哈利,你在干什么?他不在,我觉得你不应该四处走动。"

CHAPTER TWENTY-ONE The Tale of the Three Brothers

But Harry had already reached the next level.

Luna had decorated her bedroom ceiling with five beautifully painted faces: Harry, Ron, Hermione, Ginny and Neville. They were not moving as the portraits at Hogwarts moved, but there was a certain magic about them all the same: Harry thought they breathed. What appeared to be fine golden chains wove around the pictures, linking them together, but after examining them for a minute or so, Harry realised that the chains were actually one word, repeated a thousand times in golden ink: *friends ... friends ... friends ...*

Harry felt a great rush of affection for Luna. He looked around the room. There was a large photograph beside the bed, of a young Luna and a woman who looked very like her. They were hugging. Luna looked rather better-groomed in this picture than Harry had ever seen her in life. The picture was dusty. This struck Harry as slightly odd. He stared around.

Something was wrong. The pale blue carpet was also thick with dust. There were no clothes in the wardrobe, whose doors stood ajar. The bed had a cold, unfriendly look, as though it had not been slept in for weeks. A single cobweb stretched over the nearest window, across a blood-red sky.

'What's wrong?' Hermione asked, as Harry descended the staircase, but before he could respond, Xenophilius reached the top of the stairs from the kitchen, now holding a tray laden with bowls.

'Mr Lovegood,' said Harry. 'Where's Luna?'

'Excuse me?'

'Where's Luna?'

Xenophilius halted on the top step.

'I – I've already told you. She is down at Bottom Bridge, fishing for Plimpies.'

'So why have you only laid that tray for four?'

Xenophilius tried to speak, but no sound came out. The only noise was the continued chugging of the printing press, and a slight rattle from the tray as Xenophilius's hands shook.

'I don't think Luna's been here for weeks,' said Harry. 'Her clothes are gone, her bed hasn't been slept in. Where is she? And why do you keep looking out of the window?'

Xenophilius dropped the tray: the bowls bounced and smashed. Harry, Ron and Hermione drew their wands: Xenophilius froze, his hand about to

第21章 三兄弟的传说

但是哈利已经到了楼上。

卢娜在她卧室的天花板上装饰了五张画得很漂亮的脸：哈利、罗恩、赫敏、金妮、纳威。它们不像霍格沃茨里的肖像那样会动，但也有一定的魔力：哈利觉得它们有呼吸。肖像周围有精细的金链子把它们连在一起。但仔细看了一两分钟后，哈利意识到链子实际上都是一个词，用金色墨水写了上千遍：朋友……朋友……朋友……

哈利心头涌上一股对卢娜的好感。他环顾四周，床边有一张很大的照片，是幼年的卢娜和一位与她很像的女士拥抱在一起。照片中的卢娜打扮得比哈利见过的任何一次都漂亮。照片上满是灰尘，这让哈利觉得有点蹊跷，他仔细审视着这个房间。

一定出问题了。淡蓝色的地毯上也落满了灰尘，衣柜门微微开着，柜里没有衣服，床上看起来冷清清的，好像几星期没有人睡过了。一张孤零零的蜘蛛网结在近旁的窗户上，后面是血红色的天空。

"出什么问题了？"当哈利走下楼梯时，赫敏问道。他还没来得及回答，谢诺菲留斯已经从厨房楼梯上来了，手里端着个托盘，里面有几只碗。

"洛夫古德先生，"哈利说，"卢娜在哪儿？"

"什么？"

"卢娜在哪儿？"

谢诺菲留斯停在了最上面一级楼梯上。

"我——我已经告诉你们了。她在下面的谷底桥，正在捕彩球鱼呢。"

"那您托盘里为什么只放四个碗？"

谢诺菲留斯试图说话，但是没有声音出来，只听见印刷机连续的咔啦咔啦声，以及托盘发出的轻微的咯嗒声——他的手在颤抖。

"我看卢娜都好几个星期不在家了，"哈利说，"她的衣服不见了，床也好久没有睡过。她在哪儿？您又为什么一直朝窗外张望？"

托盘从谢诺菲留斯手里滑落，碗弹了几下后摔碎了。哈利、罗恩和赫敏都掏出了魔杖。谢诺菲留斯呆住了，手刚要伸进口袋。就在那

CHAPTER TWENTY-ONE   The Tale of the Three Brothers

enter his pocket. At that moment, the printing press gave a huge bang and numerous *Quibblers* came streaming across the floor from underneath the tablecloth; the press fell silent at last.

Hermione stooped down and picked up one of the magazines, her wand still pointing at Mr Lovegood.

'Harry, look at this.'

He strode over to her as quickly as he could through all the clutter. The front of *The Quibbler* carried his own picture, emblazoned with the words *Undesirable Number One*, and captioned with the reward money.

'*The Quibbler*'s going for a new angle, then?' Harry asked coldly, his mind working very fast. 'Is that what you were doing when you went into the garden, Mr Lovegood? Sending an owl to the Ministry?'

Xenophilius licked his lips.

'They took my Luna,' he whispered. 'Because of what I've been writing. They took my Luna and I don't know where she is, what they've done to her. But they might give her back to me if I – if I –'

'Hand over Harry?' Hermione finished for him.

'No deal,' said Ron flatly. 'Get out of the way, we're leaving.'

Xenophilius looked ghastly, a century old, his lips drawn back into a dreadful leer.

'They will be here at any moment. I must save Luna. I cannot lose Luna. You must not leave.'

He spread his arms in front of the staircase, and Harry had a sudden vision of his mother doing the same thing in front of his cot.

'Don't make us hurt you,' Harry said. 'Get out of the way, Mr Lovegood.'

'HARRY!' Hermione screamed.

Figures on broomsticks were flying past the windows. As the three of them looked away from him, Xenophilius drew his wand. Harry realised their mistake just in time: he launched himself sideways, shoving Ron and Hermione out of harm's way as Xenophilius's Stunning Spell soared across the room and hit the Erumpent Horn.

There was a colossal explosion. The sound of it seemed to blow the room apart: fragments of wood and paper and rubble flew in all directions, along with an impenetrable cloud of thick, white dust. Harry flew through the

第 21 章 三兄弟的传说

一刻，印刷机发出一声巨响，大量的《唱唱反调》杂志从桌布下涌到地板上，印刷机终于没有声息了。

赫敏弯腰捡起一本杂志，魔杖仍指着洛夫古德先生。

"哈利，你瞧这个。"

哈利尽量迅速地从乱糟糟的地上走过去。《唱唱反调》的封面上是他的照片，醒目地写着头号不良分子并注有悬赏金额。

"《唱唱反调》换了一个角度看问题，啊？"哈利冷冷地问，脑子转得飞快，"洛夫古德先生，刚才你去花园，是派猫头鹰给魔法部送信了吧？"

谢诺菲留斯舔了舔嘴唇。

"他们带走了我的卢娜，"他低声说道，"因为我写的东西。他们带走了我的卢娜，我不知道她在哪儿，他们对她做了什么。但他们有可能会把她还给我，只要我——只要我——"

"把哈利交给他们？"赫敏替他说完。

"没门儿。"罗恩断然说道，"闪开，我们要走了。"

谢诺菲留斯看起来面如死灰，苍老得像有一百岁，他牵动嘴角，露出一丝严酷的冷笑。

"他们马上就到，我必须救卢娜，我不能没卢娜，你们不准离开。"

他伸开双臂挡在了楼梯前，此时哈利眼前突然闪现出自己母亲在婴儿床前做的同样动作。

"不要逼我们伤害你，"哈利说，"闪开，洛夫古德先生。"

"**哈利！**"赫敏尖叫道。

骑着飞天扫帚的身影从窗口掠过。趁他们三人朝外看时，谢诺菲留斯拔出了魔杖。哈利及时意识到了错误，他纵身向外一跃，同时猛推了罗恩和赫敏一把，谢诺菲留斯发射的昏迷咒呼啸而过，穿过屋子击中了毒角兽的角。

巨大的爆炸声惊天动地，响得似乎把屋子炸开了花，木头、碎纸和石块四处乱飞，伴随着无法穿透的厚厚的白色尘雾。哈利飞了起来，重重地摔在地板上，胳膊护着脑袋，碎片像下雨一样砸在他身上，什

CHAPTER TWENTY-ONE   The Tale of the Three Brothers

air, then crashed to the floor, unable to see as debris rained upon him, his arms over his head. He heard Hermione's scream, Ron's yell and a series of sickening metallic thuds, which told him that Xenophilius had been blasted off his feet and fallen backwards down the spiral stairs.

Half buried in rubble, Harry tried to raise himself: he could barely breathe or see for dust. Half of the ceiling had fallen in and the end of Luna's bed was hanging through the hole. The bust of Rowena Ravenclaw lay beside him with half its face missing, fragments of torn parchment were floating through the air and most of the printing press lay on its side, blocking the top of the staircase to the kitchen. Then another white shape moved close by and Hermione, coated in dust like a second statue, pressed her finger to her lips.

The door downstairs crashed open.

'Didn't I tell you there was no need to hurry, Travers?' said a rough voice. 'Didn't I tell you this nutter was just raving as usual?'

There was a bang and a scream of pain from Xenophilius.

'No ... no ... upstairs ... Potter!'

'I told you last week, Lovegood, we weren't coming back for anything less than some solid information! Remember last week? When you wanted to swap your daughter for that stupid bleeding headdress? And the week before –' another bang, another squeal '– when you thought we'd give her back if you offered us proof there are Crumple –' *bang* '– Headed –' *bang* '– Snorkacks?'

'No – no – I beg you!' sobbed Xenophilius. 'It really is Potter! Really!'

'And now it turns out you only called us here to try and blow us up!' roared the Death Eater, and there was a volley of bangs interspersed with squeals of agony from Xenophilius.

'The place looks like it's about to fall in, Selwyn,' said a cool second voice, echoing up the mangled staircase. 'The stairs are completely blocked. Could try clearing it? Might bring the place down.'

'You lying piece of filth,' shouted the wizard named Selwyn. 'You've never seen Potter in your life, have you? Thought you'd lure us here to kill us, did you? And you think you'll get your girl back like this?'

'I swear ... I swear ... Potter's upstairs!'

'*Homenum revelio*,' said the voice at the foot of the stairs.

第21章 三兄弟的传说

么都看不见。他听到了赫敏的尖叫，罗恩的高喊，还有一连串令人发晕的金属撞击声，他知道谢诺菲留斯也被炸飞了，顺着螺旋形楼梯滚了下去。

哈利半个身子被埋在碎石中，他试图站起来。由于灰尘，他几乎不能呼吸或睁眼。半个天花板掉了下来，卢娜的床脚悬在豁口处。拉文克劳的半身石像躺在他身边，少了半张脸，空气里飘浮着羊皮纸碎片，印刷机大部分侧倒过来，堵住了通往厨房的楼梯口。旁边另一个白色的身影动了起来，是赫敏，满身是灰，仿佛一座雕像，一根手指放在嘴唇上。

楼底下的门被撞开了。

"我没告诉过你不用着急吗，特拉弗斯？"一个粗暴的声音说，"我没告诉过你这个疯子又在胡说吗？"

砰的一声，谢诺菲留斯痛苦地尖叫起来。

"不……不……在楼上……波特！"

"上星期我告诉过你，洛夫古德，如果没有可靠的消息，我们是不会来的！还记得上星期的事吗？你想用那个愚蠢的破头饰换回你的女儿？还有上上星期——"砰，又一声惨叫，"——你以为如果你能证明有弯角——"砰，"——鼾兽——"砰，"——我们就会把她还给你吗？"

"不——不——我求求你！"谢诺菲留斯哭诉着，"真的是波特！真的！"

"现在证明了你叫我们来就是想把我们炸死！"食死徒咆哮着，一连串的砰砰声，夹杂着谢诺菲留斯痛苦的尖叫。

"这地方看上去要塌了，塞尔温，"一个冷静的声音从炸坏的楼梯传上来，"楼梯都堵死了，能清通吗？可能会把房子搞塌的。"

"你这撒谎的狗东西，"那个名叫塞尔温的巫师大喊道，"你这辈子从没见过波特，是不是？你想把我们骗过来杀死，是吗？你以为这样会弄回你的女儿？"

"我发誓……我发誓……波特在楼上！"

"人形显身。"楼梯底下的声音说道。

CHAPTER TWENTY-ONE The Tale of the Three Brothers

Harry heard Hermione gasp, and he had the odd sensation that something was swooping low over him, immersing his body in its shadow.

'There's someone up there all right, Selwyn,' said the second man sharply.

'It's Potter, I tell you, it's Potter!' sobbed Xenophilius. 'Please ... please ... give me Luna, just let me have Luna ...'

'You can have your little girl, Lovegood,' said Selwyn, 'if you get up those stairs and bring me down Harry Potter. But if this is a plot, if it's a trick, if you've got an accomplice waiting up there to ambush us, we'll see if we can spare a bit of your daughter for you to bury.'

Xenophilius gave a wail of fear and despair. There were scurryings and scrapings: Xenophilius was trying to get through the debris on the stairs.

'Come on,' Harry whispered, 'we've got to get out of here.'

He started to dig himself out under cover of all the noise Xenophilius was making on the staircase. Ron was buried deepest: Harry and Hermione climbed, as quietly as they could, over all the wreckage to where he lay, trying to prise a heavy chest of drawers off his legs. While Xenophilius's banging and scraping drew nearer and nearer, Hermione managed to free Ron with the use of a Hover Charm.

'All right,' breathed Hermione, as the broken printing press blocking the top of the stairs began to tremble; Xenophilius was feet away from them. She was still white with dust. 'Do you trust me, Harry?'

Harry nodded.

'OK then,' Hermione whispered, 'give me the Invisibility Cloak. Ron, you're going to put it on.'

'Me? But Harry –'

'*Please Ron!* Harry, hold on tight to my hand, Ron, grab my shoulder.'

Harry held out his left hand. Ron vanished beneath the Cloak. The printing press blocking the stairs was vibrating: Xenophilius was trying to shift it using a Hover Charm. Harry did not know what Hermione was waiting for.

'Hold tight,' she whispered. 'Hold tight ... any second ...'

Xenophilius's paper-white face appeared over the top of the sideboard.

'*Obliviate!*' cried Hermione, pointing her wand first into his face, then at the floor beneath them: '*Deprimo!*'

第 21 章　三兄弟的传说

哈利听到赫敏惊叫一声，他有一种奇怪的感觉，有什么东西低低地朝他飞来，把他的身体笼罩在它的影子里。

"上面确实有人，塞尔温。"第二个人急速地说道。

"是波特，我说了，是波特！"谢诺菲留斯呜咽道，"请……请……把卢娜还给我，给我卢娜……"

"你可以要回你的女儿，洛夫古德，"塞尔温说，"如果你到楼上把哈利·波特给带下来的话。但如果这是一个阴谋，一个诡计，如果楼上埋伏着你的帮凶，我们会考虑是否给你一点你女儿的尸骨让你埋葬。"

谢诺菲留斯发出一声充满恐惧和绝望的哀号，然后是急促的脚步声和刨挖声：谢诺菲留斯正在试图穿过楼梯上的废墟。

"快点儿，"哈利悄声道，"我们必须离开这里。"

以谢诺菲留斯在楼梯上弄出的声响为掩护，哈利开始把自己刨出来。罗恩被埋得最深，哈利和赫敏尽可能轻地从废墟中爬到他身边，试图撬开压在他腿上的沉重的五斗橱。谢诺菲留斯的撞击声和刨挖声越来越近，赫敏用悬停咒帮助罗恩脱出身来。

"好了。"赫敏压着嗓子说，此时遮住楼梯口的破印刷机开始摇动，谢诺菲留斯离他们只有几步之遥了。赫敏仍然满身白灰。"你相信我吗，哈利？"

哈利点点头。

"那好，"赫敏小声道，"给我隐形衣。罗恩，你穿上它。"

"我？那哈利——"

"拜托，罗恩！哈利，抓紧我的手，罗恩，抓住我的肩膀。"

哈利用左手抓住了她。罗恩消失在隐形衣下面。堵住楼梯口的印刷机在振动，谢诺菲留斯正试图用悬停咒搬开它。哈利不知道赫敏还在等什么。

"抓紧，"她低语道，"抓紧……随时……"

谢诺菲留斯那纸一般煞白的脸从餐具柜顶上露了出来。

"一忘皆空！"赫敏用魔杖指着他的脸大声喊道，然后指向脚下的地板，"房塌地陷！"

CHAPTER TWENTY-ONE

The Tale of the Three Brothers

She had blasted a hole in the sitting-room floor. They fell like boulders, Harry still holding on to her hand for dear life, there was a scream from below and he glimpsed two men trying to get out of the way as vast quantities of rubble and broken furniture rained all around them from the shattered ceiling. Hermione twisted in mid-air and the thundering of the collapsing house rang in Harry's ears as she dragged him once more into darkness.

第21章 三兄弟的传说

她在起居室的地板上炸开一个洞,他们像大石头一样跌落下去。哈利仍然拼命紧紧抓住她的手。底下一声尖叫,他瞥见两个大汉在慌忙躲闪,大量碎石和破家具从粉碎的天花板上纷纷坠落。赫敏在半空中旋转起来,房屋倒塌的声音回响在哈利耳际,赫敏拉着他,再次消失在黑暗里。

CHAPTER TWENTY-TWO

The Deathly Hallows

Harry fell, panting, on to grass and scrambled up at once. They seemed to have landed in the corner of a field at dusk; Hermione was already running in a circle around them, waving her wand.

'*Protego totalum ... Salvio hexia ...*'

'That treacherous old bleeder!' Ron panted, emerging from beneath the Invisibility Cloak and throwing it to Harry. 'Hermione, you're a genius, a total genius, I can't believe we got out of that!'

'*Cave inimicum* ... didn't I *say* it was an Erumpent horn? Didn't I tell him? And now his house has been blown apart!'

'Serves him right,' said Ron, examining his torn jeans and the cuts to his legs. 'What d'you reckon they'll do to him?'

'Oh, I hope they don't kill him!' groaned Hermione. 'That's why I wanted the Death Eaters to get a glimpse of Harry before we left, so they knew Xenophilius hadn't been lying!'

'Why hide me, though?' asked Ron.

'You're supposed to be in bed with spattergroit, Ron! They've kidnapped Luna because her father supported Harry! What would happen to your family if they knew you're with him?'

'But what about *your* mum and dad?'

'They're in Australia,' said Hermione. 'They should be all right. They don't know anything.'

'You're a genius,' Ron repeated, looking awed.

'Yeah, you are, Hermione,' agreed Harry fervently, 'I don't know what we'd do without you.'

第 22 章

死亡圣器

哈利喘着粗气跌坐在草地上,又马上爬了起来。时已黄昏,他们似乎落在一块田地的角落,赫敏已经挥动魔杖在他们周围绕圈子奔跑。

"统统加护……平安镇守……"

"那个背信弃义的老家伙!"罗恩喘息着,从隐形衣下钻出来,把它扔给了哈利,"赫敏,你是天才,绝对的天才,真不敢相信我们跑出来了!"

"降敌陷阱……我没有说那是毒角兽的角吗,我没有告诉他吗?现在他的家被炸毁了。"

"活该。"罗恩说,一边检查着撕坏的牛仔裤和腿上的伤口,"你猜他们会怎么处置他?"

"哦,我希望他们不要杀了他!"赫敏呻吟道,"所以我才让食死徒在我们离开时瞥见哈利一眼,这样他们就知道谢诺菲留斯没有撒谎。"

"但是为什么把我藏起来呢?"罗恩问。

"你应该是得了散花痘卧床不起的,罗恩!他们绑架卢娜是因为她爸爸支持哈利!如果他们知道你和哈利在一起,又会怎样对待你的家人呢?"

"那你的爸爸妈妈呢?"

"他们在澳大利亚,"赫敏说,"应该没事。他们什么也不知道。"

"你太有才了。"罗恩再次赞叹,满脸敬畏。

"对,没错,赫敏,"哈利热忱地赞同道,"如果没有你,我真不知道我们会怎么办。"

CHAPTER TWENTY-TWO   The Deathly Hallows

She beamed, but became solemn at once.

'What about Luna?'

'Well, if they're telling the truth and she's still alive –' began Ron.

'Don't say that, don't say it!' squealed Hermione. 'She must be alive, she must!'

'Then she'll be in Azkaban, I expect,' said Ron. 'Whether she survives the place, though ... loads don't ...'

'She will,' said Harry. He could not bear to contemplate the alternative. 'She's tough, Luna, much tougher than you'd think. She's probably teaching all the inmates about Wrackspurts and Nargles.'

'I hope you're right,' said Hermione. She passed a hand over her eyes. 'I'd feel so sorry for Xenophilius if –'

'– if he hadn't just tried to sell us to the Death Eaters, yeah,' said Ron.

They put up the tent and retreated inside it, where Ron made them tea. After their narrow escape, the chilly, musty old place felt like home, safe, familiar and friendly.

'Oh, why did we go there?' groaned Hermione after a few minutes' silence. 'Harry, you were right, it was Godric's Hollow all over again, a complete waste of time! The Deathly Hallows ... such rubbish ... although actually,' a sudden thought seemed to have struck her, 'he might have made it all up, mightn't he? He probably doesn't believe in the Deathly Hallows at all, he just wanted to keep us talking until the Death Eaters arrived!'

'I don't think so,' said Ron. 'It's a damn' sight harder making stuff up when you're under stress than you'd think. I found that out when the Snatchers caught me. It was much easier pretending to be Stan, because I knew a bit about him, than inventing a whole new person. Old Lovegood was under loads of pressure, trying to make sure we stayed put. I reckon he told us the truth, or what he thinks is the truth, just to keep us talking.'

'Well, I don't suppose it matters,' sighed Hermione. 'Even if he was being honest, I never heard such a lot of nonsense in all my life.'

'Hang on, though,' said Ron. 'The Chamber of Secrets was supposed to be a myth, wasn't it?'

'But the Deathly Hallows *can't* exist, Ron!'

第22章 死亡圣器

赫敏开颜一笑，但马上又严肃起来。

"卢娜会怎样呢？"

"嗯，如果他们说的是实话，那么她还活着——"罗恩说。

"别那么说，别说了！"赫敏尖叫道，"她一定还活着，一定！"

"那么她会进阿兹卡班的，我猜。"罗恩说，"她是不是能在那里活下来呢……许多人都不能……"

"她会活下来的。"哈利说，他无法忍受去设想别的可能，"卢娜，她很坚强，比你想象的坚强得多。她可能正在给犯人们讲骚扰虻和蛹钩呢。"

"我希望你是对的。"赫敏说着，用手擦了一下眼睛，"我本来会为谢诺菲留斯感到很伤心的，如果——"

"——如果他刚才没有试图把我们出卖给食死徒的话，是啊。"罗恩说。

他们搭起帐篷，钻了进去。罗恩给大家泡了茶。惊险逃生后，这个寒冷的、发霉的老地方感觉像家一样：安全、熟悉和温馨。

"哦，我们为什么去那儿？"几分钟的沉默之后，赫敏叹息道，"哈利，还是你说得对，又是一个戈德里克山谷，完全是浪费时间！死亡圣器……真是胡扯……不过，"她似乎突然冒出了新的想法，"不过这一切可能是他捏造的，不是吗？他很可能根本不相信死亡圣器，只是为了等食死徒到来，拖着我们不停地说话！"

"我不这么认为。"罗恩说，"在那种紧急关头，现编一套故事要比你想象的困难得多。我是在被搜捕队抓住之后体会到这点的。跟捏造一个新人比起来，冒充斯坦就容易得多，因为我对他有点了解。老洛夫古德当时的压力非常大，要想办法把我们拖住。为了跟我们不停地交谈，我想他对我们讲了真话，或者说他认为那是真的。"

"嗯，我认为这都无关紧要，"赫敏叹了口气，"就算他当时是诚实的，我一生也从来没听过这么多的无稽之谈。"

"等一等，"罗恩说，"密室就曾被当成一个传说，不是吗？"

"但是死亡圣器不可能存在，罗恩！"

CHAPTER TWENTY-TWO   The Deathly Hallows

'You keep saying that, but one of them can,' said Ron. 'Harry's Invisibility Cloak —'

'"The Tale of the Three Brothers" is a story,' said Hermione firmly. 'A story about how humans are frightened of death. If surviving was as simple as hiding under the Invisibility Cloak, we'd have everything we need already!'

'I don't know. We could do with an unbeatable wand,' said Harry, turning the blackthorn wand he so disliked over in his fingers.

'There's no such thing, Harry!'

'You said there have been loads of wands — the Deathstick and whatever they were called —'

'All right, even if you want to kid yourself the Elder Wand's real, what about the Resurrection Stone?' Her fingers sketched quotation marks around the name, and her tone dripped sarcasm. 'No magic can raise the dead, and that's that!'

'When my wand connected with You-Know-Who's, it made my mum and dad appear ... and Cedric ...'

'But they weren't really back from the dead, were they?' said Hermione. 'Those kinds of — of pale imitations aren't the same as truly bringing someone back to life.'

'But she, the girl in the tale, didn't really come back, did she? The story says that once people are dead, they belong with the dead. But the second brother still got to see her and talk to her, didn't he? He even lived with her for a while ...'

He saw concern and something less easily definable in Hermione's expression. Then, as she glanced at Ron, Harry realised that it was fear: he had scared her with his talk of living with dead people.

'So that Peverell bloke who's buried in Godric's Hollow,' he said hastily, trying to sound robustly sane, 'you don't know anything about him, then?'

'No,' she replied, looking relieved at the change of subject. 'I looked him up after I saw the mark on his grave; if he'd been anyone famous or done anything important, I'm sure he'd be in one of our books. The only place I've managed to find the name "Peverell" is *Nature's Nobility: A Wizarding Genealogy*. I borrowed it from Kreacher,' she explained, as Ron raised his eyebrows. 'It lists the pure-blood families that are now extinct in the male line. Apparently the Peverells were one of the earliest families to vanish.'

第22章 死亡圣器

"你一直那么说，但是其中一个是可能存在的，"罗恩说，"哈利的隐形衣——"

"三兄弟的传说只是个故事，"赫敏坚定地说，"一个关于人类如何害怕死亡的故事。如果活着仅仅是藏在隐形衣里面那么简单，那我们就已经拥有需要的一切了！"

"这很难说。有一根永不会输的魔杖也不错。"哈利说，一边在手指上转着他不喜欢的那根黑刺李木魔杖。

"没有那样的东西，哈利！"

"你说过曾经有过好多魔杖——死亡棒和别的什么——"

"好了，即使你想骗自己相信老魔杖是真的，那么复活石呢？"赫敏用手指在这个词两边打着引号，声音里透着挖苦的味道，"没有一种魔法可以起死回生，就是这样！"

"当我的魔杖跟神秘人的连接上，我的爸爸妈妈就会出现……还有塞德里克……"

"但是他们并没有真的从阴间回来呀，是不是？"赫敏说，"这些——苍白的代用品并不是真正让人复活。"

"但是她，故事里的那个女孩，也没有真的回来，不是吗？故事说人一旦去世，就属于阴间了。但是，那个老二仍然看到了女孩，和她说话，不是吗？甚至还和她一起生活了一段时间……"

他看见赫敏有点担忧，还有一点不易描述的表情。后来赫敏瞥了一眼罗恩，哈利才意识到那是恐惧：他谈论与死去的人一同生活的话吓着了她。

"埋在戈德里克山谷的那个佩弗利尔，"哈利急忙说，努力使自己听上去头脑清醒，"你对他一点都不了解吗？"

"是啊，"赫敏答道，似乎因转换话题而松了口气，"在他的墓上看到那个标志后，我查过他。如果他有名气或者做过什么重要的事情，一定会出现在我们的某一本书里。但唯一提到过'佩弗利尔'的书是《生而高贵：巫师家谱》，我从克利切那里借的。"看到罗恩扬起了眉毛，她解释道，"那本书里列的都是父系血统已经绝种的纯血统家族。很明显，佩弗利尔家族是最早消失的家族之一。"

CHAPTER TWENTY-TWO The Deathly Hallows

'"Extinct in the male line"?' repeated Ron.

'It means the name's died out,' said Hermione, 'centuries ago, in the case of the Peverells. They could still have descendants, though, they'd just be called something different.'

And then it came to Harry in one shining piece, the memory that had stirred at the sound of the name Peverell: a filthy old man brandishing an ugly ring in the face of a Ministry official, and he cried aloud, 'Marvolo Gaunt!'

'Sorry?' said Ron and Hermione together.

'*Marvolo Gaunt!* You-Know-Who's grandfather! In the Pensieve! With Dumbledore! Marvolo Gaunt said he was descended from the Peverells!'

Ron and Hermione looked bewildered.

'The ring, the ring that became the Horcrux, Marvolo Gaunt said it had the Peverell coat of arms on it! I saw him waving it in the bloke from the Ministry's face, he nearly shoved it up his nose!'

'The Peverell coat of arms?' said Hermione sharply. 'Could you see what it looked like?'

'Not really,' said Harry, trying to remember. 'There was nothing fancy on there, as far as I could see; maybe a few scratches. I only ever saw it really close up after it had been cracked open.'

Harry saw Hermione's comprehension in the sudden widening of her eyes. Ron was looking from one to the other, astonished.

'Blimey ... you reckon it was this sign again? The sign of the Hallows?'

'Why not?' said Harry excitedly. 'Marvolo Gaunt was an ignorant old git who lived like a pig, all he cared about was his ancestry. If that ring had been passed down through the centuries, he might not have known what it really was. There were no books in that house, and trust me, he wasn't the type to read fairy tales to his kids. He'd have loved to think the scratches on the stone were a coat of arms, because as far as he was concerned, having pure blood made you practically royal.'

'Yes ... and that's all very interesting,' said Hermione cautiously, 'but Harry, if you're thinking what I think you're think—'

'Well, why not? *Why not?*' said Harry, abandoning caution. 'It was a stone, wasn't it?' He looked at Ron for support. 'What if it was the Resurrection Stone?'

Ron's mouth fell open. 'Blimey – but would it still work if Dumbledore

"'父系血统已经绝种'?"罗恩重复了一遍。

"就是说那个姓氏没有了,"赫敏说,"佩弗利尔那个姓氏消失有几个世纪了。他们可能仍有后代存在,只不过不再拥有那个姓氏。"

这时,哈利脑海里灵光一闪,被"佩弗利尔"这个名字触动的记忆跳了出来:一个肮脏的老头子,在魔法部官员面前挥舞着一枚丑陋的戒指。哈利大声叫道:"马沃罗·冈特!"

"什么?"罗恩和赫敏一起问。

"马沃罗·冈特!神秘人的外祖父!在冥想盆里!和邓布利多一起!马沃罗·冈特说过他是佩弗利尔的后代!"

罗恩和赫敏看起来都很迷惑。

"戒指,变为魂器的戒指,马沃罗·冈特说上面有佩弗利尔的饰章。我看到他在魔法部官员的面前挥舞着它,差点要碰到那人的鼻梁了!"

"佩弗利尔的饰章?"赫敏忙问,"你看见它是什么样子了吗?"

"其实没有,"哈利说,努力回忆着,"我只看到,上面没有什么花哨的东西,可能有一些刮痕。只是在它被劈开以后,我才靠近看过。"

从赫敏突然瞪大的双眼,哈利看出她顿悟了。罗恩来回看着他们两个,满脸惊讶。

"我的天哪……你认为又是这个标志?圣器的标志?"

"为什么不会呢?"哈利激动地说,"马沃罗·冈特是个愚昧的老饭桶,活得像猪一样,唯一关心的就是他的血统。如果那枚戒指已经传了好几个世纪,他很可能不知道那到底是什么。那个家里没有书,相信我,他不是那种读童话给自己孩子听的人。他肯定很乐意把那石头上的刮痕说成是饰章,因为对他来说,拥有纯血统就意味着身份高贵。"

"对……那是很有趣,"赫敏谨慎地说道,"但是哈利,如果你真的如我所想在转那种念头——"

"为什么不能?为什么不能?"哈利顾不上谨慎了,"它也是块石头,不是吗?"他看着罗恩,希望得到支持,"如果它就是复活石呢?"

罗恩张大了嘴巴:"我的天哪——但是被邓布利多打坏了,还会有

CHAPTER TWENTY-TWO   The Deathly Hallows

broke –'

'*Work*? *Work*? Ron, it never worked! *There's no such thing as a Resurrection Stone!*' Hermione had leapt to her feet, looking exasperated and angry. 'Harry, you're trying to fit everything into the Hallows story –'

'*Fit everything in?*' he repeated. 'Hermione, it fits of its own accord! I know the sign of the Deathly Hallows was on that stone! Gaunt said he was descended from the Peverells!'

'A minute ago you told us you never saw the mark on the stone properly!'

'Where d'you reckon the ring is now?' Ron asked Harry. 'What did Dumbledore do with it after he broke it open?'

But Harry's imagination was racing ahead, far beyond Ron and Hermione's ...

Three objects, or Hallows, which, if united, will make the possessor master of Death ... master ... conqueror ... vanquisher ... the last enemy that shall be destroyed is death ...

And he saw himself, possessor of the Hallows, facing Voldemort, whose Horcruxes were no match ... *neither can live while the other survives* ... was this the answer? Hallows versus Horcruxes? Was there a way, after all, to ensure that he was the one who triumphed? If he were the master of the Deathly Hallows, would he be safe?

'Harry?'

But he scarcely heard Hermione: he had pulled out his Invisibility Cloak and was running it through his fingers, the cloth supple as water, light as air. He had never seen anything to equal it in his nearly seven years in the wizarding world. The Cloak was exactly what Xenophilius had described: *a cloak that really and truly renders the wearer completely invisible, and endures eternally, giving constant and impenetrable concealment, no matter what spells are cast at it ...*

And then, with a gasp, he remembered –

'Dumbledore had my Cloak, the night my parents died!'

His voice shook and he could feel the colour in his face, but he did not care. 'My mum told Sirius Dumbledore borrowed the Cloak! This is why! He wanted to examine it, because he thought it was the third Hallow! Ignotus Peverell is buried in Godric's Hollow ...' Harry was walking blindly around the tent, feeling as though great new vistas of truth were opening all around him. 'He's my ancestor! I'm descended from the third brother! It all makes sense!'

第22章 死亡圣器

效吗——?"

"有效?有效?罗恩,它从来就不曾有效过!根本就没有复活石这种东西!"赫敏蹦了起来,又急又怒,"哈利,你是在把什么都往死亡圣器的故事里套——"

"往里套?"哈利争辩道,"赫敏,那是自然吻合!我知道那块石头上有死亡圣器的标志!冈特说他是佩弗利尔的后代!"

"一分钟前,你还说你从没真正看清那石头上的标志!"

"你猜那枚戒指这会儿在哪儿?"罗恩问哈利,"邓布利多劈开它后,又把它怎么处置了?"

但是哈利的想象已经飞到前面,远远超过了罗恩和赫敏的思路……

三件东西,或圣器,合在一起,就会使拥有者成为死神的主人……主人……征服者……胜利者……最后一个要消灭的敌人是死亡……

然后他看到自己,死亡圣器的拥有者,面对着伏地魔,他的魂器根本不是对手……两个人不能都活着,只有一个生存下来……这就是答案吗?圣器对魂器?难道有办法保证他最终获胜?如果他是死亡圣器的拥有者,就会安全吗?

"哈利?"

他几乎没有听见赫敏的叫声:他掏出隐形衣,让它从指缝间流过,织物像水一样软,像空气一样轻。哈利在魔法世界生活了快七年,还从没见过与它匹敌的东西。这隐形衣完全符合谢诺菲留斯的描述:一件让人真真正正、完完全全隐身的斗篷,永久有效,持续隐形,无论用什么咒语都不可破解……

这时,他猛吸一口气,记起来了——

"我父母死的那天晚上,隐形衣在邓布利多那里!"

他声音发抖,能感觉到自己脸色发红,但他顾不得了。"我妈妈告诉小天狼星,邓布利多借走了隐形衣!这就是原因!他想研究它,怀疑它就是第三件圣器!伊格诺图斯·佩弗利尔埋在戈德里克山谷……"哈利在帐篷里忘乎所以地走着,感觉壮丽的、全新的真相画卷正在四周展开,"他是我的祖先!我是第三个兄弟的后代!全讲通了!"

CHAPTER TWENTY-TWO   The Deathly Hallows

He felt armed in certainty, in his belief in the Hallows, as if the mere idea of possessing them was giving him protection, and he felt joyous as he turned back to the other two.

'Harry,' said Hermione again, but he was busy undoing the pouch around his neck, his fingers shaking hard.

'Read it,' he told her, pushing his mother's letter into her hand. 'Read it! Dumbledore had the Cloak, Hermione! Why else would he want it? He didn't need a Cloak, he could perform a Disillusionment Charm so powerful that he made himself completely invisible without one!'

Something fell to the floor and rolled, glittering, under a chair: he had dislodged the Snitch when he pulled out the letter. He stooped to pick it up, and then the newly tapped spring of fabulous discoveries threw him another gift, and shock and wonder erupted inside him so that he shouted out.

'IT'S IN HERE! He left me the ring – it's in the Snitch!'

'You – you reckon?'

He could not understand why Ron looked taken aback. It was so obvious, so clear to Harry: everything fitted, everything ... his Cloak was the third Hallow, and when he discovered how to open the Snitch he would have the second, and then all he needed to do was find the first Hallow, the Elder Wand, and then –

But it was as though a curtain fell on a lit stage: all his excitement, all his hope and happiness were extinguished at a stroke, and he stood alone in the darkness, and the glorious spell was broken.

'That's what he's after.'

The change in his voice made Ron and Hermione look even more scared.

'You-Know-Who's after the Elder Wand.'

He turned his back on their strained, incredulous faces. He knew it was the truth. It all made sense. Voldemort was not seeking a new wand; he was seeking an old wand, a very old wand indeed. Harry walked to the entrance of the tent, forgetting about Ron and Hermione as he looked out into the night, thinking ...

Voldemort had been raised in a Muggle orphanage. Nobody could have told him *The Tales of Beedle the Bard* when he was a child, any more than Harry had heard them. Hardly any wizards believed in the Deathly Hallows. Was it likely that Voldemort knew about them?

第22章 死亡圣器

他胸中充满信心，对死亡圣器深信不疑，好像只要在脑子里拥有它们就能给他保护。他转过身对着两个同伴，满心喜悦。

"哈利。"赫敏又叫他，但他正忙着打开脖子上的皮袋，手指抖得厉害。

"读一读，"哈利把他母亲的信塞到赫敏手里，"读一读！邓布利多拿了隐形衣，赫敏！还能有什么别的原因呢？他不需要隐形衣，他可以用强大的幻身咒使自己完全隐形的呀！"

有个东西掉在地板上，闪闪发光地滚到了椅子下面：他掏信时带出了金色飞贼。哈利弯腰捡起了它，这时，新打开的神奇的发现之泉又抛给了他一件礼物，他心里又惊又喜，大声喊道：

"**在这儿**！他把戒指留给我了——在金色飞贼里！"

"你——你这么想？"

他不能理解罗恩为什么看起来大吃一惊。哈利觉得这个推测如此顺理成章，如此清晰：一切都相吻合，一切……他的隐形衣是第三件死亡圣器，等到设法打开了金色飞贼，他就会有第二件，然后要做的就是找到第一件圣器，老魔杖，然后——

但是，就像闪亮的舞台突然落下了帷幕一样，所有的激动、所有的希望和幸福在瞬间泯灭，他独自站在黑暗中，辉煌的咒语被打破了。

"那也是他寻找的东西。"

他声音的改变让罗恩和赫敏越发恐惧。

"神秘人在寻找老魔杖。"

他转过身，背朝着他们俩紧张、惊疑的面孔。他知道这就是真相，全都讲通了。伏地魔不是在找一根新魔杖，而是在找一根老魔杖，一根很老很老的魔杖。哈利走到帐篷门口，望着外面的夜幕，完全忘记了罗恩和赫敏，他思考着……

伏地魔是在麻瓜孤儿院长大的，小时候没人会给他讲《诗翁彼豆故事集》，就像哈利一样。几乎没有巫师相信死亡圣器的存在，伏地魔会有可能知道吗？

CHAPTER TWENTY-TWO   The Deathly Hallows

Harry gazed into the darkness ... if Voldemort had known about the Deathly Hallows, surely he would have sought them, done anything to possess them: three objects that made the possessor master of Death? If he had known about the Deathly Hallows, he might not have needed Horcruxes in the first place. Didn't the simple fact that he had taken a Hallow, and turned it into a Horcrux, demonstrate that he did not know this last great wizarding secret?

Which meant that Voldemort sought the Elder Wand without realising its full power, without understanding that it was one of three ... for the wand was the Hallow that could not be hidden, whose existence was best known ... *the bloody trail of the Elder Wand is splattered across the pages of wizarding history ...*

Harry watched the cloudy sky, curves of smoke-grey and silver sliding over the face of the white moon. He felt light-headed with amazement at his discoveries.

He turned back into the tent. It was a shock to see Ron and Hermione standing exactly where he had left them, Hermione still holding Lily's letter, Ron at her side looking slightly anxious. Didn't they realise how far they had travelled in the last few minutes?

'This is it,' Harry said, trying to bring them inside the glow of his own astonished certainty. 'This explains everything. The Deathly Hallows are real, and I've got one – maybe two –'

He held up the Snitch.

'– and You-Know-Who's chasing the third, but he doesn't realise ... he just thinks it's a powerful wand –'

'Harry,' said Hermione, moving across to him and handing him back Lily's letter, 'I'm sorry, but I think you've got this wrong, all wrong.'

'But don't you see? It all fits –'

'No, it doesn't,' she said. 'It *doesn't*, Harry, you're just getting carried away. Please,' she said, as he started to speak, 'please just answer me this. If the Deathly Hallows really existed, and Dumbledore knew about them, knew that the person who possessed all three of them would be master of Death – Harry, why wouldn't he have told you? Why?'

He had his answer ready.

'But you said it, Hermione! You've got to find out about them for yourself! It's a Quest!'

第22章 死亡圣器

哈利凝视着黑暗……如果伏地魔听说过死亡圣器，他肯定会寻找它们，不顾一切地去占有它们：三件能让拥有者成为死神的主人的东西？如果他听说过死亡圣器，也许一开始他就不需要魂器了。他得到过一件死亡圣器，却把它变成了魂器，这不正说明他并不知道这最伟大的魔法秘密吗？

也就是说，伏地魔寻找老魔杖，并不知道它的全部功能，并不了解它是三件宝物之一……因为魔杖是最不可能被隐藏的一件圣器，它的存在最广为人知……老魔杖的血腥踪迹溅满了整部魔法史……

哈利看着多云的天空，烟灰色和银色的云边滑过月亮的白色面庞。他为自己的发现而惊愕，感到头有点晕。

转身回到帐篷里，令他震惊的是，两个同伴还站在原地，赫敏仍然拿着莉莉的信，罗恩在她旁边，看起来有点担忧。难道他们没有意识到刚才这几分钟里有了多大的进展吗？

"就是这样，"哈利说，努力让同伴跟他一起相信这个惊人而确凿的事实，"这解释了一切，死亡圣器真的存在，我已经有了一件——或许两件——"

他举起金色飞贼。

"——神秘人在追寻第三件，但是他没有意识到……他仅仅认为那是一根强大的魔杖——"

"哈利，"赫敏走了过来，把莉莉的信还给他，"对不起，但是我想你一定是搞错了，全搞错了。"

"但是你看不见吗？一切都吻合——"

"不，不吻合，"她说，"不吻合，哈利，你是激动过了头。请你，"她打断了正要说话的哈利，"请你回答我这个问题。如果死亡圣器真的存在，并且邓布利多知道这些，知道拥有三件圣器就可以成为死神的主人——哈利，他为什么没有告诉你？为什么？"

他已经准备好了答案。

"你说的呀，赫敏！这需要你自己去弄清！这是一种探求！"

CHAPTER TWENTY-TWO   The Deathly Hallows

'But I only said that to try and persuade you to come to the Lovegoods'!' cried Hermione in exasperation. 'I didn't really believe it!'

Harry took no notice.

'Dumbledore usually let me find out stuff for myself. He let me try my strength, take risks. This feels like the kind of thing he'd do.'

'Harry, this isn't a game, this isn't practice! This is the real thing, and Dumbledore left you very clear instructions: find and destroy the Horcruxes! That symbol doesn't mean anything, forget the Deathly Hallows, we can't afford to get sidetracked –'

Harry was barely listening to her. He was turning the Snitch over and over in his hands, half expecting it to break open, to reveal the Resurrection Stone, to prove to Hermione that he was right, that the Deathly Hallows were real.

She appealed to Ron.

'You don't believe in this, do you?'

Harry looked up. Ron hesitated.

'I dunno ... I mean ... bits of it sort of fit together,' said Ron awkwardly. 'But when you look at the whole thing ...' He took a deep breath. 'I think we're supposed to get rid of Horcruxes, Harry. That's what Dumbledore told us to do. Maybe ... maybe we should forget about this Hallows business.'

'Thank you, Ron,' said Hermione. 'I'll take first watch.'

And she strode past Harry and sat down in the tent entrance, turning the action into a fierce full stop.

But Harry hardly slept that night. The idea of the Deathly Hallows had taken possession of him, and he could not rest while agitating thoughts whirled through his mind: the wand, the stone and the Cloak, if he could just possess them all ...

I open at the close ... but what was the close? Why couldn't he have the stone now? If only he had the stone, he could ask Dumbledore these questions in person ... and Harry murmured words to the Snitch in the darkness, trying everything, even Parseltongue, but the golden ball would not open ...

And the wand, the Elder Wand, where was that hidden? Where was Voldemort searching now? Harry wished his scar would burn and show him Voldemort's thoughts, because for the first time ever, he and Voldemort were united in wanting the very same thing ... Hermione would not like that idea,

第22章 死亡圣器

"我那么说只是为了说服你去洛夫古德家！"赫敏气得叫了起来，"我并不真正相信！"

哈利没有理会。

"邓布利多通常让我自己去弄清问题。他让我考验自己的力量，去冒险。这似乎也像是他让我做的事情。"

"哈利，这不是游戏，也不是练习。这是真实的事情，并且邓布利多给你留了很清楚的指示：找到并且摧毁魂器！那个符号不代表任何东西，忘了死亡圣器吧，我们经不起再走弯路了——"

哈利几乎没有听她说话。他把金色飞贼拿在手里翻过来转过去，似乎希望它能裂开，露出复活石，向赫敏证明他是正确的，死亡圣器真的存在。

赫敏向罗恩求助。

"你不相信这些，是吧？"

哈利抬头看了一下。罗恩犹豫了。

"我不知……我的意思是……有一点点的地方似乎吻合，"罗恩尴尬地说，"但是当你全盘考虑时……"他深吸了一口气，"我想我们应该去摧毁魂器，哈利。那是邓布利多的嘱托。或许……或许我们应该忘了圣器这回事。"

"谢谢你，罗恩。"赫敏说，"我第一个放哨。"

她大步从哈利旁边走过去，坐到了帐篷口，使这次讨论戛然而止。

那晚哈利几乎没有睡着。死亡圣器这个想法萦绕在他心头，激动的思绪在他脑海中回旋，使他无法休息：魔杖、石头和隐形衣，如果他能全部拥有……

我在结束时打开……什么是"结束时"？他为什么不能现在就拿到那块石头？如果有了复活石多好啊，他就可以亲自问邓布利多了……哈利在黑暗中对着飞贼小声念念有词，什么都试了，甚至用上了蛇佬腔，可那个金色小球就是不肯打开……

还有那根魔杖，老魔杖，它藏在哪儿呢？伏地魔此刻在哪儿搜寻呢？哈利希望伤疤会刺痛，让他看到伏地魔的思想，因为这是他第一

CHAPTER TWENTY-TWO The Deathly Hallows

of course ... but then, she did not believe ... Xenophilius had been right, in a way ... *Limited. Narrow. Close-minded.* The truth was that she was scared of the idea of the Deathly Hallows, especially of the Resurrection Stone ... and Harry pressed his mouth again to the Snitch, kissing it, nearly swallowing it, but the cold metal did not yield ...

It was nearly dawn when he remembered Luna, alone in a cell in Azkaban, surrounded by Dementors, and he suddenly felt ashamed of himself. He had forgotten all about her in his feverish contemplation of the Hallows. If only they could rescue her, but Dementors in those numbers would be virtually unassailable. Now he came to think about it, he had not yet tried casting a Patronus with the blackthorn wand ... he must try that in the morning ...

If only there was a way of getting a better wand ...

And desire for the Elder Wand, the Deathstick, unbeatable, invincible, swallowed him once more ...

They packed up the tent next morning and moved on through a dreary shower of rain. The downpour pursued them to the coast, where they pitched the tent that night, and persisted through the whole week, through sodden landscapes which Harry found bleak and depressing. He could think only of the Deathly Hallows. It was as though a flame had been lit inside him that nothing, not Hermione's flat disbelief nor Ron's persistent doubts, could extinguish. And yet the fiercer the longing for the Hallows burned inside him, the less joyful it made him. He blamed Ron and Hermione: their determined indifference was as bad as the relentless rain for dampening his spirits, but neither could erode his certainty, which remained absolute. Harry's belief in and longing for the Hallows consumed him so much that he felt quite isolated from the other two and their obsession with the Horcruxes.

'Obsession?' said Hermione, in a low, fierce voice, when Harry was careless enough to use the word one evening, after Hermione had told him off for his lack of interest in locating more Horcruxes. 'We're not the ones with an obsession, Harry! We're the ones trying to do what Dumbledore wanted us to do!'

But he was impervious to the veiled criticism. Dumbledore had left the sign of the Hallows for Hermione to decipher and he had also, Harry remained convinced of it, left the Resurrection Stone hidden in the golden Snitch. *Neither can live while the other survives ... master of death ...* why didn't Ron and Hermione understand?

第22章 死亡圣器

次和伏地魔同时想要一件东西……赫敏当然不会喜欢这个想法……何况她也不相信……谢诺菲留斯在某种程度上还是对的……狭隘、眼光短浅、思维封闭。事实上赫敏是被"死亡圣器"这个概念吓着了,特别是复活石……哈利把嘴贴在飞贼上,亲吻它,差点把它吞下去,但冷冰冰的金属就是不投降……

快到破晓的时候,他想起了卢娜,独自一人被关在阿兹卡班的监狱里,周围都是摄魂怪。此时他突然感到很羞愧。他只顾狂热地思考圣器而完全忘记了卢娜。要是能把她救出来多好啊,但那么多的摄魂怪几乎是攻不破的。现在哈利想起来了,他还从未试过用黑刺李木魔杖召唤出守护神……早上一定要试一下……

要是有办法弄到一根更好的魔杖就好了……

想着老魔杖、死亡棒,永不会输的无敌魔杖,欲望再一次淹没了他……

第二天早上,他们收起帐篷,在阴凄凄的阵雨中出发了。倾盆大雨一直追到晚上他们搭帐篷的海岸边,然后延续了整个星期。到处都是湿漉漉的景物,让哈利感到阴冷和抑郁。他满脑子里只有死亡圣器,就好像他身体内一个火苗被点燃了,不论是赫敏的坚决不信,还是罗恩的不断怀疑,都不能使它熄灭。可是对圣器的渴望在心中燃烧得越强烈,就越使他不快乐。他怪罪于罗恩和赫敏,他们决意的漠视就像无情的大雨一样令他沮丧,但都不能削弱他的信心,他依然是那么确信无疑。对圣器的信念和渴望占据了哈利的心思,使他觉得跟那两个对魂器着魔的同伴有了很大的隔膜。

"着魔?"赫敏情绪激烈地低声问道——这天晚上,当赫敏责备哈利对寻找魂器缺乏兴趣时,他一不留神说出了那个词,"着魔的不是我们,哈利!我们才是在努力照着邓布利多的要求去做的人!"

但是哈利对于含蓄的批评无动于衷。邓布利多把圣器的标志留给赫敏去破译,他同时也把复活石藏在了金色飞贼里,对此哈利仍然坚信不疑。两个人不能都活着,只有一个生存下来……死神的主人……为什么罗恩和赫敏不明白呢?

CHAPTER TWENTY-TWO   The Deathly Hallows

'"*The last enemy that shall be destroyed is death*",' Harry quoted calmly.

'I thought it was You-Know-Who we were supposed to be fighting?' Hermione retorted, and Harry gave up on her.

Even the mystery of the silver doe, which the other two insisted on discussing, seemed less important to Harry now, a vaguely interesting sideshow. The only other thing that mattered to him was that his scar had begun to prickle again, although he did all he could to hide this fact from the other two. He sought solitude whenever it happened, but was disappointed by what he saw. The visions he and Voldemort were sharing had changed in quality; they had become blurred, shifting as though they were moving in and out of focus. Harry was just able to make out the indistinct features of an object that looked like a skull, and something like a mountain that was more shadow than substance. Used to images sharp as reality, Harry was disconcerted by the change. He was worried that the connection between himself and Voldemort had been damaged, a connection that he both feared and, whatever he had told Hermione, prized. Somehow Harry connected these unsatisfying, vague images with the destruction of his wand, as if it was the blackthorn wand's fault that he could no longer see into Voldemort's mind as well as before.

As the weeks crept on, Harry could not help but notice, even through his new self-absorption, that Ron seemed to be taking charge. Perhaps because he was determined to make up for having walked out on them: perhaps because Harry's descent into listlessness galvanised his dormant leadership qualities, Ron was the one now encouraging and exhorting the other two into action.

'Three Horcruxes left,' he kept saying. 'We need a plan of action, come on! Where haven't we looked? Let's go through it again. The orphanage ...'

Diagon Alley, Hogwarts, the Riddle House, Borgin and Burkes, Albania, every place that they knew Tom Riddle had ever lived or worked, visited or murdered in, Ron and Hermione raked over them again, Harry joining in only to stop Hermione pestering him. He would have been happy to sit alone in silence, trying to read Voldemort's thoughts, to find out more about the Elder Wand, but Ron insisted on journeying to ever more unlikely places simply, Harry was aware, to keep them moving.

'You never know,' was Ron's constant refrain. 'Upper Flagley is a wizarding village, he might've wanted to live there. Let's go and have a poke around.'

These frequent forays into wizarding territory brought them within

第22章 死亡圣器

"最后一个要消灭的敌人是死亡。"哈利平静地引述道。

"我们要斗的不是神秘人吗？"赫敏反驳道，哈利放弃了与她争论。

就连两个同伴坚持要讨论的银色牝鹿之谜，对哈利来说似乎也不再重要，只是一个比较有趣的插曲罢了。对他来说唯一要紧的另一件事，就是伤疤又开始刺痛了。但他努力掩饰着不让同伴知道。每次疼痛时他都找机会独处，但是看到的东西却令他失望。他和伏地魔共享的图像质量变差了，变得模糊了，好像焦距老是不准。哈利只能看到一个模糊的、头盖骨似的物体，还有似乎是一座山的影子，而以前的图像都是清晰逼真的。这个变化让哈利有点不安，担心自己和伏地魔之间的联系已经被破坏了。不管他对赫敏是怎么说的，他心里其实一直既害怕又珍惜这种联系。不知怎的，哈利觉得之所以图像模糊、不如人意，与他的魔杖损坏有关，似乎都是黑刺李木魔杖的错，使他不再能够像以前一样清楚地看到伏地魔的心思。

一星期又一星期过去了，哈利尽管沉浸在自己新的心事中，却也不能不注意到罗恩似乎正在担负起责任。可能因为决心要弥补自己出走的过错，也可能因为哈利情绪日渐低落而激起了罗恩潜在的领导才能，现在是他在鼓励和敦促另外两个人行动。

"就剩三个魂器了，"他总是说，"我们需要一个行动计划，加油啊！还有哪儿没找过？我们再查一遍，孤儿院……"

对角巷、霍格沃茨、里德尔老宅、博金-博克商店、阿尔巴尼亚，凡是他们知道汤姆·里德尔曾经住过、工作过、造访过或杀过人的地方，罗恩和赫敏又全部梳理了一遍。哈利怕赫敏不依不饶，只好也参加进去。其实他倒乐意一个人默默地坐着，试图读取伏地魔的想法，发现更多有关老魔杖的信息。哈利明白，罗恩坚持寻访一些越来越不可能的地方，仅仅是为了不停下来。

"谁知道呢，"这成了罗恩的口头禅，"上弗莱格利是一个巫师村，他没准儿在那儿住过。我们过去找找。"

如此频繁地涉足巫师的地盘，他们偶尔会撞见搜捕队。

CHAPTER TWENTY-TWO   The Deathly Hallows

occasional sight of Snatchers.

'Some of them are supposed to be as bad as Death Eaters,' said Ron. 'The lot that got me were a bit pathetic, but Bill reckons some of them are really dangerous. They said on *Potterwatch* –'

'On what?' said Harry.

'*Potterwatch*, didn't I tell you that's what it was called? The programme I keep trying to get on the radio, the only one that tells the truth about what's going on! Nearly all the programmes are following You-Know-Who's line, all except *Potterwatch*. I really want you to hear it, but it's tricky tuning in ...'

Ron spent evening after evening using his wand to beat out various rhythms on top of the wireless while the dials whirled. Occasionally they would catch snatches of advice on how to treat dragon pox, and once, a few bars of 'A Cauldron Full of Hot, Strong Love'. While he tapped, Ron continued to try to hit on the correct password, muttering strings of random words under his breath.

'They're normally something to do with the Order,' he told them. 'Bill had a real knack for guessing them. I'm bound to get one in the end ...'

But not until March did luck favour Ron at last. Harry was sitting in the tent entrance, on guard duty, staring idly at a clump of grape hyacinths that had forced their way through the chilly ground, when Ron shouted excitedly from inside the tent.

'I've got it, I've got it! Password was "Albus"! Get in here, Harry!'

Roused for the first time in days from his contemplation of the Deathly Hallows, Harry hurried back inside the tent to find Ron and Hermione kneeling on the floor beside the little radio. Hermione, who had been polishing the sword of Gryffindor just for something to do, was sitting open-mouthed, staring at the tiny speaker, from which a most familiar voice was issuing.

'... apologise for our temporary absence from the airwaves, which was due to a number of house-calls in our area by those charming Death Eaters.'

'But that's Lee Jordan!' said Hermione.

'I know!' beamed Ron. 'Cool, eh?'

'... now found ourselves another secure location,' Lee was saying, 'and I'm pleased to tell you that two of our regular contributors have joined me here this evening. Evening, boys!'

'Hi.'

第22章 死亡圣器

"其中有一些据说和食死徒一样坏，"罗恩说，"我碰到的那批有点蠢得可怜，但是比尔认为有一些十分危险。波特瞭望站说——"

"什么？"哈利说。

"波特瞭望站，我没有告诉过你它叫这个？就是我一直想调到的那个电台，是唯一真实报道当前局势的电台！现在几乎所有的电台都和神秘人保持一致，除了波特瞭望站。我真想让你听一下，但是不容易调到……"

罗恩花了一个又一个晚上，用魔杖在收音机顶上敲出各种节拍，把调谐钮旋来旋去。偶尔能听见几句如何医治龙痘疮的建议，有时是几小节《一埚火热的爱》。罗恩边敲边继续尝试找到正确的暗号，低声念出一串串连蒙带猜的词语。

"一般都是和凤凰社有关的词，"他告诉他们，"比尔猜这个特别快。我肯定早晚也能蒙中一个……"

直到三月，幸运女神才最终垂青了罗恩。当罗恩在帐篷里激动地大喊时，哈利正坐在帐篷口放哨，懒洋洋地瞅着一丛勇敢地钻出寒冷地面的麝香兰。

"我找到了，找到了！暗号是'阿不思'！快进来，哈利！"

多少天来只关心死亡圣器的哈利第一次兴奋起来，他迅速返回到帐篷里，看见罗恩和赫敏正跪在小收音机旁的地板上。刚才无事可做而在擦拭格兰芬多宝剑的赫敏，张嘴坐在那里盯着小小的扬声器，里面正传来一个最熟悉的声音。

"……为我们短暂的停播抱歉，都是因为那些迷人的食死徒，在我们地区搞了多次登门搜查。"

"是李·乔丹呀！"赫敏说。

"我知道！"罗恩笑了笑，"酷吧？"

"……现在我们找到了另一个安全的地方，"李说，"我很高兴地告诉大家，本台两位固定的供稿人今晚也在我旁边。晚上好，小伙子们！"

"嘿！"

CHAPTER TWENTY-TWO   The Deathly Hallows

'Evening, River.'

'"River", that's Lee,' Ron explained. 'They've all got code names, but you can usually tell –'

'Shh!' said Hermione.

'But before we hear from Royal and Romulus,' Lee went on, 'let's take a moment to report those deaths that the *Wizarding Wireless Network News* and the *Daily Prophet* don't think important enough to mention. It is with great regret that we inform our listeners of the murders of Ted Tonks and Dirk Cresswell.'

Harry felt a sick swooping in his belly. He, Ron and Hermione gazed at one another in horror.

'A goblin by the name of Gornuk was also killed. It is believed that Muggle-born Dean Thomas and a second goblin, both believed to have been travelling with Tonks, Cresswell and Gornuk, may have escaped. If Dean is listening, or if anyone has any knowledge of his whereabouts, his parents and sisters are desperate for news.

'Meanwhile, in Gaddley, a Muggle family of five has been found dead in their home. Muggle authorities are attributing the deaths to a gas leak, but members of the Order of the Phoenix inform me that it was the Killing Curse – more evidence, as if it were needed, of the fact that Muggle slaughter is becoming little more than a recreational sport under the new regime.

'Finally, we regret to inform our listeners that the remains of Bathilda Bagshot have been discovered in Godric's Hollow. The evidence is that she died several months ago. The Order of the Phoenix informs us that her body showed unmistakeable signs of injuries inflicted by Dark Magic.

'Listeners, I'd like to invite you now to join us in a minute's silence in memory of Ted Tonks, Dirk Cresswell, Bathilda Bagshot, Gornuk and the unnamed, but no less regretted, Muggles murdered by the Death Eaters.'

Silence fell, and Harry, Ron and Hermione did not speak. Half of Harry yearned to hear more, half of him was afraid of what might come next. It was the first time he had felt fully connected to the outside world for a long time.

'Thank you,' said Lee's voice. 'And now we turn to regular contributor, Royal, for an update on how the new wizarding order is affecting the Muggle world.'

'Thanks, River,' said an unmistakeable voice, deep, measured, reassuring.

'Kingsley!' burst out Ron.

第22章 死亡圣器

"晚上好,老江。"

"老江就是李,"罗恩解释道,"他们都有代号,但你通常可以听出来——"

"嘘!"赫敏说。

"但是在听老帅和老将讲话之前,"李接着说,"让我们先花点时间报道一下'巫师无线新闻联播'和《预言家日报》认为不值得一提的死讯。我们沉痛地通知听众们,泰德·唐克斯和德克·克莱斯韦遭到谋杀。"

哈利感到心猛地往下一沉,三人恐惧地对望着。

"一个名叫戈努克的妖精也被杀了。据信,与唐克斯、克莱斯韦、戈努克同行的麻瓜出身的迪安·托马斯和另一个妖精很可能逃了出来。如果迪安正在收听,或有任何人知道他的下落,请注意,他的父母和姐妹们迫切希望得到他的消息。

"同时,在加德里,有麻瓜一家五口死在家中。麻瓜官方把死因归于煤气泄漏,而凤凰社的成员告诉我们是杀戮咒所致——又一个证据,好像证据还不够多似的!这些事件都证明在新政权下,屠杀麻瓜正变成一种娱乐活动。

"最后,我们遗憾地通知听众们,在戈德里克山谷发现了巴希达·巴沙特的遗体,看样子是几个月前去世的。凤凰社告诉我们,她身上有确凿无误的、被黑魔法击中的伤口。

"听众们,现在请跟我们一起,为死难者默哀一分钟:悼念泰德·唐克斯、德克·克莱斯韦、巴希达·巴沙特、戈努克,以及所有无名的被食死徒暗杀的麻瓜们。"

默哀开始,哈利、罗恩和赫敏都肃穆不语。哈利既渴望听到更多,又害怕可能听到的内容。这么久以来,他第一次感觉到和外面的世界紧密相连。

"谢谢大家。"李说道,"现在,我们请固定供稿人老帅给大家讲讲巫师界的新秩序对麻瓜世界的最新影响。"

"谢谢,老江。"一个不可能听错的声音,深沉稳重,令人安心。

"金斯莱!"罗恩大喊道。

CHAPTER TWENTY-TWO   The Deathly Hallows

'We know!' said Hermione, hushing him.

'Muggles remain ignorant of the source of their suffering as they continue to sustain heavy casualties,' said Kingsley. 'However, we continue to hear truly inspirational stories of wizards and witches risking their own safety to protect Muggle friends and neighbours, often without the Muggles' knowledge. I'd like to appeal to all our listeners to emulate their example, perhaps by casting a protective charm over any Muggle dwellings in your street. Many lives could be saved if such simple measures are taken.'

'And what would you say, Royal, to those listeners who reply that in these dangerous times, it should be "wizards first"?' asked Lee.

'I'd say that it's one short step from "wizards first" to "pure-bloods first", and then to "Death Eaters",' replied Kingsley. 'We're all human, aren't we? Every human life is worth the same, and worth saving.'

'Excellently put, Royal, and you've got my vote for Minister for Magic if ever we get out of this mess,' said Lee. 'And now, over to Romulus for our popular feature: Pals of Potter.'

'Thanks, River,' said another very familiar voice; Ron started to speak, but Hermione forestalled him in a whisper.

'*We know it's Lupin!*'

'Romulus, do you maintain, as you have every time you've appeared on our programme, that Harry Potter is still alive?'

'I do,' said Lupin firmly. 'There is no doubt at all in my mind that his death would be proclaimed as widely as possible by the Death Eaters if it had happened, because it would strike a deadly blow at the morale of those resisting the new regime. The "Boy Who Lived" remains a symbol of everything for which we are fighting: the triumph of good, the power of innocence, the need to keep resisting.'

A mixture of gratitude and shame welled up in Harry. Had Lupin forgiven him, then, for the terrible things he had said when they had last met?

'And what would you say to Harry if you knew he was listening, Romulus?'

'I'd tell him we're all with him in spirit,' said Lupin, then hesitated slightly. 'And I'd tell him to follow his instincts, which are good and nearly always right.'

Harry looked at Hermione, whose eyes were full of tears.

'Nearly always right,' she repeated.

第22章 死亡圣器

"我们知道!"赫敏说,示意他安静。

"麻瓜们继续遭受惨重的伤亡,却还不知道造成他们苦难的原因。"金斯莱说,"不过,我们也不断听到真正鼓舞人心的故事,巫师们冒着危险保护麻瓜朋友和邻居,经常是在麻瓜们不知道的情况下。我想呼吁所有的听众都这样做,可以对你们街上的麻瓜住所施一个防护咒。这些简单的措施可能挽救很多条性命。"

"老帅,对于那些声称在这危险的时代应该'巫师第一'的听众,你会怎么说呢?"李问道。

"我会说'巫师第一'与'纯血统第一'仅有一小步之遥,再往前一步就是'食死徒'。"金斯莱答道,"我们都是人,不是吗?每个人的生命都一样珍贵,都值得保护。"

"讲得太好了,老帅,一旦我们摆脱了这个混乱局面,我就选你做魔法部长。"李说,"现在请听老将带给我们的热门节目:波特之友。"

"谢谢你,老江。"另一个非常熟悉的声音说。罗恩刚要说话,赫敏轻声阻止了他。

"*我们知道是卢平!*"

"老将,你是不是还和每次来本节目时一样,认为哈利·波特仍然活着?"

"是的,"卢平坚定地说,"我深信不疑,如果他死了,食死徒一定会大肆宣扬,因为这对于抵抗新政权的人将是一个致命的打击。'大难不死的男孩'仍然象征着我们为之奋斗的一切:正义的胜利,纯洁的力量,以及继续抵抗的必要性。"

感激和羞愧一起涌上哈利心头。上次见面时,哈利说过那些伤人的话,难道卢平已经原谅了他?

"如果哈利正在收听的话,老将,你会对他说些什么?"

"我会对他说:我们和你同在。"卢平说,然后稍微犹豫了一下,"还会对他说:跟着你的直觉走,你的直觉都是好的,并且几乎总是正确的。"

哈利看着满眼是泪的赫敏。

"几乎总是正确的。"她重复道。

'Oh, didn't I tell you?' said Ron in surprise. 'Bill told me Lupin's living with Tonks again! And apparently she's getting pretty big too.'

'... and our usual update on those friends of Harry Potter's who are suffering for their allegiance?' Lee was saying.

'Well, as regular listeners will know, several of the more outspoken supporters of Harry Potter have now been imprisoned, including Xenophilius Lovegood, erstwhile editor of *The Quibbler* –' said Lupin.

'At least he's still alive!' muttered Ron.

'We have also heard within the last few hours that Rubeus Hagrid –' all three of them gasped, and so nearly missed the rest of the sentence '– well-known gamekeeper at Hogwarts School, has narrowly escaped arrest within the grounds of Hogwarts, where he is rumoured to have hosted a "Support Harry Potter" party in his house. However, Hagrid was not taken into custody, and is, we believe, on the run.'

'I suppose it helps, when escaping from Death Eaters, if you've got a sixteen-foot-high half-brother?' asked Lee.

'It would tend to give you an edge,' agreed Lupin gravely. 'May I just add that while we here at *Potterwatch* applaud Hagrid's spirit, we would urge even the most devoted of Harry's supporters against following Hagrid's lead. "Support Harry Potter" parties are unwise in the present climate.'

'Indeed they are, Romulus,' said Lee, 'so we suggest that you continue to show your devotion to the man with the lightning scar by listening to *Potterwatch*! And now let's move to news concerning the wizard who is proving just as elusive as Harry Potter. We like to refer to him as the Chief Death Eater, and here to give his views on some of the more insane rumours circulating about him, I'd like to introduce a new correspondent: Rodent.'

'"*Rodent*"?' said yet another familiar voice, and Harry, Ron and Hermione cried out together: 'Fred!'

'No – is it George?'

'It's Fred, I think,' said Ron, leaning in closer, as whichever twin it was said, 'I'm not being "Rodent", no way, I told you I wanted to be "Rapier"!'

'Oh, all right then. "Rapier", could you please give us your take on the various stories we've been hearing about the Chief Death Eater?'

第22章 死亡圣器

"哦,我没有告诉你们?"罗恩惊讶地说,"比尔跟我说,卢平和唐克斯又生活在一起了!而且唐克斯的肚子很明显了。"

"……下面照例要问一下,有没有哈利·波特的朋友因为忠诚而受难的新消息?"李说。

"嗯,老听众们都会知道,好几位坦言支持哈利·波特的朋友被捕入狱了,包括《唱唱反调》的主编谢诺菲留斯·洛夫古德——"卢平说。

"至少他还活着!"罗恩低语道。

"几小时前,我们得到消息说鲁伯·海格——"三个人都倒吸了一口气,差点没听到下半句话"——大家熟知的霍格沃茨学校的猎场看守,在校内勉强逃脱了抓捕。抓捕原因是据传他在家中举办了一个'支持哈利·波特'的聚会。但海格没有被拘押,我们相信他在逃亡中。"

"我猜想,在逃避食死徒的追捕时,如果你有个身高十六英尺的同母异父兄弟,应该有点帮助吧?"李问道。

"可能会有一点优势。"卢平严肃地答道,"我们波特瞭望站虽然赞赏海格的精神,但是请允许我补充一句,即使是哈利的最忠诚的拥护者,也切勿学习海格的做法。在当前这种气候下,举办'支持哈利·波特'的聚会是不明智的。"

"确实是的,老将,"李说道,"所以建议大家继续收听波特瞭望站,以表达对带有闪电形伤疤的那个人的热爱!现在来关注一下那位同哈利·波特一样行踪不定的巫师,我们喜欢称他为'头号食死徒'。为了分析关于他的一些比较疯狂的谣言,我要介绍一位新的通讯员:老鼠。"

"老鼠?"一个熟悉的声音说。哈利、罗恩和赫敏同时喊道:"弗雷德!"

"不对——是乔治?"

"我认为是弗雷德。"罗恩说,一边靠近了些。不管到底是双胞胎中的哪一个,只听那声音说道:"我不是老鼠,绝对不是,我跟你说了我要叫老剑!"

"哦,那好吧。老剑,你能否给我们说说,对于外面流传的有关头号食死徒的各种故事,你是怎么想的?"

CHAPTER TWENTY-TWO The Deathly Hallows

'Yes, River, I can,' said Fred. 'As our listeners will know, unless they've taken refuge at the bottom of a garden pond or somewhere similar, You-Know-Who's strategy of remaining in the shadows is creating a nice little climate of panic. Mind you, if all the alleged sightings of him are genuine, we must have a good nineteen You-Know-Whos running around the place.'

'Which suits him, of course,' said Kingsley. 'The air of mystery is creating more terror than actually showing himself.'

'Agreed,' said Fred. 'So, people, let's try and calm down a bit. Things are bad enough without inventing stuff as well. For instance, this new idea that You-Know-Who can kill with a single glance from his eyes. That's a *Basilisk*, listeners. One simple test: check whether the thing that's glaring at you has got legs. If it has, it's safe to look into its eyes, although if it really is You-Know-Who, that's still likely to be the last thing you ever do.'

For the first time in weeks and weeks, Harry was laughing: he could feel the weight of tension leaving him.

'And the rumours that he keeps being sighted abroad?' asked Lee.

'Well, who wouldn't want a nice little holiday after all the hard work he's been putting in?' asked Fred. 'Point is, people, don't get lulled into a false sense of security, thinking he's out of the country. Maybe he is, maybe he isn't, but the fact remains he can move faster than Severus Snape confronted with shampoo when he wants to, so don't count on him being a long way away if you're planning on taking any risks. I never thought I'd hear myself say it, but safety first!'

'Thank you very much for those wise words, Rapier,' said Lee. 'Listeners, that brings us to the end of another *Potterwatch*. We don't know when it will be possible to broadcast again, but you can be sure we shall be back. Keep twiddling those dials: the next password will be "Mad-Eye". Keep each other safe: keep faith. Goodnight.'

The radio's dial twirled and the lights behind the tuning panel went out. Harry, Ron and Hermione were still beaming. Hearing familiar, friendly voices was an extraordinary tonic; Harry had become so used to their isolation he had nearly forgotten that other people were resisting Voldemort. It was like waking from a long sleep.

'Good, eh?' said Ron happily.

第22章 死亡圣器

"好的，老江。"弗雷德说，"听众朋友只要不是躲在花园池塘底部之类的地方，就会知道，神秘人继续藏在暗处的策略正在造成一点点可爱的恐慌气氛。请注意，如果所有声称见到他的人说的都是真话，我们周围起码有十九个神秘人。"

"这当然很合他的意，"金斯莱说，"神秘的气氛比他亲自现身更加令人恐惧。"

"同意。"弗雷德说，"因此，朋友们，让我们努力镇静一点儿。不要添加虚构的东西，情况已经够糟糕的了。譬如有种新说法认为，被神秘人看一眼就会死。那是蛇怪，听众朋友们。一个简单的鉴别方法：检查一下那个瞪着你的东西是否有脚。如果有，看它的眼睛就是安全的，不过如果真是神秘人，那仍然可能是你做的最后一件事情。"

好多好多个星期以来，哈利第一次大笑：他感到紧张的压力离他而去。

"还有人谣传说经常在国外看到他呢？"李问道。

"在奋斗了这么久之后，谁不想有一个小小的、美好的假期呢？"弗雷德问道，"问题是，朋友们，不要以为他出国了，我们就安全了。他可能出国了，也可能没有，但事实是他如果愿意的话，会比西弗勒斯·斯内普见到洗发水时跑得还要快。如果要策划什么冒险行动，别指望他会离得很远很远。我从没想过我会听到自己说出这一番话，不管怎样，安全第一！"

"十分感谢你的这些金玉良言，老剑！"李说，"听众朋友们，又到了本期波特瞭望站和大家说再见的时候了。不知道何时才能再次广播，但是请放心，我们会回来的。请经常转动调谐钮：下一次的暗号是'疯眼汉'。大家注意安全，坚定信心。晚安。"

收音机的调谐钮转动了一下，面板上的指示灯熄灭了。哈利、罗恩和赫敏仍然微笑着。听到熟悉、友善的声音真是令人无比振奋。哈利已与外面的世界隔绝太久，几乎忘记了其他人仍在抵抗伏地魔。他好像刚从一个长觉中醒来。

"不错吧？"罗恩高兴地问。

CHAPTER TWENTY-TWO   The Deathly Hallows

'Brilliant,' said Harry.

'It's so brave of them,' sighed Hermione admiringly. 'If they were found ...'

'Well, they keep on the move, don't they?' said Ron. 'Like us.'

'But did you hear what Fred said?' asked Harry excitedly; now the broadcast was over, his thoughts turned again towards his all-consuming obsession. 'He's abroad! He's still looking for the wand, I knew it!'

'Harry –'

'Come on, Hermione, why are you so determined not to admit it? Vol–'

'HARRY, NO!'

'–demort's after the Elder Wand!'

'The name's Taboo!' Ron bellowed, leaping to his feet as a loud crack sounded outside the tent. 'I told you, Harry, I told you, we can't say it any more – we've got to put the protection back around us – quickly – it's how they find –'

But Ron stopped talking, and Harry knew why. The Sneakoscope on the table had lit up and begun to spin; they could hear voices coming nearer and nearer: rough, excited voices. Ron pulled the Deluminator out of his pocket and clicked it: their lamps went out.

'Come out of there with your hands up!' came a rasping voice through the darkness. 'We know you're in there! You've got half a dozen wands pointing at you and we don't care who we curse!'

第22章 死亡圣器

"太精彩了。"哈利说。

"他们真勇敢，"赫敏赞叹道，"要是被发现了……"

"他们经常换地方，不是吗？"罗恩说，"就像我们。"

"但是你们听到弗雷德说的了吗？"哈利激动地问，广播结束后，他的心思又回到那执着的念头上，"他在国外！他还在寻找那根魔杖，我就知道是这样！"

"哈利——"

"哎呀，赫敏，你为什么这么坚决不肯承认呢？伏——"

"**哈利，别说！**"

"——地魔在找老魔杖！"

"那个名字是禁忌！"罗恩大吼一声，跳了起来，帐篷外传来一声震耳的爆响，"我告诉过你，哈利，我告诉过你，不能再说它——我们得赶紧修复防护魔法——快——他们就是这样发现——"

罗恩突然住口，哈利知道是为什么。桌上的窥镜亮了，并开始旋转。他们听见说话声越来越近：粗鲁、兴奋的声音。罗恩从口袋里掏出熄灯器摁了一下，灯灭了。

"举起双手，从里面出来！"黑夜里传来刺耳的声音，"我们知道你们在里面！有六七根魔杖正指着你们，我们可不管咒语会打到谁！"

CHAPTER TWENTY-THREE

Malfoy Manor

Harry looked round at the other two, now mere outlines in the darkness. He saw Hermione point her wand, not towards the outside, but into his face; there was a bang, a burst of white light, and he buckled in agony, unable to see. He could feel his face swelling rapidly under his hands, as heavy footfalls surrounded him.

'Get up, vermin.'

Unknown hands dragged Harry roughly off the ground. Before he could stop them, someone had rummaged through his pockets and removed the blackthorn wand. Harry clutched at his excruciatingly painful face, which felt unrecognisable beneath his fingers, tight, swollen and puffy as though he had suffered some violent allergic reaction. His eyes had been reduced to slits through which he could barely see; his glasses fell off as he was bundled out of the tent; all he could make out were the blurred shapes of four or five people wrestling Ron and Hermione outside too.

'Get – off – her!' Ron shouted. There was the unmistakeable sound of knuckles hitting flesh: Ron grunted in pain and Hermione screamed, 'No! Leave him alone, leave him alone!'

'Your boyfriend's going to have worse than that done to him if he's on my list,' said the horribly familiar, rasping voice. 'Delicious girl … what a treat … I do enjoy the softness of the skin …'

Harry's stomach turned over. He knew who this was: Fenrir Greyback, the werewolf who was permitted to wear Death Eater robes in return for his hired savagery.

'Search the tent!' said another voice.

Harry was thrown, face down, on to the ground. A thud told him that Ron had been cast down beside him. They could hear footsteps and crashes; the men were pushing over chairs inside the tent as they searched.

第 23 章

马尔福庄园

哈利看了一下两个同伴,黑暗中只能看到轮廓。只见赫敏的魔杖指向他的脸,而不是指着外面。砰的一声,一道白光炸裂,他痛得弯下腰,睁不开眼,感觉双手捂着的脸正在迅速胀大,而此时沉重的脚步声已经围住了他。

"起来,害虫!"

陌生的手粗暴地把哈利从地上拉了起来。他还没来得及阻止,就有人搜了他的口袋,拿走了黑刺李木魔杖。哈利紧捂住疼痛难忍的脸颊,感觉手指下的面部已经无法辨认,紧绷绷、胀鼓鼓的,好像发生了严重的过敏反应。他的双眼只剩下了一条缝,几乎看不到外面。眼镜在他被推出帐篷时掉落了,他只能模糊地看到四五个人影和罗恩、赫敏在外面扭打在一起。

"别——碰——她!"罗恩喊道。然后清楚地响起拳头击打身体的声音,罗恩痛得哼了一声,赫敏尖叫:"不!别打他,别打他!"

"如果你男朋友的名字在我的名单上,他会更惨。"一个熟悉得可怕的刺耳声音说道,"香喷喷的小妞儿……多好的美餐呀……我最喜欢细皮嫩肉的……"

哈利胃里面一阵恶心。他知道那是谁了:芬里尔·格雷伯克,那个因为残暴而受雇佣,被允许穿上食死徒袍子的狼人。

"搜搜帐篷里面!"另一个声音说。

哈利被脸朝下扔在地上。一声闷响告诉他,罗恩也被扔到了旁边。他们听见了脚步声和撞击声,那些在帐篷里搜查的人推翻了椅子。

CHAPTER TWENTY-THREE Malfoy Manor

'Now, let's see who we've got,' said Greyback's gloating voice from overhead, and Harry was rolled over on to his back. A beam of wandlight fell into his face and Greyback laughed.

'I'll be needing Butterbeer to wash this one down. What happened to you, ugly?'

Harry did not answer immediately.

'I *said*,' repeated Greyback, and Harry received a blow to the diaphragm that made him double over in pain, 'what happened to you?'

'Stung,' Harry muttered. 'Been stung.'

'Yeah, looks like it,' said a second voice.

'What's your name?' snarled Greyback.

'Dudley,' said Harry.

'And your first name?'

'I – Vernon. Vernon Dudley.'

'Check the list, Scabior,' said Greyback, and Harry heard him move sideways to look down at Ron, instead. 'And what about you, Ginger?'

'Stan Shunpike,' said Ron.

'Like 'ell you are,' said the man called Scabior. 'We know Stan Shunpike, 'e's put a bit of work our way.'

There was another thud.

'I'b Bardy,' said Ron, and Harry could tell that his mouth was full of blood. 'Bardy Weadley.'

'A Weasley?' rasped Greyback. 'So you're related to blood traitors even if you're not a Mudblood. And lastly, your pretty little friend ...' The relish in his voice made Harry's flesh crawl.

'Easy, Greyback,' said Scabior, over the jeering of the others.

'Oh, I'm not going to bite just yet. We'll see if she's a bit quicker at remembering her name than Barny. Who are you, girly?'

'Penelope Clearwater,' said Hermione. She sounded terrified, but convincing.

'What's your Blood Status?'

'Half-blood,' said Hermione.

'Easy enough to check,' said Scabior. 'But the 'ole lot of 'em look like they could still be 'Ogwarts age –'

第23章 马尔福庄园

"好了,来看看我们抓到了谁。"格雷伯克得意的声音从头顶传来,哈利被翻过身来。一道魔杖的亮光照在他的脸上,格雷伯克笑了起来。

"看来我要就着黄油啤酒才咽得下这个了。你是怎么搞的,丑八怪?"

哈利没有马上回答。

"问你呢,"格雷伯克冲着哈利的胸前就是一拳,痛得哈利弓起身子,"你是怎么搞的?"

"蜇的,"哈利咕哝道,"被蜇了。"

"对,看起来像。"另一个声音说道。

"你叫什么名字?"格雷伯克吼道。

"达力。"哈利说。

"全名?"

"我——弗农。弗农·达力。"

"查一下名单,斯卡比奥。"格雷伯克说,哈利听见他走到旁边去俯视罗恩,"那么你呢,红毛?"

"斯坦·桑帕克。"罗恩说。

"见你的鬼吧,"那个叫斯卡比奥的说,"我们知道斯坦·桑帕克,他给我们找了点麻烦。"

又是砰的一声。

"我唔巴迪,"罗恩说,哈利听得出他满嘴是血,"巴迪·韦德莱。"

"韦斯莱?"格雷伯克粗声粗气道,"那么,就算你不是泥巴种,也是和纯血统的叛徒沾亲了。最后一个,美丽的小朋友……"他垂涎欲滴的声音让哈利汗毛直竖。

"慢点,格雷伯克。"在其他人的哄笑声中,斯卡比奥说。

"哦,我现在还不准备咬她呢。我们瞧瞧,她想起自己名字的速度是不是比巴尼快一点儿。你是谁,小妞儿?"

"佩内洛·克里瓦特。"赫敏说,声音中充满恐惧,但还是很可信。

"你的血统呢?"

"混血。"赫敏说。

"容易检查。"斯卡比奥说,"但是他们看起来都还是霍格沃茨的年龄——"

CHAPTER TWENTY-THREE   Malfoy Manor

'We'b lebt,' said Ron.

'Left, 'ave you, Ginger?' said Scabior. 'And you decided to go camping? And you thought, just for a laugh, you'd use the Dark Lord's name?'

'Nod a laugh,' said Ron. 'Aggiden.'

'Accident?' There was more jeering laughter.

'You know who used to like using the Dark Lord's name, Weasley?' growled Greyback. 'The Order of the Phoenix. Mean anything to you?'

'Doh.'

'Well, they don't show the Dark Lord proper respect, so the name's been Tabooed. A few Order members have been tracked that way. We'll see. Bind them up with the other two prisoners!'

Someone yanked Harry up by the hair, dragged him a short way, pushed him down into a sitting position, then started binding him back-to-back with other people. Harry was still half-blind, barely able to see anything through his puffed-up eyes. When at last the man tying them had walked away, Harry whispered to the other prisoners.

'Anyone still got a wand?'

'No,' said Ron and Hermione from either side of him.

'This is all my fault. I said the name, I'm sorry –'

'Harry?'

It was a new, but familiar, voice, and it came from directly behind Harry, from the person tied to Hermione's left.

'*Dean?*'

'It *is* you! If they find out who they've got –! They're Snatchers, they're only looking for truants to sell for gold –'

'Not a bad little haul for one night,' Greyback was saying, as a pair of hobnailed boots marched close by Harry and they heard more crashes from inside the tent. 'A Mudblood, a runaway goblin and three truants. You checked their names on the list yet, Scabior?' he roared.

'Yeah. There's no Vernon Dudley on 'ere, Greyback.'

'Interesting,' said Greyback. 'That's interesting.'

He crouched down beside Harry, who saw, through the infinitesimal gap left between his swollen eyelids, a face covered in matted, grey hair and whiskers, with pointed brown teeth and sores at the corners of his mouth.

第23章 马尔福庄园

"我们不汪了。"罗恩说。

"不上学了,红毛?"斯卡比奥说,"所以你们决定来露营?然后觉得可以用黑魔王的名字开个玩笑?"

"不唔玩笑,"罗恩说,"呕误。"

"口误?"又是一阵哄笑。

"你知道什么人常说黑魔王的名字吗,韦斯莱?"格雷伯克咆哮道,"凤凰社。和你有关吗?"

"没。"

"哼,他们对黑魔王不够尊敬,所以这个名字被列为禁忌。有些凤凰社成员就是这样被抓到的。走着瞧。把他们和另外两个犯人绑在一起!"

有人揪住哈利的头发把他拽起来,拖着走了一小段路,又把他推坐到地上,跟别人背靠背绑在一起。哈利仍然像个瞎子,肿起的双眼几乎看不到东西。当绑他们的人终于离开后,哈利低声对其他犯人说道:

"谁还有魔杖?"

"没有。"罗恩和赫敏的声音分别从他的两边传来。

"都是我的错。我说了那个名字,对不起——"

"哈利?"

一个新的但是熟悉的声音直接从哈利身后传来,是绑在赫敏左边的那个人发出的。

"迪安?"

"真是你!如果他们发现抓到的是谁——!他们是搜捕队,只是抓逃学的人去卖钱的——"

"这个晚上的收获不赖,"格雷伯克说着,一双大马钉靴走近了哈利,帐篷里传来了更多的撞击声,"一个泥巴种、一个逃跑的妖精和三个逃学的。你在名单上查过他们的名字了吗,斯卡比奥?"他吼道。

"查过了,那上面没有弗农·达力,格雷伯克。"

"有趣,"格雷伯克说,"这倒有趣。"

他在哈利的旁边蹲了下来,哈利透过肿胀的眼皮间极小的缝隙看到了一张脸,乱蓬蓬的灰发和胡须,尖尖的黄牙,嘴角长着口疮。格

CHAPTER TWENTY-THREE   Malfoy Manor

Greyback smelled as he had done at the top of the Tower where Dumbledore had died: of dirt, sweat and blood.

'So you aren't wanted, then, Vernon? Or are you on that list under a different name? What house were you in at Hogwarts?'

'Slytherin,' said Harry automatically.

'Funny 'ow they all thinks we wants to 'ear that,' jeered Scabior out of the shadows. 'But none of 'em can tell us where the common room is.'

'It's in the dungeons,' said Harry clearly. 'You enter through the wall. It's full of skulls and stuff and it's under the lake, so the light's all green.'

There was a short pause.

'Well, well, looks like we really 'ave caught a little Slytherin,' said Scabior. 'Good for you, Vernon, 'cause there ain't a lot of Mudblood Slytherins. Who's your father?'

'He works at the Ministry,' Harry lied. He knew that his whole story would collapse with the smallest investigation, but on the other hand, he only had until his face regained its usual appearance before the game was up in any case. 'Department of Magical Accidents and Catastrophes.'

'You know what, Greyback,' said Scabior. 'I think there *is* a Dudley in there.'

Harry could barely breathe: could luck, sheer luck, get them safely out of this?

'Well, well,' said Greyback, and Harry could hear the tiniest note of trepidation in that callous voice, and knew that Greyback was wondering whether he had indeed just attacked and bound the son of a Ministry official. Harry's heart was pounding against the ropes around his ribs; he would not have been surprised to know that Greyback could see it. 'If you're telling the truth, ugly, you've got nothing to fear from a trip to the Ministry. I expect your father'll reward us just for picking you up.'

'But,' said Harry, his mouth bone dry, 'if you just let us –'

'Hey!' came a shout from inside the tent. 'Look at this, Greyback!'

A dark figure came bustling towards them, and Harry saw a glint of silver in the light of their wands. They had found Gryffindor's sword.

'Ve-e-ry nice,' said Greyback appreciatively, taking it from his companion. 'Oh, very nice indeed. Looks goblin-made, that. Where did you get something like this?'

第23章 马尔福庄园

雷伯克身上散发出一股怪味,和他当时在邓布利多丧生的塔顶上一样:混合着灰尘、汗水、鲜血的气味。

"这么说你不是我们要抓的人喽,弗农?或者你在名单上,但不是这个名字?你上的是霍格沃茨哪个学院?"

"斯莱特林。"哈利想也不想地说。

"滑稽,他们怎么都以为我们想听这个,"斯卡比奥在黑暗中讥笑道,"但是他们没有一个知道公共休息室在哪儿。"

"在地牢里,"哈利清晰地说,"要穿墙进去,里面都是头盖骨之类的东西,而且它在湖底,所以光都是绿色的。"

短暂的静默。

"好的,好的,看来我们的确抓到了一个小斯莱特林。"斯卡比奥说,"你很幸运,弗农,因为没有几个泥巴种的斯莱特林。你爸爸是谁?"

"他在魔法部工作,"哈利扯着谎,知道只要他们稍微调查一下,他的整个故事就会瞬间瓦解,不过,反正他面目一恢复游戏也就结束了,"魔法事故和灾害司。"

"格雷伯克,"斯卡比奥说,"我想那里面是有一个叫达力的。"

哈利几乎不敢呼吸:运气,纯粹的运气,确实会让他们安全逃脱吗?

"好的,好的。"格雷伯克说,哈利从那冷酷的声音里听出了极其细微的颤抖,知道格雷伯克在想自己是否真的殴打并捆绑了魔法部官员的儿子。哈利的心脏怦怦地撞着肋骨周围的绳子,他觉得格雷伯克应该看出来了。"如果你说的是真话,丑八怪,去一趟魔法部也没什么好害怕的。我猜你爸爸会奖励我们送你回去呢。"

"但是,"哈利说,嘴巴发干,"你得让我们——"

"嘿!"帐篷里传来一声大喊,"看看这个,格雷伯克!"

一个黑影奔跑过来,在魔杖的照耀下,哈利看见一道银光,他们找到了格兰芬多的宝剑。

"非——常漂亮,"格雷伯克满意地说,从同伴手里拿过宝剑,"哦,确实是很漂亮。看起来是妖精造的。你们从哪儿弄来的?"

CHAPTER TWENTY-THREE Malfoy Manor

'It's my father's,' Harry lied, hoping against hope that it was too dark for Greyback to see the name etched just below the hilt. 'We borrowed it to cut firewood –'

"'Ang on a minute, Greyback! Look at this, in the *Prophet*!'

As Scabior said it, Harry's scar, which was stretched tight across his distended forehead, burned savagely. More clearly than he could make out anything around him, he saw a towering building, a grim fortress, jet black and forbidding; Voldemort's thoughts had suddenly become razor-sharp again; he was gliding towards the gigantic building with a sense of calmly euphoric purpose ...

So close ... so close ...

With a huge effort of will, Harry closed his mind to Voldemort's thoughts, pulling himself back to where he sat, tied to Ron, Hermione, Dean and Griphook in the darkness, listening to Greyback and Scabior.

"'*Ermione Granger*,'" Scabior was saying, "'*the Mudblood who is known to be travelling with 'Arry Potter.*'"

Harry's scar burned in the silence, but he made a supreme effort to keep himself present, not to slip into Voldemort's mind. He heard the creak of Greyback's boots as he crouched down in front of Hermione.

'You know what, little girly? This picture looks a hell of a lot like you.'

'It isn't! It isn't me!'

Hermione's terrified squeak was as good as a confession.

"'... *known to be travelling with Harry Potter*",' repeated Greyback quietly.

A stillness had settled over the scene. Harry's scar was exquisitely painful, but he struggled with all his strength against the pull of Voldemort's thoughts: it had never been so important to remain in his own right mind.

'Well, this changes things, doesn't it?' whispered Greyback.

Nobody spoke: Harry sensed the gang of Snatchers watching, frozen, and felt Hermione's arm trembling against his. Greyback got up and took a couple of steps to where Harry sat, crouching down again to stare closely at his misshapen features.

'What's that on your forehead, Vernon?' he asked softly, his breath foul in Harry's nostrils as he pressed a filthy finger to the taut scar.

'Don't touch it!' Harry yelled; he could not stop himself; he thought he might be sick from the pain of it.

第23章　马尔福庄园

"是我爸爸的,"哈利撒谎道,拼命祈求昏暗中格雷伯克看不到剑柄下方刻的名字,"我们借来砍木柴的——"

"等一下,格雷伯克!看这个,《预言家日报》!"

斯卡比奥说话时,哈利额头上肿胀而绷紧的伤疤猛烈地灼痛起来,眼前出现了一幅画面,比身边的任何东西都要清晰:那是一座乌黑的、令人生畏的高耸建筑,一座阴森的堡垒,伏地魔的思维又突然变得异常清晰:他正飘向那座巨型建筑,目标明确,内心平静而喜悦……

这么近……这么近……

哈利用了巨大的自制力,不再去观看伏地魔的思维,把自己拽回到坐着的地方。他同罗恩、赫敏、迪安和拉环绑在一起,在黑暗中听着格雷伯克和斯卡比奥说话。

"'赫敏·格兰杰,'"斯卡比奥在说,"'据知是与哈利·波特同行的泥巴种。'"

哈利的伤疤在寂静中灼痛,但是他用惊人的毅力使自己保持神志清楚,免得滑进伏地魔的思维里。哈利听见了靴子的吱吱响声,格雷伯克蹲到了赫敏面前。

"你知道吗,小妞?这张照片看上去很像你哟。"

"不是!不是我!"

赫敏惊恐的尖叫等于是在招认。

"'……据知是与哈利·波特同行……'"格雷伯克轻轻又念了一遍。

周围鸦雀无声。哈利的伤疤疼痛难当,他竭尽全力抵御伏地魔思维的吸引。保持神志清楚从来没有像现在这样重要。

"这么说,情况改变了,是不是?"格雷伯克低语道。

没有人说话,哈利感觉到搜捕队的人在一旁呆呆地看着,也感觉到身边赫敏的胳膊在颤抖。格雷伯克站了起来,几步走到哈利面前,再次蹲了下来,仔细地瞅着他变了形的脸。

"你的额头上是什么,弗农?"他轻声问道,把一只肮脏的手指按在哈利紧绷的伤疤上,臭烘烘的呼吸喷进了哈利的鼻孔。

"别碰!"哈利大喊。他控制不住自己,痛得简直要呕吐了。

CHAPTER TWENTY-THREE   Malfoy Manor

'I thought you wore glasses, Potter?' breathed Greyback.

'I found glasses!' yelped one of the Snatchers skulking in the background. 'There was glasses in the tent, Greyback, wait –'

And seconds later Harry's glasses had been rammed back on to his face. The Snatchers were closing in, now, peering at him.

'It is!' rasped Greyback. 'We've caught Potter!'

They all took several steps backwards, stunned by what they had done. Harry, still fighting to remain present inside his own splitting head, could think of nothing to say: fragmented visions were breaking across the surface of his mind –

... he was gliding around the high walls of the black fortress –

No, he was Harry, tied up and wandless, in grave danger –

... looking up, up to the topmost window, the highest tower –

He was Harry, and they were discussing his fate in low voices –

... time to fly –

'... to the Ministry?'

'To hell with the Ministry,' growled Greyback. 'They'll take the credit, and we won't get a look in. I say we take him straight to You-Know-Who.'

'Will you summon 'im? *'Ere?*' said Scabior, sounding awed, terrified.

'No,' snarled Greyback, 'I haven't got – they say he's using the Malfoys' place as a base. We'll take the boy there.'

Harry thought he knew why Greyback was not calling Voldemort. The werewolf might be allowed to wear Death Eater robes when they wanted to use him, but only Voldemort's inner circle were branded with the Dark Mark: Greyback had not been granted this highest honour.

Harry's scar seared again –

... and he rose into the night, flying straight up to the window at the very top of the tower –

'... completely sure it's 'im? 'Cause if it ain't, Greyback, we're dead.'

'Who's in charge here?' roared Greyback, covering his moment of inadequacy. 'I say that's Potter, and him plus his wand, that's two hundred thousand Galleons right there! But if you're too gutless to come along, any of you, it's all for me, and with any luck, I'll get the girl thrown in!'

第23章 马尔福庄园

"我想你是戴眼镜的吧,波特?"格雷伯克轻声说。

"我找到眼镜了!"一个躲在后面的搜捕队员嚷道,"帐篷里有眼镜,格雷伯克,等等——"

几秒钟后,哈利的眼镜被强行架在他的脸上。现在搜捕队的人都走近了,盯着他看。

"是他!"格雷伯克吼道,"我们抓住了波特!"

他们都退了几步,为自己的收获而感到惊讶。而哈利头痛欲裂,仍在努力维持着不走神,却想不出一句可说的话。片断的景象不断从他的脑海中跳出——

……他正在黑色堡垒的高墙周围飘行——

不,他是哈利,被绑着,没有魔杖,处境极其危险——

……仰望着最顶层的窗户,最高的塔楼——

他是哈利,他们正在小声讨论他的命运——

……该起飞了……

"……去魔法部?"

"去个屁魔法部,"格雷伯克吼道,"他们会抢了功劳,让我们看都看不到一眼。依我说,就直接把他交给神秘人吧。"

"你要把他召来?召到这儿?"斯卡比奥充满敬畏和惊恐地说。

"不,"格雷伯克咆哮道,"我还没有——据说他把马尔福家作为基地。我们就把这男孩带到那儿去。"

哈利猜到格雷伯克为什么没有召唤伏地魔。食死徒为了利用狼人,让他穿上了他们的袍子,但只有伏地魔的核心集团才会有黑魔标记,格雷伯克还没有获得这个最高荣誉。

哈利的伤疤又灼痛起来——

……他跃进了黑夜,向上直飞,到了塔楼最高的窗口——

"……肯定是他吗?如果不是的话,格雷伯克,我们就死定了。"

"这里谁是头儿?"格雷伯克咆哮道,掩盖着自己刚才的窘迫,"我说这个就是波特,他加上他的魔杖,一共二十万加隆!如果你们胆小不想去,就都是我的了,而且运气好的话,这个小妞儿还可能送给我。"

CHAPTER TWENTY-THREE   Malfoy Manor

... the window was the merest slit in the black rock, not big enough for a man to enter ... a skeletal figure was just visible through it, curled beneath a blanket ... dead, or sleeping ...?

'All right!' said Scabior. 'All right, we're in! And what about the rest of 'em, Greyback, what'll we do with 'em?'

'Might as well take the lot. We've got two Mudbloods, that's another ten Galleons. Give me the sword, as well. If they're rubies, that's another small fortune right there.'

The prisoners were dragged to their feet. Harry could hear Hermione's breathing, fast and terrified.

'Grab hold, and make it tight. I'll do Potter!' said Greyback, seizing a fistful of Harry's hair; Harry could feel his long, yellow nails scratching his scalp. 'On three! One – two – three –'

They Disapparated, pulling the prisoners with them. Harry struggled, trying to throw off Greyback's hand, but it was hopeless: Ron and Hermione were squeezed tightly against him on either side, he could not separate from the group, and as the breath was squeezed out of him his scar seared more painfully still –

... as he forced himself through the slit of a window like a snake and landed, lightly as vapour, inside the cell-like room –

The prisoners lurched into one another as they landed in a country lane. Harry's eyes, still puffy, took a moment to acclimatise, then he saw a pair of wrought-iron gates at the foot of what looked like a long drive. He experienced the tiniest trickle of relief. The worst had not happened yet: Voldemort was not here. He was, Harry knew, for he was fighting to resist the vision, in some strange, fortress-like place, at the top of a tower. How long it would take Voldemort to get to this place, once he knew that Harry was here, was another matter ...

One of the Snatchers strode to the gates and shook them.

'How do we get in? They're locked, Greyback, I can't – blimey!'

He whipped his hands away in fright. The iron was contorting, twisting itself out of the abstract furls and coils into a frightening face, which spoke in a clanging, echoing voice: 'State your purpose!'

'We've got Potter!' Greyback roared triumphantly. 'We've captured Harry Potter!'

第23章 马尔福庄园

……窗户是黑石块上极窄的缝隙,人钻不进去……透过它刚刚能看到一个瘦骨嶙峋的身影,蜷曲在毯子下面……是死了,还是睡着了……?

"好吧!"斯卡比奥说,"好吧,我们跟着你!那么另外几个呢,格雷伯克,怎么处置?"

"一起带上。有两个泥巴种,又是十加隆。把那把剑也给我,如果是红宝石的,又能发一笔小财。"

犯人们被拽了起来。哈利能听到赫敏急促、恐惧的呼吸声。

"抓住,弄紧点。我来对付波特。"格雷伯克说着,一把揪住哈利的头发,哈利感到那长长的黄指甲划破了他的头皮,"数到三!——一——二——三——"

他们拖着犯人幻影移形。哈利挣扎着,试图甩开格雷伯克的手,但是毫无希望:罗恩和赫敏被紧紧地挤压在他的两边,他抽不出身。他肺里的空气被挤了出来,伤疤灼痛得更加厉害——

……他像蛇一样挤进窄窄的窗口,轻雾一般飘落到小牢房似的屋子里——

他们降落在一条乡间小路上,犯人们跟跄地撞到一起。哈利仍然肿着双眼。适应了一会儿后,他看到一副锻铁大门,后面似乎是一条长长的车道。他心中微微地松了一口气,最糟糕的事还没有发生,伏地魔不在这里。在哈利努力抵御的那幅画面里,伏地魔还在一个陌生的、堡垒般的地方,一座塔楼的顶上。至于伏地魔得知哈利在这里后,要多长时间才会赶到,就是另一回事了……

一个搜捕队员大步走上前摇晃铁门。

"我们怎么进去?门是锁着的,格雷伯克,我不能——啊呀!"

他吓得往回一缩手。锻铁正在变形,抽象的卷花图形扭曲成一张可怕的面孔,用回音铿锵的声音说:"说明来访目的。"

"我们抓到了波特!"格雷伯克耀武扬威地咆哮道,"我们逮住了哈利·波特!"

CHAPTER TWENTY-THREE   Malfoy Manor

The gates swung open.

'Come on!' said Greyback to his men, and the prisoners were shunted through the gates and up the drive, between high hedges that muffled their footsteps. Harry saw a ghostly white shape above him, and realised it was an albino peacock. He stumbled and was dragged on to his feet by Greyback; now he was staggering along sideways, tied back-to-back to the four other prisoners. Closing his puffy eyes he allowed the pain in his scar to overcome him for a moment, wanting to know what Voldemort was doing, whether he knew yet that Harry was caught –

... the emaciated figure stirred beneath its thin blanket and rolled over towards him, eyes opening in a skull of a face ... the frail man sat up, great sunken eyes fixed upon him, upon Voldemort, and then he smiled. Most of his teeth were gone ...

'So, you have come. I thought you would ... one day. But your journey was pointless. I never had it.'

'You lie!'

As Voldemort's anger throbbed inside him, Harry's scar threatened to burst with pain, and he wrenched his mind back to his own body, fighting to remain present as the prisoners were pushed over gravel.

Light spilled out over all of them.

'What is this?' said a woman's cold voice.

'We're here to see He Who Must Not Be Named!' rasped Greyback.

'Who are you?'

'You know me!' There was resentment in the werewolf's voice, 'Fenrir Greyback! We've caught Harry Potter!'

Greyback seized Harry and dragged him round to face the light, forcing the other prisoners to shuffle round too.

'I know 'e's swollen, ma'am, but it's 'im!' piped up Scabior. 'If you look a bit closer, you'll see 'is scar. And this 'ere, see the girl? The Mudblood who's been travelling around with 'im, ma'am. There's no doubt it's 'im, and we've got 'is wand as well! 'Ere, ma'am –'

Harry saw Narcissa Malfoy scrutinising his swollen face. Scabior thrust the blackthorn wand at her. She raised her eyebrows.

第23章 马尔福庄园

大门立刻打开了。

"跟上!"格雷伯克朝手下说道。犯人们被推过大门,押上了车道,两旁高高的树篱掩住了他们的脚步声。哈利看到他的头顶上空有个幽灵般的白色影子,接着发现那是一只白孔雀。他绊了一下,被格雷伯克拽了起来。他侧着身子跟跟跄跄,和另外四个犯人背靠背地绑在一起。他闭上肿胀的双眼,让伤疤的疼痛暂时战胜自己,想知道伏地魔此刻在做什么,是否已经知道哈利被抓到了——

……薄毯子下面瘦弱的身躯动了一下,转过来朝着他,骷髅般的面孔,眼睛睁开了……那个虚弱的人坐了起来,深陷的双眼盯着他,盯着伏地魔,然后笑了,牙齿几乎掉光……

"你来了。我想你会来的……总有一天。但是你此行毫无意义。我从没拥有过它。"

"你撒谎!"

伏地魔的愤怒在他体内跳动,哈利的伤疤痛得似乎要炸裂了。他把思维猛拉回来,努力维持着不走神,犯人们被推搡着行走在碎石路上。

光线照在所有的人身上。

"怎么回事?"一个妇人冷冷的声音问道。

"我们是来见神秘人的!"格雷伯克粗声回答。

"你是谁?"

"你知道我!"狼人的声音里透露出愤恨,"芬里尔·格雷伯克!我们抓住了哈利·波特!"

格雷伯克揪住哈利,把他拖过来面朝着灯光,迫使别的犯人也跟着转了方位。

"我知道他脸肿了,夫人,但就是他!"斯卡比奥说道,"如果您靠近点看,可以看到他的伤疤。还有这儿,看这个女孩,就是一直跟他同行的那个泥巴种,夫人。毫无疑问就是他,我们还拿到了他的魔杖!在这儿,夫人——"

从肿胀的眼皮的缝隙间,哈利看到纳西莎·马尔福正在查看他肿起的脸。斯卡比奥把黑刺李木魔杖塞给了她。她扬起了眉毛。

CHAPTER TWENTY-THREE Malfoy Manor

'Bring them in,' she said.

Harry and the others were shoved and kicked up broad stone steps, into a hallway lined with portraits.

'Follow me,' said Narcissa, leading the way across the hall. 'My son, Draco, is home for his Easter holidays. If that is Harry Potter, he will know.'

The drawing room dazzled after the darkness outside; even with his eyes almost closed Harry could make out the wide proportions of the room. A crystal chandelier hung from the ceiling, more portraits against the dark purple walls. Two figures rose from chairs in front of an ornate marble fireplace as the prisoners were forced into the room by the Snatchers.

'What is this?'

The dreadfully familiar, drawling voice of Lucius Malfoy fell on Harry's ears. He was panicking now: he could see no way out, and it was easier, as his fear mounted, to block out Voldemort's thoughts, though his scar was still burning.

'They say they've got Potter,' said Narcissa's cold voice. 'Draco, come here.'

Harry did not dare look directly at Draco, but saw him obliquely: a figure slightly taller than he was, rising from an armchair, his face a pale and pointed blur beneath white-blond hair.

Greyback forced the prisoners to turn again so as to place Harry directly beneath the chandelier.

'Well, boy?' rasped the werewolf.

Harry was facing a mirror over the fireplace, a great gilded thing with an intricately scrolled frame. Through the slits of his eyes, he saw his own reflection for the first time since leaving Grimmauld Place.

His face was huge, shiny and pink, every feature distorted by Hermione's jinx. His black hair reached his shoulders and there was a dark shadow around his jaw. Had he not known that it was he who stood there, he would have wondered who was wearing his glasses. He resolved not to speak, for his voice was sure to give him away; yet he still avoided eye contact with Draco as the latter approached.

'Well, Draco?' said Lucius Malfoy. He sounded avid. 'Is it? Is it Harry Potter?'

"带进来吧。"她说道。

哈利等人被连推带踹地押上宽阔的石阶,进了两边挂着肖像的门厅。

"跟我来。"纳西莎说,领着他们穿过门厅,"我儿子德拉科复活节放假在家。如果真是哈利·波特,他会认得的。"

在外面的黑暗里待久了,客厅里的灯光使人眼花。哈利的眼睛尽管都快闭上了,但也能看得出房间的宽敞气派。天花板上挂着水晶的枝形吊灯,深紫色的墙壁上挂着更多的肖像。犯人们被搜捕队员强行推进去时,两个身影从华丽的大理石壁炉前的座椅上站了起来。

"怎么回事?"

一个熟悉得可怕的懒洋洋的声音钻入了哈利的耳朵,是卢修斯·马尔福。哈利现在惊慌起来,看来是没有出路了。当恐惧增加时,抵挡伏地魔的思维就变得比较容易了,尽管伤疤还在灼痛。

"他们说抓到了波特,"纳西莎冷冷的声音说,"德拉科,过来。"

哈利不敢正视德拉科,斜着眼看到了他:一个比他稍高的身影从扶手椅上站了起来,淡金色头发下是一张苍白尖细的模糊脸庞。

格雷伯克又推着犯人们转了起来,让哈利站在枝形吊灯的正下方。

"怎么样,男孩?"狼人用刺耳的声音说。

哈利正对着壁炉上的镜子,那是一面镀金大镜,镜框上有精美的涡卷纹饰。透过双眼的缝隙,他看到了镜中的自己,这是自离开格里莫广场后的第一次。

他的脸硕大无比,亮晶晶、红通通的,所有的面部特征都被赫敏的咒语扭曲了。黑发披到了肩膀上,嘴巴周围有一片黑色阴影。若不是知道自己站在这里,哈利可能会纳闷是谁戴着他的眼镜。他下定决心不说话,因为声音肯定会使他暴露。德拉科走近了,哈利仍避免与他目光接触。

"怎么样,德拉科?"卢修斯·马尔福急切地问,"是吗?是哈利·波特吗?"

'I can't – I can't be sure,' said Draco. He was keeping his distance from Greyback, and seemed as scared of looking at Harry as Harry was of looking at him.

'But look at him carefully, look! Come closer!'

Harry had never heard Lucius Malfoy so excited.

'Draco, if we are the ones who hand Potter over to the Dark Lord, everything will be forgiv–'

'Now, we won't be forgetting who actually caught him, I hope, Mr Malfoy?' said Greyback menacingly.

'Of course not, of course not!' said Lucius impatiently. He approached Harry himself, came so close that Harry could see the usually languid, pale face in sharp detail even through his swollen eyes. With his face a puffy mask, Harry felt as though he was peering out from between the bars of a cage.

'What did you do to him?' Lucius asked Greyback. 'How did he get into this state?'

'That wasn't us.'

'Looks more like a Stinging Jinx to me,' said Lucius.

His grey eyes raked Harry's forehead.

'There's something there,' he whispered, 'it could be the scar, stretched tight ... Draco, come here, look properly! What do you think?'

Harry saw Draco's face up close, now, right beside his father's. They were extraordinarily alike, except that while his father looked beside himself with excitement, Draco's expression was full of reluctance, even fear.

'I don't know,' he said, and he walked away towards the fireplace where his mother stood watching.

'We had better be certain, Lucius,' Narcissa called to her husband in her cold, clear voice. 'Completely sure that it is Potter, before we summon the Dark Lord ... They say this is his,' she was looking closely at the blackthorn wand, 'but it does not resemble Ollivander's description ... If we are mistaken, if we call the Dark Lord here for nothing ... remember what he did to Rowle and Dolohov?'

'What about the Mudblood, then?' growled Greyback. Harry was nearly thrown off his feet as the Snatchers forced the prisoners to swivel around again, so that the light fell on Hermione instead.

第23章 马尔福庄园

"我不能——不能确定。"德拉科说。他和格雷伯克保持着一段距离，而且似乎像哈利不敢看他一样不敢看哈利。

"仔细看，看呀！走近点儿！"

哈利从没见过卢修斯·马尔福如此激动。

"德拉科，如果是我们把波特交给了黑魔王，一切都会被原谅——"

"我希望我们不要忘了是谁抓到他的，马尔福先生？"格雷伯克威胁道。

"当然不会，当然不会！"卢修斯不耐烦地说。他自己靠近了哈利，一向没精打采的苍白面孔凑得这么近，哈利从肿眼皮的缝隙中也能清晰地看到那张脸的细部。哈利的肿脸像戴着面具，他觉得自己是在隔着笼子的栅栏朝外面窥视。

"你对他做了什么？"卢修斯问格雷伯克，"他是怎么搞成这样的？"

"不是我们搞的。"

"我看，很像是蜇人咒。"卢修斯说。

他的灰眼睛扫视着哈利的前额。

"那里有东西，"他小声说，"可能是伤疤，绷得很紧……德拉科，过来，好好看看！你是怎么想的？"

哈利看到德拉科的脸凑到了自己的眼前，在他父亲的面孔旁边。两张脸非常相像，只是父亲激动得难以自制，而德拉科的表情是很不情愿，甚至有点害怕。

"我不知道。"他说，然后朝站在壁炉边观看的妈妈走去。

"我们最好搞清楚，卢修斯，"纳西莎用她那冷冷的声音清楚地对丈夫说，"完全确认是波特之后，再召唤黑魔王……他们说这是他的——"她正在仔细查看黑刺李木魔杖，"——但是它不像奥利凡德描述的……如果我们搞错了，把黑魔王白白叫过来……记得他是怎么对待罗尔和多洛霍夫的吗？"

"那么这个泥巴种呢？"格雷伯克吼道。搜捕队员又把犯人们推得转了过去，让灯光照着赫敏，哈利几乎被拽得摔了一跤。

'Wait,' said Narcissa sharply. 'Yes – yes, she was in Madam Malkin's with Potter! I saw her picture in the *Prophet*! Look, Draco, isn't it the Granger girl?'

'I ... maybe ... yeah.'

'But then, that's the Weasley boy!' shouted Lucius, striding round the bound prisoners to face Ron. 'It's them, Potter's friends – Draco look at him, isn't it Arthur Weasley's son, what's his name –?'

'Yeah,' said Draco again, his back to the prisoners. 'It could be.'

The drawing-room door opened behind Harry. A woman spoke, and the sound of the voice wound Harry's fear to an even higher pitch.

'What is this? What's happened, Cissy?'

Bellatrix Lestrange walked slowly around the prisoners, and stopped on Harry's right, staring at Hermione through her heavily lidded eyes.

'But surely,' she said quietly, 'this is the Mudblood girl? This is Granger?'

'Yes, yes, it's Granger!' cried Lucius. 'And beside her, we think, Potter! Potter and his friends, caught at last!'

'Potter?' shrieked Bellatrix, and she backed away, the better to take in Harry. 'Are you sure? Well, then, the Dark Lord must be informed at once!'

She dragged back her left sleeve: Harry saw the Dark Mark burned into the flesh of her arm, and knew that she was about to touch it, to summon her beloved master –

'I was about to call him!' said Lucius, and his hand actually closed upon Bellatrix's wrist, preventing her from touching the Mark. '*I* shall summon him, Bella, Potter has been brought to my house, and it is therefore upon my authority –'

'Your authority!' she sneered, attempting to wrench her hand from his grasp. 'You lost your authority when you lost your wand, Lucius! How dare you! Take your hands off me!'

'This is nothing to do with you, you did not capture the boy –'

'Begging your pardon, *Mr* Malfoy,' interjected Greyback, 'but it's us that caught Potter, and it's us that'll be claiming the gold –'

第23章 马尔福庄园

"等一下,"纳西莎尖叫道,"对——对,她和波特一起去过摩金夫人长袍专卖店!我在《预言家日报》上见过她的照片!德拉科,看,这是那个姓格兰杰的女孩吗?"

"我……可能……是吧。"

"那么,那个就是韦斯莱家的男孩!"卢修斯喊道,大步绕过绑着的犯人,站到罗恩面前,"是他们,波特的朋友们——德拉科,你看,他不是亚瑟·韦斯莱的儿子吗,他叫什么——?"

"嗯,"德拉科又说,背朝着犯人,"可能是吧。"

哈利后面的客厅门打开了。一个妇人的说话声把哈利的恐慌推向了更高点。

"怎么啦?发生什么事了,西茜?"

贝拉特里克斯·莱斯特兰奇绕着犯人们缓缓地走过来,停在哈利的右边,透过她的肿眼皮盯着赫敏看。

"哎哟,"她轻声说,"这不就是那个泥巴种女孩吗?这不就是格兰杰吗?"

"是的,是的,是格兰杰!"卢修斯叫喊道,"我们认为她旁边是波特!波特和他的朋友们,终于抓到了!"

"波特?"贝拉特里克斯尖叫道,退后了几步,上下打量着哈利,"你确定吗?那么,必须马上通知黑魔王!"

她捋起了左袖,哈利看见了手臂上烙进肉里的黑魔标记,知道她就要触摸它,召唤她心爱的主人——

"我刚才正要召唤他!"卢修斯说着,居然一把抓住了贝拉特里克斯的手腕,阻止她触摸黑魔标记,"应该由我来召唤他,贝拉。波特是带到我家的,因此我应该有权利——"

"你有权利!"贝拉特里克斯嘲笑道,试着甩开他的手,"你失去了魔杖,你就没有权利了,卢修斯!你竟敢!把手拿开!"

"这和你没有关系,抓到这男孩的不是你——"

"对不起,马尔福先生,"格雷伯克插话道,"波特是我们抓住的,赏金也应该归我们——"

CHAPTER TWENTY-THREE   Malfoy Manor

'Gold!' laughed Bellatrix, still attempting to throw off her brother-in-law, her free hand groping in her pocket for her wand. 'Take your gold, filthy scavenger, what do I want with gold? I seek only the honour of his – of –'

She stopped struggling, her dark eyes fixed upon something Harry could not see. Jubilant at her capitulation, Lucius threw her hand from him and ripped up his own sleeve –

'STOP!' shrieked Bellatrix. 'Do not touch it, we shall all perish if the Dark Lord comes now!'

Lucius froze, his index finger hovering over his own Mark. Bellatrix strode out of Harry's limited line of vision.

'What is that?' he heard her say.

'Sword,' grunted an out-of-sight Snatcher.

'Give it to me.'

'It's not yorn, Missus, it's mine, I reckon I found it.'

There was a bang and a flash of red light: Harry knew that the Snatcher had been Stunned. There was a roar of anger from his fellows: Scabior drew his wand.

'What d'you think you're playing at, woman?'

'*Stupefy*,' she screamed, '*stupefy!*'

They were no match for her, even though there were four of them against one of her: she was a witch, as Harry knew, with prodigious skill and no conscience. They fell where they stood, all except Greyback, who had been forced into a kneeling position, his arms outstretched. Out of the corners of his eyes, Harry saw Bellatrix bearing down upon the werewolf, the sword of Gryffindor gripped tightly in her hand, her face waxen.

'Where did you get this sword?' she whispered to Greyback as she pulled his wand out of his unresisting grip.

'How dare you?' he snarled, his mouth the only thing that could move as he was forced to gaze up at her. He bared his pointed teeth. 'Release me, woman!'

'Where did you find this sword?' she repeated, brandishing it in his face. 'Snape sent it to my vault in Gringotts!'

'It was in their tent,' rasped Greyback. 'Release me, I say!'

She waved her wand and the werewolf sprang to his feet, but appeared

第23章 马尔福庄园

"赏金!"贝拉特里克斯大笑道,一边仍然试图摆脱妹夫,一边用另一只手在口袋里摸索着魔杖,"拿你的金子吧,肮脏的食腐动物,我要金子干什么?我只追求荣誉——"

她停止了挣扎,一双黑眼睛盯着哈利看不见的东西。卢修斯见她投降了,兴奋地甩开她的手,卷起自己的袖子——

"住手!"贝拉特里克斯尖叫道,"别碰它,如果黑魔王现在就来,我们都会死!"

卢修斯愣住了,食指悬在他的黑魔标记上方。贝拉特里克斯大步走出了哈利有限的视线范围。

"那是什么?"他听见她问。

"宝剑。"一个视线外的搜捕队员嘟囔道。

"把它给我。"

"不是你的,夫人,它是我的,是我发现它的。"

砰的一声,伴随着一道红光,哈利知道那个搜捕队员被施了昏迷咒。他的同伙们怒吼起来,斯卡比奥拔出魔杖。

"你以为你在玩什么,娘儿们?"

"昏昏倒地,"贝拉特里克斯尖叫道,"昏昏倒地!"

搜捕队的人根本不是她的对手,尽管他们是四个对她一个。哈利知道她是一个法术高强而且心狠手辣的女巫。其他人都原地倒下了,只有格雷伯克是跪在地上,双臂张开。哈利眼角的余光看到贝拉特里克斯冲向了狼人,她手里紧握着格兰芬多宝剑,脸色蜡白。

"你们是从哪儿拿到这宝剑的?"她低声问格雷伯克,一边从他无力的手中拿走了魔杖。

"你怎么敢?"格雷伯克咆哮道,被迫抬头看着她,只剩下嘴能动了。他龇着尖牙说:"放开我,娘儿们!"

"你们是从哪儿拿到这宝剑的?"贝拉特里克斯又问,在他面前挥了挥宝剑,"斯内普把它送到古灵阁我的金库里了呀!"

"是在他们的帐篷里。"格雷伯克嘶吼道,"放开我,听见没有!"

贝拉特里克斯一挥魔杖,狼人就跳了起来,但似乎心存戒备,不

too wary to approach her. He prowled behind an armchair, his filthy, curved nails clutching its back.

'Draco, move this scum outside,' said Bellatrix, indicating the unconscious men. 'If you haven't got the guts to finish them, then leave them in the courtyard for me.'

'Don't you dare speak to Draco like –' said Narcissa furiously, but Bellatrix screamed, 'Be quiet! The situation is graver than you can possibly imagine, Cissy! We have a very serious problem!'

She stood, panting slightly, looking down at the sword, examining its hilt. Then she turned to look at the silent prisoners.

'If it is indeed Potter, he must not be harmed,' she muttered, more to herself than to the others. 'The Dark Lord wishes to dispose of Potter himself ... but if he finds out ... I must ... I must know ...'

She turned back to her sister again.

'The prisoners must be placed in the cellar, while I think what to do!'

'This is my house, Bella, you don't give orders in my –'

'Do it! You have no idea of the danger we are in!' shrieked Bellatrix: she looked frightening, mad; a thin stream of fire issued from her wand and burned a hole in the carpet.

Narcissa hesitated for a moment, then addressed the werewolf.

'Take these prisoners down to the cellar, Greyback.'

'Wait,' said Bellatrix sharply. 'All except ... except for the Mudblood.'

Greyback gave a grunt of pleasure.

'No!' shouted Ron. 'You can have me, keep me!'

Bellatrix hit him across the face; the blow echoed around the room.

'If she dies under questioning, I'll take you next,' she said. 'Blood traitor is next to Mudblood in my book. Take them downstairs, Greyback, and make sure they are secure, but do nothing more to them – yet.'

She threw Greyback's wand back to him, then took a short silver knife from under her robes. She cut Hermione free from the other prisoners, then dragged her by the hair into the middle of the room while Greyback forced the rest of them to shuffle across to another door, into a dark passageway, his wand held out in front of him, projecting an invisible and irresistible force.

第23章 马尔福庄园

敢靠近她。他走到一把扶手椅后面,用肮脏的、弯曲的指甲抓着椅背。

"德拉科,把这些渣滓弄出去。"贝拉特里克斯说,指着那些昏迷的搜捕队员,"如果你没有胆子干掉他们,就给我先把他们扔在院子里。"

"你竟敢这样对德拉科说话——"纳西莎大怒道,但是贝拉特里克斯尖叫起来,"安静!情况比你想象的严重得多,西茜!我们遇到大麻烦了!"

她站了起来,轻轻喘着气,低头看着宝剑,研究着剑柄,然后转身望着默不作声的犯人们。

"如果他真是波特,就绝不能让他受伤。"她嘟囔道,更像是自言自语,"黑魔王想亲自干掉波特……如果他发现……我必须……我必须知道……"

她再次转向她妹妹。

"必须先把犯人关进地牢,等我想想该怎么办!"

"这是我的家,贝拉,你不能这样发号施令——"

"快干!你根本就不知道我们有多危险!"贝拉特里克斯尖叫道。她看起来恐怖而疯狂,一条细细的火苗蹿出她的魔杖,把地毯烧了一个洞。

纳西莎犹豫了片刻,然后对狼人说:

"把这些犯人带到地牢里去,格雷伯克。"

"等一下,"贝拉特里克斯尖声说道,"除了……除了这个泥巴种。"

格雷伯克满意地哼了一声。

"不!"罗恩大叫道,"可以留下我,留下我!"

贝拉特里克斯一拳砸在他的脸上,击打声在屋里回响。

"如果她在审讯中死了,下一个就是你。"贝拉特里克斯说,"在我的黑名单上,泥巴种下面就是纯血统的叛徒。格雷伯克,把他们带下去,看牢了,但是别动他们——暂时别动。"

贝拉特里克斯把格雷伯克的魔杖扔给了他,然后从袍子底下掏出一把银色的小刀,把赫敏与其他犯人割开,揪着头发把她拉到屋子中央。格雷伯克则押着其他犯人慢慢走向另一道门,进入了一条黑暗的过道。他的魔杖举在前面,发出一股无形的、不可抗拒的力量。

CHAPTER TWENTY-THREE   Malfoy Manor

'Reckon she'll let me have a bit of the girl when she's finished with her?' Greyback crooned, as he forced them along the corridor. 'I'd say I'll get a bite or two, wouldn't you, Ginger?'

Harry could feel Ron shaking. They were forced down a steep flight of stairs, still tied back-to-back and in danger of slipping and breaking their necks at any moment. At the bottom was a heavy door. Greyback unlocked it with a tap of his wand, then forced them into a dank and musty room and left them in total darkness. The echoing bang of the slammed cellar door had not died away before there was a terrible, drawn-out scream from directly above them.

'HERMIONE!' Ron bellowed, and he started to writhe and struggle against the ropes tying them together, so that Harry staggered. 'HERMIONE!'

'Be quiet!' Harry said. 'Shut up, Ron, we need to work out a way –'

'HERMIONE! HERMIONE!'

'We need a plan, stop yelling – we need to get these ropes off –'

'Harry?' came a whisper through the darkness. 'Ron? Is that you?'

Ron stopped shouting. There was a sound of movement close by them, then Harry saw a shadow moving closer.

'Harry? Ron?'

'*Luna?*'

'Yes, it's me! Oh, no, I didn't want you to be caught!'

'Luna, can you help us get these ropes off?' said Harry.

'Oh, yes, I expect so ... there's an old nail we use if we need to break anything ... just a moment ...'

Hermione screamed again from overhead, and they could hear Bellatrix screaming too, but her words were inaudible, for Ron shouted again, 'HERMIONE! HERMIONE!'

'Mr Ollivander?' Harry could hear Luna saying. 'Mr Ollivander, have you got the nail? If you just move over a little bit ... I think it was beside the water jug ...'

She was back within seconds.

'You'll need to stay still,' she said.

Harry could feel her digging at the rope's tough fibres to work the knots free. From upstairs they heard Bellatrix's voice.

第23章 马尔福庄园

"她审讯完了之后,会把那小妞儿分一点给我吗?"格雷伯克轻声哼道,一边顺着走廊驱赶他们,"我说我会吃上一两口的,你说呢,红毛?"

哈利可以感觉到罗恩在发抖。他们被押着走过一段极陡的楼梯,仍然背靠背地绑着,随时都有可能失足摔断脖子。底下是一扇沉重的门。格雷伯克用魔杖轻轻一敲,打开了门,把他们推进了一个潮湿发霉的房间,里面一片漆黑。牢门重重关上引起的回声还没有完全消失,正上方就传来了一声恐怖的、拖长了的尖叫。

"**赫敏!**"罗恩吼道,拼命扭动想挣开把他们捆在一起的绳索,拽得哈利趔趔趄趄,"**赫敏!**"

"安静!"哈利说,"别出声,罗恩,我们需要想个办法——"

"**赫敏!赫敏!**"

"我们需要一个计划,别喊了——得把绳子解开——"

"哈利?"黑暗中传来一声低语,"罗恩?是你们吗?"

罗恩停止了嘶喊。旁边好像有东西在移动,然后哈利见到一个影子正在靠近。

"哈利?罗恩?"

"卢娜?"

"是,是我!哦,不,我不希望你们被抓到!"

"卢娜,你能帮我们把绳子解开吗?"哈利说。

"哦,我想可以……我们有一个旧钉子可以用来割东西……稍等一下……"

楼上的赫敏又在尖叫了,他们听见贝拉特里克斯也在尖叫,但听不清她在说什么,因为罗恩又喊了起来:"**赫敏!赫敏!**"

"奥利凡德先生?"哈利听见卢娜在说,"奥利凡德先生,钉子在您那儿吗?您能挪动一点点吗……我想它在水壶旁边……"

几秒钟后,她走了回来。

"你们不要动。"她说。

哈利能感觉到她在戳那结实的绳子,努力把绳结磨断。楼上传来贝拉特里克斯的声音。

CHAPTER TWENTY-THREE   Malfoy Manor

'I'm going to ask you again! Where did you get this sword? *Where?*'

'We found it – we found it – PLEASE!' Hermione screamed again; Ron struggled harder than ever and the rusty nail slipped on to Harry's wrist.

'Ron, please stay still!' Luna whispered. 'I can't see what I'm doing –'

'My pocket!' said Ron. 'In my pocket, there's a Deluminator, and it's full of light!'

A few seconds later, there was a click and the luminescent spheres the Deluminator had sucked from the lamps in the tent flew into the cellar: unable to rejoin their sources they simply hung there, like tiny suns, flooding the underground room with light. Harry saw Luna, all eyes in her white face, and the motionless figure of Ollivander the wandmaker, curled up on the floor in the corner. Craning round, he caught sight of their fellow prisoners: Dean and Griphook the goblin, who seemed barely conscious, kept standing by the ropes that bound him to the humans.

'Oh, that's much easier, thanks Ron,' said Luna, and she began hacking at their bindings again. 'Hello, Dean!'

From above came Bellatrix's voice.

'You are lying, filthy Mudblood, and I know it! You have been inside my vault at Gringotts! Tell the truth, *tell the truth!*'

Another terrible scream –

'HERMIONE!'

'What else did you take? What else have you got? Tell me the truth or, I swear, I shall run you through with this knife!'

'There!'

Harry felt the ropes fall away and turned, rubbing his wrists, to see Ron running around the cellar, looking up at the low ceiling, searching for a trapdoor. Dean, his face bruised and bloody, said, 'Thanks,' to Luna and stood there, shivering, but Griphook sank on to the cellar floor looking groggy and disorientated, many welts across his swarthy face.

Ron was now trying to Disapparate without a wand.

'There's no way out, Ron,' said Luna, watching his fruitless efforts. 'The cellar is completely escape-proof. I tried, at first. Mr Ollivander has been here for a long time, he's tried everything.'

"我再问你一次！你们是从哪儿弄到这宝剑的？哪儿？"

"我们捡到的——捡到的——**拜托了**！"赫敏再次尖叫。罗恩比以前更猛烈地挣扎着，锈钉子滑到了哈利的手腕上。

"罗恩，请别动！"卢娜低声说，"我看不见——"

"我的口袋！"罗恩说，"在我口袋里，有熄灯器，它里面有好多灯光！"

几秒钟后，随着咔嗒一声，熄灯器从帐篷里吸走的光球飞进了地牢。由于找不到原来的光源，它们只是悬挂在那里，像一个个小太阳，把地下室照得亮堂堂的。哈利看见了卢娜，苍白的脸上好像只剩下一双眼睛，还看到了魔杖制作人奥利凡德的身影，他一动不动地蜷缩在墙角的地板上。哈利扭头张望，看到了其他难友：迪安和妖精拉环。拉环都快晕过去了，只因为绑在别人身上才没有倒下。

"哦，这就容易多了，谢谢你，罗恩。"卢娜说，一边接着对付绳结，"你好，迪安！"

上面传来贝拉特里克斯的声音。

"你在撒谎，龌龊的泥巴种，我知道！你去过我古灵阁的金库！老实交代，老实交代！"

又是一声恐怖的尖叫——

"**赫敏**！"

"你们还拿了什么？还拿了什么？老实交代，不然，我发誓我要用这把刀把你刺穿！"

"好了！"

哈利感到绳子掉了，他揉揉手腕转过身，看到罗恩正绕着地牢乱跑，抬头望着低矮的天花板，希望找到一个活板门。满脸青肿和血迹的迪安向卢娜说了声"谢谢"，站在那里浑身发抖。拉环则瘫在了地上，似乎头晕目眩辨不清方向，黝黑的脸上满是伤痕。

罗恩正在尝试不用魔杖幻影移形。

"没有出口，罗恩。"卢娜看着他毫无结果的努力，说，"这地牢根本逃不出去。起先我也试过。奥利凡德先生在这儿已经很久了，他什么都试过了。"

CHAPTER TWENTY-THREE   Malfoy Manor

Hermione was screaming again: the sound went through Harry like physical pain. Barely conscious of the fierce prickling of his scar, he, too, started to run around the cellar, feeling the walls for he hardly knew what, knowing in his heart that it was useless.

'What else did you take, what else? ANSWER ME! CRUCIO!'

Hermione's screams echoed off the walls upstairs, Ron was half sobbing as he pounded the walls with his fists, and Harry, in utter desperation, seized Hagrid's pouch from around his neck and groped inside it: he pulled out Dumbledore's Snitch and shook it, hoping for he did not know what – nothing happened; he waved the broken halves of the phoenix wand, but they were lifeless – the mirror fragment fell sparkling to the floor, and he saw a gleam of brightest blue –

Dumbledore's eye was gazing at him out of the mirror.

'Help us!' he yelled at it in mad desperation. 'We're in the cellar of Malfoy Manor, help us!'

The eye blinked, and was gone.

Harry was not even sure that it had really been there. He tilted the shard of mirror this way and that, and saw nothing reflected there but the walls and ceiling of their prison, and upstairs Hermione was screaming worse than ever, and next to him, Ron was bellowing, 'HERMIONE! HERMIONE!'

'How did you get into my vault?' they heard Bellatrix scream. 'Did that dirty little goblin in the cellar help you?'

'We only met him tonight!' Hermione sobbed. 'We've never been inside your vault ... it isn't the real sword! It's a copy, just a copy!'

'A copy?' screeched Bellatrix. 'Oh, a likely story!'

'But we can find out easily!' came Lucius's voice. 'Draco, fetch the goblin, he can tell us whether the sword is real or not!'

Harry dashed across the cellar to where Griphook was huddled on the floor.

'Griphook,' he whispered into the goblin's pointed ear, 'you must tell them that sword's a fake, they mustn't know it's the real one, Griphook, please –'

He could hear someone scuttling down the cellar steps; next moment, Draco's shaking voice spoke from behind the door.

'Stand back. Line up against the back wall. Don't try anything, or I'll kill you!'

第23章 马尔福庄园

赫敏再次尖叫起来，那声音好像刀子捅在哈利身上一般。他几乎已经感觉不到伤疤的剧烈刺痛，也开始绕着地牢跑动，盲目地摸着墙壁，虽然心里知道这毫无用处。

"你们还拿了什么，还有什么？**回答我！钻心剜骨！**"

赫敏的尖叫声在楼上回响，罗恩用拳头砸墙，抽噎着，而哈利绝望中抓住了海格给他的皮袋，在里面摸索着，掏出了邓布利多给他的金色飞贼，摇晃着，希望会发生什么——什么也没有发生。他挥动着折断的凤凰尾羽魔杖，但它毫无生气——镜子的碎片掉在地上闪闪发光，他看见了一道明亮的蓝光——

邓布利多的眼睛正从镜子里凝视着他。

"救救我们！"他万分绝望地喊道，"我们在马尔福庄园的地牢里，救救我们！"

那眼睛眨了一下，消失了。

哈利甚至不能确定刚才看到过它。他拿着镜子碎片从各个角度看，什么也没有，只有地牢的墙壁和天花板映在里面。楼上赫敏的尖叫声更加惨烈，罗恩在旁边咆哮着：**"赫敏！赫敏！"**

"你们是怎么闯进我的金库的？"他们听见贝拉特里克斯尖叫道，"是不是地牢里那个肮脏的小妖精帮助你们的？"

"我们今天晚上才碰到他！"赫敏抽泣道，"我们从没进过你的金库……这不是那把真的宝剑！是仿制品，只是仿制品！"

"仿制品？"贝拉特里克斯尖声喊道，"哼，编得倒像！"

"这很容易查明！"卢修斯说道，"德拉科，把那个妖精抓来，他可以鉴定宝剑是真的还是假的！"

哈利冲到蜷缩在地上的拉环身边。

"拉环，"他对着妖精的尖耳朵低语道，"你必须说宝剑是假的，千万不能让他们知道是真的，拉环，求你了——"

哈利听见有人急速奔下地牢楼梯，随即德拉科颤抖的声音从牢门外传来。

"朝后站，靠墙站成一排，别想轻举妄动，否则就杀了你们！"

CHAPTER TWENTY-THREE   Malfoy Manor

They did as they were bidden; as the lock turned Ron clicked the Deluminator and the lights whisked back into his pocket, restoring the cellar's darkness. The door flew open; Malfoy marched inside, wand held out in front of him, pale and determined. He seized the little goblin by the arm and backed out again, dragging Griphook with him. The door slammed shut and at the same moment a loud *crack* echoed inside the cellar.

Ron clicked the Deluminator. Three balls of light flew back into the air from his pocket, revealing Dobby the house-elf, who had just Apparated into their midst.

'DOB–!'

Harry hit Ron on the arm to stop him shouting, and Ron looked terrified at his mistake. Footsteps crossed the ceiling overhead: Draco marching Griphook to Bellatrix.

Dobby's enormous, tennis-ball-shaped eyes were wide; he was trembling from his feet to the tips of his ears. He was back in the home of his old masters, and it was clear that he was petrified.

'Harry Potter,' he squeaked, in the tiniest quiver of a voice, 'Dobby has come to rescue you.'

'But how did you –?'

An awful scream drowned Harry's words: Hermione was being tortured again. He cut to the essentials.

'You can Disapparate out of this cellar?' he asked Dobby, who nodded, his ears flapping.

'And you can take humans with you?'

Dobby nodded again.

'Right. Dobby, I want you to grab Luna, Dean and Mr Ollivander, and take them – take them to –'

'Bill and Fleur's,' said Ron. 'Shell Cottage on the outskirts of Tinworth!'

The elf nodded for a third time.

'And then come back,' said Harry. 'Can you do that, Dobby?'

'Of course, Harry Potter,' whispered the little elf. He hurried over to Mr Ollivander, who appeared to be barely conscious. He took one of the wandmaker's hands in his own, then held out the other to Luna and Dean, neither of whom moved.

第 23 章 马尔福庄园

他们照办了。当锁孔转动时,罗恩一摁熄灯器,光球迅速飞回了他的口袋里,地牢里重又一片漆黑。门开了,德拉科大步走了进来,魔杖举在身前,看上去脸色苍白而坚决。他抓住拉环的胳膊,拖着小妖精退了出去。牢门重重地关上了,同时啪的一声爆响回荡在地牢里。

罗恩摁了一下熄灯器,三个光球又从口袋里飞到空中,照亮了刚刚幻影显形到他们中间的家养小精灵多比。

"多——!"

哈利打了一下罗恩的手臂,没让他喊出声来。罗恩似乎也为自己的错误而害怕。天花板顶上有脚步声走过,德拉科把拉环押送到贝拉特里克斯跟前。

多比网球般的大眼睛睁得圆圆的,从脚到耳朵尖都在颤抖。他回到了旧主人的家里,显然吓呆了。

"哈利·波特,"他吱吱地发出十分微弱的颤声,"多比救你来了。"

"可你是怎么——?"

一声恐怖的尖叫淹没了哈利的声音:赫敏又在遭受酷刑。他赶快捡最要紧的说。

"你可以幻影移形离开这个地牢吗?"他问,多比点点头,耳朵拍打了几下。

"你可以带人出去吗?"

多比再次点点头。

"好的。多比,我要你带上卢娜、迪安和奥利凡德先生,把他们带到——带到——"

"比尔和芙蓉家,"罗恩说,"丁沃斯郊区的贝壳小屋。"

小精灵第三次点点头。

"然后再回来。"哈利说,"你能做到吗,多比?"

"当然,哈利·波特。"小精灵低语道。他匆匆赶到几乎人事不省的奥利凡德先生面前,抓住了魔杖制作人的手,然后把另一只手伸给了卢娜和迪安,两人都没有动。

CHAPTER TWENTY-THREE Malfoy Manor

'Harry, we want to help you!' Luna whispered.

'We can't leave you here,' said Dean.

'Go, both of you! We'll see you at Bill and Fleur's.'

As Harry spoke, his scar burned worse than ever, and for a few seconds he looked down, not upon the wandmaker, but on another man who was just as old, just as thin, but laughing scornfully.

'Kill me, then, Voldemort, I welcome death! But my death will not bring you what you seek ... there is so much you do not understand ...'

He felt Voldemort's fury, but as Hermione screamed again he shut it out, returning to the cellar and the horror of his own present.

'Go!' Harry beseeched Luna and Dean. 'Go! We'll follow, just go!'

They caught hold of the elf's outstretched fingers. There was another loud *crack*, and Dobby, Luna, Dean and Ollivander vanished.

'What was that?' shouted Lucius Malfoy from over their heads. 'Did you hear that? What was that noise in the cellar?'

Harry and Ron stared at each other.

'Draco – no, call Wormtail! Make him go and check!'

Footsteps crossed the room overhead, then there was silence. Harry knew that the people in the drawing room were listening for more noises from the cellar.

'We're going to have to try and tackle him,' he whispered to Ron. They had no choice: the moment anyone entered the room and saw the absence of three prisoners, they were lost. 'Leave the lights on,' Harry added, and as they heard someone descending the steps outside the door, they backed against the wall on either side of it.

'Stand back,' came Wormtail's voice. 'Stand away from the door. I am coming in.'

The door flew open. For a split second Wormtail gazed into the apparently empty cellar, ablaze with light from the three miniature suns floating in mid-air. Then Harry and Ron launched themselves upon him. Ron seized Wormtail's wand arm and forced it upwards; Harry slapped a hand to his mouth, muffling his voice. Silently they struggled: Wormtail's wand emitted sparks; his silver hand closed around Harry's throat.

'What is it, Wormtail?' called Lucius Malfoy from above.

第23章　马尔福庄园

"哈利，我们想帮助你！"卢娜轻声说。

"我们不能把你留在这儿。"迪安说。

"快走，你们两个！我们在比尔和芙蓉的家里见。"

哈利说话的时候，他的伤疤前所未有地灼痛起来，有那么几秒钟，他低头看到的不是奥利凡德，而是另一个人，同样苍老，同样瘦削，但却在轻蔑地笑着。

"杀了我吧，伏地魔，我很高兴去死！但是我的死不会带来你所寻找的东西……有很多事情你不明白……"

他感到了伏地魔的愤怒，但赫敏再次尖叫起来，他便不再观看那一幕，回到了地牢和他自己当前的恐怖处境中。

"走吧！"哈利恳求卢娜和迪安，"走吧！我们随后就来，快走！"

他们俩抓住了小精灵伸出的手。又是啪的一声爆响，多比、卢娜、迪安和奥利凡德消失不见了。

"那是什么？"卢修斯·马尔福在上面大喊道，"你们听到了吗？地牢里的那个响声是怎么回事？"

哈利和罗恩惊恐地对视着。

"德拉科——不，叫虫尾巴！让他去检查一下！"

脚步声穿过楼上的房间，然后是一阵沉寂。哈利知道客厅内的人正静听着地牢里再发出声响。

"必须想办法对付他。"他小声对罗恩说。他们别无选择，只要有人走进这个房间发现三个犯人失踪，他们俩就死定了。"不要关灯。"哈利补充道。听到有人从门外的楼梯下来，他们俩分别靠在门两边的墙上。

"靠后站，"门外传来了虫尾巴的声音，"离门远一点儿，我进来了。"

门开了。短暂的一瞬间，虫尾巴凝视着看似空无一人的地牢，三个小太阳耀眼地悬在空中。哈利和罗恩扑了上去，罗恩抓住虫尾巴握着魔杖的手臂，迫使它举向上方，哈利用手捂住他的嘴，不让他出声。三人默默地搏斗，虫尾巴的魔杖发出火花，他那只银手掐住了哈利的喉咙。

"怎么啦，虫尾巴？"卢修斯·马尔福在上面喊道。

CHAPTER TWENTY-THREE   Malfoy Manor

'Nothing!' Ron called back, in a passable imitation of Wormtail's wheezy voice. 'All fine!'

Harry could barely breathe.

'You're going to kill me?' Harry choked, attempting to prise off the metal fingers. 'After I saved your life? You owe me, Wormtail!'

The silver fingers slackened. Harry had not expected it: he wrenched himself free, astonished, keeping his hand over Wormtail's mouth. He saw the rat-like man's small, watery eyes widen with fear and surprise: he seemed just as shocked as Harry at what his hand had done, at the tiny, merciful impulse it had betrayed, and he continued to struggle more powerfully, as though to undo that moment of weakness.

'And we'll have that,' whispered Ron, tugging Wormtail's wand from his other hand.

Wandless, helpless, Pettigrew's pupils dilated in terror. His eyes had slid from Harry's face to something else. His own silver fingers were moving inexorably towards his own throat.

'No—'

Without pausing to think, Harry tried to drag back the hand, but there was no stopping it. The silver tool that Voldemort had given his most cowardly servant had turned upon its Disarmed and useless owner; Pettigrew was reaping his reward for his hesitation, his moment of pity; he was being strangled before their eyes.

'No!'

Ron had released Wormtail too, and together he and Harry tried to pull the crushing metal fingers from around Wormtail's throat, but it was no use. Pettigrew was turning blue.

'*Relashio!* ' said Ron, pointing the wand at the silver hand, but nothing happened; Pettigrew dropped to his knees, and at the same moment, Hermione gave a dreadful scream from overhead. Wormtail's eyes rolled upwards in his purple face, he gave a last twitch and was still.

Harry and Ron looked at each other, then, leaving Wormtail's body on the floor behind them, ran up the stairs and back into the shadowy passageway leading to the drawing room. Cautiously they crept along it, until they reached the drawing-room door, which was ajar. Now they had a clear view of Bellatrix looking down at Griphook, who was holding Gryffindor's sword

第23章 马尔福庄园

"没事!"罗恩大声答道,差强人意地模仿着虫尾巴呼哧呼哧的声音,"一切正常!"

哈利几乎不能呼吸了。

"你要掐死我?"哈利艰难地说,试图掰开那些金属手指,"在我救过你的命之后?你还欠我人情呢,虫尾巴!"

银手指松了一下。哈利没有料到:他一下子挣脱出来,十分诧异,但手仍然捂着虫尾巴的嘴。他看到这老鼠一般的男人水汪汪的小眼睛睁大了,里面满是恐惧和惊讶,似乎和哈利一样诧异于他自己那只手的行为,对它暴露出的那一点点仁慈的冲动感到震惊。他更加猛烈地搏斗,似乎想抵消那一刻软弱造成的后果。

"给我们吧。"罗恩轻声说,拽出了虫尾巴另一只手中的魔杖。

丢了魔杖,无计可施,小矮星的瞳孔因恐惧而张大了。他的目光从哈利的脸上滑向别处,银手无情地移向自己的喉咙。

"不——"

哈利来不及思考,急忙去拉他的手,但没有办法阻止。伏地魔赐予他最怯懦的侍从的银质工具,突然开始攻击那失去武器的无用的主人。小矮星由于他的犹豫,由于那瞬间的怜悯而受到惩罚,他就要在哈利和罗恩眼前被活活地扼死了。

"不!"

罗恩也松开了虫尾巴,他和哈利一同试图拉开那只紧扼着虫尾巴喉咙的金属手指,然而没有用了,小矮星脸色已经变青。

"力松劲泄!"罗恩用魔杖指着银手说,但是毫无效果。小矮星跪倒在地。与此同时,赫敏在上面发出了一声可怕的尖叫。虫尾巴的眼睛向上翻着,脸色发紫,最后他抽搐了一下,一动不动了。

哈利和罗恩对视了一眼,然后把虫尾巴的尸体留在地上,冲上了楼梯,到了通往客厅的昏暗过道里。他们小心地悄悄往前移动,来到了客厅门口。门微开着,现在可以清楚地看到贝拉特里克斯低头看着拉环,后者的长手里正拿着格兰芬多宝剑。赫敏躺在贝拉特里克斯的

in his long-fingered hands. Hermione was lying at Bellatrix's feet. She was barely stirring.

'Well?' Bellatrix said to Griphook. 'Is it the true sword?'

Harry waited, holding his breath, fighting against the prickling of his scar.

'No,' said Griphook. 'It is a fake.'

'Are you sure?' panted Bellatrix. 'Quite sure?'

'Yes,' said the goblin.

Relief broke across her face, all tension drained from it.

'Good,' she said, and with a casual flick of her wand she slashed another deep cut into the goblin's face, and he dropped with a yell at her feet. She kicked him aside. 'And now,' she said, in a voice that burst with triumph, 'we call the Dark Lord!'

And she pushed back her sleeve and touched her forefinger to the Dark Mark.

At once, Harry's scar felt as though it had split open again. His true surroundings vanished: he was Voldemort, and the skeletal wizard before him was laughing toothlessly at him; he was enraged at the summons he felt – he had warned them, he had told them to summon him for nothing less than Potter. If they were mistaken ...

'*Kill me, then!*' demanded the old man. '*You will not win, you cannot win! That wand will never, ever be yours –*'

And Voldemort's fury broke: a burst of green light filled the prison room and the frail old body was lifted from its hard bed and then fell back, lifeless, and Voldemort returned to the window, his wrath barely controllable ... they would suffer his retribution if they had no good reason for calling him back ...

'And I think,' said Bellatrix's voice, 'we can dispose of the Mudblood. Greyback, take her if you want her.'

'NOOOOOOOOOOOO!'

Ron had burst into the drawing room; Bellatrix looked round, shocked; she turned her wand to face Ron instead –

'*Expelliarmus!*' he roared, pointing Wormtail's wand at Bellatrix, and hers flew into the air and was caught by Harry, who had sprinted after Ron. Lucius, Narcissa, Draco and Greyback wheeled about; Harry yelled, '*Stupefy!*' and Lucius Malfoy collapsed on to the hearth. Jets of light flew from Draco's,

第23章 马尔福庄园

脚边，几乎不动弹了。

"怎么样？"贝拉特里克斯问拉环，"宝剑是真的吗？"

哈利屏住呼吸，努力抵御着伤疤的刺痛，等着他回答。

"不是，"拉环说，"这是赝品。"

"你有把握？"贝拉特里克斯喘着气问，"真的有把握？"

"对。"妖精说道。

贝拉特里克斯的面孔松弛下来，所有的紧张消失殆尽。

"很好。"她说，随手一挥魔杖，又在那妖精脸上抽了一道深深的口子。他大叫一声倒在她脚边，被她踢开了。"好了，"她说道，胜利的喜悦溢于言表，"我们召唤黑魔王吧！"

她捋起袖子，食指按向了黑魔标记。

顿时，哈利的伤疤好像再次被撕裂。周围真实的景物消失了，他是伏地魔，骨瘦如柴的老巫师对他张口大笑，满嘴无牙。他感觉到了召唤，十分恼怒——他警告过他们，至少要抓到波特才能召唤他，如果他们弄错了……

"杀了我吧！"那个老人要求道，"你不会赢的，你不可能赢的！那根魔杖绝不会，永远不会是你的——"

伏地魔的愤怒爆发了，突然一道绿光充满了牢房，老头虚弱的身体从硬板床上被抛向空中，然后落了下来，毫无生气。伏地魔返回到窗前，他的愤怒几乎不可控制……如果他们没有充足的理由就把他召唤回去，将统统遭受惩罚……

"我想，"贝拉特里克斯的声音说，"我们可以除掉这个泥巴种了。格雷伯克，你想要就拿去吧。"

"不——！"

罗恩冲进了客厅。贝拉特里克斯吃惊地回过头来，转而把魔杖指向了罗恩的脸——

"除你武器！"罗恩咆哮道，用虫尾巴的魔杖指向贝拉特里克斯，她的魔杖飞向空中，被飞奔在罗恩身后的哈利接住。卢修斯、纳西莎、德拉科和格雷伯克急速转过身，哈利大喊一声："昏昏倒地！"卢修斯·马

CHAPTER TWENTY-THREE   Malfoy Manor

Narcissa's and Greyback's wands; Harry threw himself to the floor, rolling behind a sofa to avoid them.

'STOP OR SHE DIES!'

Panting, Harry peered round the edge of the sofa. Bellatrix was supporting Hermione, who seemed to be unconscious, and was holding her short silver knife to Hermione's throat.

'Drop your wands,' she whispered. 'Drop them, or we'll see exactly how filthy her blood is!'

Ron stood rigid, clutching Wormtail's wand. Harry straightened up, still holding Bellatrix's.

'I said, drop them!' she screeched, pressing the blade into Hermione's throat: Harry saw beads of blood appear there.

'All right!' he shouted, and he dropped Bellatrix's wand on to the floor at his feet. Ron did the same with Wormtail's. Both raised their hands to shoulder height.

'Good!' she leered. 'Draco, pick them up! The Dark Lord is coming, Harry Potter! Your death approaches!'

Harry knew it; his scar was bursting with the pain of it, and he could feel Voldemort flying through the sky from far away, over a dark and stormy sea, and soon he would be close enough to Apparate to them, and Harry could see no way out.

'Now,' said Bellatrix softly, as Draco hurried back with the wands, 'Cissy, I think we ought to tie these little heroes up again, while Greyback takes care of Miss Mudblood. I am sure the Dark Lord will not begrudge you the girl, Greyback, after what you have done tonight.'

At the last word there was a peculiar grinding noise from above. All of them looked upwards in time to see the crystal chandelier tremble; then, with a creak and an ominous jingling, it began to fall. Bellatrix was directly beneath it; dropping Hermione, she threw herself aside with a scream. The chandelier crashed to the floor in an explosion of crystal and chains, falling on top of Hermione and the goblin, who still clutched the sword of Gryffindor. Glittering shards of crystal flew in all directions: Draco doubled over, his hands covering his bloody face.

As Ron ran to pull Hermione out of the wreckage, Harry took his chance;

第 23 章 马尔福庄园

尔福倒在了炉边。一道道光束从德拉科、纳西莎和格雷伯克的魔杖里喷出,哈利扑倒在地,滚到一个沙发后面躲避。

"**住手,不然就让她死!**"

哈利喘着气,从沙发边缘往外望去。贝拉特里克斯正挟着似乎毫无知觉的赫敏,手持小银刀指着赫敏的喉咙。

"放下魔杖,"她轻声说道,"放下,否则我们就看看她的血到底有多脏!"

罗恩拿着虫尾巴的魔杖,呆若木鸡。哈利直起身,手里仍然攥着贝拉特里克斯的魔杖。

"我说了,放下!"贝拉特里克斯尖叫道,把刀刃抵在赫敏的咽喉上,哈利看到血珠冒了出来。

"好吧!"他喊道,把贝拉特里克斯的魔杖丢在了脚边的地上。罗恩也扔下了虫尾巴的魔杖。两人都举起了双手。

"很好!"贝拉特里克斯邪恶地笑着,"德拉科,去捡起来!黑魔王就要来了,哈利·波特!你死到临头了!"

哈利知道这点。伤疤一阵爆裂般的剧痛,他能感觉到伏地魔正在遥远的地方飞行,越过一片黑色的、波涛汹涌的海洋,很快就要近到可以使用幻影显形了,哈利想不到任何出路。

"现在,"贝拉特里克斯柔声说道,德拉科捡了魔杖匆匆回到她跟前,"西茜,我想我们应该把这些小英雄重新绑起来,让格雷伯克照顾泥巴种小姐。格雷伯克,你今晚功劳这么大,我相信黑魔王不会舍不得给你这个女孩的。"

在她说最后一个词时,她的头顶上传来一种奇异的摩擦声。所有的人都抬起头,看到水晶枝形吊灯在颤抖,随着一阵吱吱声和不祥的叮叮当当声,吊灯开始往下坠落。贝拉特里克斯就在它的正下方,她扔下赫敏,尖叫着扑向一边。枝形吊灯坠落在地板上,水晶和链子噼里啪啦,正砸在赫敏和仍然握着格兰芬多宝剑的妖精身上。闪闪发光的水晶碎片四处飞溅,德拉科弯下腰,双手捂着血淋淋的脸。

罗恩跑过去从一片狼藉中把赫敏拉了出来,哈利也抓住机会,飞

he leapt over an armchair and wrested the three wands from Draco's grip, pointed all of them at Greyback and yelled: '*Stupefy!*' The werewolf was lifted off his feet by the triple spell, flew up to the ceiling and then smashed to the ground.

As Narcissa dragged Draco out of the way of further harm, Bellatrix sprang to her feet, her hair flying as she brandished the silver knife; but Narcissa had directed her wand at the doorway.

'Dobby!' she screamed, and even Bellatrix froze. 'You! *You* dropped the chandelier –?'

The tiny elf trotted into the room, his shaking finger pointing at his old mistress.

'You must not hurt Harry Potter,' he squeaked.

'Kill him, Cissy!' shrieked Bellatrix, but there was another loud *crack*, and Narcissa's wand, too, flew into the air and landed on the other side of the room.

'You dirty little monkey!' bawled Bellatrix. 'How dare you take a witch's wand, how dare you defy your masters?'

'Dobby has no master!' squealed the elf. 'Dobby is a free elf, and Dobby has come to save Harry Potter and his friends!'

Harry's scar was blinding him with pain. Dimly, he knew that they had moments, seconds before Voldemort was with them.

'Ron, catch – and GO!' he yelled, throwing one of the wands to him; then he bent down to tug Griphook out from under the chandelier. Hoisting the groaning goblin, who still clung to the sword, over one shoulder, Harry seized Dobby's hand and he spun on the spot to Disapparate.

As he turned into darkness, he caught one last view of the drawing room: of the pale, frozen figures of Narcissa and Draco, of the streak of red that was Ron's hair, and a blur of flying silver, as Bellatrix's knife flew across the room at the place where he was vanishing –

Bill and Fleur's ... Shell Cottage ... Bill and Fleur's ...

He had disappeared into the unknown; all he could do was repeat the name of the destination and hope that it would suffice to take him there. The pain in his forehead pierced him and the weight of the goblin bore down upon him; he could feel the blade of Gryffindor's sword bumping against his back; Dobby's hand jerked in his; he wondered whether the elf was trying to take charge, to pull them in the right direction, and tried, by squeezing the fingers, to indicate that that was fine with him ...

身跃过扶手椅,夺过德拉科手中的三根魔杖,全部指向格雷伯克,大喊:"昏昏倒地!"狼人被三重咒语抛起,飞向天花板,然后重重地砸在地板上。

纳西莎拉开了德拉科,免得他再次受伤。贝拉特里克斯一跃而起,头发飞扬,挥舞着小银刀,而纳西莎把魔杖指向了门口。

"多比!"她尖叫道,连贝拉特里克斯都呆住了,"你!是你打落了枝形吊灯——?"

小精灵跑进屋,用颤抖的手指点着他以前的女主人。

"你不可以伤害哈利·波特。"他尖叫道。

"杀了他,西茜!"贝拉特里克斯厉声喊道,然而又是啪的一声爆响,纳西莎的魔杖也飞到空中,落在了客厅的另一边。

"你这个肮脏的小猢狲!"贝拉特里克斯叫骂道,"你竟敢夺走女巫的魔杖,你竟敢违抗主人?"

"多比没有主人!"小精灵尖声说道,"多比是一个自由的小精灵,多比是来营救哈利·波特和他的朋友们的!"

哈利的伤疤痛得他眼前发黑。他隐约地知道,伏地魔再有片刻或几秒钟就会出现了。

"罗恩,接着——**快走**!"哈利喊道,扔给罗恩一根魔杖,然后弯腰用力把拉环从枝形吊灯底下拉出来。那妖精呻吟着,仍然紧握着宝剑。哈利把妖精扛到肩上,抓住多比的手,原地旋转着幻影移形。

在进入黑暗前,他最后看了一眼客厅:纳西莎和德拉科凝固的苍白身影,罗恩头发的红色,一道模糊的银光掠过,是贝拉特里克斯的小刀飞向他正在消失的地方——

比尔和芙蓉的家……贝壳小屋……比尔和芙蓉的家……

他消失进未知的空间,所能做的就是一遍遍重复目的地的名字,希望这样能确保把他带到那里。前额剧烈地刺痛着,妖精的体重压在他的身上,格兰芬多宝剑的剑刃撞着他的后背。多比的手在他手里抽动了一下,他猜想小精灵是不是想要掌控,把他们拉到正确的方向,哈利试着捏了一下他的手表示同意……

CHAPTER TWENTY-THREE   Malfoy Manor

And then they hit solid earth and smelled salty air. Harry fell to his knees, relinquished Dobby's hand and attempted to lower Griphook gently to the ground.

'Are you all right?' he said, as the goblin stirred, but Griphook merely whimpered.

Harry squinted around through the darkness. There seemed to be a cottage a short way away under the wide, starry sky, and he thought he saw movement outside it.

'Dobby, is this Shell Cottage?' he whispered, clutching the two wands he had brought from the Malfoys', ready to fight if he needed to. 'Have we come to the right place? Dobby?'

He looked around. The little elf stood feet from him.

'DOBBY!'

The elf swayed slightly, stars reflected in his wide, shining eyes. Together, he and Harry looked down at the silver hilt of the knife protruding from the elf's heaving chest.

'Dobby – no – HELP!' Harry bellowed towards the cottage, towards the people moving there. 'HELP!'

He did not know or care whether they were wizards or Muggles, friends or foes; all he cared about was that a dark stain was spreading across Dobby's front, and that he had stretched out his thin arms to Harry with a look of supplication. Harry caught him and laid him sideways on the cool grass.

'Dobby, no, don't die, don't die –'

The elf's eyes found him, and his lips trembled with the effort to form words.

'Harry ... Potter ...'

And then with a little shudder the elf became quite still, and his eyes were nothing more than great, glassy orbs sprinkled with light from the stars they could not see.

第23章　马尔福庄园

而后他们落到了坚实的地面上,空气的味道咸咸的。哈利双膝着地,松开了多比的手,轻轻地把拉环放到地上。

妖精动了动,哈利问:"你还好吗?"但拉环只是呜咽了一声。

哈利朝黑暗中眯眼张望。广袤的星空下,不远处似乎有一座小屋,他觉得好像看到那边有动静。

"多比,这是贝壳小屋吗?"他轻声问,紧握着从马尔福家抢来的两根魔杖,随时准备战斗,"我们走对了吗?多比?"

他回过头,小精灵站在几步之外。

"多比!"

小精灵微微晃了一下,星星映在他闪亮的大眼睛里。他和哈利同时低头看到了银色的刀柄,插在小精灵起伏的胸口。

"多比——不——**救命啊!**"哈利朝着小屋狂喊,朝着那边走动的人们狂喊,"**救命啊!**"

他不知道也不关心那些人是巫师还是麻瓜,是敌还是友。他唯一关心的是一片深色正在多比胸前洇开,小精灵细细的手臂伸向哈利,眼中露出一丝恳求。哈利抱住他,把他侧身放在清凉的草地上。

"多比,不,不要死,不要死——"

小精灵的眼睛找到了他,嘴唇颤抖着,努力想说话。

"哈利……波特……"

然后小精灵微微战栗了一下,变得无比的安静,他的眼睛像两个大大的玻璃球,里面映着他再也看不到的闪烁星光。

CHAPTER TWENTY-FOUR

The Wandmaker

It was like sinking into an old nightmare; for an instant he knelt again beside Dumbledore's body at the foot of the tallest tower at Hogwarts, but in reality he was staring at a tiny body curled upon the grass, pierced by Bellatrix's silver knife. Harry's voice was still saying 'Dobby ... *Dobby* ...' even though he knew that the elf had gone where he could not call him back.

After a minute or so, he realised that they had, after all, come to the right place, for here were Bill and Fleur, Dean and Luna, gathering round him as he knelt over the elf.

'Hermione?' he said suddenly. 'Where is she?'

'Ron's taken her inside,' said Bill. 'She'll be all right.'

Harry looked back down at Dobby. He stretched out a hand and pulled the sharp blade from the elf's body, then dragged off his own jacket and covered Dobby in it like a blanket.

The sea was rushing against rock somewhere nearby; Harry listened to it while the others talked, discussing matters in which he could take no interest, making decisions. Dean carried the injured Griphook into the house, Fleur hurrying with them; now Bill was making suggestions about burying the elf. Harry agreed without really knowing what he was saying. As he did so, he gazed down at the tiny body, and his scar prickled and burned, and in one part of his mind, viewed as if from the wrong end of a long telescope, he saw Voldemort punishing those they had left behind at Malfoy Manor. His rage was dreadful and yet Harry's grief for Dobby seemed to diminish it, so that it became a distant storm that reached Harry from across a vast, silent ocean.

'I want to do it properly,' were the first words which Harry was fully conscious of speaking. 'Not by magic. Have you got a spade?'

第 24 章

魔杖制作人

像是陷入了一个以前的噩梦，一瞬间哈利仿佛又跪在邓布利多的遗体旁边，在霍格沃茨最高的塔楼下面，但现实是他正凝视着蜷曲在草地上的小小身体，被贝拉特里克斯的银刀刺中的身体。哈利的声音仍在叫着："多比……多比……"尽管他知道小精灵已经逝去，再也叫不回来了。

过了一两分钟，他意识到他们终于走对了地方，比尔和芙蓉、迪安和卢娜都聚在他周围，而他跪在小精灵的旁边。

"赫敏？"他突然问道，"她在哪儿？"

"罗恩带她进屋了，"比尔说，"她会好的。"

哈利又低头看着多比。他伸出一只手，从小精灵的身体里拔出了锋利的刀子，然后脱下自己的外套，把它像毯子一样盖在多比身上。

海水在近处冲击着岩石，哈利聆听着波涛声，其他人在说话，讨论着哈利没有心思去听的事情，做着决定。迪安把受伤的拉环抱进了屋里，芙蓉匆匆跟了进去。比尔提议埋葬小精灵，哈利同意了，其实并没有意识到自己在说什么。他低头凝视着那具小小的身体，伤疤刺痛着，火烧火燎。在脑海中的某个地方，像是从长长的望远镜倒着看过去似的，他看到伏地魔正在惩罚那些留在马尔福庄园的人，狂怒的样子极其恐怖，但是哈利对多比之死的哀伤似乎减轻了那场雷霆大怒的影响，就像一场遥远的风暴隔着辽阔、沉寂的海洋传来。

"我想好好安葬他，"这是哈利完全清醒后说的第一句话，"不用魔法。有铲子吗？"

CHAPTER TWENTY-FOUR   The Wandmaker

And shortly afterwards he had set to work, alone, digging the grave in the place that Bill had shown him at the end of the garden, between bushes. He dug with a kind of fury, relishing the manual work, glorying in the non-magic of it, for every drop of his sweat and every blister felt like a gift to the elf who had saved their lives.

His scar burned, but he was master of the pain; he felt it, yet was apart from it. He had learned control at last, learned to shut his mind to Voldemort, the very thing Dumbledore had wanted him to learn from Snape. Just as Voldemort had not been able to possess Harry while Harry was consumed with grief for Sirius, so his thoughts could not penetrate Harry now, while he mourned Dobby. Grief, it seemed, drove Voldemort out ... though Dumbledore, of course, would have said that it was love ...

On Harry dug, deeper and deeper into the hard, cold earth, subsuming his grief in sweat, denying the pain in his scar. In the darkness, with nothing but the sound of his own breath and the rushing sea to keep him company, the things that had happened at the Malfoys' returned to him, the things he had heard came back to him, and understanding blossomed in the darkness ...

The steady rhythm of his arms beat time with his thoughts. Hallows ... Horcruxes ... Hallows ... Horcruxes ... yet he no longer burned with that weird, obsessive longing. Loss and fear had snuffed it out: he felt as though he had been slapped awake again.

Deeper and deeper Harry sank into the grave, and he knew where Voldemort had been tonight, and whom he had killed in the topmost cell of Nurmengard, and why ...

And he thought of Wormtail, dead because of one, small, unconscious impulse of mercy ... Dumbledore had foreseen that ... how much more had he known?

Harry lost track of time. He knew only that the darkness had lightened a few degrees when he was rejoined by Ron and Dean.

'How's Hermione?'

'Better,' said Ron. 'Fleur's looking after her.'

Harry had his retort ready for when they asked him why he had not simply created a perfect grave with his wand, but he did not need it. They jumped down into the hole he had made with spades of their own, and together they worked in silence until the hole seemed deep enough.

第24章 魔杖制作人

片刻之后,他独自一人干了起来,在比尔指给的花园尽头的灌木丛中间,开始挖掘墓穴。他有些疯狂地挖着,体验着手工劳动的快慰,为不用魔法而感到自豪。他觉得每一滴汗水,每一个水泡,都是献给拯救了他们生命的小精灵的礼物。

伤疤灼痛着,但他能够战胜疼痛了,虽然仍能感觉到,但有了距离。他最终学会了控制,学会了把伏地魔关在大脑之外,这正是邓布利多要他向斯内普学习的东西。就像哈利为小天狼星悲伤的时候,伏地魔的思维无法控制哈利一样,现在哈利正在哀悼多比,伏地魔的思维也无法穿透哈利。似乎是悲伤把伏地魔赶了出去……邓布利多当然会说那是爱……

哈利在又冷又硬的泥土中越挖越深,化悲痛为汗水,毫不理会伤疤的疼痛。黑暗中,只有他自己的呼吸声与海涛为伴。马尔福家发生的一切一幕幕重现,他又想起了听到的那些事情,他在黑暗中突然醒悟……

手臂的节奏为他的思考打着拍子。圣器……魂器……圣器……魂器……但是他内心不再燃烧着那种怪异的、着迷的渴望。哀悼和恐惧使它熄灭,他好像被一巴掌扇醒了。

墓穴越挖越深,哈利知道伏地魔今晚去了哪儿,知道在纽蒙迦德最高的牢房里被杀的那个人是谁,也知道为什么……

他想到了虫尾巴,只因为一个小小的、无意识的仁慈冲动而丧命……邓布利多预见到了……他还知道些什么呢?

哈利已经没有时间概念,他只知道,当罗恩和迪安回到他身边时,黑暗减了几分。

"赫敏怎么样?"

"好些了,"罗恩说,"芙蓉在照料她。"

如果他们问他为什么不直接用魔杖营造一个完美的墓穴,哈利已经准备好了答案,但是没有用上。他们俩都拿着铲子,跳进了哈利挖的墓穴,一起默默地挖掘,直到墓穴看起来足够深了。

CHAPTER TWENTY-FOUR   The Wandmaker

Harry wrapped the elf more snugly in his jacket. Ron sat on the edge of the grave and stripped off his shoes and socks, which he placed upon the elf's bare feet. Dean produced a woollen hat, which Harry placed carefully upon Dobby's head, muffling his bat-like ears.

'We should close his eyes.'

Harry had not heard the others coming through the darkness. Bill was wearing a travelling cloak; Fleur a large, white apron, from the pocket of which protruded a bottle of what Harry recognised to be Skele-Gro. Hermione was wrapped in a borrowed dressing gown, pale and unsteady on her feet; Ron put an arm around her when she reached him. Luna, who was huddled in one of Fleur's coats, crouched down and placed her fingers tenderly upon each of the elf's eyelids, sliding them over his glassy stare.

'There,' she said softly. 'Now he could be sleeping.'

Harry placed the elf into the grave, arranged his tiny limbs so that he might have been resting, then climbed out and gazed for the last time upon the little body. He forced himself not to break down as he remembered Dumbledore's funeral, and the rows and rows of golden chairs, and the Minister for Magic in the front row, the recitation of Dumbledore's achievements, the stateliness of the white marble tomb. He felt that Dobby deserved just as grand a funeral, and yet here the elf lay between bushes in a roughly dug hole.

'I think we ought to say something,' piped up Luna. 'I'll go first, shall I?'

And as everybody looked at her, she addressed the dead elf at the bottom of the grave.

'Thank you so much, Dobby, for rescuing me from that cellar. It's so unfair that you had to die, when you were so good and brave. I'll always remember what you did for us. I hope you're happy now.'

She turned and looked expectantly at Ron, who cleared his throat and said in a thick voice, 'Yeah ... thanks Dobby.'

'Thanks,' muttered Dean.

Harry swallowed.

'Goodbye, Dobby,' he said. It was all he could manage, but Luna had said it all for him. Bill raised his wand, and the pile of earth beside the grave rose up into the air and fell neatly upon it, a small, reddish mound.

第24章 魔杖制作人

哈利用他的外套把小精灵包裹得更舒适一些。罗恩坐在墓穴边，脱掉鞋袜，给光脚的小精灵穿上。迪安拿出一顶羊毛帽子，哈利小心地把它戴在多比的头上，包住了那对蝙蝠般的耳朵。

"让他瞑目吧。"

哈利没有听见其他人已从黑暗中走了过来。比尔穿着一件旅行斗篷，芙蓉系了条白色的大围裙，兜里插着一个瓶子，哈利认出是生骨灵。赫敏裹在一件借来的晨衣里，脸色苍白，站立不稳，勉强走到罗恩身边，罗恩伸手搂住了她。卢娜蜷缩在芙蓉的外套里，蹲下来，手指温柔地抚着小精灵的眼皮，合上了那双玻璃球般的眼睛。

"好了，"她轻轻地说道，"现在他可以安睡了。"

哈利把小精灵放进了墓穴，摆好纤细的四肢，让他看上去像是在休息一样，然后爬出来，最后一次凝视着他小小的身体。哈利强忍着不让自己崩溃，他想起了邓布利多的葬礼，一排排的金椅子，魔法部长坐在前排，悼词里宣读着邓布利多的成就，白色的大理石坟墓庄严气派。他觉得多比也应该得到那样盛大的葬礼，然而小精灵却躺在灌木丛间一个草草挖掘的土坑里。

"我想我们应该说点什么。"卢娜提议道，"我先来，可以吗？"

大家都看着她，卢娜向墓穴里死去的小精灵致辞。

"十分感谢你，多比，把我从那个地牢里救了出来。你是那么善良和勇敢，却被迫献出生命，这太不公平了。我会永远记得你为我们所做的一切。愿你现在是幸福的。"

她转过身，期待地看着罗恩。罗恩清了清嗓子，声音沙哑地说道："对……谢谢多比。"

"谢谢。"迪安喃喃道。

哈利哽咽了一下。

"别了，多比。"他只能说这么多，好在卢娜已经全替他说了。比尔举起魔杖，墓穴旁的那堆泥土升到空中，又整齐地落下，堆成一个小小的红土丘。

CHAPTER TWENTY-FOUR   The Wandmaker

'D'you mind if I stay here a moment?' he asked the others.

They murmured words he did not catch; he felt gentle pats upon his back, and then they all traipsed back towards the cottage, leaving Harry alone beside the elf.

He looked around: there were a number of large, white stones, smoothed by the sea, marking the edge of the flowerbeds. He picked up one of the largest and laid it, pillow-like, over the place where Dobby's head now rested. He then felt in his pocket for a wand.

There were two in there. He had forgotten, lost track; he could not now remember whose wands these were; he seemed to remember wrenching them out of someone's hand. He selected the shorter of the two, which felt friendlier in his hand, and pointed it at the rock.

Slowly, under his murmured instruction, deep cuts appeared upon the rock's surface. He knew that Hermione could have done it more neatly, and probably more quickly, but he wanted to mark the spot as he had wanted to dig the grave. When Harry stood up again, the stone read:

HERE LIES DOBBY, A FREE ELF.

He looked down at his handiwork for a few more seconds, then walked away, his scar still prickling a little and his mind full of those things that had come to him in the grave, ideas that had taken shape in the darkness, ideas both fascinating and terrible.

They were all sitting in the living room when he entered the little hall, their attention focused upon Bill, who was talking. The room was light-coloured, pretty, with a small fire of driftwood burning brightly in the fireplace. Harry did not want to drop mud upon the carpet, so he stood in the doorway, listening.

'... lucky that Ginny's on holiday. If she'd been at Hogwarts, they could have taken her before we reached her. Now we know she's safe too.'

He looked round and saw Harry standing there.

'I've been getting them all out of The Burrow,' he explained. 'Moved them to Muriel's. The Death Eaters know Ron's with you now, they're bound to target the family — don't apologise,' he added, at the sight of Harry's expression. 'It was always a matter of time, Dad's been saying so for months. We're the biggest blood traitor family there is.'

第 24 章 魔杖制作人

"我在这儿多待一会儿行吗?"哈利问大家。

他们的低语哈利没有听清,他感到有人轻轻拍了拍他的后背,然后他们全都慢步走回了小屋,把他独自留在了小精灵旁边。

他看了一下四周,花圃边沿围着许多被海水冲圆了的白色大石头。他捡了一块大的,像枕头一样安放在多比头部的位置,然后伸手到口袋里去摸魔杖。

魔杖有两根。他已经忘记了,脑子断了片儿,现在已想不起这些是谁的魔杖,只记得仿佛是从某个人手里抢过来的。他选了短的那根,因为拿着舒服一些,然后用它指着那块石头。

在他轻声的指令下,深深的刻痕慢慢出现在石头表面。他知道赫敏可以做得更漂亮,而且可能更麻利,但是他想亲自做,就像他想亲自挖墓穴一样。当哈利站起来时,石头上刻着:

这里安睡着多比,一个自由的小精灵。

他又低头看了一会儿自己的手艺,才转身走开,伤疤仍然有一点刺痛,脑海里净是他在挖墓穴时想到的那些事情,在黑暗中形成的念头,既令人着迷又令人恐惧。

他走进小门厅,众人都坐在起居室里,正在专心地听比尔说话。屋里色彩淡雅,装饰漂亮,一小块海边捡的浮木在壁炉里燃烧,放出明亮的光芒。哈利不想把泥巴弄在地毯上,便站在门口聆听。

"……幸好金妮在放假。如果她在霍格沃茨,很可能没等我们联系上就被抓走了,现在我们知道她也没事。"

他扫视了一圈,发现哈利站在那里。

"我已经把他们都从陋居转移出来,"他解释道,"藏到穆丽尔姨婆家了。现在食死徒知道罗恩和你在一起,肯定会去找我们的家人——不要抱歉,"他看到哈利的表情,补充道,"这只是时间问题,爸爸已经说过好几个月了,我们是最大的纯血统叛徒家族。"

CHAPTER TWENTY-FOUR   The Wandmaker

'How are they protected?' asked Harry.

'Fidelius Charm. Dad's Secret Keeper. And we've done it on this cottage too; I'm Secret Keeper here. None of us can go to work, but that's hardly the most important thing now. Once Ollivander and Griphook are well enough, we'll move them to Muriel's too. There isn't much room here, but she's got plenty. Griphook's legs are on the mend, Fleur's given him Skele-Gro: we could probably move them in an hour or –'

'No,' Harry said, and Bill looked startled. 'I need both of them here. I need to talk to them. It's important.'

He heard the authority in his own voice, the conviction, the sense of purpose that had come to him as he dug Dobby's grave. All of their faces were turned towards him, looking puzzled.

'I'm going to wash,' Harry told Bill, looking down at his hands, still covered in mud and Dobby's blood. 'Then I'll need to see them, straight away.'

He walked into the little kitchen, to the basin beneath a window overlooking the sea. Dawn was breaking over the horizon, shell pink and faintly gold, as he washed, again following the train of thought that had come to him in the dark garden ...

Dobby would never be able to tell them who had sent him to the cellar, but Harry knew what he had seen. A piercing blue eye had looked out of the mirror fragment, and then help had come. *Help will always be given at Hogwarts to those who ask for it.*

Harry dried his hands, impervious to the beauty of the scene outside the window and to the murmuring of the others in the sitting room. He looked out over the ocean and felt closer, this dawn, than ever before, closer to the heart of it all.

And still his scar prickled, and he knew that Voldemort was getting there too. Harry understood, and yet did not understand. His instinct was telling him one thing, his brain quite another. The Dumbledore in Harry's head smiled, surveying Harry over the tips of his fingers, pressed together as if in prayer.

You gave Ron the Deluminator. You understood him ... you gave him a way back ...

And you understood Wormtail too ... you knew there was a bit of regret there, somewhere ...

And if you knew them ... what did you know about me, Dumbledore?

Am I meant to know, but not to seek? Did you know how hard I'd find that? Is that why

第24章 魔杖制作人

"怎么保护他们的？"哈利问。

"赤胆忠心咒，爸爸是保密人。这所小屋也用了同样的方法，我是这里的保密人。我们谁也不能去上班，但现在这不是最重要的事情了。奥利凡德和拉环康复以后，也会被转移到穆丽尔姨婆家。这里房间不多，但她那儿多的是。拉环的腿正在恢复，芙蓉给他用了生骨灵，他们很快就能转移，也许再过一小时或——"

"不！"哈利说，比尔似乎吃了一惊，"我需要他们俩都在这儿，我要和他们谈谈，这很重要。"

他从自己的声音里听出了威严，带着给多比挖掘墓穴时产生的信念与决心。大家都转过脸来看着他，疑惑不解。

"我去洗洗，"哈利告诉比尔，低头看着自己沾满泥巴和多比血迹的双手，"然后我需要马上见他们。"

他走进小厨房，水池上方的窗户面临大海，曙光正在冲破地平线，天空是贝壳般的粉红色和朦胧的金色。洗手的时候，他继续顺着在黑暗花园中得到的思路想下去……

多比永远不可能说出是谁派他去地牢的了，但是哈利知道他看到了什么，一只锐利的蓝眼睛从镜子碎片中向外看了一眼，然后帮助就来了。在霍格沃茨，那些请求帮助的人总是能得到帮助的。

哈利擦干了手，顾不上注意窗外的美景和起居室里人们的低语。他凝视着海面，在这个黎明，他感到自己比任何时候都更接近一切的核心。

伤疤仍然刺痛着，他知道伏地魔也想到了。哈利明白了，却又没有明白。他的直觉这样讲，而大脑却那样讲。哈利脑海中的邓布利多微笑着，手指合在一起像是在祈祷，目光越过指尖审视着他。

你给了罗恩熄灯器。你了解他……你给了他一条回来的路……

你也了解虫尾巴……你知道他内心某个地方有一点点忏悔……

既然你了解他们……那么你了解我什么呢，邓布利多？

我是否注定会知道，而不是去谋求？你是否知道我会觉得这有多

CHAPTER TWENTY-FOUR   The Wandmaker

you made it this difficult? So I'd have time to work that out?

Harry stood quite still, eyes glazed, watching the place where a bright gold rim of dazzling sun was rising over the horizon. Then he looked down at his clean hands, and was momentarily surprised to see the cloth he was holding in them. He set it down and returned to the hall, and as he did so, he felt his scar pulse angrily, and there flashed across his mind, swift as the reflection of a dragonfly over water, the outline of a building he knew extremely well.

Bill and Fleur were standing at the foot of the stairs.

'I need to speak to Griphook and Ollivander,' Harry said.

'No,' said Fleur. 'You will 'ave to wait, 'Arry. Zey are both ill, tired –'

'I'm sorry,' he said, without heat, 'but it can't wait. I need to talk to them now. Privately – and separately. It's urgent.'

'Harry, what the hell's going on?' asked Bill. 'You turn up here with a dead house-elf and a half-conscious goblin, Hermione looks as though she's been tortured and Ron's just refused to tell me anything –'

'We can't tell you what we're doing,' said Harry flatly. 'You're in the Order, Bill, you know Dumbledore left us a mission. We're not supposed to talk about it to anyone else.'

Fleur made an impatient noise, but Bill did not look at her; he was staring at Harry. His deeply scarred face was hard to read. Finally, Bill said, 'All right. Who do you want to talk to first?'

Harry hesitated. He knew what hung on his decision. There was hardly any time left: now was the moment to decide: Horcruxes or Hallows?

'Griphook,' Harry said. 'I'll speak to Griphook first.'

His heart was racing, as if he had been sprinting and had just cleared an enormous obstacle.

'Up here, then,' said Bill, leading the way.

Harry had walked up several steps before stopping and looking back.

'I need you two, as well!' he called to Ron and Hermione, who had been skulking, half concealed, in the doorway of the sitting room.

They both moved into the light, looking oddly relieved.

'How are you?' Harry asked Hermione. 'You were amazing – coming up with that story when she was hurting you like that –'

第24章 魔杖制作人

难？是否正因为如此，你才把它安排得如此困难？让我有时间领悟？

哈利静静地站在那里，目光凝滞地望着远方，太阳的金边正从海平面上升起，明亮耀眼。他低头看着洁净的双手，惊讶地发现手里还拿着擦布。他放下它返回到门厅，感到伤疤愤怒地跳动着，脑海中有什么东西一闪，宛如蜻蜓点水的掠影，是一座他极其熟悉的建筑物的轮廓。

比尔和芙蓉站在楼梯下。

"我需要跟拉环和奥利凡德谈谈。"哈利说。

"不行，"芙蓉说，"你必须等一等，哈利。他们俩都病了，累了——"

"对不起，"哈利心平气和地说，"但是我不能等。我要马上跟他们谈谈。密谈——并且分别谈。很紧急。"

"哈利，究竟发生了什么？"比尔问道，"你带着一个死去的家养小精灵和一个半昏迷的妖精来到这里，赫敏看起来好像被折磨过，罗恩什么也不肯告诉我——"

"我们不能告诉你我们在做什么。"哈利斩钉截铁地说，"你是凤凰社成员，比尔，你知道邓布利多给我们留下一个任务，不许我们告诉任何人。"

芙蓉发出不耐烦的声音，但是比尔没有看她，只是盯着哈利，但他那伤疤很深的脸上表情难以看透。最后，比尔说："好吧。你想先跟谁谈？"

哈利犹豫了。他知道这决定意味着什么。没有多少时间了，现在就要做出选择：魂器还是圣器？

"拉环，"哈利说，"我先跟拉环谈。"

他心跳得很快，好像他一直在狂奔，刚刚越过一个巨大的障碍。

"那么，上来吧。"比尔说，在前面领路。

哈利爬了几级楼梯后停住了，向身后看了看。

"我也需要你们两个！"他朝偷偷摸摸躲在起居室门口的罗恩和赫敏叫了一声。

两人走到亮处，似乎莫名地松了口气。

"你好吗？"哈利问赫敏，"你真是太神奇了——当她那样折磨你的时候，还能编出那么一个故事——"

CHAPTER TWENTY-FOUR

The Wandmaker

Hermione gave a weak smile as Ron gave her a one-armed squeeze.

'What are we doing now, Harry?' he asked.

'You'll see. Come on.'

Harry, Ron and Hermione followed Bill up the steep stairs, on to a small landing. Three doors led off it.

'In here,' said Bill, opening the door to his and Fleur's room. It, too, had a view of the sea, now flecked with gold in the sunrise. Harry moved to the window, turned his back on the spectacular view and waited, his arms folded, his scar prickling. Hermione took the chair beside the dressing table; Ron sat on the arm.

Bill reappeared, carrying the little goblin, whom he set down carefully upon the bed. Griphook grunted thanks and Bill left, closing the door upon them all.

'I'm sorry to take you out of bed,' said Harry. 'How are your legs?'

'Painful,' replied the goblin. 'But mending.'

He was still clutching the sword of Gryffindor, and wore a strange look; half truculent, half intrigued. Harry noted the goblin's sallow skin, his long, thin fingers, his black eyes. Fleur had removed his shoes: his long feet were dirty. He was larger than a house-elf, but not by much. His domed head was much bigger than a human's.

'You probably don't remember –' Harry began.

'– that I was the goblin who showed you to your vault, the first time you ever visited Gringotts?' said Griphook. 'I remember, Harry Potter. Even amongst goblins, you are very famous.'

Harry and the goblin looked at each other, sizing each other up. Harry's scar was still prickling. He wanted to get through this interview with Griphook quickly, and at the same time was afraid of making a false move. While he tried to decide on the best way to approach his request, the goblin broke the silence.

'You buried the elf,' he said, sounding unexpectedly rancorous. 'I watched you, from the window of the bedroom next door.'

'Yes,' said Harry.

Griphook looked at him out of the corners of his slanting black eyes.

'You are an unusual wizard, Harry Potter.'

第24章 魔杖制作人

赫敏虚弱地一笑，罗恩用一只胳膊紧搂了她一下。

"我们现在要做什么，哈利？"罗恩问道。

"你们会看到的。快上来。"

哈利、罗恩和赫敏跟着比尔爬上很陡的楼梯，来到一个小平台上。这里有三扇门。

"这边。"比尔打开了他和芙蓉的房间。从这儿也能望见大海，此时的海面在朝阳的照耀下金光斑驳。哈利走到窗前，抱着手臂，背对壮丽的景色等待着，伤疤在刺痛。赫敏坐到梳妆台旁边的椅子里，罗恩坐在椅子扶手上。

比尔抱着小妖精回来了，把他轻轻地放在床上，拉环咕哝了一声谢谢。比尔走出去，关上了房门。

"对不起，把你从床上弄过来了。"哈利说，"你的腿怎么样了？"

"很痛，"妖精回答，"但是在恢复中。"

他仍然紧握着格兰芬多宝剑，脸上的表情很奇怪：有点凶狠，又有点好奇。哈利看到了妖精灰黄的皮肤、细长的手指和黑色的眼睛。他的鞋子已经被芙蓉脱掉了，两只长脚脏兮兮的。他比家养小精灵大不了多少，一颗圆脑袋却比人类的脑袋大得多。

"你可能不记得了——"哈利说道。

"——在你第一次去古灵阁时，就是我领你们去金库的，是不是？"拉环说，"我记得，哈利·波特。即使是在妖精中间，你也是很出名的。"

哈利和妖精对视，互相打量。哈利的伤疤还在刺痛，他想尽快跟拉环谈完，同时又担心一步走错。当他在斟酌怎样提出请求最为明智时，妖精打破了沉默。

"你埋葬了小精灵，"他说，语气里透着令人吃惊的恶意，"我从隔壁卧室的窗户看到的。"

"是的。"哈利说。

拉环用他斜吊的黑眼睛的眼角瞟着他。

"你是个不同一般的巫师，哈利·波特。"

CHAPTER TWENTY-FOUR   The Wandmaker

'In what way?' asked Harry, rubbing his scar absently.

'You dug the grave.'

'So?'

Griphook did not answer. Harry rather thought he was being sneered at for acting like a Muggle, but it did not much matter to him whether Griphook approved of Dobby's grave or not. He gathered himself for the attack.

'Griphook, I need to ask –'

'You also rescued a goblin.'

'What?'

'You brought me here. Saved me.'

'Well, I take it you're not sorry?' said Harry, a little impatiently.

'No, Harry Potter,' said Griphook, and with one finger he twisted the thin, black beard upon his chin, 'but you are a very odd wizard.'

'Right,' said Harry. 'Well, I need some help, Griphook, and you can give it to me.'

The goblin made no sign of encouragement, but continued to frown at Harry as though he had never seen anything like him.

'I need to break into a Gringotts vault.'

Harry had not meant to say it so baldly; the words were forced from him as pain shot through his lightning scar and he saw, again, the outline of Hogwarts. He closed his mind firmly. He needed to deal with Griphook first. Ron and Hermione were staring at Harry as though he had gone mad.

'Harry –' said Hermione, but she was cut off by Griphook.

'Break into a Gringotts vault?' repeated the goblin, wincing a little as he shifted his position upon the bed. 'It is impossible.'

'No, it isn't,' Ron contradicted him. 'It's been done.'

'Yeah,' said Harry. 'The same day I first met you, Griphook. My birthday, seven years ago.'

'The vault in question was empty at the time,' snapped the goblin, and Harry understood that even though Griphook had left Gringotts, he was offended at the idea of its defences being breached. 'Its protection was minimal.'

'Well, the vault we need to get into isn't empty, and I'm guessing its

第24章 魔杖制作人

"怎么不同?"哈利问道,下意识地揉着伤疤。

"你挖了墓穴。"

"那又怎么样?"

拉环没有回答,哈利觉得对方是在嘲笑他的行为像个麻瓜。但是拉环是否赞同多比的墓穴已不要紧,哈利集中精力发起进攻。

"拉环,我要问你——"

"你还救了一个妖精。"

"什么?"

"你把我带到这里,救了我。"

"我想你不是感到遗憾吧?"哈利说,有点不耐烦了。

"不是,哈利·波特。"拉环说,一根手指绞着下巴上细细的黑胡须,"但你是一个很奇特的巫师。"

"好吧。"哈利说,"是这样,我需要一些帮助,拉环,你可以提供。"

妖精没有任何表示,而是继续对着哈利皱眉头,似乎从没见过他这样的怪物。

"我需要潜入古灵阁的金库。"

哈利并没有打算这么突兀地说出来。这句话是被挤出来的,因为闪电形的伤疤一阵剧痛,霍格沃茨的轮廓再次闪现。他坚决地关闭了这一幕,首先得对付拉环。罗恩和赫敏瞪着哈利,好像觉得他疯了。

"哈利——"赫敏说,但被拉环打断了。

"潜入古灵阁的金库?"妖精说,在床上换了个姿势,痛得缩了一下,"这不可能。"

"不,有可能,"罗恩反驳,"曾经发生过。"

"是的,"哈利说,"在我第一次遇到你的那一天,拉环。是我的生日,七年以前。"

"当时那个金库是空的,"妖精严厉地说,哈利明白了,尽管拉环离开了古灵阁,但想到古灵阁的防御被突破也会令他不快,"所以保卫措施是最低标准的。"

"我们要进去的金库不是空的,我猜保卫措施会很强大。"哈利说,

CHAPTER TWENTY-FOUR The Wandmaker

protection will be pretty powerful,' said Harry. 'It belongs to the Lestranges.'

He saw Hermione and Ron look at each other, astonished, but there would be time enough to explain after Griphook had given his answer.

'You have no chance,' said Griphook flatly. 'No chance at all. "*If you seek beneath our floors, a treasure that was never yours —*"'

'"*Thief, you have been warned, beware —*" yeah, I know, I remember,' said Harry. 'But I'm not trying to get myself any treasure, I'm not trying to take anything for personal gain. Can you believe that?'

The goblin looked slantwise at Harry, and the lightning scar on Harry's forehead prickled, but he ignored it, refusing to acknowledge its pain or its invitation.

'If there was a wizard of whom I would believe that they did not seek personal gain,' said Griphook finally, 'it would be you, Harry Potter. Goblins and elves are not used to the protection, or the respect, that you have shown this night. Not from wand-carriers.'

'Wand-carriers,' repeated Harry: the phrase fell oddly upon his ears as his scar prickled, as Voldemort turned his thoughts northwards, and as Harry burned to question Ollivander, next door.

'The right to carry a wand,' said the goblin quietly, 'has long been contested between wizards and goblins.'

'Well, goblins can do magic without wands,' said Ron.

'That is immaterial! Wizards refuse to share the secrets of wandlore with other magical beings, they deny us the possibility of extending our powers!'

'Well, goblins won't share any of their magic, either,' said Ron. 'You won't tell us how to make swords and armour the way you do. Goblins know how to work metal in a way wizards have never —'

'It doesn't matter,' said Harry, noting Griphook's rising colour. 'This isn't about wizards versus goblins or any other sort of magical creature —'

Griphook gave a nasty laugh.

'But it is, it is about precisely that! As the Dark Lord becomes ever more powerful, your race is set still more firmly above mine! Gringotts falls under wizarding rule, house-elves are slaughtered, and who amongst the wand-carriers protests?'

'We do!' said Hermione. She had sat up straight, her eyes bright. 'We protest!

第24章 魔杖制作人

"是莱斯特兰奇家的金库。"

他看到赫敏和罗恩惊讶地对视,没关系,等拉环回答过后,他会有充足的时间来解释。

"你根本没戏,"拉环坚决地说,"根本没戏。如果你想从我们的地下金库取走/一份从来不属于你的财富——"

"窃贼啊,你已经受到警告/当心——是的,我知道,我记得。"哈利说,"但我不是想为自己谋取任何财富,不是想将任何东西占为己有。你相信吗?"

妖精斜眼看着哈利,哈利前额闪电形的伤疤又刺痛起来,但是他不予理睬,拒绝理会它的疼痛和它的邀请。

"如果我相信有哪个巫师不为自己谋求任何利益,"最后拉环说道,"那就是你,哈利·波特。妖精和小精灵很少得到你今晚给予的保护和尊敬——从带魔杖的人那里。"

"带魔杖的人。"哈利重复了一遍,觉得这个说法听起来很古怪。这时伤疤又在刺痛,伏地魔的思想飘向了北方,哈利迫切地想请教隔壁的奥利凡德。

"带魔杖的权利,"妖精轻声说,"是巫师与妖精争夺已久的。"

"妖精可以不用魔杖而施魔法呀。"罗恩说。

"那不是实质!巫师拒绝让其他魔法生物分享魔杖学问的秘密,不让我们扩大势力!"

"妖精也不肯透露自己的魔法呀,"罗恩说,"你们不会告诉我们如何制作宝剑和盔甲。妖精锻造金属的特殊方法,是巫师从未——"

"这不相干,"哈利说,他注意到拉环面带怒色,"问题不是巫师对妖精或别的魔法生物——"

拉环恶意地笑了一声。

"错了,问题正在这里!当黑魔头变得日益强大,你们的种族更加巩固地凌驾于我们之上!古灵阁被巫师控制了,家养小精灵被屠杀,有哪个带魔杖的人抗议了?"

"我们抗议了!"赫敏说,她身体坐直了,眼睛明亮,"我们抗议了!

CHAPTER TWENTY-FOUR   The Wandmaker

And I'm hunted quite as much as any goblin or elf, Griphook! I'm a Mudblood!'

'Don't call yourself –' Ron muttered.

'Why shouldn't I?' said Hermione. 'Mudblood, and proud of it! I've got no higher position under this new order than you have, Griphook! It was me they chose to torture, back at the Malfoys'!'

As she spoke, she pulled aside the neck of the dressing gown to reveal the thin cut Bellatrix had made, scarlet against her throat.

'Did you know that it was Harry who set Dobby free?' she asked. 'Did you know that we've wanted elves to be freed for years?' (Ron fidgeted uncomfortably on the arm of Hermione's chair.) 'You can't want You-Know-Who defeated more than we do, Griphook!'

The goblin gazed at Hermione with the same curiosity he had shown Harry.

'What do you seek within the Lestranges' vault?' he asked abruptly. 'The sword that lies inside it is a fake. This is the real one.' He looked from one to the other of them. 'I think that you already know this. You asked me to lie for you back there.'

'But the fake sword isn't the only thing in that vault, is it?' asked Harry. 'Perhaps you've seen the other things in there?'

His heart was pounding harder than ever. He redoubled his efforts to ignore the pulsing of his scar.

The goblin twisted his beard around his finger again.

'It is against our code to speak of the secrets of Gringotts. We are the guardians of fabulous treasures. We have a duty to the objects placed in our care, which were, so often, wrought by our fingers.'

The goblin stroked the sword, and his black eyes roved from Harry, to Hermione, to Ron and then back again.

'So young,' he said finally, 'to be fighting so many.'

'Will you help us?' said Harry. 'We haven't got a hope of breaking in without a goblin's help. You're our one chance.'

'I shall ... think about it,' said Griphook maddeningly.

'But –' Ron started angrily; Hermione nudged him in the ribs.

'Thank you,' said Harry.

The goblin bowed his great, domed head in acknowledgement, then flexed

第24章 魔杖制作人

我和妖精或小精灵一样被搜捕，拉环！我是泥巴种！"

"别叫你自己——"罗恩咕哝道。

"为什么不能？"赫敏说，"我是泥巴种，并为此感到自豪！在这个新秩序下，我的地位不比你高，拉环！在马尔福家，他们挑选了我来折磨！"

她一边说一边拉开晨衣领子，露出咽喉处被贝拉特里克斯刺出的细细的伤口，颜色鲜红。

"你知道是哈利释放了多比吗？"她问道，"你知道我们多年来一直希望解放小精灵吗？"（罗恩在赫敏的椅子扶手上有点坐不住了。）"你不会比我们更希望打败神秘人，拉环！"

妖精注视着赫敏，和刚才打量哈利时一样好奇。

"你们要在莱斯特兰奇家的金库里找什么？"他突然问道，"那里面的宝剑是假的，这把才是真的。"他挨个儿地看着他们，"我以为你们已经知道了。你们还在那儿让我替你们撒了谎。"

"但是那个金库里面不仅有假宝剑，是不是？"哈利问道，"也许你见过里面别的东西？"

他的心跳从没有这样剧烈过。他加倍努力来抵御伤疤的阵阵剧痛。

妖精再次用手指绞着胡须。

"泄露古灵阁里的秘密是违反规定的。我们是巨大财富的守护者，要对看护的东西负责，那些东西往往是我们亲手制造的。"

妖精抚摸着宝剑，黑眼睛滴溜溜地把哈利、赫敏和罗恩看了一遍，又回到哈利身上。

"太年轻了，"他最后说，"可要对抗的东西那么多。"

"你会帮助我们吗？"哈利说，"如果没有妖精帮忙，我们不可能闯进去。你是我们唯一的希望。"

"我会……想一想。"拉环令人恼火地说道。

"但是——"罗恩生气地说，赫敏轻轻捅了他一下。

"谢谢你。"哈利说。

妖精低了一下巨大的圆脑袋接受了谢意，然后活动了一下短短的

CHAPTER TWENTY-FOUR The Wandmaker

his short legs.

'I think,' he said, settling himself ostentatiously upon Bill and Fleur's bed, 'that the Skele-Gro has finished its work. I may be able to sleep at last. Forgive me ...'

'Yeah, of course,' said Harry, but before leaving the room he leaned forwards and took the sword of Gryffindor from beside the goblin. Griphook did not protest, but Harry thought he saw resentment in the goblin's eyes as he closed the door upon him.

'Little git,' whispered Ron. 'He's enjoying keeping us hanging.'

'Harry,' whispered Hermione, pulling them both away from the door, into the middle of the still dark landing, 'are you saying what I think you're saying? Are you saying there's a Horcrux in the Lestranges' vault?'

'Yes,' said Harry. 'Bellatrix was terrified when she thought we'd been in there, she was beside herself. Why? What did she think we'd seen, what else did she think we might have taken? Something she was petrified You-Know-Who would find out about.'

'But I thought we were looking for places You-Know-Who's been, places he's done something important?' said Ron, looking baffled. 'Was he ever inside the Lestranges' vault?'

'I don't know whether he was ever inside Gringotts,' said Harry. 'He never had gold there when he was younger, because nobody left him anything. He would have seen the bank from the outside, though, the first time he ever went to Diagon Alley.'

Harry's scar throbbed, but he ignored it; he wanted Ron and Hermione to understand about Gringotts before they spoke to Ollivander.

'I think he would have envied anyone who had a key to a Gringotts vault. I think he'd have seen it as a real symbol of belonging to the wizarding world. And don't forget, he trusted Bellatrix and her husband. They were his most devoted servants before he fell, and they went looking for him after he vanished. He said it the night he came back, I heard him.'

Harry rubbed his scar.

'I don't think he'd have told Bellatrix it was a Horcrux, though. He never told Lucius Malfoy the truth about the diary. He probably told her it was a treasured possession and asked her to place it in her vault. The safest place in the world for anything you want to hide, Hagrid told me ... except for Hogwarts.'

第24章 魔杖制作人

双腿。

"我想,"他大模大样地在比尔和芙蓉的床上躺了下来,"生骨灵已经发挥完了作用,我终于能睡个觉了。请原谅……"

"好的,当然。"哈利说,离开屋子之前,他欠身从妖精身旁拿走了格兰芬多宝剑。拉环没有抗议,但是哈利在关门时好像看到了妖精眼里的愤恨。

"小坏蛋,"罗恩小声说,"吊我们的胃口,他觉得很开心。"

"哈利,"赫敏低语道,一边把他们俩从门口拉走,回到依然黑暗的平台中央,"你是那个意思吗?你是说莱斯特兰奇家的金库中有魂器?"

"是的,"哈利说,"贝拉特里克斯一想到我们去过那儿就惊恐万分,简直歇斯底里了。为什么?她以为我们看到了什么?她以为我们还可能拿走了什么?她特别害怕神秘人发现那东西不在了。"

"可是,我原以为要找的是神秘人去过或做过什么重要事情的地方,"罗恩说,看起来有点困惑,"他进过莱斯特兰奇家的金库吗?"

"我不知道他是不是进过古灵阁,"哈利说,"他年轻时从没在那儿存过金子,因为没人给他留下任何东西。但他第一次去对角巷时,可能从外面看见过那家银行。"

哈利的伤疤突突地痛着,但他没去理会。他希望在和奥利凡德交谈之前,能让罗恩和赫敏明白古灵阁的事。

"我想他可能会羡慕有古灵阁金库钥匙的人,他可能认为这是魔法界成员的真正标志。别忘了,他很信任贝拉特里克斯和她丈夫。他们是他倒台前最忠诚的仆人,在他消失后还出去找他。这是他复出的那天晚上说的,我亲耳听见的。"

哈利揉了揉伤疤。

"不过,我认为他不可能告诉贝拉特里克斯那是魂器。他没有对卢修斯·马尔福说过那本日记的真相。他可能告诉贝拉特里克斯那是一件珍贵的宝物,要寄存在她的金库里。海格告诉过我,如果你想藏什么东西,那是世界上最安全的地方……除了霍格沃茨之外。"

CHAPTER TWENTY-FOUR The Wandmaker

When Harry had finished speaking, Ron shook his head.

'You really understand him.'

'Bits of him,' said Harry. 'Bits ... I just wish I'd understood Dumbledore as much. But we'll see. Come on – Ollivander now.'

Ron and Hermione looked bewildered, but impressed, as they followed him across the little landing and knocked upon the door opposite Bill and Fleur's. A weak 'Come in!' answered them.

The wandmaker was lying on the twin bed furthest from the window. He had been held in the cellar for more than a year, and tortured, Harry knew, on at least one occasion. He was emaciated, the bones of his face sticking out sharply against the yellowish skin. His great, silver eyes seemed vast in their sunken sockets. The hands that lay upon the blanket could have belonged to a skeleton. Harry sat down on the empty bed, beside Ron and Hermione. The rising sun was not visible here. The room faced the cliff-top garden and the freshly dug grave.

'Mr Ollivander, I'm sorry to disturb you,' Harry said.

'My dear boy.' Ollivander's voice was feeble. 'You rescued us. I thought we would die in that place. I can never thank you ... *never* thank you ... enough.'

'We were glad to do it.'

Harry's scar throbbed. He knew, he was certain, that there was hardly any time left in which to beat Voldemort to his goal, or else to attempt to thwart him. He felt a flutter of panic ... yet he had made his decision when he chose to speak to Griphook first. Feigning a calm he did not feel, he groped in the pouch around his neck and took out the two halves of his broken wand.

'Mr Ollivander, I need some help.'

'Anything. Anything,' said the wandmaker weakly.

'Can you mend this? Is it possible?'

Ollivander held out a trembling hand and Harry placed the two barely connected halves into his palm.

'Holly and phoenix feather,' said Ollivander in a tremulous voice. 'Eleven inches. Nice and supple.'

'Yes,' said Harry. 'Can you –?'

'No,' whispered Ollivander. 'I am sorry, very sorry, but a wand that has suffered this degree of damage cannot be repaired by any means that I know of.'

第24章 魔杖制作人

哈利说完后，罗恩摇了摇头。

"你真是了解他。"

"了解他的一点点，"哈利说，"一点点……我只希望我也能那样了解邓布利多。等着瞧吧。快——轮到奥利凡德了。"

罗恩和赫敏看起来又困惑又钦佩，跟着他穿过小平台，敲了敲比尔和芙蓉对面房间的门。一声微弱的"请进！"回答了他们。

屋里是一对单人床，魔杖制作人躺在远离窗户的那张床上。他在地牢里关了一年多，哈利还知道他至少有一次惨遭折磨。他很憔悴，脸上的骨头全都突了出来，皮肤蜡黄。银色的大眼睛深陷在眼窝里，显得更加巨大。放在毛毯上的双手像是骷髅的一般。哈利坐在那张空床上，挨着罗恩和赫敏。在这里看不到初升的太阳，这房间朝着悬崖顶上的花园和刚挖的坟墓。

"奥利凡德先生，对不起，打扰您了。"哈利说。

"我亲爱的孩子，"奥利凡德的声音很虚弱，"你解救了我们。我原以为我们会死在那里。我怎么谢你……怎么谢你……也不够啊。"

"我们很高兴能帮您。"

哈利的伤疤突突地痛。他知道，他可以肯定，几乎不可能赶在伏地魔前面，来不及去阻挠他了。他感到一阵惊慌……然而是他决定先跟拉环谈的。他假装很镇定，从脖子上挂的皮袋里摸出那根断成两截的魔杖。

"奥利凡德先生，我需要一些帮助。"

"在所不辞，在所不辞。"魔杖制作人无力地说。

"您能修好这个吗？有可能吗？"

奥利凡德伸出一只颤抖的手，哈利把勉强相连的两截魔杖放到他的掌心里。

"冬青木和凤凰羽毛，"奥利凡德颤巍巍地说，"十一英寸，漂亮，柔韧。"

"是的，"哈利说，"您能——？"

"不能，"奥利凡德轻声说，"我很抱歉，非常抱歉。魔杖遭受了这么严重的损伤，据我所知没有任何办法能够修好。"

CHAPTER TWENTY-FOUR

The Wandmaker

Harry had been braced to hear it, but it was a blow nevertheless. He took the wand halves back and replaced them in the pouch around his neck. Ollivander stared at the place where the shattered wand had vanished, and did not look away until Harry had taken from his pocket the two wands he had brought from the Malfoys'.

'Can you identify these?' Harry asked.

The wandmaker took the first of the wands and held it close to his faded eyes, rolling it between his knobble-knuckled fingers, flexing it slightly.

'Walnut and dragon heartstring,' he said. 'Twelve and three-quarter inches. Unyielding. This wand belonged to Bellatrix Lestrange.'

'And this one?'

Ollivander performed the same examination.

'Hawthorn and unicorn hair. Ten inches precisely. Reasonably springy. This was the wand of Draco Malfoy.'

'Was?' repeated Harry. 'Isn't it still his?'

'Perhaps not. If you took it –'

'– I did –'

'– then it may be yours. Of course, the manner of taking matters. Much also depends upon the wand itself. In general, however, where a wand has been won, its allegiance will change.'

There was silence in the room, except for the distant rushing of the sea.

'You talk about wands like they've got feelings,' said Harry, 'like they can think for themselves.'

'The wand chooses the wizard,' said Ollivander. 'That much has always been clear to those of us who have studied wandlore.'

'A person can still use a wand that hasn't chosen them, though?' asked Harry.

'Oh yes, if you are any wizard at all you will be able to channel your magic through almost any instrument. The best results, however, must always come where there is the strongest affinity between wizard and wand. These connections are complex. An initial attraction, and then a mutual quest for experience, the wand learning from the wizard, the wizard from the wand.'

The sea gushed forwards and backwards; it was a mournful sound.

第24章 魔杖制作人

哈利已有思想准备，但这话对他还是一个巨大的打击。他拿回断成两截的魔杖，放回脖子上的皮袋里。奥利凡德盯着断魔杖消失的地方，一直没有移开视线，直到哈利从口袋里取出了从马尔福家夺来的两根魔杖。

"您能鉴定一下吗？"哈利问。

魔杖制作人拿起第一根魔杖，举到昏花的老眼前，用他指节突起的手指旋转着，轻轻弯折着。

"胡桃木和火龙的心脏神经，"他说，"十二又四分之三英寸，不易弯曲，这根魔杖是贝拉特里克斯·莱斯特兰奇的。"

"这根呢？"

奥利凡德做了同样的检查。

"山楂木和独角兽毛。刚好十英寸，弹性尚可，这曾是德拉科·马尔福的魔杖。"

"曾是？"哈利重复道，"难道现在不是了？"

"可能不是了，如果被你夺到——"

"——是啊——"

"——那么它就可能是你的了。当然，夺的方式很重要，另外也取决于魔杖本身。通常说来，一根魔杖被赢取后，它效忠的对象就会改变。"

房间里一片沉寂，只听见遥远的海涛声。

"您把魔杖说得好像有感情一样，"哈利说，"好像它们可以自己思考。"

"魔杖选择巫师，"奥利凡德说，"对于我们研究魔杖学问的人来说，这一直是显而易见的。"

"不过，人还是可以使用一根没有选择他的魔杖的吧？"哈利问道。

"哦，是的，只要你是个巫师，就应该差不多能用任何工具表现你的魔法。但最佳效果一定是来自巫师和魔杖间最紧密的结合。这些联系是复杂的，最初是相互吸引，继而相互探求经验，魔杖向巫师学习，巫师也向魔杖学习。"

潮起潮落，像悲哀的挽歌。

CHAPTER TWENTY-FOUR The Wandmaker

'I took this wand from Draco Malfoy by force,' said Harry. 'Can I use it safely?'

'I think so. Subtle laws govern wand ownership, but the conquered wand will usually bend its will to its new master.'

'So I should use this one?' said Ron, pulling Wormtail's wand out of his pocket and handing it to Ollivander.

'Chestnut and dragon heartstring. Nine and a quarter inches. Brittle. I was forced to make this, shortly after my kidnap, for Peter Pettigrew. Yes, if you won it, it is more likely to do your bidding, and do it well, than another wand.'

'And this holds true for all wands, does it?' asked Harry.

'I think so,' replied Ollivander, his protuberant eyes upon Harry's face. 'You ask deep questions, Mr Potter. Wandlore is a complex and mysterious branch of magic.'

'So, it isn't necessary to kill the previous owner to take true possession of a wand?' asked Harry.

Ollivander swallowed.

'Necessary? No, I should not say that it is necessary to kill.'

'There are legends, though,' said Harry, and as his heart rate quickened, the pain in his scar became more intense; he was sure that Voldemort had decided to put his idea into action. 'Legends about a wand – or wands – that have passed from hand to hand by murder.'

Ollivander turned pale. Against the snowy pillow he was light grey, and his eyes were enormous, bloodshot and bulging with what looked like fear.

'Only one wand, I think,' he whispered.

'And You-Know-Who is interested in it, isn't he?' asked Harry.

'I – how?' croaked Ollivander, and he looked appealingly at Ron and Hermione for help. 'How do you know this?'

'He wanted you to tell him how to overcome the connection between our wands,' said Harry.

Ollivander looked terrified.

'He tortured me, you must understand that! The Cruciatus Curse, I – I had no choice but to tell him what I knew, what I guessed!'

第24章 魔杖制作人

"我是用咒语从德拉科·马尔福手中夺到这根魔杖的,"哈利说,"我可以安全地使用它吗?"

"我想可以。魔杖的所有权遵循精细的规则,但是被征服的魔杖通常会服从新的主人。"

"那么我也能用这根吗?"罗恩说,一边从口袋里拿出虫尾巴的魔杖,递给了奥利凡德。

"栗木和火龙的心脏神经,九又四分之一英寸,质地坚脆,是我被绑架后不久,被迫为小矮星彼得制作的。不错,如果是你赢来的,它会比别的魔杖更愿意执行你的命令,并且执行得很好。"

"所有的魔杖都是这样的,对吗?"哈利问。

"我想是的。"奥利凡德回答,他的凸眼睛盯着哈利的脸,"你问的问题很深奥,波特先生。魔杖学是一门复杂而神秘的魔法学科。"

"那么,要真正拥有一根魔杖,并不一定要杀死它的前任主人,对吗?"哈利问道。

奥利凡德咽了咽口水。

"一定?不,我认为不一定要杀人。"

"但是,有一些传说。"哈利说,心跳加快的同时,伤疤疼得越加厉害。他相信伏地魔已经决定把想法付诸行动。"传说有一根魔杖——或一些魔杖——是通过谋杀而转手的。"

奥利凡德脸色一变。在雪白的枕头上,他面如纸灰,眼睛显得特别大,充血而凸出,似乎充满恐惧。

"只有一根魔杖,我想。"他低声说。

"神秘人对它很感兴趣,对吗?"哈利问。

"我——你是怎么——?"奥利凡德用低沉沙哑的声音问,求助地看着罗恩和赫敏,"你是怎么知道这个的?"

"他希望您告诉他,如何克服我们俩魔杖之间的联系。"哈利说。

奥利凡德似乎吓呆了。

"他拷问我,你必须理解!钻心咒,我——我别无选择,只能对他说出我知道的,我猜测的!"

CHAPTER TWENTY-FOUR   The Wandmaker

'I understand,' said Harry. 'You told him about the twin cores? You said he just had to borrow another wizard's wand?'

Ollivander looked horrified, transfixed, by the amount that Harry knew. He nodded slowly.

'But it didn't work,' Harry went on. 'Mine still beat the borrowed wand. Do you know why that is?'

Ollivander shook his head as slowly as he had just nodded.

'I had ... never heard of such a thing. Your wand performed something unique that night. The connection of the twin cores is incredibly rare, yet why your wand should have snapped the borrowed wand, I do not know ...'

'We were talking about the other wand, the wand that changes hands by murder. When You-Know-Who realised my wand had done something strange, he came back and asked about that other wand, didn't he?'

'How do you know this?'

Harry did not answer.

'Yes, he asked,' whispered Ollivander. 'He wanted to know everything I could tell him about the wand variously known as the Deathstick, the Wand of Destiny or the Elder Wand.'

Harry glanced sideways at Hermione. She looked flabbergasted.

'The Dark Lord,' said Ollivander, in hushed and frightened tones, 'had always been happy with the wand I made him – yew and phoenix feather, thirteen and a half inches – until he discovered the connection of the twin cores. Now he seeks another, more powerful, wand, as the only way to conquer yours.'

'But he'll know soon, if he doesn't already, that mine's broken beyond repair,' said Harry quietly.

'No!' said Hermione, sounding frightened. 'He can't know that, Harry, how could he –?'

'*Priori Incantatem*,' said Harry. 'We left your wand and the blackthorn wand at the Malfoys', Hermione. If they examine them properly, make them recreate the spells they've cast lately, they'll see that yours broke mine, they'll see that you tried and failed to mend it, and they'll realise that I've been using the blackthorn one ever since.'

第24章 魔杖制作人

"我理解，"哈利说，"您对他说了孪生杖芯的事吧？您说他只需向别的巫师借一根魔杖？"

奥利凡德没想到哈利知道得这么多，他又害怕又惊诧，慢慢地点点头。

"但是那没有用，"哈利继续说，"我的魔杖仍然打败了他借来的那根魔杖。您知道那是为什么吗？"

奥利凡德慢慢地摇摇头，和刚才点头时一样慢。

"我……从没听说过这样的事。你的魔杖那天晚上的表现很奇特。孪生杖芯的联系极其罕见，然而为什么你的魔杖竟会折断借来的魔杖，我不知道……"

"我们刚才讨论到了另一根魔杖，那根靠谋杀转手的魔杖。当神秘人意识到我的魔杖表现奇特后，他回来问到了那根魔杖，是不是？"

"你是怎么知道的？"

哈利没有回答。

"是的，他问了，"奥利凡德低声说道，"他想知道我能告诉他的一切，关于那根有着不同名称的魔杖——死亡棒、命运杖或老魔杖。"

哈利瞥了一眼旁边的赫敏，她看起来目瞪口呆。

"黑魔头，"奥利凡德压低声音恐惧地说，"一直对我给他做的魔杖很满意——紫杉木和凤凰羽毛，十三又二分之一英寸——直到他发现了孪生杖芯之间的联系。现在他要寻找另一根更加强大的魔杖，作为征服你的魔杖的唯一办法。"

"但是，即使他现在还不知道，他也很快会知道我的魔杖坏了，修不好了。"哈利轻声说。

"不！"赫敏惊恐地说，"他不可能知道这个，哈利，他怎么可能——？"

"闪回咒。"哈利说，"我们把你的魔杖和黑刺李木魔杖丢在马尔福家了，赫敏。如果他们仔细检查，让它们重现最近施过的咒语，就会看到你的魔杖打断了我的，也会看到你试图修复它而没有成功，然后他们就会想到我从那时起就一直使用黑刺李木魔杖了。"

CHAPTER TWENTY-FOUR   The Wandmaker

The little colour she had regained since their arrival had drained from her face. Ron gave Harry a reproachful look, and said, 'Let's not worry about that now –'

But Mr Ollivander intervened.

'The Dark Lord no longer seeks the Elder Wand only for your destruction, Mr Potter. He is determined to possess it, because he believes it will make him truly invulnerable.'

'And will it?'

'The owner of the Elder Wand must always fear attack,' said Ollivander, 'but the idea of the Dark Lord in possession of the Deathstick is, I must admit ... formidable.'

Harry was suddenly reminded of how he had been unsure, when they first met, of how much he liked Ollivander. Even now, having been tortured and imprisoned by Voldemort, the idea of the Dark wizard in possession of this wand seemed to enthral him as much as it repulsed him.

'You – you really think this wand exists, then, Mr Ollivander?' asked Hermione.

'Oh yes,' said Ollivander. 'Yes, it is perfectly possible to trace the wand's course through history. There are gaps, of course, and long ones, where it vanishes from view, temporarily lost or hidden; but always it resurfaces. It has certain identifying characteristics that those who are learned in wandlore recognise. There are written accounts, some of them obscure, that I and other wandmakers have made it our business to study. They have the ring of authenticity.'

'So you – you don't think it can be a fairy tale, or a myth?' Hermione asked hopefully.

'No,' said Ollivander. 'Whether it *needs* to pass by murder, I do not know. Its history is bloody, but that may be simply due to the fact that it is such a desirable object, and arouses such passions in wizards. Immensely powerful, dangerous in the wrong hands, and an object of incredible fascination to all of us who study the power of wands.'

'Mr Ollivander,' said Harry, 'you told You-Know-Who that Gregorovitch had the Elder Wand, didn't you?'

Ollivander turned, if possible, even paler. He looked ghostly as he gulped.

'But how – how do you –?'

第24章 魔杖制作人

赫敏来到这里后脸上恢复的一点血色又消失殆尽。罗恩责备地瞥了哈利一眼，说道："现在别担心那个——"

但是奥利凡德先生插话了。

"黑魔头寻找老魔杖，不再仅仅是为了打败你，波特先生。他决心要拥有它，因为他相信老魔杖会让他变得无懈可击。"

"会吗？"

"老魔杖的拥有者总是担心受到攻击，"奥利凡德说，"但是黑魔头拥有死亡棒，我必须承认……这个想法令人生畏。"

哈利突然想起他们第一次见面时，他就不能确定是不是喜欢奥利凡德。现在，即使在被伏地魔拷问和关押之后，老头儿对于黑巫师拥有老魔杖的这件事，似乎仍是既反感又着迷。

"您——您真的认为这根魔杖是存在的吗，奥利凡德先生？"赫敏问道。

"哦，是的，"奥利凡德说，"是的。在历史上完全有踪迹可寻。当然其间会有中断，很长时间的中断，它会从人们的视野里消失，暂时丢失或者隐藏起来，但总会重新出现。它有某些可识别的特征，研究过魔杖学的人会认得出来。有一些书面的记录，有的很隐晦，我和其他魔杖制作人专门研究过。那些记录有一定的真实性。"

"那么您——您不认为它可能是一个传说，或是虚构的故事？"赫敏带着希望问。

"不。"奥利凡德说，"至于它是否需要靠谋杀来转手，我不知道。它的历史是血腥的，但那可能只是因为这样一件如此令人觊觎的器物，在巫师间引起了强烈的欲望。它无比强大，在不适当的人手中会很危险，而对于我们研究魔杖能力的人来说，它是一件有莫大诱惑力的器物。"

"奥利凡德先生，"哈利说，"您告诉了神秘人，老魔杖在格里戈维奇那里，是不是？"

奥利凡德的脸色变得——如果可能的话——更加灰白，看起来像鬼一样，他惊得倒吸了一口气。

"不过你——你是怎么——"

CHAPTER TWENTY-FOUR   The Wandmaker

'Never mind how I know it,' said Harry, closing his eyes momentarily as his scar burned and he saw, for mere seconds, a vision of the main street in Hogsmeade, still dark, because it was so much further north. 'You told You-Know-Who that Gregorovitch had the wand?'

'It was a rumour,' whispered Ollivander. 'A rumour, years and years ago, long before you were born! I believe Gregorovitch himself started it. You can see how good it would be for business: that he was studying, and duplicating, the qualities of the Elder Wand!'

'Yes, I can see that,' said Harry. He stood up. 'Mr Ollivander, one last thing, and then we'll let you get some rest. What do you know about the Deathly Hallows?'

'The – the what?' asked the wandmaker, looking utterly bewildered.

'The Deathly Hallows.'

'I'm afraid I don't know what you're talking about. Is this still something to do with wands?'

Harry looked into the sunken face and believed that Ollivander was not acting. He did not know about the Hallows.

'Thank you,' said Harry. 'Thank you very much. We'll leave you to get some rest now.'

Ollivander looked stricken.

'He was torturing me!' he gasped. 'The Cruciatus Curse ... you have no idea ...'

'I do,' said Harry. 'I really do. Please get some rest. Thank you for telling me all of this.'

He led Ron and Hermione down the staircase. Harry caught a glimpse of Bill, Fleur, Luna and Dean sitting at the table in the kitchen, cups of tea in front of them. They all looked up at Harry as he appeared in the doorway, but he merely nodded to them, and continued into the garden, Ron and Hermione behind him. The reddish mound of earth that covered Dobby lay ahead, and Harry walked back to it, as the pain in his head built more and more powerfully. It was a huge effort, now, to close down the visions that were forcing themselves upon him, but he knew that he would have to resist only a little longer. He would yield very soon, because he needed to know that his theory was right. He must make only one more, short effort, so that he could explain to Ron and Hermione.

第24章　魔杖制作人

"别管我是怎么知道的。"哈利说,他的伤疤灼痛起来,他稍稍闭了一下眼睛。仅仅几秒钟,他看到了霍格莫德大马路的景象,仍然是黑夜,因为是在很远的北方。"您告诉神秘人老魔杖在格里戈维奇那里,是吗?"

"那是一个谣传,"奥利凡德轻声说,"一个谣传,许多年前,早在你出生以前!我相信是格里戈维奇自己说出去的。你可以想见,如果传说他在研究和复制老魔杖的特性,这对他的生意多么有利啊。"

"是的,可以想见。"哈利说着站了起来,"奥利凡德先生,再问最后一件事,然后我们就让您休息了。关于死亡圣器您知道些什么?"

"关于——关于什么?"奥利凡德问道,看起来十分困惑。

"死亡圣器。"

"我恐怕不知道你在说些什么,仍然和魔杖有关吗?"

哈利观察了一下那凹陷的面孔,相信奥利凡德没有假装,他不知道圣器的事。

"谢谢您,"哈利说,"非常感谢您。我们这就离开,让您好好休息。"

奥利凡德显得十分痛苦。

"他折磨我!"他气喘吁吁地说,"钻心咒……你是不知道……"

"我知道,"哈利说,"我真的知道。请好好休息。谢谢您告诉我们这一切。"

他领着罗恩和赫敏下了楼,瞥见比尔、芙蓉、卢娜和迪安坐在厨房的桌旁,面前放着茶杯。当哈利走过门口时,他们都抬起头,但他只是点了点头,继续往花园里走,罗恩和赫敏跟在后面。埋着多比的红色土丘就在前方,哈利朝它走去,额头的疼痛愈发剧烈。现在他需要用巨大的毅力来关闭闯入脑海的景象,但他知道只需再忍耐一小会儿,很快他就会放弃,他必须去验证自己的推理是否正确。他必须再坚持片刻,好向罗恩和赫敏解释。

CHAPTER TWENTY-FOUR The Wandmaker

'Gregorovitch had the Elder Wand, a long time ago,' he said. 'I saw You-Know-Who trying to find him. When he tracked him down, he found that Gregorovitch didn't have it any more: it was stolen from him by Grindelwald. How Grindelwald found out that Gregorovitch had it, I don't know – but if Gregorovitch was stupid enough to spread the rumour, it can't have been that difficult.'

Voldemort was at the gates of Hogwarts; Harry could see him standing there, and see, too, the lamp bobbing in the pre-dawn, coming closer and closer.

'And Grindelwald used the Elder Wand to become powerful. And at the height of his power, when Dumbledore knew he was the only one who could stop him, he duelled Grindelwald, and beat him, and he took the Elder Wand.'

'*Dumbledore* had the Elder Wand?' said Ron. 'But then – where is it now?'

'At Hogwarts,' said Harry, fighting to remain with them in the cliff-top garden.

'But then, let's go!' said Ron urgently. 'Harry, let's go and get it, before he does!'

'It's too late for that,' said Harry. He could not help himself, but clutched his head, trying to help it resist. 'He knows where it is. He's there now.'

'Harry!' Ron said, furiously. 'How long have you known this – why have we been wasting time? Why did you talk to Griphook first? We could have gone – we could still go –'

'No,' said Harry, and he sank to his knees in the grass. 'Hermione's right. Dumbledore didn't want me to have it. He didn't want me to take it. He wanted me to get the Horcruxes.'

'The unbeatable wand, Harry!' moaned Ron.

'I'm not supposed to … I'm supposed to get the Horcruxes …'

And now everything was cool and dark: the sun was barely visible over the horizon as he glided alongside Snape, up through the grounds towards the lake.

'I shall join you in the castle shortly,' he said, in his high, cold voice. 'Leave me now.'

Snape bowed and set off back up the path, his black cloak billowing

第24章 魔杖制作人

"格里戈维奇得到过老魔杖,在很久以前。"他说,"我看到神秘人在找他,可是找到之后,却发现魔杖已经不在格里戈维奇那里,被格林德沃偷走了。至于格林德沃是怎么知道格里戈维奇有老魔杖的,我就不清楚了——但如果格里戈维奇愚蠢得四处吹嘘,别人应该不难知道吧。"

伏地魔在霍格沃茨的大门口,哈利能看见他站在那里,也能看见灯光在黎明前的空气中浮动,越来越近了。

"格林德沃凭借老魔杖使自己变得强大起来。在他鼎盛的时候,邓布利多知道自己是唯一能够阻止他的人,就去和格林德沃决斗,并且战胜了他,拿走了老魔杖。"

"邓布利多拥有过老魔杖?"罗恩问,"那么——它现在呢?"

"在霍格沃茨。"哈利说,努力控制着,不让自己的思维离开悬崖顶上的花园,离开他们俩。

"那我们去吧!"罗恩急切地说,"哈利,去拿到老魔杖,赶在他之前。"

"已经太迟了,"哈利说,忍不住抱紧了脑袋,试图帮它一起抵御,"他知道老魔杖在哪儿,他已经在那里了。"

"哈利!"罗恩生气地说,"你知道这个多久了——为什么我们一直在浪费时间?为什么你要先跟拉环谈?不然我们已经去了——我们还可以去——"

"不,"哈利说,他跪倒在草地上,"赫敏是对的。邓布利多不希望我拥有它。他不希望我拿走它。他希望我去找魂器。"

"永不会输的魔杖,哈利!"罗恩抱怨道。

"我不应该……我应该去找魂器……"

此刻周围的一切又冷又暗,太阳还没有在地平线上显露,他在斯内普的旁边飘然而行,穿过操场向着湖边飘去。

"稍后我在城堡里和你会合,"他用那高亢、冷酷的声音说道,"现在你去吧。"

斯内普鞠了个躬,沿小路返回,黑色的斗篷在身后飘扬。哈利慢

CHAPTER TWENTY-FOUR   The Wandmaker

behind him. Harry walked slowly, waiting for Snape's figure to disappear. It would not do for Snape, or indeed anyone else, to see where he was going. But there were no lights in the castle windows, and he could conceal himself ... and in a second he had cast upon himself a Disillusionment Charm that hid him even from his own eyes.

And he walked on, around the edge of the lake, taking in the outlines of the beloved castle, his first kingdom, his birthright ...

And here it was, beside the lake, reflected in the dark waters. The white marble tomb, an unnecessary blot on the familiar landscape. He felt again that rush of controlled euphoria, that heady sense of purpose in destruction. He raised the old yew wand: how fitting that this would be its last great act.

The tomb split open from head to foot. The shrouded figure was as long and thin as it had been in life. He raised the wand again.

The wrappings fell open. The face was translucent, pale, sunken, yet almost perfectly preserved. They had left his spectacles on the crooked nose: he felt amused derision. Dumbledore's hands were folded upon his chest, and there it lay, clutched beneath them, buried with him.

Had the old fool imagined that marble or death would protect the wand? Had he thought that the Dark Lord would be scared to violate his tomb? The spider-like hand swooped and pulled the wand from Dumbledore's grasp, and as he took it, a shower of sparks flew from its tip, sparkling over the corpse of its last owner, ready to serve a new master at last.

第24章 魔杖制作人

慢走着,等待斯内普的身影消失。不能让斯内普看到他往哪里走,不能让任何人看到。城堡的窗户里没有灯光,而且他可以把自己隐藏起来……他立刻施了一个幻身咒,就连自己都看不见自己了。

他继续走着,环湖边而行,看着他心爱的城堡的轮廓,他的第一个王国,他与生俱来的权利……

到了,就在湖边,倒映在黑色的湖水里,白色的大理石坟墓,熟悉的风景中一个多余的污点。他再次感到那种有节制的喜悦冲动,那种制造毁灭的振奋感觉。他举起了那根旧的紫杉木魔杖:这将是它的最后一个壮举,多么合适呀。

坟墓从头到脚被劈开,包裹在布中的躯体和生前一样瘦长,他再次举起了魔杖。

包裹布散开了,脸是半透明的,苍白凹陷,然而保存得近乎完美。眼镜还架在弯鼻子上,真是滑稽可笑。邓布利多双手交握在胸前,魔杖就在那儿,抓在手里,同他一道被埋葬了。

这个老傻瓜以为大理石或死亡会保护这根魔杖吗?他以为黑魔王不敢侵犯他的坟墓吗?蜘蛛般的手猛地伸下去,从邓布利多手中抽出魔杖,一大串火花从杖尖迸出,在前主人的尸体上方闪闪发光,老魔杖终于要为一位新主人效劳了。

CHAPTER TWENTY-FIVE

Shell Cottage

Bill and Fleur's cottage stood alone on a cliff overlooking the sea, its walls embedded with shells and whitewashed. It was a lonely and beautiful place. Wherever Harry went inside the tiny cottage or its garden, he could hear the constant ebb and flow of the sea, like the breathing of some great, slumbering creature. He spent much of the next few days making excuses to escape the crowded cottage, craving the cliff-top view of open sky and wide, empty sea, and the feel of cold, salty wind on his face.

The enormity of his decision not to race Voldemort to the wand still scared Harry. He could not remember, ever before, choosing *not* to act. He was full of doubts, doubts that Ron could not help voicing whenever they were together.

'What if Dumbledore wanted us to work out the symbol in time to get the wand?' 'What if working out what the symbol meant made you "worthy" to get the Hallows?' 'Harry, if that really is the Elder Wand, how the hell are we supposed to finish off You-Know-Who?'

Harry had no answers: there were moments when he wondered whether it had been outright madness not to try to prevent Voldemort breaking open the tomb. He could not even explain satisfactorily why he had decided against it: every time he tried to reconstruct the internal arguments that had led to his decision, they sounded feebler to him.

The odd thing was that Hermione's support made him feel just as confused as Ron's doubts. Now forced to accept that the Elder Wand was real, she maintained that it was an evil object, and that the way Voldemort had taken possession of it was repellent, not to be considered.

'You could never have done that, Harry,' she said again and again. 'You couldn't have broken into Dumbledore's grave.'

第25章

贝壳小屋

比尔和芙蓉的小屋孤零零地屹立在悬崖之上，俯视着大海，墙壁是贝壳嵌成的，刷成了白色。这是一个孤独而美丽的地方。哈利在小屋和花园中无论走到哪儿，都能听到持续的潮起潮落的声音，像某个巨大的怪物沉睡时的呼吸。在接下来的几天里，他一直在寻找借口逃离拥挤的小屋，渴望感受悬崖顶上辽阔的天空和宽广空寂的大海，让冰冷的、咸咸的海风吹拂面颊。

没有试图赶在伏地魔的前面去拿老魔杖，这个沉重的决定仍然让哈利心有余悸。他不记得自己以前什么时候选择过不行动。他内心充满怀疑，而每当他和罗恩在一起时，罗恩也总是忍不住会表达出这些怀疑。

"如果邓布利多希望我们及时弄懂那个标志并拿到老魔杖，怎么办？""如果弄懂那个标志就意味着你'有资格'去获取圣器，怎么办？""哈利，如果那真的是老魔杖，我们还有什么办法干掉神秘人呢？"

哈利没有答案：有的时候他在疑惑，没有试图阻止伏地魔砸开坟墓，是不是十分愚蠢的行为。他甚至不能令人满意地解释为什么他决定不去反抗：每一次他试图推想导致他做出决定的内心依据，都觉得它们越来越站不住脚。

奇怪的是，赫敏的支持和罗恩的怀疑同样让他感到困惑。在被迫承认老魔杖真的存在后，赫敏坚持认为它是一个邪恶的东西，认为伏地魔占有它的方式是令人厌恶的，是想都不该想的。

"你绝不会那样做的，哈利，"她说了一遍又一遍，"你绝不可能闯进邓布利多的坟墓。"

CHAPTER TWENTY-FIVE   Shell Cottage

But the idea of Dumbledore's corpse frightened Harry much less than the possibility that he might have misunderstood the living Dumbledore's intentions. He felt that he was still groping in the dark; he had chosen his path but kept looking back, wondering whether he had misread the signs, whether he should not have taken the other way. From time to time, anger at Dumbledore crashed over him again, powerful as the waves slamming themselves against the cliff beneath the cottage, anger that Dumbledore had not explained before he died.

'But *is* he dead?' said Ron, three days after they had arrived at the cottage. Harry had been staring out over the wall that separated the cottage garden from the cliff when Ron and Hermione had found him; he wished they had not, having no wish to join in with their argument.

'Yes, he is, Ron, *please* don't start that again!'

'Look at the facts, Hermione,' said Ron, speaking across Harry, who continued to gaze at the horizon. 'The silver doe. The sword. The eye Harry saw in the mirror –'

'Harry admits he could have imagined the eye! Don't you, Harry?'

'I could have,' said Harry, without looking at her.

'But you don't think you did, do you?' asked Ron.

'No, I don't,' said Harry.

'There you go!' said Ron quickly, before Hermione could carry on. 'If it wasn't Dumbledore, explain how Dobby knew we were in the cellar, Hermione?'

'I can't – but can you explain how Dumbledore sent him to us if he's lying in a tomb at Hogwarts?'

'I dunno, it could've been his ghost!'

'Dumbledore wouldn't come back as a ghost,' said Harry. There was little about Dumbledore he was sure of, now, but he knew that much. 'He would have gone on.'

'What d'you mean, "gone on"?' asked Ron, but before Harry could say any more, a voice behind them said, ''Arry?'

Fleur had come out of the cottage, her long, silver hair flying in the breeze.

''Arry, Grip'ook would like to speak to you. 'E eez in ze smallest bedroom, 'e says 'e does not want to be over 'eard.'

Her dislike of the goblin sending her to deliver messages was clear; she looked irritable as she walked back round the house.

第25章 贝壳小屋

但是哈利觉得，比起可能误解邓布利多生前的意图，面对邓布利多的遗体倒并没有那么可怕。他感到自己仍然在黑暗中摸索，选择了一条路却不停地回头看，怀疑是否读错了路标，是否本该走另外一条路。对邓布利多的恼恨不时地再次涌上他的心头，就像小屋下的海水击打悬崖一般强烈，他恼恨邓布利多在去世前没有解释清楚。

"但是他真的死了吗？"在他们抵达小屋三天后，罗恩说。刚才哈利正凝望着花园与悬崖之间的隔墙，两个同伴找到了他。哈利不想加入他们的争辩，满心希望他们没有找来。

"是的，他死了。罗恩，求你不要再说那个啦！"

"看看事实，赫敏，"罗恩隔着哈利说道，哈利继续凝视着天边，"银色的牡鹿。宝剑。哈利在镜子里看到的眼睛——"

"哈利承认眼睛可能是他的错觉！不是吗，哈利？"

"可能是。"哈利说，但没有看赫敏。

"但是你认为不是错觉，对吗？"罗恩问。

"对。"哈利说。

"这就对了！"罗恩赶紧说道，不让赫敏插话，"如果那不是邓布利多，请解释一下多比是怎么知道我们在地牢里的，赫敏？"

"我不能——但是你能解释邓布利多是怎么派多比来救我们的吗？如果他躺在霍格沃茨的坟墓里的话？"

"我不知道，可能是他的幽灵！"

"邓布利多不会变成幽灵回来的。"哈利说。关于邓布利多，他现在有把握的事已寥寥无几，但这一点他是知道的："他会继续。"

"'继续'是什么意思？"罗恩问。哈利刚要回答，一个声音从后面传来："哈利？"

芙蓉从小屋里出来了，银色的长发在微风中飘舞。

"哈利，拉环想要和你谈谈。他在最小的卧室里。他说不希望有人偷听。"

芙蓉显然很讨厌妖精派她来传递消息，绕着小屋走回去时，她看上去脾气很不好。

CHAPTER TWENTY-FIVE Shell Cottage

Griphook was waiting for them, as Fleur had said, in the tiniest of the cottage's three bedrooms, in which Hermione and Luna slept by night. He had drawn the red cotton curtains against the bright, cloudy sky, which gave the room a fiery glow at odds with the rest of the airy, light cottage.

'I have reached my decision, Harry Potter,' said the goblin, who was sitting cross-legged in a low chair, drumming its arms with his spindly fingers. 'Though the goblins of Gringotts will consider it base treachery, I have decided to help you –'

'That's great!' said Harry, relief surging through him. 'Griphook, thank you, we're really –'

'– in return,' said the goblin firmly, 'for payment.'

Slightly taken aback, Harry hesitated.

'How much do you want? I've got gold.'

'Not gold,' said Griphook. 'I have gold.'

His black eyes glittered; there were no whites to his eyes.

'I want the sword. The sword of Godric Gryffindor.'

Harry's spirits plummeted.

'You can't have that,' he said. 'I'm sorry.'

'Then,' said the goblin softly, 'we have a problem.'

'We can give you something else,' said Ron eagerly. 'I'll bet the Lestranges have got loads of stuff, you can take your pick once we get into the vault.'

He had said the wrong thing. Griphook flushed angrily.

'I am not a thief, boy! I am not trying to procure treasures to which I have no right!'

'The sword's ours –'

'It is not,' said the goblin.

'We're Gryffindors, and it was Godric Gryffindor's –'

'And before it was Gryffindor's, whose was it?' demanded the goblin, sitting up straight.

'No one's,' said Ron, 'it was made for him, wasn't it?'

'No!' cried the goblin, bristling with anger as he pointed a long finger at Ron. 'Wizarding arrogance again! That sword was Ragnuk the First's, taken from him by Godric Gryffindor! It is a lost treasure, a masterpiece of goblinwork! It belongs with the goblins! The sword is the price of my hire, take it or leave it!'

第25章 贝壳小屋

正如芙蓉所说,拉环在贝壳小屋三间卧室中最小的一间里等着他们。赫敏和卢娜晚上就睡在这里。妖精拉上了红色棉布窗帘,外面的天空明亮而多云,透过窗帘给房间里映入火红的光,与小屋淡雅的风格很不谐调。

"我已经做出决定,哈利·波特。"妖精跷着脚坐在一张矮椅子上,细长的手指敲打着扶手,"尽管古灵阁的妖精们会认为这是卑鄙的背叛,但我决定帮助你——"

"太棒了!"哈利说,轻松的感觉涌遍全身,"拉环,谢谢你,我们真的——"

"——是有偿的,"妖精坚定地说,"要有报酬。"

哈利有点吃惊,犹豫了。

"你要多少?我有金子。"

"不要金子。"拉环说,"金子我有。"

他的黑眼睛闪闪发光,没有眼白。

"我要宝剑。戈德里克·格兰芬多的宝剑。"

哈利的心猛地沉了下去。

"这个不行,"他说,"对不起。"

"那么,"妖精轻声说,"事情就麻烦了。"

"我们可以给你别的,"罗恩急切地说,"我打赌莱斯特兰奇夫妇有大量的好东西,只要我们进了金库,你可以随便挑。"

他说错了话。拉环气得满脸通红。

"我不是窃贼,小子!我不会图谋我无权占有的财富!"

"宝剑是我们的——"

"不是。"妖精说。

"我们是格兰芬多学院的,而宝剑是戈德里克·格兰芬多的——"

"那么在格兰芬多之前,它是谁的?"妖精坐直了身子质问道。

"没有谁,"罗恩说,"那宝剑是为他定制的,不是吗?"

"不是!"妖精喊道,用长手指点着罗恩,气得毛发竖立,"又是巫师的狂傲自大!那宝剑是莱格纳克一世的,被格兰芬多拿走了!这是一件丢失的宝物,妖精的杰作!它属于妖精!那把宝剑就是雇佣我的代价,不同意就拉倒!"

CHAPTER TWENTY-FIVE   Shell Cottage

Griphook glared at them. Harry glanced at the other two, then said, 'We need to discuss this, Griphook, if that's all right. Could you give us a few minutes?'

The goblin nodded, looking sour.

Downstairs in the empty sitting room, Harry walked to the fireplace, brow furrowed, trying to think what to do. Behind him, Ron said, 'He's having a laugh. We can't let him have that sword.'

'It is true?' Harry asked Hermione. 'Was the sword stolen by Gryffindor?'

'I don't know,' she said hopelessly. 'Wizarding history often skates over what the wizards have done to other magical races, but there's no account that I know of that says Gryffindor stole the sword.'

'It'll be one of those goblin stories,' said Ron, 'about how the wizards are always trying to get one over on them. I suppose we should think ourselves lucky he hasn't asked for one of our wands.'

'Goblins have got good reason to dislike wizards, Ron,' said Hermione. 'They've been treated brutally in the past.'

'Goblins aren't exactly fluffy little bunnies, though, are they?' said Ron. 'They've killed plenty of us. They've fought dirty too.'

'But arguing with Griphook about whose race is most underhand and violent isn't going to make him more likely to help us, is it?'

There was a pause while they tried to think of a way round the problem. Harry looked out of the window at Dobby's grave. Luna was arranging sea lavender in a jam jar beside the headstone.

'OK,' said Ron, and Harry turned back to face him, 'how's this? We tell Griphook we need the sword until we get inside the vault, and then he can have it. There's a fake in there, isn't there? We switch them, and give him the fake.'

'Ron, he'd know the difference better than we would!' said Hermione. 'He's the only one who realised there had been a swap!'

'Yeah, but we could scarper before he realises –'

He quailed beneath the look Hermione was giving him.

'That,' she said quietly, 'is despicable. Ask for his help, then double-cross him? And you wonder why goblins don't like wizards, Ron?'

Ron's ears had turned red.

'All right, all right! It was the only thing I could think of! What's your solution, then?'

第 25 章 贝壳小屋

拉环对他们怒目而视。哈利看看两个同伴，然后说："拉环，我们需要商量一下。你能给我们几分钟吗？"

妖精阴沉着脸点点头。

到了楼下无人的起居室，哈利走到壁炉前，紧锁眉头，努力想着对策。罗恩在他身后说："他在开玩笑吧，我们不能让他占有宝剑。"

"是真的吗？"哈利问赫敏，"宝剑是格兰芬多偷来的？"

"我不知道，"赫敏无奈地说，"魔法史常常把巫师对其他魔法种族做的事情一笔带过。据我了解，记载中没有提到格兰芬多偷了宝剑。"

"这又是妖精编的一个故事，"罗恩说，"说巫师总是试图欺骗他们。我想我们应该觉得幸运，他没有要我们的魔杖。"

"妖精有理由讨厌巫师，罗恩，"赫敏说，"他们过去遭受过残酷的待遇。"

"可是，妖精并不是毛茸茸的小兔子，不是吗？"罗恩说，"他们杀死了我们很多人。他们的手段也很卑鄙。"

"但是跟拉环争论哪个种族更阴险残暴，并不会让他更乐意帮助我们，不是吗？"

一阵沉默，三人试图想出解决问题的办法。哈利朝窗外多比的坟墓望去。卢娜正在墓碑旁，把插在果酱瓶里的紫花匙叶草放到那里。

"好吧，"罗恩说，哈利转过来看着他，"这样行不行？告诉拉环我们需要那把宝剑，要等进了金库才能给他。那里面不是有个假货吗？我们悄悄换一下，把假的给他。"

"罗恩，他比我们更能区别真伪！"赫敏说，"他是唯一发现宝剑调包的人！"

"对，但是我们可以在他发现之前溜掉——"

他在赫敏的眼神面前畏缩了。

"那是卑鄙的。"赫敏轻声说，"请求帮助，然后欺骗他？你还奇怪为什么妖精不喜欢巫师吗，罗恩？"

罗恩的耳朵红了。

"好吧，好吧！我只能想到这个主意！那你有什么办法？"

'We need to offer him something else, something just as valuable.'

'Brilliant. I'll go and get one of our other ancient goblin-made swords and you can gift-wrap it.'

Silence fell between them again. Harry was sure that the goblin would accept nothing but the sword, even if they had something as valuable to offer him. Yet the sword was their one, indispensable weapon against the Horcruxes.

He closed his eyes for a moment or two and listened to the rush of the sea. The idea that Gryffindor might have stolen the sword was unpleasant to him; he had always been proud to be a Gryffindor; Gryffindor had been the champion of Muggle-borns, the wizard who had clashed with the pure-blood-loving Slytherin ...

'Maybe he's lying,' Harry said, opening his eyes again. 'Griphook. Maybe Gryffindor didn't take the sword. How do we know the goblin version of history's right?'

'Does it make a difference?' asked Hermione.

'Changes how I feel about it,' said Harry.

He took a deep breath.

'We'll tell him he can have the sword after he's helped us get into that vault – but we'll be careful to avoid telling him exactly *when* he can have it.'

A grin spread slowly across Ron's face. Hermione, however, looked alarmed.

'Harry, we can't –'

'He can have it,' Harry went on, 'after we've used it on all of the Horcruxes. I'll make sure he gets it then. I'll keep my word.'

'But that could be years!' said Hermione.

'I know that, but *he* needn't. I won't be lying ... really.'

Harry met her eyes with a mixture of defiance and shame. He remembered the words that had been engraved over the gateway to Nurmengard: *For the Greater Good*. He pushed the idea away. What choice did they have?

'I don't like it,' said Hermione.

'Nor do I, much,' Harry admitted.

'Well, I think it's genius,' said Ron, standing up again. 'Let's go and tell him.'

第25章 贝壳小屋

"我们需要给他别的东西，一件同样贵重的东西。"

"妙极了。我再去在咱们那些妖精制作的古老宝剑里头挑一把，你用礼品纸包装一下。"

又是一阵沉默。哈利相信妖精除了那把宝剑，别的什么都不会接受，即使他们能有同样贵重的东西给他。然而，宝剑是他们对付魂器时必不可少的武器。

他闭了一会儿眼睛，倾听着海浪拍岸的声音。想到格兰芬多有可能偷了宝剑，他心里不大舒服。哈利一直以自己是格兰芬多学院的学生为荣。格兰芬多努力维护麻瓜出身者的权益，曾与迷恋纯血统的斯莱特林有过激烈冲突……

"拉环可能在撒谎，"哈利说，睁开了眼睛，"格兰芬多可能并没有偷那把宝剑。我们怎么知道妖精讲的历史就是真实的呢？"

"这有关系吗？"赫敏问。

"会改变我的感受。"哈利说。

他深吸了一口气。

"我们就对拉环说，等他帮助我们进入金库之后，就可以拥有这把宝剑——但是要说得很小心，别告诉他可以拿到宝剑的确切时间。"

罗恩慢慢地咧嘴一笑，但是赫敏显得很不安。

"哈利，我们不能——"

"拉环可以得到它，"哈利接着说，"在我们用它对付完所有的魂器之后。我保证拉环那时候会得到它。我会守信用的。"

"但那可能是很多年之后！"赫敏说。

"这我知道，但是他不必知道。我不会说谎的……真的。"

哈利倔强而又羞愧地迎视着赫敏的目光，想起刻在纽蒙迦德大门上的那句话：为了更伟大的利益。他抛开了那个念头。他们还有什么选择呢？

"我不喜欢。"赫敏说。

"我也不大喜欢。"哈利承认。

"哦，我认为这主意妙极了。"罗恩说着站起身，"我们去告诉他吧。"

CHAPTER TWENTY-FIVE   Shell Cottage

Back in the smallest bedroom, Harry made the offer, careful to phrase it so as not to give any definite time for the handover of the sword. Hermione frowned at the floor while he was speaking; he felt irritated at her, afraid that she might give the game away. However, Griphook had eyes for nobody but Harry.

'I have your word, Harry Potter, that you will give me the sword of Gryffindor if I help you?'

'Yes,' said Harry.

'Then shake,' said the goblin, holding out his hand.

Harry took it and shook. He wondered whether those black eyes saw any misgivings in his own. Then Griphook relinquished him, clapped his hands together and said, 'So. We begin!'

It was like planning to break into the Ministry all over again. They settled to work in the smallest bedroom, which was kept, according to Griphook's preference, in semi-darkness.

'I have visited the Lestranges' vault only once,' Griphook told them, 'on the occasion I was told to place inside it the false sword. It is one of the most ancient chambers. The oldest wizarding families store their treasures at the deepest level, where the vaults are largest and best protected ...'

They remained shut in the cupboard-like room for hours at a time. Slowly, the days stretched into weeks. There was problem after problem to overcome, not least of which was that their store of Polyjuice Potion was greatly depleted.

'There's really only enough left for one of us,' said Hermione, tilting the thick mud-like Potion against the lamplight.

'That'll be enough,' said Harry, who was examining Griphook's hand-drawn map of the deepest passageways.

The other inhabitants of Shell Cottage could hardly fail to notice that something was going on now that Harry, Ron and Hermione only emerged for mealtimes. Nobody asked questions, although Harry often felt Bill's eyes on the three of them at the table, thoughtful, concerned.

The longer they spent together, the more Harry realised that he did not much like the goblin. Griphook was unexpectedly bloodthirsty, laughed at the idea of pain in lesser creatures and seemed to relish the possibility that they might have to hurt other wizards to reach the Lestranges' vault. Harry could tell that his distaste was shared by the other two, but they did not discuss it: they needed Griphook.

第25章 贝壳小屋

回到那间最小的卧室，哈利答应把宝剑给拉环，他措辞很小心，没有说出移交宝剑的确切时间。他说话的时候，赫敏皱眉看着地板，哈利很是恼火，怕她泄露了秘密。还好，拉环只盯着哈利，没有看别人。

"向我保证，哈利·波特，如果我帮助了你，你会给我格兰芬多的宝剑，是吗？"

"是的。"哈利说。

"那么握手。"妖精说着伸出手来。

哈利握住妖精的手，不知那双黑眼睛是否在他眼中看出了几分疑虑。拉环松开他的手，双手合在一起，说道："那么，我们开始吧！"

就像当初策划潜入魔法部一样，他们在最小的卧室里开始工作。依着拉环的偏好，屋里保持着半黑暗状态。

"我只去过莱斯特兰奇的金库一次，"拉环对他们说，"就是奉命把假宝剑放进去的那次。那是最古老的密室之一。最古老巫师家族的财物储存在最深的一层，那里的金库最大，并且保护最好……"

他们把自己关在衣柜般的小房间里，一待就是好几个小时。渐渐地，几天过去了，几星期过去了，要攻克的难题一个接一个，其中包括复方汤剂快用光了。

"只够一个人用的了。"赫敏说，一边对着灯光斜举着泥浆般浓稠的汤剂。

"那就够了。"哈利说，他正在研究拉环手绘的最深处的过道地图。

贝壳小屋的其他人不可能不发现异常，因为哈利、罗恩和赫敏只在吃饭的时候出现。没有人问起，但哈利经常感觉到比尔在饭桌上端详他们三个，关切而若有所思。

在一起的时间越长，哈利越觉得他不太喜欢那个妖精。拉环是出奇的残忍，他把低等物种的痛苦当成笑谈，而对于进入莱斯特兰奇的金库可能需要伤害其他巫师，他似乎津津乐道。哈利看得出来自己的两个同伴也感到厌恶，但是他们没有讨论这个，他们需要拉环。

CHAPTER TWENTY-FIVE Shell Cottage

The goblin ate only grudgingly with the rest of them. Even after his legs had mended, he continued to request trays of food in his room, like the still frail Ollivander, until Bill (following an angry outburst from Fleur) went upstairs to tell him that the arrangement could not continue. Thereafter, Griphook joined them at the overcrowded table, although he refused to eat the same food, insisting, instead, on lumps of raw meat, roots and various fungi.

Harry felt responsible: it was, after all, he who had insisted that the goblin remain at Shell Cottage so that he could question him; his fault that the whole Weasley family had been driven into hiding, that Bill, Fred, George and Mr Weasley could no longer work.

'I'm sorry,' he told Fleur, one blustery April evening as he helped her prepare dinner. 'I never meant you to have to deal with all of this.'

She had just set some knives to work, chopping up steaks for Griphook and Bill, who had preferred his meat bloody ever since he had been attacked by Greyback. While the knives sliced away behind her, her somewhat irritable expression softened.

''Arry, you saved my sister's life, I do not forget.'

This was not, strictly speaking, true, but Harry decided against reminding her that Gabrielle had never been in real danger.

'Anyway,' Fleur went on, pointing her wand at a pot of sauce on the stove, which began to bubble at once, 'Mr Ollivander leaves for Muriel's zis evening. Zat will make things easier. Ze goblin,' she scowled a little at the mention of him, 'can move downstairs, and you, Ron and Dean can take zat room.'

'We don't mind sleeping in the living room,' said Harry, who knew that Griphook would think poorly of having to sleep on the sofa; keeping Griphook happy was essential to their plans. 'Don't worry about us.' And when she tried to protest he went on, 'We'll be off your hands soon, too, Ron, Hermione and I. We won't need to be here much longer.'

'But what do you mean?' she said, frowning at him, her wand pointing at the casserole dish now suspended in mid-air. 'Of course, you must not leave, you are safe 'ere!'

She looked rather like Mrs Weasley as she said it, and he was glad that the back door opened at that moment. Luna and Dean entered, their hair damp from the rain outside and their arms full of driftwood.

第 25 章 贝壳小屋

妖精满不情愿地和其他人一道吃饭。腿伤治好以后，他仍然要求与还很虚弱的奥利凡德一样享受饭菜送到房间的待遇，直到比尔（在芙蓉的愤怒爆发后）上楼告诉他不能再那样安排。从那以后，拉环加入到拥挤的餐桌前，但拒绝吃同样的食物，坚持要吃大块的生肉、根茎和各种蘑菇。

哈利感到自己有责任，毕竟是他坚持让那妖精留在贝壳小屋，以便向他提问的。是他的错误导致了韦斯莱一家被迫隐藏，使比尔、弗雷德、乔治和韦斯莱先生不能继续上班。

"对不起，"在四月一个狂风大作的夜晚，他帮芙蓉准备晚餐时说，"我真不想让你们承受这一切。"

芙蓉刚安排几把刀子自动为拉环和比尔切牛排，比尔自从被格雷伯克咬伤后，也喜欢吃带血的肉了。刀子在身后切着肉，芙蓉有点烦躁的表情缓和了下来。

"哈利，你救过我妹妹的命，我不会忘记的。"

严格说来，那不是真的，但是哈利决定不提醒她加布丽从未真的有过危险。

"不管怎样，"芙蓉接着说，一边用魔杖指着炉子上的一锅调味汁，它马上开始冒泡，"奥利凡德先生今晚就要搬去穆丽尔姨婆家，这样就会方便一些了。那个妖精，"提到拉环时芙蓉微微皱了一下眉头，"可以搬到楼下来，这样你、罗恩和迪安就可以住那间屋了。"

"我们不介意睡在客厅里。"哈利说，他知道拉环要是睡沙发会不痛快，而保持拉环心情愉快对于他们的计划至关重要。"不用担心我们，"看到芙蓉要反对，哈利接着说，"我和罗恩、赫敏很快也要走了，我们不会再待多久。"

"你在说什么呀？"芙蓉皱着眉头对他说，魔杖指着悬在半空中的砂锅，"你们当然不能离开，你们在这儿是安全的！"

她说这话时的样子很像韦斯莱夫人，哈利很高兴后门这时开了，卢娜和迪安走了进来，头发被雨水打湿了，怀里抱满浮木。

CHAPTER TWENTY-FIVE   Shell Cottage

'... and tiny little ears,' Luna was saying, 'a bit like a hippo's, Daddy says, only purple and hairy. And if you want to call them, you have to hum; they prefer a waltz, nothing too fast ...'

Looking uncomfortable, Dean shrugged at Harry as he passed, following Luna into the combined dining and sitting room where Ron and Hermione were laying the dinner table. Seizing the chance to escape Fleur's questions, Harry grabbed two jugs of pumpkin juice and followed them.

'... and if you ever come to our house I'll be able to show you the horn, Daddy wrote to me about it but I haven't seen it yet, because the Death Eaters took me from the Hogwarts Express and I never got home for Christmas,' Luna was saying, as she and Dean relaid the fire.

'Luna, we told you,' Hermione called over to her. 'That horn exploded. It came from an Erumpent, not a Crumple-Horned Snorkack –'

'No, it was definitely a Snorkack horn,' said Luna serenely. 'Daddy told me. It will probably have reformed by now, they mend themselves, you know.'

Hermione shook her head and continued laying down forks as Bill appeared, leading Mr Ollivander down the stairs. The wandmaker still looked exceptionally frail, and he clung to Bill's arm as the latter supported him, carrying a large suitcase.

'I'm going to miss you, Mr Ollivander,' said Luna, approaching the old man.

'And I you, my dear,' said Ollivander, patting her on the shoulder. 'You were an inexpressible comfort to me in that terrible place.'

'So, *au revoir*, Mr Ollivander,' said Fleur, kissing him on both cheeks. 'And I wonder whezzer you could oblige me by delivering a package to Bill's Auntie Muriel? I never returned 'er tiara.'

'It will be an honour,' said Ollivander, with a little bow, 'the very least I can do in return for your generous hospitality.'

Fleur drew out a worn velvet case, which she opened to show the wandmaker. The tiara sat glittering and twinkling in the light from the low-hanging lamp.

'Moonstones and diamonds,' said Griphook, who had sidled into the room without Harry noticing. 'Made by goblins, I think?'

'And paid for by wizards,' said Bill quietly, and the goblin shot him a look that was both furtive and challenging.

第25章 贝壳小屋

"……还有小小的耳朵，"卢娜正说着，"有一点儿像河马的，爸爸说，不过是紫色的，而且有毛。如果你想呼唤它们，必须哼歌，它们喜欢华尔兹，节奏不要太快……"

迪安看起来不大自在，朝哈利耸了耸肩，跟着卢娜走进餐厅兼客厅，罗恩和赫敏正在布置餐桌。哈利抓住机会回避了芙蓉的问题，抄起两壶南瓜汁跟了过去。

"……如果你来我家，我可以给你看那只兽角，爸爸写信告诉我的，我还没有看到呢，因为食死徒把我从霍格沃茨特快列车上带走了，我没能回家过圣诞节。"卢娜说着，和迪安一起把火续上。

"卢娜，我们告诉过你，"赫敏冲她叫道，"那个兽角爆炸了，它是毒角兽的角，不是弯角鼾兽的——"

"不，肯定是鼾兽的角，"卢娜不为所动地说，"爸爸告诉我的。这会儿可能已经变好了，知道吗，它们会自我修复。"

赫敏摇了摇头，继续摆放叉子，这时比尔带着奥利凡德先生走下楼梯。魔杖制作人看起来仍然异常虚弱，紧抓着比尔的手臂，比尔一边扶着他，一边还提着个大箱子。

"我会想念您的，奥利凡德先生。"卢娜走到老人跟前说。

"我也会想念你，亲爱的。"奥利凡德说，拍了拍她的肩膀，"在那个可怕的地方，你对我是一个莫大的安慰。"

"那么，再会，奥利凡德先生。"芙蓉亲了亲他的双颊说，"不知道您能不能帮我带一个包裹给比尔的穆丽尔姨婆？我还没有把她的头饰还给她呢。"

"很荣幸。"奥利凡德微鞠一躬说，"感谢你的盛情款待，这点回报不足挂齿。"

芙蓉取出一个磨破的天鹅绒箱子，打开来给魔杖制作人看了一下，头饰在低悬的吊灯下闪闪发光。

"月长石和钻石，"拉环刚才悄悄走了进来，哈利没有注意到，"我想是妖精做的吧？"

"巫师花钱买的。"比尔平静地说。妖精迅速看了他一眼，目光鬼祟而含有挑衅意味。

CHAPTER TWENTY-FIVE Shell Cottage

A strong wind gusted against the cottage windows as Bill and Ollivander set off into the night. The rest of them squeezed in around the table; elbow to elbow and with barely enough room to move, they started to eat. The fire crackled and popped in the grate beside them. Fleur, Harry noticed, was merely playing with her food; she glanced at the window every few minutes; however, Bill returned before they had finished their first course, his long hair tangled by the wind.

'Everything fine,' he told Fleur. 'Ollivander settled in, Mum and Dad say hello. Ginny sends you all her love. Fred and George are driving Muriel up the wall, they're still operating an Owl Order business out of her back room. It cheered her up to have her tiara back, though. She said she thought we'd stolen it.'

'Ah, she eez *charmante*, your aunt,' said Fleur crossly, waving her wand and causing the dirty plates to rise and form a stack in mid-air. She caught them and marched out of the room.

'Daddy's made a tiara,' piped up Luna. 'Well, more of a crown, really.'

Ron caught Harry's eye and grinned; Harry knew that he was remembering the ludicrous headdress they had seen on their visit to Xenophilius.

'Yes, he's trying to recreate the lost diadem of Ravenclaw. He thinks he's identified most of the main elements now. Adding the Billywig wings really made a difference –'

There was a bang on the front door. Everyone's heads turned towards it. Fleur came running out of the kitchen, looking frightened; Bill jumped to his feet, his wand pointing at the door; Harry, Ron and Hermione did the same. Silently, Griphook slipped beneath the table out of sight.

'Who is it?' Bill called.

'It is I, Remus John Lupin!' called a voice over the howling wind. Harry experienced a thrill of fear; what had happened? 'I am a werewolf, married to Nymphadora Tonks, and you, the Secret Keeper of Shell Cottage, told me the address and bade me come in an emergency!'

'Lupin,' muttered Bill, and he ran to the door and wrenched it open.

Lupin fell over the threshold. He was white-faced, wrapped in a travelling cloak, his greying hair windswept. He straightened up, looked around the room, making sure of who was there, then cried aloud, 'It's a boy! We've named him Ted, after Dora's father!'

第25章 贝壳小屋

大风刮着小屋的窗户，比尔和奥利凡德朝着黑夜出发了。其他人挤在餐桌周围，开始吃饭，胳膊碰着胳膊，几乎没有空间可以活动。旁边壁炉里的火焰噼啪作响。哈利注意到芙蓉几乎没吃东西，只是不停地拨弄盘中的食物，每隔几分钟就看一眼窗户。还好，他们刚吃完第一道菜，比尔就回来了，长发被风吹得缠在一起。

"一切都好。"他告诉芙蓉，"奥利凡德安顿好了，爸爸妈妈向大家问好，金妮说她爱你们。弗雷德和乔治让穆丽尔姨婆很生气，他们仍然在她的后屋承接猫头鹰订单业务。不过，归还头饰令她很高兴，她说还以为被我们贪污了呢。"

"啊，你的姨婆她很可爱。"芙蓉气呼呼地说，一边挥舞着魔杖使脏盘子在半空中摞在一起，她接住它们走出了房间。

"我爸爸做了一个头饰，"卢娜说，"噢，实际上更像一个王冠。"

罗恩看到哈利的目光后咧嘴一笑，哈利知道他想起了在谢诺菲留斯家看到的滑稽头饰。

"是的，他在试着重做失踪的拉文克劳冠冕，认为他已经确定了大多数主要成分，加上比利威格虫的翅膀后确实不一样了——"

前门砰的一响，大家都转过头去，芙蓉惊恐地从厨房里跑了出来。比尔一跃而起，用魔杖指着门口。哈利、罗恩和赫敏也是一样。拉环悄悄地钻到了桌子底下。

"是谁？"比尔喊道。

"是我，莱姆斯·卢平！"一个声音在呼啸的风声中喊道。哈利感到一阵心惊肉跳，出什么事了？"我是狼人，我妻子叫尼法朵拉·唐克斯，你是贝壳小屋的保密人，告诉了我这个地址，叫我有紧急情况就过来！"

"卢平。"比尔咕哝道，跑过去拧开了门。

卢平跌进门内，脸色苍白，裹着一件旅行斗篷，灰白的头发被风刮乱了。他站起来，环顾四周，确认屋里有谁，然后大声喊道："是个男孩！我们给他起名叫泰德，用了朵拉父亲的名字！"

CHAPTER TWENTY-FIVE   Shell Cottage

Hermione shrieked.

'Wha–? Tonks – Tonks has had the baby?'

'Yes, yes, she's had the baby!' shouted Lupin. All around the table came cries of delight, sighs of relief: Hermione and Fleur both squealed, 'Congratulations!' and Ron said, 'Blimey, a baby!' as if he had never heard of such a thing before.

'Yes – yes – a boy,' said Lupin again, who seemed dazed by his own happiness. He strode round the table and hugged Harry; the scene in the basement of Grimmauld Place might never have happened.

'You'll be godfather?' he said, as he released Harry.

'M – me?' stammered Harry.

'You, yes, of course – Dora quite agrees, no one better –'

'I – yeah – blimey –'

Harry felt overwhelmed, astonished, delighted: now Bill was hurrying to fetch wine and Fleur was persuading Lupin to join them for a drink.

'I can't stay long, I must get back,' said Lupin, beaming around at them all: he looked years younger than Harry had ever seen him. 'Thank you, thank you, Bill.'

Bill had soon filled all of their goblets; they stood and raised them high in a toast.

'To Teddy Remus Lupin,' said Lupin, 'a great wizard in the making!'

''Oo does 'e look like?' Fleur enquired.

'I think he looks like Dora, but she thinks he is like me. Not much hair. It looked black when he was born, but I swear it's turned ginger in the hour since. Probably be blond by the time I get back. Andromeda says Tonks's hair started changing colour the day that she was born.' He drained his goblet. 'Oh, go on then, just one more,' he added, beaming, as Bill made to fill it again.

The wind buffeted the little cottage and the fire leapt and crackled, and Bill was soon opening another bottle of wine. Lupin's news seemed to have taken them out of themselves, removed them for a while from their state of siege: tidings of new life were exhilarating. Only the goblin seemed untouched by the suddenly festive atmosphere, and after a while he slunk back to the bedroom he now occupied alone. Harry thought he was the only one who had noticed this, until he saw Bill's eyes following the goblin

第25章 贝壳小屋

赫敏尖叫起来。

"什么——？唐克斯——唐克斯生了？"

"生了，生了！生了小宝宝！"卢平喊道。餐桌周围一片欢呼声和欣慰的叹息声。赫敏和芙蓉都尖叫道："恭喜恭喜！"罗恩说："我的天哪，一个新生儿！"好像以前从没听说过这种事似的。

"是的——是的——是个男孩。"卢平又说了一遍，似乎高兴得飘飘然了。他大步走过来和哈利拥抱，格里莫广场地下室里的那一幕好像从未发生过。

"你愿意当教父吗？"他松开哈利，问道。

"我——我？"哈利结结巴巴地说。

"对，是你，当然——朵拉完全同意，没有人更合适了——"

"我——好的——天哪——"

哈利惊喜交加，激动得不知所措。现在比尔忙着去拿酒，芙蓉劝卢平跟大家一起喝点。

"我不能待得太久，必须回去。"卢平说，冲着大家眉开眼笑，看上去比哈利见过的任何时候都年轻了好几岁，"谢谢你，谢谢你，比尔。"

比尔很快就给所有的酒杯倒满了酒，大家站了起来，高高地举杯庆祝。

"为了泰德·莱姆斯·卢平，"卢平说，"一个正在成长的伟大巫师！"

"他长得像谁？"芙蓉问道。

"我认为他像朵拉，可是朵拉认为像我。头发不多，刚出生时看上去是黑色的，但是我发誓一小时后就变成了红色，很可能到我回去时就是金黄色了。安多米达说唐克斯出生第一天头发就开始变色。"卢平把酒一饮而尽，"哦，再来点，再来一杯。"他笑眯眯地添了一句，比尔又给他加了酒。

狂风吹打着小屋，炉火跳跃着，噼啪作响，比尔很快又打开了一瓶酒。卢平带来的消息似乎让他们都忘记了自我，暂时从被困的状态中释放了出来：新生命诞生的喜讯令人振奋。唯有那个妖精似乎对突如其来的欢庆气氛无动于衷，不一会儿就溜回他现在独住的卧室去了。

CHAPTER TWENTY-FIVE   Shell Cottage

up the stairs.

'No ... no ... I really must get back,' said Lupin at last, declining yet another goblet of wine. He got to his feet and pulled his travelling cloak back around himself. 'Goodbye, goodbye – I'll try and bring some pictures in a few days' time – they'll all be so glad to know that I've seen you –'

He fastened his cloak and made his farewells, hugging the women and grasping hands with the men, then, still beaming, returned into the wild night.

'Godfather, Harry!' said Bill, as they walked into the kitchen together, helping clear the table. 'A real honour! Congratulations!'

As Harry set down the empty goblets he was carrying, Bill pulled the door behind him closed, shutting out the still voluble voices of the others, who were continuing to celebrate even in Lupin's absence.

'I wanted a private word, actually, Harry. It hasn't been easy to get an opportunity with the cottage this full of people.'

Bill hesitated.

'Harry, you're planning something with Griphook.'

It was a statement, not a question, and Harry did not bother to deny it. He merely looked at Bill, waiting.

'I know goblins,' said Bill. 'I've worked for Gringotts ever since I left Hogwarts. As far as there can be friendship between wizards and goblins, I have goblin friends – or, at least, goblins I know well, and like.' Again, Bill hesitated. 'Harry, what do you want from Griphook, and what have you promised him in return?'

'I can't tell you that,' said Harry. 'Sorry, Bill.'

The kitchen door opened behind them; Fleur was trying to bring through more empty goblets.

'Wait,' Bill told her. 'Just a moment.'

She backed out and he closed the door again.

'Then I have to say this,' Bill went on. 'If you have struck any kind of bargain with Griphook, and most particularly if that bargain involves treasure, you must be exceptionally careful. Goblin notions of ownership, payment and repayment are not the same as human ones.'

Harry felt a slight squirm of discomfort, as though a small snake had stirred inside him.

第25章 贝壳小屋

哈利原以为只有他一个人注意到,忽然发现比尔的目光盯着妖精上了楼梯。

"不……不……我真的必须回去了。"卢平终于说道,谢绝了又一次斟酒。他站起身,将旅行斗篷裹到身上。"再见,再见——过几天我想办法带些照片来——他们知道我见到了你们,都会非常高兴的——"

他系好斗篷后开始道别,和女士们拥抱,和男士们握手,仍然眉开眼笑,返回了狂风呼啸的黑夜里。

"教父,哈利!"比尔说,他们帮着清理餐桌,一起走进了厨房,"真是荣幸啊!恭喜!"

哈利放下端着的空酒杯,比尔顺手拉上了身后的门,把仍在大声说话的其他人隔在外面。尽管卢平已经离开,他们还在继续庆祝。

"哈利,其实我想和你单独谈谈。小屋里人太多,找这么一个机会不容易。"

比尔犹豫了一下。

"哈利,你们和拉环在计划着什么事情。"

这是一个陈述,不是一个问句,哈利也就不必否认。他只是看着比尔,等待下文。

"我了解妖精,"比尔说,"我离开霍格沃茨后就一直为古灵阁工作。如果说巫师和妖精之间能有友谊的话,那么我有妖精朋友——或者至少,有一些我很了解也很喜欢的妖精。"比尔再次犹豫了一下,"哈利,你想从拉环那儿得到什么,你又答应回报他什么?"

"这个我不能告诉你,"哈利说,"对不起,比尔。"

厨房的门开了,芙蓉端着更多的空酒杯要进来。

"等一下,"比尔对她说,"就一会儿。"

芙蓉退了出去,比尔把门重新关上了。

"那么我不得不说一句,"比尔接着说,"如果你和拉环订了任何协议,尤其是如果那协议涉及财宝,你必须格外小心。妖精概念中的所有权、报酬与补偿跟人类的不同。"

哈利感到一阵不安,好像一条小蛇在他体内搅动。

CHAPTER TWENTY-FIVE   Shell Cottage

'What do you mean?' he asked.

'We are talking about a different breed of being,' said Bill. 'Dealings between wizards and goblins have been fraught for centuries – but you'll know all that from History of Magic. There has been fault on both sides, I would never claim that wizards have been innocent. However, there is a belief among some goblins, and those at Gringotts are perhaps most prone to it, that wizards cannot be trusted in matters of gold and treasure, that they have no respect for goblin ownership.'

'I respect –' Harry began, but Bill shook his head.

'You don't understand, Harry, nobody could understand unless they have lived with goblins. To a goblin, the rightful and true master of any object is the maker, not the purchaser. All goblin-made objects are, in goblin eyes, rightfully theirs.'

'But if it was bought –'

'– then they would consider it rented by the one who had paid the money. They have, however, great difficulty with the idea of goblin-made objects passing from wizard to wizard. You saw Griphook's face when the tiara passed under his eyes. He disapproves. I believe he thinks, as do the fiercest of his kind, that it ought to have been returned to the goblins once the original purchaser died. They consider our habit of keeping goblin-made objects, passing them from wizard to wizard without further payment, little more than theft.'

Harry had an ominous feeling now; he wondered whether Bill guessed more than he was letting on.

'All I am saying,' said Bill, setting his hand on the door back into the sitting room, 'is to be very careful what you promise goblins, Harry. It would be less dangerous to break into Gringotts than to renege on a promise to a goblin.'

'Right,' said Harry, as Bill opened the door, 'yeah. Thanks. I'll bear that in mind.'

As he followed Bill back to the others, a wry thought came to him, born no doubt of the wine he had drunk. He seemed set on course to become just as reckless a godfather to Teddy Lupin as Sirius Black had been to him.

第25章 贝壳小屋

"什么意思?"他问。

"我们是在讨论另一种生物。"比尔说,"许多个世纪以来,巫师和妖精间的交往充满矛盾——这些你都可以从魔法史中去了解。双方都曾有过错,我绝不会说巫师清白无辜。然而,一些妖精认为——古灵阁的妖精也许更容易认为:涉及金子和财宝时,巫师就不可信任,并且巫师不尊重妖精的所有权。"

"我尊重——"哈利说,但是比尔摇了摇头。

"你不理解,哈利,没人能够理解,除非和妖精在一起生活过。对于妖精来说,任何一件东西真正且正当的主人都是它的制造者,而不是购买者。凡是妖精制造的东西,在妖精看来,都理当归他们所有。"

"但如果是买来——"

"——妖精们会认为那是付钱者租用的。他们最难接受的,就是妖精制作的东西由巫师传给巫师。当头饰在拉环眼皮下传递时,你看到了他的脸色。他很不满。我相信拉环会像他同类中的极端者一样,认为原来的购买者死后,那东西就应该归还给妖精。他们认为我们这样习惯于占有妖精制造的东西,由巫师传给巫师而不再付钱,比偷窃好不到哪里去。"

哈利现在有了一种不祥的感觉,他怀疑比尔猜到了更多的事情。

"我要说的,"比尔把手伸到厨房的门上,"就是你在对妖精做出承诺时要格外小心,哈利。对一个妖精食言要比闯进古灵阁更危险。"

"好的。"哈利说,比尔打开了门,"好的。谢谢。我会记在心上的。"

跟着比尔回到大家中间时,哈利突然产生了一个怪异的念头,无疑是喝酒引起的。他觉得对于小泰德·卢平来说,自己正要变成一个像小天狼星布莱克一样鲁莽的教父。

CHAPTER TWENTY-SIX

Gringotts

Their plans were made, their preparations complete; in the smallest bedroom a single long, coarse, black hair (plucked from the sweater Hermione had been wearing at Malfoy Manor) lay curled in a small glass phial on the mantelpiece.

'And you'll be using her actual wand,' said Harry, nodding towards the walnut wand, 'so I reckon you'll be pretty convincing.'

Hermione looked frightened that the wand might sting or bite her as she picked it up.

'I hate this thing,' she said in a low voice. 'I really hate it. It feels all wrong, it doesn't work properly for me ... it's like a bit of *her*.'

Harry could not help but remember how Hermione had dismissed his loathing of the blackthorn wand, insisting that he was imagining things when it did not work as well as his own, telling him to simply practise. He chose not to repeat her own advice back to her, however; the eve of their attempted assault on Gringotts felt like the wrong moment to antagonise her.

'It'll probably help you get in character, though,' said Ron. 'Think what that wand's done!'

'But that's my point!' said Hermione. 'This is the wand that tortured Neville's mum and dad, and who knows how many other people? This is the wand that killed Sirius!'

Harry had not thought of that: he looked down at the wand and was visited by a brutal urge to snap it, to slice it in half with Gryffindor's sword, which was propped against the wall beside him.

'I miss *my* wand,' Hermione said miserably. 'I wish Mr Ollivander could have made me another one too.'

Mr Ollivander had sent Luna a new wand that morning. She was out on

第26章

古灵阁

计划已经定好,准备已经完成,在那间最小卧室的壁炉架上,一根长长的粗糙的黑头发(是从赫敏在马尔福庄园穿的那件毛衣上摘下的)卷缩在一个小玻璃药瓶里。

"你拿着她本人的魔杖,"哈利朝胡桃木魔杖点了点头说,"我想应该是很令人信服的。"

赫敏战战兢兢地拿起魔杖,好像害怕魔杖会蜇她或咬她一样。

"我讨厌这个东西,"她低声说道,"真心讨厌。感觉很糟糕,用起来很不顺手……有点像她的一部分。"

哈利忍不住想起赫敏当初怎样驳斥他对黑刺李木魔杖的嫌恶,当他认为那根魔杖不如自己的好用时,赫敏坚持认为那只是心理作用,对他说只要多加练习就好。然而哈利决定不再重提她当初的建议,在偷袭古灵阁的前夜跟她作对似乎不是时候。

"不过,它可能会帮助你进入角色,"罗恩说,"想想那根魔杖做了些什么吧!"

"这正是我要说的!"赫敏说,"就是这根魔杖摧残过纳威的父母,谁知道还有多少人被它折磨过?就是这根魔杖杀死了小天狼星!"

哈利没有想到这一点。他低头看着魔杖,有一种强烈的冲动想把它折断,想用靠在身旁墙上的格兰芬多宝剑把它砍成两截。

"我怀念我的魔杖,"赫敏可怜地说,"真希望奥利凡德先生也给我另外做一根。"

那天早上,奥利凡德先生给卢娜寄来了一根新魔杖。此刻卢娜正

CHAPTER TWENTY-SIX Gringotts

the back lawn at that moment, testing its capabilities in the late afternoon sun. Dean, who had lost his wand to the Snatchers, was watching rather gloomily.

Harry looked down at the hawthorn wand that had once belonged to Draco Malfoy. He had been surprised, but pleased, to discover that it worked for him at least as well as Hermione's had done. Remembering what Ollivander had told them of the secret workings of wands, Harry thought he knew what Hermione's problem was: she had not won the walnut wand's allegiance by taking it personally from Bellatrix.

The door of the bedroom opened and Griphook entered. Harry reached instinctively for the hilt of the sword and drew it close to him, but regretted his action at once: he could tell that the goblin had noticed. Seeking to gloss over the sticky moment he said, 'We've just been checking the last-minute stuff, Griphook. We've told Bill and Fleur we're leaving tomorrow, and we've told them not to get up to see us off.'

They had been firm on this point, because Hermione would need to transform into Bellatrix before they left, and the less that Bill and Fleur knew or suspected about what they were about to do, the better. They had also explained that they would not be returning. As they had lost Perkins's old tent on the night that the Snatchers caught them, Bill had lent them another one. It was now packed inside the beaded bag, which, Harry was impressed to learn, Hermione had protected from the Snatchers by the simple expedient of stuffing it down her sock.

Though he would miss Bill, Fleur, Luna and Dean, not to mention the home comforts they had enjoyed over the last few weeks, Harry was looking forward to escaping the confinement of Shell Cottage. He was tired of trying to make sure that they were not overheard, tired of being shut in the tiny, dark bedroom. Most of all, he longed to be rid of Griphook. However, precisely how and when they were to part from the goblin without handing over Gryffindor's sword remained a question to which Harry had no answer. It had been impossible to decide how they were going to do it, because the goblin rarely left Harry, Ron and Hermione alone together for more than five minutes at a time; 'He could give my mother lessons,' growled Ron, as the goblin's long fingers kept appearing around the edges of doors. With Bill's warning in mind, Harry could not help suspecting that Griphook was on the watch for possible skulduggery. Hermione disapproved so heartily of the planned double-cross that Harry had given up attempting to pick her brains on how best to do it; Ron, on the rare occasions that they had been able to

第26章 古灵阁

在屋后的草坪上,在傍晚的阳光下试验它的性能。迪安的魔杖也被搜捕队夺去了,他在一旁郁闷地看着。

哈利低头注视着曾经属于德拉科·马尔福的山楂木魔杖。他惊讶但庆幸地发现,这根魔杖用起来至少跟赫敏的那根一样顺手。哈利记起了奥利凡德说过的魔杖性能的秘密,他估计赫敏的问题是:她没有战胜胡桃木魔杖效忠的对象,没有直接从贝拉特里克斯的手上夺得它。

卧室的门开了,拉环走了进来。哈利本能地伸手抓住剑柄,把宝剑揽到自己的身边,但马上又后悔了:他能看出妖精注意到了这个动作。为了掩饰刚才的尴尬,哈利说:"我们正在做最后的检查,拉环。我们已经告诉比尔和芙蓉我们明天离开,并且叫他们不要起床送我们。"

他们离开之前,赫敏要化装成贝拉特里克斯,这件事让比尔和芙蓉知道或猜到得越少越好,所以哈利等坚决不要他们送,并讲明了不再返回这里。珀金斯的旧帐篷在遭遇搜捕队的那天晚上弄丢了,比尔又借给他们一个,现在就放在串珠小包里。赫敏那天情急之下,居然把小包塞进袜子里躲过了搜捕队的搜查,哈利得知后十分佩服。

哈利会想念比尔、芙蓉、卢娜以及迪安,更不必说这几个星期来享受到的家的舒适,但他仍然期待着逃离贝壳小屋的禁锢。他已经厌倦了总要确保他和罗恩、赫敏说话时不会被别人听见,厌倦了把他们自己关在狭小黑暗的卧室里。尤其是他想摆脱拉环。然而,在不交出格兰芬多宝剑的情况下,怎样以及什么时候才能与那个妖精分手,哈利一直想不出答案。妖精很少让哈利、罗恩和赫敏单独待在一起五分钟以上,他们三人不可能商量出办法。"他都可以给我妈妈上上课了。"罗恩埋怨道,因为妖精的长手指不停地出现在门边。有比尔的警告在脑海里,哈利不禁怀疑拉环随时都在提防他们使诈。赫敏强烈反对计划中的骗局,哈利只好放弃了同她商量如何行动。

CHAPTER TWENTY-SIX   Gringotts

snatch a few Griphook-free moments, had come up with nothing better than 'We'll just have to wing it, mate.'

Harry slept badly that night. Lying awake in the early hours, he thought back to the way he had felt the night before they had infiltrated the Ministry of Magic and remembered a determination, almost an excitement. Now he was experiencing jolts of anxiety, nagging doubts: he could not shake off the fear that it was all going to go wrong. He kept telling himself that their plan was good, that Griphook knew what they were facing, that they were well-prepared for all the difficulties they were likely to encounter; yet still he felt uneasy. Once or twice he heard Ron stir, and was sure that he, too, was awake, but they were sharing the sitting room with Dean, so Harry did not speak.

It was a relief when six o'clock arrived and they could slip out of their sleeping bags, dress in the semi-darkness, then creep out into the garden, where they were to meet Hermione and Griphook. The dawn was chilly, but there was little wind now that it was May. Harry looked up at the stars still glimmering palely in the dark sky and listened to the sea washing backwards and forwards against the cliff: he was going to miss the sound.

Small green shoots were forcing their way up through the red earth of Dobby's grave now; in a year's time the mound would be covered in flowers. The white stone that bore the elf's name had already acquired a weathered look. He realised now that they could hardly have laid Dobby to rest in a more beautiful place, but Harry ached with sadness to think of leaving him behind. Looking down on the grave, he wondered yet again how the elf had known where to come to rescue them. His fingers moved absent-mindedly to the little pouch still strung around his neck, through which he could feel the jagged mirror fragment in which he had been sure he had seen Dumbledore's eye. Then the sound of a door opening made him look round.

Bellatrix Lestrange was striding across the lawn towards them, accompanied by Griphook. As she walked, she was tucking the small beaded bag into the inside pocket of another set of the old robes they had taken from Grimmauld Place. Though Harry knew perfectly well that it was really Hermione, he could not suppress a shiver of loathing. She was taller than he was, her long, black hair rippling down her back, her heavily lidded eyes disdainful as they rested upon him; but then she spoke, and he heard Hermione through Bellatrix's low voice.

第26章 古灵阁

而在难得几次没有拉环的自由时间里，罗恩所能想到的也就是："我们见机行事吧，伙计。"

那个晚上哈利睡得很糟糕。开始几小时一直醒着，回想起潜入魔法部之前那天晚上的感受。记得当时他是满怀决心，几乎是兴奋的，而现在他却感到一阵阵焦虑和痛苦的怀疑，摆脱不掉对于彻底失败的恐惧。他不停地告诉自己计划很周密，对可能遭遇的所有困难都做了充分准备，而且拉环很熟悉情况。可是他心里仍然不踏实，有一两次听到罗恩那边有动静，他断定罗恩也醒着，但他们是和迪安一起睡在起居室里，所以哈利没有说话。

谢天谢地，六点钟到了，他们钻出睡袋，在昏暗中穿上衣服，轻手轻脚地走到花园里，等待同赫敏和拉环会合。黎明很寒冷，但由于是五月了，没有什么风。哈利抬头看着仍在黑色夜空中闪烁微光的星星，听着海水一遍遍冲击峭壁——他将会怀念这声音。

现在，绿色的小嫩芽已经从多比坟上的红土中钻出，一年之后这个土丘将被鲜花覆盖。刻有多比名字的白石头已经有点风化的痕迹。他现在才意识到，再也找不到一个比这里更美丽的地方让多比安息了。然而，想到就要离开多比，哈利悲伤得有点心痛。他低头看着坟墓，再次疑惑小精灵是怎么知道去哪里营救他们的。他的手指不经意间伸向挂在脖子上的小皮袋，摸到了边缘不齐的镜子碎片，他曾相信在里面见到了邓布利多的眼睛。这时，开门声一响，他回过头来。

贝拉特里克斯·莱斯特兰奇大步跨过草坪朝他们走来，拉环陪在旁边。贝拉特里克斯穿着一件从格里莫广场带来的旧袍子，边走边把串珠小包塞进袍子里面的口袋。哈利明知道那其实是赫敏，却仍然抑制不住一阵厌恶的战栗。她的个头比他还高，长长的波浪形黑发披在背后，肿眼皮的眼睛轻蔑地看着他。但她说话时，哈利从贝拉特里克斯低沉的声音中听出了赫敏的风格。

'She tasted *disgusting*, worse than Gurdyroots! OK, Ron, come here so I can do you ...'

'Right, but remember, I don't like the beard too long –'

'Oh, for heaven's sake, this isn't about looking handsome –'

'It's not that, it gets in the way! But I liked my nose a bit shorter, try and do it the way you did last time.'

Hermione sighed and set to work, muttering under her breath as she transformed various aspects of Ron's appearance. He was to be given a completely fake identity, and they were trusting to the malevolent aura cast by Bellatrix to protect him. Meanwhile, Harry and Griphook were to be concealed under the Invisibility Cloak.

'There,' said Hermione, 'how does he look, Harry?'

It was just possible to discern Ron under his disguise, but only, Harry thought, because he knew him so well. Ron's hair was now long and wavy, he had a thick, brown beard and moustache, no freckles, a short, broad nose and heavy eyebrows.

'Well, he's not my type, but he'll do,' said Harry. 'Shall we go, then?'

All three of them glanced back at Shell Cottage, lying dark and silent under the fading stars, then turned and began to walk towards the point, just beyond the boundary wall, where the Fidelius Charm stopped working and they would be able to Disapparate. Once past the gate, Griphook spoke.

'I should climb up now, Harry Potter, I think?'

Harry bent down and the goblin clambered on to his back, his hands linked in front of Harry's throat. He was not heavy, but Harry disliked the feeling of the goblin and the surprising strength with which he clung on. Hermione pulled the Invisibility Cloak out of the beaded bag and threw it over them both.

'Perfect,' she said, bending down to check Harry's feet. 'I can't see a thing. Let's go.'

Harry turned on the spot with Griphook on his shoulders, concentrating with all his might on the Leaky Cauldron, the inn that was the entrance to Diagon Alley. The goblin clung even tighter as they moved into the compressing darkness, and seconds later Harry's feet found pavement and he opened his eyes on Charing Cross Road. Muggles bustled past wearing the hangdog expressions of early morning, quite unconscious of the little inn's existence.

第26章 古灵阁

"她的味道令人作呕，比戈迪根还难喝！好，罗恩，过来让我给你弄……"

"好吧，但是记住，我不喜欢胡子太长——"

"哦，看在老天爷的分上，这不是好看不好看的问题——"

"不是的，它碍事儿！不过我喜欢我的鼻子变短一点儿，就照你上次弄的那样。"

赫敏叹了口气，开始工作，嘴里喃喃地念着，帮罗恩改变容貌。罗恩被赋予了一个完全是捏造的身份，他们指望贝拉特里克斯那股邪恶的霸气会保护他。哈利和拉环将藏在隐形衣下面。

"好了。"赫敏说，"他看起来怎样，哈利？"

伪装过的罗恩还能勉强辨认出来，但哈利想那仅仅是因为他和罗恩太熟悉了。罗恩现在头发长而拳曲，下巴上有一把浓密的棕色胡须，上唇也留着小胡子，脸上没有了雀斑，眉毛很浓，鼻子又短又宽。

"嗯，不是我喜欢的类型，但是还凑合。"哈利说，"我们可以走了吗？"

三人都回头看了一眼贝壳小屋，它黑乎乎地静卧在渐渐黯淡下去的星星下。他们转身朝外走，只要过了界墙，赤胆忠心咒就不再有效，他们便可以幻影移形了。一出大门，拉环便说话了。

"现在我该爬上了吧，哈利·波特？"

哈利弯下腰，妖精爬到他背上，双手相扣抱住哈利的喉咙口。他并不重，但哈利不喜欢碰到妖精，也不喜欢他那样紧抱着自己，力气大得惊人。赫敏从串珠小包里取出隐形衣盖住了他们俩。

"好极了，"她说道，一边俯身检查哈利的脚，"我什么也看不到。走吧。"

哈利背着拉环原地旋转，拼命集中意念想着破釜酒吧——那是对角巷的入口。当他们进入压得人透不过气来的黑暗时，妖精抱得更紧了。几秒钟后，哈利的双脚踏到了地面，睁眼一看是查令十字街。麻瓜们匆匆走过，带着大清早那种没精打采的表情，丝毫没有意识到小旅馆的存在。

CHAPTER TWENTY-SIX

Gringotts

The bar of the Leaky Cauldron was nearly deserted. Tom, the stooped and toothless landlord, was polishing glasses behind the bar counter; a couple of warlocks having a muttered conversation in the far corner glanced at Hermione and drew back into the shadows.

'Madam Lestrange,' murmured Tom, and as Hermione passed he inclined his head subserviently.

'Good morning,' said Hermione, and as Harry crept past, still carrying Griphook piggyback under the Cloak, he saw Tom look surprised.

'Too polite,' Harry whispered in Hermione's ear as they passed out of the inn into the tiny backyard. 'You need to treat people like they're scum!'

'OK, OK!'

Hermione drew out Bellatrix's wand and tapped a brick in the nondescript wall in front of them. At once the bricks began to whirl and spin: a hole appeared in the middle of them, which grew wider and wider, finally forming an archway on to the narrow cobbled street that was Diagon Alley.

It was quiet, barely time for the shops to open, and there were hardly any shoppers abroad. The crooked, cobbled street was much altered, now, from the bustling place Harry had visited before his first term at Hogwarts so many years before. More shops than ever were boarded-up, though several new establishments dedicated to the Dark Arts had been created since his last visit. Harry's own face glared down at him from posters plastered over many windows, always captioned with the words *Undesirable Number One*.

A number of ragged people sat huddled in doorways. He heard them moaning to the few passers-by, pleading for gold, insisting that they were really wizards. One man had a bloody bandage over his eye.

As they set off along the street, the beggars glimpsed Hermione. They seemed to melt away before her, drawing hoods over their faces and fleeing as fast as they could. Hermione looked after them curiously, until the man with the bloodied bandage came staggering right across her path.

'My children!' he bellowed, pointing at her. His voice was cracked, high-pitched, he sounded distraught. 'Where are my children? What has he done with them? You know, *you know!*'

'I – I really –' stammered Hermione.

The man lunged at her, reaching for her throat: then, with a bang and a burst of red light he was thrown backwards on to the ground, unconscious.

第26章 古灵阁

破釜酒吧里几乎没人。汤姆,那个驼背又没牙的老板,正在吧台后面擦拭玻璃杯;几个在远处墙角里窃窃私语的巫师瞥了一眼赫敏,退到了暗处。

"莱斯特兰奇夫人。"汤姆低声说道,当赫敏走过时,他恭敬地低下了头。

"早上好。"赫敏说,在隐形衣下背着拉环轻轻走过的哈利看出汤姆有些惊讶。

"太有礼貌了,"从旅馆进入小小的后院时,哈利对赫敏耳语道,"你对他们要像对待垃圾一样。"

"好,好!"

赫敏抽出贝拉特里克斯的魔杖,在面前看似普通的墙上轻敲一块砖头。墙砖马上开始旋转,中间的地方出现一个小洞,洞口越变越大,最后形成一个拱洞,通向一条鹅卵石铺砌的狭窄街道,那就是对角巷。

街上静悄悄的,刚到店铺开门的时间,外面几乎还没有顾客。蜿蜒曲折的卵石小巷变化很大,当年哈利初进霍格沃茨之前来这里的时候,小巷中熙熙攘攘,何等热闹。而现在这么多的店铺都用木板封上了,倒是新建了几家经营黑魔法物品的店面,哈利上一次来时还没有呢。哈利自己的面孔从许多窗口张贴的海报上瞪着他,下面写着头号不良分子。

许多衣衫褴褛的人挤坐在各家店铺的门口。哈利听到他们在向寥寥无几的过客哀诉,乞讨金币,并强调自己是真正的巫师。有个男人一只眼睛上蒙着染血的绷带。

当他们沿着街道往前走时,乞丐们瞥见了赫敏,顿时作鸟兽散,都拉起兜帽遮着脸尽快逃离。赫敏好奇地目送他们,直到眼睛上蒙绷带的男人蹒跚地走到她面前。

"我的孩子们!"他指着她咆哮道,声音沙哑刺耳,听起来有点精神错乱,"我的孩子们在哪儿?他把他们怎么样了?你知道的,你知道的!"

"我——我真的——"赫敏结结巴巴地说。

男人突然冲向她,伸手来抓她的喉咙。随着砰的一声和一道红光,他向后摔倒在地,不省人事。罗恩站在那儿,魔杖仍举在手里,胡子

Ron stood there, his wand still outstretched and a look of shock visible behind his beard. Faces appeared at the windows on either side of the street, while a little knot of prosperous-looking passers-by gathered their robes about them and broke into gentle trots, keen to vacate the scene.

Their entrance into Diagon Alley could hardly have been more conspicuous; for a moment Harry wondered whether it might not be better to leave, now, and try to think of a different plan. Before they could move or consult one another, however, they heard a cry from behind them.

'Why, Madam Lestrange!'

Harry whirled round and Griphook tightened his hold around Harry's neck: a tall, thin wizard with a crown of bushy, grey hair and a long, sharp nose was striding towards them.

'It's Travers,' hissed the goblin into Harry's ear, but at that moment Harry could not think who Travers was. Hermione had drawn herself up to her fullest height and said, with as much contempt as she could muster, 'and what do you want?'

Travers stopped in his tracks, clearly affronted.

'*He's another Death Eater!*' breathed Griphook, and Harry sidled sideways to repeat the information into Hermione's ear.

'I merely sought to greet you,' said Travers coolly, 'but if my presence is not welcome ...'

Harry recognised his voice now; Travers was one of the Death Eaters who had been summoned to Xenophilius's house.

'No, no, not at all, Travers,' said Hermione quickly, trying to cover up her mistake. 'How are you?'

'Well, I confess I am surprised to see you out and about, Bellatrix.'

'Really? Why?' asked Hermione.

'Well,' Travers coughed, 'I *heard* that the inhabitants of Malfoy Manor were confined to the house, after the ... ah ... *escape*.'

Harry willed Hermione to keep her head. If this was true, and Bellatrix was not supposed to be out in public –

'The Dark Lord forgives those who have served him most faithfully in the past,' said Hermione, in a magnificent imitation of Bellatrix's most contemptuous manner. 'Perhaps your credit is not as good with him as mine is, Travers.'

第26章 古灵阁

后面的脸上满是惊讶。街道两边的窗户里露出了人脸,一小群衣着体面的过路人拉起长袍小跑起来,急于离开现场。

这样进入对角巷实在太惹人注目了,哈利一时犹豫是否现在就撤离,重新再制订一个计划。可是他们还没来得及挪动脚步或商量,就听到身后传来一声叫喊。

"咦,莱斯特兰奇夫人!"

哈利急转过身,拉环把他的脖子抱得更紧了。一个瘦高个的巫师大步向他们走来,一头浓密的灰发,鼻子又长又尖。

"是特拉弗斯。"妖精在哈利耳边嘶嘶地说,但是哈利一时想不起特拉弗斯是谁。赫敏挺直了身子,带着她所能装出来的最大轻蔑问道:"你想干吗?"

特拉弗斯停住脚步,显然觉得受到了冒犯。

"他也是食死徒!"拉环耳语道,哈利悄悄靠过去,把这个信息传进了赫敏的耳朵。

"我只是想和你打个招呼,"特拉弗斯冷冷地说道,"但是如果不受欢迎的话……"

哈利现在听出他的声音了,特拉弗斯是被召唤到谢诺菲留斯家的食死徒之一。

"不,不,哪里,特拉弗斯。"赫敏忙说,试图掩盖刚才的错误,"你好吗?"

"嗯,我承认见到你出来走动我很惊讶,贝拉特里克斯。"

"是吗?为什么?"赫敏问。

"嗯,"特拉弗斯咳嗽了一下,"我听说马尔福庄园的人都被禁闭在屋子里了,在那个……啊……逃脱之后。"

哈利祈求赫敏保持镇静。如果这消息是真的,如果贝拉特里克斯不该在公共场合出现——

"黑魔王原谅了那些在过去对他最忠诚的人,"赫敏说,惟妙惟肖地模仿贝拉特里克斯最傲慢时的态度,"也许你在他那里的信用没有我好,特拉弗斯。"

Though the Death Eater looked offended, he also seemed less suspicious. He glanced down at the man Ron had just Stunned.

'How did it offend you?'

'It does not matter, it will not do so again,' said Hermione coolly.

'Some of these Wandless can be troublesome,' said Travers. 'While they do nothing but beg I have no objection, but one of them actually asked me to plead her case at the Ministry last week. *"I'm a witch, sir, I'm a witch, let me prove it to you!"*' he said, in a squeaky impersonation. 'As if I was going to give her my wand – but whose wand,' said Travers curiously, 'are you using at the moment, Bellatrix? I heard that your own was –'

'I have my wand here,' said Hermione coldly, holding up Bellatrix's wand. 'I don't know what rumours you have been listening to, Travers, but you seem sadly misinformed.'

Travers seemed a little taken aback at that, and he turned instead to Ron.

'Who is your friend? I do not recognise him.'

'This is Dragomir Despard,' said Hermione; they had decided that a fictional foreigner was the safest cover for Ron to assume. 'He speaks very little English, but he is in sympathy with the Dark Lord's aims. He has travelled here from Transylvania to see our new regime.'

'Indeed? How do you do, Dragomir?'

''Ow you?' said Ron, holding out his hand.

Travers extended two fingers and shook Ron's hand as though frightened of dirtying himself.

'So what brings you and your – ah – sympathetic friend to Diagon Alley this early?' asked Travers.

'I need to visit Gringotts,' said Hermione.

'Alas, I also,' said Travers. 'Gold, filthy gold! We cannot live without it, yet I confess I deplore the necessity of consorting with our long-fingered friends.'

Harry felt Griphook's clasped hands tighten momentarily around his neck.

'Shall we?' said Travers, gesturing Hermione forwards.

Hermione had no choice but to fall into step beside him and head along the crooked, cobbled street towards the place where the snowy-white Gringotts stood towering over the other little shops. Ron sloped along beside them, and Harry and Griphook followed.

第26章 古灵阁

食死徒又好像受到了冒犯,但似乎也少了些怀疑。他低头看了一眼刚被罗恩击昏的那个男人。

"这东西怎么得罪了你?"

"没关系,不会再这样了。"赫敏冷冷地说。

"这些没有魔杖的东西有时很麻烦。"特拉弗斯说,"如果他们只是乞讨我倒不介意,但有一个竟然要我到魔法部去为她辩护。'我是个女巫,先生,我是个女巫,让我证明给你看!'"他尖叫着模仿道,"好像我会把我的魔杖给她——可是,"特拉弗斯好奇地说,"你现在用的是谁的魔杖呀,贝拉特里克斯?我听说你自己的被——"

"这就是我自己的魔杖。"赫敏冷冷地说,一边举起贝拉特里克斯的魔杖,"我不知道你听到了什么谣言,特拉弗斯,你似乎被很可悲地误导了。"

特拉弗斯显得有点吃惊,他转向罗恩。

"你的朋友是谁?我不认识他。"

"他是德拉哥米尔·德斯帕德,"赫敏说,他们商议计划时决定,一个虚构的外国名字对于罗恩是最安全的掩护,"他几乎不会说英语,但是很支持黑魔王的目标。他是从特兰西瓦尼亚来观摩我们新政权的。"

"是吗?你好,德拉哥米尔。"

"你好。"罗恩伸出手说。

特拉弗斯伸出两根手指与罗恩握手,似乎担心自己被弄脏似的。

"那么,你和你的——啊——这位支持我们的朋友这么早就到对角巷来有何贵干呀?"特拉弗斯问道。

"我要去古灵阁。"赫敏说。

"哎呀,我也要去。"特拉弗斯说,"金子,肮脏的金子!我们活着离不开它,但是我承认,我很遗憾我必须跟那些长手指的朋友打交道。"

哈利感到拉环的手一时勒紧了他的脖子。

"请吧?"特拉弗斯说着,示意赫敏向前走。

赫敏别无选择,只好跟在他的身边,沿着蜿蜒曲折的鹅卵石街道,朝高高耸立在小店铺之上的那座雪白的建筑——古灵阁走去。罗恩走在他们身旁,哈利和拉环跟在后面。

CHAPTER TWENTY-SIX   Gringotts

A watchful Death Eater was the very last thing they needed, and the worst of it was, with Travers marching at what he believed to be Bellatrix's side, there was no means for Harry to communicate with Hermione or Ron. All too soon they arrived at the foot of the marble steps leading up to the great bronze doors. As Griphook had already warned them, the liveried goblins who usually flanked the entrance had been replaced by two wizards, both of whom were clutching long, thin golden rods.

'Ah, Probity Probes,' sighed Travers theatrically, 'so crude – but effective!'

And he set off up the steps, nodding left and right to the wizards, who raised the golden rods and passed them up and down his body. The Probes, Harry knew, detected spells of concealment and hidden magical objects. Knowing that he had only seconds, Harry pointed Draco's wand at each of the guards in turn and murmured, '*Confundo*,' twice. Unnoticed by Travers, who was looking through the bronze doors at the inner hall, each of the guards gave a little start as the spells hit them.

Hermione's long, black hair rippled behind her as she climbed the steps.

'One moment, Madam,' said the guard, raising his Probe.

'But you've just done that!' said Hermione, in Bellatrix's commanding, arrogant voice. Travers looked round, eyebrows raised. The guard was confused. He stared down at the thin, golden Probe and then at his companion, who said in a slightly dazed voice, 'Yeah, you've just checked them, Marius.'

Hermione swept forwards, Ron by her side, Harry and Griphook trotting invisibly behind them. Harry glanced back as they crossed the threshold: the wizards were both scratching their heads.

Two goblins stood before the inner doors, which were made of silver and which carried the poem warning of dire retribution to potential thieves. Harry looked up at it, and all of a sudden a knife-sharp memory came to him: standing on this very spot on the day that he had turned eleven, the most wonderful birthday of his life, and Hagrid standing beside him saying, '*Like I said, yeh'd be mad ter try an' rob it.*' Gringotts had seemed a place of wonder that day, the enchanted repository of a trove of gold he had never known he possessed, and never for an instant could he have dreamed that he would return to steal ... But within seconds they were standing in the vast marble hall of the bank.

第26章 古灵阁

他们最不希望出现的就是一个警惕的食死徒，最糟糕的是，特拉弗斯陪伴在他以为的贝拉特里克斯身旁，哈利就没有办法同赫敏和罗恩交流了。很快，他们到了通往青铜大门的大理石台阶底部。正如拉环警告过的那样，大门两侧穿制服的妖精已经换成了两个巫师，各持一根细长的金棒。

"啊，诚实探测器，"特拉弗斯夸张地叹了口气，"很原始——但很有效！"

他走上台阶，朝大门左右的巫师点了点头，他们举起金棒在他周身上下移动。哈利知道这种仪器会探测到隐藏的魔咒和暗藏的魔法物件。哈利知道只有几秒钟的机会，他迅速举起德拉科的魔杖点了点两个门卫，低声念了两遍混淆视听。两个门卫被咒语击中，都微微一震，特拉弗斯正看着铜门里面的内厅，没有注意到。

赫敏登上台阶，长长的黑发在身后如波浪般飘荡。

"等一等，夫人。"门卫举起探测器说道。

"你刚刚已经查过了！"赫敏用贝拉特里克斯那傲慢的、盛气凌人的口吻说。特拉弗斯回过头，扬起眉毛。门卫迷惑了，低头盯着细细的金色探测器，然后盯着他的同伴，后者有点茫然地说："是的，你刚才查过他们了，马里厄斯。"

赫敏大步往前走，罗恩跟在她身边，隐形的哈利和拉环紧随其后。过了门口，哈利回头瞥了一眼：两个巫师都在挠脑袋。

第二道门前站着两个妖精，银质大门上镌刻着窃贼必受恶报的诗句。哈利抬头看着它，突然一个如刀刻般鲜明的记忆浮现在他眼前：他刚满十一岁的那天，他一生中最奇妙的生日那天，就是站在这里，海格在他旁边说："就像我说的，你要是想抢这个银行，那你就是疯了。"那天，古灵阁在他看来是一个神奇的地方，是施了魔法的宝库，里面藏着那么多他根本不知道在他名下的金子。他从没想到过自己会回来偷盗……但几秒钟后，他们已站在了巨大的大理石门厅里。

The long counter was manned by goblins sitting on high stools, serving the first customers of the day. Hermione, Ron and Travers headed towards an old goblin who was examining a thick gold coin through an eyeglass. Hermione allowed Travers to step ahead of her on the pretext of explaining features of the hall to Ron.

The goblin tossed the coin he was holding aside, said to nobody in particular, 'Leprechaun,' and then greeted Travers, who passed over a tiny golden key, which was examined and given back to him.

Hermione stepped forwards.

'Madam Lestrange!' said the goblin, evidently startled. 'Dear me! How – how may I help you today?'

'I wish to enter my vault,' said Hermione.

The old goblin seemed to recoil a little. Harry glanced around. Not only was Travers hanging back, watching, but several other goblins had looked up from their work to stare at Hermione.

'You have ... identification?' asked the goblin.

'Identification? I – I have never been asked for identification before!' said Hermione.

'*They know!*' whispered Griphook in Harry's ear. '*They must have been warned there might be an impostor!*'

'Your wand will do, Madam,' said the goblin. He held out a slightly trembling hand, and in a dreadful blast of realisation Harry knew that the goblins of Gringotts were aware that Bellatrix's wand had been stolen.

'*Act now, act now,*' whispered Griphook in Harry's ear, '*the Imperius Curse!*'

Harry raised the hawthorn wand beneath the Cloak, pointed it at the old goblin and whispered, for the first time in his life, '*Imperio!*'

A curious sensation shot down Harry's arm, a feeling of tingling warmth that seemed to flow from his mind, down the sinews and veins connecting him to the wand and the curse it had just cast. The goblin took Bellatrix's wand, examined it closely and then said, 'Ah, you have had a new wand made, Madam Lestrange!'

'What?' said Hermione, 'no, no, that's mine –'

'A new wand?' said Travers, approaching the counter again; still the goblins all around were watching. 'But how could you have done, which wandmaker did you use?'

第26章 古灵阁

长长的柜台后面,妖精们坐在高凳上,接待当天的第一批顾客。赫敏、罗恩和特拉弗斯朝着一个年长的妖精走去,他正在透过镜片检查一块厚厚的金币。赫敏借口要向罗恩介绍大厅的特色,让特拉弗斯走在她的前面。

年长的妖精把手里的金币丢到一边,随口说了声"小矮妖",然后向特拉弗斯问好,接过他递上去的一把小金钥匙,检查过后又还给了他。

赫敏跨步向前。

"莱斯特兰奇夫人!"妖精说道,显然很吃惊,"啊呀!您——今天我能为您做点什么?"

"我想进入我的金库。"赫敏说。

年长的妖精似乎退缩了一下。哈利瞥了一眼四周。不仅特拉弗斯停下来看着她,好几个妖精都抬起头盯着赫敏。

"您有……身份证明吗?"那个妖精问。

"身份证明?我——我——以前从没有向我要过什么身份证明!"赫敏说。

"他们知道了!"拉环在哈利的耳边轻声低语,"他们一定得到警告,说有人会冒名顶替!"

"您的魔杖就可以证明,夫人。"那妖精说着,伸出了微微颤抖的手。哈利突然产生了一个可怕的念头,他意识到古灵阁的妖精们知道贝拉特里克斯的魔杖已经失窃。

"马上动手,马上动手,"拉环耳语道,"用夺魂咒!"

哈利在隐形衣下面举起山楂木魔杖,指向那个年长的妖精,平生第一次轻声念道:"魂魄出窍!"

一种奇特的感觉迅速传入哈利的手臂,一股麻刺刺的暖流似乎从他的脑海里流出,顺着肌肉和血管把他与魔杖和刚施的咒语连接在一起。那个妖精接过贝拉特里克斯的魔杖,仔细检查过后说:"啊,您又做了一根新魔杖,莱斯特兰奇夫人!"

"什么?"赫敏说,"不,不,那是我的——"

"新魔杖?"特拉弗斯又走回柜台前,周围的妖精仍在注视着,"但你是怎么做到的呢?找了哪一位魔杖制作人?"

CHAPTER TWENTY-SIX   Gringotts

Harry acted without thinking: pointing his wand at Travers, he muttered, '*Imperio!*' once more.

'Oh, yes, I see,' said Travers, looking down at Bellatrix's wand, 'yes, very handsome. And is it working well? I always think wands require a little breaking in, don't you?'

Hermione looked utterly bewildered, but to Harry's enormous relief she accepted the bizarre turn of events without comment.

The old goblin behind the counter clapped his hands and a younger goblin approached.

'I shall need the clankers,' he told the goblin, who dashed away and returned a moment later with a leather bag that seemed to be full of jangling metal, which he handed to his senior. 'Good, good! So, if you will follow me, Madam Lestrange,' said the old goblin, hopping down off his stool and vanishing from sight, 'I shall take you to your vault.'

He appeared around the end of the counter, jogging happily towards them, the contents of the leather bag still jingling. Travers was now standing quite still with his mouth hanging wide open. Ron was drawing attention to this odd phenomenon by regarding Travers with confusion.

'Wait – Bogrod!'

Another goblin came scurrying around the counter.

'We have instructions,' he said, with a bow to Hermione, 'forgive me, Madam Lestrange, but there have been special orders regarding the vault of Lestrange.'

He whispered urgently in Bogrod's ear, but the Imperiused goblin shook him off.

'I am aware of the instructions. Madam Lestrange wishes to visit her vault ... very old family ... old clients ... this way, please ...'

And, still clanking, he hurried towards one of the many doors leading off the hall. Harry looked back at Travers, who was still rooted to the spot looking abnormally vacant, and made his decision: with a flick of his wand he made Travers come with them, walking meekly in their wake as they reached the door and passed into the rough stone passageway beyond, which was lit with flaming torches.

'We're in trouble, they suspect,' said Harry, as the door slammed behind them and he pulled off the Invisibility Cloak. Griphook jumped down from

第26章 古灵阁

哈利不假思索地采取行动:他将魔杖指向特拉弗斯,再次低声喝道:"魂魄出窍!"

"哦,是,我看到了,"特拉弗斯低头看着贝拉特里克斯的魔杖说,"是的,很漂亮。好用吗？我一直认为魔杖需要一点时间来磨合,你认为呢？"

赫敏似乎完全被搞糊涂了,但是她一言不发地接受了这些古怪的变化,哈利深深地松了口气。

柜台后面那位年长的妖精拍了一下手,一个年纪稍轻的妖精走了过来。

"我要用叮当片。"年长的妖精对他说,年轻的妖精迅速离去,不一会儿就拿来一个小皮包交给了年长的妖精,小包里似乎装满了叮当作响的金属。"好的,好的! 请跟我来吧,莱斯特兰奇夫人,"年长的妖精说着,从凳子上跳下去不见了,"我带您去您的金库。"

他出现在柜台的尽头,很高兴地朝他们跑过来,小皮包里的东西仍在叮当作响。特拉弗斯现在很安静地站在那里,嘴巴张得大大的。罗恩困惑地看着特拉弗斯,这等于在吸引别人注意这个怪现象。

"等等——鲍格罗德!"

另一个妖精急忙绕过柜台跑来。

"我们有指示。"他说,同时向赫敏鞠了一躬,"请原谅,莱斯特兰奇夫人。关于莱斯特兰奇的金库,我们得到过特殊的指示。"

他在鲍格罗德的耳边急急地低语了几句,但是被施了夺魂咒的妖精推开了他。

"我知道有指示。莱斯特兰奇夫人希望看看她的金库……很古老的家族……老顾客……这边走,请……"

他仍然叮当作响地匆匆朝大厅的一扇门走去。哈利回头一看,特拉弗斯还像生了根一样站在原地,眼神茫然而不正常。哈利做出决定:轻挥魔杖让特拉弗斯跟了过来。那巫师温顺地紧跟在他们后面,他们穿过那扇门进了粗糙的石廊,里面有燃烧的火把照明。

"有麻烦,他们怀疑了。"当他们身后的那扇门重重地关上后,哈利扯下隐形衣说道。拉环从他背上跳了下来。看到哈利·波特突然出

his shoulders; neither Travers nor Bogrod showed the slightest surprise at the sudden appearance of Harry Potter in their midst. 'They're Imperiused,' he added, in response to Hermione and Ron's confused queries about Travers and Bogrod, who were both now standing there looking blank. 'I don't think I did it strongly enough, I don't know ...'

And another memory darted through his mind, of the real Bellatrix Lestrange shrieking at him when he had first tried to use an Unforgivable Curse: *'You need to mean them, Potter!'*

'What do we do?' asked Ron. 'Shall we get out now, while we can?'

'If we can,' said Hermione, looking back towards the door into the main hall, beyond which who knew what was happening.

'We've got this far, I say we go on,' said Harry.

'Good!' said Griphook. 'So, we need Bogrod to control the cart; I no longer have the authority. But there will not be room for the wizard.'

Harry pointed his wand at Travers.

'Imperio!'

The wizard turned and set off along the dark track at a smart pace.

'What are you making him do?'

'Hide,' said Harry, as he pointed his wand at Bogrod, who whistled to summon a little cart which came trundling along the tracks towards them out of the darkness. Harry was sure he could hear shouting behind them in the main hall as they all clambered into it, Bogrod in front with Griphook, Harry, Ron and Hermione crammed together in the back.

With a jerk the cart moved off, gathering speed: they hurtled past Travers, who was wriggling into a crack in the wall, then the cart began twisting and turning through the labyrinthine passages, sloping downwards all the time. Harry could not hear anything over the rattling of the cart on the tracks: his hair flew behind him as they swerved between stalactites, flying ever deeper into the earth, but he kept glancing back. They might as well have left enormous footprints behind them; the more he thought about it, the more foolish it seemed to have disguised Hermione as Bellatrix, to have brought along Bellatrix's wand, when the Death Eaters knew who had stolen it –

They were deeper than Harry had ever penetrated within Gringotts; they took a hairpin bend at speed and saw ahead of them, with seconds to spare, a waterfall pounding over the track. Harry heard Griphook shout, 'No!'

第26章 古灵阁

现在他们中间，特拉弗斯和鲍格罗德都没有表现出一点点惊奇，只是呆呆地站在那里。"他们被施了夺魂咒，"哈利解释道，回答赫敏和罗恩困惑的询问，"我想我的魔咒可能不够强，我不知道……"

又一段记忆闪过他的脑海，是真的贝拉特里克斯·莱斯特兰奇，在他第一次尝试使用不可饶恕咒后冲他尖叫："你需要发自内心，波特！"

"我们怎么办？"罗恩问，"趁现在还有可能，赶紧出去吧？"

"有可能吗？"赫敏说，回头看着通往大厅的门，谁知道那扇门后正在发生什么。

"已经到这里了，我看就往前走吧。"哈利说。

"好！"拉环说，"那么，我们需要鲍格罗德来控制小推车，我已经没有这个权限。但是车上没有那个巫师的位置了。"

哈利用魔杖指着特拉弗斯。

"*魂魄出窍！*"

巫师转过身，沿着黑黑的轨道步履轻快地离开了。

"你让他做什么？"

"藏起来。"哈利说，一边将魔杖指向鲍格罗德，那妖精吹了声口哨，一辆小推车从黑暗中沿着轨道滚来。他们爬进小推车，鲍格罗德和拉环在前面，哈利、罗恩和赫敏挤在后排，这时哈利确定他听见了身后大厅里的叫喊声。

小推车猛然启动，速度越来越快：呼啸着超过了特拉弗斯，他正扭动着身体钻进墙上的一个缝隙中。然后小推车开始沿着迷宫似的甬道拐来拐去地向下冲，在轨道上发出咔嗒咔嗒的声音，哈利什么也听不见。他们在钟乳石间不停地急转弯，朝地球深处飞驰。哈利的头发向后飞扬，但他还在不时地回头扫视。他们很可能在身后留下了太多可疑的踪迹。哈利越想越觉得愚蠢，把赫敏化装成贝拉特里克斯，还带着贝拉特里克斯的魔杖，而食死徒已经知道是谁偷走了它——

他们下到哈利以前在古灵阁从没到过的深度，快速拐了一个急弯，只见前面一道瀑布哗哗地冲泻在轨道上。只有几秒钟的反应时间，哈利听见拉环大喊一声："不！"但是无法刹车，他们飞驰而过。水灌满

CHAPTER TWENTY-SIX Gringotts

but there was no braking: they zoomed through it. Water filled Harry's eyes and mouth: he could not see or breathe: then, with an awful lurch, the cart flipped over and they were all thrown out of it. Harry heard the cart smash into pieces against the passage wall, heard Hermione shriek something and felt himself glide back towards the ground as though weightless, landing painlessly on the rocky passage floor.

'C – Cushioning Charm,' Hermione spluttered, as Ron pulled her to her feet: but to Harry's horror he saw that she was no longer Bellatrix; instead she stood there in overlarge robes, sopping wet and completely herself; Ron was red-haired and beardless again. They were realising it as they looked at each other, feeling their own faces.

'The Thief's Downfall!' said Griphook, clambering to his feet and looking back at the deluge on to the tracks, which Harry knew, now, had been more than water. 'It washes away all enchantment, all magical concealment! They know there are impostors in Gringotts, they have set off defences against us!'

Harry saw Hermione checking that she still had the beaded bag, and hurriedly thrust his own hand under his jacket to make sure he had not lost the Invisibility Cloak. Then he turned to see Bogrod shaking his head in bewilderment: the Thief's Downfall seemed to have lifted the Imperius Curse.

'We need him,' said Griphook, 'we cannot enter the vault without a Gringotts goblin. And we need the Clankers!'

'*Imperio!*' Harry said again; his voice echoed through the stone passage as he felt again the sense of heady control that flowed from brain to wand. Bogrod submitted once more to his will, his befuddled expression changing to one of polite indifference, as Ron hurried to pick up the leather bag of metal tools.

'Harry, I think I can hear people coming!' said Hermione, and she pointed Bellatrix's wand at the waterfall and cried, '*Protego!*' They saw the Shield Charm break the flow of enchanted water as it flew up the passageway.

'Good thinking,' said Harry, 'lead the way, Griphook!'

'How are we going to get out again?' Ron asked, as they hurried on foot into the darkness after the goblin, Bogrod panting in their wake like an old dog.

'Let's worry about that when we have to,' said Harry. He was trying to listen: he thought he could hear something clanking and moving around nearby. 'Griphook, how much further?'

'Not far, Harry Potter, not far ...'

第26章 古灵阁

哈利的眼睛和嘴巴,他不能睁眼,也无法呼吸。突然小推车猛地一斜,翻倒了,他们都被甩出了车外。哈利听见小推车撞在甬道的墙壁上摔成了碎片,又听见赫敏尖叫了几声,然后感觉自己在滑行,好像没有重量一样飘落到石头地面上,一点也没摔疼。

"减——减震咒。"赫敏呛着说,罗恩把她拉了起来。但哈利惊恐地看到她不再是贝拉特里克斯,站在那里的完全就是赫敏自己,穿着过大的长袍,浑身湿透。罗恩又变成红头发,胡须没有了。他们俩对视之后也意识到了,摸着自己的面颊。

"防贼瀑布!"拉环说,一边爬了起来,回头看着倾注在轨道上的水帘,哈利这才知道那不仅仅是水,"它会洗掉所有的魔咒,所有的魔法伪装!他们知道有人冒名闯入古灵阁,他们已经启动了防卫装置!"

哈利看见赫敏在检查她的串珠小包还在不在,也赶忙把手伸进自己外套里,确认隐形衣有没有丢。他一转身,看见鲍格罗德疑惑地摇着头,防贼瀑布似乎消除了夺魂咒。

"我们需要他,"拉环说,"没有古灵阁的妖精就进不了金库,而且我们需要叮当片!"

"魂魄出窍!"哈利又说道,声音在石头甬道里回响,他再次觉得那使人飘飘然的控制感从脑部流向了他的魔杖。鲍格罗德再次顺从了他的意愿,迷惑的表情变成了一种礼貌的淡漠,罗恩急忙捡起了装有金属工具的小皮包。

"哈利,我好像听见有人来了!"赫敏说,她举起贝拉特里克斯的魔杖指向瀑布喊道,"盔甲护身!"只见铁甲咒沿着甬道飞去,截住了魔法瀑布。

"想得好。"哈利说,"带路,拉环!"

他们急忙跟着妖精走入黑暗中,鲍格罗德像老狗一样喘着气跟在后面。"我们待会儿怎么出去呢?"罗恩问。

"到时候再担心吧。"哈利说,他正努力聆听,好像附近有东西在铿锵作响地走来走去。"拉环,还有多远?"

"不远了,哈利·波特,不远了……"

CHAPTER TWENTY-SIX   Gringotts

And they turned a corner and saw the thing for which Harry had been prepared, but which still brought all of them to a halt.

A gigantic dragon was tethered to the ground in front of them, barring access to four or five of the deepest vaults in the place. The beast's scales had turned pale and flaky during its long incarceration under the ground; its eyes were milkily pink: both rear legs bore heavy cuffs from which chains led to enormous pegs driven deep into the rocky floor. Its great, spiked wings, folded close to its body, would have filled the chamber if it spread them, and when it turned its ugly head towards them, it roared with a noise that made the rock tremble, opened its mouth and spat a jet of fire that sent them running back up the passageway.

'It is partially blind,' panted Griphook, 'but even more savage for that. However, we have the means to control it. It has learned what to expect when the Clankers come. Give them to me.'

Ron passed the bag to Griphook and the goblin pulled out a number of small metal instruments that when shaken made a loud, ringing noise like miniature hammers on anvils. Griphook handed them out: Bogrod accepted his meekly.

'You know what to do,' Griphook told Harry, Ron and Hermione. 'It will expect pain when it hears the noise: it will retreat, and Bogrod must place his palm upon the door of the vault.'

They advanced round the corner again, shaking the Clankers and the noise echoed off the rocky walls, grossly magnified, so that the inside of Harry's skull seemed to vibrate with the din. The dragon let out another hoarse roar, then retreated. Harry could see it trembling, and as they drew nearer he saw the scars made by vicious slashes across its face, and guessed that it had been taught to fear hot swords when it heard the sound of the Clankers.

'Make him press his hand to the door!' Griphook urged Harry, who turned his wand again upon Bogrod. The old goblin obeyed, pressing his palm to the wood, and the door of the vault melted away to reveal a cave-like opening crammed from floor to ceiling with golden coins and goblets, silver armour, the skins of strange creatures, some with long spines, others with drooping wings, potions in jewelled flasks, and a skull still wearing a crown.

'Search, fast!' said Harry, as they all hurried inside the vault.

第26章 古灵阁

他们转过一个拐角,眼前所见虽然是哈利已经做好准备应付的,但还是让所有的人猛然止住了脚步。

一条巨大的火龙拴在前面的地上,阻止人们接近那里的四五个最深的金库。由于禁闭在地下太久,巨龙身上的鳞片已经变得苍白松动了,它的眼睛是浑浊的粉红色,两条后腿都戴着沉重的镣铐,上面的粗链子连着深深打进石头地的巨桩。它那带尖刺的巨翅收拢在身体两侧,如果展开将会充满整个地下室。巨龙朝他们转过丑陋的脑袋,发出一声让石头都发抖的巨吼,张开大口喷出一股烈火,逼得他们顺着过道往回跑。

"它的眼睛不行了,"拉环喘息着说,"但这使它更加残暴。不过我们有办法控制它。它已经对叮当片形成了条件反射。拿给我吧。"

罗恩把那个小包递给了拉环,妖精从里面拿出一些小小的金属器具,摇起来发出响亮而清脆的叮当声,就像小铁锤砸在铁砧上。拉环把它们发给大家,鲍格罗德也很温顺地接了过去。

"你们知道要做什么。"拉环告诉哈利、罗恩和赫敏,"它一听到这个声音就会想到疼痛,就会撤退,然后鲍格罗德必须把手掌放在金库的门上。"

他们摇着叮当片再次转过拐角,噪音在石壁间回响,被放大了许多倍,吵得哈利的脑浆似乎都在振动。巨龙又发出一声嘶哑的吼叫,朝后退去。哈利能看到它在颤抖,靠得更近时,他看到了它脸上一道道被劈出来的可怕的伤疤,猜测它是被训练得一听到叮当片响就惧怕火热的宝剑砍来。

"让他把手按在门上!"拉环催促哈利,哈利把他的魔杖再次指向了鲍格罗德。年长的妖精服从了,把手掌按在木头上,金库的门随之消失了,露出一个洞口。洞里从地面到天花板塞满了金币和金酒杯、银盔甲、长着脊刺或垂着翅膀的各种奇异动物的毛皮、装在宝瓶里的魔药,还有一个仍然戴着王冠的头盖骨。

"快找!"哈利说,他们一起冲进了金库。

He had described Hufflepuff's cup to Ron and Hermione, but if it was the other, unknown Horcrux that resided in this vault, he did not know what it looked like. He barely had time to glance around, however, before there was a muffled clunk from behind them: the door had reappeared, sealing them inside the vault, and they were plunged into total darkness.

'No matter, Bogrod will be able to release us!' said Griphook, as Ron gave a shout of surprise. 'Light your wands, can't you? And hurry, we have very little time!'

'*Lumos!*'

Harry shone his lit wand around the vault: its beam fell upon glittering jewels, he saw the fake sword of Gryffindor lying on a high shelf amongst a jumble of chains. Ron and Hermione had lit their wands too, and were now examining the piles of objects surrounding them.

'Harry, could this be –? Aargh!'

Hermione screamed in pain and Harry turned his wand on her in time to see a jewelled goblet tumbling from her grip: but as it fell it split, and became a shower of goblets, so that a second later, with a great clatter, the floor was covered in identical cups rolling in every direction, the original impossible to discern amongst them.

'It burned me!' moaned Hermione, sucking her blistered fingers.

'They have added Gemino and Flagrante Curses!' said Griphook. 'Everything you touch will burn and multiply, but the copies are worthless – and if you continue to handle the treasure, you will eventually be crushed to death by the weight of expanding gold!'

'OK, don't touch anything!' said Harry desperately, but even as he said it, Ron accidentally nudged one of the fallen goblets with his foot, and twenty more exploded into being while Ron hopped on the spot, part of his shoe burned away by contact with the hot metal.

'Stand still, don't move!' said Hermione, clutching at Ron.

'Just look around!' said Harry. 'Remember, the cup's small and gold, it's got a badger engraved on it, two handles – otherwise see if you can spot Ravenclaw's symbol anywhere, the eagle –'

They directed their wands into every nook and crevice, turning cautiously on the spot. It was impossible not to brush up against anything; Harry sent a great cascade of fake Galleons on to the ground where they joined the goblets, and now there was scarcely room to place their feet, and the glowing

第26章 古灵阁

他曾向罗恩和赫敏描述过赫奇帕奇的金杯,但如果藏在这个金库里的是别的魂器,他就不知道是什么样子的了。他几乎还没来得及环顾四周,身后就传来一声沉闷的金属撞击声:门重新出现,把他们都封在了金库里,四下一片漆黑。罗恩吃惊地大喊了一声。

"没关系,鲍格罗德能够把我们放出去!"拉环说,"点亮你们的魔杖,行吗?快点,我们只有一点点时间!"

"荧光闪烁!"

哈利用自己点亮的魔杖照着金库四周:荧光照在闪烁的珠宝上,他看见假的格兰芬多宝剑躺在高处架子上的一堆链子中间。罗恩和赫敏也点亮了魔杖,正在检查他们周围成堆的物品。

"哈利,这是不是——?啊!"

赫敏痛得尖叫一声,哈利及时把魔杖照向了她,看到一个嵌有宝石的酒杯从她手中滑落:但它落下时裂开了,变成了好多酒杯,一秒钟之后,随着一连串噼里啪啦的响声,地板上滚满了同样的酒杯,分不出哪个是原来的那个。

"它烫伤了我!"赫敏呻吟道,一边吮吸着起泡的手指。

"他们添加了烈火咒和复制咒!"拉环说,"任何东西你们碰到后都会灼烧和复制,但是复制品毫无价值——如果你们继续触摸财宝,最终会被金子压死!"

"好,不要碰任何东西!"哈利绝望地说,但是就在他提醒时,罗恩的脚无意间触到一个跌落的酒杯,烫得他跳了起来,鞋子被炙热的金属烧掉了一块,而原地又迸出了二十多个酒杯。

"站住,别动!"赫敏说,一边抓住罗恩。

"只用眼睛看!"哈利说,"记住,杯子很小,是金的,上面刻着一只獾,有两个柄——或者找拉文克劳的标志,老鹰——"

他们极其小心地原地转动,把魔杖指向每一个角落、每一道缝隙,然而不碰到任何东西是不可能的。哈利弄得一大堆假加隆瀑布似的洒落在地上,跟酒杯混在一起,现在几乎没有地方落脚了。炽热的金子散发着高温,整个金库感觉就像个火炉。哈利魔杖的光束移过盾牌和

gold blazed with heat, so that the vault felt like a furnace. Harry's wandlight passed over shields and goblin-made helmets set on shelves rising to the ceiling. Higher and higher he raised the beam, until suddenly it found an object that made his heart skip and his hand tremble.

'*It's there, it's up there!*'

Ron and Hermione pointed their wands at it too, so that the little golden cup sparkled in a three-way spotlight: the cup that had belonged to Helga Hufflepuff, which had passed into the possession of Hepzibah Smith, from whom it had been stolen by Tom Riddle.

'And how the hell are we going to get up there without touching anything?' asked Ron.

'*Accio cup!*' cried Hermione, who had evidently forgotten, in her desperation, what Griphook had told them during their planning sessions.

'No use, no use!' snarled the goblin.

'Then what do we do?' said Harry, glaring at the goblin. 'If you want the sword, Griphook, then you'll have to help us more than – wait! Can I touch stuff with the sword? Hermione, give it here!'

Hermione fumbled inside her robes, drew out the beaded bag, rummaged for a few seconds, then removed the shining sword. Harry seized it by its rubied hilt and touched the tip of the blade to a silver flagon nearby, which did not multiply.

'If I can just poke the sword through a handle – but how am I going to get up there?'

The shelf on which the cup reposed was out of reach for any of them, even Ron, who was tallest. The heat from the enchanted treasure rose in waves, and sweat ran down Harry's face and back as he struggled to think of a way up to the cup; and then he heard the dragon roar on the other side of the vault door, and the sound of clanking growing louder and louder.

They were truly trapped now: there was no way out except through the door, and a horde of goblins seemed to be approaching on the other side. Harry looked at Ron and Hermione and saw terror in their faces.

'Hermione,' said Harry, as the clanking grew louder, 'I've got to get up there, we've got to get rid of it –'

She raised her wand, pointed it at Harry and whispered, '*Levicorpus.*'

Hoisted into the air by his ankle, Harry hit a suit of armour and replicas burst out of it like white-hot bodies, filling the cramped space. With screams

第26章 古灵阁

妖精制作的头盔,那一层层的架子一直顶到天花板,他的魔杖越举越高,突然照到了一个物体,他的心猛地一跳,手抖了起来。

"在那儿,在上面!"

罗恩和赫敏也将魔杖指向了它,小金杯在三道聚光灯下闪闪发光:那杯子曾经属于赫尔加·赫奇帕奇,后来传到赫普兹巴·史密斯手里,然后被汤姆·里德尔偷去了。

"见鬼,怎么才能上到那儿,而不碰到任何东西呢?"罗恩问。

"金杯飞来!"赫敏喊道,显然是在情急之中忘记了拉环在商议计划时的提醒。

"没有用,没有用!"拉环咆哮道。

"那怎么办呢?"哈利瞪着妖精说道,"如果你要那把宝剑,拉环,就必须帮助我们而不只是——等等!我能用宝剑碰东西吗?赫敏,快拿过来!"

赫敏从袍子里摸出串珠小包,翻找了几秒钟,取出了闪光的宝剑。哈利抓住嵌红宝石的剑柄,用剑尖碰了一下旁边的一个银酒壶,它没有复制。

"要是我只用宝剑穿进杯柄——可是,怎么能上到那里去呢?"

他们谁也够不着放金杯的架子,连个子最高的罗恩也不行。施有魔法的财宝散发出滚滚热浪,哈利拼命思考着拿杯子的办法,汗水顺着他的面颊和脊背直往下淌。这时他听见了金库门外巨龙的咆哮,叮当声越来越响。

他们现在真的是被困住了:那扇门是出去的唯一通道,然而似乎有一群妖精正在门外靠近。哈利望望罗恩和赫敏,在他们俩的脸上看到了恐慌。

"赫敏,"哈利说,外面的叮当声更响了,"我必须上去,我们必须消灭它——"

赫敏举起魔杖,指着哈利念道:"倒挂金钟。"

哈利被提着脚踝升上空中,碰到了一副盔甲,复制品迸发出来,像一具具白热的躯体,塞满了狭小的空间。罗恩、赫敏和两个妖精被

of pain Ron, Hermione and the two goblins were knocked aside into other objects, which also began to replicate. Half buried in a rising tide of red-hot treasure, they struggled and yelled as Harry thrust the sword through the handle of Hufflepuff's cup, hooking it on to the blade.

'*Impervius!*' screeched Hermione, in an attempt to protect herself, Ron and the goblins from the burning metal.

Then the worst scream yet made Harry look down: Ron and Hermione were waist-deep in treasure, struggling to keep Bogrod from slipping beneath the rising tide, but Griphook had sunk out of sight and nothing but the tips of a few long fingers were left in view.

Harry seized Griphook's fingers and pulled. The blistered goblin emerged by degrees, howling.

'*Liberacorpus!*' yelled Harry, and with a crash he and Griphook landed on the surface of the swelling treasure, and the sword flew out of Harry's hand.

'Get it!' Harry yelled, fighting the pain of the hot metal on his skin, as Griphook clambered on to his shoulders again, determined to avoid the swelling mass of red-hot objects. 'Where's the sword? It had the cup on it!'

The clanking on the other side of the door was growing deafening – it was too late –

'There!'

It was Griphook who had seen it and Griphook who lunged, and in that instant Harry knew that the goblin had never expected them to keep their word. One hand holding tightly to a fistful of Harry's hair to make sure he did not fall into the heaving sea of burning gold, Griphook seized the hilt of the sword and swung it high out of Harry's reach.

The tiny golden cup, skewered by the handle on the sword's blade, was flung into the air. The goblin still astride him, Harry dived and caught it, and although he could feel it scalding his flesh he did not relinquish it, even while countless Hufflepuff cups burst from his fist, raining down upon him as the entrance of the vault opened up again and he found himself sliding uncontrollably on an expanding avalanche of fiery gold and silver that bore him, Ron and Hermione into the outer chamber.

Hardly aware of the pain from the burns covering his body, and still borne along on the swell of replicating treasure, Harry shoved the cup into his pocket and reached up to retrieve the sword, but Griphook was gone. Sliding

第26章 古灵阁

挤得碰到其他物品上，痛得大叫，而被碰到的物品也开始复制。他们几乎半个身子都埋在潮水般上涌的炽热财宝中。他们挣扎着，叫喊着。哈利忙用宝剑插入赫奇帕奇金杯的杯柄，将它挑在剑刃上。

"水火不侵！"赫敏尖叫着，试图保护自己、罗恩和妖精不被炽热的金属烫伤。

突然传来一声最恐怖的尖叫，哈利低头看去：罗恩和赫敏站在齐腰深的财宝中，拼命拽着鲍格罗德不让他整个儿陷进去，但是拉环已经被埋得看不见了，只剩下一点手指尖露在外面。

哈利抓住拉环的手指往外拉，满身水泡的妖精渐渐浮出来，嗷嗷号叫。

"金钟落地！"哈利高喊，他和拉环一起摔在不停膨胀的财宝上面，宝剑脱手飞出。

"抓住它！"哈利忍着滚烫的金属接触皮肤的灼痛大喊道，而拉环再次爬到他背上，一心躲避着越涨越高的炽热物体，"宝剑在哪儿？上面挂着金杯呢！"

门外面的叮当声变得震耳欲聋——来不及了——

"那儿！"

是拉环看到的，拉环突然往前一冲。一刹那间哈利意识到这妖精从没指望过他们信守诺言。妖精一手紧抓着哈利的一撮头发，确保自己不掉进汹涌炽热的金子的海洋，另一只手抓住了宝剑的剑柄，高高扬起不让哈利够到。

剑上挑着的小金杯被抛向了空中，但妖精仍然骑在哈利身上。哈利向下猛扑抓到了金杯，尽管感觉到皮肉被它烫伤，尽管无数的赫奇帕奇金杯从他手中迸出，像雨点一样砸在身上，他都没有松手。就在这时，金库的门打开了，哈利发现自己无法控制地滑行在炽热的金银洪流上，与罗恩、赫敏一起被冲到了金库的外面。

哈利几乎没意识到全身烧伤的灼痛，他一边随着那些不停复制的财宝往外冲，一边把小金杯塞进口袋，伸手想拿回宝剑，但是拉环不见了。他一找到机会就从哈利背上溜了下去，撒腿逃向周围的妖精中间，

CHAPTER TWENTY-SIX   Gringotts

from Harry's shoulders the moment he could, he had sprinted for cover amongst the surrounding goblins, brandishing the sword and crying, 'Thieves! Thieves! Help! Thieves!' He vanished into the midst of the advancing crowd, all of whom were holding daggers and who accepted him without question.

Slipping on the hot metal, Harry struggled to his feet and knew that the only way out was through.

'*Stupefy!* ' he bellowed, and Ron and Hermione joined in: jets of red light flew into the crowd of goblins and some toppled over, but others advanced, and Harry saw several wizard guards running round the corner.

The tethered dragon let out a roar, and a gush of flame flew over the goblins: the wizards fled, doubled-up, back the way they had come, and inspiration, or madness, came to Harry. Pointing his wand at the thick cuffs chaining the beast to the floor he yelled, '*Relashio!* '

The cuffs broke open with loud bangs.

'This way!' Harry yelled, and still shooting Stunning Spells at the advancing goblins he sprinted towards the blind dragon.

'Harry – Harry – what are you doing?' cried Hermione.

'Get up, climb up, come on –'

The dragon had not realised that it was free: Harry's foot found the crook of its hind leg and he pulled himself up on to its back. The scales were hard as steel: it did not even seem to feel him. He stretched out an arm; Hermione hoisted herself up; Ron climbed on behind them, and a second later the dragon became aware that it was untethered.

With a roar it reared: Harry dug in his knees, clutching as tightly as he could to the jagged scales as the wings opened, knocking the shrieking goblins aside like skittles, and it soared into the air. Harry, Ron and Hermione, flat on its back, scraped against the ceiling as it dived towards the passage opening, while the pursuing goblins hurled daggers that glanced off its flanks.

'We'll never get out, it's too big!' Hermione screamed, but the dragon opened its mouth and belched flame again, blasting the tunnel, whose floors and ceiling cracked and crumbled. By sheer force the dragon clawed and fought its way through. Harry's eyes were tight shut against the heat and dust: deafened by the crashing of rock and the dragon's roars, he could only cling to its back, expecting to be shaken off at any moment; then he heard Hermione yelling, '*Defodio!* '

第26章 古灵阁

挥舞着宝剑叫喊道:"有贼！有贼！救命啊！有贼！"他转眼消失在涌上前来的那群妖精里,他们都手持短剑,毫无异议地接纳了他。

哈利在炽热的金属上趔趔趄趄,努力站了起来,他知道唯一的出路就是冲过去。

"昏昏倒地！"他大吼道,罗恩和赫敏也大吼起来。一道道红光飞入妖精群中,有些妖精栽倒了,但其余的继续前进,哈利还看到好几个巫师警卫从拐角处跑了过来。

被拴住的巨龙一声怒吼,一股火焰从妖精头上飞过,巫师们弯着身子退了回去。哈利突然来了灵感,或者说产生了一个疯狂的念头。他举起魔杖对着巨兽厚重的脚镣大喊一声:"力松劲泄！"

随着几声巨响,脚镣断开了。

"这边！"哈利大喊,一边继续向逼近的妖精们发射昏迷咒,一边朝瞎眼的火龙奔去。

"哈利——哈利——你在干什么？"赫敏叫道。

"上来,爬上来,快点儿——"

巨龙还没有意识到它已经自由了。哈利踩着它的后腿弯曲处爬到了龙背上。鳞片硬得像钢铁一样,巨龙似乎都没有感觉到他。哈利伸出一只手臂,赫敏拽着它跃了上去,罗恩也爬上去坐在了他们后面。一秒钟后,巨龙意识到了锁链已经断开。

一声怒吼,巨龙立了起来,张开翅膀,升向了空中。哈利夹紧膝盖,死命地牢牢抓住锯齿状的龙鳞,尖叫着的妖精们像保龄球瓶一样被撞倒在一边。巨龙向甬道出口冲去,哈利、罗恩和赫敏趴在龙背上,身子擦到了甬道顶。追赶的妖精们纷纷向巨龙投掷短剑,一把把短剑擦着它的身体掠过。

"我们根本出不去,它太大了！"赫敏尖叫道,但是巨龙张开大嘴喷出火焰,炸开了隧洞,洞顶碎裂坍塌了。巨龙使用蛮力抓刨着,一路往外冲去。哈利紧闭双眼避开灰尘和热浪,石头的爆裂声和巨龙的吼叫声震耳欲聋。他只能紧紧抓住龙背,担心随时会被甩下去。正在这时,他听见赫敏大喊道:"掘进三尺！"

CHAPTER TWENTY-SIX   Gringotts

She was helping the dragon enlarge the passageway, carving out the ceiling as it struggled upwards, towards the fresher air, away from the shrieking and clanking goblins: Harry and Ron copied her, blasting the ceiling apart with more gouging spells. They passed the underground lake, and the great crawling, snarling beast seemed to sense freedom and space ahead of it, and behind them the passage was full of the dragon's thrashing, spiked tail, of great lumps of rock, gigantic, fractured stalactites, and the clanking of the goblins seemed to be growing more muffled, while ahead, the dragon's fire kept their progress clear –

And then at last, by the combined force of their spells and the dragon's brute strength, they had blasted their way out of the passage into the marble hallway. Goblins and wizards shrieked and ran for cover, and finally the dragon had room to stretch its wings: turning its horned head towards the cool outside air it could smell beyond the entrance, it took off, and with Harry, Ron and Hermione still clinging to its back, it forced its way through the metal doors, leaving them buckled and hanging from their hinges as it staggered into Diagon Alley and launched itself into the sky.

第26章 古灵阁

她在帮助巨龙扩大通道，挖开洞顶，让它冲向上面新鲜的空气里，离开那些尖叫着的叮当作响的妖精。哈利和罗恩也学着她，用更多的挖掘咒来炸开洞顶。他们经过了地下湖，缓缓前进的巨龙咆哮着，似乎感觉到了自由，感觉到了前方的空间，而他们身后的甬道，被巨龙扫动的带尖刺的尾巴、大堆的石块，以及碎裂的巨大钟乳石塞得满满的。妖精们发出的叮当声似乎减弱了，而在前方，巨龙的火焰为他们扫清了道路——

终于，靠着巨龙的蛮力和咒语的作用，他们炸开甬道进入了大理石门厅，妖精和巫师们尖叫着奔逃躲藏。巨龙终于找到了可以展翅的空间，它有角的脑袋转向门口，闻到了外面凉爽的空气。它迈步而出，用力挤出金属门，哈利、罗恩和赫敏仍然紧紧抓着它的后背。变了形的门在铰链上摇摇晃晃，巨龙蹒跚着走进了对角巷，然后腾空而起。

CHAPTER TWENTY-SEVEN

The Final Hiding Place

There was no means of steering; the dragon could not see where it was going, and Harry knew that if it turned sharply or rolled in mid-air they would find it impossible to cling on to its broad back. Nevertheless, as they climbed higher and higher, London unfurling below them like a grey and green map, Harry's overwhelming feeling was of gratitude for an escape that had seemed impossible. Crouching low over the beast's neck, he clung tight to the metallic scales, and the cool breeze was soothing on his burned and blistered skin, the dragon's wings beating the air like the sails of a windmill. Behind him, whether from delight or fear he could not tell, Ron kept swearing at the top of his voice, and Hermione seemed to be sobbing.

After five minutes or so, Harry lost some of his immediate dread that the dragon was going to throw them off, for it seemed intent on nothing but getting as far away from its underground prison as possible, but the question of how and when they were to dismount remained rather frightening. He had no idea how long dragons could fly without landing, nor how this particular dragon, which could barely see, would locate a good place to put down. He glanced around constantly, imagining that he could feel his scar prickling ...

How long would it be before Voldemort knew that they had broken into the Lestranges' vault? How soon would the goblins of Gringotts notify Bellatrix? How quickly would they realise what had been taken? And then, when they discovered that the golden cup was missing? Voldemort would know, at last, that they were hunting Horcruxes ...

The dragon seemed to crave cooler and fresher air: it climbed steadily until they were flying through wisps of chilly cloud and Harry could no longer make out the little coloured dots which were cars pouring in and out of the capital. On and on they flew, over countryside parcelled out in patches of green and brown, over roads and rivers winding through the landscape like strips of matt and glossy ribbon.

第 27 章

最后的隐藏之处

无法驾驭巨龙，它看不见方向，哈利知道如果巨龙在半空中翻身或急转弯的话，他们就不可能继续抱着它宽阔的后背了。然而，当他们越升越高，伦敦像一张灰绿相间的地图展现在下方时，哈利心中涨满了绝处逢生后的感激之情。他伏在巨龙的颈部，紧紧抓着金属般的龙鳞，凉爽的清风抚慰着他烫起水泡的皮肤，龙的翅膀像风车的叶片拍打着空气。在他背后，不知是由于高兴还是恐惧，罗恩不停地高声诅咒，赫敏则似乎在抽泣。

过了大约五分钟，哈利不再那么担心巨龙会把他们扔下去了，巨龙似乎一心只想远离地牢。但是怎样离开巨龙以及什么时候才能离开的问题仍然十分可怕。他不知道巨龙能持续飞行多久，也不知道这条几乎瞎了的巨龙能不能找到一个好的地方着陆。他不停地扫视四周，隐约感觉到伤疤在刺痛……

伏地魔要过多久才知道他们闯入了莱斯特兰奇家的金库？古灵阁的妖精多快会通知贝拉特里克斯？他们多快会发现被拿走了什么？然后，当他们发现金杯不见了呢？伏地魔最终会知道他们在搜寻魂器……

巨龙似乎渴求更凉爽、更清新的空气。它不断上升，直到飞行在一丝丝寒冷的轻云间，哈利再也看不清进出首都的汽车变成的彩色小点。他们不停地飞呀飞，飞过一片片绿色和棕色交织的乡间，地面上蜿蜒的公路与河流宛如一条条暗淡或光滑的丝带。

CHAPTER TWENTY-SEVEN   The Final Hiding Place

'What do you reckon it's looking for?' Ron yelled, as they flew further and further north.

'No idea,' Harry bellowed back. His hands were numb with cold but he did not dare attempt to shift his grip. He had been wondering for some time what they would do if they saw the coast sail beneath them, if the dragon headed for open sea: he was cold and numb, not to mention desperately hungry and thirsty. When, he wondered, had the beast itself last eaten? Surely it would need sustenance before long? And what if, at that point, it realised it had three highly edible humans sitting on its back?

The sun slipped lower in the sky, which was turning indigo; and still the dragon flew, cities and towns gliding out of sight beneath them, its enormous shadow sliding over the earth like a great, dark cloud. Every part of Harry ached with the effort of holding on to the dragon's back.

'Is it my imagination,' shouted Ron, after a considerable stretch of silence, 'or are we losing height?'

Harry looked down and saw deep-green mountains and lakes, coppery in the sunset. The landscape seemed to grow larger and more detailed as he squinted over the side of the dragon and he wondered whether it had divined the presence of fresh water by the flashes of reflected sunlight.

Lower and lower the dragon flew, in great, spiralling circles, honing in, it seemed, upon one of the smaller lakes.

'I say we jump when it gets low enough!' Harry called back to the others. 'Straight into the water before it realises we're here!'

They agreed, Hermione a little faintly: and now Harry could see the dragon's wide, yellow underbelly rippling in the surface of the water.

'NOW!'

He slithered over the side of the dragon and plummeted, feet first, towards the surface of the lake; the drop was greater than he had estimated and he hit the water hard, plunging like a stone into a freezing, green, reed-filled world. He kicked towards the surface and emerged, panting, to see enormous ripples emanating in circles from the places where Ron and Hermione had fallen. The dragon did not seem to have noticed anything: it was already fifty feet away, swooping low over the lake to scoop up water in its scarred snout. As Ron and Hermione emerged, spluttering and gasping from the depths of the lake, the dragon flew on, its wings beating hard, and landed at last on a distant bank.

第27章 最后的隐藏之处

"你猜它在找什么？"罗恩大喊道，他们正往北飞得越来越远。

"不知道。"哈利叫道。手冻得都麻木了，但是他紧抓着龙鳞不敢动一下。他已经担心了有一段时间，如果看到海岸线在下面飘移，如果巨龙朝着远海飞去，他们该怎么办？他浑身寒冷发木，更不用说极度饥渴。他不知道巨龙上一次吃东西是什么时候，它肯定要不多久就会需要食物了吧？如果到时候它意识到背上有三个相当可口的活人，又该怎么办？

太阳又滑下去一些，天空变成了靛蓝色。巨龙仍在飞行，它巨大的影子像一大块乌云掠过地面，城市和集镇在他们下方远去。由于一直死命抓着龙背，哈利感到浑身疼痛。

"是我的错觉吗，"在一段长时间的沉默后罗恩喊道，"还是我们真的在下降？"

哈利低头看到了深绿色的山脉和湖泊，在夕阳下泛着紫铜的光泽。他眯眼顺着巨龙的侧面向下看去，地面的景物似乎在变大，并且显出了更多的细节。他怀疑巨龙是由于太阳的反光而感到了湖水的存在。

巨龙飞得越来越低，绕着大圈盘旋下降，似乎对准的是一个较小的湖泊。

"听着，等它飞得够低了我们就跳！"哈利招呼两个同伴，"在它感觉到我们之前，直接跳进水里！"

他们同意了，赫敏答应的声音有点虚弱。现在哈利能看到巨龙宽阔的黄肚皮在水波中晃动。

"跳！"

他从巨龙的侧面滑了下去，脚朝下垂直地向湖面坠落。落水的过程比他想象的猛烈，他重重地击中水面，像一块石头落进了一个冰冷的满是芦苇的绿色世界。他蹬腿游向湖面，浮了上来，喘着粗气，看到大圈的涟漪从罗恩和赫敏落水的地方扩散开来。巨龙似乎什么也没有注意到，它已经在五十英尺外，正俯冲到湖面上用伤疤累累的口鼻饮水。罗恩和赫敏从湖水深处浮上来，吐着水，大口吸气。巨龙接着飞行，猛烈地拍打着翅膀，最后停在了远处的湖岸上。

CHAPTER TWENTY-SEVEN   The Final Hiding Place

Harry, Ron and Hermione struck out for the opposite shore. The lake did not seem to be deep: soon it was more a question of fighting their way through reeds and mud than swimming, and finally they flopped, sodden, panting and exhausted, on to slippery grass.

Hermione collapsed, coughing and shuddering. Though Harry could have happily lain down and slept, he staggered to his feet, drew out his wand and started casting the usual protective spells around them.

When he had finished, he joined the others. It was the first time that he had seen them properly since escaping from the vault. Both had angry red burns all over their faces and arms, and their clothing was singed away in places. They were wincing as they dabbed essence of dittany on to their many injuries. Hermione handed Harry the bottle, then pulled out three bottles of pumpkin juice she had brought from Shell Cottage and clean, dry robes for all of them. They changed and then gulped down the juice.

'Well, on the up side,' said Ron finally, who was sitting watching the skin on his hands regrow, 'we got the Horcrux. On the down side –'

'– no sword,' said Harry through gritted teeth, as he dripped dittany through the singed hole in his jeans on to the angry burn beneath.

'No sword,' repeated Ron. 'That double-crossing little scab ...'

Harry pulled the Horcrux from the pocket of the wet jacket he had just taken off and set it down on the grass in front of them. Glinting in the sun, it drew their eyes as they swigged their bottles of juice.

'At least we can't wear it this time, that'd look a bit weird hanging round our necks,' said Ron, wiping his mouth on the back of his hand.

Hermione looked across the lake to the far bank, where the dragon was still drinking.

'What'll happen to it, do you think?' she asked. 'Will it be all right?'

'You sound like Hagrid,' said Ron. 'It's a dragon, Hermione, it can look after itself. It's us we need to worry about.'

'What do you mean?'

'Well, I don't know how to break this to you,' said Ron, 'but I think they *might* have noticed we broke into Gringotts.'

All three of them started to laugh, and once started, it was difficult to stop. Harry's ribs ached, he felt light-headed with hunger, but he lay back on the grass beneath the reddening sky and laughed until his throat was raw.

第 27 章　最后的隐藏之处

哈利、罗恩和赫敏使劲游向它的对岸。湖水似乎并不深，他们很快就由游泳变成了在芦苇和淤泥中奋力前行。最后他们喘着粗气跌坐在滑溜溜的草地上，浑身透湿，精疲力竭。

赫敏瘫倒了，咳嗽着，浑身发抖。哈利尽管巴不得幸福地躺下睡一会儿，但还是挣扎着站起来，抽出魔杖，开始在他们周围施布常用的防护咒。

完成之后，他回到了两个同伴身边。这是逃出金库后他第一次细看他们俩。罗恩和赫敏的脸上和手臂上到处都是红肿的烫伤，衣服多处被烧焦。他们正在往数不清的伤处抹白鲜香精，痛得直皱眉头。赫敏把药瓶递给哈利，又掏出她从贝壳小屋带来的三瓶南瓜汁和干净的袍子。三人换了衣服，开始大口地喝南瓜汁。

"我说，好的一面是，"罗恩最后说道，他坐在那里看着手上的皮肤重新长出来，"我们拿到了魂器。坏的一面是——"

"——丢了宝剑。"哈利咬着牙说，一边透过牛仔裤上烧焦的破洞往红肿的烫伤处滴白鲜香精。

"丢了宝剑。"罗恩重复道，"那个骗人的小无赖……"

哈利从他刚脱下的湿外套口袋里掏出那个魂器，放在面前的草地上。它在阳光下闪闪发亮，正在痛饮南瓜汁的罗恩和赫敏被吸引住了。

"至少这回不能戴着它了，把它挂在脖子上会显得有点怪异。"罗恩说，一边用手背擦了擦嘴。

赫敏看了一眼湖对岸，巨龙还在那里饮水。

"你们说，它会怎么样呢？"她问道，"它会有事吗？"

"你说起话来像海格。"罗恩说，"它是一条火龙，赫敏，它能够照料自己的。需要担心的是我们。"

"什么意思？"

"啊，我不知道怎么委婉地告诉你，"罗恩说，"我想那些家伙可能已经发现我们闯进了古灵阁。"

三个人都笑了起来，而且笑得一发不可收拾。哈利饿得头昏眼花，肋骨疼痛，但是他躺在草地上和泛红的天空下一直笑到喉咙发疼。

CHAPTER TWENTY-SEVEN   The Final Hiding Place

'What are we going to do, though?' said Hermione finally, hiccoughing herself back to seriousness. 'He'll know, won't he? You-Know-Who will know we know about his Horcruxes!'

'Maybe they'll be too scared to tell him?' said Ron hopefully. 'Maybe they'll cover up –'

The sky, the smell of lake water, the sound of Ron's voice were extinguished: pain cleaved Harry's head like a sword stroke. He was standing in a dimly lit room, and a semi-circle of wizards faced him, and on the floor at his feet knelt a small, quaking figure.

'What did you say to me?' His voice was high and cold, but fury and fear burned inside him. The one thing he had dreaded – but it could not be true, he could not see how …

The goblin was trembling, unable to meet the red eyes high above his.

'Say it again!' murmured Voldemort. '*Say it again!*'

'M – my Lord,' stammered the goblin, its black eyes wide with terror, 'm – my Lord … we t – tried t – to st – stop them … im – impostors, my Lord … broke – broke into the – into the Lestranges' v – vault …'

'Impostors? What impostors? I thought Gringotts had ways of revealing impostors? Who were they?'

'It was … it was … the P – Potter b – boy and t – two accomplices …'

'*And they took?*' he said, his voice rising, a terrible fear gripping him. 'Tell me! *What did they take?*'

'A … a s – small golden c – cup m – my Lord …'

The scream of rage, of denial, left him as if it were a stranger's: he was crazed, frenzied, it could not be true, it was impossible, nobody had ever known: how was it possible that the boy could have discovered his secret?

The Elder Wand slashed through the air and green light erupted through the room, the kneeling goblin rolled over, dead, the watching wizards scattered before him, terrified: Bellatrix and Lucius Malfoy threw others behind them in their race for the door, and again and again his wand fell, and those who were left were slain, all of them, for bringing him this news, for hearing about the golden cup –

Alone amongst the dead, he stormed up and down, and they passed before him in vision: his treasures, his safeguards, his anchors to immortality – the

第 27 章 最后的隐藏之处

"那么,我们该干什么呢?"赫敏最后说道,打着嗝严肃起来,"他会知道,不是吗?神秘人会知道我们在了解他的魂器!"

"也许他们会吓得不敢告诉他?"罗恩心存侥幸地说,"也许他们会掩盖——"

天空、湖水的气味、罗恩的说话声突然消失了:疼痛像剑一般刺进哈利的脑袋。他正站在一个灯光昏暗的房间里,巫师们面向他围成半圆,他脚边的地板上跪着一个颤抖的矮小身影。

"你说什么?"他的声音高亢而冷酷,但是愤怒和恐惧在内心灼烧。他畏惧的唯一一件事——但那不可能是真的,他搞不懂怎么会……

那个妖精在发抖,不敢正视高高在上的那双红眼睛。

"再说一遍!"伏地魔嘟囔道,"再说一遍!"

"主—主人,"妖精结结巴巴地说,黑眼睛睁得圆圆的,充满了恐惧,"主—主人……我们试—试图阻—阻止他们……冒—冒名顶替者,主人……闯—闯进了—莱斯特兰奇家的金—金库……"

"冒名顶替者?什么冒名顶替者?我以为古灵阁是有办法识别冒名顶替者的,难道不是?他们是谁?"

"是……是……叫波—波特的男—男孩和两—两个同伙……"

"那么他们拿东西了?"他说,声音越来越高,一种可怕的预感攫住了他,"告诉我!他们拿走了什么?"

"一个……一个小金—小金杯,主—主人……"

愤怒与不相信的尖叫声从他口里发出,像是陌生人的声音。他发狂了,暴怒了,这不可能是真的,不可能,没有人知道!那个男孩怎么可能发现他的秘密?

老魔杖猛地从空中劈下,绿光喷射而出,跪着的妖精滚到地上,死了。那些观看的巫师吓得四散而逃。贝拉特里克斯和卢修斯·马尔福拼命冲向门口,把别人都甩在后面。他的魔杖一次一次地劈下,没跑掉的都被杀死了,一个没留,因为他们给他带来了这个消息,因为他得知金杯——

独自站在死尸中间,他暴跳如雷。一切都在他的眼前——出现:他

CHAPTER TWENTY-SEVEN   The Final Hiding Place

diary was destroyed and the cup was stolen; what if, *what if,* the boy knew about the others? Could he know, had he already acted, had he traced more of them? Was Dumbledore at the root of this? Dumbledore, who had always suspected him, Dumbledore, dead on his orders, Dumbledore, whose wand was his now, yet who reached out from the ignominy of death through the boy, *the boy* –

But surely if the boy had destroyed any of his Horcruxes, he, Lord Voldemort, would have known, would have felt it? He, the greatest wizard of them all, he, the most powerful, he, the killer of Dumbledore and of how many other worthless, nameless men: how could Lord Voldemort not have known, if he, himself, most important and precious, had been attacked, mutilated?

True, he had not felt it when the diary had been destroyed, but he had thought that was because he had no body to feel, being less than ghost ... no, surely, the rest were safe ... the other Horcruxes must be intact ...

But he must know, he must be sure ... He paced the room, kicking aside the goblin's corpse as he passed, and the pictures blurred and burned in his boiling brain: the lake, the shack, and Hogwarts –

A modicum of calm cooled his rage now: how could the boy know that he had hidden the ring in the Gaunt shack? No one had ever known him to be related to the Gaunts, he had hidden the connection, the killings had never been traced to him: the ring, surely, was safe.

And how could the boy, or anybody else, know about the cave or penetrate its protection? The idea of the locket being stolen was absurd ...

As for the school: he alone knew where in Hogwarts he had stowed the Horcrux, because he alone had plumbed the deepest secrets of that place ...

And there was still Nagini, who must remain close now, no longer sent to do his bidding, under his protection ...

But to be sure, to be utterly sure, he must return to each of his hiding places, he must redouble protection around each of his Horcruxes ... a job, like the quest for the Elder Wand, that he must undertake alone ...

Which should he visit first, which was in most danger? An old unease flickered inside him. Dumbledore had known his middle name ... Dumbledore might have made the connection with the Gaunts ... their abandoned home was, perhaps, the least secure of his hiding places, it was there that he would go first ...

第27章 最后的隐藏之处

的珍宝、他的护卫、他长生不死的希望——日记已经被毁，金杯又被偷走。假如，假如，那个男孩还知道别的？他会知道吗？他已经动手了吗？他找到了更多吗？邓布利多是这一切的根源吗？邓布利多，那老家伙总是怀疑他；邓布利多，那老家伙已经按他的指令被杀死，连魔杖都归了他；然而那老家伙却在可鄙的阴间，通过那个男孩来报复，那个男孩——

但是，如果那男孩销毁了他的某个魂器，他，黑魔王伏地魔，肯定会知道，肯定会感觉到的吧？他是世界上最伟大的巫师；他的强大无人能及；他杀死了邓布利多和其他许多无名鼠辈。如果他——他自己，最重要的和最珍贵的自己受到攻击、损伤，他黑魔王伏地魔怎么可能不知道？

是的，日记被毁时他没有感觉，但他一直认为那是由于他当时连幽灵都不如，没有身体来感觉……不，另外几个肯定是安全的……其余的魂器肯定完好无损……

但是他必须知道，他必须确定……他在屋里踱着步，把妖精的尸体踢到一边，他沸腾的脑海里是一幅幅烧灼而模糊的画面：湖、小屋、霍格沃茨——

他暴怒的头脑稍稍冷静了一些：那个男孩怎么可能知道他把戒指藏在冈特小屋？从没有人知道他和冈特家是亲戚，他一直隐瞒着这层关系，对谋杀案的追查从未有线索指向他：戒指肯定是安全的。

那个男孩，或不管是谁，又怎么可能知道那个山洞或穿透它的防护呢？挂坠盒被偷的想法很荒谬……

至于学校，他在霍格沃茨隐藏魂器的地方只有他一个人知道，因为只有他一个人探测到了霍格沃茨最深的秘密……

还有纳吉尼，它现在必须留在身边，时刻处在他的保护之下，不能再被派去执行命令了……

但是为了万无一失，完全万无一失，他必须返回每一个隐藏地点，他必须加固每一个魂器的防护措施……这个任务，像搜寻老魔杖一样，必须由他独自完成……

CHAPTER TWENTY-SEVEN   The Final Hiding Place

The lake, surely impossible ... though was there a slight possibility that Dumbledore might have known some of his past misdeeds, through the orphanage.

And Hogwarts ... but he knew that his Horcrux there was safe, it would be impossible for Potter to enter Hogsmeade without detection, let alone the school. Nevertheless, it would be prudent to alert Snape to the fact that the boy might try to re-enter the castle ... to tell Snape why the boy might return would be foolish, of course; it had been a grave mistake to trust Bellatrix and Malfoy: didn't their stupidity and carelessness prove how unwise it was, ever, to trust?

He would visit the Gaunt shack first, then, and take Nagini with him: he would not be parted from the snake any more ... And he strode from the room, through the hall and out into the dark garden where the fountain played; he called the snake in Parseltongue and it slithered out to join him like a long shadow ...

Harry's eyes flew open as he wrenched himself back to the present: he was lying on the bank of the lake in the setting sun, and Ron and Hermione were looking down at him. Judging by their worried looks, and by the continued pounding of his scar, his sudden excursion into Voldemort's mind had not passed unnoticed. He struggled up, shivering, vaguely surprised that he was still wet to his skin, and saw the cup lying innocently in the grass before him and the lake, deep-blue shot with gold in the failing sun.

'He knows.' His own voice sounded strange and low after Voldemort's high screams. 'He knows, and he's going to check where the others are, and the last one,' he was already on his feet, 'is at Hogwarts. I knew it. I *knew* it.'

'What?'

Ron was gaping at him; Hermione knelt up, looking worried.

'But what did you see? How do you know?'

'I saw him find out about the cup, I – I was in his head, he's –' Harry remembered the killings, 'he's seriously angry, and scared too, he can't understand how we knew, and now he's going to check the others are safe, the ring first. He thinks the Hogwarts one is safest, because Snape's there,

第 27 章　最后的隐藏之处

他应该先去看哪一个呢？哪一个最有危险？一种熟悉的不安在他心头闪现。邓布利多知道他的中间名字……邓布利多也许把他和冈特家联系在一起了……也许废弃的冈特老宅是最不安全的隐藏地点，他首先要去的就是那里……

湖，肯定不可能……尽管邓布利多也许有一点儿可能会通过孤儿院知道他过去的一些劣迹。

还有霍格沃茨……但是他知道魂器在那里是安全的。波特进入霍格莫德都不可能不被察觉，更不用说学校了。不过，最好还是警告一下斯内普，说那男孩会设法潜入城堡……当然，告诉斯内普那男孩为什么会回去是不明智的。信任贝拉特里克斯和马尔福就是重大的失误，他们的愚蠢和大意，不是证明了相信别人是多么不明智吗？

那么，他要先去冈特小屋，把纳吉尼带在身边：他不能再和蛇分开了……他大步跨出房间，走出门厅，进入了喷泉声中黑暗的花园。他用蛇佬腔呼叫大蛇，它游了出来，像长长的影子贴向他身边……

哈利突然睁开眼睛，把自己猛拉回当前的现实中。他躺在夕阳下的湖岸上，罗恩和赫敏低头看着他。从他们焦急的表情和伤疤连续的剧痛判断，他们已经注意到他刚才突然闯入了伏地魔的思想。哈利战栗着挣扎起来，发现身上仍然透湿，略微有些惊讶。小金杯看似毫无危险地放在他面前的草丛里，深蓝色的湖面在落日的余晖中金光闪闪。

"他知道了。"在伏地魔的高声尖叫之后，他自己的声音听起来陌生而低沉，"他知道了，而且他要检查另外几个在哪里。最后一个，"他已经站了起来，"在霍格沃茨。我猜到了。我猜到了。"

"什么？"

罗恩冲他张着嘴巴，赫敏跪起身，看起来很担心。

"你看到什么了？你是怎么知道的？"

"我看到了他发现金杯的事，我——我在他的脑海里，他——"哈利想起了那场杀戮，"他气得要命，也吓坏了，他想不通我们怎么知道的，现在他要去检查另外几个是否安全，第一个是戒指。他认为霍格沃茨的那个是最安全的，因为斯内普在那里，我们要混进去很难不

CHAPTER TWENTY-SEVEN   The Final Hiding Place

because it'll be so hard not to be seen getting in, I think he'll check that one last, but he could still be there within hours —'

'Did you see where in Hogwarts it is?' asked Ron, now scrambling to his feet too.

'No, he was concentrating on warning Snape, he didn't think about exactly where it is —'

'Wait, *wait!*' cried Hermione, as Ron caught up the Horcrux and Harry pulled out the Invisibility Cloak again. 'We can't just *go*, we haven't got a plan, we need to —'

'We need to get going,' said Harry firmly. He had been hoping to sleep, looking forward to getting into the new tent, but that was impossible now. 'Can you imagine what he's going to do once he realises the ring and the locket are gone? What if he moves the Hogwarts Horcrux, decides it isn't safe enough?'

'But how are we going to get in?'

'We'll go to Hogsmeade,' said Harry, 'and try to work something out once we see what the protection around the school's like. Get under the Cloak, Hermione, I want to stick together this time.'

'But we don't really fit —'

'It'll be dark, no one's going to notice our feet.'

The flapping of enormous wings echoed across the black water: the dragon had drunk its fill and risen into the air. They paused in their preparations to watch it climb higher and higher, now black against the rapidly darkening sky, until it vanished over a nearby mountain. Then Hermione walked forwards and took her place between the other two. Harry pulled the Cloak down as far as it would go, and together they turned on the spot into the crushing darkness.

第 27 章 最后的隐藏之处

被发现。我想他会最后检查那一个，但是他仍然可能在几小时内赶到那里——"

"那你看到在霍格沃茨的什么地方了吗？"罗恩问道，也爬了起来。

"没有，他在考虑要警告斯内普，没有想那东西确切在哪儿——"

"等等，等等！"当罗恩抓起魂器，哈利再次掏出隐形衣时，赫敏大喊道，"不能就这样去，没有一个计划，我们需要——"

"我们需要采取行动。"哈利坚定地说。他本来希望睡一觉，盼着钻进新帐篷，但现在不可能了。"一旦他发现戒指和挂坠盒都不见了，你能想象出他会做什么吗？如果他认为霍格沃茨都不够安全，把魂器转移了怎么办？"

"但是我们怎么进去呢？"

"我们先去霍格莫德，"哈利说，"看看学校周围的警戒是什么样的，然后再想办法。到隐形衣下面来，赫敏，我希望这次我们不要分开。"

"但是它恐怕装不下我们——"

"天快黑了，没人会注意到我们的脚。"

巨翅的拍打声在黑色的湖面上回响：火龙已经喝足了水，飞入空中。他们暂时停止了准备工作，看着它越飞越高，黑色的身影映在迅速暗下来的天空中，直到消失在不远处的山峰后。然后，赫敏走过来站在他们俩中间，哈利把隐形衣尽量往下拉了拉。他们一同原地旋转，进入了压迫身心的黑暗中。

CHAPTER TWENTY-EIGHT

The Missing Mirror

Harry's feet touched road. He saw the achingly familiar Hogsmeade High Street: dark shop fronts, and the outline of black mountains beyond the village, and the curve in the road ahead that led off towards Hogwarts, and light spilling from the windows of the Three Broomsticks, and with a lurch of the heart, he remembered, with piercing accuracy, how he had landed here, nearly a year before, supporting a desperately weak Dumbledore; all this in a second, upon landing – and then, even as he relaxed his grip upon Ron and Hermione's arms, it happened.

The air was rent by a scream that sounded like Voldemort's when he had realised the cup had been stolen: it tore at every nerve in Harry's body, and he knew immediately that their appearance had caused it. Even as he looked at the other two beneath the Cloak, the door of the Three Broomsticks burst open and a dozen cloaked and hooded Death Eaters dashed into the street, their wands aloft.

Harry seized Ron's wrist as he raised his wand. There were too many of them to Stun: even attempting it would give away their position. One of the Death Eaters waved his wand and the scream stopped, still echoing around the distant mountains.

'*Accio Cloak!*' roared one of the Death Eaters.

Harry seized its folds, but it made no attempt to escape: the Summoning Charm had not worked on it.

'Not under your wrapper, then, Potter?' yelled the Death Eater who had tried the charm, and then, to his fellows, 'Spread out. He's here.'

Six of the Death Eaters ran towards them: Harry, Ron and Hermione backed, as quickly as possible, down the nearest side street and the Death Eaters missed them by inches. They waited in the darkness, listening to the

第 28 章

丢失的镜子

哈利的脚触到了路面。他看见了熟悉得令他心痛的霍格莫德大街：漆黑的店面，村外远处黑黢黢的群山轮廓，前方通往霍格沃茨的弯道，还有三把扫帚酒吧窗户里透出的灯光。他的心猛地抽搐了一下，想起就在差不多一年前，他搀扶着奄奄一息的邓布利多降落在这里，那一幕情景如刀刻一般清晰地留在他的脑海里。所有这些都是在降落的一瞬间感到的——就在他松开罗恩和赫敏的胳膊时，出事了。

一声尖叫划破了夜空，听着像是伏地魔发现金杯被盗时的喊叫，这声音折磨着哈利全身的神经，他立刻明白这是他们引起的。就在他看着隐形衣下的另外两个人时，三把扫帚的门突然打开，十几个穿斗篷、戴兜帽的食死徒高举着魔杖冲到了街上。

罗恩举起魔杖，哈利一把抓住他的手腕。敌人太多，不能使用昏迷咒，就连试一试都会暴露他们的方位。一个食死徒挥了挥魔杖，尖叫声停止了，但仍在远处的群山间回荡不绝。

"隐形衣飞来！"一个食死徒吼道。

哈利揪住斗篷，但它并没有溜走的意思：召唤咒对它不起作用。

"这么说你没包裹着，波特？"念召唤咒的那个食死徒喊道，然后又对同伙说，"小心散开。他就在这儿。"

六个食死徒朝他们跑来，哈利、罗恩和赫敏迅速后退，拐进了最近的一条小街，仅差几英寸就被他们撞上了。他们在黑暗中等待着，听着脚步声跑过来跑过去，食死徒举着魔杖搜寻，一道道魔杖的光在

CHAPTER TWENTY-EIGHT   The Missing Mirror

footsteps running up and down, beams of light flying along the street from the Death Eaters' searching wands.

'Let's just leave!' Hermione whispered. 'Disapparate now!'

'Great idea,' said Ron, but before Harry could reply, a Death Eater shouted, 'We know you're here, Potter, and there's no getting away! We'll find you!'

'They were ready for us,' whispered Harry. 'They set up that spell to tell them we'd come. I reckon they've done something to keep us here, trap us –'

'What about Dementors?' called another Death Eater. 'Let 'em have free rein, they'd find him quick enough!'

'The Dark Lord wants Potter dead by no hand but his –'

'– an' Dementors won't kill him! The Dark Lord wants Potter's life, not his soul. He'll be easier to kill if he's been kissed first!'

There were noises of agreement. Dread filled Harry: to repel Dementors they would have to produce Patronuses, which would give them away immediately.

'We're going to have to try to Disapparate, Harry!' Hermione whispered.

Even as she said it, he felt the unnatural cold begin to steal over the street. Light was sucked from the environment right up to the stars, which vanished. In the pitch blackness, he felt Hermione take hold of his arm and together, they turned on the spot.

The air through which they needed to move seemed to have become solid: they could not Disapparate; the Death Eaters had cast their charms well. The cold was biting deeper and deeper into Harry's flesh. He, Ron and Hermione retreated down the side street, groping their way along the wall, trying not to make a sound. Then, round the corner, gliding noiselessly, came Dementors, ten or more of them, visible because they were of a denser darkness than their surroundings, with their black cloaks and their scabbed and rotting hands. Could they sense fear in the vicinity? Harry was sure of it: they seemed to be coming more quickly now, taking those dragging, rattling breaths he detested, tasting despair on the air, closing in –

He raised his wand: he could not, would not, suffer the Dementor's Kiss, whatever happened afterwards. It was of Ron and Hermione that he thought as he whispered, '*Expecto patronum!*'

The silver stag burst from his wand and charged: the Dementors scattered

第28章 丢失的镜子

街上穿梭扫射。

"我们离开吧!"赫敏小声说,"现在就幻影移形!"

"好主意。"罗恩说。没等哈利回答,一个食死徒就叫了起来:"我们知道你在这儿,波特,你逃不了啦!我们会找到你的!"

"他们早有准备,"哈利小声说,"弄了那个咒语,我们一来就发出警报。我想他们肯定也采取了什么办法要把我们留在这里,困在这里——"

"摄魂怪怎么样?"另一个食死徒大声喊道,"把它们放出来吧,它们会很快找到他的!"

"黑魔王想要亲手杀死波特——"

"——摄魂怪不会杀死他的!黑魔王要的是波特的命,不是他的灵魂。如果他先被吻过,再要杀死他就容易了!"

食死徒们嚷嚷着表示同意。哈利心头掠过一阵恐惧:驱散摄魂怪必须召来守护神,那样立刻就会暴露自己。

"只能试试幻影移形了,哈利!"赫敏小声说。

她话音没落,哈利就感到一股不同寻常的寒意从街上袭来。四周的灯光都被吸走了,就连星星也消失了。在伸手不见五指的黑暗中,他感到赫敏抓住了他的胳膊,他们一起原地旋转。

需要穿越的空气似乎变成了坚实的固体:他们不能幻影移形了。食死徒的魔咒还真厉害。寒意一点一点地渗透进哈利的肌肤。他和罗恩、赫敏在小街上一步一步后退,顺着墙壁摸索,尽量不发出一点声音。接着,摄魂怪在街角出现了,有十多个,无声无息地飘移过来。哈利之所以能看得到它们,是因为它们黑色的斗篷、结痂腐烂的手比周围的黑暗更加深浓。它们能感觉到附近的恐惧吗?哈利知道肯定能。它们现在似乎移动得更快了,发出令他憎恶的那种又长又慢、咯咯作响的呼吸声,品尝着空气里的绝望,围拢过来——

他举起了魔杖。不管后面会发生什么事,他都不能也不愿经受摄魂怪的吻。"呼神护卫!"他小声说,心里想的是罗恩和赫敏。

银色的牡鹿从他的魔杖里奔出来往前冲去。摄魂怪四散逃开,从

CHAPTER TWENTY-EIGHT   The Missing Mirror

and there was a triumphant yell from somewhere out of sight.

'It's him, down there, down there, I saw his Patronus, it was a stag!'

The Dementors had retreated, the stars were popping out again, and the footsteps of the Death Eaters were becoming louder; but before Harry in his panic could decide what to do, there was a grinding of bolts nearby, a door opened on the left-hand side of the narrow street and a rough voice said, 'Potter, in here, quick!'

He obeyed without hesitation: the three of them hurtled through the open doorway.

'Upstairs, keep the Cloak on, keep quiet!' muttered a tall figure, passing them on his way into the street and slamming the door behind him.

Harry had had no idea where they were, but now he saw, by the stuttering light of a single candle, the grubby, sawdust-strewn bar of the Hog's Head. They ran behind the counter and through a second doorway, which led to a rickety wooden staircase, which they climbed as fast as they could. The stairs opened on to a sitting room with a threadbare carpet and a small fireplace, above which hung a single large oil painting of a blonde girl who gazed out at the room with a kind of vacant sweetness.

Shouts reached them from the street below. Still wearing the Invisibility Cloak, they crept towards the grimy window and looked down. Their saviour, whom Harry now recognised as the Hog's Head's barman, was the only person not wearing a hood.

'So what?' he was bellowing into one of the hooded faces. 'So what? You send Dementors down my street, I'll send a Patronus back at 'em! I'm not having 'em near me, I've told you that, I'm not having it!'

'That wasn't your Patronus!' said a Death Eater. 'That was a stag, it was Potter's!'

'Stag!' roared the barman, and he pulled out a wand. 'Stag! You idiot – *expecto patronum!*'

Something huge and horned erupted from the wand: head down it charged towards the High Street and out of sight.

'That's not what I saw –' said the Death Eater, though with less certainty.

'Curfew's been broken, you heard the noise,' one of his companions told the barman. 'Someone was out in the street against regulations –'

'If I want to put my cat out, I will, and be damned to your curfew!'

第28章 丢失的镜子

看不见的地方传来一声得意的叫嚷。

"是他,就在那儿,就在那儿,我看见他的守护神了,是一头牡鹿!"

摄魂怪退去了,星星又开始眨动眼睛,食死徒的脚步声越来越响。情急之下,哈利一时不知如何应对。就在这时,旁边传来门闩吱吱嘎嘎的声音,小街左侧的一扇门打开了,一个粗哑的声音说:"波特,快进来,快!"

哈利毫不犹豫地照办,三个人冲进了敞开的门。

"上楼,别脱隐形衣,别出声!"一个高高的身影说,从他们身边走到小街上,重重地关上了门。

哈利刚才不知道他们身在何处,此刻在一根孤零零的蜡烛摇曳的微光下,他看见了猪头酒吧那破烂肮脏、散着锯末的吧台。他们跑到柜台后面,又穿过一扇门,那里有一道摇摇晃晃的木头楼梯,他们尽快爬了上去。楼梯顶上是客厅,铺着破旧的地毯,还有个小小的壁炉,壁炉上方挂着一幅很大的油画,画上是一个金发的姑娘茫然而温柔地望着屋内。

下面的街道上传来喊叫声。他们仍然披着隐形衣,悄悄走到满是污垢的窗前向下张望。他们的救命恩人——这时哈利认出他是猪头酒吧的老板——是唯一没戴兜帽的人。

"怎么啦?"他朝一个戴兜帽的面孔吼道,"怎么啦?你们敢把摄魂怪弄到我的小街上来,我就要召守护神来对付它们!我不能让它们靠近我,我跟你们说过的,绝对不能!"

"那不是你的守护神!"一个食死徒说,"那是一头牡鹿,是波特的!"

"牡鹿!"酒店老板大吼一声,抽出魔杖,"牡鹿!你这个白痴——呼神护卫!"

他的杖尖冒出一个长着犄角的大家伙:它埋着脑袋冲向大街,消失不见了。

"我看见的不是这个——"那个食死徒说,但不像刚才那么肯定了。

"有人违反了宵禁,你听见声音了,"他的一个同伙对酒吧老板说,"有人违反规定跑到了街上——"

"如果我想把猫放出去,我自然要放,去你妈的什么宵禁!"

CHAPTER TWENTY-EIGHT   The Missing Mirror

'*You* set off the Caterwauling Charm?'

'What if I did? Going to cart me off to Azkaban? Kill me for sticking my nose out my own front door? Do it, then, if you want to! But I hope for your sakes you haven't pressed your little Dark Marks and summoned him. He's not going to like being called here for me and my old cat, is he, now?'

'Don't you worry about us,' said one of the Death Eaters, 'worry about yourself, breaking curfew!'

'And where will you lot traffic potions and poisons when my pub's closed down? What'll happen to your little sidelines then?'

'Are you threatening –?'

'I keep my mouth shut, it's why you come here, isn't it?'

'I still say I saw a stag Patronus!' shouted the first Death Eater.

'Stag?' roared the barman. 'It's a *goat*, idiot!'

'All right, we made a mistake,' said the second Death Eater. 'Break curfew again and we won't be so lenient!'

The Death Eaters strode back towards the High Street. Hermione moaned with relief, wove out from under the Cloak and sat down on a wobble-legged chair. Harry drew the curtains tight shut, then pulled the Cloak off himself and Ron. They could hear the barman down below, rebolting the door of the bar, then climbing the stairs.

Harry's attention was caught by something on the mantelpiece: a small, rectangular mirror propped on top of it, right beneath the portrait of the girl.

The barman entered the room.

'You bloody fools,' he said gruffly, looking from one to the other of them. 'What were you thinking, coming here?'

'Thank you,' said Harry, 'we can't thank you enough. You saved our lives.'

The barman grunted. Harry approached him, looking up into the face, trying to see past the long, stringy, wire-grey hair and beard. He wore spectacles. Behind the dirty lenses, the eyes were a piercing, brilliant blue.

'It's your eye I've been seeing in the mirror.'

There was silence in the room. Harry and the barman looked at each other.

'You sent Dobby.'

第28章 丢失的镜子

"是你触响了啸叫咒？"

"是我又怎么样？要把我押到阿兹卡班去吗？就因为我把鼻子探出了自己的家门而杀死我吗？好吧，想这么做，你们尽管动手吧！不过为你们考虑，我奉劝你们不要去摁你们的黑魔小标记把他召来。他来了只看见我和我的老猫，肯定不会高兴的，是不是？"

"你就别替我们操心了，"一个食死徒说，"还是考虑考虑你自己吧，违反宵禁！"

"如果我的酒吧关门了，你们这帮人上哪儿去倒卖魔药和毒品呢？你们的小副业怎么办呢？"

"你胆敢威胁——？"

"我向来守口如瓶，你们就是为了这个来的，是不是？"

"我还是认为我看见了一头牡鹿守护神！"第一个食死徒大喊。

"牡鹿？"酒吧老板吼道，"那是只山羊，白痴！"

"好了好了，我们弄错了。"第二个食死徒说，"再敢违反宵禁，我们就不会这么客气了！"

食死徒们转身返回到大街上。赫敏放心地舒了口气，从隐形衣下面钻了出来，坐在一张摇摇晃晃的椅子上。哈利把窗帘拉严了，把隐形衣从自己和罗恩身上脱下来。他们听见酒吧老板在下面闩上酒吧的门，走上了楼梯。

哈利的注意力被壁炉台上的一个东西吸引住了：一面长方形的小镜子支在台上，就在那个姑娘肖像的下面。

酒吧老板进了房间。

"你们这些该死的傻瓜，"他粗暴地说，挨个儿看看他们三个，"你们是怎么想的，竟然跑到这儿来了？"

"谢谢你，"哈利说，"真不知该怎么感谢你。你救了我们的命。"

酒吧老板气哼哼地嘟囔着。哈利走上前去，抬头端详着他的脸，努力透过一缕缕金属丝般的灰色头发和胡须看清他的模样。他戴着眼镜，在脏兮兮的镜片后面，一双蓝色的眼睛明亮、锐利。

"我在镜子里看见的就是你的眼睛。"

房间里一片寂静。哈利和酒吧老板互相对视着。

"多比是你派来的。"

CHAPTER TWENTY-EIGHT   The Missing Mirror

The barman nodded and looked around for the elf.

'Thought he'd be with you. Where've you left him?'

'He's dead,' said Harry. 'Bellatrix Lestrange killed him.'

The barman's face was impassive. After a few moments, he said, 'I'm sorry to hear it. I liked that elf.'

He turned away, lighting lamps with prods of his wand, not looking at any of them.

'You're Aberforth,' said Harry, to the man's back.

He neither confirmed nor denied it, but bent to light the fire.

'How did you get this?' Harry asked, walking across to Sirius's mirror, the twin of the one he had broken nearly two years before.

'Bought it from Dung 'bout a year ago,' said Aberforth. 'Albus told me what it was. Been trying to keep an eye out for you.'

Ron gasped.

'The silver doe!' he said excitedly. 'Was that you too?'

'What are you talking about?' said Aberforth.

'Someone sent a doe Patronus to us!'

'Brains like that, you could be a Death Eater, son. Haven't I just proved my Patronus is a goat?'

'Oh,' said Ron. 'Yeah ... well, I'm hungry!' he added defensively, as his stomach gave an enormous rumble.

'I got food,' said Aberforth, and he sloped out of the room, reappearing moments later with a large loaf of bread, some cheese and a pewter jug of mead, which he set upon a small table in front of the fire. Ravenous, they ate and drank, and for a while there was silence but for the crackle of the fire, the clink of goblets and the sound of chewing.

'Right then,' said Aberforth, when they had eaten their fill, and Harry and Ron sat slumped dozily in their chairs. 'We need to think of the best way to get you out of here. Can't be done by night, you heard what happens if anyone moves outdoors during darkness: Caterwauling Charm's set off, they'll be on to you like Bowtruckles on Doxy eggs. I don't reckon I'll be able to pass off a stag as a goat a second time. Wait for daybreak, when curfew lifts, then you can put your Cloak back on and set out on foot. Get right out

第 28 章 丢失的镜子

酒吧老板点点头,左右张望着寻找那个小精灵。

"我以为他会和你在一起。你把他留在哪儿了?"

"他死了,"哈利说,"贝拉特里克斯·莱斯特兰奇杀死了他。"

酒吧老板的脸上毫无表情。过了片刻,他说:"这消息让我很难过。我喜欢那个小精灵。"

他转过身,不再看他们三个,兀自用魔杖把一盏盏灯点亮了。

"你是阿不福思。"哈利对着他的后背说。

他不置可否,弯腰去点炉火。

"你是怎么弄到这个的?"哈利问,一边走到小天狼星的镜子跟前,它跟将近两年前被哈利打碎的那面镜子是一对。

"大约一年前从蒙顿格斯手里买的。"阿不福思说,"阿不思跟我讲过。我一直在密切注意你。"

罗恩吃惊得喘不过气来。

"那头银色的牝鹿!"他激动地说,"也是你吗?"

"你在说什么呀?"阿不福思问。

"有人派了一头牝鹿守护神来找我们!"

"这种脑子,可以去当食死徒了,小子。我不是刚证实我的守护神是只山羊吗?"

"噢,"罗恩说,"是啊……唉,我饿了!"他的肚子突然咕噜咕噜叫起来,他便像是替自己辩护似的说。

"我有吃的。"阿不福思说。他走出房间,片刻之后又回来了,拿来了一大块面包、几片奶酪和一壶蜂蜜酒,放在炉火前的一张小桌上。三个人狼吞虎咽地又吃又喝,房间里一时安静下来,只有炉火的噼啪声、高脚酒杯的碰撞声,以及咀嚼食物的声音。

"好了,"阿不福思说,这时他们已经吃饱喝足,哈利和罗恩昏昏欲睡地瘫坐在椅子上,"需要想个最好的办法把你们从这里转移出去。夜里不行,你们刚才也听见了,如果有人夜里在户外活动会怎么样:触响啸叫咒,他们就会像护树罗锅扑向狐媚子蛋一样扑向你们。我恐怕不能第二次再用山羊去冒充牝鹿了。等到天亮吧,宵禁解除后,你

CHAPTER TWENTY-EIGHT   The Missing Mirror

of Hogsmeade, up into the mountains, and you'll be able to Disapparate there. Might see Hagrid. He's been hiding in a cave up there with Grawp ever since they tried to arrest him.'

'We're not leaving,' said Harry. 'We need to get into Hogwarts.'

'Don't be stupid, boy,' said Aberforth.

'We've got to,' said Harry.

'What you've got to do,' said Aberforth, leaning forwards, 'is to get as far from here as you can.'

'You don't understand. There isn't much time. We've got to get into the castle. Dumbledore – I mean, your brother – wanted us –'

The firelight made the grimy lenses of Aberforth's glasses momentarily opaque, a bright, flat white, and Harry remembered the blind eyes of the giant spider, Aragog.

'My brother Albus wanted a lot of things,' said Aberforth, 'and people had a habit of getting hurt while he was carrying out his grand plans. You get away from this school, Potter, and out of the country if you can. Forget my brother and his clever schemes. He's gone where none of this can hurt him, and you don't owe him anything.'

'You don't understand,' said Harry again.

'Oh, don't I?' said Aberforth quietly. 'You don't think I understood my own brother? Think you knew Albus better than I did?'

'I didn't mean that,' said Harry, whose brain felt sluggish with exhaustion and from the surfeit of food and wine. 'It's ... he left me a job.'

'Did he, now?' said Aberforth. 'Nice job, I hope? Pleasant? Easy? Sort of thing you'd expect an unqualified wizard kid to be able to do without overstretching themselves?'

Ron gave a rather grim laugh. Hermione was looking strained.

'I – it's not easy, no,' said Harry. 'But I've got to –'

'"Got to"? Why "*got to*"? He's dead, isn't he?' said Aberforth roughly. 'Let it go, boy, before you follow him! Save yourself!'

'I can't.'

'Why not?'

第28章 丢失的镜子

们可以重新穿上隐形衣，步行出发。赶快离开霍格莫德，到大山里去，在那里可以幻影移形，说不定还会看见海格。自从他们想要抓他，他就和格洛普一起躲在了一个山洞里。"

"我们不离开，"哈利说，"我们需要进入霍格沃茨。"

"别犯傻，孩子。"阿不福思说。

"我们必须去。"哈利说。

"你们必须做的，"阿不福思向前探着身子说，"是尽量远远地离开这儿。"

"你不了解。时间不多了，我们必须进入城堡。邓布利多——我是说你哥哥——想要我们——"

火光照在阿不福思的眼镜上，满是污垢的镜片突然变成不透明的纯白色，哈利想起了巨蜘蛛阿拉戈克的那双瞎眼。

"我哥哥阿不思想要许多东西，"阿不福思说，"在他贯彻他的宏伟计划时，人们经常受到伤害。波特，你快离开这所学校，如果可能的话，离开这个国家。忘记我的哥哥和他那些巧妙的计划吧。他去了一个这些都伤害不了他的地方，你并不欠他任何东西。"

"你不了解。"哈利又说。

"哦，是吗？"阿不福思小声说，"你认为我不了解我自己的哥哥？你认为你比我还要了解阿不思？"

"我不是那个意思，"哈利说，疲惫再加上酒足饭饱，他的脑袋显得有些迟钝，"是……他留给了我一项任务。"

"哦，是吗？"阿不福思说，"一桩美差，是吗？令人愉快？简单易行？一个资历不够的小巫师不用勉为其难就能完成的事情？"

罗恩不自然地冷笑一声。赫敏看上去有些紧张。

"我——事情不容易，不容易，"哈利说，"但我非做不可——"

"'非做不可'？为什么'非做不可'？他已经死了，不是吗？"阿不福思粗暴地说，"别想这事了，孩子，免得你也步他的后尘！保住你的命吧！"

"我不能。"

"为什么？"

CHAPTER TWENTY-EIGHT   The Missing Mirror

'I –' Harry felt overwhelmed; he could not explain, so he took the offensive instead. 'But you're fighting too, you're in the Order of the Phoenix –'

'I was,' said Aberforth. 'The Order of the Phoenix is finished. You-Know-Who's won, it's over, and anyone who's pretending different's kidding themselves. It'll never be safe for you here, Potter, he wants you too badly. So go abroad, go into hiding, save yourself. Best take these two with you.' He jerked a thumb at Ron and Hermione. 'They'll be in danger long as they live now everyone knows they've been working with you.'

'I can't leave,' said Harry. 'I've got a job –'

'Give it to someone else!'

'I can't. It's got to be me, Dumbledore explained it all –'

'Oh, did he, now? And did he tell you everything, was he honest with you?'

Harry wanted with all his heart to say 'yes', but somehow the simple word would not rise to his lips. Aberforth seemed to know what he was thinking.

'I knew my brother, Potter. He learned secrecy at our mother's knee. Secrets and lies, that's how we grew up, and Albus ... he was a natural.'

The old man's eyes travelled to the painting of the girl over the mantelpiece. It was, now Harry looked around properly, the only picture in the room. There was no photograph of Albus Dumbledore, nor of anyone else.

'Mr Dumbledore?' said Hermione rather timidly. 'Is that your sister? Ariana?'

'Yes,' said Aberforth tersely. 'Been reading Rita Skeeter, have you, missy?'

Even by the rosy light of the fire it was clear that Hermione had turned red.

'Elphias Doge mentioned her to us,' said Harry, trying to spare Hermione.

'That old berk,' muttered Aberforth, taking another swig of mead. 'Thought the sun shone out of my brother's every orifice, he did. Well, so did plenty of people, you three included, by the looks of it.'

Harry kept quiet. He did not want to express the doubts and uncertainties about Dumbledore that had riddled him for months now. He had made his choice while he dug Dobby's grave; he had decided to continue along the winding, dangerous path indicated for him by Albus Dumbledore, to accept that he had not been told everything that he wanted to know, but simply to trust. He had no desire to doubt again, he did not want to hear anything that would deflect him from his purpose. He met Aberforth's gaze, which was so

第28章 丢失的镜子

"我——"哈利觉得无言以对，他没法解释，便转守为攻，"可是你也在战斗呀，你是凤凰社成员——"

"现在不是了，"阿不福思说，"凤凰社完了，神秘人赢了，大势已去，那些假装不承认这些的人是在欺骗自己。波特，你待在这里永远不会安全，他急不可待地想抓住你。所以，到国外去吧，躲藏起来吧，保全自己的性命吧。最好把这两个也带上，"他用大拇指点了点罗恩和赫敏，"他们只要活着就有危险，现在大家都知道他们跟你一起做事。"

"我不能离开，"哈利说，"我有任务——"

"交给别人！"

"不能，必须是我，邓布利多解释得很清楚——"

"哦，是吗？那么，他把一切都告诉你了吗，他对你开诚布公了吗？"

哈利多么想说"是的"，然而不知怎么，这个简单的词就是不肯来到他的嘴边。阿不福思似乎知道他在想什么。

"我了解我的哥哥，波特。他在我母亲的膝头就学会了保密。秘密和谎言，我们就是这样成长起来的，而阿不思……他天生如此。"

老人的目光转向壁炉台上的那幅少女画像。此刻哈利已经把周围打量清楚了，知道这是房间里唯一的一幅画。这里没有阿不思·邓布利多和别人的照片。

"邓布利多先生，"赫敏有点胆怯地说，"这是你的妹妹？阿利安娜？"

"对，"阿不福思简短地说，"读了丽塔·斯基特写的东西，是吗，小姑娘？"

即使在红红的火光映照下，也能看出赫敏的脸红了。

"埃非亚斯·多吉向我们提到过她。"哈利说，想替赫敏解围。

"那个老傻瓜，"阿不福思低声说，又喝了一大口蜂蜜酒，"他认为我哥哥每一个毛孔都放射出阳光，哼，许多人都那么想，看样子，你们三个也不例外。"

哈利没有说话。他不想说出几个月来困扰心头的对邓布利多的怀疑和犹豫。他为多比掘墓时就做出了选择，他已经决定沿着阿不思·邓布利多指点的危险、曲折的道路继续前行，虽然邓布利多没有把他需

CHAPTER TWENTY-EIGHT   The Missing Mirror

strikingly like his brother's: the bright blue eyes gave the same impression that they were X-raying the object of their scrutiny, and Harry thought that Aberforth knew what he was thinking, and despised him for it.

'Professor Dumbledore cared about Harry, very much,' said Hermione in a low voice.

'Did he, now?' said Aberforth. 'Funny thing, how many of the people my brother cared about very much, ended up in a worse state than if he'd left 'em well alone.'

'What do you mean?' asked Hermione breathlessly.

'Never you mind,' said Aberforth.

'But that's a really serious thing to say!' said Hermione. 'Are you – are you talking about your sister?'

Aberforth glared at her: his lips moved as if he were chewing the words he was holding back. Then he burst into speech.

'When my sister was six years old, she was attacked, set upon, by three Muggle boys. They'd seen her doing magic, spying through the back garden hedge: she was a kid, she couldn't control it, no witch or wizard can at that age. What they saw scared them, I expect. They forced their way through the hedge, and when she couldn't show them the trick, they got a bit carried away trying to stop the little freak doing it.'

Hermione's eyes were huge in the firelight: Ron looked slightly sick. Aberforth stood up, tall as Albus, and suddenly terrible in his anger and the intensity of his pain.

'It destroyed her, what they did: she was never right again. She wouldn't use magic, but she couldn't get rid of it: it turned inwards and drove her mad, it exploded out of her when she couldn't control it, and at times she was strange and dangerous. But mostly she was sweet, and scared, and harmless.

'And my father went after the bastards that did it,' said Aberforth, 'and attacked them. And they locked him up in Azkaban for it. He never said why he'd done it, because if the Ministry had known what Ariana had become, she'd have been locked up in St Mungo's for good. They'd have seen her as a serious threat to the International Statute of Secrecy, unbalanced like she was, with magic exploding out of her at moments when she couldn't keep it in any longer.

第28章 丢失的镜子

要知道的事情都告诉他,但他只有深信不疑。他不愿意再去怀疑,他不想听到任何会使他偏离目标的东西。哈利碰到了阿不福思的目光,跟他哥哥的目光惊人地相似:都是明亮的蓝眼睛,都像在透视被审视的对象。哈利觉得阿不福思知道他在想什么,并因此而看不起他。

"邓布利多教授关心哈利,非常关心。"赫敏低声说。

"哦,是吗?"阿不福思说,"真是可笑,有多少我哥哥非常关心的人最后下场可悲,他当初还不如不管他们呢。"

"什么意思?"赫敏屏住呼吸问。

"不关你的事。"阿不福思说。

"但是这句话真的说得很重!"赫敏说,"你——你说的是你妹妹吗?"

阿不福思狠狠地瞪着她,嘴唇嚅动着,像是在咀嚼他忍住不说的话。然后,他突然打开了话匣子。

"我妹妹六岁时,遭到三个麻瓜男孩的袭击。他们透过后花园的树篱看见她在变魔法。她还是个孩子,还不能收放自如,那个年纪的巫师都不能。我猜,那些男孩是被眼前的情景吓着了。他们从树篱中挤了进来,我妹妹没法告诉他们魔法是怎么变的,他们就失去控制,想阻止小怪物再变魔法。"

火光里,赫敏的眼睛睁得大大的,罗恩看上去有点不舒服。阿不福思站了起来,和阿不思一样高大,因为愤怒,因为剧烈的痛苦,他突然显得很可怕。

"他们做的事情把她毁了,她再也没有恢复正常。她不愿意使用魔法,但又没法摆脱。魔法转入了她的内心,把她逼疯了,在她不能控制的时候,魔法就会在她身上发作。她有时候又古怪又危险,但大多数时候很可爱,怯生生的,对人没有伤害。

"我父亲去找那几个混蛋算账,"阿不福思说,"把他们教训了一顿,结果被关进了阿兹卡班。他从来没说他为什么那么做,如果魔法部知道了阿利安娜的状况,她将被终身囚禁在圣芒戈医院里。他们会把她看作是对《国际保密法》的一个严重威胁,因为她精神错乱,在无法控制的时候她内在的魔法就会爆发出来。

CHAPTER TWENTY-EIGHT — The Missing Mirror

'We had to keep her safe, and quiet. We moved house, put it about she was ill, and my mother looked after her, and tried to keep her calm and happy.

'*I* was her favourite,' he said, and as he said it, a grubby schoolboy seemed to look out through Aberforth's wrinkles and tangled beard. 'Not Albus, he was always up in his bedroom when he was home, reading his books and counting his prizes, keeping up with his correspondence with "the most notable magical names of the day",' Aberforth sneered, '*he* didn't want to be bothered with her. She liked me best. I could get her to eat when she wouldn't do it for my mother, I could get her to calm down when she was in one of her rages, and when she was quiet, she used to help me feed the goats.

'Then, when she was fourteen ... see, I wasn't there,' said Aberforth. 'If I'd been there, I could have calmed her down. She had one of her rages, and my mother wasn't as young as she was, and ... it was an accident. Ariana couldn't control it. But my mother was killed.'

Harry felt a horrible mixture of pity and repulsion; he did not want to hear any more, but Aberforth kept talking and Harry wondered how long it had been since he had spoken about this; whether, in fact, he had ever spoken about it.

'So that put paid to Albus's trip round the world with little Doge. The pair of 'em came home for my mother's funeral and then Doge went off on his own, and Albus settled down as head of the family. Ha!'

Aberforth spat into the fire.

'I'd have looked after her, I told him so, I didn't care about school, I'd have stayed home and done it. He told me I had to finish my education and *he'd* take over from my mother. Bit of a comedown for Mr Brilliant, there's no prizes for looking after your half-mad sister, stopping her blowing up the house every other day. But he did all right for a few weeks ... 'til *he* came.'

And now a positively dangerous look crept over Aberforth's face.

'Grindelwald. And at last, my brother had an *equal* to talk to, someone just as bright and talented as *he* was. And looking after Ariana took a back seat then, while they were hatching all their plans for a new wizarding order, and looking for *Hallows*, and whatever else it was they were so interested in. Grand plans for the benefit of all wizardkind, and if one young girl got neglected, what did that matter, when Albus was working for *the greater good*?

第28章 丢失的镜子

"我们必须保证她的安全,并把她隐藏起来。我们搬了家,谎称她病了,我母亲负责照料她,尽量使她平静、快乐。"

"她最喜欢我,"阿不福思说,他说这话的时候,似乎一个邋遢的男生正在透过阿不福思满脸的皱纹和纠结的胡子朝外窥视,"而不是阿不思。阿不思在家时总待在楼上自己的卧室里,读他的书,数他的奖状,跟'当时最有名的魔法大师'通信,"阿不福思讥笑地说,"他根本不愿意为她操心。她最喜欢我。我母亲没法让她吃饭时,我能哄她吃下去;她脾气发作时,我能让她平静下来;她安静时,经常帮我一起喂羊。

"后来,她十四岁了……唉,当时我不在,"阿不福思说,"如果我在,就会让她平静下来。她脾气又发作了,我母亲已不像以前那么年轻,结果……那是个意外,阿利安娜没法控制自己,我母亲被杀死了。"

哈利感到一种强烈的同情和抵触情绪,他不想再听了。可是阿不福思还在继续往下说,哈利心想老人不知多长时间没有说过这件事了,也许他从来就没对人说起过。

"这样,阿不思和小多吉一起周游世界的计划就破灭了。他们俩回来参加了我母亲的葬礼,然后多吉独自出发了,阿不思作为一家之长留了下来。呸!"

阿不福思朝火里啐了一口。

"我对他说,我愿意照顾妹妹,我不在乎上学的事,我可以待在家里自学。他却说我必须完成学业,他会留下来接替我母亲。这对于精英先生来说是有点失落的。照顾一个半疯的妹妹,每隔一天就要阻止她把房子炸飞,这可没人给他发奖。不过最初几个星期他做得挺好……后来那个人来了。"

这时,阿不福思脸上露出了一种十分危险的神情。

"格林德沃。终于,我哥哥有了个谈话的对手,有了个跟他一样聪明、有才华的人。照顾阿利安娜就成了第二位的了,他们整天都在酝酿建立新巫师秩序的计划,寻找圣器,做他们非常感兴趣的所有事情。为了宏伟的计划,为了整个巫师界的利益,一个小姑娘受到忽视又有什么关系?阿不思在为更伟大的利益工作呢!"

CHAPTER TWENTY-EIGHT

The Missing Mirror

'But after a few weeks of it, I'd had enough, I had. It was nearly time for me to go back to Hogwarts, so I told 'em, both of 'em, face to face, like I am to you, now,' and Aberforth looked down at Harry, and it took little imagination to see him as a teenager, wiry and angry, confronting his elder brother. 'I told him, you'd better give it up, now. You can't move her, she's in no fit state, you can't take her with you, wherever it is you're planning to go, when you're making your clever speeches, trying to whip yourselves up a following. He didn't like that,' said Aberforth, and his eyes were briefly occluded by the firelight on the lenses of his glasses: they shone white and blind again. 'Grindelwald didn't like that at all. He got angry. He told me what a stupid little boy I was, trying to stand in the way of him and my brilliant brother ... didn't I *understand*, my poor sister wouldn't have to be hidden once they'd changed the world, and led the wizards out of hiding, and taught the Muggles their place?

'And there was an argument ... and I pulled out my wand, and he pulled out his, and I had the Cruciatus Curse used on me by my brother's best friend – and Albus was trying to stop him, and then all three of us were duelling, and the flashing lights and the bangs set her off, she couldn't stand it –'

The colour was draining from Aberforth's face as though he had suffered a mortal wound.

'– and I think she wanted to help, but she didn't really know what she was doing, and I don't know which of us did it, it could have been any of us – and she was dead.'

His voice broke on the last word and he dropped down into the nearest chair. Hermione's face was wet with tears and Ron was almost as pale as Aberforth. Harry felt nothing but revulsion: he wished he had not heard it, wished he could wash his mind clean of it.

'I'm so ... I'm so sorry,' Hermione whispered.

'Gone,' croaked Aberforth. 'Gone forever.'

He wiped his nose on his cuff, and cleared his throat.

''Course, Grindelwald scarpered. He had a bit of a track record already, back in his own country, and he didn't want Ariana set to his account too. And Albus was free, wasn't he? Free of the burden of his sister, free to become the greatest wizard of the –'

第28章 丢失的镜子

"几个星期后,我受够了,真是受够了。那时我快要回霍格沃茨了,于是我告诉他们,告诉他们两个,面对面地,就像我现在对着你一样。"阿不福思低头看着哈利,不难想象他十几岁时的模样,精瘦结实,满腔怒火,和自己的哥哥对质。"我告诉他,你最好趁早放弃。你不能转移她,她的状态不行,你不能带她一起走,去你打算去的地方,发表你那些聪明的讲话,给自己煽动起一批追随者。他不爱听。"阿不福思说,火光照在他的镜片上,暂时遮住了他的眼睛,镜片上又是白光一片,"格林德沃听了很不高兴,他生气了,说我是个愚蠢的小男孩,想当他和我那出色的哥哥的绊脚石……还说难道我不明白,一旦他们改变了世界,让巫师们不再躲躲藏藏,让麻瓜们安分守己,我那可怜的妹妹就再也不用东躲西藏了。

"我们争论起来……我抽出我的魔杖,他也抽出了他的,我中了钻心咒,是我哥哥最好的朋友下的手——阿不思试图阻止他。于是我们三个展开了决斗,一道道闪光和一声声巨响刺激了我妹妹,她无法承受——"

阿不福思的脸上突然没了血色,仿佛受了致命的创伤。

"——我猜她是想来帮忙,但她不清楚自己在做什么,我不知道究竟是我们中间谁干的,谁都有可能——她死了。"

说到最后一句,他声音哽咽了,扑通跌坐在最近的那把椅子上。赫敏满脸泪水,罗恩的脸色几乎和阿不福思的一样苍白。哈利只感到一阵难受:他希望自己没有听见,希望能把这件事从脑子里洗掉。

"我……我很抱歉。"赫敏小声说。

"没了,"阿不福思哑着嗓子说,"永远没了。"

他用袖口擦擦鼻子,清了清嗓子。

"当然啦,格林德沃逃跑了。他在自己国内已经有了点前科,可不希望把阿利安娜的账也算在他头上。阿不思解脱了,不是吗?摆脱了妹妹这个负担,可以无牵无挂地去做最伟大的巫师——"

CHAPTER TWENTY-EIGHT   The Missing Mirror

'He was never free,' said Harry.

'I beg your pardon?' said Aberforth.

'Never,' said Harry. 'The night that your brother died he drank a potion that drove him out of his mind. He started screaming, pleading with someone who wasn't there. "*Don't hurt them, please ... hurt me instead.*"'

Ron and Hermione were staring at Harry. He had never gone into details about what had happened on the island on the lake: the events that had taken place after he and Dumbledore had returned to Hogwarts had eclipsed it so thoroughly.

'He thought he was back there with you and Grindelwald, I know he did,' said Harry, remembering Dumbledore whimpering, pleading. 'He thought he was watching Grindelwald hurting you and Ariana ... it was torture to him, if you'd seen him then, you wouldn't say he was free.'

Aberforth seemed lost in contemplation of his own knotted and veined hands. After a long pause, he said, 'How can you be sure, Potter, that my brother wasn't more interested in the greater good than in you? How can you be sure you aren't dispensable, just like my little sister?'

A shard of ice seemed to pierce Harry's heart.

'I don't believe it. Dumbledore loved Harry,' said Hermione.

'Why didn't he tell him to hide, then?' shot back Aberforth. 'Why didn't he say to him, take care of yourself, here's how to survive?'

'Because,' said Harry, before Hermione could answer, 'sometimes you've *got* to think about more than your own safety! Sometimes you've *got* to think about the greater good! This is war!'

'You're seventeen, boy!'

'I'm of age, and I'm going to keep fighting even if you've given up!'

'Who says I've given up?'

'"The Order of the Phoenix is finished,"' Harry repeated. '"You-Know-Who's won, it's over, and anyone who's pretending different's kidding themselves."'

'I don't say I like it, but it's the truth!'

'No, it isn't,' said Harry. 'Your brother knew how to finish You-Know-Who and he passed the knowledge on to me. I'm going to keep going until I succeed – or I die. Don't think I don't know how this might end. I've known

第28章 丢失的镜子

"他从来没有解脱。"哈利说。

"你说什么？"阿不福思说。

"从来没有。"哈利说，"你哥哥死去的那天夜里喝了一种毒药，变得精神错乱。他开始喊叫，向一个不在场的人发出恳求：'别伤害他们，求求你……冲我来吧。'"

罗恩和赫敏都吃惊地看着哈利。他从来没有跟他们讲过在湖心小岛的具体细节。他和邓布利多回到霍格沃茨后发生的事情，使那一幕显得毫不重要了。

"他以为自己回到了从前，跟你和格林德沃在一起，我知道是这样。"哈利说，想起了邓布利多带着呜咽的恳求，"他以为自己正眼看着格林德沃伤害你和阿利安娜……这对他来说太痛苦了，如果当时你看见他，就不会说他已经解脱。"

阿不福思出神地盯着自己骨节突出、布满青筋的手。过了良久，他说："波特，你怎么能够确定，我哥哥更感兴趣的不是更伟大的利益而是你呢？你怎么能确定你不像我的小妹妹一样是可有可无的呢？"

似乎有锋利的冰碴刺中了哈利的心。

"我不相信。邓布利多是爱哈利的。"赫敏说。

"那他为什么不叫哈利躲藏起来？"阿不福思反驳道，"为什么不叫哈利好好地照顾自己，保全性命？"

"因为，"哈利抢在赫敏前面回答，"有时候必须考虑比自身安全更多的东西！有时候必须考虑更伟大的利益！这是战争！"

"你才十七岁，孩子！"

"我成人了，我要继续战斗，即使你已经放弃！"

"谁说我放弃了？"

"'凤凰社完了，'"哈利重复着他的话，"'神秘人赢了，大势已去，那些假装不承认这些的人是在欺骗自己。'"

"我没有说我愿意这样，但这是事实！"

"不，不是。"哈利说，"你哥哥知道怎么干掉神秘人，他把情况告诉了我。我要继续下去，直到成功——或者死去。别以为我不知道最

CHAPTER TWENTY-EIGHT   The Missing Mirror

it for years.'

He waited for Aberforth to jeer or to argue, but he did not. He merely scowled.

'We need to get into Hogwarts,' said Harry again. 'If you can't help us, we'll wait 'til daybreak, leave you in peace and try to find a way in ourselves. If you *can* help us – well, now would be a great time to mention it.'

Aberforth remained fixed in his chair, gazing at Harry with the eyes that were so extraordinarily like his brother's. At last he cleared his throat, got to his feet, walked around the little table and approached the portrait of Ariana.

'You know what to do,' he said.

She smiled, turned and walked away, not as people in portraits usually did, out of the sides of their frames, but along what seemed to be a long tunnel painted behind her. They watched her slight figure retreating until finally she was swallowed by the darkness.

'Er – what –?' began Ron.

'There's only one way in, now,' said Aberforth. 'You must know they've got all the old secret passageways covered at both ends, Dementors all around the boundary walls, regular patrols inside the school from what my sources tell me. The place has never been so heavily guarded. How you expect to do anything once you get inside it, with Snape in charge and the Carrows as his Deputies ... well, that's your lookout, isn't it? You say you're prepared to die.'

'But what ...?' said Hermione, frowning at Ariana's picture.

A tiny white dot had reappeared at the end of the painted tunnel, and now Ariana was walking back towards them, growing bigger and bigger as she came. But there was somebody else with her now, someone taller than she was, who was limping along looking excited. His hair was longer than Harry had ever seen it: he appeared to have suffered several gashes to his face and his clothes were ripped and torn. Larger and larger the two figures grew, until only their heads and shoulders filled the portrait. Then the whole thing swung forwards on the wall like a little door, and the entrance to a real tunnel was revealed. And out of it, his hair overgrown, his face cut, his robes ripped, clambered the real Neville Longbottom, who gave a roar of delight, leapt down from the mantelpiece and yelled, 'I knew you'd come! *I knew it, Harry!*'

第28章 丢失的镜子

后可能会是什么结局。早在几年前我就知道了。"

哈利等待着阿不福思的讥笑或者反驳，但他没有，他只是阴沉着脸。

"我们需要进入霍格沃茨，"哈利又说道，"如果你不能帮忙，我们就等到天亮，自己想办法，不再麻烦你。如果你能帮忙——现在正好可以说出来。"

阿不福思仍然一动不动地坐在椅子上，怔怔地盯着哈利，那双眼睛像极了他哥哥的。最后，他清清嗓子，站了起来，绕过小桌子，走向阿利安娜的肖像。

"你知道该怎么做。"他说。

那少女微微一笑，转身走远了，她不像平常肖像里的人那样消失在相框旁边，而似乎是顺着画在她身后的一条长长的隧道走去。他们注视着她纤弱的身影越走越远，最后被黑暗吞没。

"呃——这是怎么——？"罗恩想问个究竟。

"现在只有一条路能进去。"阿不福思说，"你们必须知道，整个学校从来没有这样严防死守过。据我得到的消息，他们已经把所有古老的秘密通道的两头都堵死了，围墙边都是摄魂怪，校内固定有人巡逻。斯内普独掌大权，卡罗兄妹当他的左膀右臂，你就是进了学校，又能有什么作为呢……唉，那是你自己的事了，对吗？你说你已经做好赴死的准备。"

"可是……"赫敏皱眉望着阿利安娜的画像，说道。

一个小白点在画中的隧道尽头出现了，阿利安娜朝他们走了回来，越来越近，越来越大。但她身边还有一个人，个子比她高，走路一瘸一拐的，满脸的兴奋。他的头发比哈利以前见过的任何时候都长，脸上似乎划了几道口子，衣服也被撕扯得不像样子。两个人影越来越大，最后他们的脑袋和肩膀占满了整个肖像。这时，墙上的肖像如同一扇小门一样打开了，露出一条真正的隧道的入口。真正的纳威·隆巴顿从隧道里爬出来，头发长得出奇，满脸伤痕，长袍被扯烂了。他狂喜地大吼一声，从壁炉台上跳了下来，嚷道："我知道你会来！我早就知道，哈利！"

CHAPTER TWENTY-NINE

The Lost Diadem

'Neville – what the – how –?'

But Neville had spotted Ron and Hermione, and with yells of delight was hugging them too. The longer Harry looked at Neville, the worse he appeared: one of his eyes was swollen, yellow and purple, there were gouge marks on his face, and his general air of unkemptness suggested that he had been living rough. Nevertheless, his battered visage shone with happiness as he let go of Hermione and said again, 'I knew you'd come! Kept telling Seamus it was a matter of time!'

'Neville, what's happened to you?'

'What? This?' Neville dismissed his injuries with a shake of the head. 'This is nothing. Seamus is worse. You'll see. Shall we get going, then? Oh,' he turned to Aberforth, 'Ab, there might be a couple more people on the way.'

'Couple more?' repeated Aberforth ominously. 'What d'you mean, a couple more, Longbottom? There's a curfew and a Caterwauling Charm on the whole village!'

'I know, that's why they'll be Apparating directly into the bar,' said Neville. 'Just send them down the passage when they get here, will you? Thanks a lot.'

Neville held out his hand to Hermione and helped her to climb up on to the mantelpiece and into the tunnel; Ron followed, then Neville. Harry addressed Aberforth.

'I don't know how to thank you. You've saved our lives, twice.'

'Look after 'em, then,' said Aberforth gruffly. 'I might not be able to save 'em a third time.'

Harry clambered up on to the mantelpiece and through the hole behind Ariana's portrait. There were smooth stone steps on the other side: it looked

第29章

失踪的冠冕

"纳威——真是——怎么会——？"

纳威又看见了罗恩和赫敏，欣喜若狂地尖叫着，也挨个儿把他们抱了抱。哈利越看纳威，越觉得他的模样惨不忍睹：一只眼睛肿了，又青又紫，脸上有许多深深的伤口，整个人蓬头垢面，说明他的日子过得很糟糕。不过，他伤痕累累的脸上洋溢着喜悦。他放开赫敏，又说道："我知道你们会来！一直对西莫说这是迟早的事！"

"纳威，你这是怎么啦？"

"什么？这个？"纳威摇摇脑袋，没把自己的伤当回事，"没什么，西莫比我还惨呢。你们会看到的。我们现在就走吧？哦，"他转向阿不福思，"阿不，可能还有两个人要过来。"

"还有两个？"阿不福思凶巴巴地说，"你说什么，隆巴顿，还有两个？外面在宵禁，整个村子都布了啸叫咒！"

"我知道，所以他们会直接幻影显形到酒吧里。"纳威说，"来了就让他们从通道过去，好吗？多谢了。"

纳威把手伸给赫敏，扶她爬上壁炉台，钻进了隧道。罗恩跟了上去，纳威紧随其后。

哈利对阿不福思说："真不知道怎么感谢你，你救了我们的命，两次。"

"好好照顾他们吧，"阿不福思粗声粗气地说，"我恐怕救不了他们三次。"

哈利爬到壁炉台上，穿过了阿利安娜肖像后面的那个洞。洞的那

CHAPTER TWENTY-NINE The Lost Diadem

as though the passageway had been there for years. Brass lamps hung from the walls and the earthy floor was worn and smooth; as they walked, their shadows rippled, fan-like, across the wall.

'How long's this been here?' Ron asked, as they set off. 'It isn't on the Marauder's Map, is it, Harry? I thought there were only seven passages in and out of school?'

'They sealed off all of those before the start of the year,' said Neville. 'There's no chance of getting through any of them now, not with curses over the entrances and Death Eaters and Dementors waiting at the exits.' He started walking backwards, beaming, drinking them in. 'Never mind that stuff ... is it true? Did you break into Gringotts? Did you escape on a dragon? It's everywhere, everyone's talking about it, Terry Boot got beaten up by Carrow for yelling about it in the Great Hall at dinner!'

'Yeah, it's true,' said Harry.

Neville laughed gleefully.

'What did you do with the dragon?'

'Released it into the wild,' said Ron. 'Hermione was all for keeping it as a pet —'

'Don't exaggerate, Ron —'

'But what have you been doing? People have been saying you've just been on the run, Harry, but I don't think so. I think you've been up to something.'

'You're right,' said Harry, 'but tell us about Hogwarts, Neville, we haven't heard anything.'

'It's been ... well, it's not really like Hogwarts any more,' said Neville, the smile fading from his face as he spoke. 'Do you know about the Carrows?'

'Those two Death Eaters who teach here?'

'They do more than teach,' said Neville. 'They're in charge of all discipline. They like punishment, the Carrows.'

'Like Umbridge?'

'Nah, they make her look tame. The other teachers are all supposed to refer us to the Carrows if we do anything wrong. They don't, though, if they can avoid it. You can tell they all hate them as much as we do.

第29章 失踪的冠冕

边是光滑的石头台阶,似乎这条通道已经存在了许多年。墙壁上挂着黄铜灯,泥土地面被踩得平平实实。他们走在通道里,影子投在墙壁上,像扇子一样摇摆着。

"这通道有多长时间了?"罗恩边走边问,"活点地图上没有吧,哈利?我原来以为只有七条通道进出学校呢。"

"开学前他们就把那些通道全封死了,"纳威说,"入口施了魔咒,出口有食死徒和摄魂怪把守,现在根本不可能从那里进出了。"他开始倒退着走,笑容满面地细细端详他们。"别管那些事啦……是真的吗?你们真的闯进了古灵阁?真的骑着火龙逃走了?事情都传开了,大家都在说,泰瑞·布特吃饭时在礼堂里大声嚷嚷这事儿,被卡罗兄妹打了一顿!"

"对,是真的。"哈利说。

纳威高兴地笑了起来。

"后来你们把那条火龙怎么样了?"

"在野外放掉了,"罗恩说,"赫敏一心想把它当宠物养着——"

"不许夸张,罗恩——"

"可是你们在做什么呢?人们都说你在四处逃窜,哈利,但我认为不会。我想你肯定在做什么事情。"

"你说得对。"哈利说,"快跟我们说说霍格沃茨吧,纳威,我们什么消息都没有。"

"学校……唉,它现在已经不像霍格沃茨了。"纳威说着,脸上的笑容隐去了,"你们知道卡罗兄妹吗?"

"就是在这里教书的那两个食死徒?"

"他们不光教书,"纳威说,"纪律也归他们管。这两个卡罗,最喜欢惩罚学生。"

"像乌姆里奇一样?"

"哪里,乌姆里奇跟他们一比,还算是温和的。如果我们做了错事,别的老师都得把我们交给他们俩。不过,老师们只要能躲得过去就不这么做。看得出来,他们也像我们一样恨那两个人。"

CHAPTER TWENTY-NINE The Lost Diadem

'Amycus, the bloke, he teaches what used to be Defence Against the Dark Arts, except now it's just the Dark Arts. We're supposed to practise the Cruciatus Curse on people who've earned detentions –'

'*What?*'

Harry, Ron and Hermione's united voices echoed up and down the passage.

'Yeah,' said Neville. 'That's how I got this one,' he pointed at a particularly deep gash in his cheek, 'I refused to do it. Some people are into it, though; Crabbe and Goyle love it. First time they've ever been top in anything, I expect.

'Alecto, Amycus's sister, teaches Muggle Studies, which is compulsory for everyone. We've all got to listen to her explain how Muggles are like animals, stupid and dirty, and how they drove wizards into hiding by being vicious towards them, and how the natural order is being re-established. I got this one,' he indicated another slash to his face, 'for asking her how much Muggle blood she and her brother have got.'

'Blimey, Neville,' said Ron, 'there's a time and a place for getting a smart mouth.'

'You didn't hear her,' said Neville. 'You wouldn't have stood it either. The thing is, it helps when people stand up to them, it gives everyone hope. I used to notice that when you did it, Harry.'

'But they've used you as a knife sharpener,' said Ron, wincing slightly as they passed a lamp and Neville's injuries were thrown into even greater relief.

Neville shrugged.

'Doesn't matter. They don't want to spill too much pure blood, so they'll torture us a bit if we're mouthy but they won't actually kill us.'

Harry did not know what was worse, the things that Neville was saying or the matter-of-fact tone in which he said them.

'The only people in real danger are the ones whose friends and relatives on the outside are giving trouble. They get taken hostage. Old Xeno Lovegood was getting a bit too outspoken in *The Quibbler*, so they dragged Luna off the train on the way back for Christmas.'

'Neville, she's all right, we've seen her –'

'Yeah, I know, she managed to get a message to me.'

第29章 失踪的冠冕

"阿米库斯，那个男的，教以前的那门黑魔法防御术课，现在其实就是赤裸裸的黑魔法了。要我们在那些被关禁闭的人身上练习钻心咒——"

"什么？"

哈利、罗恩和赫敏异口同声的惊叫在整个通道里回荡。

"是啊，"纳威说，"我这个伤就是这么来的。"他指指面颊上一道特别深的伤口，"我不肯做。不过有些人兴趣倒挺大，克拉布和高尔可喜欢了。这大概是他们第一次在什么事情上冒了尖儿。"

"阿莱克托，阿米库斯的妹妹，教麻瓜研究课，这现在是每个人的必修课了。我们都得听她说，麻瓜就像动物一样，又脏又蠢，对巫师凶恶残暴，逼得巫师四处躲藏，她还说现在正常秩序得到了重新建立。这道伤口，"他指指脸上的另一条口子，"是我问她和她哥哥手上沾了多少麻瓜鲜血时留下的。"

"天哪，纳威，"罗恩说，"说话放肆也要分时间地点呀。"

"你没听到她说话，"纳威说，"不然你也受不了。关键是，有人站出来跟他们对抗是有用的，这使大家看到了希望。哈利，当初你这么做的时候我就注意到了。"

"可他们这是在拿你磨刀呀。"罗恩说。他们从一盏灯下走过时，灯光照得纳威的伤口更加触目惊心，罗恩看了不禁一哆嗦。

纳威耸了耸肩膀。

"没关系。他们舍不得糟蹋太多纯血统巫师的血，所以只在我们说话放肆时稍稍折磨我们一下，不会真要我们的命。"

哈利不知道到底哪一个更糟糕，是纳威所说的事情，还是他说这些事情时那副无所谓的口吻。

"真正有危险的，是那些有亲戚朋友在外面惹了麻烦的同学，他们会被当成人质。老谢诺·洛夫古德在《唱唱反调》上说话太坦率，他们就在卢娜回去过圣诞节时把她从火车上抓走了。"

"纳威，卢娜没事儿，我们看见她了——"

"是啊，我知道，她给我送了个信儿。"

CHAPTER TWENTY-NINE The Lost Diadem

From his pocket he pulled a golden coin, and Harry recognised it as one of the fake Galleons that Dumbledore's Army had used to send one another messages.

'These have been great,' said Neville, beaming at Hermione. 'The Carrows never rumbled how we were communicating, it drove them mad. We used to sneak out at night and put graffiti on the walls: *Dumbledore's Army, Still Recruiting*, stuff like that. Snape hated it.'

'You *used to?*' said Harry, who had noticed the past tense.

'Well, it got more difficult as time went on,' said Neville. 'We lost Luna at Christmas and Ginny never came back after Easter, and the three of us were sort of the leaders. The Carrows seemed to know I was behind a lot of it, so they started coming down on me hard, and then Michael Corner went and got caught releasing a first-year they'd chained up, and they tortured him pretty badly. That scared people off.'

'No kidding,' muttered Ron, as the passage began to slope upwards.

'Yeah, well, I couldn't ask people to go through what Michael did, so we dropped those kinds of stunts. But we were still fighting, doing underground stuff, right up until a couple of weeks ago. That's when they decided there was only one way to stop me, I suppose, and they went for Gran.'

'They *what?*' said Harry, Ron and Hermione together.

'Yeah,' said Neville, panting a little now, because the passage was climbing so steeply, 'well, you can see their thinking. It had worked really well, kidnapping kids to force their relatives to behave, I s'pose it was only a matter of time before they did it the other way round. Thing was,' he faced them, and Harry was astonished to see that he was grinning, 'they bit off a bit more than they could chew with Gran. Little old witch living alone, they probably thought they didn't need to send anyone particularly powerful. Anyway,' Neville laughed, 'Dawlish is still in St Mungo's and Gran's on the run. She sent me a letter,' he clapped a hand to the breast pocket of his robes, 'telling me she was proud of me, that I'm my parents' son, and to keep it up.'

'Cool,' said Ron.

'Yeah,' said Neville happily. 'Only thing was, once they realised they had no hold over me, they decided Hogwarts could do without me after all. I don't know whether they were planning to kill me or send me to Azkaban, either way, I knew it was time to disappear.'

第 29 章 失踪的冠冕

纳威从口袋里掏出一枚金币，哈利认出是邓布利多军用来互相传递消息的那种假加隆。

"这玩意儿太棒了。"纳威笑嘻嘻地对赫敏说，"卡罗兄妹一直没发现我们是用什么方式联系的，简直都要气疯了。那会儿我们经常半夜溜出去，在墙上涂写邓布利多军仍在招募新兵之类的话。斯内普恨死了。"

"那会儿？"哈利注意到他用的是过去时，问道。

"唉，后来形势越来越严峻了，"纳威说，"圣诞节时失去了卢娜，金妮复活节后再没回来，而当时我们三个相当于是领头的。卡罗兄妹似乎知道许多事情都是我在后面策划，开始狠狠地惩罚我，后来迈克尔·科纳去释放一个被他们锁住的一年级新生时不幸被发现，他们把他折磨得可惨了。这把许多人都吓跑了。"

"真不敢相信。"罗恩低声嘟囔道，这时通道开始变成上坡。

"是啊，我不能要求别人经受迈克尔的那种遭遇，所以就放弃了那些危险的做法。但我们仍在战斗，做一些地下工作，直到两个星期前。那时他们大概断定只有一个办法能让我收敛，就去找我奶奶了。"

"什么？"哈利、罗恩和赫敏同时问道。

"是啊。"纳威说，通道的坡度很陡，他说话微微带喘，"哼，可以看得出他们的想法。绑架孩子让亲属循规蹈矩，这一招一直很灵，我就猜到他们早晚会把这招儿反过来用。问题是，"他面对着他们，哈利惊讶地看到他竟然满脸笑容，"他们太不自量力了。奶奶，一个不起眼的老女巫，独自一人过活，他们大概以为用不着派个特别厉害的人去。结果，"纳威大笑起来，"德力士这会儿还在圣芒戈医院躺着呢，奶奶逃走了。她给我捎了封信，"他用手拍拍长袍胸前的口袋，"告诉我说她为我骄傲，还说我不愧是我父母的儿子，叫我坚持下去。"

"真了不起。"罗恩说。

"是啊。"纳威高兴地说，"问题是，他们意识到威胁不了我，就决定霍格沃茨可以不再有我这个人。我不知道他们是打算杀死我还是把我送到阿兹卡班，不管怎么样，我知道我应该消失了。"

CHAPTER TWENTY-NINE The Lost Diadem

'But,' said Ron, looking thoroughly confused, 'aren't – aren't we heading straight back into Hogwarts?'

''Course,' said Neville. 'You'll see. We're here.'

They turned a corner and there ahead of them was the end of the passage. Another short flight of steps led to a door just like the one hidden behind Ariana's portrait. Neville pushed it open and climbed through. As Harry followed, he heard Neville call out to unseen people: 'Look who it is! Didn't I tell you?'

As Harry emerged into the room beyond the passage, there were several screams and yells –

'HARRY!'

'It's Potter, it's POTTER!'

'Ron!'

'*Hermione!*'

He had a confused impression of coloured hangings, of lamps and many faces. The next moment, he, Ron and Hermione were engulfed, hugged, pounded on the back, their hair ruffled, their hands shaken, by what seemed to be more than twenty people: they might just have won a Quidditch final.

'OK, OK, calm down!' Neville called, and as the crowd backed away, Harry was able to take in their surroundings.

He did not recognise the room at all. It was enormous, and looked rather like the interior of a particularly sumptuous tree house, or perhaps a gigantic ship's cabin. Multicoloured hammocks were strung from the ceiling and from a balcony that ran around the dark wood-panelled and windowless walls, which were covered in bright tapestry hangings: Harry saw the gold Gryffindor lion, emblazoned on scarlet; the black badger of Hufflepuff, set against yellow, and the bronze eagle of Ravenclaw, on blue. The silver and green of Slytherin alone were absent. There were bulging bookcases, a few broomsticks propped against the walls, and in the corner, a large wooden-cased wireless.

'Where are we?'

'Room of Requirement, of course!' said Neville. 'Surpassed itself, hasn't it? The Carrows were chasing me, and I knew I had just one chance for a hideout: I managed to get through the door and this is what I found! Well, it

第29章 失踪的冠冕

"可是，"罗恩似乎完全被弄糊涂了，说，"我们——我们不是正往霍格沃茨去吗？"

"当然，"纳威说，"你会明白的。我们到了。"

他们拐过一个弯，前面就是通道的尽头。又是一道短短的石头台阶通向一扇门，跟阿利安娜肖像后面的那扇门一模一样。纳威推开门，爬了进去。哈利也跟了过去，只听纳威朝一些看不见的人喊道："快看谁来了！我怎么跟你们说的？"

哈利一钻进通道那头的房间，就听见好几个人尖叫、高喊起来——

"**哈利！**"

"是波特，是**波特**！"

"罗恩！"

"赫敏！"

五颜六色的帷帐，一盏盏灯，还有许多张脸，看得哈利眼花缭乱。接着，他、罗恩和赫敏就被大约二十多个人团团围住了。那些人搂抱他们，跟他们握手，捶他们的后背，揉他们的头发，就好像他们刚赢了一场魁地奇决赛。

"好了，好了，安静点儿！"纳威喊道，人群退去，哈利这才看清周围的情况。

哈利根本不认识这个房间。它大极了，看上去像一座特别考究的树屋，又像一艘大船的船舱。不同颜色的吊床吊在天花板上，吊在环绕着没有窗户的深色镶木墙壁的楼厅上，墙上挂满了各种鲜艳的挂毯，哈利看见了格兰芬多的金色狮子，在深红的底子上分外醒目，还有赫奇帕奇的黑獾，底色是黄的，以及拉文克劳的青铜老鹰，被蓝色衬托着，唯独不见斯莱特林的银色和绿色。房间里有塞得满满当当的书架，墙上靠着几把飞天扫帚，墙角还有一台大大的木头收音机。

"我们这是在哪儿？"

"有求必应屋呀，这还用问！"纳威说，"它超水平发挥了，是不是？当时卡罗兄妹在追我，我知道要找到藏身之处只有一个机会：还好，我终于进了门，发现了这里！当然啦，我刚来的时候这里可不是这样的，

CHAPTER TWENTY-NINE   The Lost Diadem

wasn't exactly like this when I arrived, it was a load smaller, there was only one hammock and just Gryffindor hangings. But it's expanded as more and more of the DA have arrived.'

'And the Carrows can't get in?' asked Harry, looking around for the door.

'No,' said Seamus Finnigan, whom Harry had not recognised until he spoke: Seamus's face was bruised and puffy. 'It's a proper hideout, as long as one of us stays in here, they can't get at us, the door won't open. It's all down to Neville. He really *gets* this room. You've got to ask it for *exactly* what you need – like, "I don't want any Carrow supporters to be able to get in" – and it'll do it for you! You've just got to make sure you close the loopholes! Neville's the man!'

'It's quite straightforward, really,' said Neville modestly. 'I'd been in here about a day and a half, and getting really hungry, and wishing I could get something to eat, and that's when the passage to the Hog's Head opened up. I went through it and met Aberforth. He's been providing us with food, because for some reason, that's the one thing the room doesn't really do.'

'Yeah, well, food's one of the five exceptions to Gamp's Law of Elemental Transfiguration,' said Ron, to general astonishment.

'So we've been hiding out here for nearly two weeks,' said Seamus, 'and it just makes more hammocks every time we need them, and it even sprouted a pretty good bathroom once girls started turning up –'

'– and thought they'd quite like to wash, yes,' supplied Lavender Brown, whom Harry had not noticed until that point. Now that he looked around properly, he recognised many familiar faces. Both Patil twins were there, as were Terry Boot, Ernie Macmillan, Anthony Goldstein and Michael Corner.

'Tell us what you've been up to, though,' said Ernie, 'there've been so many rumours, we've been trying to keep up with you on *Potterwatch*.' He pointed at the wireless. 'You didn't break into Gringotts?'

'They did!' said Neville. 'And the dragon's true too!'

There was a smattering of applause and a few whoops; Ron took a bow.

'What were you after?' asked Seamus eagerly.

Before any of them could parry the question with one of their own, Harry felt a terrible, scorching pain in the lightning scar. As he turned his back

第29章 失踪的冠冕

要小得多，而且只有一个吊床，只有格兰芬多的帷帐。后来随着越来越多的D.A.成员加入进来，它就拓展开了。"

"卡罗兄妹进不来吗？"哈利张望着寻找房门，问道。

"进不来。"西莫·斐尼甘说，他说话时哈利才认出他来。西莫的脸肿了，伤痕累累。"真是个理想的藏身之处，只要我们有一个人在这里，他们就进不来，门打不开。多亏了纳威。他真正知道如何利用这个房间。你得向它索要你真正需要的东西——比如，'我不希望卡罗兄妹的追随者能够进来'——它就会为你办到！不过你必须保证把漏洞堵上！纳威最拿手！"

"其实很简单。"纳威谦虚地说，"当时我在这里躲了一天半，饿得实在受不了，希望能有点吃的，结果通向猪头酒吧的通道就在那时候打开了。我穿过通道，遇到了阿不福思。从那以后，他一直在给我们提供食物，不知为什么，这房子居然做不到这一点。"

"是啊，食物是'甘普基本变形法则'的五大例外之一。"罗恩的话使大家吃惊不小。

"我们在这里躲了将近两个星期。"西莫说，"每当我们需要的时候，它就会变出更多的吊床，后来女生也开始加入，它还冒出了一间挺不错的盥洗室呢——"

"——因为女生很想洗洗涮涮，没错。"拉文德·布朗接着说，哈利这才注意到她。哈利仔细望望周围，认出了许多张熟悉的面孔。佩蒂尔孪生姐妹都在，还有泰瑞·布特、厄尼·麦克米兰、安东尼·戈德斯坦和迈克尔·科纳。

"快说说你们在干些什么吧。"厄尼说，"外面传闻很多，我们一直靠波特瞭望站跟踪你的最新消息。"他指指收音机，"你们没有真的闯进古灵阁吧？"

"闯进去了！"纳威说，"那条火龙也是真的！"

一阵掌声，几声欢呼，罗恩鞠了一躬。

"你们去那儿找什么？"西莫急切地问。

没等他们三个有谁打岔来回避这个问题，哈利就感到闪电形伤疤

CHAPTER TWENTY-NINE The Lost Diadem

hastily on the curious and delighted faces, the Room of Requirement vanished, and he was standing inside a ruined stone shack, and the rotting floorboards were ripped apart at his feet, a disinterred golden box lay open and empty beside the hole, and Voldemort's scream of fury vibrated inside his head.

With an enormous effort, he pulled out of Voldemort's mind again, back to where he stood, swaying, in the Room of Requirement, sweat pouring from his face and Ron holding him up.

'Are you all right, Harry?' Neville was saying. 'Want to sit down? I expect you're tired, aren't –?'

'No,' said Harry. He looked at Ron and Hermione, trying to tell them without words that Voldemort had just discovered the loss of one of the other Horcruxes. Time was running out fast: if Voldemort chose to visit Hogwarts next they would miss their chance.

'We need to get going,' he said, and their expressions told him that they understood.

'What are we going to do, then, Harry?' asked Seamus. 'What's the plan?'

'Plan?' repeated Harry. He was exercising all his will power to prevent himself succumbing again to Voldemort's rage: his scar was still burning. 'Well, there's something we – Ron, Hermione and I – need to do, and then we'll get out of here.'

Nobody was laughing or whooping any more. Neville looked confused.

'What d'you mean, "get out of here"?'

'We haven't come back to stay,' said Harry, rubbing his scar, trying to soothe the pain. 'There's something important we need to do –'

'What is it?'

'I – I can't tell you.'

There was a ripple of muttering at this: Neville's brows contracted.

'Why can't you tell us? It's something to do with fighting You-Know-Who, right?'

'Well, yeah –'

'Then we'll help you.'

The other members of Dumbledore's Army were nodding, some enthusiastically, others solemnly. A couple of them rose from their chairs to demonstrate their willingness for immediate action.

第29章 失踪的冠冕

一阵突如其来的剧烈灼痛。他赶紧转过身,背对着那些好奇而兴奋的面孔。有求必应屋突然消失了,他站在一座破败的石屋里,脚边腐烂的地板被扯开了,一只挖出来的金盒子放在洞边,盖子开着,里面是空的,伏地魔愤怒的叫声在他脑海里震荡。

他使出全部的力气,从伏地魔的思维中挣脱出来,重新回到了有求必应屋,微微摇晃着站在那里,脸上汗如雨下,罗恩在一旁扶着他。

"你还好吗,哈利?"是纳威在说话,"想坐下来吗?我猜你是累了,对吗——?"

"不。"哈利说。他看着罗恩和赫敏,试图无声地告诉他们伏地魔刚才又发现他的一个魂器不见了。剩下的时间不多了:如果伏地魔选择下一步就来霍格沃茨,他们就会错过机会。

"我们要走了。"他说,两个同伴的表情告诉他,他们已经心领神会。

"那我们怎么做呢,哈利?"西莫问,"计划是什么?"

"计划?"哈利重复了一遍。他用全部的意志力量阻止自己再次陷入伏地魔的暴怒:伤疤仍然火烧火燎地疼。"是这样,我们——罗恩、赫敏和我——需要做一件事,然后我们就离开这里。"

不再有人大笑或尖叫了。纳威显得很困惑。

"你说什么,'离开这里'?"

"我们这次不能久留,"哈利一边说,一边揉着伤疤缓解疼痛,"有一件重要的事需要我们去做——"

"什么事?"

"我——我不能告诉你们。"

听了这话,人们纷纷小声嘟囔起来,纳威的眉头皱在了一起。

"为什么不能告诉我们?是跟抗击神秘人有关的事,对吗?"

"嗯,是啊——"

"那我们可以帮助你呀。"

邓布利多军的其他成员也都点头称是,有的摩拳擦掌,有的表情严肃,有两个还从椅子上站了起来,表达了他们想立刻采取行动的愿望。

CHAPTER TWENTY-NINE   The Lost Diadem

'You don't understand.' Harry seemed to have said that a lot in the last few hours. 'We – we can't tell you. We've got to do it – alone.'

'Why?' asked Neville.

'Because …' In his desperation to start looking for the missing Horcrux, or at least to have a private discussion with Ron and Hermione about where they might commence their search, Harry found it difficult to gather his thoughts. His scar was still searing. 'Dumbledore left the three of us a job,' he said carefully, 'and we weren't supposed to tell – I mean, he wanted us to do it, just the three of us.'

'We're his Army,' said Neville. 'Dumbledore's Army. We were all in it together, we've been keeping it going while you three have been off on your own –'

'It hasn't exactly been a picnic, mate,' said Ron.

'I never said it had, but I don't see why you can't trust us. Everyone in this Room's been fighting and they've been driven in here because the Carrows were hunting them down. Everyone in here's proven they're loyal to Dumbledore – loyal to you.'

'Look,' Harry began, without knowing what he was going to say, but it did not matter: the tunnel door had just opened behind him.

'We got your message, Neville! Hello you three, I thought you must be here!'

It was Luna and Dean. Seamus gave a great roar of delight and ran to hug his best friend.

'Hi, everyone!' said Luna happily. 'Oh, it's great to be back!'

'Luna,' said Harry distractedly, 'what are you doing here? How did you –?'

'I sent for her,' said Neville, holding up the fake Galleon. 'I promised her and Ginny that if you turned up I'd let them know. We all thought that if you came back, it would mean revolution. That we were going to overthrow Snape and the Carrows.'

'Of course that's what it means,' said Luna brightly. 'Isn't it, Harry? We're going to fight them out of Hogwarts?'

'Listen,' said Harry, with a rising sense of panic, 'I'm sorry, but that's not what we came back for. There's something we've got to do, and then –'

'You're going to leave us in this mess?' demanded Michael Corner.

第29章 失踪的冠冕

"你们不了解,"在最近几个小时里,哈利似乎把这句话说了许多遍,"我们——我们不能说。我们必须——独立完成。"

"为什么?"纳威问。

"因为……"哈利急不可耐地想开始寻找失踪的魂器,或至少跟罗恩和赫敏单独谈谈从何处着手搜寻,但他发现自己很难集中思想。伤疤仍然火辣辣地疼。"邓布利多留给我们三个人一项任务,"他小心地斟词酌句,"我们不能告诉——我是说,他希望我们去完成,就我们三个人。"

"我们是他的军队,"纳威说,"邓布利多的军队。我们都是一起的,而且你们三个不在的时候,我们一直保留着这个组织——"

"伙计,我们也不是去野餐了呀。"罗恩说。

"我没那么说,但我不明白你们为什么不能信任我们。这房间里的每个人都一直在战斗,他们被逼到了这里,因为卡罗兄妹在追捕他们。事实证明,这里的每个人都是忠实于邓布利多——忠实于你的。"

"是这样……"哈利开了个头,但不知道该怎么往下说,不过没关系了,隧道的门在他身后打开了。

"我们接到你的消息了,纳威!嘿,你们三个,我就知道你们肯定在这儿!"

是卢娜和迪安。西莫欣喜若狂地大喊一声,冲过去拥抱他最好的朋友。

"嘿,大家好!"卢娜高兴地说,"噢,回来真是太好了!"

"卢娜,"哈利心烦意乱地说,"你来这里做什么?你是怎么——?"

"是我叫她来的,"纳威说着,举起那枚假加隆,"我向她和金妮保证过,你们一露面就通知她们。我们都以为你们回来就意味着造反,意味着推翻斯内普和卡罗兄妹。"

"当然是这样,"卢娜神采飞扬地说,"对吗,哈利?我们要把他们赶出霍格沃茨,对吗?"

"听着,"哈利说,心头越来越紧张,"对不起,但我们回来不是为了这个。我们必须做一件事,然后——"

"然后就离开,把我们留在这水深火热之中?"迈克尔·科纳质问。

CHAPTER TWENTY-NINE The Lost Diadem

'No!' said Ron. 'What we're doing will benefit everyone in the end, it's all about trying to get rid of You-Know-Who –'

'Then let us help!' said Neville angrily. 'We want to be a part of it!'

There was another noise behind them, and Harry turned. His heart seemed to fail: Ginny was now climbing through the hole in the wall, closely followed by Fred, George and Lee Jordan. Ginny gave Harry a radiant smile: he had forgotten, or had never fully appreciated, how beautiful she was, but he had never been less pleased to see her.

'Aberforth's getting a bit ratty,' said Fred, raising his hand in answer to several cries of greeting. 'He wants a kip, and his bar's turned into a railway station.'

Harry's mouth fell open. Right behind Lee Jordan came Harry's old girlfriend, Cho Chang. She smiled at him.

'I got the message,' she said, holding up her own fake Galleon, and she walked over to sit beside Michael Corner.

'So what's the plan, Harry?' said George.

'There isn't one,' said Harry, still disorientated by the sudden appearance of all these people, unable to take everything in while his scar was still burning so fiercely.

'Just going to make it up as we go along, are we? My favourite kind,' said Fred.

'You've got to stop this!' Harry told Neville. 'What did you call them all back for? This is insane –'

'We're fighting, aren't we?' said Dean, taking out his fake Galleon. 'The message said Harry was back, and we were going to fight! I'll have to get a wand, though –'

'You haven't got a *wand* –?' began Seamus.

Ron turned suddenly to Harry.

'Why can't they help?'

'What?'

'They can help.' He dropped his voice and said, so that none of them could hear but Hermione, who stood between them. 'We don't know where it is. We've got to find it fast. We don't have to tell them it's a Horcrux.'

Harry looked from Ron to Hermione, who murmured, 'I think Ron's

第29章 失踪的冠冕

"不!"罗恩说,"我们要做的事情最终会给大家带来好处,是关于怎样除掉神秘人——"

"那让我们帮忙呀!"纳威生气地说,"我们也想尽自己的一份力!"

身后又传来动静,哈利转身一看,心脏似乎停止了跳动:金妮正从墙上的洞口爬进来,后面紧跟着弗雷德、乔治和李·乔丹。金妮朝哈利绽开一个灿烂的微笑,哈利这才感觉到——也许以前从未充分认识到——金妮有多么美丽,但他从没像现在这样不乐意看见她。

"阿不福思有点冒火了,"弗雷德说,一边举起手回应几个人的大声问候,"他想睡觉,他的酒吧变成火车站了。"

哈利的嘴张得老大。哈利以前的女朋友秋·张出现在李·乔丹的身后,朝他嫣然一笑。

"我接到了消息。"秋·张举起她那枚假加隆说,然后走过去坐在迈克尔·科纳身边。

"快说吧,哈利,计划是什么?"乔治问。

"没有什么计划。"哈利说,这么多人突然出现仍使他感到晕头转向,而额头的伤疤还是火辣辣地剧痛,他一时有些应付不过来。

"边干边定计划,对吗?我最喜欢这样。"弗雷德说。

"你必须阻止他们!"哈利对纳威说,"你把他们都叫回来做什么?这是愚蠢的——"

"我们要战斗,不是吗?"迪安说着,把他那枚假加隆掏了出来,"消息说哈利回来了,我们要开始战斗!不过我得弄到一根魔杖——"

"你没有魔杖——?"西莫奇怪地问。

罗恩突然转向哈利。

"为什么不能让他们帮忙?"

"什么?"

"他们可以帮忙,"罗恩压低了声音,除了站在他和哈利中间的赫敏,谁也听不见他说话,"我们不知道那东西在哪儿,又必须赶快找到它。我们用不着说那是魂器。"

哈利的目光从罗恩移向了赫敏,她喃喃地说:"我认为罗恩说得对。

CHAPTER TWENTY-NINE The Lost Diadem

right. We don't even know what we're looking for, we need them.' And when Harry looked unconvinced, 'You don't have to do everything alone, Harry.'

Harry thought fast, his scar still prickling, his head threatening to split again. Dumbledore had warned him against telling anyone but Ron and Hermione about the Horcruxes. *Secrets and lies, that's how we grew up, and Albus ... he was a natural ...* Was he turning into Dumbledore, keeping his secrets clutched to his chest, afraid to trust? But Dumbledore had trusted Snape, and where had that led? To murder at the top of the highest tower ...

'All right,' he said quietly to the other two. 'OK,' he called to the Room at large, and all noise ceased: Fred and George, who had been cracking jokes for the benefit of those nearest, fell silent, and all of them looked alert, excited.

'There's something we need to find,' Harry said. 'Something – something that'll help us overthrow You-Know-Who. It's here at Hogwarts, but we don't know where. It might have belonged to Ravenclaw. Has anyone heard of an object like that? Has anyone ever come across something with her eagle on it, for instance?'

He looked hopefully towards the little group of Ravenclaws, to Padma, Michael, Terry and Cho, but it was Luna who answered, perched on the arm of Ginny's chair.

'Well, there's her lost diadem. I told you about it, remember, Harry? The lost diadem of Ravenclaw? Daddy's trying to duplicate it.'

'Yeah, but the lost diadem,' said Michael Corner, rolling his eyes, 'is *lost*, Luna. That's sort of the point.'

'When was it lost?' asked Harry.

'Centuries ago, they say,' said Cho, and Harry's heart sank. 'Professor Flitwick says the diadem vanished with Ravenclaw herself. People have looked, but,' she appealed to her fellow Ravenclaws, 'nobody's ever found a trace of it, have they?'

They all shook their heads.

'Sorry, but what *is* a diadem?' asked Ron.

'It's a kind of crown,' said Terry Boot. 'Ravenclaw's was supposed to have magical properties, enhance the wisdom of the wearer.'

'Yes, Daddy's Wrackspurt siphons –'

第29章 失踪的冠冕

我们连要找什么东西都不知道,我们需要他们。"看到哈利还在迟疑,她又说:"你用不着每件事都一个人去做,哈利。"

哈利在飞快地思索,伤疤仍在刺痛,脑袋又像是要裂开似的。邓布利多警告过他,魂器的事除了罗恩和赫敏谁也不能说。秘密和谎言,我们就是这样成长起来的,而阿不思……他天生如此……莫非他正在变成邓布利多,把秘密紧紧地锁在自己心里,不敢信任别人?可是邓布利多信任过斯内普,结果又怎么样呢?导致了高塔顶上的谋杀……

"好吧。"他轻声对两个同伴说,"听我说。"他对房间里所有的人宣布,嘈杂声立刻平息下来,正在给周围人说笑话的弗雷德和乔治也不作声了,一个个都显得警觉而兴奋。

"我们需要找到一件东西,"哈利说,"一件——一件能够帮助我们推翻神秘人的东西。就在霍格沃茨,但不知道具体在什么地方。它可能是属于拉文克劳的。有没有人听说过这样一件东西?有没有人碰到过,比如,上面带着拉文克劳老鹰标志的东西?"

他满怀希望地看着那一小群拉文克劳的学生,从帕德玛、迈克尔、泰瑞,到秋·张,不料却是坐在金妮椅子扶手上的卢娜做出了回答。

"对了,她那失踪的冠冕。我跟你说过的,记得吗,哈利?拉文克劳失踪的冠冕?我爸爸想复制来着。"

"对,可是那失踪的冠冕,"迈克尔·科纳翻着眼睛说,"已经失踪了呀,卢娜。这似乎才是关键呢。"

"它是什么时候失踪的?"哈利问。

"听说是许多世纪以前。"秋·张说,哈利的心往下一沉,"弗立维教授说冠冕是跟拉文克劳本人一起消失的。人们找过,可是,"她求援地看了看她的拉文克劳同学,"谁也没有发现一点线索,是不是?"

他们都点了点头。

"对不起,什么是冠冕呀?"罗恩问。

"就是一种王冠。"泰瑞·布特说,"据说拉文克劳的冠冕具有魔法特性,能增加佩戴者的智慧。"

"对,我爸爸的骚扰虻虹吸管——"

CHAPTER TWENTY-NINE The Lost Diadem

But Harry cut across Luna.

'And none of you have ever seen anything that looks like it?'

They all shook their heads again. Harry looked at Ron and Hermione and his own disappointment was mirrored back at him. An object that had been lost this long, and apparently without trace, did not seem like a good candidate for the Horcrux hidden in the castle ... before he could formulate a new question, however, Cho spoke again.

'If you'd like to see what the diadem's supposed to look like, I could take you up to our common room and show you, Harry? Ravenclaw's wearing it in her statue.'

Harry's scar scorched again: for a moment the Room of Requirement swam before him, and he saw instead the dark earth soaring beneath him and felt the great snake wrapped around his shoulders. Voldemort was flying again, whether to the underground lake or here, to the castle, he did not know: either way, there was hardly any time left.

'He's on the move,' he said quietly to Ron and Hermione. He glanced at Cho and then back at them. 'Listen, I know it's not much of a lead, but I'm going to go and look at this statue, at least find out what the diadem looks like. Wait for me here and keep, you know – the other one – safe.'

Cho had got to her feet, but Ginny said rather fiercely, 'No, Luna will take Harry, won't you, Luna?'

'Oooh, yes, I'd like to,' said Luna happily, and Cho sat down again, looking disappointed.

'How do we get out?' Harry asked Neville.

'Over here.'

He led Harry and Luna to a corner, where a small cupboard opened on to a steep staircase.

'It comes out somewhere different every day, so they've never been able to find it,' he said. 'Only trouble is, we never know exactly where we're going to end up when we go out. Be careful, Harry, they're always patrolling the corridors at night.'

'No problem,' said Harry. 'See you in a bit.'

He and Luna hurried up the staircase, which was long, lit by torches and turned corners in unexpected places. At last they reached what appeared to be solid wall.

第29章 失踪的冠冕

哈利打断了卢娜的话。

"你们谁也没见过类似的东西吗?"

他们又都摇了摇头。哈利看看罗恩和赫敏,在两人脸上看到了跟他同样的失望。一件失踪了这么久的东西,看样子又没有任何线索,似乎不太可能是那个藏在城堡里的魂器……然而,没等他提出新的问题,秋·张又说话了。

"如果你想看看冠冕是什么样子的,我可以带你上我们的公共休息室去指给你看,好吗,哈利?拉文克劳的塑像上戴着它呢。"

哈利的伤疤又开始烧灼:一时间,有求必应屋在他面前浮动起来,他看见漆黑的大地在他身下飞掠而过,感觉到巨蛇盘绕在他的肩头。伏地魔又在飞了,是飞向地下湖泊,还是飞向这里——霍格沃茨城堡,他不知道,但不管怎样,他们的时间不多了。

"他在路上。"哈利小声对罗恩和赫敏说。他扫了一眼秋·张,又转过来对着他们俩。"听我说,我知道这不算什么线索,但还是想去看看这座塑像,至少可以弄清冠冕是什么样子。你们在这里等我,要保证那一件的安全——你们知道。"

秋·张已经站起来了,但金妮很不客气地说:"不用,卢娜会带哈利去的,对吗,卢娜?"

"噢,对,我很乐意。"卢娜高兴地说,秋·张重新坐了下去,显得很失望。

"我们怎么出去?"哈利问纳威。

"就在这儿。"

他把哈利和卢娜领到一个墙角,一个小碗柜通向一道很陡的楼梯。

"它每天都通向不同的地方,所以一直没被他们发现。"他说,"唯一的麻烦是你永远不知道最后会从什么地方出来。小心点儿,哈利,他们夜里总在走廊上巡逻。"

"没问题,"哈利说,"待会儿见。"

他和卢娜匆匆走上楼梯,楼梯很长,映着火把的光,经常会有出其不意的拐弯。最后,他们像是来到了一堵结实的墙前。

CHAPTER TWENTY-NINE   The Lost Diadem

'Get under here,' Harry told Luna, pulling out the Invisibility Cloak and throwing it over both of them. He gave the wall a little push.

It melted away at his touch and they slipped outside: Harry glanced back and saw that it had resealed itself at once. They were standing in a dark corridor: Harry pulled Luna back into the shadows, fumbled in the pouch around his neck and took out the Marauder's Map. Holding it close to his nose, he searched and located his and Luna's dots at last.

'We're up on the fifth floor,' he whispered, watching Filch moving away from them, a corridor ahead. 'Come on, this way.'

They crept off.

Harry had prowled the castle at night many times before, but never had his heart hammered this fast, never had so much depended on his safe passage through the place. Through squares of moonlight upon the floor, past suits of armour whose helmets creaked at the sound of their soft footsteps, around corners beyond which who knew what lurked, Harry and Luna walked, checking the Marauder's Map whenever light permitted, twice pausing to allow a ghost to pass without drawing attention to themselves. He expected to encounter an obstacle at any moment; his worst fear was Peeves, and he strained his ears with every step to hear the first, telltale signs of the poltergeist's approach.

'This way, Harry,' breathed Luna, plucking his sleeve and pulling him towards a spiral staircase.

They climbed in tight, dizzying circles; Harry had never been up here before. At last they reached a door. There was no handle and no keyhole: nothing but a plain expanse of aged wood, and a bronze knocker in the shape of an eagle.

Luna reached out a pale hand, which looked eerie floating in mid-air, unconnected to arm or body. She knocked once, and in the silence it sounded to Harry like a cannon blast. At once the beak of the eagle opened, but instead of a bird's call, a soft, musical voice said, 'Which came first, the phoenix or the flame?'

'Hmm ... what do you think, Harry?' said Luna, looking thoughtful.

'What? Isn't there just a password?'

'Oh, no, you've got to answer a question,' said Luna.

第29章 失踪的冠冕

"钻进来。"哈利对卢娜说,一边抽出隐形衣披在两人身上。他轻轻推了推墙。

墙立刻融化了,他们闪身来到外面。哈利朝后看了一眼,发现墙又封死了。他们站在一道昏暗的走廊里,哈利拉着卢娜退到阴影里,从脖子上挂的皮袋里摸索着掏出活点地图,凑在鼻子跟前仔细搜寻,终于找到了他和卢娜的那两个小点。

"我们在六楼。"他小声说,一边注视着费尔奇在前面那道走廊上越走越远,"来,这边走。"

他们蹑手蹑脚地走开了。

哈利以前曾经多次在城堡夜游,但他的心从没跳得这么剧烈过,他深知自己这次行动关系重大,必须做到万无一失。哈利和卢娜走过地板上的一方方月光,经过一套套铠甲——轻轻的脚步声震得那些头盔嘎嘎作响,转过一个个弯——天知道那后面会躲藏着什么。每当光线稍亮一点,他们就查看一下活点地图,有两次还停下脚步让一个幽灵通过,以免引起他的注意。哈利时刻提防着遇到障碍,他最担心的是皮皮鬼,每走一步都竖起耳朵,倾听有没有那个恶作剧精灵走近的最轻微的声响。

"这边走,哈利。"卢娜轻声说,拉着哈利的衣袖把他拖向一道旋转楼梯。

他们转着令人头晕目眩的小圈往上走。哈利以前没有来过这上面。最后他们来到一扇门前。门上没有把手,也没有钥匙孔,只有一块上了年头的光光的木板,上面有个鹰状的青铜门环。

卢娜伸出一只苍白的手,这只手在半空中移动,没有胳膊和身体与之相连,显得十分怪异。她敲了一下门,在一片寂静中,哈利觉得这声音简直就像炮弹炸响。鹰嘴立刻张开了,但没有发出鸟叫,而是用一个温柔的、音乐般的声音说:"凤凰和火,先有哪一个?"

"嗯……你说呢,哈利?"卢娜若有所思地说。

"什么?不只是口令?"

"哦,是的,必须回答一个问题。"卢娜说。

CHAPTER TWENTY-NINE The Lost Diadem

'What if you get it wrong?'

'Well, you have to wait for somebody who gets it right,' said Luna. 'That way you learn, you see?'

'Yeah ... trouble is, we can't really afford to wait for anyone else, Luna.'

'No, I see what you mean,' said Luna seriously. 'Well then, I think the answer is that a circle has no beginning.'

'Well reasoned,' said the voice, and the door swung open.

The deserted Ravenclaw common room was a wide, circular room, airier than any Harry had ever seen at Hogwarts. Graceful arched windows punctuated the walls, which were hung with blue and bronze silks: by day, the Ravenclaws would have a spectacular view of the surrounding mountains. The ceiling was domed and painted with stars, which were echoed in the midnight-blue carpet. There were tables, chairs and bookcases, and in a niche opposite the door stood a tall statue of white marble.

Harry recognised Rowena Ravenclaw from the bust he had seen at Luna's house. The statue stood beside a door which led, he guessed, to dormitories above. He strode right up to the marble woman and she seemed to look back at him with a quizzical half smile on her face, beautiful yet slightly intimidating. A delicate-looking circlet had been reproduced in marble on top of her head. It was not unlike the tiara Fleur had worn at her wedding. There were tiny words etched into it. Harry stepped out from under the Cloak and climbed up on to Ravenclaw's plinth to read them.

'"*Wit beyond measure is man's greatest treasure.*"'

'Which makes you pretty skint, witless,' said a cackling voice.

Harry whirled round, slipped off the plinth and landed on the floor. The sloping-shouldered figure of Alecto Carrow was standing before him, and even as Harry raised his wand, she pressed a stubby forefinger to the skull and snake branded on her forearm.

第29章 失踪的冠冕

"如果答错了呢?"

"那就只好等着别人来答对了,"卢娜说,"这样可以学到知识,明白吗?"

"明白……问题是,我们可等不起别人呀,卢娜。"

"对,我懂你的意思。"卢娜认真地说,"好吧,我想答案是一个循环,没有起点。"

"有道理。"那声音说完,门就开了。

空无一人的拉文克劳公共休息室是一间很大的圆形屋子,比哈利在霍格沃茨看见的所有房间都更显空灵。墙上开着一扇扇雅致的拱形窗户,挂着蓝色和青铜色的丝绸:白天,拉文克劳的同学可以看见周围的群山,风景优美。天花板是穹顶的,上面绘着星星,下面深蓝色的地毯上也布满星星。房间里有桌椅、书架,门对面的壁龛里立着一尊高高的白色大理石塑像。

哈利认出这就是罗伊纳·拉文克劳,因为他在卢娜家看到过那座半身石像。塑像旁边是一扇门,他猜是通向上面的宿舍的。他大步走到大理石塑像跟前,那女人似乎在望着他,脸上带着若有似无的揶揄的微笑,美丽,却有些令人生畏。她的头顶上有一个用大理石复制的精致圆环,有点像芙蓉在婚礼上戴的那种头饰。圆环上刻着细小的文字。哈利从隐形衣下面钻出来,爬到拉文克劳塑像的底座上去读那些文字。

"过人的聪明才智是人类最大的财富。"

"会让你变成穷光蛋,傻瓜!"一个声音尖笑着说。

哈利猛一转身,从底座上滑下来摔在了地上,他面前站着削肩膀的阿莱克托·卡罗。就在哈利举起魔杖的一刹那,她用短粗的食指按住了烙在她小臂上的骷髅和蛇。

CHAPTER THIRTY

The Sacking of Severus Snape

The moment her finger touched the Mark, Harry's scar burned savagely, the starry room vanished from sight, and he was standing upon an outcrop of rock beneath a cliff, and the sea was washing around him and there was triumph in his heart – *they have the boy*.

A loud *bang* brought Harry back to where he stood: disorientated, he raised his wand, but the witch before him was already falling forwards; she hit the ground so hard that the glass in the bookcases tinkled.

'I've never Stunned anyone except in our DA lessons,' said Luna, sounding mildly interested. 'That was noisier than I thought it would be.'

And sure enough, the ceiling had begun to tremble. Scurrying, echoing footsteps were growing louder from behind the door leading to the dormitories: Luna's spell had woken Ravenclaws sleeping above.

'Luna, where are you? I need to get under the Cloak!'

Luna's feet appeared out of nowhere; he hurried to her side and she let the Cloak fall back over them as the door opened and a stream of Ravenclaws, all in their nightclothes, flooded into the common room. There were gasps and cries of surprise as they saw Alecto lying there unconscious. Slowly, they shuffled in around her, a savage beast that might wake at any moment and attack them. Then one brave little first-year darted up to her and prodded her backside with his big toe.

'I think she might be dead!' he shouted with delight.

'Oh, look,' whispered Luna happily, as the Ravenclaws crowded in around Alecto. 'They're pleased!'

'Yeah ... great ...'

第 30 章

西弗勒斯·斯内普被赶跑

阿莱克托的手指一碰到黑魔标记，哈利的伤疤就如着了火一般剧痛起来，群星密布的房间从他眼前消失了。他站在悬崖下一块突出的岩石上，周围海浪汹涌，内心一阵狂喜——他们抓住了那男孩。

砰的一声巨响，哈利又回到他置身的地方，他茫然地举起魔杖，可是面前的女巫已经向前扑倒。她重重地摔倒在地，震得书柜的玻璃叮当作响。

"我以前只在 D.A. 训练时练习过昏迷咒，"卢娜饶有兴趣地说，"没想到会发出这么大的声音。"

果然，天花板开始颤抖。通向宿舍的门后面传来越来越响的奔跑声：卢娜的咒语惊醒了睡在上面的拉文克劳学生。

"卢娜，你在哪儿？我需要钻到隐形衣下面！"

卢娜的脚突然出现了，哈利赶紧跑到她身边。她刚把隐形衣披到两人身上，门就开了，一群穿着睡衣的拉文克劳学生拥进了公共休息室。他们看见阿莱克托不省人事地躺在地上，都倒抽了一口冷气，发出惊讶的尖叫。慢慢地，他们蹭过去围在她身边，看着这头随时都会醒来、向他们发起进攻的猛兽。然后，一个勇敢的一年级新生冲过去用大脚趾顶了顶她的屁股。

"我想她可能死了！"他高兴地喊了起来。

"哦，看，"卢娜看见拉文克劳的同学们把阿莱克托团团围住，开心地小声说，"他们多高兴呀！"

"是啊……太棒了……"

CHAPTER THIRTY   The Sacking of Severus Snape

Harry closed his eyes, and as his scar throbbed he chose to sink again into Voldemort's mind ... he was moving along the tunnel into the first cave ... he had chosen to make sure of the locket before coming ... but that would not take him long ...

There was a rap on the common-room door and every Ravenclaw froze. From the other side, Harry heard the soft, musical voice that issued from the eagle doorknocker: 'Where do vanished objects go?'

'I dunno, do I? Shut it!' snarled an uncouth voice that Harry knew was that of the Carrow brother, Amycus. 'Alecto? *Alecto?* Are you there? Have you got him? Open the door!'

The Ravenclaws were whispering amongst themselves, terrified. Then, without warning, there came a series of loud bangs, as though somebody was firing a gun into the door.

'*ALECTO!* If he comes, and we haven't got Potter – d'you want to go the same way as the Malfoys? ANSWER ME!' Amycus bellowed, shaking the door for all he was worth, but still, it did not open. The Ravenclaws were all backing away, and some of the most frightened began scampering back up the staircase to their beds. Then, just as Harry was wondering whether he ought not to blast open the door and Stun Amycus before the Death Eater could do anything else, a second, most familiar voice rang out beyond the door.

'May I ask what you are doing, Professor Carrow?'

'Trying – to get – through this damned – door!' shouted Amycus. 'Go and get Flitwick! Get him to open it, now!'

'But isn't your sister in there?' asked Professor McGonagall. 'Didn't Professor Flitwick let her in, earlier this evening, at your urgent request? Perhaps she could open the door for you? Then you needn't wake up half the castle.'

'She ain't answering, you old besom! *You* open it! Garn! Do it, now!'

'Certainly, if you wish it,' said Professor McGonagall, with awful coldness. There was a genteel tap of the knocker and the musical voice asked, again, 'Where do vanished objects go?'

'Into non-being, which is to say, everything,' replied Professor McGonagall.

'Nicely phrased,' replied the eagle doorknocker, and the door swung open.

第30章 西弗勒斯·斯内普被赶跑

哈利闭上眼睛,伤疤突突地跳疼,他主动地再次陷入了伏地魔的思想……他行走在通往第一个山洞的地道里……他决定先检查了挂坠盒再过来……那也不会要多长时间……

公共休息室门外传来敲门声,拉文克劳的同学们都怔住了。哈利听见门外的鹰形门环又发出那音乐般的温柔声音:"消失的东西去了哪儿?"

"不知道!你给我闭嘴!"一个粗鲁的声音吼道,哈利知道是阿莱克托的哥哥——阿米库斯。"阿莱克托?阿莱克托?你在吗?你抓住他了吗?快开门!"

拉文克劳的同学们都吓坏了,聚在一起窃窃私语。随即,突如其来地传来一连串巨响,好像有人在朝门开枪。

"**阿莱克托**!如果他来了,我们却没有抓住波特——你想遭到跟马尔福一家同样的下场吗?**快回答我**!"阿米库斯大声咆哮着,一边拼命推搡着门,可是门没有开。拉文克劳的同学们纷纷后退,最害怕的几个开始匆匆跑回楼上的卧室。哈利犹豫着是不是应该把门炸开,击昏阿米库斯,不让他再做别的。就在这时,门外又响起一个极为熟悉的声音。

"请问你在做什么呢,卡罗教授?"

"我想——穿过——这扇该死的——门!"阿米库斯喊道,"去把弗立维叫来!叫他来开门,快!"

"但你妹妹不是在里面吗?"麦格教授问,"今天晚上早些时候,弗立维不是在你的紧急请求下放你妹妹进去了吗?或许她可以替你开门?你就用不着把半个城堡的人都吵醒了。"

"她不应声儿,你这个老娘们!你给我把门打开!快!快打开!"

"没问题,如果你愿意这样。"麦格教授说,声音里透着可怕的寒意。只听门环轻轻响了一下,那个音乐般的声音又问道:"消失的东西去了哪儿?"

"化为虚无,也就是说,化为万物。"麦格教授回答。

"说得好。"鹰形门环说,门一下子打开了。

CHAPTER THIRTY   The Sacking of Severus Snape

The few Ravenclaws who had remained behind sprinted for the stairs as Amycus burst over the threshold, brandishing his wand. Hunched like his sister, he had a pallid, doughy face and tiny eyes, which fell at once on Alecto, sprawled motionless on the floor. He let out a yell of fury and fear.

'What've they done, the little whelps?' he screamed. 'I'll Cruciate the lot of 'em 'til they tell me who did it – and what's the Dark Lord going to say?' he shrieked, standing over his sister and smacking himself on the forehead with his fist. 'We haven't got him, and they've gorn and killed her!'

'She's only Stunned,' said Professor McGonagall impatiently, who had stooped down to examine Alecto. 'She'll be perfectly all right.'

'No she bludgering well won't!' bellowed Amycus. 'Not after the Dark Lord gets hold of her! She's gorn and sent for him, I felt me Mark burn, and he thinks we've got Potter!'

'"Got Potter"?' said Professor McGonagall sharply. 'What do you mean, "got Potter"?'

'He told us Potter might try and get inside Ravenclaw Tower, and to send for him if we caught him!'

'Why would Harry Potter try to get inside Ravenclaw Tower? Potter belongs in my house!'

Beneath the disbelief and anger, Harry heard a little strain of pride in her voice, and affection for Minerva McGonagall gushed up inside him.

'We was told he might come in here!' said Carrow. 'I dunno why, do I?'

Professor McGonagall stood up and her beady eyes swept the room. Twice they passed right over the place where Harry and Luna stood.

'We can push it off on the kids,' said Amycus, his pig-like face suddenly crafty. 'Yeah, that's what we'll do. We'll say Alecto was ambushed by the kids, them kids up there,' he looked up at the starry ceiling towards the dormitories, 'and we'll say they forced her to press her Mark, and that's why he got a false alarm ... he can punish them. Couple of kids more or less, what's the difference?'

'Only the difference between truth and lies, courage and cowardice,' said Professor McGonagall, who had turned pale, 'a difference, in short, which you and your sister seem unable to appreciate. But let me make one thing very clear. You are not going to pass off your many ineptitudes on the

第30章 西弗勒斯·斯内普被赶跑

阿米库斯挥舞着魔杖冲进门来，落在后面的几个拉文克劳同学仓皇地朝楼梯奔去。阿米库斯和他妹妹一样是个驼背，长着一张苍白的面团般的脸和一双小绿豆眼。这双眼睛立刻看见了瘫在地板上一动不动的阿莱克托。他发出一声愤怒和惊恐的喊叫。

"他们干了什么？这帮小崽子！"他嚷道，"我要给他们念钻心咒，让他们告诉我是谁干的——黑魔王会怎么说呢？"阿米库斯站在他妹妹跟前，用拳头砸着自己的脑门，尖声大叫，"我们没有抓到那小子，他们竟然把我妹妹给杀了！"

"她只是被击昏了，"麦格教授蹲下身查看了阿莱克托一番，不耐烦地说，"她不会有什么事的。"

"呸，她的麻烦大了！"阿米库斯咆哮道，"被黑魔王抓住她就完了！她竟然把他给召来了，我感到我的标记烧起来了，黑魔王还以为我们抓住了波特呢！"

"'抓住了波特'？"麦格教授警觉地说，"你说什么，'抓住了波特'？"

"他告诉我们波特可能会闯进拉文克劳塔楼，要我们一抓住波特就把他召来！"

"哈利·波特为什么要闯进拉文克劳塔楼？波特是我们学院的！"

在麦格教授疑惑和愤怒的声音里，哈利听出了一丝骄傲的口气，他内心立刻涌起对米勒娃·麦格的爱戴。

"他就告诉我们波特会来这里！"卡罗说，"我哪知道是怎么回事？"

麦格教授站起身，锐利的眼睛在房间里扫视着，目光两次从哈利和卢娜站的地方扫过。

"我们可以推到那些毛孩子身上，"阿米库斯说，那张胖猪脸突然变得狡猾起来，"对呀，就这么做。我们就说阿莱克托遭到毛孩子的偷袭，就是住在上面的那些毛孩子，"他抬头看向宿舍的位置，望着布满星星的天花板，"我们就说是他们逼着她按了标记，让黑魔王得到了假情报……他可以惩罚他们。多几个毛孩子少几个毛孩子又有什么差别？"

"这是事实与谎言、勇气与懦弱之间的差别！"麦格教授脸色变白了，说道，"总之，看来这是你和你妹妹不能理解的一种差别。但有一

CHAPTER THIRTY   The Sacking of Severus Snape

students of Hogwarts. I shall not permit it.'

'Excuse me?'

Amycus moved forwards until he was offensively close to Professor McGonagall, his face within inches of hers. She refused to back away, but looked down at him as if he were something disgusting she had found stuck to a lavatory seat.

'It's not a case of what *you'll* permit, Minerva McGonagall. Your time's over. It's us what's in charge here now, and you'll back me up or you'll pay the price.'

And he spat in her face.

Harry pulled the Cloak off himself, raised his wand and said, 'You shouldn't have done that.'

As Amycus spun round, Harry shouted, '*Crucio!*'

The Death Eater was lifted off his feet. He writhed through the air like a drowning man, thrashing and howling in pain, and then, with a crunch and a shattering of glass, he smashed into the front of a bookcase and crumpled, insensible, to the floor.

'I see what Bellatrix meant,' said Harry, the blood thundering through his brain, 'you need to really mean it.'

'Potter!' whispered Professor McGonagall, clutching her heart. 'Potter – you're here! What –? How –?' She struggled to pull herself together. 'Potter, that was foolish!'

'He spat at you,' said Harry.

'Potter, I – that was very – very *gallant* of you – but don't you realise –?'

'Yeah, I do,' Harry assured her. Somehow her panic steadied him. 'Professor McGonagall, Voldemort's on the way.'

'Oh, are we allowed to say the name now?' asked Luna with an air of interest, pulling off the Invisibility Cloak. This appearance of a second outlaw seemed to overwhelm Professor McGonagall, who staggered backwards and fell into a nearby chair, clutching at the neck of her old tartan dressing gown.

'I don't think it makes any difference what we call him,' Harry told Luna, 'he already knows where I am.'

In a distant part of Harry's brain, that part connected to the angry,

点我必须说明白:绝不能把你们的许多愚蠢行为嫁祸到霍格沃茨的学生身上。我不允许。"

"你说什么?"

阿米库斯向前逼近,一副咄咄逼人的样子,他的脸离麦格教授只差几寸。麦格教授没有退缩,而是以一种鄙夷的目光看着他,就好像他是沾在马桶圈上的令人恶心的东西。

"这可不是你允许不允许的事,米勒娃·麦格。你的日子结束了。现在是我们在这儿掌权,你必须支持我,不然你吃不了兜着走。"

他朝麦格教授脸上啐了一口。

哈利一把扯掉身上的隐形衣,举起魔杖说道:"你不该这样做!"就在阿米库斯转过身来的一刹那,哈利大喊一声:"钻心剜骨!"

食死徒一下子悬了起来,像个落水者一样在空中扭动翻转,痛苦地扑打、号叫。随着哗啦一声巨响和碎玻璃溅落的声音,他砸在一个书架的门上,然后不省人事地摔倒在地。

"我明白贝拉特里克斯的意思了,"哈利说,血液在脑子里涌动,轰轰作响,"你需要真正下得了狠心才行。"

"波特!"麦格教授抓住自己的胸口,小声说道,"波特——你在这儿!真——怎么会——?"她努力使自己镇静下来,"波特,这太愚蠢了!"

"他朝你吐唾沫。"哈利说。

"波特,我——你真是——真是见义勇为——但你难道没有想到——?"

"噢,我知道。"哈利安慰她道。不知怎的,她的紧张倒让他镇定了下来。"麦格教授,伏地魔要来了。"

"怎么,现在可以说这个名字了?"卢娜兴趣盎然地问,一把扯掉了隐形衣。看到又出现一个在逃的学生,麦格教授再也承受不住了,她跟跟跄跄地后退几步,跌坐在近旁的一把椅子上,紧紧地揪住她那旧格子呢晨衣的领口。

"我想,我们叫他什么已经没有多大关系了,"哈利对卢娜说,"他已经知道我在哪儿了。"

在哈利脑海里某个遥远的角落——那个角落连接着烧灼、暴怒的

CHAPTER THIRTY The Sacking of Severus Snape

burning scar, he could see Voldemort sailing fast over the dark lake in the ghostly green boat ... he had nearly reached the island where the stone basin stood ...

'You must flee,' whispered Professor McGonagall. 'Now, Potter, as quickly as you can!'

'I can't,' said Harry. 'There's something I need to do. Professor, do you know where the diadem of Ravenclaw is?'

'The d – diadem of Ravenclaw? Of course not – hasn't it been lost for centuries?' She sat up a little straighter. 'Potter, it was madness, utter madness, for you to enter this castle –'

'I had to,' said Harry. 'Professor, there's something hidden here that I'm supposed to find, and it *could* be the diadem – if I could just speak to Professor Flitwick –'

There was a sound of movement, of clinking glass: Amycus was coming round. Before Harry or Luna could act, Professor McGonagall rose to her feet, pointed her wand at the groggy Death Eater and said, '*Imperio.*'

Amycus got up, walked over to his sister, picked up her wand, then shuffled obediently to Professor McGonagall and handed it over along with his own. Then he lay down on the floor beside Alecto. Professor McGonagall waved her wand again, and a length of shimmering silver rope appeared out of thin air and snaked around the Carrows, binding them tightly together.

'Potter,' said Professor McGonagall, turning to face him again with superb indifference to the Carrows' predicament, 'if He Who Must Not Be Named does indeed know that you are here –'

As she said it, a wrath that was like physical pain blazed through Harry, setting his scar on fire, and for a second he looked down upon a basin whose potion had turned clear, and saw that no golden locket lay safe beneath the surface –

'Potter, are you all right?' said a voice, and Harry came back: he was clutching Luna's shoulder to steady himself.

'Time's running out, Voldemort's getting nearer. Professor, I'm acting on Dumbledore's orders, I must find what he wanted me to find! But we've got to get the students out while I'm searching the castle – it's me Voldemort wants, but he won't care about killing a few more or less, not now –' *Not now*

第30章 西弗勒斯·斯内普被赶跑

伤疤,他看见伏地魔坐着阴森可怖的绿船,在漆黑的湖面上飞快地掠行……他很快就要到达石盆所在的小岛了……

"你必须逃走,"麦格教授轻声说,"快,波特,越快越好!"

"我不能,"哈利说,"我还有一件事情要做。教授,你知道拉文克劳的冠冕在哪儿吗?"

"拉——拉文克劳的冠冕?我怎么会知道——不是失踪好多个世纪了吗?"她微微直起些身子,"波特,你进入这座城堡真是愚蠢,太愚蠢了——"

"我必须这么做,"哈利说,"教授,有一件东西藏在这里,我要把它找到,可能是那个冠冕——要是我能跟弗立维教授说说——"

突然传来动静和碎玻璃的碰撞声:阿米库斯醒过来了。没等哈利或卢娜做出反应,麦格教授忽地站起,用魔杖指着那个摇摇晃晃的食死徒,说了声:"魂魄出窍。"

阿米库斯爬起来走到他妹妹身边,捡起她的魔杖,老老实实地拖着脚步走到麦格教授面前,连同自己的魔杖一起递了过来,然后在地板上阿莱克托的身边躺下了。麦格教授又一挥魔杖,凭空变出一根银光闪烁的绳子,像蛇一般绕过卡罗兄妹,把他们俩结结实实地捆在了一起。

"波特,"麦格教授对卡罗兄妹的处境完全不予理会,又把脸转向哈利说,"如果那个连名字都不能提的人真的知道你在这里——"

她的话还没说完,一阵剧痛般的怒火冲上哈利的头顶,使他的伤疤如同着了火一样。刹那间,他低头看见一只石盆,里面的药水已经变清,他看到药水下面的金挂坠盒不见了——

"波特,你没事吧?"一个声音说,哈利回过神来:他正抓住卢娜的肩膀稳住身子。

"时间不多了,伏地魔越来越近了。教授,我是在按照邓布利多的吩咐行动,我必须找到他要我找的东西!不过当我在城堡里搜寻的时候,必须把同学们都疏散出去——伏地魔要的是我,但他是不会介意多杀几个人的,尤其现在——"尤其现在他已经知道我在偷袭魂器了,

CHAPTER THIRTY   The Sacking of Severus Snape

he knows I'm attacking Horcruxes, Harry finished the sentence in his head.

'You're acting on *Dumbledore's* orders?' she repeated, with a look of dawning wonder. Then she drew herself up to her fullest height.

'We shall secure the school against He Who Must Not Be Named while you search for this – this object.'

'Is that possible?'

'I think so,' said Professor McGonagall drily, 'we teachers are rather good at magic, you know. I am sure we will be able to hold him off for a while if we all put our best efforts into it. Of course, something will have to be done about Professor Snape –'

'Let me –'

'– and if Hogwarts is about to enter a state of siege, with the Dark Lord at the gates, it would indeed be advisable to take as many innocent people out of the way as possible. With the Floo Network under observation and Apparition impossible within the grounds –'

'There's a way,' said Harry quickly, and he explained about the passageway leading into the Hog's Head.

'Potter, we're talking about hundreds of students –'

'I know, Professor, but if Voldemort and the Death Eaters are concentrating on the school boundaries they won't be interested in anyone who's Disapparating out of the Hog's Head.'

'There's something in that,' she agreed. She pointed her wand at the Carrows, and a silver net fell upon their bound bodies, tied itself around them and hoisted them into the air, where they dangled beneath the blue and gold ceiling, like two large, ugly sea creatures. 'Come. We must alert the other Heads of House. You'd better put that Cloak back on.'

She marched towards the door, and as she did so she raised her wand. From the tip burst three silver cats with spectacle markings around their eyes. The Patronuses ran sleekly ahead, filling the spiral staircase with silvery lights, as Professor McGonagall, Harry and Luna hurried back down.

Along the corridors they raced, and one by one the Patronuses left them; Professor McGonagall's tartan dressing gown rustled over the floor and Harry and Luna jogged behind her under the Cloak.

They had descended two more floors when another set of quiet footsteps joined theirs. Harry, whose scar was still prickling, heard them first: he felt in the pouch around his neck for the Marauder's Map, but before he could take

第30章 西弗勒斯·斯内普被赶跑

哈利在脑子里说完了这句话。

"你在按照邓布利多的吩咐行动?"麦格教授重复了一句,脸上慢慢露出惊异的神情,然后直直地站了起来。

"你搜寻这件——这件东西的时候,我们会抵挡那个连名字都不能提的人,保护学校的安全。"

"有可能吗?"

"我认为有,"麦格教授淡淡地说,"你知道,我们教师都很擅长魔法。如果大家全力以赴,我相信肯定能把他拖住一段时间。当然啦,必须对斯内普教授采取一点行动——"

"让我——"

"——如果黑魔头就在门口,霍格沃茨要被围攻,确实需要把无辜者尽可能地转移出去。飞路网受到了监视,学校里又不能幻影移形——"

"有一条路。"哈利立刻说道,他仔细讲了通向猪头酒吧的那条通道。

"波特,我们说的是成百上千个学生——"

"我知道,教授,但如果伏地魔和食死徒都把注意力放在学校边上,他们不会关心有谁从猪头酒吧幻影移形的。"

"这倒有点道理。"麦格教授表示赞同。她用魔杖一指卡罗兄妹,一张银色的网立刻落到两人被捆绑的身体上,把他们兜起来吊到了半空,像两只巨大而丑陋的海底生物一样悬挂在蓝底缀金的天花板下。"走吧,我们必须叫醒其他院长。你最好把那隐形衣穿上。"

她大步朝门口走去,一边举起魔杖,杖尖蹿出三只银色的猫,它们的眼睛周围都有眼镜形状的斑纹。三个守护神敏捷地往前跑去,只见旋转楼梯上洒满了银光,麦格教授、哈利和卢娜匆匆奔下楼。

他们跑过一道道走廊,守护神一个个离开了。麦格教授的格子呢晨衣在地板上沙沙作响,隐形衣下的哈利和卢娜小跑着跟在后面。

又下了两层楼,突然多了一个人轻轻的脚步声。是哈利先听到的,他的伤疤仍在刺痛。他在脖子上的皮袋里摸索活点地图,可没等他掏

CHAPTER THIRTY   The Sacking of Severus Snape

it out, McGonagall, too, seemed to become aware of their company. She halted, raised her wand ready to duel, and said, 'Who's there?'

'It is I,' said a low voice.

From behind a suit of armour stepped Severus Snape.

Hatred boiled up in Harry at the sight of him: he had forgotten the details of Snape's appearance in the magnitude of his crimes, forgotten how his greasy, black hair hung in curtains around his thin face, how his black eyes had a dead, cold look. He was not wearing nightclothes, but was dressed in his usual black cloak and he, too, was holding his wand ready for a fight.

'Where are the Carrows?' he asked quietly.

'Wherever you told them to be, I expect, Severus,' said Professor McGonagall.

Snape stepped nearer, and his eyes flitted over Professor McGonagall into the air around her, as if he knew that Harry was there. Harry held his wand up too, ready to attack.

'I was under the impression,' said Snape, 'that Alecto had apprehended an intruder.'

'Really?' said Professor McGonagall. 'And what gave you that impression?'

Snape made a slight flexing movement of his left arm, where the Dark Mark was branded into his skin.

'Oh, but naturally,' said Professor McGonagall. 'You Death Eaters have your own private means of communication, I forgot.'

Snape pretended not to have heard her. His eyes were still probing the air all about her and he was moving gradually closer, with an air of hardly noticing what he was doing.

'I did not know that it was your night to patrol the corridors, Minerva.'

'You have some objection?'

'I wonder what could have brought you out of your bed at this late hour?'

'I thought I heard a disturbance,' said Professor McGonagall.

'Really? But all seems calm.'

Snape looked into her eyes.

'Have you seen Harry Potter, Minerva? Because if you have, I must insist —'

Professor McGonagall moved faster than Harry could have believed: her wand slashed through the air and for a split second Harry thought that

第30章 西弗勒斯·斯内普被赶跑

出来,麦格教授似乎也发现了有人。她停住脚步,举起魔杖准备战斗,一边问道:"谁在那儿?"

"是我。"一个低沉的声音说。

从一套铠甲后面,走出了西弗勒斯·斯内普。

哈利一看见他,心里就冒出仇恨的怒火。哈利只记得斯内普罪大恶极,几乎忘记了他的具体模样,忘记了他油腻腻的黑发像窗帘一样耷拉在枯瘦的面孔周围,忘记了他那双黑眼睛有着怎样冷酷无情的目光。他没穿睡衣,而是穿着平常的黑色斗篷,手里也举着魔杖准备战斗。

"卡罗兄妹呢?"他轻声问。

"大概在你叫他们去的地方吧,西弗勒斯。"麦格教授说。

斯内普走近前来,目光从麦格教授周围迅速掠过,似乎知道哈利就在那里。哈利也举起了魔杖,随时准备出击。

"我有种感觉,"斯内普说,"阿莱克托抓到了一个闯入者。"

"真的吗?"麦格教授说,"这种感觉从何而来?"

斯内普微微活动了一下左臂,那里的皮肤上烙着黑魔标记。

"哦,当然,"麦格教授说,"我忘记了,你们食死徒有自己的秘密联系方式。"

斯内普假装没有听见麦格教授的话,目光仍然在她周围的空气里搜寻,同时一点点地向她逼近,而看他的神情,仿佛并没发觉自己在这么做。

"我记得今天夜里不该是你在走廊里巡逻,米勒娃。"

"你有意见?"

"我只是奇怪,这么晚了,是什么让你从床上爬起来的?"

"我好像听到了动静。"麦格教授说。

"真的吗?似乎到处都很安静呀。"

斯内普直视着她的眼睛。

"你看见哈利·波特了吗,米勒娃?如果你看见了,我必须强调——"

麦格教授出手之快,简直令哈利难以相信。她的魔杖在空中嗖嗖挥砍,哈利一时以为斯内普肯定会神志不清地瘫倒在地,不料他的铁

CHAPTER THIRTY The Sacking of Severus Snape

Snape must crumple, unconscious, but the swiftness of his Shield Charm was such that McGonagall was thrown off balance. She brandished her wand at a torch on the wall and it flew out of its bracket: Harry, about to curse Snape, was forced to pull Luna out of the way of the descending flames, which became a ring of fire that filled the corridor and flew like a lasso at Snape –

Then it was no longer fire, but a great, black serpent that McGonagall blasted to smoke, which reformed and solidified in seconds to become a swarm of pursuing daggers: Snape avoided them only by forcing the suit of armour in front of him, and with echoing clangs the daggers sank, one after another, into its breast –

'Minerva!' said a squeaky voice, and looking behind him, still shielding Luna from flying spells, Harry saw Professors Flitwick and Sprout sprinting up the corridor towards them in their nightclothes, with the enormous Professor Slughorn panting along at the rear.

'No!' squealed Flitwick, raising his wand. 'You'll do no more murder at Hogwarts!'

Flitwick's spell hit the suit of armour behind which Snape had taken shelter: with a clatter it came to life. Snape struggled free of the crushing arms and sent it flying back towards his attackers: Harry and Luna had to dive sideways to avoid it as it smashed into the wall and shattered. When Harry looked up again, Snape was in full flight, McGonagall, Flitwick and Sprout all thundering after him: Snape hurtled through a classroom door and, moments later, Harry heard McGonagall cry, 'coward! *COWARD!*'

'What's happened, what's happened?' asked Luna.

Harry dragged her to her feet and they raced along the corridor, trailing the Invisibility Cloak behind them, into the deserted classroom where Professors McGonagall, Flitwick and Sprout were standing at a smashed window.

'He jumped,' said Professor McGonagall, as Harry and Luna ran into the room.

'You mean he's *dead*?' Harry sprinted to the window, ignoring Flitwick and Sprout's yells of shock at his sudden appearance.

'No, he's not dead,' said McGonagall bitterly. 'Unlike Dumbledore, he was still carrying a wand ... and he seems to have learned a few tricks from his master.'

With a tingle of horror, Harry saw in the distance a huge, bat-like shape flying through the darkness towards the perimeter wall.

第30章 西弗勒斯·斯内普被赶跑

甲咒实在太敏捷,震得麦格失去了平衡。她朝墙上的一支火把挥舞着魔杖,火把立刻从支架上飞了出来。正准备给斯内普念咒的哈利只好赶紧把卢娜拖到一边,躲避落下来的火焰。火焰变成一个火环,占满整个走廊,像绳套一样朝斯内普飞去——

接着它不再是火,而是一条巨大的黑蛇,麦格把它炸成了黑烟。几秒钟内,黑烟变形、凝固,成为密密麻麻的匕首追了过去。斯内普只好把那套铠甲挡在身前,一把把匕首插在铠甲的护胸上,当当不绝——

"米勒娃!"一个尖细的声音说,哈利一边仍替卢娜遮挡着穿梭的魔咒,一边回头看去,只见弗立维和斯普劳特教授穿着睡衣从走廊里匆匆跑来,身材臃肿的斯拉格霍恩教授气喘吁吁地跟在后面。

"住手!"弗立维举着魔杖尖叫,"不许你再在霍格沃茨杀人!"

弗立维的魔咒击中了斯内普当作盾牌的铠甲,哗啦一声,铠甲变活了。斯内普拼命挣脱把他死死挤压住的铁臂,并把铠甲朝袭击他的人飞掷过去。哈利和卢娜赶紧闪身扑倒,铠甲撞在墙上,成为碎片。等哈利再抬头看时,斯内普正在拼命逃跑,麦格、弗立维和斯普劳特都嗵嗵地追了上去。斯内普飞快地跑进一间教室,片刻之后,哈利听见麦格大喊:"懦夫!**懦夫!**"

"怎么啦?怎么啦?"卢娜问。

哈利把她从地上拉了起来,两人把隐形衣拖在身后,顺着走廊奔进那个空荡荡的教室,麦格、弗立维和斯普劳特教授都站在一扇打碎的窗户前。

"他跳下去了。"哈利和卢娜冲进教室时,麦格教授说。

"你是说他死了?"哈利三步并作两步奔到窗口,没有理睬弗立维和斯普劳特看到他突然出现时发出的惊愕的喊叫。

"不,他没有死,"麦格教授愤愤地说,"他不像邓布利多,他手里还拿着魔杖……而且,他似乎从他主子那里学了几手。"

哈利看见远处有一个很大的、蝙蝠般的身影,正穿过黑暗朝围墙飞去,他不由得心生恐惧。

CHAPTER THIRTY — The Sacking of Severus Snape

There were heavy footfalls behind them, and a great deal of puffing: Slughorn had just caught up.

'Harry!' he panted, massaging his immense chest beneath his emerald-green silk pyjamas. 'My dear boy ... what a surprise ... Minerva, do please explain ... Severus ... what ...?'

'Our Headmaster is taking a short break,' said Professor McGonagall, pointing at the Snape-shaped hole in the window.

'Professor!' Harry shouted, his hands at his forehead. He could see the Inferi-filled lake sliding beneath him, and he felt the ghostly green boat bump into the underground shore, and Voldemort leapt from it with murder in his heart –

'Professor, we've got to barricade the school, he's coming now!'

'Very well. He Who Must Not Be Named is coming,' she told the other teachers. Sprout and Flitwick gasped; Slughorn let out a low groan. 'Potter has work to do in the castle on Dumbledore's orders. We need to put in place every protection of which we are capable, while Potter does what he needs to do.'

'You realise, of course, that nothing we do will be able to keep out You-Know-Who indefinitely?' squeaked Flitwick.

'But we can hold him up,' said Professor Sprout.

'Thank you, Pomona,' said Professor McGonagall, and between the two witches there passed a look of grim understanding. 'I suggest we establish basic protection around the place, then gather our students and meet in the Great Hall. Most must be evacuated, though if any of those who are over-age wish to stay and fight, I think they ought to be given the chance.'

'Agreed,' said Professor Sprout, already hurrying towards the door. 'I shall meet you in the Great Hall in twenty minutes with my house.'

And as she jogged out of sight, they could hear her muttering, 'Tentacula. Devil's Snare. And Snargaluff pods ... yes, I'd like to see the Death Eaters fighting those.'

'I can act from here,' said Flitwick, and although he could barely see out of it, he pointed his wand through the smashed window and started muttering incantations of great complexity. Harry heard a weird rushing noise, as though Flitwick had unleashed the power of the wind into the grounds.

第 30 章　西弗勒斯·斯内普被赶跑

身后传来重重的脚步声和呼哧呼哧的喘气声：斯拉格霍恩追了过来。

"哈利！"他气喘吁吁地说，按摩着鲜绿色丝绸睡衣下的肥大胸脯，"我亲爱的孩子……多么令人意外……米勒娃，请解释一下……西弗勒斯……怎么……？"

"我们的校长暂时休息了。"麦格教授指着窗户上那个斯内普形状的大洞说道。

"教授！"哈利双手捂着额头大喊一声。他看见布满阴尸的湖水在他身下掠过，感觉到阴森可怖的绿船轻轻撞在地下湖的岸边，伏地魔杀气腾腾地从船上跳下来——

"教授，我们必须封锁学校，他这就来了！"

"很好。那个连名字都不能提的人来了。"麦格教授对另外几个教师说。斯普劳特和弗立维倒抽了一口冷气，斯拉格霍恩低低呻吟了一声。"波特按照邓布利多的吩咐，在城堡里有工作要做。我们必须尽力提供各种掩护，让波特完成他要做的事情。"

"你肯定知道，不管我们做什么，都不可能把神秘人长久地挡在门外，是不是？"弗立维尖着嗓子说。

"但我们可以把他牵制住。"斯普劳特教授说。

"谢谢你，波莫娜。"麦格教授说，两位女巫严肃地交换了一个会意的目光，"我建议在学校周围设立基本的警戒，然后把学生召集起来，在大礼堂会合。大多数学生都必须疏散出去，但若有成年的学生愿意留下来作战，我认为应该给他们这个机会。"

"同意。"斯普劳特教授说着已朝门口匆匆走去，"二十分钟后，我带着我院的学生在大礼堂跟你们碰头。"

她小跑着远去了，他们听见她嘴里念念有词："毒触手，魔鬼网，疙瘩藤的荚果……对，我倒要看看食死徒怎么对付这些。"

"我可以从这里着手。"弗立维说，他虽然看不到外面，但用魔杖指着打碎的玻璃窗外，低声念起了十分复杂的咒语。哈利听到了一种古怪的呼呼声，似乎弗立维把风的力量释放到了学校场地上。

CHAPTER THIRTY

The Sacking of Severus Snape

'Professor,' Harry said, approaching the little Charms master, 'Professor, I'm sorry to interrupt, but this is important. Have you got any idea where the diadem of Ravenclaw is?'

'... *Protego horribilis* – the diadem of Ravenclaw?' squeaked Flitwick. 'A little extra wisdom never goes amiss, Potter, but I hardly think it would be much use in *this* situation!'

'I only meant – do you know where it is? Have you ever seen it?'

'Seen it? Nobody has seen it in living memory! Long since lost, boy!'

Harry felt a mixture of desperate disappointment and panic. What, then, was the Horcrux?

'We shall meet you and your Ravenclaws in the Great Hall, Filius!' said Professor McGonagall, beckoning to Harry and Luna to follow her.

They had just reached the door when Slughorn rumbled into speech.

'My word,' he puffed, pale and sweaty, his walrus moustache aquiver. 'What a to-do! I'm not at all sure whether this is wise, Minerva. He is bound to find a way in, you know, and anyone who has tried to delay him will be in most grievous peril –'

'I shall expect you and the Slytherins in the Great Hall in twenty minutes, also,' said Professor McGonagall. 'If you wish to leave with your students, we shall not stop you. But if any of you attempt to sabotage our resistance, or take up arms against us within this castle, then, Horace, we duel to kill.'

'Minerva!' he said, aghast.

'The time has come for Slytherin House to decide upon its loyalties,' interrupted Professor McGonagall. 'Go and wake your students, Horace.'

Harry did not stay to watch Slughorn splutter: he and Luna ran after Professor McGonagall, who had taken up a position in the middle of the corridor and raised her wand.

'*Piertotum* – oh, for heaven's sake, Filch, not *now* –'

The aged caretaker had just come hobbling into view, shouting, 'Students out of bed! Students in the corridors!'

'They're supposed to be, you blithering idiot!' shouted McGonagall. 'Now go and do something constructive! Find Peeves!'

'P – Peeves?' stammered Filch, as though he had never heard the name before.

第30章 西弗勒斯·斯内普被赶跑

"教授,"哈利走到小个子的魔咒课教师面前,说道,"教授,很抱歉打断你,但事情很重要。你知道拉文克劳的冠冕在哪儿吗?"

"……超强盔甲护身——拉文克劳的冠冕?"弗立维用尖细的嗓音说,"多一点智慧总不会有错,波特,但我认为在这种形势下恐怕用处不大!"

"我只是问——你知道它在哪儿吗?你见过它吗?"

"见过它?在活着的人的记忆中谁也没见过它!早就失踪了,孩子!"

哈利感到了一种绝望和紧张。那么,魂器到底是什么呢?

"菲利乌斯,我们在大礼堂里跟你和拉文克劳的学生会合!"麦格教授说完,示意哈利和卢娜跟她一起走。

他们刚走到门口,斯拉格霍恩吭哧吭哧地说话了。

"哎呀,"他喘着气说,苍白的脸上汗涔涔的,海象胡须微微发颤,"真是够乱的!我可不知道这么做是不是明智,米勒娃。他肯定有办法闯进来,谁想阻拦他,肯定会非常危险——"

"我也希望你和斯莱特林的学生二十分钟后到大礼堂集合。"麦格教授说,"如果你愿意和你的学生一起离开,我们不会阻拦。但如果你们有谁想破坏抵抗活动,或在城堡内部拿起武器跟我们对抗,那么,霍拉斯,我们将决一死战。"

"米勒娃!"斯拉格霍恩惊骇地说。

"斯莱特林学院应该决定为谁效忠了。"麦格教授打断了他,"去把你的学生叫醒吧,霍拉斯。"

哈利没有留下来看斯拉格霍恩支支吾吾,他和卢娜跟着麦格教授冲了出去。麦格教授在走廊中央站好位置,举起魔杖。

"石磙——哦,看在老天的分上,费尔奇,现在别——"

年迈的管理员蹒跚地出现了,嘴里大喊:"学生下床啦!学生跑到走廊里来啦!"

"他们应该这样,你这白痴!"麦格喊道,"快去做一些有用的事情!去把皮皮鬼找来!"

"皮——皮皮鬼?"费尔奇结结巴巴地说,似乎从没听说过这个名字。

CHAPTER THIRTY — The Sacking of Severus Snape

'Yes, *Peeves*, you fool, *Peeves!* Haven't you been complaining about him for a quarter of a century? Go and fetch him, at once!'

Filch evidently thought Professor McGonagall had taken leave of her senses, but hobbled away, hunch-shouldered, muttering under his breath.

'And now – *piertotum locomotor!*' cried Professor McGonagall.

And all along the corridor the statues and suits of armour jumped down from their plinths, and from the echoing crashes from the floors above and below, Harry knew that their fellows throughout the castle had done the same.

'Hogwarts is threatened!' shouted Professor McGonagall. 'Man the boundaries, protect us, do your duty to our school!'

Clattering and yelling, the horde of moving statues stampeded past Harry: some of them smaller, others larger than life. There were animals too, and the clanking suits of armour brandished swords and spiked balls on chains.

'Now, Potter,' said McGonagall, 'you and Miss Lovegood had better return to your friends and bring them to the Great Hall – I shall rouse the other Gryffindors.'

They parted at the top of the next staircase: Harry and Luna running back towards the concealed entrance to the Room of Requirement. As they ran, they met crowds of students, most wearing travelling cloaks over their pyjamas, being shepherded down to the Great Hall by teachers and prefects.

'That was Potter!'

'*Harry Potter!*'

'It was him, I swear, I just saw him!'

But Harry did not look back, and at last they reached the entrance to the Room of Requirement. Harry leaned against the enchanted wall, which opened to admit them, and he and Luna sped back down the steep staircase.

'Wh–?'

As the room came into view, Harry slipped down a few stairs in shock. It was packed, far more crowded than when he had last been in there. Kingsley and Lupin were looking up at him, as were Oliver Wood, Katie Bell, Angelina Johnson and Alicia Spinnet, Bill and Fleur, and Mr and Mrs Weasley.

第30章 西弗勒斯·斯内普被赶跑

"对，皮皮鬼，你这个傻瓜，皮皮鬼！二十多年来你不是一直在抱怨他吗？去把他找来，快！"

费尔奇显然觉得麦格教授失去了理智，但他还是耸着肩膀，蹒跚地走开了，嘴里不出声地嘟囔着。

"好了——石礅出动！"麦格教授大喊一声。

说时迟那时快，整个走廊上的塑像和铠甲都从底座上跳了下来，哈利听见楼上楼下传来轰隆轰隆的撞击声，知道它们在整个城堡的同伴都采取了同样的行动。

"霍格沃茨受到威胁！"麦格教授高声说道，"守住边界，保卫我们，为学校尽你们的义务！"

随着一片碰撞声和呐喊声，一群活动的塑像步伐沉重地走过哈利身边，有的稍小一些，有的比真人还大，还有一些是动物。那些铿铿作响的铠甲挥舞着宝剑和带链子的狼牙球。

"好了，波特，"麦格说，"你和洛夫古德小姐最好回去找你们的朋友，把他们带到大礼堂来——我去叫醒格兰芬多的其他学生。"

他们在下一个楼梯口分手了，哈利和卢娜向有求必应屋的秘密入口跑去，路上遇到了一群群的学生，大多数都在睡衣外面套着旅行斗篷，由教师和级长护送着赶往大礼堂。

"刚才那是波特！"

"哈利·波特！"

"是他，我敢发誓，我刚才看见他了！"

可是哈利没有回头，一路来到了有求必应屋的入口。哈利往施了魔法的墙上一靠，墙立刻分开让他们进去了，他和卢娜匆匆奔下很陡的楼梯。

"怎么——？"

看到屋子里面，哈利大吃一惊，滑下了几级楼梯。屋里挤满了人，比他刚才在这里时还要拥挤得多。金斯莱和卢平正抬头看着他，还有奥利弗·伍德、凯蒂·贝尔、安吉利娜·约翰逊和艾丽娅·斯平内特、比尔和芙蓉，以及韦斯莱夫妇。

CHAPTER THIRTY

The Sacking of Severus Snape

'Harry, what's happening?' said Lupin, meeting him at the foot of the stairs.

'Voldemort's on his way, they're barricading the school – Snape's run for it – what are you doing here? How did you know?'

'We sent messages to the rest of Dumbledore's Army,' Fred explained. 'You couldn't expect everyone to miss the fun, Harry, and the DA let the Order of the Phoenix know, and it all kind of snowballed.'

'What first, Harry?' called George. 'What's going on?'

'They're evacuating the younger kids and everyone's meeting in the Great Hall to get organised,' Harry said. 'We're fighting.'

There was a great roar and a surge towards the foot of the stairs; he was pressed back against the wall as they ran past him, the mingled members of the Order of the Phoenix, Dumbledore's Army and Harry's old Quidditch team, all with their wands drawn, heading up into the main castle.

'Come on, Luna,' Dean called as he passed, holding out his free hand; she took it and followed him back up the stairs.

The crowd was thinning: only a little knot of people remained below in the Room of Requirement and Harry joined them. Mrs Weasley was struggling with Ginny. Around them stood Lupin, Fred, George, Bill and Fleur.

'You're under-age!' Mrs Weasley shouted at her daughter as Harry approached. 'I won't permit it! The boys, yes, but you, you've got to go home!'

'I won't!'

Ginny's hair flew as she pulled her arm out of her mother's grip.

'I'm in Dumbledore's Army –'

'– a teenagers' gang!'

'A teenagers' gang that's about to take him on, which no one else has dared to do!' said Fred.

'She's sixteen!' shouted Mrs Weasley. 'She's not old enough! What you two were thinking, bringing her with you –'

Fred and George looked slightly ashamed of themselves.

'Mum's right, Ginny,' said Bill gently. 'You can't do this. Everyone under-age will have to leave, it's only right.'

第30章 西弗勒斯·斯内普被赶跑

"哈利,怎么回事?"卢平在楼梯下迎住哈利,问道。

"伏地魔要来了,学校要封锁——斯内普逃命去了——你们在这里做什么?你们怎么知道的?"

"我们给邓布利多军的其他人发了消息,"弗雷德解释说,"谁都不愿意错过这份乐趣,哈利。然后 D.A. 又通知了凤凰社,就跟滚雪球似的越滚越大。"

"先干什么,哈利?"乔治喊道,"情况怎么样?"

"他们在疏散小一点的学生,大家都到大礼堂集合,听候安排,"哈利说,"我们准备战斗。"

吼叫声排山倒海,人们朝楼梯脚下涌来。哈利紧贴在墙上,让他们从他身边跑过,有凤凰社和邓布利多军的成员,还有哈利以前的魁地奇球队的队员,他们都抽出了魔杖,朝城堡主楼冲去。

"走吧,卢娜。"迪安走过时伸出手喊道。卢娜握住他的手,跟他上了楼梯。

人群渐渐稀少,只有一小伙人还留在下面的有求必应屋里,哈利走了过去。韦斯莱夫人正在跟金妮争吵,周围站着卢平、弗雷德、乔治、比尔和芙蓉。

"你还不够年龄!"哈利走近时,韦斯莱夫人正冲着女儿喊道,"我不允许!男孩子可以,但你,必须回家!"

"我不!"

金妮头发一甩,把胳膊从母亲手里挣脱出来。

"我是邓布利多军的——"

"——那是一个少年团伙!"

"一个准备同神秘人较量的少年团伙,别人谁有胆量这么做!"弗雷德说。

"她才十六岁!"韦斯莱夫人大声说,"她还太小!你们俩是怎么想的,竟然把她带来——"

弗雷德和乔治显出有点羞愧的样子。

"妈妈说得对,金妮,"比尔温和地说,"你不能这么做。不到年龄的人都必须离开,这是对的。"

CHAPTER THIRTY   The Sacking of Severus Snape

'I can't go home!' Ginny shouted, angry tears sparkling in her eyes. 'My whole family's here, I can't stand waiting there alone and not knowing and –'

Her eyes met Harry's for the first time. She looked at him beseechingly, but he shook his head and she turned away bitterly.

'Fine,' she said, staring at the entrance to the tunnel back to the Hog's Head. 'I'll say goodbye now, then, and –'

There was a scuffling and a great thump: someone else had clambered out of the tunnel, overbalanced slightly and fallen. He pulled himself up on the nearest chair, looked around through lopsided horn-rimmed glasses and said, 'Am I too late? Has it started? I only just found out, so I – I –'

Percy spluttered into silence. Evidently he had not expected to run into most of his family. There was a long moment of astonishment, broken by Fleur turning to Lupin and saying, in a wildly transparent attempt to break the tension, 'So – 'ow eez leetle Teddy?'

Lupin blinked at her, startled. The silence between the Weasleys seemed to be solidifying, like ice.

'I – oh yes – he's fine!' Lupin said loudly. 'Yes, Tonks is with him – at her mother's.'

Percy and the other Weasleys were still staring at one another, frozen.

'Here, I've got a picture!' Lupin shouted, pulling a photograph from inside his jacket and showing it to Fleur and Harry, who saw a tiny baby with a tuft of bright turquoise hair, waving fat fists at the camera.

'I was a fool!' Percy roared, so loudly that Lupin nearly dropped his photograph. 'I was an idiot, I was a pompous prat, I was a – a –'

'Ministry-loving, family-disowning, power-hungry moron,' said Fred.

Percy swallowed.

'Yes, I was!'

'Well, you can't say fairer than that,' said Fred, holding out his hand to Percy.

Mrs Weasley burst into tears. She ran forwards, pushed Fred aside and pulled Percy into a strangling hug, while he patted her on the back, his eyes on his father.

'I'm sorry, Dad,' Percy said.

第30章 西弗勒斯·斯内普被赶跑

"我不能回家！"金妮喊道，眼里闪着愤怒的泪光，"我们全家都在这儿，我不能独自在那边等着，什么也不知道——"

她的目光第一次与哈利相遇。她恳求地望着哈利，可是哈利摇了摇头，她气愤地回过头去。

"好吧，"她望着通向猪头酒吧的通道入口，说道，"我现在就告别，以后——"

忽听一阵窸窸窣窣，然后是扑通一声，又有一个人从通道里爬了出来，身体摇晃几下，摔倒了。然后，他爬起来坐到近旁的椅子上，透过歪斜的角质架眼镜望望周围，说道："我来晚了吗？已经开始了吗？我刚知道，就——就——"

珀西结结巴巴地说不下去了。他显然没有料到会碰见这么多亲人。长时间的惊愕，最后芙蓉转向卢平，用明显试图打破僵局的口吻说道："对了——小泰迪怎么样啊？"

卢平惊讶地朝她眨眨眼睛。韦斯莱一家的沉默正在凝固，像冰一样。

"我——哦，对了——他很好！"卢平大声说，"是的，唐克斯陪着他——在她母亲家。"

珀西和韦斯莱家的其他人仍然在那里对视、僵持。

"看，我带了照片来！"卢平喊道，从上衣里面抽出一张照片给芙蓉和哈利看，照片上是一个长着一簇青绿色头发的小宝宝，正冲着镜头挥动胖胖的小拳头。

"我是个傻瓜！"珀西吼了起来，声音真大，吓得卢平差点把照片掉在地上，"我是个白痴，我是个爱虚荣的笨蛋，我是个——是个——"

"是个只爱魔法部、跟亲人脱离关系、野心勃勃的混蛋。"弗雷德说。

珀西咽了口唾沫。

"对，没错！"

"行了，不可能说得比这更清楚了。"弗雷德说着，把手伸给了珀西。

韦斯莱夫人哭了起来，她跑上前，把弗雷德推到一边，把珀西拉到怀里紧紧地搂住。珀西拍着母亲的后背，眼睛望着父亲。

"对不起，爸爸。"珀西说。

CHAPTER THIRTY   The Sacking of Severus Snape

Mr Weasley blinked rather rapidly, then he, too, hurried to hug his son.

'What made you see sense, Perce?' enquired George.

'It's been coming on for a while,' said Percy, mopping his eyes under his glasses with a corner of his travelling cloak. 'But I had to find a way out and it's not so easy at the Ministry, they're imprisoning traitors all the time. I managed to make contact with Aberforth and he tipped me off ten minutes ago that Hogwarts was going to make a fight of it, so here I am.'

'Well, we do look to our prefects to take a lead at times such as these,' said George, in a good imitation of Percy's most pompous manner. 'Now let's get upstairs and fight, or all the good Death Eaters'll be taken.'

'So, you're my sister-in-law now?' said Percy, shaking hands with Fleur as they hurried off towards the staircase with Bill, Fred and George.

'Ginny!' barked Mrs Weasley.

Ginny had been attempting, under cover of the reconciliation, to sneak upstairs too.

'Molly, how about this,' said Lupin. 'Why doesn't Ginny stay here, then at least she'll be on the scene and know what's going on, but she won't be in the middle of the fighting?'

'I –'

'That's a good idea,' said Mr Weasley firmly. 'Ginny, you stay in this room, you hear me?'

Ginny did not seem to like the idea much, but under her father's unusually stern gaze she nodded. Mr and Mrs Weasley and Lupin headed off for the stairs as well.

'Where's Ron?' asked Harry. 'Where's Hermione?'

'They must have gone up to the Great Hall already,' Mr Weasley called over his shoulder.

'I didn't see them pass me,' said Harry.

'They said something about a bathroom,' said Ginny, 'not long after you left.'

'A bathroom?'

Harry strode across the room to an open door leading off the Room of Requirement and checked the bathroom beyond. It was empty.

'You're sure they said bath–?'

第30章 西弗勒斯·斯内普被赶跑

韦斯莱先生快速地眨眨眼睛，然后也冲过去搂抱住自己的儿子。

"你是怎么明白过来的，珀西？"乔治问。

"已经有一阵子了，"珀西说着，把旅行斗篷的一角伸到眼镜后面擦了擦眼泪，"但我必须想办法逃出来，这在部里可不容易，他们一直在把反叛者抓去坐牢。后来我总算跟阿不福思联系上了，他十分钟前向我透露了霍格沃茨要全力抵抗，所以我就来了。"

"是啊，我们确实希望级长在这样的关键时候能起表率作用。"乔治说，惟妙惟肖地模仿着珀西那副十足的假正经派头，"我们赶紧上楼战斗吧，不然所有像样的食死徒都被抓住了。"

"这么说，我现在可以叫你嫂子了？"珀西说着，跟芙蓉握了握手，两人和比尔、弗雷德和乔治一起朝楼梯冲去。

"金妮！"韦斯莱夫人大吼一声。

金妮趁着全家人和解的工夫，也试图偷偷溜上楼去。

"莫丽，你看这样如何，"卢平说，"不妨就让金妮留在这里，这样她至少能在现场，知道事情的进展，但又不在战斗的中心，怎么样？"

"我——"

"这个办法不错。"韦斯莱先生坚决地说，"金妮，你就留在这间屋里，听见了吗？"

金妮似乎不大喜欢这个主意，但在父亲异常严厉的目光下，她只好点了点头。韦斯莱夫妇和卢平也朝楼梯口冲去。

"罗恩呢？"哈利问，"赫敏呢？"

"肯定已经去大礼堂了。"韦斯莱先生扭头喊道。

"我路上没看见他们呀。"哈利说。

"他们好像说是去盥洗室，"金妮说，"就在你离开后不久。"

"盥洗室？"

哈利大步穿过房间，走到有求必应屋边上一扇敞开的门前，察看了一下那边的盥洗室。里面没人。

"你确定他们说的是盥洗——？"

CHAPTER THIRTY

The Sacking of Severus Snape

But then his scar seared and the Room of Requirement vanished: he was looking through the high, wrought-iron gates, with winged boars on pillars at either side, looking through the dark grounds towards the castle, which was ablaze with lights. Nagini lay draped over his shoulders. He was possessed of that cold, cruel sense of purpose that preceded murder.

第30章　西弗勒斯·斯内普被赶跑

就在这时，他的伤疤突然烧灼起来，有求必应屋消失了，他的目光掠过高高的铸铁大门——两边是顶上有带翼野猪的石柱，掠过漆黑的场地，望向那灯火通明的城堡。纳吉尼懒散地耷拉在他的肩头。他内心充满了大开杀戒前的冷酷和决绝。

CHAPTER THIRTY-ONE

The Battle of Hogwarts

The enchanted ceiling of the Great Hall was dark and scattered with stars, and below it the four long house tables were lined with dishevelled students, some in travelling cloaks, others in dressing gowns. Here and there shone the pearly-white figures of the school ghosts. Every eye, living and dead, was fixed upon Professor McGonagall, who was speaking from the raised platform at the top of the Hall. Behind her stood the remaining teachers, including the palomino centaur, Firenze, and the members of the Order of the Phoenix who had arrived to fight.

'... evacuation will be overseen by Mr Filch and Madam Pomfrey. Prefects, when I give the word, you will organise your house and take your charges, in an orderly fashion, to the evacuation point.'

Many of the students looked petrified. However, as Harry skirted the walls, scanning the Gryffindor table for Ron and Hermione, Ernie Macmillan stood up at the Hufflepuff table and shouted, 'And what if we want to stay and fight?'

There was a smattering of applause.

'If you are of age, you may stay,' said Professor McGonagall.

'What about our things?' called a girl at the Ravenclaw table. 'Our trunks, our owls?'

'We have no time to collect possessions,' said Professor McGonagall. 'The important thing is to get you out of here safely.'

'Where's Professor Snape?' shouted a girl from the Slytherin table.

'He has, to use the common phrase, done a bunk,' replied Professor McGonagall, and a great cheer erupted from the Gryffindors, Hufflepuffs and Ravenclaws.

第 31 章

霍格沃茨的战斗

大礼堂里那被施了魔法的天花板黑蒙蒙的,闪烁着点点星光,下面的四张长桌旁坐着衣冠不整、头发蓬乱的学生,有的披着旅行斗篷,有的穿着晨衣。这里那里不时闪过校内那些幽灵的乳白色身影。无论是死人还是活人,每双眼睛都盯着麦格教授,她正站在礼堂前高高的讲台上对大家讲话,身后站着留下来的教师们,包括银鬃马人费伦泽,还有赶来参加战斗的凤凰社成员。

"……疏散工作由费尔奇先生和庞弗雷女士负责监督。级长听到我的命令后,组织你们学院的学生,负责将他们井然有序地送到疏散地点。"

许多学生都是一副吓呆了的样子。不过,当哈利贴着墙根移动,在格兰芬多桌旁寻找罗恩和赫敏时,厄尼·麦克米兰从赫奇帕奇桌旁站起来大声喊道:"如果我们想留下来参加战斗呢?"

他的话赢得了一些人的喝彩。

"如果够年龄,可以留下。"麦格教授说。

"我们的东西呢?"拉文克劳桌旁的一位女生大声问道,"我们的箱子,还有猫头鹰呢?"

"来不及收拾财物了,"麦格教授说,"最重要的是把你们从这里安全地转移出去。"

"斯内普教授呢?"斯莱特林桌旁的一位女生喊了起来。

"用一句通俗的话来说,他溜了。"麦格教授说,格兰芬多、赫奇帕奇和拉文克劳桌旁爆发出一片欢呼。

CHAPTER THIRTY-ONE The Battle of Hogwarts

Harry moved up the Hall alongside the Gryffindor table, still looking for Ron and Hermione. As he passed, faces turned in his direction, and a great deal of whispering broke out in his wake.

'We have already placed protection around the castle,' Professor McGonagall was saying, 'but it is unlikely to hold for very long unless we reinforce it. I must ask you, therefore, to move quickly and calmly, and do as your prefects —'

But her final words were drowned as a different voice echoed throughout the Hall. It was high, cold and clear: there was no telling from where it came; it seemed to issue from the walls themselves. Like the monster it had once commanded, it might have lain dormant there for centuries.

'I know that you are preparing to fight.' There were screams amongst the students, some of whom clutched each other, looking around in terror for the source of the sound. 'Your efforts are futile. You cannot fight me. I do not want to kill you. I have great respect for the teachers of Hogwarts. I do not want to spill magical blood.'

There was silence in the Hall now, the kind of silence that presses against the eardrums, that seems too huge to be contained by walls.

'Give me Harry Potter,' said Voldemort's voice, 'and none shall be harmed. Give me Harry Potter, and I shall leave the school untouched. Give me Harry Potter, and you will be rewarded.

'You have until midnight.'

The silence swallowed them all again. Every head turned, every eye in the place seemed to have found Harry, to hold him frozen in the glare of thousands of invisible beams. Then a figure rose from the Slytherin table and he recognised Pansy Parkinson as she raised a shaking arm and screamed, 'But he's there! Potter's *there*! Someone grab him!'

Before Harry could speak, there was a massive movement. The Gryffindors in front of him had risen and stood facing, not Harry, but the Slytherins. Then the Hufflepuffs stood, and, almost at the same moment, the Ravenclaws, all of them with their backs to Harry, all of them looking towards Pansy instead, and Harry, awestruck and overwhelmed, saw wands emerging everywhere, pulled from beneath cloaks and from under sleeves.

'Thank you, Miss Parkinson,' said Professor McGonagall in a clipped voice.

第31章 霍格沃茨的战斗

哈利顺着格兰芬多的桌子往前走,仍在寻找罗恩和赫敏。他走动时,许多人朝他这边转过脸来,他身后响起一片窃窃私语声。

"我们已经在城堡周围布下防御,"麦格教授说,"但不可能守住很长时间,除非我们不断加固这种防御。因此,我要求你们必须迅速而沉着地行动,听级长的——"

突然,另一个声音响彻了大礼堂,把她的话淹没了。那声音高亢、冷酷、清晰,说不清从什么地方传来,似乎是墙壁本身发出来的。这声音就像它曾经指挥过的蛇怪一样,仿佛也在那里沉睡了好几个世纪。

"我知道你们在准备抵抗。"学生们中间发出尖叫,有些人搂作一团,惊恐地四处张望,寻找声音发出的地方。"你们的努力是没有用的。你们不是我的对手。我不想杀死你们。我对霍格沃茨的教师十分尊敬。我不想让巫师流血。"

大礼堂里一片寂静,这寂静压迫着人们的耳膜,这寂静如此巨大,大得似乎整个礼堂都盛载不下。

"把哈利·波特交出来,"伏地魔的声音说,"你们谁也不会受伤。把哈利·波特交出来,我会让学校安然无恙。把哈利·波特交出来,你们会得到奖赏。"

"我等到午夜。"

寂静再次把他们全部吞没。每个人都转过脑袋,每双眼睛似乎都找到了哈利,千百道目光死死地盯着他,使他动弹不得。然后,斯莱特林桌旁站起一个身影,哈利认出是潘西·帕金森,只见她举起颤抖的胳膊尖叫道:"他在那儿!波特在那儿!快把他抓住!"

哈利还没来得及说话,同学们已经采取行动。他面前的格兰芬多学生站了起来,不是面对哈利,而是面对斯莱特林。接着赫奇帕奇学生也纷纷起立,拉文克劳学生几乎在同时也采取了同样的行动。他们全都背对哈利,他们全都面朝潘西,哈利百感交集,既敬畏又感动。他看见四面八方都有魔杖被抽出来,有从斗篷底下,有从袖子里面。

"谢谢你,帕金森小姐,"麦格教授清楚而干脆地说,"你和费尔奇

CHAPTER THIRTY-ONE   The Battle of Hogwarts

'You will leave the Hall first with Mr Filch. If the rest of your house could follow.'

Harry heard the grinding of benches and then the sound of the Slytherins trooping out on the other side of the Hall.

'Ravenclaws, follow on!' cried Professor McGonagall.

Slowly, the four tables emptied. The Slytherin table was completely deserted, but a number of older Ravenclaws remained seated while their fellows filed out: even more Hufflepuffs stayed behind, and half of Gryffindor remained in their seats, necessitating Professor McGonagall's descent from the teachers' platform to chivvy the under-age on their way.

'Absolutely not, Creevey, go! *And* you, Peakes!'

Harry hurried over to the Weasleys, all sitting together at the Gryffindor table.

'Where are Ron and Hermione?'

'Haven't you found –?' began Mr Weasley, looking worried.

But he broke off as Kingsley had stepped forwards on the raised platform to address those who had remained behind.

'We've only got half an hour until midnight, so we need to act fast! A battle plan has been agreed between the teachers of Hogwarts and the Order of the Phoenix. Professors Flitwick, Sprout and McGonagall are going to take groups of fighters up to the three highest Towers – Ravenclaw, Astronomy and Gryffindor – where they'll have a good overview, excellent positions from which to work spells. Meanwhile, Remus,' he indicated Lupin, 'Arthur,' he pointed towards Mr Weasley, sitting at the Gryffindor table, 'and I will take groups into the grounds. We'll need somebody to organise defence of the entrances of the passageways into the school –'

'– sounds like a job for us,' called Fred, indicating himself and George, and Kingsley nodded his approval.

'All right, leaders up here and we'll divide up the troops!'

'Potter,' said Professor McGonagall, hurrying up to him, as students flooded the platform, jostling for position, receiving instructions, '*aren't you supposed to be looking for something?*'

'What? Oh,' said Harry, 'oh yeah!'

He had almost forgotten about the Horcrux, almost forgotten that the battle was being fought so that he could search for it: the inexplicable absence of Ron and Hermione had momentarily driven every other thought from his mind.

先生一起先离开礼堂。你们学院的其他同学也可以跟上。"

哈利听见了板凳的碰撞摩擦声,斯莱特林们纷纷从礼堂另一边离开了。

"拉文克劳,跟上!"麦格教授大声说。

四张桌子渐渐地空了。斯莱特林桌旁空无一人;而拉文克劳鱼贯而出时,一些年纪较大的同学坐着没动;赫奇帕奇留下来的就更多了;格兰芬多更是有一半的同学都待在座位上。麦格教授只好从讲台上下来,强行驱赶不到年龄的学生。

"绝对不行,克里维,快走!还有你,珀克斯!"

哈利匆匆走向坐在格兰芬多桌旁的韦斯莱一家。

"罗恩和赫敏呢?"

"你还没有找到——?"韦斯莱先生很担忧地问。

他的话没有说完,因为金斯莱已经走到讲台上,向留下来的人发表讲话。

"到午夜只有半个小时了,我们需要迅速行动!霍格沃茨教师和凤凰社成员联合拟定了一个作战方案。弗立维、斯普劳特和麦格教授分别带领战斗队登上三个最高的塔楼——拉文克劳塔、天文塔和格兰芬多塔——那里视野开阔,位置有利,便于施魔法。莱姆斯,"他指指卢平,"亚瑟,"他指指坐在格兰芬多桌旁的韦斯莱先生,"和我带领队伍进入场地。我们需要有人组织把守进入学校的各个通道入口——"

"听着像是我们的活儿。"弗雷德指指他自己和乔治大声说,金斯莱点头同意。

"好了,领队的到上面来,我们分一下队伍!"

"波特,"麦格教授说着匆匆向他走来,这时同学们都朝讲台拥去,推推搡搡地抢位置,接受指令,"你不是要寻找什么东西吗?"

"什么?噢,"哈利说,"噢,对了!"

他几乎忘记了魂器,几乎忘记了作战的目的是让他能够寻找魂器。罗恩和赫敏的离奇失踪暂时赶跑了他脑子里所有的其他念头。

CHAPTER THIRTY-ONE

The Battle of Hogwarts

'Then go, Potter, go!'

'Right – yeah –'

He sensed eyes following him as he ran out of the Great Hall again, into the Entrance Hall still crowded with evacuating students. He allowed himself to be swept up the marble staircase with them, but at the top he hurried off along a deserted corridor. Fear and panic were clouding his thought processes. He tried to calm himself, to concentrate on finding the Horcrux, but his thoughts buzzed as frantically and fruitlessly as wasps trapped beneath a glass. Without Ron and Hermione to help him, he could not seem to marshal his ideas. He slowed down, coming to a halt halfway along an empty passage, where he sat down upon the plinth of a departed statue and pulled the Marauder's Map out of the pouch around his neck. He could not see Ron or Hermione's names anywhere on it, though the density of the crowd of dots now making its way to the Room of Requirement might, he thought, be concealing them. He put the map away, pressed his hands over his face and closed his eyes, trying to concentrate ...

Voldemort thought I'd go to Ravenclaw Tower.

There it was: a solid fact, the place to start. Voldemort had stationed Alecto Carrow in the Ravenclaw common room, and there could only be one explanation: Voldemort feared that Harry already knew his Horcrux was connected to that house.

But the only object anyone seemed to associate with Ravenclaw was the lost diadem ... and how could the Horcrux be the diadem? How was it possible that Voldemort, the Slytherin, had found the diadem that had eluded generations of Ravenclaws? Who could have told him where to look, when nobody had seen the diadem in living memory?

In living memory ...

Beneath his fingers, Harry's eyes flew open again. He leapt up from the plinth and tore back the way he had come, now in pursuit of his one last hope. The sound of hundreds of people marching towards the Room of Requirement grew louder and louder as he returned to the marble stairs. Prefects were shouting instructions, trying to keep track of the students in their own houses; there was much pushing and shoving; Harry saw Zacharias Smith bowling over first-years to get to the front of the queue; here and there younger students were in tears, while older ones called desperately for friends or siblings ...

第31章 霍格沃茨的战斗

"那就去吧,波特,快去吧!"

"行——好的——"

他从大礼堂里跑了出去,感觉到后面有许多双眼睛跟着他。门厅里仍然挤着正在疏散的学生。哈利被他们挟裹着上了大理石楼梯,到了顶上他立刻顺着一条空荡荡的走廊跑去。恐慌和紧张使他的思绪混乱不清。他试着平静下来,集中思想考虑怎么找到魂器,可是思想像关在玻璃罩里的黄蜂一样,疯狂而徒劳地嗡嗡乱飞。没有罗恩和赫敏在旁相助,他似乎理不清自己的思路。他放慢脚步,在空无一人的过道中间停了下来,坐在一个塑像离开后留下的底座上,从脖子上的皮袋里掏出活点地图。他在地图上怎么也找不到罗恩和赫敏的名字,不过,它们可能藏在那片拥向有求必应屋的密密麻麻的小点当中了。他把地图收了起来,用两只手捂住脸,闭上眼睛,努力集中思绪……

伏地魔认为我会去拉文克劳塔。

没错,这是一个可靠的事实,就从这里开始吧。伏地魔派阿莱克托·卡罗驻守在拉文克劳公共休息室,这只能有一个解释:伏地魔担心哈利已经知道他的魂器跟那个学院有关。

可是,唯一能跟拉文克劳联系在一起的似乎只有失踪的冠冕……魂器怎么可能是冠冕呢?伏地魔是斯莱特林的学生,怎么可能找到拉文克劳多少代人都没见过的冠冕呢?是谁告诉他上哪儿去寻找的呢?活着的人记忆中谁也没有见过那个冠冕呀。

活着的人记忆中……

哈利用手捂着的眼睛突然睁开了。他从底座上一跃而起,顺着原路往回跑,追逐他的最后一个希望。回到大理石楼梯时,成百上千的人朝有求必应屋进发的声音越来越响。大家纷纷推搡着,级长们大声喊着指令,努力分辨自己学院的学生。哈利看见扎卡赖斯·史密斯为了抢到队伍前面而把一年级新生撞得东倒西歪。随处可见年纪较小的学生在哭鼻子,年纪较大的学生焦急地呼唤朋友或兄弟姐妹……

CHAPTER THIRTY-ONE The Battle of Hogwarts

Harry caught sight of a pearly-white figure drifting across the Entrance Hall below and yelled as loudly as he could over the clamour.

'Nick! NICK! I need to talk to you!'

He forced his way back through the tide of students, finally reaching the bottom of the stairs where Nearly Headless Nick, ghost of Gryffindor Tower, stood waiting for him.

'Harry! My dear boy!'

Nick made to grasp Harry's hands with both of his own: Harry's felt as though they had been thrust into icy water.

'Nick, you've got to help me. Who's the ghost of Ravenclaw Tower?'

Nearly Headless Nick looked surprised, and a little offended.

'The Grey Lady, of course; but if it is ghostly services you require –?'

'It's got to be her – d'you know where she is?'

'Let's see …'

Nick's head wobbled a little on his ruff as he turned hither and thither, peering over the heads of the swarming students.

'That's her over there, Harry, the young woman with the long hair.'

Harry looked in the direction of Nick's transparent, pointing finger and saw a tall ghost who caught sight of Harry looking at her, raised her eyebrows, and drifted away through a solid wall.

Harry ran after her. Once through the door of the corridor into which she had disappeared, he saw her at the very end of the passage, still gliding smoothly away from him.

'Hey – wait – come back!'

She consented to pause, floating a few inches from the ground. Harry supposed that she was beautiful, with her waist-length hair and floor-length cloak, but she also looked haughty and proud. Close to, he recognised her as a ghost he had passed several times in the corridor, but to whom he had never spoken.

'You're the Grey Lady?'

She nodded but did not speak.

'The ghost of Ravenclaw Tower?'

'That is correct.'

Her tone was not encouraging.

第31章 霍格沃茨的战斗

哈利看见一个乳白色的身影在下面的门厅里飘然而过,他赶紧在喧闹声中扯足嗓子大喊起来。

"尼克!**尼克**!我有话对你说!"

他在拥挤的人流中拼命往下挤,终于到了楼梯脚下,格兰芬多塔楼的幽灵——差点没头的尼克正站在那里等他。

"哈利!我亲爱的孩子!"

尼克用双手攥住哈利的两只手,哈利立刻觉得双手像是插进了冰水里。

"尼克,你一定得帮帮我。拉文克劳塔楼的幽灵是谁?"

差点没头的尼克显得又吃惊又有点儿生气。

"是格雷女士,这还用问。但如果你需要幽灵为你服务——?"

"必须是她——你知道她在哪儿吗?"

"让我看看……"

尼克东张张西望望,在人头攒动的学生中间寻找,他的脑袋在轮状皱领上微微摇晃。

"她在那儿,哈利,那个长头发的年轻女人。"

哈利循着尼克透明的手指所指的方向望去,看见一个身材修长的幽灵。她发现哈利在看她,便扬起眉毛,然后转身飘然穿墙而去。

哈利追了过去,冲进那道走廊的门,看见她在通道尽头,仍然幽幽地越飘越远。

"喂——等等——回来!"

她总算停了下来,悬在离地几英寸高的地方。哈利猜想她长得很美,长发齐腰,长袍及地,但她同时又显得很傲慢,目中无人。待走近一些,哈利认出自己曾几次在走廊里碰见过这个幽灵,但一次也没跟她说过话。

"你是格雷女士?"

她点点头,没有说话。

"是拉文克劳塔楼的幽灵?"

"不错。"

她的口气一点也不热情。

CHAPTER THIRTY-ONE The Battle of Hogwarts

'Please: I need some help. I need to know anything you can tell me about the lost diadem.'

A cold smile curved her lips.

'I am afraid,' she said, turning to leave, 'that I cannot help you.'

'WAIT!'

He had not meant to shout, but anger and panic were threatening to overwhelm him. He glanced at his watch as she hovered in front of him: it was a quarter to midnight.

'This is urgent,' he said fiercely. 'If that diadem's at Hogwarts, I've got to find it, fast.'

'You are hardly the first student to covet the diadem,' she said disdainfully. 'Generations of students have badgered me –'

'This isn't about trying to get better marks!' Harry shouted at her. 'It's about Voldemort – defeating Voldemort – or aren't you interested in that?'

She could not blush, but her transparent cheeks became more opaque, and her voice was heated as she replied, 'Of course I – how dare you suggest –?'

'Well, help me, then!'

Her composure was slipping.

'It – it is not a question of –' she stammered. 'My mother's diadem –'

'Your *mother's*?'

She looked angry with herself.

'When I lived,' she said stiffly, 'I was Helena Ravenclaw.'

'You're her *daughter*? But then, you must know what happened to it!'

'While the diadem bestows wisdom,' she said, with an obvious effort to pull herself together, 'I doubt that it would greatly increase your chances of defeating the wizard who calls himself Lord –'

'Haven't I just told you, I'm not interested in wearing it!' Harry said fiercely. 'There's no time to explain – but if you care about Hogwarts, if you want to see Voldemort finished, you've got to tell me anything you know about the diadem!'

She remained quite still, floating in mid-air, staring down at him, and a sense of hopelessness engulfed Harry. Of course, if she had known anything, she would have told Flitwick or Dumbledore, who had surely asked her the same question. He had shaken his head, and made to turn away, when she

第31章 霍格沃茨的战斗

"求求你,我需要帮助。我需要你把失踪的冠冕的情况都告诉我。"

她的嘴唇扭曲成一个冷笑。

"恐怕,"她说着转身要离开,"我帮不了你。"

"等等!"

哈利并没打算叫嚷,但愤怒和紧张几乎把他压垮了。幽灵在他面前悬着不动,他着急地看看表:离午夜只有一刻钟了。

"事情很紧急,"哈利焦躁地说,"如果那个冠冕在霍格沃茨,我必须找到它,马上。"

"你不是第一个垂涎冠冕的学生,"她轻蔑地说,"一代一代的学生都缠着我——"

"这不是为了得到好分数!"哈利朝她嚷道,"是为了伏地魔——打败伏地魔——难道你对这个不感兴趣?"

她不会脸红,但透明的面颊似乎变得不那么透明了,回答时声音里透着激动:"我当然——你怎么敢说——?"

"那就快帮助我吧!"

她不像刚才那么镇静了。

"这——这问题不是——"她结结巴巴地说,"我母亲的冠冕——"

"你母亲的?"

她似乎对自己感到很恼火。

"我活着的时候,"她生硬地说,"是海莲娜·拉文克劳。"

"你是她的女儿?那你肯定知道冠冕的下落!"

"虽然冠冕赐予人智慧,"她说,显然想使自己重新镇静下来,"但我怀疑它不会帮助你打败那个自称是黑——"

"我不是跟你说了吗,我感兴趣的不是自己戴它!"哈利激烈地说,"没时间解释了——如果你关心霍格沃茨,如果你希望看到伏地魔完蛋,就必须把你知道的关于冠冕的事情都告诉我!"

她还是不动声色,在空中飘飘荡荡,低头望着哈利。一种绝望的情绪把哈利淹没了。她如果知道一些情况,肯定早就告诉弗立维或邓布利多了,他们想必问过她同样的问题。哈利摇了摇头,正转身要走,

CHAPTER THIRTY-ONE   The Battle of Hogwarts

spoke in a low voice.

'I stole the diadem from my mother.'

'You – you did what?'

'*I stole the diadem*,' repeated Helena Ravenclaw in a whisper. 'I sought to make myself cleverer, more important than my mother. I ran away with it.'

He did not know how he had managed to gain her confidence, and did not ask: he simply listened, hard, as she went on, 'My mother, they say, never admitted that the diadem was gone, but pretended that she had it still. She concealed her loss, my dreadful betrayal, even from the other founders of Hogwarts.

'Then my mother fell ill – fatally ill. In spite of my perfidy, she was desperate to see me one more time. She sent a man who had long loved me, though I spurned his advances, to find me. She knew that he would not rest until he had done so.'

Harry waited. She drew a deep breath and threw back her head.

'He tracked me to the forest where I was hiding. When I refused to return with him, he became violent. The Baron was always a hot-tempered man. Furious at my refusal, jealous of my freedom, he stabbed me.'

'The *Baron*? You mean –?'

'The Bloody Baron, yes,' said the Grey Lady, and she lifted aside the cloak she wore to reveal a single dark wound in her white chest. 'When he saw what he had done, he was overcome with remorse. He took the weapon that had claimed my life, and used it to kill himself. All these centuries later, he wears his chains as an act of penitence ... as he should,' she added bitterly.

'And ... and the diadem?'

'It remained where I had hidden it when I heard the Baron blundering through the forest towards me. Concealed inside a hollow tree.'

'A hollow tree?' repeated Harry. 'What tree? Where was this?'

'A forest in Albania. A lonely place I thought was far beyond my mother's reach.'

'Albania,' repeated Harry. Sense was emerging miraculously from confusion, and now he understood why she was telling him what she had denied Dumbledore and Flitwick. 'You've already told someone this story, haven't you? Another student?'

第31章 霍格沃茨的战斗

她却低声说话了。

"我从我母亲那里偷走了冠冕。"

"你——你做了什么?"

"我偷了冠冕,"海莲娜·拉文克劳又轻声说了一遍,"我想让自己比母亲更聪明,更有名望。我带着冠冕逃走了。"

哈利不知道自己怎么赢得了她的信任,他没有问,只是仔细地听她往下说:"他们说,我母亲始终没有承认冠冕不见了,她一直假装冠冕还在。她甚至对霍格沃茨的另外几个创办人也隐瞒了她的损失,隐瞒了我可怕的背叛。

"后来我母亲病了——病得很重。虽然我做了不孝不义的事,她仍然迫切地想再见我一面。她派了一个男人来找我,那人爱了我很久,但我拒绝了他。我母亲知道那人不找到我是不肯罢休的。"

哈利等着。她深深吸了口气,把脑袋往后一仰。

"他找到了我藏身的森林。我不肯跟他回去,他就暴怒起来。巴罗一向是个脾气暴躁的人。他恨我拒绝了他,嫉妒我的自由,就把我给刺死了。"

"巴罗?你是说——?"

"血人巴罗,是的。"格雷女士说着撩起斗篷,露出雪白的胸脯上一道黑色的伤口,"他醒过神来后,痛悔莫及,拿起他索取了我性命的武器,自杀了。这么多世纪过去了,他为了悔罪,至今还戴着镣铐……他是活该。"她愤愤地加了一句。

"那么……那么冠冕呢?"

"当时我听见巴罗在森林里跌跌撞撞地向我走来,就把冠冕藏了起来,后来一直留在那里。藏在一棵空心树里。"

"一棵空心树?"哈利追问道,"什么树?在哪儿?"

"在阿尔巴尼亚的一座森林里。一个荒凉的地方,我以为我母亲鞭长莫及。"

"阿尔巴尼亚。"哈利重复道,奇迹般地从一片混乱中理清了思绪,他现在明白她为什么把没有告诉邓布利多和弗立维的事情告诉他了,"你已经跟人讲过这个故事,对吗?跟另一个学生?"

CHAPTER THIRTY-ONE   The Battle of Hogwarts

She closed her eyes and nodded.

'I had ... no idea ... he was ... flattering. He seemed to ... to understand ... to sympathise ...'

Yes, Harry thought, Tom Riddle would certainly have understood Helena Ravenclaw's desire to possess fabulous objects to which she had little right.

'Well, you weren't the first person Riddle wormed things out of,' Harry muttered. 'He could be charming when he wanted ...'

So Voldemort had managed to wheedle the location of the lost diadem out of the Grey Lady. He had travelled to that far-flung forest and retrieved the diadem from its hiding place, perhaps as soon as he left Hogwarts, before he even started work at Borgin and Burkes.

And wouldn't those secluded Albanian woods have seemed an excellent refuge when, so much later, Voldemort had needed a place to lie low, undisturbed, for ten long years?

But the diadem, once it became his precious Horcrux, had not been left in that lowly tree ... no, the diadem had been returned secretly to its true home, and Voldemort must have put it there –

'– the night he asked for a job!' said Harry, finishing his thought.

'I beg your pardon?'

'He hid the diadem in the castle, the night he asked Dumbledore to let him teach!' said Harry. Saying it out loud enabled him to make sense of it all. 'He must've hidden the diadem on his way up to, or down from, Dumbledore's office! But it was still worth trying to get the job – then he might've got the chance to nick Gryffindor's sword as well – thank you, thanks!'

Harry left her floating there, looking utterly bewildered. As he rounded the corner back into the Entrance Hall, he checked his watch. It was five minutes until midnight, and though he now knew *what* the last Horcrux was, he was no closer to discovering *where* it was ...

Generations of students had failed to find the diadem; that suggested that it was not in the Ravenclaw Tower – but if not there, where? What hiding place had Tom Riddle discovered inside Hogwarts castle, that he believed would remain secret forever?

Lost in desperate speculation, Harry turned a corner, but he had taken only a few steps down the new corridor when the window to his left broke

第 31 章 霍格沃茨的战斗

她闭上眼睛，点了点头。

"我……我不知道……他……很会讨人喜欢。他似乎……似乎善解人意……有同情心……"

没错，哈利想，海莲娜·拉文克劳想要霸占她无权获得的宝物的欲望，汤姆·里德尔当然能够理解。

"唉，被里德尔花言巧语骗去东西的，可不止你一个人。"哈利嘟囔道，"需要的时候，他可以使自己变得很迷人……"

这么说，伏地魔从格雷女士那里套出了失踪的冠冕的下落。他去了那座遥远的森林，把藏着的冠冕取了回来，那时他大概离开霍格沃茨不久，还没有开始在博金-博克商店工作。

多年以后，当伏地魔需要一个地方潜伏下来，不受打扰地度过漫长的十年时，那些荒凉偏僻的阿尔巴尼亚森林不正是他理想的避难所吗？

可是，冠冕一旦成为他宝贵的魂器，就不会留在那棵卑微的树里了……不，冠冕已被秘密送回它真正的家，伏地魔肯定把它放在了那里——

"——他来申请工作的那天夜里！"哈利终于理清了思路。

"你说什么？"

"他来请求邓布利多让他教书的那天晚上，把冠冕藏在了城堡里！"哈利说，把想法大声说出来使推理变得更清晰了，"他上楼或下楼到邓布利多的办公室去时，肯定顺路把冠冕藏了起来！但他仍然想争取到那份工作——那样他就有机会把格兰芬多的宝剑也偷到手了——谢谢你，太感谢了！"

哈利转身离去，只留下幽灵飘飘悠悠地浮荡在那里，一脸迷惑。哈利转弯返回门厅时看了看表：离午夜还差五分钟了，他虽然弄清了最后一个魂器是什么，但它究竟藏在哪里，他仍然一无所知……

多少代学生都没能找到冠冕，这就说明它不在拉文克劳塔楼里——但不在那里，又在哪里呢？汤姆·里德尔在霍格沃茨城堡里找到了怎样的秘密场所，并且相信那个地方永远不为人知呢？

哈利一边拼命思索，一边又拐过一个弯，但他在这条新的走廊里

CHAPTER THIRTY-ONE   The Battle of Hogwarts

open with a deafening, shattering crash. As he leapt aside, a gigantic body flew in through the window and hit the opposite wall. Something large and furry detached itself, whimpering, from the new arrival and flung itself at Harry.

'Hagrid!' Harry bellowed, fighting off Fang the boarhound's attentions as the enormous bearded figure clambered to his feet. 'What the –?'

'Harry, yer here! *Yer here!*'

Hagrid stooped down, bestowed upon Harry a cursory and rib-cracking hug, then ran back to the shattered window.

'Good boy, Grawpy!' he bellowed through the hole in the window. 'I'll see yer in a moment, there's a good lad!'

Beyond Hagrid, out in the dark night, Harry saw bursts of light in the distance and heard a weird, keening scream. He looked down at his watch: it was midnight. The battle had begun.

'Blimey, Harry,' panted Hagrid, 'this is it, eh? Time ter fight?'

'Hagrid, where have you come from?'

'Heard You-Know-Who from up in our cave,' said Hagrid grimly. 'Voice carried, didn' it? "Yeh got 'til midnight ter gimme Potter." knew yeh mus' be here, knew what mus' be happenin'. Get *down*, Fang. So we come ter join in, me an' Grawpy an' Fang. Smashed our way through the boundary by the forest, Grawpy was carryin' us, Fang an' me. Told him ter let me down at the castle so he shoved me through the window, bless him. Not exac'ly what I meant, bu' – where's Ron an' Hermione?'

'That,' said Harry, 'is a really good question. Come on.'

They hurried together along the corridor, Fang lolloping beside them. Harry could hear movement through the corridors all around: running footsteps, shouts; through the windows, he could see more flashes of light in the dark grounds.

'Where're we goin'?' puffed Hagrid, pounding along at Harry's heels, making the floorboards quake.

'I dunno exactly,' said Harry, making another random turn, 'but Ron and Hermione must be around here somewhere.'

第31章 霍格沃茨的战斗

没走几步，就听到哗啦一声巨响，左边的窗户突然爆开。他赶紧跳到一边，一个庞然大物从窗户外飞了进来，撞在对面的墙上。紧接着又见一个毛茸茸的大东西从这庞然大物身上挣脱出来，低声吠叫着朝哈利扑来。

"海格！"哈利大吼一声，拼命摆脱猎狗牙牙的殷勤，那个胡子拉碴的庞然大物费力地站了起来，"怎么——？"

"哈利，你在这儿！你在这儿！"

海格弯下腰匆匆抱了一下哈利，几乎勒断了他的肋骨，然后又跑回打碎的窗户前。

"好孩子，格洛普！"他对着窗户上的窟窿喊道，"待会儿见，乖孩子！"

在海格身后漆黑的夜色中，哈利看见远处突然射出几道强光，又听见一声古怪的、哀恸的尖叫。他低头看了看表：正是午夜。战斗开始了。

"天哪，哈利，"海格喘着气说，"这就来了，是不？开战了？"

"海格，你从哪儿来的？"

"我们在上面山洞里听见了神秘人的声音，"海格神色严峻地说，"那声音传得真远，是不？'午夜之前你们必须把波特交出来。'我就知道你肯定在这儿，就知道发生了什么事。下来，牙牙。所以我们就来参战了，我和格洛普还有牙牙。格洛普驮着我和牙牙，从森林里突破了学校的边界。我叫他在城堡里把我放下来，结果他就把我从窗口塞了进来，真有他的！其实我不是那个意思，可——罗恩和赫敏呢？"

"嘿，"哈利说，"可真让你问着了。走吧。"

他们一起在走廊上匆匆往前走，牙牙蹦蹦跳跳地跟在旁边。哈利听见四下的走廊里响声杂沓：奔跑声，喊叫声。他透过窗户看见漆黑的场地上闪烁着一道道强光。

"我们去哪儿？"海格气喘吁吁地问，他脚步沉重地跟着哈利，震得地板都在颤抖。

"我也不知道。"哈利说着，又盲目地拐了个弯，"但罗恩和赫敏肯定在这附近的什么地方。"

CHAPTER THIRTY-ONE   The Battle of Hogwarts

The first casualties of the battle were already strewn across the passage ahead: the two stone gargoyles that usually guarded the entrance to the staff room had been smashed apart by a jinx that had sailed through another broken window. Their remains stirred feebly on the floor, and as Harry leapt over one of their disembodied heads it moaned faintly, 'Oh, don't mind me ... I'll just lie here and crumble ...'

Its ugly stone face made Harry think suddenly of the marble bust of Rowena Ravenclaw at Xenophilius's house, wearing that mad headdress – and then of the statue in Ravenclaw Tower, with the stone diadem upon her white curls ...

And as he reached the end of the passage, the memory of a third stone effigy came back to him: that of an ugly old warlock, on to whose head Harry himself had placed a wig and a battered, old tiara. The shock shot through Harry with the heat of Firewhisky, and he nearly stumbled.

He knew, at last, where the Horcrux sat waiting for him ...

Tom Riddle, who confided in no one and operated alone, might have been arrogant enough to assume that he, and only he, had penetrated the deepest mysteries of Hogwarts Castle. Of course, Dumbledore and Flitwick, those model pupils, had never set foot in that particular place, but he, Harry, had strayed off the beaten track in his time at school – here at last was a secret he and Voldemort knew, that Dumbledore had never discovered –

He was roused by Professor Sprout, who was thundering past followed by Neville and half a dozen others, all of them wearing earmuffs and carrying what appeared to be large potted plants.

'Mandrakes!' Neville bellowed at Harry over his shoulder as he ran. 'Going to lob them over the walls – they won't like this!'

Harry knew, now, where to go: he sped off, with Hagrid and Fang galloping behind him. They passed portrait after portrait, and the painted figures raced alongside them, wizards and witches in ruffs and breeches, in armour and cloaks, cramming themselves into each other's canvases, screaming news from other parts of the castle. As they reached the end of this corridor, the whole castle shook and Harry knew, as a gigantic vase blew off its plinth with explosive force, that it was in the grip of enchantments more sinister than those of the teachers and the Order.

第31章 霍格沃茨的战斗

前面的通道里已经躺着战场上的第一批伤亡者：平时看守教工休息室入口的两个滴水嘴石兽，已被从另一扇破窗户射进来的恶咒击中，变得四分五裂，残片在地板上有气无力地蠕动着。哈利从一个与身体分家的脑袋上一跃而过时，它虚弱地呻吟道："哦，别管我……就让我躺在这儿，自生自灭吧……"

那张丑陋的石脸使哈利突然想起了谢诺菲留斯家那尊罗伊纳·拉文克劳的大理石半身像，戴着那个可笑的头饰——接着又想起拉文克劳塔楼里的那尊塑像，白色的鬈发上戴着石头冠冕……

跑到通道尽头时，他又想起第三尊石像：一个丑陋的老男巫，哈利亲手给他脑袋上戴了一个旧发套和一个破烂的冠冕。哈利突然打了一个激灵，就像受了火焰威士忌的刺激，差点跌倒在地。

他终于知道了，知道魂器在什么地方等着他……

汤姆·里德尔一向独来独往，不相信任何人，他是那么傲慢，大概以为他——只有他一个人——了解霍格沃茨城堡里隐藏的最深的秘密。邓布利多和弗立维这些模范学生无疑从不涉足那个特殊的场所，然而哈利，在校时曾经光顾常人没去过的地方——终于，有了一个唯独他和伏地魔知道而邓布利多从未发现的秘密——

斯普劳特教授把他从沉思中惊醒，她脚步重重地走了过去，后面跟着纳威和六七个其他同学，都戴着耳套，手里拎着像是大型的盆栽植物。

"曼德拉草！"纳威一边跑，一边扭头对哈利喊道，"准备把它们抛出墙去——让他们尝尝滋味！"

现在哈利知道该往哪儿去了。他撒腿就跑，海格和牙牙跟在后面。他们经过一幅又一幅肖像，画中人也跟着他们一起跑，那些戴轮状皱领、穿马裤、套铠甲、披斗篷的男女巫师，乱纷纷地挤进别人的相框，大声通报着城堡别处的消息。他们跑到这条走廊的尽头时，整个城堡都在颤抖，一只巨大的花瓶突然爆裂，从底座炸碎了，于是哈利知道此刻控制城堡的是另一种魔法，比教师和凤凰社成员的咒语要邪恶得多。

CHAPTER THIRTY-ONE The Battle of Hogwarts

'It's all righ', Fang – it's all righ'!' yelled Hagrid, but the great boarhound had taken flight as slivers of china flew like shrapnel through the air, and Hagrid pounded off after the terrified dog, leaving Harry alone.

He forged on through the trembling passages, his wand at the ready, and for the length of one corridor the little painted knight, Sir Cadogan, rushed from painting to painting beside him, clanking along in his armour, screaming encouragement, his fat little pony cantering behind him.

'Braggarts and rogues, dogs and scoundrels, drive them out, Harry Potter, see them off!'

Harry hurtled round a corner and found Fred and a small knot of students, including Lee Jordan and Hannah Abbott, standing beside another empty plinth, whose statue had concealed a secret passageway. Their wands were drawn and they were listening at the concealed hole.

'Nice night for it!' Fred shouted, as the castle quaked again, and Harry sprinted by, elated and terrified in equal measure. Along yet another corridor he dashed, and then there were owls everywhere, and Mrs Norris was hissing and trying to bat them with her paws, no doubt to return them to their proper place ...

'Potter!'

Aberforth Dumbledore stood blocking the corridor ahead, his wand held ready.

'I've had hundreds of kids thundering through my pub, Potter!'

'I know, we're evacuating,' Harry said. 'Voldemort's –'

'– attacking because they haven't handed you over, yeah,' said Aberforth, 'I'm not deaf, the whole of Hogsmeade heard him. And it never occurred to any of you to keep a few Slytherins hostage? There are kids of Death Eaters you've just sent to safety. Wouldn't it have been a bit smarter to keep 'em here?'

'It wouldn't stop Voldemort,' said Harry, 'and your brother would never have done it.'

Aberforth grunted and tore away in the opposite direction.

Your brother would never have done it ... well, it was the truth, Harry thought, as he ran on again; Dumbledore, who had defended Snape for so long, would never have held students ransom ...

第 31 章 霍格沃茨的战斗

"没关系,牙牙——没关系!"海格大声喊道,可是破碎的瓷片像榴霰弹一样在空中飞溅,吓得大猎狗惊慌逃窜。海格嗵嗵嗵地跑去追它,留下了哈利一个人。

他举着魔杖,稳住脚步穿过一条条颤抖的通道,一个肖像中人——小个子骑士卡多根爵士,陪在哈利身旁从一幅肖像冲进另一幅肖像,大声喊着一些鼓励的话,一直跑了整整一条走廊。他的铠甲铿锵作响,那匹肥胖的小矮马小跑着跟在后面。

"吹牛大王、混蛋、流氓、无赖,把他们赶出去,哈利·波特,把他们打退!"

哈利快速拐过一个弯,发现弗雷德和一小伙学生,包括李·乔丹和汉娜·艾博,站在另一个空底座旁边,那上面的雕像原来掩藏着一个秘密通道。这些人都拿着魔杖,聚在隐蔽的洞口倾听动静。

"这个夜晚真过瘾!"弗雷德喊道。城堡又震颤起来,哈利既兴奋又害怕地冲了过去。他在另一条走廊里奔跑时,到处都是猫头鹰在飞,洛丽丝夫人嘶嘶叫着用爪子去拍打,无疑是想把它们赶回合适的地方……

"波特!"

阿不福思·邓布利多挡在了前面的走廊上,手里举着魔杖。

"几百个孩子闹纷纷地穿过我的酒吧,波特!"

"我知道,我们在疏散,"哈利说,"伏地魔——"

"——在进攻,因为他们没有把你交出去,我知道。"阿不福思说,"我不是聋子,整个霍格莫德村都听见了他的话。难道你们谁都没想到留下几个斯莱特林当人质吗?刚才被安全疏散的就有食死徒的孩子。把他们留在这里岂不更高明一些?"

"那也挡不住伏地魔,"哈利说,"而且你哥哥绝不会这么做。"

阿不福思不满地嘟囔着,大步朝另一个方向走远了。

你哥哥绝不会这么做……没错,正是这样,哈利一边想一边继续往前跑。邓布利多维护了斯内普那么长时间,他绝不会把学生扣作人质……

CHAPTER THIRTY-ONE The Battle of Hogwarts

And then he skidded round a final corner and with a yell of mingled relief and fury he saw them: Ron and Hermione, both with their arms full of large, curved, dirty yellow objects, Ron with a broomstick under his arm.

'Where the *hell* have you been?' Harry shouted.

'Chamber of Secrets,' said Ron.

'Chamber – *what?*' said Harry, coming to an unsteady halt before them.

'It was Ron, all Ron's idea!' said Hermione breathlessly. 'Wasn't it absolutely brilliant? There we were, after you left, and I said to Ron, even if we find the other one, how are we going to get rid of it? We still hadn't got rid of the cup! And then he thought of it! The Basilisk!'

'What the –?'

'Something to get rid of Horcruxes,' said Ron simply.

Harry's eyes dropped to the objects clutched in Ron and Hermione's arms: great, curved fangs torn, he now realised, from the skull of a dead Basilisk.

'But how did you get in there?' he asked, staring from the fangs to Ron. 'You need to speak Parseltongue!'

'He did!' whispered Hermione. 'Show him, Ron!'

Ron made a horrible, strangled hissing noise.

'It's what you did to open the locket,' he told Harry apologetically. 'I had to have a few goes to get it right, but,' he shrugged modestly, 'we got there in the end.'

'He was *amazing*!' said Hermione. 'Amazing!'

'So ...' Harry was struggling to keep up. 'So ...'

'So we're another Horcrux down,' said Ron, and from under his jacket he pulled the mangled remains of Hufflepuff's cup. 'Hermione stabbed it. Thought she should. She hasn't had the pleasure yet.'

'Genius!' yelled Harry.

'It was nothing,' said Ron, though he looked delighted with himself. 'So what's new with you?'

As he said it, there was an explosion from overhead: all three of them looked up as dust fell from the ceiling and they heard a distant scream.

'I know what the diadem looks like, and I know where it is,' said Harry, talking fast. 'He hid it exactly where I hid my old Potions book, where

第 31 章 霍格沃茨的战斗

哈利脚步打滑地拐过最后一个弯，顿时既放心又恼火地喊了起来。他看见他们了，罗恩和赫敏，两人怀里都抱着又大又弯、黄乎乎、脏兮兮的东西，罗恩胳膊底下还夹着一把扫帚。

"你们俩到底上哪儿去了？"哈利喊道。

"密室。"罗恩说。

"密——什么？"哈利说着，在他们面前摇摇晃晃地刹住脚步。

"是罗恩，都是罗恩的主意！"赫敏激动得气喘吁吁，"真是绝妙，不是吗？你走了以后，我就对罗恩说，即使找到了另一个魂器，又怎么毁掉它呢？那个金杯还没能毁掉呢！于是他就想起来了！蛇怪！"

"什么——？"

"除掉魂器的东西。"罗恩简单地说。

哈利的目光落在罗恩和赫敏怀里抱的那些东西上，才发现是从一个死去的蛇怪头上掰下来的弯曲的巨牙。

"你们怎么进去的呢？"哈利把目光从巨牙挪到罗恩身上，问道，"需要说蛇佬腔呀！"

"他说了！"赫敏小声说，"说给他听听，罗恩！"

罗恩发出一种难听的、窒息般的嘶嘶声。

"你打开挂坠盒时就这么说的。"他带点歉意地对哈利说，"我试了几次才说对，不过，"他谦虚地耸了耸肩，"我们总算进去了。"

"他真神！"赫敏说，"太神了！"

"所以……"哈利努力跟上他们的思路，"所以……"

"所以我们又干掉了一个魂器。"罗恩说着，从外衣里掏出赫奇帕奇金杯的残片，"是赫敏刺的，觉得应该由她来，她还没享受过这份乐趣呢。"

"你太有才了！"哈利喊道。

"没什么。"罗恩说，不过看上去对自己还是挺满意的，"你怎么样？"

他话音未落，他们的头顶上突然响起爆炸声。三人抬头看去，灰尘从天花板上纷纷撒落，接着远处传来一声喊叫。

"我知道冠冕是什么样子了，也知道它在哪儿。"哈利快速地说，"他

CHAPTER THIRTY-ONE The Battle of Hogwarts

everyone's been hiding stuff for centuries. He thought he was the only one to find it. Come on.'

As the walls trembled again, he led the other two back through the concealed entrance and down the staircase into the Room of Requirement. It was empty except for three women: Ginny, Tonks, and an elderly witch wearing a moth-eaten hat, whom Harry recognised immediately as Neville's grandmother.

'Ah, Potter,' she said crisply, as if she had been waiting for him. 'You can tell us what's going on.'

'Is everyone OK?' said Ginny and Tonks together.

''S far as we know,' said Harry. 'Are there still people in the passage to the Hog's Head?'

He knew that the Room would not be able to transform while there were still users inside it.

'I was the last to come through,' said Mrs Longbottom. 'I sealed it, I think it unwise to leave it open now Aberforth has left his pub. Have you seen my grandson?'

'He's fighting,' said Harry.

'Naturally,' said the old lady proudly. 'Excuse me, I must go and assist him.'

With surprising speed, she trotted off towards the stone steps.

Harry looked at Tonks.

'I thought you were supposed to be with Teddy at your mother's?'

'I couldn't stand not knowing —' Tonks looked anguished. 'She'll look after him — have you seen Remus?'

'He was planning to lead a group of fighters into the grounds —'

Without another word, Tonks sped off.

'Ginny,' said Harry, 'I'm sorry, but we need you to leave too. Just for a bit. Then you can come back in.'

Ginny looked simply delighted to leave her sanctuary.

'And then you can come back in!' he shouted after her, as she ran up the steps after Tonks. '*You've got to come back in!*'

'Hang on a moment!' said Ron sharply. 'We've forgotten someone!'

'Who?' asked Hermione.

第31章 霍格沃茨的战斗

把它藏在了我藏那本旧魔药课本的地方,好多世纪的人都把东西藏在那儿。他以为只有他一个人才能找到。走吧。"

墙壁又在颤抖,哈利领着两个同伴穿过隐蔽的入口,下楼来到有求必应屋。里面空荡荡的,只有三个女人:金妮、唐克斯,和一位头戴一顶虫蛀的帽子的老女巫,哈利一眼认出是纳威的奶奶。

"啊,波特,"她脆嘣嘣地说,似乎一直在等着他,"你可以跟我们说说情况了。"

"大家都好吗?"金妮和唐克斯同时问道。

"据我们所知还行。"哈利说,"通往猪头酒吧的通道里还有人吗?"

哈利知道,如果还有人在有求必应屋里面,它就不能变形。

"我是最后一个过来的,"隆巴顿夫人说,"我把它封上了。我想,现在阿不福思已经离开酒吧,再让通道敞着就不妥当了。你看见我孙子了吗?"

"他在战斗呢。"哈利说。

"那是当然。"老太太自豪地说,"请原谅,我得去帮他。"

随后,她以惊人的速度奔向了石阶。

哈利看着唐克斯。

"你不是在你母亲家里陪着小泰迪吗?"

"我受不了蒙在鼓里的滋味——"唐克斯显得很痛苦,"我母亲会照顾他的——你看见莱姆斯了吗?"

"他要领一支队伍去场地作战——"

唐克斯二话没说就跑了。

"金妮,"哈利说,"对不起,我们需要你也离开一下。就一会儿,然后你可以再进来。"

金妮似乎正巴不得离开她的庇护所呢。

"然后你可以再进来!"哈利看见金妮跟着唐克斯跑上石阶,忙冲着她的背影喊道,"你一定要再进来!"

"等等!"罗恩突然说道,"我们把谁给忘记了!"

"谁?"赫敏问。

CHAPTER THIRTY-ONE   The Battle of Hogwarts

'The house-elves, they'll all be down in the kitchen, won't they?'

'You mean we ought to get them fighting?' asked Harry.

'No,' said Ron seriously, 'I mean we should tell them to get out. We don't want any more Dobbys, do we? We can't order them to die for us –'

There was a clatter as the Basilisk fangs cascaded out of Hermione's arms. Running at Ron, she flung them around his neck and kissed him full on the mouth. Ron threw away the fangs and broomstick he was holding and responded with such enthusiasm that he lifted Hermione off her feet.

'Is this the moment?' Harry asked weakly, and when nothing happened except that Ron and Hermione gripped each other still more firmly and swayed on the spot, he raised his voice. 'OI! There's a war going on here!'

Ron and Hermione broke apart, their arms still around each other.

'I know, mate,' said Ron, who looked as though he had recently been hit on the back of the head with a Bludger, 'so it's now or never, isn't it?'

'Never mind that, what about the Horcrux?' Harry shouted. 'D'you think you could just – just hold it in until we've got the diadem?'

'Yeah – right – sorry –' said Ron, and he and Hermione set about gathering up fangs, both pink in the face.

It was clear, as the three of them stepped back into the corridor upstairs, that in the minutes that they had spent in the Room of Requirement the situation within the castle had deteriorated severely: the walls and ceiling were shaking worse than ever; dust filled the air and through the nearest window Harry saw bursts of green and red light so close to the foot of the castle that he knew the Death Eaters must be very near to entering the place. Looking down, Harry saw Grawp the giant meandering past, swinging what looked like a stone gargoyle torn from the roof and roaring his displeasure.

'Let's hope he steps on some of them!' said Ron, as more screams echoed from close by.

'As long as it's not any of our lot!' said a voice: Harry turned and saw Ginny and Tonks, both with their wands drawn at the next window, which was missing several panes. Even as he watched, Ginny sent a well-aimed jinx into a crowd of fighters below.

'Good girl!' roared a figure running through the dust towards them, and Harry saw Aberforth again, his grey hair flying as he led a small group of students past. 'They look like they might be breaching the North Battlements, they've brought giants of their own!'

第 31 章 霍格沃茨的战斗

"家养小精灵,他们都在下面的厨房里,不是吗?"

"你是说应该让他们参加战斗?"哈利问。

"不,"罗恩严肃地说,"我是说应该叫他们赶紧逃走。我们不想再出现更多的多比,对吗?不能要求他们为我们去死——"

哗啦啦,赫敏怀里的蛇怪牙齿纷纷落在地上。她奔向罗恩,一把搂紧他的脖子,吻住他的嘴唇。罗恩丢掉手里的蛇牙和扫帚,以火热的激情做出回应,把赫敏抱得双脚离地。

"这时间合适吗?"哈利底气不足地说,罗恩和赫敏却搂得更紧了,在那里相拥着微微摇晃,哈利提高了声音,"喂!这里正打仗呢!"

罗恩和赫敏猛地松开,但胳膊还搂着对方。

"我知道,伙计,"罗恩说,他的模样就像被一个游走球砸中了后脑勺,"机不可失,时不再来嘛,对吧?"

"这事先放一放吧,魂器怎么办?"哈利大声说,"你们能不能——能不能先忍一忍,等我们找到冠冕再说?"

"噢——好的——对不起——"罗恩说,然后开始和赫敏捡起蛇怪的牙齿,两个人的脸都红红的。

三个人回到楼上的走廊里,才发现就在刚才进入有求必应屋的几分钟内,城堡里的局势严重恶化:墙壁和天花板抖得更厉害了,空气里灰尘弥漫。哈利透过近旁的窗户看见一道道绿光和红光在城堡脚下很近的地方飞射,他知道食死徒肯定很快就要冲进来了。哈利往下望去,巨人格洛普漫无目的地走过,一边甩着一个像是从房顶上拽下来的滴水嘴石兽,一边不高兴地吼叫着。

"但愿他能踩倒几个人!"罗恩说,旁边又传来几声惨叫。

"只要不是我们自己人就行!"一个声音说,哈利一扭头,看见金妮和唐克斯都已拔出魔杖,站在旁边缺了几块玻璃的窗户前。就在他注视她们的当儿,金妮朝下面一群搏斗的人发了个恶咒,打得很准。

"好姑娘!"尘土中一个身影朝他们跑过来吼道,哈利又看见了阿不福思,他灰色的头发四下飘舞,领着一小群学生匆匆而过,"看样子他们要攻破北面的墙垛,他们也带了巨人!"

CHAPTER THIRTY-ONE   The Battle of Hogwarts

'Have you seen Remus?' Tonks called after him.

'He was duelling Dolohov,' shouted Aberforth, 'haven't seen him since!'

'Tonks,' said Ginny, 'Tonks, I'm sure he's OK –'

But Tonks had run off into the dust after Aberforth.

Ginny turned, helpless, to Harry, Ron and Hermione.

'They'll be all right,' said Harry, though he knew they were empty words. 'Ginny, we'll be back in a moment, just keep out of the way, keep safe – come on!' he said to Ron and Hermione, and they ran back to the stretch of wall beyond which the Room of Requirement was waiting to do the bidding of the next entrant.

I need the place where everything is hidden, Harry begged of it, inside his head, and the door materialised on their third run past.

The furore of the battle died the moment they crossed the threshold and closed the door behind them: all was silent. They were in a place the size of a cathedral with the appearance of a city, its towering walls built of objects hidden by thousands of long-gone students.

'And he never realised *anyone* could get in?' said Ron, his voice echoing in the silence.

'He thought he was the only one,' said Harry. 'Too bad for him I've had to hide stuff in my time ... this way,' he added, 'I think it's down here ...'

He passed the stuffed troll and the Vanishing Cabinet Draco Malfoy had mended last year with such disastrous consequences, then hesitated, looking up and down aisles of junk; he could not remember where to go next ...

'*Accio diadem*,' cried Hermione in desperation, but nothing flew through the air towards them. It seemed that, like the vault at Gringotts, the room would not yield its hidden objects that easily.

'Let's split up,' Harry told the other two. 'Look for a stone bust of an old man wearing a wig and a tiara! It's standing on a cupboard and it's definitely somewhere near here ...'

They sped off up adjacent aisles; Harry could hear the others' footsteps echoing through the towering piles of junk, of bottles, hats, crates, chairs, books, weapons, broomsticks, bats ...

'Somewhere near here,' Harry muttered to himself. 'Somewhere ... somewhere ...'

第31章 霍格沃茨的战斗

"你看见莱姆斯了吗?"唐克斯冲着他的背影大声问。

"刚才他在和多洛霍夫决斗,"阿不福思喊道,"后来就没看见他了!"

"唐克斯,"金妮说,"唐克斯,我相信他没事的——"

可是唐克斯已经在飞扬的尘土中跑去追赶阿不福思了。

金妮无奈地转过身,看着哈利、罗恩和赫敏。

"他们不会有事的。"哈利说,但也知道这句话空洞无力,"金妮,我们过一会儿就回来,你要远离危险,注意安全——走吧!"他对罗恩、赫敏说,三个人跑回那面墙,墙后面就是有求必应屋,正等着执行进入者的吩咐。

我需要那个藏东西的地方,哈利在脑海里恳求道,当他们第三次跑过时,门出现了。

他们跨过门槛,把门关上,战斗的喧闹声立刻就听不见了,四下里一片寂静。这地方有教堂那么大,周围的景物看着像一座城市,那些林立的高墙,是由成千上万个早已不在人世的学生所藏的东西组成的。

"他从来不知道任何人都能进来?"罗恩说,声音在寂静中回响。

"他以为只有他能进来,"哈利说,"也该他倒霉,我那时碰巧要藏东西……这边走,"他又说,"我想就在这里……"

他经过巨怪标本,又经过德拉科·马尔福去年试图修理却造成了悲惨后果的那个消失柜,然后他迟疑了,打量着垃圾堆之间的通道,不记得接下来该往哪儿走……

"冠冕飞来。"赫敏焦急地大喊一声,可是并没有东西朝他们飞来。这房间似乎也像古灵阁的地下金库一样,不肯轻易把它收藏的东西交出来。

"我们分头寻找吧,"哈利对两个同伴说,"找一个戴发套和头冠的老头儿的半身石像!它放在一个大柜子上,肯定就在这附近的什么地方……"

他们顺着邻近的几条通道迅速跑开。哈利听见两个同伴的脚步声在高高耸立的垃圾堆间回响,瓶子、帽子、箱子、椅子、书本、武器、扫帚、球棒……

"就在这附近的什么地方,"哈利喃喃自语,"就在……就在……"

CHAPTER THIRTY-ONE   The Battle of Hogwarts

Deeper and deeper into the labyrinth he went, looking for objects he recognised from his one previous trip into the room. His breath was loud in his ears, and then his very soul seemed to shiver: there it was, right ahead, the blistered old cupboard in which he had hidden his old Potions book, and on top of it, the pock-marked stone warlock wearing a dusty, old wig and what looked like an ancient, discoloured tiara.

He had already stretched out his hand, though he remained ten feet away, when a voice behind him said, 'Hold it, Potter.'

He skidded to a halt and turned round. Crabbe and Goyle were standing behind him, shoulder to shoulder, wands pointing right at Harry. Through the small space between their jeering faces, he saw Draco Malfoy.

'That's my wand you're holding, Potter,' said Malfoy, pointing his own through the gap between Crabbe and Goyle.

'Not any more,' panted Harry, tightening his grip on the hawthorn wand. 'Winners, keepers, Malfoy. Who's lent you theirs?'

'My mother,' said Draco.

Harry laughed, though there was nothing very humorous about the situation. He could not hear Ron or Hermione any more. They seemed to have run out of earshot, searching for the diadem.

'So how come you three aren't with Voldemort?' asked Harry.

'We're gonna be rewarded,' said Crabbe: his voice was surprisingly soft for such an enormous person; Harry had hardly ever heard him speak before. Crabbe was smiling like a small child promised a large bag of sweets. 'We 'ung back, Potter. We decided not to go. Decided to bring you to 'im.'

'Good plan,' said Harry in mock admiration. He could not believe that he was this close, and was going to be thwarted by Malfoy, Crabbe and Goyle. He began edging slowly backwards towards the place where the Horcrux sat lopsided upon the bust. If he could just get his hands on it before the fight broke out …

'So how did you get in here?' he asked, trying to distract them.

'I virtually lived in the Room of Hidden Things all last year,' said Malfoy, his voice brittle. 'I know how to get in.'

'We was hiding in the corridor outside,' grunted Goyle. 'We can do Disslusion Charms now! And then,' his face split into a gormless grin, 'you

第31章 霍格沃茨的战斗

他在迷宫里越走越深，寻找着上次进这个房间看见过的东西，耳边响着自己粗重的呼吸声。突然，他的灵魂似乎颤抖起来：有了，就在前面。那个表面起泡的旧柜子，他曾把那本旧魔药课本藏在了里面，而在柜子的顶上，正是那个布满麻点的男巫半身像，头上戴着灰扑扑的旧发套，还有一个古旧褪色的王冠一样的东西。

虽然还差十来步，哈利已把手伸了出去，可是突然他身后有个声音说道："站住，波特。"

哈利脚下打着滑停了下来，转身一看，克拉布和高尔并肩站在他身后，都用魔杖指着他。在两张讥讽的面孔之间狭小的空当里，他看见了德拉科·马尔福。

"你拿的是我的魔杖，波特。"马尔福说，他自己手里的魔杖从克拉布和高尔之间的空隙里指着哈利。

"已经不是了，"哈利喘着气说，一边攥紧手里的山楂木魔杖，"谁赢的归谁，马尔福。是什么人把自己的魔杖借给了你？"

"我母亲。"德拉科说。

哈利笑了起来，其实这情形并没有什么可笑的。他已经听不见罗恩和赫敏的声音，他们大概跑到远处去寻找冠冕了。

"你们三个怎么没跟伏地魔在一起？"哈利问。

"我们想得到奖赏。"克拉布说，对于这么一个大块头来说，他的声音轻柔得令人吃惊。哈利以前几乎没有听他说过话。克拉布像个将要得到一大袋糖果的小孩一样天真地笑着。"我们留下来了，波特。我们决定不走了，决定把你带去见他。"

"想得真妙。"哈利假装夸奖他。他简直不敢相信马尔福、克拉布和高尔将会使他功亏一篑。他开始慢慢地、一点一点地向后挪动，魂器就在那里，歪戴在半身像的脑袋上。只要开战前他能用手把它抓住……

"你们是怎么进来的？"他问，想转移他们的注意力。

"去年一年我几乎都住在藏宝屋里。"马尔福用尖厉的声音说，"我知道怎么进来。"

"我们刚才就躲在外面的走廊里。"高尔嘟嘟囔囔地说，"我们现在

CHAPTER THIRTY-ONE The Battle of Hogwarts

turned up right in front of us and said you was looking for a die-dum! What's a die-dum?'

'Harry?' Ron's voice echoed suddenly from the other side of the wall to Harry's right. 'Are you talking to someone?'

With a whip-like movement, Crabbe pointed his wand at the fifty-foot mountain of old furniture, of broken trunks, of old books and robes and unidentifiable junk and shouted, '*Descendo!*'

The wall began to totter, then crumbled into the aisle next door where Ron stood.

'Ron!' Harry bellowed, as somewhere out of sight Hermione screamed, and Harry heard innumerable objects crashing to the floor on the other side of the destabilised wall: he pointed his wand at the rampart, cried, '*Finite!*' and it steadied.

'No!' shouted Malfoy, staying Crabbe's arm as the latter made to repeat his spell. 'If you wreck the room, you might bury this diadem thing!'

'What's that matter?' said Crabbe, tugging himself free. 'It's Potter the Dark Lord wants, who cares about a die-dum?'

'Potter came in here to get it,' said Malfoy with ill-disguised impatience at the slow-wittedness of his colleagues, 'so that must mean –'

'"Must mean"?' Crabbe turned on Malfoy with undisguised ferocity. 'Who cares what you think? I don't take your orders no more, *Draco*. You an' your dad are finished.'

'Harry?' shouted Ron again, from the other side of the junk wall. 'What's going on?'

'Harry?' mimicked Crabbe. 'What's going – no, Potter! *Crucio!*'

Harry had lunged for the tiara; Crabbe's curse missed him but hit the stone bust, which flew into the air; the diadem soared upwards and then dropped out of sight in the mass of objects on which the bust had rested.

'STOP!' Malfoy shouted at Crabbe, his voice echoing through the enormous room. 'The Dark Lord wants him alive –'

'So? I'm not killing him, am I?' yelled Crabbe, throwing off Malfoy's restraining arm, 'but if I can, I will, the Dark Lord wants him dead anyway, what's the diff–?'

第31章 霍格沃茨的战斗

会施幻身咒啦!结果,"他绽开一个傻乎乎的笑容,"你突然在我们面前冒了出来,说要找一个冠帽!什么是冠帽?"

"哈利?"罗恩的声音突然从哈利右侧墙的另一边传来,"你在跟人说话吗?"

说时迟那时快,克拉布突然用魔杖一指那堆五十英尺高的垃圾墙——都是破旧的家具、箱子、课本、校袍,以及无法辨认的其他杂物,大喊一声:"应声落地!"

垃圾墙开始摇晃,然后倒塌在罗恩所在的隔壁通道里。

"罗恩!"哈利喊道,赫敏在看不见的地方发出尖叫,摇摆不定的垃圾墙的另一边有数不清的东西稀里哗啦落到地上。哈利用魔杖指着墙大叫:"咒立停!"垃圾墙不再摇晃了。

"别!"克拉布还想再念一遍那个咒语,马尔福大喊一声拽住他的胳膊,"如果你把这屋子毁了,那个什么冠冕就会被埋掉!"

"那有什么关系?"克拉布说着,使劲挣脱了马尔福,"黑魔王要的是波特,谁在乎一个破帽子?"

"波特到这儿来是为了找它,"马尔福勉强掩饰着对头脑迟钝的同伙的不耐烦,说道,"那肯定意味着——"

"'肯定意味着'?"克拉布带着不加掩饰的凶狠转向马尔福,"谁管你是怎么想的,我再也不听你发号施令了,德拉科。你和你爹都完蛋了。"

"哈利?"罗恩又在垃圾墙的另一边喊道,"怎么回事?"

"哈利?"克拉布学着他的腔调说,"怎么回事——不,波特!钻心剜骨!"

哈利已经冲过去拿那头冠,克拉布的咒语没有击中他,却击中了石像。石像立刻飞到空中,冠冕被抛了起来,然后随着石像落在一大堆杂物里,看不见了。

"**住手!**"马尔福冲克拉布大喊,声音在巨大的房间里回响,"黑魔王想要抓活的——"

"那又怎么样?我又没有要他的命!"克拉布嚷道,使劲挣脱马尔福拉着他的胳膊,"要是能把他干掉也好,反正黑魔王是要他死,有什么两样——?"

CHAPTER THIRTY-ONE

The Battle of Hogwarts

A jet of scarlet light shot past Harry by inches: Hermione had run round the corner behind him and sent a Stunning Spell straight at Crabbe's head. It only missed because Malfoy pulled him out of the way.

'It's that Mudblood! *Avada Kedavra!*'

Harry saw Hermione dive aside and his fury that Crabbe had aimed to kill wiped all else from his mind. He shot a Stunning Spell at Crabbe, who lurched out of the way, knocking Malfoy's wand out of his hand; it rolled out of sight beneath a mountain of broken furniture and boxes.

'Don't kill him! DON'T KILL HIM!' Malfoy yelled at Crabbe and Goyle, who were both aiming at Harry: their split second's hesitation was all Harry needed.

'*Expelliarmus!*'

Goyle's wand flew out of his hand and disappeared into the bulwark of objects beside him; Goyle leapt foolishly on the spot, trying to retrieve it; Malfoy jumped out of range of Hermione's second Stunning Spell and Ron, appearing suddenly at the end of the aisle, shot a full Body-Bind Curse at Crabbe, which narrowly missed.

Crabbe wheeled round and screamed, '*Avada Kedavra!*' again. Ron leapt out of sight to avoid the jet of green light. The wandless Malfoy cowered behind a three-legged wardrobe as Hermione charged towards them, hitting Goyle with a Stunning Spell as she came.

'It's somewhere here!' Harry yelled at her, pointing at the pile of junk into which the old tiara had fallen. 'Look for it while I go and help R—'

'HARRY!' she screamed.

A roaring, billowing noise behind him gave him a moment's warning. He turned and saw both Ron and Crabbe running as hard as they could up the aisle towards them.

'Like it hot, scum?' roared Crabbe as he ran.

But he seemed to have no control over what he had done. Flames of abnormal size were pursuing them, licking up the sides of the junk bulwarks, which were crumbling to soot at their touch.

'*Aguamenti!*' Harry bawled, but the jet of water that soared from the tip of his wand evaporated in the air.

'RUN!'

第31章 霍格沃茨的战斗

一道耀眼的红光从哈利身旁几寸的地方射过：是赫敏在他身后的拐弯处跑来，冲着克拉布的脑袋发了个昏迷咒。马尔福赶紧把克拉布拉到一边，咒语没有击中。

"是那个泥巴种！阿瓦达索命！"

哈利看见赫敏倒地躲闪。克拉布竟然起了杀心，哈利的怒火腾地冒起来，脑子里忘记了一切。他朝克拉布发了个昏迷咒，克拉布赶紧闪身躲避，把马尔福手里的魔杖撞掉了。魔杖滚到堆积如山的旧家具和破箱子下面不见了。

"**别杀死他！别杀死他！**"马尔福朝同时瞄准哈利的克拉布和高尔嚷道，他们俩略一迟疑，这对哈利来说已经够了。

"除你武器！"

高尔的魔杖从手里飞了出去，消失在他身旁的杂物堆里，高尔傻乎乎地原地跳了跳，想把魔杖找回来。马尔福蹿起来躲过赫敏的第二个昏迷咒。罗恩突然出现在通道尽头，对准克拉布发了个全身束缚咒，但偏了一点没有击中。

克拉布迅速转身，又叫了一声："阿瓦达索命！"罗恩纵身一跳，躲过了那道绿光。赫敏冲上前，边跑边用昏迷咒击中了高尔，没有魔杖的马尔福缩在一个三条腿的大衣柜后面。

"它就在这里！"哈利指着旧头冠落入的那堆垃圾对赫敏喊道，"把它找出来，我去帮罗——"

"**哈利！**"赫敏大叫一声。

哈利身后突然传来呼啸、奔涌的声音，刹那间他有了一种不祥的预感。他一转身，看见罗恩和克拉布顺着通道没命地奔了过来。

"喜欢烫的吧，废物？"克拉布边跑边吼。

但是克拉布似乎无法控制自己做的事情。熊熊的烈焰追着他们，吞噬着垃圾墙的边缘，火舌所到之处都变成了灰烬。

"清水如泉！"哈利大叫，但是杖尖喷出的水柱立刻在空气中蒸发了。

"快跑！"

CHAPTER THIRTY-ONE   The Battle of Hogwarts

Malfoy grabbed the Stunned Goyle and dragged him along: Crabbe outstripped all of them, now looking terrified; Harry, Ron and Hermione pelted along in his wake, and the fire pursued them. It was not normal fire; Crabbe had used a curse of which Harry had no knowledge: as they turned a corner the flames chased them as though they were alive, sentient, intent upon killing them. Now the fire was mutating, forming a gigantic pack of fiery beasts: flaming serpents, Chimaeras and dragons rose and fell and rose again, and the detritus of centuries on which they were feeding was thrown up in the air into their fanged mouths, tossed high on clawed feet, before being consumed by the inferno.

Malfoy, Crabbe and Goyle had vanished from view: Harry, Ron and Hermione stopped dead; the fiery monsters were circling them, drawing closer and closer, claws and horns and tails lashed, and the heat was solid as a wall around them.

'What can we do?' Hermione screamed over the deafening roars of the fire. 'What can we do?'

'Here!'

Harry seized a pair of heavy-looking broomsticks from the nearest pile of junk and threw one to Ron, who pulled Hermione on to it behind him. Harry swung his leg over the second broom and, with hard kicks to the ground, they soared up into the air, missing by feet the horned beak of a flaming raptor that snapped its jaws at them. The smoke and heat were becoming overwhelming: below them the cursed fire was consuming the contraband of generations of hunted students, the guilty outcomes of a thousand banned experiments, the secrets of the countless souls who had sought refuge in the room. Harry could not see a trace of Malfoy, Crabbe or Goyle anywhere: he swooped as low as he dared over the marauding monsters of flame to try to find them, but there was nothing but fire: what a terrible way to die ... he had never wanted this ...

'Harry, let's get out, let's get out!' bellowed Ron, though it was impossible to see where the door was through the black smoke.

And then Harry heard a thin, piteous human scream from amidst the terrible commotion, the thunder of devouring flame.

'It's – too – dangerous –!' Ron yelled, but Harry wheeled in the air. His glasses giving his eyes some small protection from the smoke, he raked the firestorm below, seeking a sign of life, a limb or a face that was not yet charred like wood ...

第31章　霍格沃茨的战斗

马尔福抓住被击昏的高尔，拖着他一起逃去，此刻已神色惊慌的克拉布跑在了最前面。哈利、罗恩和赫敏跟着他飞奔，大火追在他们身后。这不是一般的火，克拉布施了一个哈利不知道的魔咒。他们拐了个弯，火立刻追了上来，就好像这些火焰是有生命有感觉的，决意要把他们烧死。这时候，火焰开始变形，变成一大群由火组成的野兽：火蛇、客迈拉和火龙，它们腾起来，落下去，又腾起来，多少个世纪积累的破烂垃圾被抛在空中，掉进它们长着獠牙的嘴里，落在它们长着利爪的脚上，最后被地狱般的烈火吞没。

马尔福、克拉布和高尔不见了，哈利、罗恩和赫敏突然停下脚步：那些火兽把他们围在中间，越逼越近，爪子、尖角和尾巴啪啪甩动，热浪像墙壁一样围住他们。

"怎么办？"赫敏在火焰震耳欲聋的怒吼中尖叫着问，"怎么办哪？"

"给！"

哈利从最近的垃圾堆上抓过两把看着很沉重的扫帚，扔了一把给罗恩。罗恩拉过赫敏坐在他身后，哈利骑上第二把扫帚，用脚使劲踢了几下地面，飞到空中，离一只张嘴要咬他们的喷火巨鸟的利喙只差几英尺。浓烟和热浪令人窒息，在他们下面，邪恶的大火吞噬着多少代被追查的学生的非法物品，吞噬着千百个违禁试验的罪恶成果，吞噬着数不清的人藏在这个房间里的秘密。哈利四处都看不见马尔福、克拉布和高尔的影子。他在那些贪婪凶恶的火兽上方尽量飞得很低，寻找他们，但是除了火看不见别的：这样的死法太惨了……他绝不希望……

"哈利，我们出去吧，我们出去吧！"罗恩吼道，但是在黑黑的浓烟中根本看不见门在哪里。

就在这时，在可怕的混乱中，在吞噬一切的火焰的轰鸣中，哈利听见了一个人微弱的惨叫声。

"太——太——危险了——！"罗恩嚷道，可是哈利还在空中盘旋。浓烟弥漫中，他的眼镜多少对眼睛起了些保护作用。他掠过下面熊熊的火阵，寻找生命的迹象，寻找没被烧成焦炭的一只胳膊、一张脸……

CHAPTER THIRTY-ONE   The Battle of Hogwarts

And he saw them: Malfoy with his arms around the unconscious Goyle, the pair of them perched on a fragile tower of charred desks, and Harry dived. Malfoy saw him coming, and raised one arm, but even as Harry grasped it he knew at once that it was no good: Goyle was too heavy and Malfoy's hand, covered in sweat, slid instantly out of Harry's –

'IF WE DIE FOR THEM, I'LL KILL YOU, HARRY!' roared Ron's voice, and as a great, flaming Chimaera bore down upon them he and Hermione dragged Goyle on to their broom and rose, rolling and pitching, into the air once more as Malfoy clambered up behind Harry.

'The door, get to the door, the door!' screamed Malfoy in Harry's ear, and Harry sped up, following Ron, Hermione and Goyle through the billowing black smoke, hardly able to breathe: and all around them the last few objects unburned by the devouring flames were flung into the air, as the creatures of the cursed fire cast them high in celebration: cups and shields, a sparkling necklace and an old, discoloured tiara –

'*What are you doing, what are you doing? The door's that way!*' screamed Malfoy, but Harry made a hairpin swerve and dived. The diadem seemed to fall in slow motion, turning and glittering as it dropped towards the maw of a yawning serpent, and then he had it, caught it around his wrist –

Harry swerved again as the serpent lunged at him, he soared upwards and straight towards the place where, he prayed, the door stood open: Ron, Hermione and Goyle had vanished, Malfoy was screaming and holding Harry so tightly it hurt. Then, through the smoke, Harry saw a rectangular patch on the wall and steered the broom at it, and moments later clean air filled his lungs and they collided with the wall in the corridor beyond.

Malfoy fell off the broom and lay face down, gasping, coughing and retching. Harry rolled over and sat up: the door to the Room of Requirement had vanished and Ron and Hermione sat panting on the floor beside Goyle, who was still unconscious.

'C – Crabbe,' choked Malfoy, as soon as he could speak. 'C – Crabbe …'

'He's dead,' said Ron harshly.

There was silence, apart from panting and coughing. Then a number of huge bangs shook the castle, and a great cavalcade of transparent figures galloped past on horses, their heads screaming with bloodlust under their

第31章 霍格沃茨的战斗

他看见了，马尔福搂住不省人事的高尔，在烧焦的桌子堆成的摇摇欲坠的高塔上。哈利俯冲下去，马尔福看见他过来，赶紧举起一只胳膊，但哈利刚一抓住就知道没有用。高尔太重，马尔福的手上都是汗，立刻就从哈利手中滑脱了——

"如果我们被他们拖死，我就杀了你，哈利！"罗恩的声音吼道。就在一个巨大的喷火客迈拉扑过来时，他和赫敏把高尔拖到了他们的扫帚上，然后打着转儿、起伏不定地再次飞到空中，与此同时，马尔福爬到了哈利身后。

"门，往门那儿飞，门！"马尔福在哈利的耳边叫道。哈利加快速度，跟着罗恩、赫敏和高尔穿过令人窒息的滚滚黑烟。在他们周围，最后几件没被烈焰烧毁的东西，被邪恶的火中怪兽们欢庆地抛向了空中：杯子、盾牌、一串闪亮的项链，还有一个古旧而褪色的王冠——

"你干什么？你干什么？门在那边！"马尔福尖叫道，但是哈利突然一个急转弯，俯冲下去。闪闪发光的冠冕似乎在以慢动作降落，它翻转着，慢慢地落向一条巨蛇大张着的嘴里。在这千钧一发之际，哈利得手了，用手腕套住了它——

巨蛇朝他扑来，哈利又一转身飞向空中，朝着他祈祷有门开着的地方飞去。罗恩、赫敏和高尔不见了，马尔福一边尖叫，一边紧紧抓住哈利，把哈利抓得生疼。接着，哈利在浓烟中看见墙上有一块长方形的东西，便调整扫帚对准它冲去。片刻之后，新鲜的空气灌进了他的肺里，他们撞在了外面走廊的墙上。

马尔福从扫帚上摔了下去，脸朝下趴在地上，喘气、咳嗽、连连干呕。哈利翻了个身坐起来：有求必应屋的门消失了，罗恩和赫敏坐在地板上喘着粗气，旁边的高尔仍然神志不清。

"克——克拉布，"马尔福刚能说话，就哽噎着说，"克——克拉布……"

"他死了。"罗恩毫不客气地说。

沉默，只听见喘气和咳嗽声。接着一连串砰砰的巨响，震得整个城堡都在颤抖，一支由透明的人影组成的浩浩荡荡的队伍，骑着马飞

CHAPTER THIRTY-ONE   The Battle of Hogwarts

arms. Harry staggered to his feet when the Headless Hunt had passed and looked around: the battle was still going on all around him. He could hear more screams than those of the retreating ghosts. Panic flared within him.

'Where's Ginny?' he said sharply. 'She was here. She was supposed to be going back into the Room of Requirement.'

'Blimey, d'you reckon it'll still work after that fire?' asked Ron, but he, too, got to his feet, rubbing his chest and looking left and right. 'Shall we split up and look –?'

'No,' said Hermione, getting to her feet too. Malfoy and Goyle remained slumped hopelessly on the corridor floor; neither of them had wands. 'Let's stick together. I say we go – Harry, what's that on your arm?'

'What? Oh, yeah –'

He pulled the diadem from his wrist and held it up. It was still hot, blackened with soot, but as he looked at it closely he was just able to make out the tiny words etched upon it:

*Wit beyond measure
is man's greatest treasure.*

A blood-like substance, dark and tarry, seemed to be leaking from the diadem. Suddenly Harry felt the thing vibrate violently, then break apart in his hands, and as it did so, he thought he heard the faintest, most distant scream of pain, echoing not from the grounds or the castle, but from the thing that had just fragmented in his fingers.

'It must have been Fiendfyre!' whimpered Hermione, her eyes on the broken pieces.

'Sorry?'

'Fiendfyre – cursed fire – it's one of the substances that destroy Horcruxes, but I would never, ever have dared use it, it's so dangerous. How did Crabbe know how to –?'

'Must've learned from the Carrows,' said Harry grimly.

'Shame he wasn't concentrating when they mentioned how to stop it, really,' said Ron, whose hair like Hermione's was singed, and whose face was blackened. 'If he hadn't tried to kill us all, I'd be quite sorry he was dead.'

第31章 霍格沃茨的战斗

奔而过,他们的脑袋夹在胳膊底下,还在杀气腾腾地呐喊着。无头猎手队经过后,哈利摇摇晃晃地站起来,打量着四周:战斗还在进行。除了那些撤退的幽灵在尖叫,他还听到更多的喊叫声。他的内心恐慌极了。

"金妮在哪儿?"他突然说道,"她刚才在这儿,她应该回到有求必应屋的。"

"天哪,在那场大火之后,你以为那屋子还管用吗?"罗恩问,但他也站了起来,一边揉着胸口一边左右张望,"我们分头找找——?"

"不。"赫敏说着也站起身。马尔福和高尔还是无力地瘫在走廊的地板上,两人都没了魔杖。"我们不要分开。我们走吧——哈利,你胳膊上是什么?"

"什么?噢,对了——"

他把冠冕从手腕上褪下来举在手里。冠冕还是滚烫的,上面沾满黑色的烟灰,但他仔细看时,勉强辨认出了上面刻着的细小的文字:

> 过人的聪明才智
> 是人类最大的财富。

一种血一般的、乌黑黏稠的东西,似乎正从冠冕里渗透出来。突然,哈利感到冠冕在剧烈地振动,然后在他手里裂成了碎片。它裂开时,哈利隐约听见了极其微弱、极其遥远的痛苦的惨叫,不是从城堡或场地传来,而是从他手指间那个刚刚碎裂的东西里发出来的。

"肯定是厉火!"赫敏眼睛盯着那些碎片,带着哭腔说。

"你说什么?"

"厉火——邪恶的火——可以毁灭魂器的物质之一,但我一辈子也没胆量使用它,太危险了。克拉布怎么知道——?"

"肯定是从卡罗兄妹那里学来的。"哈利神色严峻地说。

"真可惜,他没有专心听他们讲怎么把火熄灭。"罗恩说,他的头发跟赫敏的一样被烤焦了,脸上黑乎乎的,"要不是他一心想杀死我们,我倒会为他的死感到难过呢。"

CHAPTER THIRTY-ONE The Battle of Hogwarts

'But don't you realise?' whispered Hermione. 'This means, if we can just get the snake –'

But she broke off as yells and shouts and the unmistakeable noises of duelling filled the corridor. Harry looked around and his heart seemed to fail: Death Eaters had penetrated Hogwarts. Fred and Percy had just backed into view, both of them duelling masked and hooded men.

Harry, Ron and Hermione ran forwards to help: jets of light flew in every direction and the man duelling Percy backed off, fast: then his hood slipped and they saw a high forehead and streaked hair –

'Hello, Minister!' bellowed Percy, sending a neat jinx straight at Thicknesse, who dropped his wand and clawed at the front of his robes, apparently in awful discomfort. 'Did I mention I'm resigning?'

'You're joking, Perce!' shouted Fred, as the Death Eater he was battling collapsed under the weight of three separate Stunning Spells. Thicknesse had fallen to the ground with tiny spikes erupting all over him; he seemed to be turning into some form of sea urchin. Fred looked at Percy with glee.

'You actually *are* joking, Perce ... I don't think I've heard you joke since you were –'

The air exploded. They had been grouped together, Harry, Ron, Hermione, Fred and Percy, the two Death Eaters at their feet, one Stunned, the other Transfigured: and in that fragment of a moment, when danger seemed, temporarily, at bay, the world was rent apart. Harry felt himself flying through the air, and all he could do was hold as tightly as possible to that thin stick of wood that was his one and only weapon, and shield his head in his arms: he heard the screams and yells of his companions without a hope of knowing what had happened to them –

And then the world resolved itself into pain and semi-darkness: he was half buried in the wreckage of a corridor that had been subjected to a terrible attack: cold air told him that the side of the castle had been blown away and hot stickiness on his cheek told him that he was bleeding copiously. Then he heard a terrible cry that pulled at his insides, that expressed agony of a kind neither flame nor curse could cause, and he stood up, swaying, more frightened than he had been that day, more frightened, perhaps, than he had been in his life ...

第31章 霍格沃茨的战斗

"可是你想没想到?"赫敏小声说,"这就是说,如果我们能把那条蛇——"

她的话没有说完,因为尖叫声、呐喊声,还有分明的格斗声响彻了整个走廊。哈利环顾四周,心里不禁一沉:食死徒已经攻进了霍格沃茨。弗雷德和珀西后退着出现了,两人都在跟戴兜帽的蒙面大汉决斗。

哈利、罗恩和赫敏跑上前去相助,一道道强光射向四面八方,跟珀西格斗的那个人快速后退,他的兜帽滑落了,他们看见他高高的额头和杂色的头发。

"你好,部长!"珀西大喊一声,冲着辛克尼斯干脆利落地发了个恶咒。辛克尼斯丢掉魔杖,用手抓住长袍的胸口处,显然难受极了。"我说过我要辞职的吧?"珀西补充了一句。

"你在说笑话,珀西!"弗雷德喊道,跟他搏斗的那个食死徒在三个昏迷咒的重击下瘫倒了。辛克尼斯倒在地上,全身冒出许多小钉子,好像正在变成一种海胆。弗雷德高兴地看着珀西。

"你真是在说笑话,珀西……我好像很久没听你说笑话了,自从你——"

空气突然爆炸了。他们刚才聚拢在一起,哈利、罗恩、赫敏、弗雷德、珀西,还有他们脚边的两个食死徒,一个中了昏迷咒,一个中了变形咒。接着,在危险似乎暂未来临的一瞬间,世界被撕裂了。哈利觉得自己飞到了空中,只能死死地抓住那根细细的木棍——他唯一的武器,并用双臂护住脑袋。他听见了同伴们的大喊和惨叫,却无法知道他们到底怎么样了——

然后,世界渐渐化为疼痛和一片模糊:他半个身子都被废墟埋住了,走廊刚才遭到了可怕的袭击。寒冷的空气告诉他,城堡的一侧被炸飞了,面颊上湿热、黏稠的感觉告诉他,他正在大量流血。接着,他听见一声令他揪心的惨叫,那叫声里所表达的痛苦,绝不是火焰或咒语能够引起的。哈利摇摇晃晃地站起身,心头极度恐惧,比他这一天,也许是这一辈子的任何时候都要恐惧……

CHAPTER THIRTY-ONE The Battle of Hogwarts

And Hermione was struggling to her feet in the wreckage, and three red-headed men were grouped on the ground where the wall had blasted apart. Harry grabbed Hermione's hand as they staggered and stumbled over stone and wood.

'No – no – no!' someone was shouting. 'No! Fred! No!'

And Percy was shaking his brother, and Ron was kneeling beside them, and Fred's eyes stared without seeing, the ghost of his last laugh still etched upon his face.

第 31 章 霍格沃茨的战斗

赫敏从废墟中挣扎着站起来,三个红头发的人聚在墙壁被炸飞的地方。哈利抓住赫敏的手,两人跌跌撞撞地走过碎石头和碎木片。

"不——不——不!"有人在大喊,"不!弗雷德!不!"

珀西摇晃着他的弟弟;罗恩跪在他们身边;弗雷德的两只眼睛空洞地瞪着,脸上还留着最后的一丝笑容。

CHAPTER THIRTY-TWO

The Elder Wand

The world had ended, so why had the battle not ceased, the castle fallen silent in horror, and every combatant laid down their arms? Harry's mind was in freefall, spinning out of control, unable to grasp the impossibility, because Fred Weasley could not be dead, the evidence of all his senses must be lying –

And then a body fell past the hole blown into the side of the school and curses flew in at them from the darkness, hitting the wall behind their heads.

'Get down!' Harry shouted, as more curses flew through the night: he and Ron had both grabbed Hermione and pulled her to the floor, but Percy lay across Fred's body, shielding it from further harm, and when Harry shouted, 'Percy, come on, we've got to move!' he shook his head.

'Percy!' Harry saw tear tracks streaking the grime coating Ron's face as he seized his elder brother's shoulders and pulled, but Percy would not budge. 'Percy, you can't do anything for him! We're going to –'

Hermione screamed, and Harry, turning, did not need to ask why. A monstrous spider the size of a small car was trying to climb through the huge hole in the wall: one of Aragog's descendants had joined the fight.

Ron and Harry shouted together; their spells collided and the monster was blown backwards, its legs jerking horribly, and vanished into the darkness.

'It brought friends!' Harry called to the others, glancing over the edge of the castle through the hole in the wall the curses had blasted: more giant spiders were climbing the side of the building, liberated from the Forbidden Forest into which the Death Eaters must have penetrated. Harry fired Stunning Spells down upon them, knocking the lead monster into its fellows, so that they rolled back down the building and out of sight. Then more curses came soaring over

第 32 章

老 魔 杖

世界终结了，为什么战斗还没有停止，城堡没有陷入恐怖的沉寂，还有人没有放下武器？哈利的思想如自由落体一般坠落，失控地旋转着，不能理解这桩不可思议的事情，弗雷德·韦斯莱不可能死，哈利所有的感官肯定都在欺骗他——

这时，一具身体从外墙上被炸开的豁口处坠下，许多咒语噼里啪啦地从黑暗中朝他们射来，击中了他们脑袋后面的墙壁。

"蹲下！"哈利大喊，又一批咒语从夜空飞来。他和罗恩同时抓住赫敏把她拖倒在地，可是珀西伏在弗雷德的遗体上，挡住弟弟不让他再受伤害。哈利嚷道："珀西，走吧，我们必须离开！"但珀西只是摇头。

"珀西！"哈利看见罗恩脸上的污泥被泪水冲出了两道沟，看见罗恩抓住哥哥的肩膀使劲地拽，可是珀西不肯动弹，"珀西，你为他做不了什么！我们要去——"

赫敏失声尖叫，哈利一转身，明白了她尖叫的原因。一只像小汽车那么大的巨蜘蛛正从墙上的大豁口爬进来：阿拉戈克的一位后代也参加了战斗。

罗恩和哈利同时大喊，两个咒语撞在一起，那个怪物被打退了，它的腿可怕地抽动着，消失在黑暗中。

"它带来了同伙！"哈利大声对其他人说。他透过墙上被咒语炸出的窟窿朝城堡外望去，又有许多巨蜘蛛从墙壁外侧爬上来。一定是食死徒闯入禁林，把它们放了出来。哈利朝它们连连发射昏迷咒，领头的蜘蛛被打倒了，摔在它的同伙身上，它们一起翻滚着掉下城堡，消

CHAPTER THIRTY-TWO The Elder Wand

Harry's head, so close he felt the force of them blow his hair.

'Let's move, NOW!'

Pushing Hermione ahead of him with Ron, Harry stooped to seize Fred's body under the armpits. Percy, realising what Harry was trying to do, stopped clinging to the body and helped; together, crouching low to avoid the curses flying at them from the grounds, they hauled Fred out of the way.

'Here,' said Harry, and they placed him in a niche where a suit of armour had stood earlier. He could not bear to look at Fred a second longer than he had to, and after making sure that the body was well hidden he took off after Ron and Hermione. Malfoy and Goyle had vanished, but at the end of the corridor, which was now full of dust and falling masonry, glass long gone from the windows, he saw many people running backwards and forwards, whether friends or foes he could not tell. Rounding the corner, Percy let out a bull-like roar, 'ROOKWOOD!' and sprinted off in the direction of a tall man, who was pursuing a couple of students.

'Harry, in here!' Hermione screamed.

She had pulled Ron behind a tapestry. They seemed to be wrestling together, and for one mad second Harry thought that they were embracing again; then he saw that Hermione was trying to restrain Ron, to stop him running after Percy.

'Listen to me – *LISTEN, RON!*'

'I wanna help – I wanna kill Death Eaters –'

His face was contorted, smeared with dust and smoke, and he was shaking with rage and grief.

'Ron, we're the only ones who can end it! Please – Ron – we need the snake, we've got to kill the snake!' said Hermione.

But Harry knew how Ron felt: pursuing another Horcrux could not bring the satisfaction of revenge; he too wanted to fight, to punish them, the people who had killed Fred, and he wanted to find the other Weasleys, and above all make sure, make quite sure, that Ginny was not – but he could not permit that idea to form in his mind –

'We *will* fight!' Hermione said. 'We'll have to, to reach the snake! But let's not lose sight, now, of what we're supposed to be d – doing! We're the only ones who can end it!'

第32章 老魔杖

失了。接着，又有咒语从哈利头顶上掠过，离得真近哪，他感到魔咒的力量把他的头发都吹动了。

"快走，**快**！"

他把赫敏推上前，让她和罗恩一起走，自己俯身拽住弗雷德的胳肢窝。珀西明白了哈利的意图，便不再紧贴在遗体上，也出手相助。他们猫腰躲避着从场地上射来的魔咒，一起拖着弗雷德离开了危险地带。

"这儿。"哈利说，他们把弗雷德放在本来有一套铠甲的壁龛里。哈利不敢再多看弗雷德一眼，在确保遗体藏好以后，他便跟着罗恩和赫敏跑开了。马尔福和高尔不见了，走廊尽头灰尘弥漫，散落着被击碎的石块，窗户上的玻璃早就没有了。哈利看见走廊尽头有许多人奔来奔去，不知是敌是友。转过一个弯，珀西像公牛一样大吼一声："**卢克伍德！**"就冲一个正在追赶两个学生的高个子男巫奔了过去。

"哈利，在这里！"赫敏尖叫道。

她刚才把罗恩拖到了一幅挂毯后面，两人似乎扭在一起。哈利一时没明白过来，以为他们俩又在拥抱，接着看见赫敏在拼命阻拦罗恩，不让他跑去追珀西。

"听我说——**听我说，罗恩！**"

"我要去帮忙——我要去杀食死徒——"

他的脸扭曲了，满是黑烟和泥灰，愤怒和悲痛使他浑身发抖。

"罗恩，只有我们能够结束这一切！求求你——罗恩——我们需要找到那条蛇，我们必须杀死那条蛇！"赫敏说。

可是哈利理解罗恩的感受。寻找另一个魂器不可能带来复仇的快感。他也想投入战斗，去惩罚他们，惩罚那些杀死弗雷德的人，他还想找到韦斯莱家的其他人，最重要的是弄清，百分之百地弄清金妮没有被——然而他不允许那个念头在脑海里成形——

"我们要战斗！"赫敏说，"我们必须战斗，才能接近那条蛇！但现在千万不能忘记我们应该做的事——事情！只有我们才能结束这一切！"

CHAPTER THIRTY-TWO The Elder Wand

She was crying too, and she wiped her face on her torn and singed sleeve as she spoke, but she took great, heaving breaths to calm herself as, still keeping a tight hold on Ron, she turned to Harry.

'You need to find out where Voldemort is, because he'll have the snake with him, won't he? Do it, Harry – look inside him!'

Why was it so easy? Because his scar had been burning for hours, yearning to show him Voldemort's thoughts? He closed his eyes on her command, and at once, the screams and the bangs and all the discordant sounds of the battle were drowned until they became distant, as though he stood far, far away from them ...

He was standing in the middle of a desolate but strangely familiar room, with peeling paper on the walls and all the windows boarded except for one. The sounds of the assault on the castle were muffled and distant. The single unblocked window revealed distant bursts of light where the castle stood, but inside the room it was dark except for a solitary oil lamp.

He was rolling his wand between his fingers, watching it, his thoughts on the Room in the castle, the secret Room only he had ever found, the Room, like the Chamber, that you had to be clever, and cunning, and inquisitive to discover ... he was confident that the boy would not find the diadem ... although Dumbledore's puppet had come much further than he had ever expected ... too far ...

'My Lord,' said a voice, desperate and cracked. He turned: there was Lucius Malfoy sitting in the darkest corner, ragged and still bearing the marks of the punishment he had received after the boy's last escape. One of his eyes remained closed and puffy. 'My Lord ... please ... my son ...'

'If your son is dead, Lucius, it is not my fault. He did not come and join me, like the rest of the Slytherins. Perhaps he has decided to befriend Harry Potter?'

'No – never,' whispered Malfoy.

'You must hope not.'

'Aren't – aren't you afraid, my Lord, that Potter might die at another hand but yours?' asked Malfoy, his voice shaking. 'Wouldn't it be ... forgive me ... more prudent to call off this battle, enter the castle and seek him y – yourself?'

'Do not pretend, Lucius. You wish the battle to cease so that you can

第32章 老魔杖

她也在哭,一边说一边用撕裂、烧焦的衣袖擦着脸,但她仍然紧紧抓着罗恩,做着深呼吸平静自己的情绪。她转身望着哈利。

"你需要弄清伏地魔在哪儿,他会把蛇带在身边的,对吗?快,哈利——到他脑子里去看看!"

为什么如此容易?是因为几小时来伤疤一直在灼痛,渴望向他展示伏地魔的思想?哈利听从赫敏的吩咐闭上了眼睛,立刻,战斗的呐喊声、撞击声,以及各种杂乱刺耳的声音都似乎被淹没了,变得若有若无。他仿佛站在离它们非常非常遥远的地方……

他站在一个破败却又异常熟悉的房间中央,周围的墙纸都剥落了,窗户都用木板封死,只留了一扇。城堡里攻击的声音隐约而遥远。透过那唯一没有封死的窗户,他可以看见远处城堡所在的地方射出道道光亮,可是房间里却黑乎乎的,只点着一盏油灯。

他手指间转动着一根魔杖,眼睛注视着它,心里却想着城堡里的那个房间,那个只有他自己发现的秘密房间。那个房间像密室一样,必须是特别聪明、机灵、好奇的人才能发现……他相信那男孩不会找到冠冕……尽管邓布利多的牵线木偶要比他原先料想的厉害得多……厉害得多……

"主人。"一个绝望而沙哑的声音说。他转过身,卢修斯·马尔福坐在最黑暗的角落里,一身破衣烂衫,脸上留着上次他在男孩逃跑后受到惩罚的痕迹,一只眼睛肿着,还不能睁开。"主人……求求您……我儿子……"

"卢修斯,如果你儿子死了,可不能怪我。他没有像其他斯莱特林一样过来投靠我。也许他决定去帮助哈利·波特了?"

"不——不可能。"马尔福小声说。

"最好没有。"

"主人,您就——您就不担心波特会死在别人手里吗?"马尔福声音颤抖地问,"如果……请您原谅……如果您下令结束战斗,亲——亲自到城堡里去找他,是不是更稳妥些?"

"别跟我来这套,卢修斯。你希望战斗停止,你就可以弄清你

CHAPTER THIRTY-TWO The Elder Wand

discover what has happened to your son. And I do not need to seek Potter. Before the night is out, Potter will have come to find me.'

Voldemort dropped his gaze once more to the wand in his fingers. It troubled him ... and those things that troubled Lord Voldemort needed to be rearranged ...

'Go and fetch Snape.'

'Snape, m – my Lord?'

'Snape. Now. I need him. There is a – service – I require from him. Go.'

Frightened, stumbling a little through the gloom, Lucius left the room. Voldemort continued to stand there, twirling the wand between his fingers, staring at it.

'It is the only way, Nagini,' he whispered, and he looked round, and there was the great, thick snake, now suspended in mid-air, twisting gracefully within the enchanted, protected space he had made for her, a starry, transparent sphere somewhere between glittering cage and tank.

With a gasp, Harry pulled back and opened his eyes; at the same moment his ears were assaulted with the screeches and cries, the smashes and bangs of battle.

'He's in the Shrieking Shack. The snake's with him, it's got some sort of magical protection around it. He's just sent Lucius Malfoy to find Snape.'

'Voldemort's sitting in the Shrieking Shack?' said Hermione, outraged. 'He's not – he's not even *fighting*?'

'He doesn't think he needs to fight,' said Harry. 'He thinks I'm going to go to him.'

'But why?'

'He knows I'm after Horcruxes – he's keeping Nagini close beside him – obviously I'm going to have to go to him to get near the thing –'

'Right,' said Ron, squaring his shoulders. 'So you can't go, that's what he wants, what he's expecting. You stay here and look after Hermione, and I'll go and get it –'

Harry cut across Ron.

'You two stay here, I'll go under the Cloak and I'll be back as soon as I –'

'No,' said Hermione, 'it makes much more sense if I take the Cloak and –'

'Don't even think about it,' Ron snarled at her.

第32章 老魔杖

儿子的下落了。我用不着去寻找波特。不出今夜,波特就会上门来找我。"

伏地魔的目光又一次落在手里的魔杖上。这魔杖让他困惑……而让伏地魔大人困惑的东西必须重新安排……

"去把斯内普叫来。"

"斯内普,主——主人?"

"斯内普。快。我需要他。有件事要他为我——效力。去吧。"

卢修斯心惊胆战,跌跌绊绊地走过黑暗的房间,离开了。伏地魔仍站在那里,转动着手指间的魔杖,眼睛也盯着它。

"只有这个办法了,纳吉尼。"他轻声说,转过目光,看着那条粗粗的大蛇。大蛇现在悬在半空中,在伏地魔为它设置的魔法保护空间里优雅地扭动着,那是一个星光闪闪的透明球体,既像一个闪光的笼子又像一个水箱。

哈利猛抽一口冷气,把思绪拉了回来,睁开眼睛,他的耳朵里立刻充满了战斗的尖叫声、呐喊声、撞击声和轰响声。

"他在尖叫棚屋。大蛇在他身边,蛇的周围好像有一层魔法保护。伏地魔刚派卢修斯·马尔福去找斯内普了。"

"伏地魔在尖叫棚屋?"赫敏气愤地说,"他没有——他甚至没有参加战斗?"

"他认为自己不用战斗,"哈利说,"他认为我会主动送上门去。"

"可是凭什么?"

"他知道我在寻找魂器——他把纳吉尼留在身边——显然我必须去找他才能接近那东西——"

"对,"罗恩说着挺起了胸脯,"所以你不能去,他正希望你去,盼着你去呢。你留在这里照顾赫敏,我去把那条——"

哈利打断了罗恩。

"你们俩留在这里,我穿着隐形衣去,很快就回来,只等我——"

"不,"赫敏说,"最妥当的办法还是我穿着隐形衣去——"

"你想都别想。"罗恩冲她吼道。

CHAPTER THIRTY-TWO The Elder Wand

Before Hermione could get further than, 'Ron, I'm just as capable –' the tapestry at the top of the staircase on which they stood was ripped open.

'POTTER!'

Two masked Death Eaters stood there, but even before their wands were fully raised, Hermione shouted, '*Glisseo!*'

The stairs beneath their feet flattened into a chute and she, Harry and Ron hurtled down it, unable to control their speed but so fast that the Death Eaters' Stunning Spells flew far over their heads. They shot through the concealing tapestry at the bottom and spun on to the floor, hitting the opposite wall.

'*Duro!*' cried Hermione, pointing her wand at the tapestry, and there were two loud, sickening crunches as the tapestry turned to stone and the Death Eaters pursuing them crumpled against it.

'Get back!' shouted Ron, and he, Harry and Hermione flattened themselves against a door as a herd of galloping desks thundered past, shepherded by a sprinting Professor McGonagall. She appeared not to notice them: her hair had come down and there was a gash on her cheek. As she turned the corner, they heard her scream: 'CHARGE!'

'Harry, you get the Cloak on,' said Hermione. 'Never mind us –'

But he threw it over all three of them; large though they were, he doubted anyone would see their disembodied feet through the dust that clogged the air, the falling stone, the shimmer of spells.

They ran down the next staircase and found themselves in a corridor full of duellers. The portraits on either side of the fighters were crammed with figures, screaming advice and encouragement, while Death Eaters both masked and unmasked duelled students and teachers. Dean had won himself a wand, for he was face to face with Dolohov, Parvati with Travers. Harry, Ron and Hermione raised their wands at once, ready to strike, but the duellers were weaving and darting around so much that there was a strong likelihood of hurting one of their own side if they cast curses. Even as they stood braced, looking for the opportunity to act, there came a great '*wheeeeeeeeeeee!*' and, looking up, Harry saw Peeves zooming over them, dropping Snargaluff pods down on to the Death Eaters, whose heads were suddenly engulfed in wriggling, green tubers like fat worms.

'Argh!'

第32章 老魔杖

赫敏刚说了半句"罗恩,我也有能力——"就见他们所在的楼梯顶上的挂毯突然被撕开了。

"**波特!**"

两个蒙面食死徒站在那里,但没等他们举起魔杖,赫敏就大喊了一声:"滑道平平!"

脚下的楼梯突然变成了平滑的斜道,赫敏、哈利和罗恩立刻往下冲去,速度太快了,根本刹不住,食死徒的昏迷咒高高地从他们头顶上掠过。他们飞速穿过楼梯底部隐藏的挂毯,在地上打了好几个滚,撞到对面的墙上。

"幻形石板!"赫敏用魔杖指着挂毯大叫,随着嘭嘭两声难听的巨响,挂毯变成了石头,追他们的两个食死徒撞在上面不省人事。

"往后退!"罗恩大喊,他和哈利、赫敏把身子贴在一扇门上,一大堆桌子轰隆隆地跑过,麦格教授在一旁飞奔着指挥它们,似乎没有发现他们三个。她头发散了下来,面颊上有一道伤口。他们听见她转过弯后大声叫道:"冲啊!"

"哈利,你穿上隐形衣,"赫敏说,"别管我们——"

可是哈利把隐形衣披在三个人身上,虽然他们个头大了,但是空气里满是灰尘、碎落的石头以及一道道咒语的闪光,他估计没人会看见他们没有身体的脚。

他们又跑下一道楼梯,发现这里的走廊上都是格斗者。蒙面和没有蒙面的食死徒在跟师生们搏斗,两边的肖像里挤满了人,都在嚷嚷着出主意,给他们鼓劲。迪安为自己赢得了一根魔杖,正面对面地跟多洛霍夫拼杀,帕瓦蒂在对付特拉弗斯。哈利、罗恩和赫敏立刻举起魔杖想投入战斗,可是那些格斗者不停地穿梭移动,如果发射咒语,很可能会伤到自己人。他们站在那里,随时准备找机会出击,这时突然传来"嘀嘀嘀嘀!"的大叫。哈利抬头一看,皮皮鬼从他们头顶上飞过,一边把疙瘩藤的荚果朝食死徒扔去,食死徒的脑袋立刻淹没在许多胖毛虫般蠕动的绿疙瘩里。

"哎哟!"

CHAPTER THIRTY-TWO The Elder Wand

A fistful of tubers had hit the Cloak over Ron's head; the slimy, green roots were suspended improbably in mid-air as Ron tried to shake them loose.

'Someone's invisible there!' shouted a masked Death Eater, pointing.

Dean made the most of the Death Eater's momentary distraction, knocking him out with a Stunning Spell; Dolohov attempted to retaliate and Parvati shot a Body-Bind Curse at him.

'LET'S GO!' Harry yelled, and he, Ron and Hermione gathered the Cloak tightly around themselves and pelted, heads down, through the midst of the fighters, slipping a little in pools of Snargaluff juice, towards the top of the marble staircase into the Entrance Hall.

'I'm Draco Malfoy, I'm Draco, I'm on your side!'

Draco was on the upper landing, pleading with another masked Death Eater. Harry Stunned the Death Eater as they passed: Malfoy looked around, beaming, for his saviour, and Ron punched him from under the Cloak. Malfoy fell backwards on top of the Death Eater, his mouth bleeding, utterly bemused.

'And that's the second time we've saved your life tonight, you two-faced bastard!' Ron yelled.

There were more duellers all over the stairs and in the Hall, Death Eaters everywhere Harry looked: Yaxley, close to the front doors, in combat with Flitwick, a masked Death Eater duelling Kingsley right beside them. Students ran in every direction, some carrying or dragging injured friends. Harry directed a Stunning Spell towards the masked Death Eater, it missed but nearly hit Neville, who had emerged from nowhere brandishing armfuls of Venomous Tentacula, which looped itself happily around the nearest Death Eater and began reeling him in.

Harry, Ron and Hermione sped down the marble staircase: glass shattered to their left and the Slytherin hourglass that had recorded house points spilled its emeralds everywhere, so that people slipped and staggered as they ran. Two bodies fell from the balcony overhead as they reached the ground and a grey blur that Harry took for an animal sped four-legged across the hall to sink its teeth into one of the fallen.

'NO!' shrieked Hermione, and with a deafening blast from her wand Fenrir Greyback was thrown backwards from the feebly stirring body of Lavender Brown. He hit the marble banisters and struggled to return to his

第32章 老魔杖

一把疙瘩扔到了披着隐形衣的罗恩脑袋上,罗恩想把它抖掉,那黏糊糊的绿色根茎荒唐地悬在半空。

"这里有个隐身人!"一个蒙面食死徒指着喊道。

迪安充分利用食死徒分神的一刹那,用一个昏迷咒把他击倒了。多洛霍夫试图报复,帕瓦蒂给了他一个全身束缚咒。

"**我们走!**"哈利大喊一声,他和罗恩、赫敏用隐形衣紧紧裹住身体,埋着脑袋,从格斗者们中间朝着通向门厅的大理石楼梯顶冲去,脚踩在疙瘩藤的黏液里直打滑。

"我是德拉科·马尔福,我是德拉科,我是你们一边的!"

德拉科在上面的楼梯平台上央求一个蒙面食死徒。他们三个跑过时,哈利把食死徒击昏了。马尔福高兴地转脸寻找他的救命恩人,罗恩从隐形衣下给了他一拳。马尔福仰面摔倒在食死徒身上,嘴里流血,神情十分困惑。

"这是今晚我们第二次救你小命了,你这个两面三刀的混蛋!"罗恩嚷道。

楼梯上、门厅里挤满了格斗者,哈利放眼看去,到处都是食死徒。靠近前门的亚克斯利正在跟弗立维搏斗。就在他们身边,一个蒙面食死徒在跟金斯莱较量。学生们四下奔跑,有的抱着、拖着受伤的朋友。哈利朝蒙面食死徒发了一个昏迷咒,没有击中他,却差点击中了纳威。纳威甩着一大堆毒触手不知从什么地方钻了出来,毒触手高兴地盘到离它最近的那个食死徒身上,开始把他缠绕起来。

哈利、罗恩和赫敏冲下大理石楼梯,左边突然传来玻璃砸碎的声音,记录学院分数的斯莱特林沙漏被打碎了,里面的绿宝石撒得到处都是,奔跑的人们脚底打滑,摇摇晃晃。他们跑到底楼时,两具人体从上面的楼厅上掉了下来,一个灰色的身影——哈利以为是一只动物,四脚着地跑过大厅,对准掉下来的一个人咬了下去。

"不!"赫敏尖叫道,她的魔杖发出震耳欲聋的一声炸响,芬里尔·格雷伯克从拉文德·布朗微微悸动的身体旁被击退了,撞到大理石扶栏上,

CHAPTER THIRTY-TWO The Elder Wand

feet. Then, with a bright white flash and a crack, a crystal ball fell on the top of his head and he crumpled to the ground and did not move.

'I have more!' shrieked Professor Trelawney from over the banisters, 'more for any who want them! Here –'

And with a movement like a tennis serve, she heaved another enormous crystal sphere from her bag, waved her wand through the air, and caused the ball to speed across the hall and smash through a window. At the same moment, the heavy wooden front doors burst open, and more of the gigantic spiders forced their way into the Entrance Hall.

Screams of terror rent the air: the fighters scattered, Death Eaters and Hogwartians alike, and red and green jets of light flew into the midst of the oncoming monsters, which shuddered and reared, more terrifying than ever.

'How do we get out?' yelled Ron over all the screaming, but before either Harry or Hermione could answer they were bowled aside: Hagrid had come thundering down the stairs, brandishing his flowery pink umbrella.

'Don't hurt 'em, don't hurt 'em!' he yelled.

'HAGRID, NO!'

Harry forgot everything else: he sprinted out from under the Cloak, running bent double to avoid the curses illuminating the whole Hall.

'HAGRID, COME BACK!'

But he was not even halfway to Hagrid when he saw it happen: Hagrid vanished amongst the spiders, and with a great scurrying, a foul swarming movement, they retreated under the onslaught of spells, Hagrid buried in their midst.

'HAGRID!'

Harry heard someone calling his own name, whether friend or foe he did not care: he was sprinting down the front steps into the dark grounds, and the spiders were swarming away with their prey, and he could see nothing of Hagrid at all.

'HAGRID!'

He thought he could make out an enormous arm waving from the midst of the spider swarm, but as he made to chase after them, his way was impeded by a monumental foot, which swung down out of the darkness and made the ground on which he stood shudder. He looked up: a giant stood

第32章 老魔杖

挣扎着站起身来。接着，一道耀眼的白光一闪，一声爆裂的脆响，一只水晶球落在他的头顶上，他立刻瘫倒在地，再也不动弹了。

"我这儿还有呢！"特里劳妮教授从上面的扶栏上叫道，"还有谁想要！给——"

她就像网球的发球员一样，又从袋子里掏出一只巨大的水晶球，并在空中挥舞着魔杖，让球飞速穿过门厅，破窗而出。就在这时，沉重的木头大门被撞开了，又一批巨蜘蛛闯进了门厅。

空气里充斥着惊恐的尖叫，那些战斗者，不管是食死徒还是霍格沃茨师生，纷纷四下逃窜，一道道红光、绿光射到逼上前来的怪物们中间。它们发着抖，用后腿站立起来，比刚才更吓人了。

"我们怎么出去呢？"罗恩在一片尖叫声中大喊，哈利和赫敏还没来得及回答，就被撞到了一边。海格轰隆轰隆地跑下楼梯，挥舞着他那把粉红色的花伞。

"别伤害它们，别伤害它们！"他嚷道。

"海格，不！"

哈利忘记了一切，他从隐形衣下冲了出去，弯腰躲避着那些把整个门厅都照亮了的魔咒。

"海格，回来！"

他朝海格跑去，但没等跑到一半，那一幕就在他眼前发生了：海格消失在蜘蛛群里。面对强大的咒语攻势，密密麻麻、臭烘烘的大蜘蛛纷纷后退，杂沓混乱，海格被埋在它们中间不见了踪影。

"海格！"

哈利听见有人在叫自己的名字，不知是敌是友，但他只顾冲下前门的台阶，冲到黑黢黢的场地上。大蜘蛛们带着它们的猎物浩浩荡荡地离开了，他根本看不见海格的影子。

"海格！"

他隐约分辨出蜘蛛群里有一条硕大的胳膊在挥动，正要追过去，却被一只巨大无比的脚挡住了去路。这只脚从黑暗中踏过来，震得土地都在颤抖。哈利抬头望去，一个巨人站在他面前，足有二十英尺高，

CHAPTER THIRTY-TWO   The Elder Wand

before him, twenty feet high, its head hidden in shadow, nothing but its tree-like, hairy shins illuminated by light from the castle doors. With one brutal, fluid movement, it smashed a massive fist through an upper window and glass rained down upon Harry, forcing him back under the shelter of the doorway.

'Oh my –!' shrieked Hermione, as she and Ron caught up with Harry and gazed upwards at the giant now trying to seize people through the window above.

'DON'T!' Ron yelled, grabbing Hermione's hand as she raised her wand. 'Stun him and he'll crush half the castle –'

'HAGGER?'

Grawp came lurching round the corner of the castle; only now did Harry realise that Grawp was, indeed, an undersized giant. The gargantuan monster trying to crush people on the upper floors looked around and let out a roar. The stone steps trembled as he stomped towards his smaller kin, and Grawp's lopsided mouth fell open, showing yellow, half-brick-sized teeth, and then they launched themselves at each other with the savagery of lions.

'RUN!' Harry roared; the night was full of hideous yells and blows as the giants wrestled, and he seized Hermione's hand and tore down the steps into the grounds, Ron bringing up the rear. Harry had not lost hope of finding and saving Hagrid; he ran so fast that they were halfway towards the Forest before they were brought up short again.

The air around them had frozen: Harry's breath caught and solidified in his chest. Shapes moved out in the darkness, swirling figures of concentrated blackness, moving in a great wave towards the castle, their faces hooded and their breath rattling …

Ron and Hermione closed in beside him as the sounds of fighting behind them grew suddenly muted, deadened, because a silence only Dementors could bring was falling thickly through the night …

'Come on, Harry!' said Hermione's voice, from a very long way away, 'Patronuses, Harry, come on!'

He raised his wand, but a dull hopelessness was spreading through him: Fred was gone, and Hagrid was surely dying or already dead; how many more lay dead that he did not yet know about; he felt as though his soul had already half left his body …

'HARRY, COME ON!' screamed Hermione.

第32章 老魔杖

脑袋隐在阴影里,只有树干般的、汗毛森森的小腿被城堡门内透出的灯光照着。巨人动作残暴而流畅,把一只大拳头猛地杵进楼上的一扇窗户,玻璃碎片雨点般落在哈利身上,迫使他退回到门口。

"哦,天——!"赫敏尖叫,她和罗恩追上哈利,抬头注视着正想从楼上窗户里往外抓人的巨人。

"别!"罗恩大喊一声,抓住赫敏举起魔杖的手,"别把他击昏,他会压塌半个城堡——"

"海格?"

格洛普摇摇晃晃地从城堡一角拐了过来。哈利这才发现格洛普实际上是个小个子巨人。那个想把楼上的人捏碎的庞然大物扭过头来,发出一声吼叫。他重重地朝他的矮个儿同类走去,石头台阶在他的脚下颤抖,格洛普的歪嘴张开了,露出黄兮兮的、半块砖那么大的牙齿,然后两个巨人像狮子一般狂野地朝对方扑去。

"快跑!"哈利大吼一声。两个巨人扭作一团,黑夜里充斥着可怕的喊叫声和重击声。哈利抓住赫敏的手奔下台阶,冲进场地里,罗恩殿后。哈利仍没有放弃寻找和拯救海格的希望,他飞快地朝禁林跑去,可是刚跑到一半,他们又被迫停住了。

周围的空气冻结了,哈利喘不过气来,胸膛里的空气好像凝固了一般。黑夜中有东西在移动,无数旋转着的浓黑身影,排山倒海似的朝城堡涌去,它们的脸被兜帽遮住了,它们的呼吸咔啦啦响……

罗恩和赫敏聚拢在哈利身边,后面作战的声音突然变得喑哑、低沉了,一种只有摄魂怪才能带来的死寂正在穿透黑夜压下来……

"快,哈利!"赫敏的声音像是从很远的地方传来,"守护神,哈利,快!"

哈利举起魔杖,可是一种灰暗的绝望在他心头扩散开来:弗雷德死了,海格肯定奄奄一息或已经毙命,还有多少人丢了性命他不知道,哈利觉得似乎他的灵魂已经离他而去……

"哈利,快呀!"赫敏在尖叫。

CHAPTER THIRTY-TWO   The Elder Wand

A hundred Dementors were advancing, gliding towards them, sucking their way closer to Harry's despair, which was like a promise of a feast ...

He saw Ron's silver terrier burst into the air, flicker feebly and expire; he saw Hermione's otter twist in mid-air and fade, and his own wand trembled in his hand, and he almost welcomed the oncoming oblivion, the promise of nothing, of no feeling ...

And then a silver hare, a boar and a fox soared past Harry, Ron and Hermione's heads: the Dementors fell back before the creatures' approach. Three more people had arrived out of the darkness to stand beside them, their wands outstretched, continuing to cast their Patronuses: Luna, Ernie and Seamus.

'That's right,' said Luna encouragingly, as if they were back in the Room of Requirement and this was simply spell practice for the DA. 'That's right, Harry ... come on, think of something happy ...'

'Something happy?' he said, his voice cracked.

'We're all still here,' she whispered, 'we're still fighting. Come on, now ...'

There was a silver spark, then a wavering light, and then, with the greatest effort it had ever cost him, the stag burst from the end of Harry's wand. It cantered forwards, and now the Dementors scattered in earnest, and immediately the night was mild again, but the sounds of the surrounding battle were loud in his ears.

'Can't thank you enough,' said Ron shakily, turning to Luna, Ernie and Seamus, 'you just saved –'

With a roar and an earthquaking tremor, another giant came lurching out of the darkness from the direction of the Forest, brandishing a club taller than any of them.

'RUN!' Harry shouted again, but the others needed no telling: they all scattered, and not a second too soon, for next moment the creature's vast foot had fallen exactly where they had been standing. Harry looked round: Ron and Hermione were following him, but the other three had vanished back into the battle.

'Let's get out of range!' yelled Ron, as the giant swung its club again and its bellows echoed through the night, across the grounds where bursts of red and green light continued to illuminate the darkness.

'The Whomping Willow,' said Harry. 'Go!'

Somehow he walled it all up in his mind, crammed it into a small space into which he could not look now: thoughts of Fred and Hagrid, and his

第32章 老魔杖

一百个摄魂怪轻快无声地飘了过来,一路哑吸着,逼近哈利的绝望,这对它们来说如同预示着一顿美餐……

哈利看见罗恩的狼犬跃入空中,微弱地闪了闪就不见了。他又看见赫敏的水獭在空中扭动,接着也消失了。他自己的魔杖在手里颤抖,他几乎巴不得自己赶快忘掉一切,坠入虚无,没有思想,没有感觉……

就在这时,一只银兔、一头公猪和一只狐狸从哈利、罗恩和赫敏的头顶飞过。面对这些逼近的灵物,摄魂怪纷纷后退。又有三个人从黑暗中出现了,站在他们身边,伸手举着魔杖,继续给守护神施魔法:是卢娜、厄尼和西莫。

"很好。"卢娜鼓励地说,就好像他们回到了有求必应屋,只是在做D.A.的魔咒练习,"很好,哈利……快,想点高兴的事儿……"

"高兴的事儿?"他声音嘶哑地说。

"我们还在这儿,"卢娜轻声说,"我们还在战斗。好了,快……"

一朵银色的火花喷了出来,接着是一道摇摆不定的光,哈利付出了前所未有的努力。终于,牡鹿从他的杖尖涌了出来。它甩开蹄子朝前奔去,这下子摄魂怪真的溃逃了,夜晚顿时又变得温暖起来,但他耳朵里却灌满了打斗的声音。

"太谢谢你们了,"罗恩声音颤抖地对卢娜、厄尼和西莫说,"你们救了——"

随着一声大吼和地震般的颤抖,又一个巨人从禁林那边的黑暗中蹒跚而出,手里挥舞着一根比他们谁的个子都长的棍棒。

"快跑!"哈利又大喊一声,别人不用他说,早就四散逃开了。真悬哪,那家伙的大脚紧接着就落在了他们刚才站立的地方。哈利望望四周,罗恩和赫敏都跟着他,但另外三个人已经又回去战斗了。

"我们快躲开!"罗恩嚷道。这时巨人又在挥舞棍棒,吼声在夜色中、在场地上空回荡,场地上一道道红光和绿光继续把黑暗照亮。

"打人柳,"哈利说,"快走!"

他似乎把一些思绪封存在脑子里,塞进了一个暂时不能去看的狭小空间,对弗雷德和海格的牵念,对所有他爱的、散落在城堡内外的

CHAPTER THIRTY-TWO

The Elder Wand

terror for all the people he loved, scattered in and outside the castle, must all wait, because they had to run, had to reach the snake, and Voldemort, because that was, as Hermione said, the only way to end it –

He sprinted, half believing he could outdistance death itself, ignoring the jets of light flying in the darkness all around him, and the sound of the lake crashing like the sea, and the creaking of the Forbidden Forest though the night was windless; through grounds that seemed, themselves, to have risen in rebellion, he ran faster than he had ever moved in his life, and it was he who saw the great tree first, the Willow that protected the secret at its roots with whip-like, slashing branches.

Panting and gasping Harry slowed down, skirting the Willow's swiping branches, peering through the darkness towards its thick trunk, trying to see the single knot in the bark of the old tree that would paralyse it. Ron and Hermione caught up, Hermione so out of breath she could not speak.

'How – how're we going to get in?' panted Ron. 'I can – see the place – if we just had – Crookshanks again –'

'Crookshanks?' wheezed Hermione, bent double, clutching her chest. '*Are you a wizard, or what?*'

'Oh – right – yeah –'

Ron looked around, then directed his wand at a twig on the ground and said, '*Wingardium Leviosa!* ' The twig flew up from the ground, spun through the air as if caught by a gust of wind, then zoomed directly at the trunk through the Willow's ominously swaying branches. It jabbed at a place near the roots and at once, the writhing tree became still.

'Perfect!' panted Hermione.

'Wait.'

For one teetering second, while the crashes and booms of the battle filled the air, Harry hesitated. Voldemort wanted him to do this, wanted him to come ... was he leading Ron and Hermione into a trap?

But then the reality seemed to close upon him, cruel and plain: the only way forwards was to kill the snake, and the snake was where Voldemort was, and Voldemort was at the end of this tunnel ...

'Harry, we're coming, just get in there!' said Ron, pushing him forwards.

Harry wriggled into the earthy passage hidden in the tree's roots. It was

第32章 老魔杖

人们的担心……都必须等一等,因为他们必须快跑,必须去接近那条蛇,接近伏地魔,因为就像赫敏说的,只有这样才能结束这一切——

他拼命狂奔,几乎觉得自己能把死亡甩在后面。他不去理会周围黑暗中射过的道道亮光,不去理会像大海一样阵阵冲刷的湖水声,也不去理会禁林里传出的吱吱嘎嘎的声响——虽然夜里并没有风。他们奔过似乎本身也在崛起反抗的场地,哈利这辈子从来没有跑得这么快过。然后,他第一个看见了那棵大树,那棵甩打着鞭子般的枝条、保护着树根底下的秘密的打人柳。

哈利上气不接下气地慢下脚步,避开打人柳嗖嗖抽打的枝条,在黑暗中仔细望着粗粗的树干,想看到老树皮上那个能使大树平静下来的节疤。罗恩和赫敏也赶了上来,赫敏喘得连话都说不出来了。

"我们——我们怎么进去呢?"罗恩喘着气说,"我能——能看见那地方——如果我们——还带着克鲁克山——"

"克鲁克山?"赫敏气喘吁吁地说,弯腰揪着自己的胸口,"你到底是不是巫师呀?"

"哦——是呀——对了——"

罗恩环顾四周,然后用魔杖指着地上的一根树枝,说道:"羽加迪姆 勒维奥萨!"树枝一下子从地上飞了起来,像被风吹着一样在空中旋转,然后嗖地穿过打人柳的那些凶险的枝条,直朝树干冲去。它捅了捅树根附近的某个地方,顿时,扭曲抽打的柳树便安静下来。

"漂亮!"赫敏喘着气说。

"等等。"

在那短暂的一瞬间,哈利迟疑了。空气里充斥着战斗的轰鸣和撞击声。伏地魔希望他这么做,希望他自己送上门来……他是不是在把罗恩和赫敏带入一个陷阱?

接着,现实似乎把他包围了,残酷而清楚:前面只有一条路,就是杀死那条蛇,而蛇是跟伏地魔在一起的,伏地魔就在这条隧道的尽头……

"哈利,我们来了,快进去吧!"罗恩说着,把他往前推了一把。

哈利扭动着身子爬进隐在树根底下的泥土隧道。这里比他们上次

CHAPTER THIRTY-TWO   The Elder Wand

a much tighter squeeze than it had been the last time they had entered it. The tunnel was low-ceilinged: they had had to double up to move through it nearly four years previously, now there was nothing for it but to crawl. Harry went first, his wand illuminated, expecting at any moment to meet barriers, but none came. They moved in silence, Harry's gaze fixed upon the swinging beam of the wand held in his fist.

At last the tunnel began to slope upwards and Harry saw a sliver of light ahead. Hermione tugged at his ankle.

'The Cloak!' she whispered. 'Put the Cloak on!'

He groped behind him and she forced the bundle of slippery cloth into his free hand. With difficulty he dragged it over himself, murmured, '*Nox,*' extinguishing his wandlight, and continued on his hands and knees, as silently as possible, all his senses straining, expecting every second to be discovered, to hear a cold clear voice, see a flash of green light.

And then he heard voices coming from the room directly ahead of them, only slightly muffled by the fact that the opening at the end of the tunnel had been blocked up by what looked like an old crate. Hardly daring to breathe, Harry edged right up to the opening and peered through a tiny gap left between crate and wall.

The room beyond was dimly lit, but he could see Nagini, swirling and coiling like a serpent underwater, safe in her enchanted, starry sphere, which floated unsupported in mid-air. He could see the edge of a table, and a long-fingered, white hand toying with a wand. Then Snape spoke, and Harry's heart lurched: Snape was inches away from where he crouched, hidden.

'... my Lord, their resistance is crumbling –'

'– and it is doing so without your help,' said Voldemort, in his high, clear voice. 'Skilled wizard though you are, Severus, I do not think you will make much difference now. We are almost there ... almost.'

'Let me find the boy. Let me bring you Potter. I know I can find him, my Lord. Please.'

Snape strode past the gap, and Harry drew back a little, keeping his eyes fixed upon Nagini, wondering whether there was any spell that might penetrate the protection surrounding her, but he could not think of anything. One failed attempt, and he would give away his position ...

第32章 老魔杖

进来时狭窄逼仄多了。隧道的顶很低,差不多四年前他们就不得不弯着身子,现在只能匍匐前进。哈利在最前面,他点亮魔杖,随时提防会遇到障碍,不料一路都很顺利。他们不出声地往前爬。哈利盯着他手里攥着的魔杖发出的那点摇摆不定的亮光。

终于,隧道开始向上升,哈利看见前面有一道狭长的亮光。赫敏拽了拽他的脚脖子。

"隐形衣!"她小声说,"把隐形衣穿上!"

哈利在身后摸索着,赫敏将那件滑溜溜的衣服塞进他没拿魔杖的手里。哈利费劲地把衣服披在身上,低声说了句"诺克斯",熄灭了魔杖的亮光,然后继续手脚并用地往前爬,尽量不发出一点声响。他绷紧了所有的神经,知道随时都可能被人发现,随时都可能听到一个冰冷而清晰的声音,看到一道耀眼的绿光。

接着,他听见从前面的房间里传来了说话声,但隧道尽头的豁口被一个旧箱子似的东西堵住了,使说话声听上去有点发闷。哈利尽量屏住呼吸,一点点地挪到豁口处,透过箱子和洞壁间的狭小缝隙望过去。

那边的屋子里光线昏暗,但他还是看见了纳吉尼。大蛇安全地待在那个飘浮在半空的星光闪闪的魔法保护球里,像在水底下一样扭动、盘绕。哈利还看见一张桌子的边缘,有一只苍白的、手指修长的手在摆弄一根魔杖。接着,斯内普说话了,哈利的心猛地一跳。斯内普距哈利蜷身躲藏的地方只有几寸。

"……主人,他们的抵抗正在瓦解——"

"——这里面并没有你的功劳。"伏地魔用他高亢、清晰的声音说,"西弗勒斯,你虽然是个高明的巫师,但我认为你现在已经没有什么用了。我们还差一点儿就要成功了……还差一点儿。"

"让我去找那个男孩。让我把波特给您带来。我知道我能找到他,主人。求求您。"

斯内普从缝隙前走过,哈利往后退了一点儿,眼睛仍盯在纳吉尼身上,心里在想有没有魔咒能够击穿大蛇周围的保护层,但一个也想不出来。他不敢轻举妄动,一旦失败,就会暴露他的位置……

CHAPTER THIRTY-TWO   The Elder Wand

Voldemort stood up. Harry could see him now, see the red eyes, the flattened, serpentine face, the pallor of him gleaming slightly in the semi-darkness.

'I have a problem, Severus,' said Voldemort softly.

'My Lord?' said Snape.

Voldemort raised the Elder Wand, holding it as delicately and precisely as a conductor's baton.

'Why doesn't it work for me, Severus?'

In the silence, Harry imagined he could hear the snake hissing slightly as it coiled and uncoiled, or was it Voldemort's sibilant sigh lingering on the air?

'My – my Lord?' said Snape blankly. 'I do not understand. You – you have performed extraordinary magic with that wand.'

'No,' said Voldemort. 'I have performed my usual magic. I am extraordinary, but this wand ... no. It has not revealed the wonders it has promised. I feel no difference between this wand and the one I procured from Ollivander all those years ago.'

Voldemort's tone was musing, calm, but Harry's scar had begun to throb and pulse: pain was building in his forehead and he could feel that controlled sense of fury building inside Voldemort.

'No difference,' said Voldemort again.

Snape did not speak. Harry could not see his face: he wondered whether Snape sensed danger, was trying to find the right words, to reassure his master.

Voldemort started to move around the room: Harry lost sight of him for seconds as he prowled, speaking in that same measured voice, while the pain and fury mounted in Harry.

'I have thought long and hard, Severus ... do you know why I have called you back from the battle?'

And for a moment Harry saw Snape's profile: his eyes were fixed upon the coiling snake in its enchanted cage.

'No, my Lord, but I beg you will let me return. Let me find Potter.'

'You sound like Lucius. Neither of you understands Potter as I do. He does not need finding. Potter will come to me. I know his weakness, you see,

第32章 老魔杖

伏地魔站了起来。哈利可以看见他了，看见他那双红眼睛，那张扁扁的、蛇一般的脸，还有他在昏暗中闪烁的苍白肤色。

"我有个难题，西弗勒斯。"伏地魔轻声说。

"主人？"斯内普说。

伏地魔举起老魔杖，细致优雅地捏在指间，像捏着一根指挥棒。

"它为什么对我不管用呢，西弗勒斯？"

静默中，哈利仿佛能听见大蛇盘绕、伸展时发出的咝咝声，或者是伏地魔那在空气中萦绕不去的咝咝叹息声。

"主——主人？"斯内普茫然地说，"我不明白。您——您用这根魔杖施出了高超非凡的魔法吧。"

"不，"伏地魔说，"我只施出了我平常的魔法。我是高超非凡的，但这根魔杖……不。它没有显示出它应该显示的奇迹。这根魔杖和我多年前从奥利凡德手里买的那根魔杖相比，我感觉不到有什么差别。"

伏地魔的语气是平静的、若有所思的，但哈利的伤疤又开始突突地跳疼。随着额头上的疼痛一点点地加剧，他感觉到伏地魔内心的怒火逐步升级了。

"没有差别。"伏地魔又说了一遍。

斯内普没有说话。哈利看不见他的脸，不知道斯内普是不是感觉到了危险，正在搜肠刮肚地寻找合适的话来使主人消除疑虑。

伏地魔开始在屋子里走来走去。哈利有几秒钟看不见他，只听见他一边踱步一边仍然用那种不紧不慢的声音说话，与此同时，哈利的疼痛和怒火还在不断加剧。

"我苦苦地想了很长时间，西弗勒斯……你知道我为什么把你从战场上叫回来吗？"

一时间，哈利看见了斯内普的侧影，斯内普的眼睛正盯着魔法笼子里盘绕的大蛇。

"不知道，主人，但我请求您让我回去，让我找到波特。"

"你说话很像卢修斯，你们谁都不如我了解波特。用不着去找。波特自己会送上门来的。我知道他的弱点，他的一个很大的缺陷。他不

his one great flaw. He will hate watching the others struck down around him, knowing that it is for him that it happens. He will want to stop it at any cost. He will come.'

'But my Lord, he might be killed accidentally by one other than yourself –'

'My instructions to my Death Eaters have been perfectly clear. Capture Potter. Kill his friends – the more, the better – but do not kill him.

'But it is of you that I wished to speak, Severus, not Harry Potter. You have been very valuable to me. Very valuable.'

'My Lord knows I seek only to serve him. But – let me go and find the boy, my Lord. Let me bring him to you. I know I can –'

'I have told you, no!' said Voldemort, and Harry caught the glint of red in his eyes as he turned again, and the swishing of his cloak was like the slithering of a snake, and he felt Voldemort's impatience in his burning scar. 'My concern at the moment, Severus, is what will happen when I finally meet the boy!'

'My Lord, there can be no question, surely –?'

'– but there *is* a question, Severus. There is.'

Voldemort halted, and Harry could see him plainly again as he slid the Elder Wand through his white fingers, staring at Snape.

'Why did both the wands I have used fail when directed at Harry Potter?'

'I – I cannot answer that, my Lord.'

'Can't you?'

The stab of rage felt like a spike driven through Harry's head: he forced his own fist into his mouth to stop himself from crying out in pain. He closed his eyes, and suddenly he was Voldemort, looking into Snape's pale face.

'My wand of yew did everything of which I asked it, Severus, except to kill Harry Potter. Twice it failed. Ollivander told me under torture of the twin cores, told me to take another's wand. I did so, but Lucius's wand shattered upon meeting Potter's.'

'I – I have no explanation, my Lord.'

Snape was not looking at Voldemort now. His dark eyes were still fixed

第32章 老魔杖

愿意看着别人在他周围被击倒，况且又知道这一切都是因他而发生。他会不惜一切代价去阻止。他会来的。"

"可是，主人，他可能会被别人失手杀死——"

"我给我那些食死徒的指令非常明确。活捉波特。杀死他的朋友——越多越好——但不许取他的性命。"

"但是，西弗勒斯，我想要谈的是你，而不是哈利·波特。你曾经对我很有价值，很有价值。"

"主人知道我甘愿为您效力。可是——让我去找那个男孩吧，主人。让我把他带来见您。我知道我能——"

"我跟你说了，不行！"伏地魔说，在他又转过身来时，哈利看见了他眼睛里闪烁的红光，听见了他的斗篷沙沙作响，就像蛇在地上爬行。哈利还从灼痛的伤疤感觉到伏地魔的不耐烦。"西弗勒斯，我目前关心的是，当我最终面对那个男孩时会怎么样！"

"主人，那当然不可能有问题——？"

"——有问题，西弗勒斯，有问题。"

伏地魔停住脚步，哈利又能清楚地看见他了，只见他用苍白的手指捋着老魔杖，眼睛盯着斯内普。

"为什么我用的两根魔杖面对哈利·波特时都不管用呢？"

"我——我回答不上来，主人。"

"是吗？"

强烈的怒火像钉子一样刺进哈利的脑袋，他把拳头塞进嘴里，免得自己疼得叫出声来。他闭上眼睛，突然他变成了伏地魔，正盯着斯内普那张惨白的脸。

"我的那根紫杉木魔杖对我百依百顺，西弗勒斯，可就是没能杀死哈利·波特。两次都失败了。奥利凡德在酷刑之下告诉了我孪生杖芯的事，叫我使用别人的魔杖。我这么做了，可是，卢修斯的魔杖一遇到波特的魔杖就成了碎片。"

"我——我也不明白，主人。"

斯内普此刻没有看着伏地魔。他那双黑眼睛仍然盯着在保护球里

CHAPTER THIRTY-TWO   The Elder Wand

upon the coiling serpent in its protective sphere.

'I sought a third wand, Severus. The Elder Wand, the Wand of Destiny, the Deathstick. I took it from its previous master. I took it from the grave of Albus Dumbledore.'

And now Snape looked at Voldemort, and Snape's face was like a death mask. It was marble white and so still that when he spoke it was a shock to see that anyone lived behind the blank eyes.

'My Lord – let me go to the boy –'

'All this long night, when I am on the brink of victory, I have sat here,' said Voldemort, his voice barely louder than a whisper, 'wondering, wondering, why the Elder Wand refuses to be what it ought to be, refuses to perform as legend says it must perform for its rightful owner ... and I think I have the answer.'

Snape did not speak.

'Perhaps you already know it? You are a clever man, after all, Severus. You have been a good and faithful servant, and I regret what must happen.'

'My Lord –'

'The Elder Wand cannot serve me properly, Severus, because I am not its true master. The Elder Wand belongs to the wizard who killed its last owner. You killed Albus Dumbledore. While you live, Severus, the Elder Wand cannot be truly mine.'

'My Lord!' Snape protested, raising his wand.

'It cannot be any other way,' said Voldemort. 'I must master the wand, Severus. Master the wand, and I master Potter at last.'

And Voldemort swiped the air with the Elder Wand. It did nothing to Snape, who for a split second seemed to think he had been reprieved: but then Voldemort's intention became clear. The snake's cage was rolling through the air, and before Snape could do anything more than yell, it had encased him, head and shoulders, and Voldemort spoke in Parseltongue.

'*Kill.*'

There was a terrible scream. Harry saw Snape's face losing the little colour it had left, it whitened as his black eyes widened, as the snake's fangs pierced his neck, as he failed to push the enchanted cage off himself, as his knees gave way, and he fell to the floor.

第32章 老魔杖

盘绕扭动的大蛇。

"我寻找到第三根魔杖,西弗勒斯。老魔杖,命运杖,死亡棒。我从它的前任主人那里把它拿来了。我从阿不思·邓布利多的坟墓里把它拿来了。"

现在斯内普看着伏地魔了,斯内普的脸如同一张死人面具,像大理石一样惨白、凝固。他开口说话时令人大吃一惊,没想到那双空洞的眼睛后面居然是个活人。

"主人——让我去找那个男孩——"

"整个漫漫长夜,眼看到了胜利的边缘,我却坐在这里,"伏地魔说,声音几近耳语,"想啊,想啊,为什么老魔杖不肯发挥它的本领,不肯像传说中那样为它的合法主人创造奇迹……现在我似乎有了答案。"

斯内普没有说话。

"也许你已经知道了?你毕竟是个聪明人,西弗勒斯。你一直是个忠心耿耿的好仆人,我为必须发生的事情感到遗憾。"

"主人——"

"老魔杖不能好好地为我效力,西弗勒斯,因为我不是它真正的主人。老魔杖属于杀死它前任主人的那位巫师。是你杀死了阿不思·邓布利多。只要你活着,西弗勒斯,老魔杖就不可能真正属于我。"

"主人!"斯内普抗议道,一边举起了魔杖。

"不可能有别的办法,"伏地魔说,"我必须征服这根魔杖,西弗勒斯。征服这根魔杖,就最终征服了波特。"

伏地魔用老魔杖猛击了一下空气。斯内普毫发未伤,刹那间,他似乎以为自己暂时被豁免了。接着,伏地魔的意图就清楚了。大蛇的笼子在空中翻滚,斯内普只发出一声尖叫,笼子就把他的脑袋和肩膀罩住,伏地魔用蛇佬腔说话了。

"杀。"

一声可怕的惨叫,哈利看见斯内普脸上仅有的一点儿血色也消失了,蛇的尖牙扎进了他的脖子。他无力地推开那带魔法的笼子,膝头一软倒在地上,脸色煞白,黑黑的眼睛睁得老大。

CHAPTER THIRTY-TWO — The Elder Wand

'I regret it,' said Voldemort coldly.

He turned away; there was no sadness in him, no remorse. It was time to leave this shack and take charge, with a wand that would now do his full bidding. He pointed it at the starry cage holding the snake, which drifted upwards, off Snape, who fell sideways on to the floor, blood gushing from the wounds in his neck. Voldemort swept from the room without a backwards glance, and the great serpent floated after him in its huge protective sphere.

Back in the tunnel and his own mind, Harry opened his eyes: he had drawn blood, biting down on his knuckles in the effort not to shout out. Now he was looking through the tiny crack between crate and wall, watching a foot in a black boot trembling on the floor.

'Harry!' breathed Hermione behind him, but he had already pointed his wand at the crate blocking his view. It lifted an inch into the air and drifted sideways, silently. As quietly as he could, he pulled himself up into the room.

He did not know why he was doing it, why he was approaching the dying man: he did not know what he felt as he saw Snape's white face, and the fingers trying to staunch the bloody wound at his neck. Harry took off the Invisibility Cloak and looked down upon the man he hated, whose widening black eyes found Harry as he tried to speak. Harry bent over him; and Snape seized the front of his robes and pulled him close.

A terrible rasping, gurgling noise issued from Snape's throat.

'Take ... it ... Take ... it ...'

Something more than blood was leaking from Snape. Silvery blue, neither gas nor liquid, it gushed from his mouth and his ears and his eyes, and Harry knew what it was, but did not know what to do –

A flask, conjured from thin air, was thrust into his shaking hands by Hermione. Harry lifted the silvery substance into it with his wand. When the flask was full to the brim, and Snape looked as though there was no blood left in him, his grip on Harry's robes slackened.

'Look ... at ... me ...' he whispered.

The green eyes found the black, but after a second something in the depths of the dark pair seemed to vanish, leaving them fixed, blank and empty. The hand holding Harry thudded to the floor, and Snape moved no more.

第32章 老魔杖

"我很遗憾。"伏地魔冷冷地说。

他转过身,内心里没有悲哀,也没有悔恨。有了绝对听从他命令的魔杖,他现在应该离开这个棚屋,去收拾局面了。他用魔杖指着星光闪闪的蛇笼,笼子飘升起来,离开了斯内普。斯内普身子一歪倒在地上,鲜血从他脖子里的伤口喷涌而出。伏地魔快速离开了屋子,没有再回头看一眼,那条关在大保护球里的巨蛇也随他飘浮而去。

哈利又回到隧道,回到他自己的思想里,他睁开了眼睛。他为了不让自己喊出声来,把手指的关节都咬出血了。此刻他透过箱子和洞壁间的狭小缝隙窥视,看见一只穿黑靴子的脚在地板上颤抖。

"哈利!"赫敏在他身后喘着气叫道,但他已将魔杖指向挡住视线的箱子。箱子悬起了一英寸,悄没声儿地飘到旁边。哈利蹑手蹑脚地爬进了那个屋子。

他不知道自己为什么要这么做,为什么要走近那个垂死的人。当他看见斯内普那张煞白的脸,看见那些手指在努力堵住脖子上喷血的伤口时,他不知道自己是何感受。哈利脱掉隐形衣,低头望着这个他仇恨的男人。斯内普睁得大大的黑眼睛看见了哈利,他挣扎着想说话。哈利俯下身,斯内普抓住哈利长袍的前襟,把他拉近自己。

斯内普的喉咙里发出呼哧呼哧、咯啦咯啦的可怕声音。

"拿……去……拿……去……"

斯内普身上流出来的不仅是血。一种银蓝色的、既不是气体也不是液体的东西,从他嘴里、耳朵里和眼睛里冒出来。哈利明白这是什么,但不知道该怎么做——

一只凭空变出的细颈瓶被赫敏塞进了他颤抖的手里。哈利用魔杖把银色物质捞取到瓶子里。瓶子满了,斯内普的血似乎也已流尽,他抓住哈利长袍的手无力地松开了。

"看……着……我……"他轻声说。

绿眼睛盯着黑眼睛,但一秒钟后,那一双黑眸深处的什么东西似乎消失了,它们变得茫然、呆滞而空洞。抓住哈利的那只手垂落在地上,斯内普不动了。

CHAPTER THIRTY-THREE

The Prince's Tale

Harry remained kneeling at Snape's side, simply staring down at him, until quite suddenly a high, cold voice spoke so close to them that Harry jumped to his feet, the flask gripped tightly in his hands, thinking that Voldemort had re-entered the room.

Voldemort's voice reverberated from the walls and floor, and Harry realised that he was talking to Hogwarts and to all the surrounding area, that the residents of Hogsmeade and all those still fighting in the castle would hear him as clearly as if he stood beside them, his breath on the back of their necks, a death blow away.

'You have fought,' said the high, cold voice, 'valiantly. Lord Voldemort knows how to value bravery.

'Yet you have sustained heavy losses. If you continue to resist me, you will all die, one by one. I do not wish this to happen. Every drop of magical blood spilled is a loss and a waste.

'Lord Voldemort is merciful. I command my forces to retreat, immediately.

'You have one hour. Dispose of your dead with dignity. Treat your injured.

'I speak now, Harry Potter, directly to you. You have permitted your friends to die for you rather than face me yourself. I shall wait for one hour in the Forbidden Forest. If, at the end of that hour, you have not come to me, have not given yourself up, then battle recommences. This time, I shall enter the fray myself, Harry Potter, and I shall find you, and I shall punish every last man, woman and child who has tried to conceal you from me. One hour.'

Both Ron and Hermione shook their heads frantically, looking at Harry.

'Don't listen to him,' said Ron.

第 33 章

"王子"的故事

  哈利久久地跪在斯内普身边，呆呆地凝望着他。突然，一个似乎近在咫尺的高亢、冷酷的声音开始说话了，哈利惊跳起来，手里紧紧攥着瓶子，以为伏地魔又返回了屋里。

  伏地魔的声音在墙壁和地板间回响，哈利这才意识到他是在对霍格沃茨及周围的所有地区说话。霍格莫德村的居民和城堡里仍在战斗的人们都能清楚地听见他的声音，如同他就站在他们身边，他的呼吸就喷在他们脖子后面，他一出手就能让他们毙命。

  "你们进行了勇敢的抵抗，"那个高亢、冷酷的声音说，"伏地魔大人知道如何欣赏勇气。

  "但是你们蒙受了沉重的损失。如果继续抵抗，你们一个接一个都会死去。我不希望发生这样的事情。巫师的血，每流一滴都是一种损失和浪费。

  "伏地魔大人是仁慈的。我命令我的队伍撤退，立即撤退。

  "给你们一个小时，体面地安置死者，治疗伤员。

  "哈利·波特，现在我直接对你说话。你听任你的朋友为你赴死，而不是挺身出来面对我。我将在禁林里等候一个小时。如果一小时后你没有来找我，没有主动投降，那么战斗还将继续。这次，我将亲自上阵，哈利·波特，我将找到你，我将惩罚每一个试图窝藏你的男人、女人和孩子，一个也不放过。一个小时。"

  罗恩和赫敏都看着哈利拼命摇头。

  "别听他的。"罗恩说。

CHAPTER THIRTY-THREE   The Prince's Tale

'It'll be all right,' said Hermione wildly. 'Let's – let's get back to the castle, if he's gone to the Forest we'll need to think of a new plan –'

She glanced at Snape's body, then hurried back to the tunnel entrance. Ron followed her. Harry gathered up the Invisibility Cloak, then looked down at Snape. He did not know what to feel, except shock at the way Snape had been killed, and the reason for which it had been done ...

They crawled back through the tunnel, none of them talking, and Harry wondered whether Ron and Hermione could still hear Voldemort ringing in their heads, as he could.

You have permitted your friends to die for you rather than face me yourself. I shall wait for one hour in the Forbidden Forest ... one hour ...

Small bundles seemed to litter the lawn at the front of the castle. It could only be an hour or so from dawn, yet it was pitch black. The three of them hurried towards the stone steps. A lone clog, the size of a small boat, lay abandoned in front of them. There was no other sign of Grawp or of his attacker.

The castle was unnaturally silent. There were no flashes of light now, no bangs or screams or shouts. The flagstones of the deserted Entrance Hall were stained with blood. Emeralds were still scattered all over the floor along with pieces of marble and splintered wood. Part of the banisters had been blown away.

'Where is everyone?' whispered Hermione.

Ron led the way to the Great Hall. Harry stopped in the doorway.

The house tables were gone and the room was crowded. The survivors stood in groups, their arms around each other's necks. The injured were being treated up on the raised platform by Madam Pomfrey and a group of helpers. Firenze was amongst the injured; his flank poured blood and he shook where he lay, unable to stand.

The dead lay in a row in the middle of the hall. Harry could not see Fred's body, because his family surrounded him. George was kneeling at his head; Mrs Weasley was lying across Fred's chest, her body shaking, Mr Weasley stroking her hair while tears cascaded down his cheeks.

Without a word to Harry, Ron and Hermione walked away. Harry saw Hermione approach Ginny, whose face was swollen and blotchy, and hug her. Ron joined Bill, Fleur and Percy, who flung an arm around Ron's shoulders.

第33章 "王子"的故事

"没关系的,"赫敏激动地说,"我们——我们回城堡去吧。如果他去了禁林,我们需要重新考虑一个计划——"

她扫了一眼斯内普的尸体,便匆匆朝隧道入口走去,罗恩也跟了过来。哈利收起隐形衣,又低头看着斯内普。他说不清内心的感受,只是为斯内普的这种死法,以及他丧命的原因而感到震惊……

他们在隧道里往外爬,谁也没有说话,哈利不知道罗恩和赫敏是不是也像他一样,脑子里仍然回响着伏地魔的声音。

你听任你的朋友为你赴死,而不是挺身出来面对我。我将在禁林里等候一个小时……一个小时……

城堡前的草地上散落着一个个小包裹似的东西。离天亮大约只有一个小时了,但四下里还是漆黑一片。他们三个急急忙忙跑向石阶。一根小船那么大的长木头横在他们面前,格洛普和刚才袭击他的那个巨人都不见了踪影。

城堡里异常寂静,此刻既看不见亮光闪烁,也听不见撞击声、尖叫声和呐喊声。空无一人的门厅里,石板上血迹斑斑,绿宝石仍然散落在地,还有破碎的大理石和劈裂的木头;一部分扶栏被炸飞了。

"人都到哪儿去了?"赫敏轻声说。

罗恩领头朝大礼堂走去。哈利在门口停住了。

学院桌子不见了,礼堂里挤满了人。幸存者三五成群地站着,互相搂抱在一起。伤员都集中在台子上,庞弗雷女士和一群助手在给他们治疗。费伦泽也受伤了,一侧身体大量出血,他已经站立不住,躺在那里瑟瑟发抖。

死者在礼堂中央躺成一排。哈利看不见弗雷德的遗体,因为他的家人把他团团围住了。乔治跪在弗雷德脑袋边,韦斯莱夫人浑身颤抖地伏在弗雷德胸上,韦斯莱先生抚摸着她的头发,泪流满面。

罗恩和赫敏没有对哈利说一句话就走开了。哈利看见赫敏走到金妮面前抱了抱她,金妮的脸肿着,满是污垢。罗恩走到比尔、芙蓉和珀西身边,珀西搂住了罗恩的肩膀。就在金妮和赫敏靠近家里其他人时,

CHAPTER THIRTY-THREE   The Prince's Tale

As Ginny and Hermione moved closer to the rest of the family, Harry had a clear view of the bodies lying next to Fred: Remus and Tonks, pale and still and peaceful-looking, apparently asleep beneath the dark, enchanted ceiling.

The Great Hall seemed to fly away, become smaller, shrink, as Harry reeled backwards from the doorway. He could not draw breath. He could not bear to look at any of the other bodies, to see who else had died for him. He could not bear to join the Weasleys, could not look into their eyes, when if he had given himself up in the first place, Fred might never have died ...

He turned away and ran up the marble staircase. Lupin, Tonks ... he yearned not to feel ... he wished he could rip out his heart, his innards, everything that was screaming inside him ...

The castle was completely empty; even the ghosts seemed to have joined the mass mourning in the Great Hall. Harry ran without stopping, clutching the crystal flask of Snape's last thoughts, and he did not slow down until he reached the stone gargoyle guarding the Headmaster's office.

'Password?'

'Dumbledore!' said Harry without thinking, because it was he whom he yearned to see, and to his surprise the gargoyle slid aside, revealing the spiral staircase behind.

But when Harry burst into the circular office, he found a change. The portraits that hung all around the walls were empty. Not a single headmaster or headmistress remained to see him; all, it seemed, had flitted away, charging through the paintings that lined the castle, so that they could have a clear view of what was going on.

Harry glanced hopelessly at Dumbledore's deserted frame, which hung directly behind the Headmaster's chair, then turned his back on it. The stone Pensieve lay in the cabinet where it had always been: Harry heaved it on to the desk and poured Snape's memories into the wide basin with its runic markings around the edge. To escape into someone else's head would be a blessed relief ... nothing that even Snape had left him could be worse than his own thoughts. The memories swirled, silver-white and strange, and without hesitating, with a feeling of reckless abandonment, as though this would assuage his torturing grief, Harry dived.

He fell headlong into sunlight, and his feet found warm ground. When

第33章 "王子"的故事

哈利看清了躺在弗雷德身边的两具遗体：莱姆斯和唐克斯，脸色苍白，一动不动，但看上去很宁静，似乎在施了魔法的漆黑的天花板下安详地睡着了。

哈利跟跟跄跄地后退着离开了门口，礼堂似乎在飞去，越缩越小。他透不过气来。他没有勇气再去看其他遗体，再去弄清还有谁为他而死。他不敢去见韦斯莱一家，不敢看他们的眼睛，如果他一开始就主动投降，弗雷德也许就不会死……

他转身顺着大理石楼梯往上跑。卢平、唐克斯……他多么希望自己没有感觉……多么希望能把他的心、他的五脏六腑都扯出来，这些东西都在他的体内尖叫……

城堡里空无一人，就连幽灵似乎也加入了礼堂里哀悼的人群。哈利不停地往前跑，手里紧紧攥着装满斯内普最后思想的水晶瓶，一直跑到校长办公室外的滴水嘴石兽跟前才放慢脚步。

"口令？"

"邓布利多！"哈利不假思索地喊道，因为他心里最想见的人就是邓布利多。令他吃惊的是，石兽竟然滑到一边，露出了后面的螺旋形楼梯。

哈利冲进圆形办公室，发现这里已经有了变化。墙上挂的肖像都空了。那些男女校长没有一个留在这里。他们似乎都溜走了，顺着城堡墙壁上排列的图画冲到了前面，想看清事态的发展。

哈利绝望地看了一眼挂在校长座椅后面的邓布利多的空肖像，然后转过身来。石头冥想盆还和往常一样放在柜子里。哈利把盆口刻有如尼文符号的大石盆搬到桌上，将斯内普的记忆倒了进去。逃到别人的思想里去也是一种解脱……即使是斯内普留给他的，也不可能比他自己的思绪更糟。记忆在旋转，银白色，形状奇异，哈利不再迟疑，抱着一种不管不顾、彻底放弃的心理，一头扎了进去，似乎这能缓解他内心刀割般的痛苦。

他头朝前落进了阳光里，双脚踏在温暖的土地上。他直起身子，

CHAPTER THIRTY-THREE   The Prince's Tale

he straightened up, he saw that he was in a nearly deserted playground. A single, huge chimney dominated the distant skyline. Two girls were swinging backwards and forwards, and a skinny boy was watching them from behind a clump of bushes. His black hair was overlong and his clothes were so mismatched that it looked deliberate: too-short jeans, a shabby, overlarge coat that might have belonged to a grown man, an odd smock-like shirt.

Harry moved closer to the boy. Snape looked no more than nine or ten years old, sallow, small, stringy. There was undisguised greed in his thin face as he watched the younger of the two girls swinging higher and higher than her sister.

'Lily, don't do it!' shrieked the elder of the two.

But the girl had let go of the swing at the very height of its arc and flown into the air, quite literally flown, launched herself skywards with a great shout of laughter, and instead of crumpling on the playground asphalt, she soared, like a trapeze artist through the air, staying up far too long, landing far too lightly.

'Mummy told you not to!'

Petunia stopped her swing by dragging the heels of her sandals on the ground, making a crunching, grinding sound, then leapt up, hands on hips.

'Mummy said you weren't allowed, Lily!'

'But I'm fine,' said Lily, still giggling. 'Tuney, look at this. Watch what I can do.'

Petunia glanced around. The playground was deserted apart from themselves and, though the girls did not know it, Snape. Lily had picked up a fallen flower from the bush behind which Snape lurked. Petunia advanced, evidently torn between curiosity and disapproval. Lily waited until Petunia was near enough to have a clear view, then held out her palm. The flower sat there, opening and closing its petals, like some bizarre, many-lipped oyster.

'Stop it!' shrieked Petunia.

'It's not hurting you,' said Lily, but she closed her hand on the blossom and threw it back to the ground.

'It's not right,' said Petunia, but her eyes had followed the flower's flight to the ground and lingered upon it. 'How do you do it?' she added, and there was definite longing in her voice.

第33章 "王子"的故事

发现自己是在一个几乎没有人的游乐场上。一个大大的烟囱赫然耸立在远处的天际。两个女孩在荡秋千,一个瘦瘦的男孩躲在灌木丛后面注视着她们。男孩的黑头发很长,身上的衣服极不协调,倒像是故意穿成这个样子的:一条过短的牛仔裤,一件又大又长、像是大人穿的破旧外衣,还有一件怪模怪样的孕妇服似的衬衫。

哈利走近男孩身边。斯内普看上去约莫九到十岁,脸色灰黄,个头矮小,体格精瘦。注视着那个较小的女孩在秋千上荡得比她姐姐越来越高,他瘦瘦的脸上露出了不加掩饰的渴慕。

"莉莉,别这样!"较大的女孩尖叫道。

可是,小女孩在秋千荡到最高处时松开手飞到了空中,真的是在飞,欢声大笑着扑向天空。她并没有重重地摔在游乐场的柏油地上,而是像杂技演员一样在空中滑翔,停留了很长时间,最后十分轻盈地落在地上。

"妈妈叫你别这么做!"

佩妮让鞋跟擦地停住秋千,发出尖厉刺耳的摩擦声,然后她又跳了起来,双手叉腰。

"妈妈说不许你这样,莉莉!"

"可是我没事儿,"莉莉说,还在咯咯笑着,"佩妮,看看这个。看我的本事。"

佩妮看了看四周,空荡荡的游乐场里只有她们俩,当然还有斯内普,不过女孩们并不知道。莉莉从斯内普藏身的灌木丛里捡起一朵枯落的花。佩妮走了上来,看上去既好奇又不满,内心十分矛盾。莉莉等佩妮走近可以看清了,就把手摊开来,花瓣在她手心里不停地一开一合,就像某种古怪的、多层的牡蛎。

"别这样!"佩妮尖叫道。

"我又没把你怎么样。"莉莉说,不过她还是把花捏成一团扔到了地上。

"这不对。"佩妮说,但她的目光追随着落地的花,并久久地停在上面,"你是怎么做的?"她又问,声音里透着掩饰不住的渴望。

CHAPTER THIRTY-THREE   The Prince's Tale

'It's obvious, isn't it?' Snape could no longer contain himself, but had jumped out from behind the bushes. Petunia shrieked and ran backwards towards the swings, but Lily, though clearly startled, remained where she was. Snape seemed to regret his appearance. A dull flush of colour mounted the sallow cheeks as he looked at Lily.

'What's obvious?' asked Lily.

Snape had an air of nervous excitement. With a glance at the distant Petunia, now hovering beside the swings, he lowered his voice and said, 'I know what you are.'

'What do you mean?'

'You're ... you're a witch,' whispered Snape.

She looked affronted.

'*That's* not a very nice thing to say to somebody!'

She turned, nose in the air, and marched off towards her sister.

'No!' said Snape. He was highly coloured now, and Harry wondered why he did not take off the ridiculously large coat, unless it was because he did not want to reveal the smock beneath it. He flapped after the girls, looking ludicrously bat-like, like his older self.

The sisters considered him, united in disapproval, both holding on to one of the swing poles as though it was the safe place in tag.

'You *are*,' said Snape to Lily. 'You *are* a witch. I've been watching you for a while. But there's nothing wrong with that. My mum's one, and I'm a wizard.'

Petunia's laugh was like cold water.

'Wizard!' she shrieked, her courage returned now that she had recovered from the shock of his unexpected appearance. '*I* know who *you* are. You're that Snape boy! They live down Spinner's End by the river,' she told Lily, and it was evident from her tone that she considered the address a poor recommendation. 'Why have you been spying on us?'

'Haven't been spying,' said Snape, hot and uncomfortable and dirty-haired in the bright sunlight. 'Wouldn't spy on *you*, anyway,' he added spitefully, '*you're a Muggle.*'

Though Petunia evidently did not understand the word, she could hardly mistake the tone.

'Lily, come on, we're leaving!' she said shrilly. Lily obeyed her sister at

第33章 "王子"的故事

"这不是很清楚的事吗?"斯内普再也克制不住,从灌木丛后面跳了出来。佩妮尖叫一声,转身向秋千跑去,莉莉显然也吓了一跳,但待在原地没动。斯内普似乎后悔自己贸然出现,他看着莉莉,灰黄的面颊上泛起淡淡的红晕。

"什么很清楚?"莉莉问。

斯内普显得又紧张又激动。他看看远处在秋千旁徘徊的佩妮,压低声音说道:"我知道你是什么人。"

"什么意思?"

"你是……你是个女巫。"斯内普轻声说。

莉莉像是受了侮辱。

"对别人说这种话是很不礼貌的!"

她转过身,仰着脸大步朝她姐姐走去。

"不!"斯内普说。他的脸已经变得通红,哈利不明白他为什么不脱掉那件可笑的超大外衣,除非是因为他不想露出下面的孕妇服。他甩着袖子去追两个女孩,那滑稽的模样活像蝙蝠,活像他成年后的样子。

姐妹俩以同样不满的目光审视着他,两人都抓着一根秋千柱子,好像那是捉人游戏中的安全地带。

"你就是,"斯内普对莉莉说,"你就是个女巫。我观察你有一阵子了。这没有什么不好的。我妈妈就是女巫,我是男巫。"

佩妮的笑声像冷水一样。

"男巫!"她尖叫一声。刚才这男孩的突然出现使她受惊不小,现在她恢复了镇静,勇气又回来了,"我知道你是谁。你是斯内普家的那个男孩!他们住在河边的蜘蛛尾巷。"她告诉莉莉,语气明显表示她认为那是个下三烂的地方,"你为什么要偷看我们?"

"我没偷看。"斯内普说,他又激动又不安,在明亮的阳光下头发显得很脏,"我才不愿意偷看你呢,"他轻蔑地接着说,"你是个麻瓜。"

佩妮显然不明白这个词的意思,但她绝不会听不懂他的语气。

"莉莉,快,我们走吧!"她尖声说。莉莉立刻听从姐姐的话动身

CHAPTER THIRTY-THREE The Prince's Tale

once, glaring at Snape as she left. He stood watching them as they marched through the playground gate, and Harry, the only one left to observe him, recognised Snape's bitter disappointment, and understood that Snape had been planning this moment for a while, and that it had all gone wrong ...

The scene dissolved, and before Harry knew it, reformed around him. He was now in a small thicket of trees. He could see a sunlit river glittering through their trunks. The shadows cast by the trees made a basin of cool, green shade. Two children sat facing each other, cross-legged on the ground. Snape had removed his coat now; his odd smock looked less peculiar in the half-light.

'... and the Ministry can punish you if you do magic outside school, you get letters.'

'But I *have* done magic outside school!'

'We're all right. We haven't got wands yet. They let you off when you're a kid and you can't help it. But once you're eleven,' he nodded importantly, 'and they start training you, then you've got to go careful.'

There was a little silence. Lily had picked up a fallen twig and twirled it in the air, and Harry knew that she was imagining sparks trailing from it. Then she dropped the twig, leaned in towards the boy, and said, 'It *is* real, isn't it? It's not a joke? Petunia says you're lying to me. Petunia says there isn't a Hogwarts. It *is* real, isn't it?'

'It's real for us,' said Snape. 'Not for her. But we'll get the letter, you and me.'

'Really?' whispered Lily.

'Definitely,' said Snape, and even with his poorly cut hair and his odd clothes, he struck an oddly impressive figure sprawled in front of her, brimful of confidence in his destiny.

'And will it really come by owl?' Lily whispered.

'Normally,' said Snape. 'But you're Muggle-born, so someone from the school will have to come and explain to your parents.'

'Does it make a difference, being Muggle-born?'

Snape hesitated. His black eyes, eager in the greenish gloom, moved over the pale face, the dark red hair.

第33章 "王子"的故事

离开了,但眼睛还瞪着斯内普。斯内普站在那里,注视着她们俩大步穿过游乐场的门,此刻只有哈利在一旁看着他。哈利看出了斯内普内心的痛苦和失望,他明白斯内普筹划这一刻有一段时间了,没想到一切都乱了套……

眼前的情景消失了,没等哈利反应过来,周围完全变了样。他现在是在一片小树林里。他看见一条阳光下的小河在树丛间流过,波光粼粼,树荫洒下一片墨绿色的清凉。两个孩子盘着腿,面对面地坐在地上。斯内普已经脱去了外衣,在半明半暗的光线里,那件古怪的孕妇服显得不那么刺眼了。

"……如果你在校外施魔法,魔法部就会惩罚你,你会收到信的。"

"可是我在校外施过魔法呀!"

"我们没关系。我们还没有魔杖呢。小孩子控制不住自己,他们不管。一旦到了十一岁,"他煞有介事地点点头,"他们开始训练你,那时你就得小心点儿了。"

两人沉默了一会儿。莉莉捡起地上的一根树枝,在空中快速地旋转,哈利知道她在想象树枝后面飘出火星。然后她扔掉树枝,探身冲着男孩说道:"这是真的,对吗?不是开玩笑?佩妮说你在骗我。佩妮说根本就没有什么霍格沃茨。这是真的,对吗?"

"对我们来说是真的,"斯内普说,"对她来说不是。我们会收到信的,你和我。"

"真的?"莉莉轻声问。

"千真万确。"斯内普说,他虽然头发参差不齐,衣服稀奇古怪,但坐在莉莉面前却显得别有一番气派,对自己的前途充满信心。

"信真的是由猫头鹰送来?"莉莉小声问。

"一般来说是这样,"斯内普说,"但你是麻瓜出身,所以学校会派人来向你父母解释一下。"

"麻瓜出身会有什么不同吗?"

斯内普迟疑着,他的黑眼睛在绿荫下显得很热切,看着莉莉那张苍白的脸和深红色的头发。

CHAPTER THIRTY-THREE The Prince's Tale

'No,' he said. 'It doesn't make any difference.'

'Good,' said Lily, relaxing: it was clear that she had been worrying.

'You've got loads of magic,' said Snape. 'I saw that. All the time I was watching you ...'

His voice trailed away; she was not listening, but had stretched out on the leafy ground and was looking up at the canopy of leaves overhead. He watched her as greedily as he had watched her in the playground.

'How are things at your house?' Lily asked.

A little crease appeared between his eyes.

'Fine,' he said.

'They're not arguing any more?'

'Oh, yes, they're arguing,' said Snape. He picked up a fistful of leaves and began tearing them apart, apparently unaware of what he was doing. 'But it won't be that long and I'll be gone.'

'Doesn't your dad like magic?'

'He doesn't like anything, much,' said Snape.

'Severus?'

A little smile twisted Snape's mouth when she said his name.

'Yeah?'

'Tell me about the Dementors again.'

'What d'you want to know about them for?'

'If I use magic outside school –'

'They wouldn't give you to the Dementors for that! Dementors are for people who do really bad stuff. They guard the wizard prison, Azkaban. You're not going to end up in Azkaban, you're too –'

He turned red again and shredded more leaves. Then a small rustling noise behind Harry made him turn: Petunia, hiding behind a tree, had lost her footing.

'Tuney!' said Lily, surprise and welcome in her voice, but Snape had jumped to his feet.

'Who's spying now?' he shouted. 'What d'you want?'

Petunia was breathless, alarmed at being caught. Harry could see her struggling for something hurtful to say.

第33章 "王子"的故事

"不会,"他说,"不会有什么不同。"

"太好了。"莉莉说,松了口气。显然她一直在为此担心。

"你会变许多魔法,"斯内普说,"我看见了。我一直在看你……"

他的声音越来越轻。莉莉没有听他说,而是四肢伸开躺在铺满绿叶的地上,望着头顶茂密的树叶。斯内普渴慕地望着她,就像在游乐场上望着她时一样。

"你家里的事情怎么样啦?"莉莉问。

斯内普微微蹙起了眉头。

"还好。"他说。

"他们不吵了?"

"噢,还吵,"斯内普说,一边抓起一把叶子,把它们撕碎,但显然并没有意识到自己在做什么,"但不会太久了,我就要走了。"

"你爸爸不喜欢魔法?"

"他什么都不太喜欢。"斯内普说。

"西弗勒斯?"

听到她叫自己的名字,斯内普的嘴角掠过一丝笑意。

"嗯?"

"再跟我说说摄魂怪的事。"

"你打听它们干什么?"

"如果我在校外使用魔法——"

"不会为了这个把你交给摄魂怪的!摄魂怪是专门对付那些真正干了坏事的人。它们看守巫师监狱——阿兹卡班。你不会进阿兹卡班的,你这么——"

他的脸又红了,撕碎了更多的树叶。就在这时,哈利身后传来沙沙的声音,他转身一看,佩妮躲在一棵树后,脚下没有站稳。

"佩妮!"莉莉说,声音里透着惊讶和欢迎,可是斯内普跳了起来。

"现在是谁在偷看?"他嚷道,"你想干吗?"

佩妮被发现后惊慌失措,几乎喘不过气来。哈利看出她在绞尽脑汁想说几句伤人的话。

CHAPTER THIRTY-THREE The Prince's Tale

'What is that you're wearing, anyway?' she said, pointing at Snape's chest. 'Your mum's blouse?'

There was a *crack*: a branch over Petunia's head had fallen. Lily screamed: the branch caught Petunia on the shoulder and she staggered backwards and burst into tears.

'Tuney!'

But Petunia was running away. Lily rounded on Snape.

'Did you make that happen?'

'No.' He looked both defiant and scared.

'You did!' She was backing away from him. 'You *did*! You hurt her!'

'No – no I didn't!'

But the lie did not convince Lily: after one last burning look she ran from the little thicket, off after her sister, and Snape looked miserable and confused …

And the scene reformed. Harry looked around: he was on platform nine and three-quarters, and Snape stood beside him, slightly hunched, next to a thin, sallow-faced, sour-looking woman who greatly resembled him. Snape was staring at a family of four a short distance away. The two girls stood a little apart from their parents. Lily seemed to be pleading with her sister; Harry moved closer to listen.

'… I'm sorry, Tuney, I'm sorry! Listen –' She caught her sister's hand and held tight to it, even though Petunia tried to pull it away. 'Maybe once I'm there – no, listen, Tuney! Maybe once I'm there, I'll be able to go to Professor Dumbledore and persuade him to change his mind!'

'I don't – want – to – go!' said Petunia, and she dragged her hand back out of her sister's grasp. 'You think I want to go to some stupid castle and learn to be a – a –'

Her pale eyes roved over the platform, over the cats mewling in their owners' arms, over the owls fluttering and hooting at each other in cages, over the students, some already in their long, black robes, loading trunks on to the scarlet steam engine or else greeting one another with glad cries after a summer apart.

'– you think I want to be a – a freak?'

Lily's eyes filled with tears as Petunia succeeded in tugging her hand away.

'I'm not a freak,' said Lily. 'That's a horrible thing to say.'

第33章 "王子"的故事

"你倒说说你穿的那是什么?"她指着斯内普的胸口说,"你妈妈的衣服?"

咔嚓一声,佩妮头顶上一根树枝突然落了下来。莉莉尖叫一声,树枝砸中了佩妮的肩膀,她踉跄着后退几步,哭了起来。

"佩妮!"

可是佩妮跑开了。莉莉朝斯内普发火了。

"是你干的吗?"

"不是。"斯内普显得既不服又害怕。

"就是你!"莉莉从他面前后退,"就是你!你伤着她了!"

"不——我没有!"

然而莉莉不相信他的谎话。她气冲冲地看了他最后一眼,就跑出小树林,追她姐姐去了,斯内普显得痛苦而困惑……

场景转换。哈利环顾四周,他是在 $9\frac{3}{4}$ 站台上,斯内普站在他旁边,微微弓着身子,紧挨着一个跟他长得很像的脸色灰黄、神情阴沉的瘦女人。斯内普正盯着不远处的一家四口。两个女孩离开她们的父母站着。莉莉似乎在央求她的姐姐。哈利凑过去听。

"……我很难过,佩妮,我很难过!你听我说——"她抓过姐姐的手紧紧地握住,佩妮则拼命想挣脱,"也许我一到那儿——不,听我说,佩妮!也许我一到那儿,就能找到邓布利多教授,说服他改变主意!"

"我才——不想——去呢!"佩妮说,使劲想把手从妹妹手里抽出来,"你以为我愿意到某个荒唐的城堡里去,学着做一个——一个——"

她浅色的眼睛扫视着站台,望着猫在主人怀里喵喵叫;望着猫头鹰在笼子里扑打翅膀,互相高叫;望着那些学生——有的已穿上黑色的长袍,他们在把行李搬上深红色的蒸汽机车,或是在分别一个暑假后高兴地大声与同学打着招呼。

"——你以为我想成为一个——一个怪物?"

佩妮终于把手抽走了,莉莉眼睛里满是泪水。

"我不是怪物,"莉莉说,"这么说真难听。"

CHAPTER THIRTY-THREE The Prince's Tale

'That's where you're going,' said Petunia with relish. 'A special school for freaks. You and that Snape boy ... weirdos, that's what you two are. It's good you're being separated from normal people. It's for our safety.'

Lily glanced towards her parents, who were looking around the platform with an air of wholehearted enjoyment, drinking in the scene. Then she looked back at her sister, and her voice was low and fierce.

'You didn't think it was such a freak's school when you wrote to the Headmaster and begged him to take you.'

Petunia turned scarlet.

'Beg? I didn't beg!'

'I saw his reply. It was very kind.'

'You shouldn't have read –' whispered Petunia. 'That was my private – how could you –?'

Lily gave herself away by half glancing towards where Snape stood, nearby. Petunia gasped.

'That boy found it! You and that boy have been sneaking in my room!'

'No – not sneaking –' Now Lily was on the defensive. 'Severus saw the envelope, and he couldn't believe a Muggle could have contacted Hogwarts, that's all! He says there must be wizards working undercover in the postal service who take care of –'

'Apparently wizards poke their noses in everywhere!' said Petunia, now as pale as she had been flushed. '*Freak!*' she spat at her sister, and she flounced off to where her parents stood ...

The scene dissolved again. Snape was hurrying along the corridor of the Hogwarts Express as it clattered through the countryside. He had already changed into his school robes, had perhaps taken the first opportunity to take off his dreadful Muggle clothes. At last he stopped, outside a compartment in which a group of rowdy boys were talking. Hunched in a corner seat beside the window was Lily, her face pressed against the window pane.

Snape slid open the compartment door and sat down opposite Lily. She glanced at him and then looked back out of the window. She had been crying.

'I don't want to talk to you,' she said in a constricted voice.

'Why not?'

第33章 "王子"的故事

"那就是你要去的地方,"佩妮来劲地说,"一个专门给怪物办的学校。你和那个姓斯内普的男孩……怪胎,你们俩都是怪胎。幸好把你们跟普通人隔开了,那是为了我们的安全。"

莉莉朝父母那边瞟了一眼,他们正带着由衷的喜悦看着站台上的情景,尽情地饱览这一幕。莉莉又回过头来看着姐姐,压低声音,语气变得很激烈。

"你给校长写信求他收下你时,可没认为这是一所怪物学校。"

佩妮的脸变得通红。

"求?我没求!"

"我看见他的回信了,写得很委婉。"

"你不应该偷看——"佩妮轻声说,"那是我的隐私——你怎么可以——?"

莉莉朝站在近旁的斯内普瞥了一眼,这一眼泄漏了秘密。佩妮倒抽了一口冷气。

"那个男孩发现的!你和那个男孩偷偷溜进了我的房间!"

"不是——不是偷偷溜进去——"现在是莉莉在辩解了,"西弗勒斯看见了一信封,他不相信麻瓜也能跟霍格沃茨取得联系,就是这样!他说邮政系统里肯定安插了巫师,他们关照了一下——"

"看来巫师到处乱管闲事!"佩妮说,刚才通红的脸现在变得煞白,"怪物!"她朝妹妹啐了一口,猛一转身,向父母跑去……

场景又消失了。斯内普在霍格沃茨特快列车的过道里匆匆往前走,列车哐当哐当地在乡野间穿行。他已经换上了校袍,这大概是他第一次有机会脱掉那身难看的麻瓜衣服。终于,他在一间包厢外停住脚步,包厢里一群吵吵闹闹的男孩正在聊天。莉莉蜷身坐在窗边角落里的一个座位上,脸贴着玻璃窗。

斯内普拉开包厢的门,坐在了莉莉对面。莉莉看了他一眼,又回过头望着窗外。她一直在哭。

"我不想跟你说话。"她声音哽咽地说。

"为什么?"

CHAPTER THIRTY-THREE The Prince's Tale

'Tuney h – hates me. Because we saw that letter from Dumbledore.'

'So what?'

She threw him a look of deep dislike.

'So she's my sister!'

'She's only a –' He caught himself quickly; Lily, too busy trying to wipe her eyes without being noticed, did not hear him.

'But we're going!' he said, unable to suppress the exhilaration in his voice. 'This is it! We're off to Hogwarts!'

She nodded, mopping her eyes, but in spite of herself, she half smiled.

'You'd better be in Slytherin,' said Snape, encouraged that she had brightened a little.

'Slytherin?'

One of the boys sharing the compartment, who had shown no interest at all in Lily or Snape until that point, looked round at the word, and Harry, whose attention had been focused entirely on the two beside the window, saw his father: slight, black-haired like Snape, but with that indefinable air of having been well cared for, even adored, that Snape so conspicuously lacked.

'Who wants to be in Slytherin? I think I'd leave, wouldn't you?' James asked the boy lounging on the seats opposite him, and with a jolt, Harry realised that it was Sirius. Sirius did not smile.

'My whole family have been in Slytherin,' he said.

'Blimey,' said James, 'and I thought you seemed all right!'

Sirius grinned.

'Maybe I'll break the tradition. Where are you heading, if you've got the choice?'

James lifted an invisible sword.

'"*Gryffindor, where dwell the brave at heart!*" Like my dad.'

Snape made a small, disparaging noise. James turned on him.

'Got a problem with that?'

'No,' said Snape, though his slight sneer said otherwise. 'If you'd rather be brawny than brainy –'

第33章 "王子"的故事

"佩妮恨——恨我,因为我们看了邓布利多的那封信。"

"那又怎么样?"

她非常嫌恶地白了他一眼。

"她是我姐姐!"

"她不过是个——"他赶紧闭了嘴。莉莉只顾忙着偷偷擦眼泪,没有听见他的话。

"可是我们出发了!"他说,声音里带着无法抑制的喜悦,"没错!我们出发去霍格沃茨了!"

莉莉点点头,擦擦眼睛,忍不住露出了一丝笑容。

"你最好进斯莱特林。"斯内普说,看到莉莉高兴了一点儿,他觉得很受鼓舞。

"斯莱特林?"

坐在包厢里的一个男孩听到这个词转过头来。他本来对莉莉和斯内普没有表示出丝毫兴趣。哈利刚才把注意力全集中在窗边的两个人身上,此刻才看见了自己的父亲:他像斯内普一样身材瘦弱,头发乌黑,但一看就知道从小备受呵护,甚至很受宠爱,这显然是斯内普极度缺乏的。

"谁想去斯莱特林?要是我的话可能会退学,你呢?"詹姆问悠闲地坐在对面座位上的男孩。哈利心头一跳,认出那是小天狼星。小天狼星没有笑。

"我们全家都是斯莱特林的。"他说。

"天哪,"詹姆说,"我还觉得你挺好的呢!"

小天狼星咧嘴笑了笑。

"说不定我会打破传统。如果让你选择,你想去哪儿?"

詹姆举起一把无形的宝剑。

"格兰芬多,那里有埋藏在心底的勇敢!像我爸爸一样。"

斯内普轻蔑地哼了一声,詹姆转头看着他。

"怎么,你有意见?"

"没有,"斯内普说,但他傲慢的讥笑却表露了相反的意思,"如果你情愿肌肉发达而不是头脑发达——"

CHAPTER THIRTY-THREE The Prince's Tale

'Where're you hoping to go, seeing as you're neither?' interjected Sirius.

James roared with laughter. Lily sat up, rather flushed, and looked from James to Sirius in dislike.

'Come on, Severus, let's find another compartment.'

'Oooooo ...'

James and Sirius imitated her lofty voice; James tried to trip Snape as he passed.

'See ya, Snivellus!' a voice called, as the compartment door slammed ...

And the scene dissolved once more ...

Harry was standing right behind Snape as they faced the candlelit house tables, lined with rapt faces. Then Professor McGonagall said, 'Evans, Lily!'

He watched his mother walk forwards on trembling legs and sit down upon the rickety stool. Professor McGonagall dropped the Sorting Hat on to her head, and barely a second after it had touched the dark red hair the Hat cried, *'Gryffindor!'*

Harry heard Snape let out a tiny groan. Lily took off the Hat, handed it back to Professor McGonagall, then hurried towards the cheering Gryffindors, but as she went she glanced back at Snape, and there was a sad little smile on her face. Harry saw Sirius move up the bench to make room for her. She took one look at him, seemed to recognise him from the train, folded her arms and firmly turned her back on him.

The roll call continued. Harry watched Lupin, Pettigrew and his father join Lily and Sirius at the Gryffindor table. At last, when only a dozen students remained to be sorted, Professor McGonagall called Snape.

Harry walked with him to the stool, watched him place the Hat upon his head. *'Slytherin!'* cried the Sorting Hat.

And Severus Snape moved off to the other side of the Hall, away from Lily, to where the Slytherins were cheering him, to where Lucius Malfoy, a prefect badge gleaming upon his chest, patted Snape on the back as he sat down beside him ...

And the scene changed ...

第33章 "王子"的故事

"那么你希望去哪儿?看样子你两样都不发达。"小天狼星突然插嘴道。

詹姆大声笑了起来。莉莉挺直身子,绯红了脸,厌恶地看看詹姆,又看看小天狼星。

"走吧,西弗勒斯,我们另外找一间包厢。"

"哦哦哦哦……"

詹姆和小天狼星模仿着莉莉高傲的声音,斯内普走过时詹姆还伸腿绊了他一下。

"回见,鼻涕精!"一个声音喊道,包厢的门重重地关上了……

场景再次消失……

哈利站在斯内普身后,面对烛光映照下的几张学院长桌,桌旁是一张张兴奋的面孔。这时,麦格教授说道:"莉莉·伊万斯!"

他注视着自己的母亲迈着颤抖的双腿走上前去,在摇摇晃晃的凳子上坐下来。麦格教授把分院帽罩在她脑袋上,帽子接触到她深红色的头发还不到一秒钟,就喊道:"格兰芬多!"

哈利听见斯内普发出一声轻轻的叹息。莉莉脱下帽子还给了麦格教授,匆匆朝热烈欢呼的格兰芬多同学们走去,但她回头看了一眼斯内普,脸上露出一丝无奈的苦笑。哈利看见小天狼星在板凳上挪了挪,给她腾出了地方。莉莉看了他一眼,似乎认出他就是火车上的那个人,立刻抱起双臂,坚定地转过身背朝着他。

点名还在继续。哈利看到卢平、小矮星和他父亲都到了格兰芬多桌旁,跟莉莉和小天狼星坐在一起。最后,只有十几个学生还没有分院,麦格教授喊到了斯内普。

哈利和他一起走到凳子旁,看着他把帽子戴在脑袋上。"斯莱特林!"分院帽喊道。

西弗勒斯·斯内普走向礼堂的另一边,离莉莉越来越远。斯莱特林同学在那里朝他欢呼,卢修斯·马尔福胸前戴着闪闪发亮的级长徽章,拍了拍在他身边坐下的斯内普……

场景变换……

CHAPTER THIRTY-THREE   The Prince's Tale

Lily and Snape were walking across the castle courtyard, evidently arguing. Harry hurried to catch up with them, to listen in. As he reached them, he realised how much taller they both were: a few years seemed to have passed since their Sorting.

'... thought we were supposed to be friends?' Snape was saying. 'Best friends?'

'We *are*, Sev, but I don't like some of the people you're hanging around with! I'm sorry, but I detest Avery and Mulciber! *Mulciber!* What do you see in him, Sev? He's creepy! D'you know what he tried to do to Mary Macdonald the other day?'

Lily had reached a pillar and leaned against it, looking up into the thin, sallow face.

'That was nothing,' said Snape. 'It was a laugh, that's all –'

'It was Dark Magic, and if you think that's funny –'

'What about the stuff Potter and his mates get up to?' demanded Snape. His colour rose again as he said it, unable, it seemed, to hold in his resentment.

'What's Potter got to do with anything?' said Lily.

'They sneak out at night. There's something weird about that Lupin. Where does he keep going?'

'He's ill,' said Lily. 'They say he's ill –'

'Every month at the full moon?' said Snape.

'I know your theory,' said Lily, and she sounded cold. 'Why are you so obsessed with them, anyway? Why do you care what they're doing at night?'

'I'm just trying to show you they're not as wonderful as everyone seems to think they are.'

The intensity of his gaze made her blush.

'They don't use Dark Magic, though.' She dropped her voice. 'And you're being really ungrateful. I heard what happened the other night. You went sneaking down that tunnel by the Whomping Willow and James Potter saved you from whatever's down there –'

Snape's whole face contorted and he spluttered, 'Saved? Saved? You think he was playing the hero? He was saving his neck and his friends' too! You're not going to – I won't let you –'

'*Let* me? *Let* me?'

Lily's bright green eyes were slits. Snape backtracked at once.

第33章 "王子"的故事

莉莉和斯内普走在城堡的院子里，显然是在吵架。哈利紧走几步，追上去偷听。等到他追近时，才发现他们俩都高了许多。似乎自分院之后已经过去了好几年。

"……以为我们应该是朋友？"斯内普在说话，"最好的朋友？"

"是这样啊，西弗，但我不喜欢跟你一起鬼混的那几个人！对不起，可是我讨厌埃弗里和穆尔塞伯！穆尔塞伯！你看出他有哪点好啊，西弗？鬼鬼祟祟的！你知道他那天想对玛丽·麦克唐纳做什么吗？"

莉莉走到一根柱子前靠了上去，抬头望着那张灰黄的瘦脸。

"那不算什么，"斯内普说，"开个玩笑而已，没什么——"

"那是黑魔法，如果你觉得那很好玩——"

"可波特和他那些朋友干的勾当呢？"斯内普质问道，血又涌到脸上，他似乎无法控制怨恨的情绪。

"波特有什么勾当？"莉莉说。

"他们晚上溜出去。那个卢平有些怪异。他总是出去，去哪儿呢？"

"他病了，"莉莉说，"他们说他病了——"

"每个月满月的时候？"斯内普说。

"我知道你的想法。"莉莉说，口气很冷，"奇怪了，你为什么对他们那么上心？你为什么关心他们在夜里做什么？"

"我只是想让你看到他们并不像大家认为的那样优秀。"

在他专注的凝视下，莉莉的脸红了。

"但他们没有使用黑魔法呀，"她降低了声音，"而且你真是忘恩负义。我听说了那天夜里的事情。你从打人柳下偷偷溜进了那条隧道，是詹姆·波特救了你，逃脱了那下面的——"

斯内普整张脸都扭曲变形了，气急败坏地说："救我？救我？你以为他是英雄？他是为了救他自己，还有他的朋友！你可不能——我不让你——"

"让我？让我？"

莉莉那双明亮的绿眼睛眯成了缝，斯内普立刻退缩了。

CHAPTER THIRTY-THREE The Prince's Tale

'I didn't mean – I just don't want to see you made a fool of – he fancies you, James Potter fancies you!' The words seemed wrenched from him against his will. 'And he's not ... everyone thinks ... Big Quidditch hero –' Snape's bitterness and dislike were rendering him incoherent, and Lily's eyebrows were travelling further and further up her forehead.

'I know James Potter's an arrogant toerag,' she said, cutting across Snape. 'I don't need you to tell me that. But Mulciber and Avery's idea of humour is just evil. *Evil*, Sev. I don't understand how you can be friends with them.'

Harry doubted that Snape had even heard her strictures on Mulciber and Avery. The moment she had insulted James Potter, his whole body had relaxed, and as they walked away there was a new spring in Snape's step ...

And the scene dissolved ...

Harry watched, again, as Snape left from the Great Hall, after sitting his O.W.L. in Defence Against the Dark Arts, watched as he wandered away from the castle and strayed, inadvertently, close to the place beneath the beech tree where James, Sirius, Lupin and Pettigrew sat together. But Harry kept his distance this time, because he knew what happened after James had hoisted Severus into the air and taunted him; he knew what had been done and said, and it gave him no pleasure to hear it again. He watched, as Lily joined the group and went to Snape's defence. Distantly he heard Snape shout at her in his humiliation and his fury, the unforgivable word: '*Mudblood*.'

The scene changed ...

'I'm sorry.'

'I'm not interested.'

'I'm sorry!'

'Save your breath.'

It was night-time. Lily, who was wearing a dressing gown, stood with her arms folded in front of the portrait of the Fat Lady, at the entrance to Gryffindor Tower.

'I only came out because Mary told me you were threatening to sleep here.'

'I was. I would have done. I never meant to call you Mudblood, it just –'

'Slipped out?' There was no pity in Lily's voice. 'It's too late. I've made excuses for you for years. None of my friends can understand why I even talk

第33章 "王子"的故事

"我不是那个意思——我只是不想看到别人把你当傻瓜——他喜欢你，詹姆·波特喜欢你！"这句话似乎是勉强从他嘴里拽出来的，"他可不是……大家都以为……了不起的魁地奇球明星——"痛苦和反感使得斯内普语无伦次，莉莉的眉毛在额头上越扬越高。

"我知道詹姆·波特是个自以为是的自大狂，"莉莉打断了斯内普，"这点不需要你告诉我。但穆尔塞伯和埃弗里的所谓幽默是邪恶的。邪恶的，西弗。我不明白你怎么能跟他们交朋友。"

哈利怀疑斯内普是否听见了莉莉对穆尔塞伯和埃弗里的批评。莉莉指责詹姆·波特的话一出口，他整个身体就放松了。当他们转身走开时，斯内普的脚步重又变得轻快起来……

场景消失了……

哈利注视着斯内普参加完黑魔法防御术课的O.W.L.考试后离开了礼堂，注视着他悠闲地走出城堡，漫无目的地逛到那棵山毛榉树附近，詹姆、小天狼星、卢平和小矮星正一起坐在树下。但哈利这次没有靠近他们，因为他知道詹姆把西弗勒斯吊在空中百般奚落之后发生了什么事情。他知道他们做了什么，说了什么，再听一遍不会使他快乐。他注视着，莉莉走到那伙人中间去替斯内普辩护。他远远地听见斯内普恼羞成怒地冲她喊出了那个不可原谅的词："泥巴种。"

场景变换……

"对不起。"

"我没兴趣。"

"对不起！"

"别白费口舌了。"

时间是晚上，莉莉穿着晨衣，抱着双臂站在格兰芬多塔楼入口处的胖夫人肖像前面。

"玛丽说你扬言要睡在这里我才出来的。"

"是啊，你要是不出来，我就要睡在这里。我绝不是故意叫你泥巴种的，我只是——"

"只是说漏了嘴？"莉莉的声音里没有半点同情，"太晚了。这么多

CHAPTER THIRTY-THREE   The Prince's Tale

to you. You and your precious little Death Eater friends – you see, you don't even deny it! You don't even deny that's what you're all aiming to be! You can't wait to join You-Know-Who, can you?'

He opened his mouth, but closed it without speaking.

'I can't pretend any more. You've chosen your way, I've chosen mine.'

'No – listen, I didn't mean –'

'– to call me Mudblood? But you call everyone of my birth Mudblood, Severus. Why should I be any different?'

He struggled on the verge of speech, but with a contemptuous look she turned and climbed back through the portrait hole …

The corridor dissolved, and the scene took a little longer to reform: Harry seemed to fly through shifting shapes and colours until his surroundings solidified again and he stood on a hilltop, forlorn and cold in the darkness, the wind whistling through the branches of a few leafless trees. The adult Snape was panting, turning on the spot, his wand gripped tightly in his hand, waiting for something or for someone … his fear infected Harry, too, even though he knew that he could not be harmed, and he looked over his shoulder, wondering what it was that Snape was waiting for –

Then a blinding, jagged jet of white light flew through the air: Harry thought of lightning, but Snape had dropped to his knees and his wand had flown out of his hand.

'Don't kill me!'

'That was not my intention.'

Any sound of Dumbledore Apparating had been drowned by the sound of the wind in the branches. He stood before Snape with his robes whipping around him, and his face was illuminated from below in the light cast by his wand.

'Well, Severus? What message does Lord Voldemort have for me?'

'No – no message – I'm here on my own account!'

Snape was wringing his hands: he looked a little mad, with his straggling, black hair flying around him.

'I – I come with a warning – no, a request – please –'

Dumbledore flicked his wand. Though leaves and branches still flew through the night air around them, silence fell on the spot where he and Snape faced each other.

第33章 "王子"的故事

年来我一直在找借口原谅你。我的朋友都不能理解我为什么还跟你说话。你和你那些亲爱的食死徒朋友——你看，你甚至都不否认！你甚至都不否认那就是你们的目标！你迫不及待地想成为神秘人的手下，对吗？"

他的嘴巴张了张，没有说话，又闭上了。

"我不能再装下去了，你选择了你的路，我选择了我的。"

"不——听我说，我不是故意——"

"——叫我泥巴种？但是你管我这类出身的人都叫泥巴种，西弗勒斯。我又有什么不同呢？"

他挣扎着还想说点什么，但莉莉轻蔑地看了他一眼，转身从肖像洞口爬了回去……

走廊消失了，这次场景变换的时间长了一些。哈利似乎飞过了许多变幻的形状和色彩，最后周围的景物才固定下来。他站在黑暗中一个荒凉、寒冷的山顶上，风嗖嗖地刮过几棵没有叶子的枯树。成年的斯内普气喘吁吁地原地转过身子，手里紧紧地捏着魔杖，似乎在等什么人或什么东西……他的恐惧也感染了哈利，虽然哈利知道自己不可能受到伤害。他纳闷斯内普在等什么呢，不禁也转过头去——

突然，空中闪过一道刺眼的、之字形的白光，哈利以为是闪电，但斯内普扑通跪倒在地，魔杖从手里飞了出去。

"别杀我！"

"那不是我的意图。"

风在树枝间呜呜作响，淹没了邓布利多刚才幻影显形的声音。他站在斯内普的面前，长袍在风里飘摆，魔杖的光从下面照着他的脸。

"怎么样，西弗勒斯？伏地魔大人有什么口信给我？"

"没有——没有口信——我是为自己来的！"

斯内普绞着双手，看上去有点心神错乱，乌黑纷乱的头发在脑袋周围飘舞。

"我——我带来了一个警报——不，一个请求——求求您——"

邓布利多一挥魔杖。虽然周围的枝叶仍在晚风里飞舞，但在他和斯内普面对面站立的地方，却是一片寂静。

CHAPTER THIRTY-THREE   The Prince's Tale

'What request could a Death Eater make of me?'

'The – the prophecy ... the prediction ... Trelawney ...'

'Ah, yes,' said Dumbledore. 'How much did you relay to Lord Voldemort?'

'Everything – everything I heard!' said Snape. 'That is why – it is for that reason – he thinks it means Lily Evans!'

'The prophecy did not refer to a woman,' said Dumbledore. 'It spoke of a boy born at the end of July –'

'You know what I mean! He thinks it means her son, he is going to hunt her down – kill them all –'

'If she means so much to you,' said Dumbledore, 'surely Lord Voldemort will spare her? Could you not ask for mercy for the mother, in exchange for the son?'

'I have – I have asked him –'

'You disgust me,' said Dumbledore, and Harry had never heard so much contempt in his voice. Snape seemed to shrink a little. 'You do not care, then, about the deaths of her husband and child? They can die, as long as you have what you want?'

Snape said nothing, but merely looked up at Dumbledore.

'Hide them all, then,' he croaked. 'Keep her – them – safe. Please.'

'And what will you give me in return, Severus?'

'In – in return?' Snape gaped at Dumbledore, and Harry expected him to protest, but after a long moment he said, 'Anything.'

The hilltop faded, and Harry stood in Dumbledore's office, and something was making a terrible sound, like a wounded animal. Snape was slumped forwards in a chair and Dumbledore was standing over him, looking grim. After a moment or two, Snape raised his face, and he looked like a man who had lived a hundred years of misery since leaving the wild hilltop.

'I thought ... you were going ... to keep her ... safe ...'

'She and James put their faith in the wrong person,' said Dumbledore. 'Rather like you, Severus. Weren't you hoping that Lord Voldemort would spare her?'

Snape's breathing was shallow.

第33章 "王子"的故事

"一个食死徒能对我有何请求？"

"那个——那个预言……那个预测……特里劳尼……"

"啊，是了，"邓布利多说，"你向伏地魔传达了多少？"

"一切——我听到的一切！"斯内普说，"所以——正因为那个——他认为指的是莉莉·伊万斯！"

"预言没有说是女人，"邓布利多说，"说的是一个七月底出生的男孩——"

"您明白我的意思！他认为指的是莉莉的儿子，他要找到莉莉——把他们全部杀掉——"

"既然莉莉对你这么重要，"邓布利多说，"伏地魔肯定会免她一死吧？你就不能求求他饶了那位母亲，拿儿子作为交换？"

"我——我求过他——"

"你令我厌恶。"邓布利多说，哈利从没听过邓布利多以这么轻蔑的口吻说话。斯内普似乎畏缩了一下。"那么，你就不关心她丈夫和孩子的死活？他们尽可以死，只要你能得到你想要的？"

斯内普什么也没说，只是抬头看着邓布利多。

"那就把他们都藏起来，"他嘶哑着声音说，"保证她——他们的——安全。求求您。"

"那你给我什么作为回报呢，西弗勒斯？"

"作为——回报？"斯内普张口结舌地看着邓布利多，哈利以为他会抗议，但良久之后，他说，"什么都行。"

山顶消失了，哈利站在邓布利多的办公室里，什么东西在发出可怕的声音，像某种受伤的动物。斯内普颓然坐在椅子上，身体前倾。邓布利多站在他面前，神色严峻。过了片刻，斯内普抬起脸，自从荒野山顶的一幕之后，他仿佛度过了一百年的苦难岁月。

"我以为……你会……保证她的……安全……"

"她和詹姆错误地信任了别人，"邓布利多说，"就像你，西弗勒斯。你不是也曾指望伏地魔会饶她一命吗？"

斯内普的呼吸虚弱无力。

CHAPTER THIRTY-THREE   The Prince's Tale

'Her boy survives,' said Dumbledore.

With a tiny jerk of the head, Snape seemed to flick off an irksome fly.

'Her son lives. He has her eyes, precisely her eyes. You remember the shape and colour of Lily Evans's eyes, I am sure?'

'DON'T!' bellowed Snape. 'Gone ... Dead ...'

'Is this remorse, Severus?'

'I wish ... I wish *I* were dead ...'

'And what use would that be to anyone?' said Dumbledore coldly. 'If you loved Lily Evans, if you truly loved her, then your way forward is clear.'

Snape seemed to peer through a haze of pain, and Dumbledore's words appeared to take a long time to reach him.

'What – what do you mean?'

'You know how and why she died. Make sure it was not in vain. Help me protect Lily's son.'

'He does not need protection. The Dark Lord has gone –'

'– the Dark Lord will return, and Harry Potter will be in terrible danger when he does.'

There was a long pause, and slowly Snape regained control of himself, mastered his own breathing. At last he said, 'Very well. Very well. But never – never tell, Dumbledore! This must be between us! Swear it! I cannot bear ... especially Potter's son ... I want your word!'

'My word, Severus, that I shall never reveal the best of you?' Dumbledore sighed, looking down into Snape's ferocious, anguished face. 'If you insist ...'

The office dissolved but reformed instantly. Snape was pacing up and down in front of Dumbledore.

'– mediocre, arrogant as his father, a determined rule-breaker, delighted to find himself famous, attention-seeking and impertinent –'

'You see what you expect to see, Severus,' said Dumbledore, without raising his eyes from a copy of *Transfiguration Today*. 'Other teachers report that the boy is modest, likeable and reasonably talented. Personally, I find him an engaging child.'

Dumbledore turned a page, and said, without looking up, 'Keep an eye on Quirrell, won't you?'

第33章 "王子"的故事

"她儿子活下来了。"邓布利多说。

斯内普猛地晃了一下脑袋,像在赶走一只讨厌的苍蝇。

"她儿子还活着,眼睛和他妈妈的一样,一模一样。我想,你肯定记得莉莉·伊万斯的眼睛,它们的形状和颜色,对吗?"

"**不要**!"斯内普吼道,"没了……死了……"

"这是悔恨吗,西弗勒斯?"

"我希望……我希望死的是我……"

"那对任何人又有什么用呢?"邓布利多冷冷地说,"如果你爱莉莉·伊万斯,如果你真心地爱她,那你面前的道路很清楚。"

斯内普眼前似乎隔着一层痛苦的迷雾,邓布利多的话仿佛过了很长时间才传到他的耳朵里。

"您——您说什么?"

"你知道她是怎么死的,为什么死的。别让她白白牺牲。帮助我保护莉莉的儿子。"

"他不需要保护。黑魔王走了——"

"——黑魔王还会回来,到那时候,哈利·波特将会面临可怕的危险。"

静默良久,斯内普慢慢控制住自己,呼吸自如了。最后他说道:"很好。很好。可是千万——千万别说出去,邓布利多!只能你知我知!您起誓!我受不了……特别是波特的儿子……我要您起誓!"

"要我起誓,西弗勒斯,永远不把你最好的一面透露出去?"邓布利多低头看着斯内普那张激动而又痛苦的脸,叹息着说,"如果你坚持……"

办公室消失了,紧接着又重新浮现。斯内普在邓布利多面前踱来踱去。

"——跟他父亲一样平庸、傲慢,专爱违反纪律,喜欢出风头,吸引别人注意,放肆无礼——"

"你看到的是你预想会看到的东西,西弗勒斯。"邓布利多在看一本《今日变形术》,头也不抬地说,"别的老师都说那男孩谦虚、随和,天资也不错。我个人也发现他是个讨人喜欢的孩子。"

邓布利多翻过一页,仍然头也不抬地说:"注意奇洛,好吗?"

CHAPTER THIRTY-THREE   The Prince's Tale

A whirl of colour, and now everything darkened, and Snape and Dumbledore stood a little apart in the Entrance Hall, while the last stragglers from the Yule Ball passed them on their way to bed.

'Well?' murmured Dumbledore.

'Karkaroff's Mark is becoming darker too. He is panicking, he fears retribution; you know how much help he gave the Ministry after the Dark Lord fell.' Snape looked sideways at Dumbledore's crooked-nosed profile. 'Karkaroff intends to flee if the Mark burns.'

'Does he?' said Dumbledore softly, as Fleur Delacour and Roger Davies came giggling in from the grounds. 'And are you tempted to join him?'

'No,' said Snape, his black eyes on Fleur and Roger's retreating figures. 'I am not such a coward.'

'No,' agreed Dumbledore. 'You are a braver man by far than Igor Karkaroff. You know, I sometimes think we Sort too soon ...'

He walked away, leaving Snape looking stricken ...

And now Harry stood in the Headmaster's office yet again. It was night-time, and Dumbledore sagged sideways in the throne-like chair behind the desk, apparently semi-conscious. His right hand dangled over the side, blackened and burned. Snape was muttering incantations, pointing his wand at the wrist of the hand, while with his left hand he tipped a goblet full of thick golden potion down Dumbledore's throat. After a moment or two, Dumbledore's eyelids fluttered and opened.

'Why,' said Snape, without preamble, '*why* did you put on that ring? It carries a curse, surely you realised that. Why even touch it?'

Marvolo Gaunt's ring lay on the desk before Dumbledore. It was cracked; the sword of Gryffindor lay beside it.

Dumbledore grimaced.

'I ... was a fool. Sorely tempted ...'

'Tempted by what?'

Dumbledore did not answer.

'It is a miracle you managed to return here!' Snape sounded furious. 'That ring carried a curse of extraordinary power, to contain it is all we can hope for; I have trapped the curse in one hand for the time being –'

第33章 "王子"的故事

色彩旋转，周围的一切都变得昏暗了，斯内普和邓布利多隔开一点儿站在门厅里。圣诞舞会上的最后一批人从他们身边走过，回去睡觉了。

"怎么样？"邓布利多轻声问。

"卡卡洛夫的标记也变黑了。他很紧张，担心会受惩罚。你知道黑魔王倒台后卡卡洛夫给了魔法部很多帮助。"斯内普侧眼看着邓布利多那长着弯鼻子的侧影，"他打算，如果标记灼痛起来，他就逃跑。"

"是吗？"邓布利多轻声说，这时芙蓉·德拉库尔和罗杰·戴维斯咯咯地笑着从操场进来了，"你也很想跟他一起去？"

"不，"斯内普说，一双黑眼睛盯着芙蓉和罗杰远去的背影，"我不是那样的胆小鬼。"

"对，"邓布利多赞同道，"到目前为止，你比伊戈尔·卡卡洛夫要勇敢得多。知道吗，我有时觉得我们的分类太草率了……"

他走开了，斯内普独自垂头丧气……

这一次，哈利还是站在校长办公室里。时间是晚上，邓布利多无力地歪在桌后宝座般的椅子上，看上去神志不清。他的右手在一侧耷拉着，被烧焦了，黑乎乎的。斯内普低声念着咒语，将魔杖对准那只手腕，左手把一杯浓浓的金色药液灌进了邓布利多的嘴里。过了片刻，邓布利多的眼皮抖动了几下，睁开了。

"你为什么，"斯内普劈头就问，"为什么要戴上那枚戒指？它上面有魔咒，你肯定知道。为什么还要碰它？"

马沃罗·冈特的戒指放在邓布利多面前的桌子上，已经破裂，旁边是格兰芬多的宝剑。

邓布利多做了个鬼脸。

"我……我做了傻事。诱惑太大了……"

"什么诱惑？"

邓布利多没有回答。

"你能够回到这里已是个奇迹！"斯内普怒气冲冲地说，"那枚戒指上有特别强大的魔咒，我们最多希望能把它遏制住。我已经把魔咒暂时囚禁在一只手里——"

CHAPTER THIRTY-THREE   The Prince's Tale

Dumbledore raised his blackened, useless hand, and examined it with the expression of one being shown an interesting curio.

'You have done very well, Severus. How long do you think I have?'

Dumbledore's tone was conversational; he might have been asking for a weather forecast. Snape hesitated, and then said, 'I cannot tell. Maybe a year. There is no halting such a spell forever. It will spread, eventually, it is the sort of curse that strengthens over time.'

Dumbledore smiled. The news that he had less than a year to live seemed a matter of little or no concern to him.

'I am fortunate, extremely fortunate, that I have you, Severus.'

'If you had only summoned me a little earlier, I might have been able to do more, buy you more time!' said Snape furiously. He looked down at the broken ring and the sword. 'Did you think that breaking the ring would break the curse?'

'Something like that ... I was delirious, no doubt ...' said Dumbledore. With an effort, he straightened himself in his chair. 'Well, really, this makes matters much more straightforward.'

Snape looked utterly perplexed. Dumbledore smiled.

'I refer to the plan Lord Voldemort is revolving around me. His plan to have the poor Malfoy boy murder me.'

Snape sat down in the chair Harry had so often occupied, across the desk from Dumbledore. Harry could tell that he wanted to say more on the subject of Dumbledore's cursed hand, but the other held it up in polite refusal to discuss the matter further. Scowling, Snape said, 'The Dark Lord does not expect Draco to succeed. This is merely punishment for Lucius's recent failures. Slow torture for Draco's parents, while they watch him fail and pay the price.'

'In short, the boy has had a death sentence pronounced upon him as surely as I have,' said Dumbledore. 'Now, I should have thought the natural successor to the job, once Draco fails, is yourself?'

There was a short pause.

'That, I think, is the Dark Lord's plan.'

'Lord Voldemort foresees a moment in the near future when he will not need a spy at Hogwarts?'

'He believes the school will soon be in his grasp, yes.'

第33章 "王子"的故事

邓布利多举起那只焦黑、无用的手，仔细端详着，就像面对一个非常有趣的收藏品。

"你干得很出色，西弗勒斯。你认为我还有多少时间？"

邓布利多的语气轻松随意，如同在询问天气预报。斯内普迟疑了一下，说道："我说不好，大概一年。没有办法永远遏制这样的魔咒。它最终总会扩散，这种魔咒会随着时间的推移不断加强。"

邓布利多露出了微笑。他只剩下不到一年的时间了，这消息对他来说似乎无足轻重。

"我很幸运，非常幸运，有你在我身边，西弗勒斯。"

"如果你早点儿把我叫来，我或许能多采取些措施，为你争取更多的时间！"斯内普恼怒地说，他低头看着破碎的戒指和那把宝剑，"你以为摧毁戒指就能破除魔咒？"

"差不多吧……我肯定是昏了头了……"邓布利多说，他吃力地在椅子上坐直身子，"也好，这样就使事情变得更简单了。"

斯内普似乎完全被弄糊涂了。邓布利多笑了笑。

"我指的是伏地魔围绕我制订的计划。他计划让马尔福家那个可怜的男孩杀死我。"

斯内普在哈利经常坐的椅子上坐了下来，隔着桌子面对邓布利多。哈利看出他还想再谈谈邓布利多那只被魔咒伤害的手，但对方举起焦手，委婉地表示不愿意继续谈论这个话题。斯内普皱着眉头说："黑魔王没指望德拉科能够得手。这只是为了惩罚卢修斯最近的失败。让德拉科的父母眼看着儿子失手，然后付出代价，这对他们来说是钝刀子割肉。"

"总之，这男孩像我一样被明确地判了死刑。"邓布利多说，"我以为，一旦德拉科失手，接替这项工作的自然是你啰？"

短暂的沉默。

"我想，黑魔王是这么设计的。"

"伏地魔是否预见在不久的将来，他在霍格沃茨将不再需要密探？"

"他相信学校很快就会被他控制，是的。"

CHAPTER THIRTY-THREE   The Prince's Tale

'And if it does fall into his grasp,' said Dumbledore, almost, it seemed, as an aside, 'I have your word that you will do all in your power to protect the students of Hogwarts?'

Snape gave a stiff nod.

'Good. Now then. Your first priority will be to discover what Draco is up to. A frightened teenage boy is a danger to others as well as to himself. Offer him help and guidance, he ought to accept, he likes you –'

'– much less since his father has lost favour. Draco blames me, he thinks I have usurped Lucius's position.'

'All the same, try. I am concerned less for myself than for accidental victims of whatever schemes might occur to the boy. Ultimately, of course, there is only one thing to be done if we are to save him from Lord Voldemort's wrath.'

Snape raised his eyebrows and his tone was sardonic as he asked, 'Are you intending to let him kill you?'

'Certainly not. *You* must kill me.'

There was a long silence, broken only by an odd clicking noise. Fawkes the phoenix was gnawing a bit of cuttlebone.

'Would you like me to do it now?' asked Snape, his voice heavy with irony. 'Or would you like a few moments to compose an epitaph?'

'Oh, not quite yet,' said Dumbledore, smiling. 'I daresay the moment will present itself in due course. Given what has happened tonight,' he indicated his withered hand, 'we can be sure that it will happen within a year.'

'If you don't mind dying,' said Snape roughly, 'why not let Draco do it?'

'That boy's soul is not yet so damaged,' said Dumbledore. 'I would not have it ripped apart on my account.'

'And my soul, Dumbledore? Mine?'

'You alone know whether it will harm your soul to help an old man avoid pain and humiliation,' said Dumbledore. 'I ask this one, great favour of you, Severus, because death is coming for me as surely as the Chudley Cannons will finish bottom of this year's league. I confess I should prefer a quick, painless exit to the protracted and messy affair it will be if, for instance, Greyback is involved – I hear Voldemort has recruited him? Or dear

第33章 "王子"的故事

"如果学校真的落到他手里,"邓布利多说,好像是临时想到插了一句,"我要你起誓你会尽全部的力量保护霍格沃茨的学生,行吗?"

斯内普僵硬地点了点头。

"很好。那么,你首先需要弄清德拉科打算干什么。一个惊慌失措的少年不仅对他自己危险,对别人也很危险。向他提供帮助和指导,他应该会接受,他喜欢你——"

"——他父亲失宠之后,他就不那么喜欢我了。德拉科怨恨我,认为我夺走了卢修斯的位置。"

"没关系,试试吧。比起我自己来,我更关心的是那男孩采取的行动计划的意外受害者。当然啦,如果要把他从伏地魔的暴怒中解救出来,最终只有一个办法。"

斯内普扬起眉毛,用讽刺的口吻问道:"你打算让他把你杀死?"

"当然不是。必须由你杀死我。"

长久的沉默,屋里只有一种奇怪的咔啦啦的声音。凤凰福克斯在啃一小块墨鱼骨头。

"你希望我现在就动手吗?"斯内普问,语气里透着浓浓的讽刺,"还是你需要一点儿时间构思一下墓志铭?"

"哦,暂时还不用,"邓布利多微笑着说,"我想,那一刻该来的时候总会来的。从今晚的事情来看,"他指指自己焦枯的手,"我们可以肯定它将在一年之内发生。"

"既然你不在乎死,"斯内普粗暴地说,"为什么不让德拉科得手呢?"

"那个男孩的灵魂还没被完全糟蹋,"邓布利多说,"我不愿意因为我的缘故把它弄得四分五裂。"

"那么我的灵魂呢,邓布利多?我的呢?"

"只有你才知道,帮助一个老人免于痛苦和耻辱会不会伤害你的灵魂。"邓布利多说,"西弗勒斯,我请求你为我完成这件大事,因为死亡对于我来说是铁板钉钉的事,就像查德里火炮队将在今年的联赛中垫底一样。说句实话,我倒愿意没有痛苦地迅速结束生命,而不愿意拖拖拉拉,死得很狼狈,比如,把格雷伯克牵扯进来——我听说伏地魔把他也招进去了?或者落到亲爱的贝拉特里克斯手里,她喜欢把食

CHAPTER THIRTY-THREE The Prince's Tale

Bellatrix, who likes to play with her food before she eats it.'

His tone was light but his blue eyes pierced Snape as they had frequently pierced Harry, as though the soul they discussed was visible to him. At last Snape gave another curt nod.

Dumbledore seemed satisfied.

'Thank you, Severus ...'

The office disappeared, and now Snape and Dumbledore were strolling together in the deserted castle grounds by twilight.

'What are you doing with Potter, all these evenings you are closeted together?' Snape asked abruptly.

Dumbledore looked weary.

'Why? You aren't trying to give him *more* detentions, Severus? The boy will soon have spent more time in detention than out.'

'He is his father over again –'

'In looks, perhaps, but his deepest nature is much more like his mother's. I spend time with Harry because I have things to discuss with him, information I must give him before it is too late.'

'Information,' repeated Snape. 'You trust him ... you do not trust me.'

'It is not a question of trust. I have, as we both know, limited time. It is essential that I give the boy enough information for him to do what he needs to do.'

'And why may I not have the same information?'

'I prefer not to put all of my secrets in one basket, particularly not a basket that spends so much time dangling on the arm of Lord Voldemort.'

'Which I do on your orders!'

'And you do it extremely well. Do not think that I underestimate the constant danger in which you place yourself, Severus. To give Voldemort what appears to be valuable information while withholding the essentials is a job I would entrust to nobody but you.'

'Yet you confide much more in a boy who is incapable of Occlumency, whose magic is mediocre and who has a direct connection into the Dark Lord's mind!'

'Voldemort fears that connection,' said Dumbledore. 'Not so long ago he had one, small taste of what truly sharing Harry's mind means to him. It

第33章 "王子"的故事

物玩够了再吃。"

他的语气很轻松,但那双蓝眼睛却犀利地望着斯内普,就像从前经常望着哈利一样,似乎能真切地看见他们所谈论的灵魂。最后,斯内普轻轻地点了点头。

邓布利多好像满意了。

"谢谢你,西弗勒斯……"

办公室消失了,暮色中,斯内普和邓布利多一起在冷清清的城堡操场上漫步。

"这些晚上你和波特两人关在屋里做什么呢?"斯内普突然问道。

邓布利多显得很疲惫。

"怎么?你不是想再让他关禁闭吧,西弗勒斯?过不了多久,这男孩关禁闭的时间会比他自由的时间还多。"

"他简直是他父亲的翻版——"

"相貌上也许是这样,但他骨子里更像他的母亲。我和哈利待在一起,是因为我有事情要跟他商量,我必须给他一些信息,不然就来不及了。"

"信息,"斯内普说,"你信任他……却不信任我。"

"这不是信任不信任的问题。你我都知道,我的时间有限。我必须给那男孩足够的信息,让他去完成需要完成的事情。"

"那为什么我不能得到同样的信息?"

"我不想把我所有的秘密都装在一个篮子里,特别是一个许多时间都挂在伏地魔胳膊上的篮子。"

"我是按你的吩咐做的!"

"你做得非常出色。不要以为我低估了你时时所处的危险,西弗勒斯。只把看似有价值的情报告诉伏地魔,而把最重要的信息留在心底,这项工作我只能交给你。"

"可是你却更信赖一个连大脑封闭术都不会的小男孩,他的魔法很平庸,而且可以直接连接黑魔王的思想!"

"伏地魔害怕那种连接,"邓布利多说,"不久以前,他稍稍领略了一番分享哈利的思想对他来说意味着什么。他从未体验过那样的痛苦。

CHAPTER THIRTY-THREE The Prince's Tale

was pain such as he has never experienced. He will not try to possess Harry again, I am sure of it. Not in that way.'

'I don't understand.'

'Lord Voldemort's soul, maimed as it is, cannot bear close contact with a soul like Harry's. Like a tongue on frozen steel, like flesh in flame –'

'Souls? We were talking of minds!'

'In the case of Harry and Lord Voldemort, to speak of one is to speak of the other.'

Dumbledore glanced around to make sure that they were alone. They were close by the Forbidden Forest, now, but there was no sign of anyone near them.

'After you have killed me, Severus –'

'You refuse to tell me everything, yet you expect that small service of me!' snarled Snape, and real anger flared in the thin face now. 'You take a great deal for granted, Dumbledore! Perhaps I have changed my mind!'

'You gave me your word, Severus. And while we are talking about services you owe me, I thought you agreed to keep a close eye on our young Slytherin friend?'

Snape looked angry, mutinous. Dumbledore sighed.

'Come to my office tonight, Severus, at eleven, and you shall not complain that I have no confidence in you …'

They were back in Dumbledore's office, the windows dark, and Fawkes sat silent as Snape sat quite still, as Dumbledore walked around him, talking.

'Harry must not know, not until the last moment, not until it is necessary, otherwise how could he have the strength to do what must be done?'

'But what must he do?'

'That is between Harry and me. Now, listen closely, Severus. There will come a time – after my death – do not argue, do not interrupt! There will come a time when Lord Voldemort will seem to fear for the life of his snake.'

'For Nagini?' Snape looked astonished.

'Precisely. If there comes a time when Lord Voldemort stops sending that snake forth to do his bidding, but keeps it safe beside him, under magical protection, then, I think, it will be safe to tell Harry.'

'Tell him what?'

第33章 "王子"的故事

他再也不会试图控制哈利了,我可以肯定,至少不是用那种方式。"

"我不明白。"

"伏地魔的灵魂如此残缺不全,它受不了接近哈利那样的灵魂,就像舌头粘在冰冻的钢上,皮肉接触火焰——"

"灵魂?我们谈的是思想!"

"在哈利和伏地魔的问题上,这两者是一回事。"

邓布利多环顾四周,确保除了他们俩之外没有别人。他们现在到了禁林附近,但周围没有一个人影。

"西弗勒斯,在你杀死我之后——"

"你什么都不肯告诉我,却还指望我帮你那个小忙!"斯内普低吼道,瘦瘦的脸上闪着真正的怒气,"你觉得许多事情都理所当然,邓布利多!说不定我改变主意了呢!"

"你发过誓的,西弗勒斯。说到你为我效力的事,我记得你答应过要密切关注我们那位年轻的斯莱特林朋友,对吗?"

斯内普显得恼怒而不服气。邓布利多叹息了一声。

"今晚十一点到我办公室来,西弗勒斯,你就不会抱怨我不信任你了……"

他们回到了邓布利多的办公室,窗外漆黑一片,福克斯安安静静地待着,斯内普坐在那里一动不动,邓布利多一边说话,一边在他周围走来走去。

"不到最后关头,不到绝对必要的时候,千万不能让哈利知道,不然他怎么有力量去做他必须要做的事情呢?"

"他必须要做什么?"

"那是哈利和我之间的事。现在,西弗勒斯,请你听仔细了。到了某个时候——在我死后——不要反驳,不要插嘴!到了某个时候,伏地魔似乎会为他那条大蛇的生命担心。"

"为纳吉尼担心?"斯内普显得很惊愕。

"不错。如果到了某个时候,伏地魔不再派那条大蛇去执行命令,而是让它守在身边,用魔法把它保护起来,到了那时,我想就可以告诉哈利了。"

"告诉他什么?"

CHAPTER THIRTY-THREE — The Prince's Tale

Dumbledore took a deep breath and closed his eyes.

'Tell him that on the night Lord Voldemort tried to kill him, when Lily cast her own life between them as a shield, the Killing Curse rebounded upon Lord Voldemort, and a fragment of Voldemort's soul was blasted apart from the whole, and latched itself on to the only living soul left in that collapsing building. Part of Lord Voldemort lives inside Harry, and it is that which gives him the power of speech with snakes, and a connection with Lord Voldemort's mind that he has never understood. And while that fragment of soul, unmissed by Voldemort, remains attached to, and protected by Harry, Lord Voldemort cannot die.'

Harry seemed to be watching the two men from one end of a long tunnel, they were so far away from him, their voices echoing strangely in his ears.

'So the boy ... the boy must die?' asked Snape, quite calmly.

'And Voldemort himself must do it, Severus. That is essential.'

Another long silence. Then Snape said, 'I thought ... all these years ... that we were protecting him for her. For Lily.'

'We have protected him because it has been essential to teach him, to raise him, to let him try his strength,' said Dumbledore, his eyes still tight shut. 'Meanwhile, the connection between them grows ever stronger, a parasitic growth: sometimes I have thought he suspects it himself. If I know him, he will have arranged matters so that when he does set out to meet his death, it will, truly, mean the end of Voldemort.'

Dumbledore opened his eyes. Snape looked horrified.

'You have kept him alive so that he can die at the right moment?'

'Don't be shocked, Severus. How many men and women have you watched die?'

'Lately, only those whom I could not save,' said Snape. He stood up. 'You have used me.'

'Meaning?'

'I have spied for you, and lied for you, put myself in mortal danger for you. Everything was supposed to be to keep Lily Potter's son safe. Now you tell me you have been raising him like a pig for slaughter –'

'But this is touching, Severus,' said Dumbledore seriously. 'Have you grown to care for the boy, after all?'

第33章 "王子"的故事

邓布利多深深吸了口气,闭上了眼睛。

"告诉他,在伏地魔试图杀死他的那天夜里,当莉莉用自己的生命挡在他们之间时,那个杀戮咒反弹到伏地魔身上,伏地魔灵魂的一个碎片被炸飞了,附着在坍塌的房子里唯一活着的灵魂上。伏地魔的一部分活在哈利体内,使哈利有了与蛇对话的能力,并可以连接伏地魔的思想,这一直令他百思不得其解。只要那个灵魂碎片没被伏地魔惦记,还依附在哈利身上,受到哈利的保护,伏地魔就不可能死。"

哈利似乎是在一条长长隧道的尽头注视着邓布利多和斯内普,他们离他那么遥远,他们的说话声在他耳朵里发出奇怪的回音。

"那么那男孩……那男孩必须死去?"斯内普很平静地问。

"而且必须由伏地魔亲自动手,西弗勒斯。那是非常重要的。"

又是长时间的沉默。然后斯内普说:"我还以为……这么多年来……我还以为我们是在保护他,为了她,为了莉莉。"

"我们保护他,是因为必须调教他,培养他,让他磨炼自己的能力,"邓布利多说,仍然紧闭着眼睛,"与此同时,他们之间的连接也变得越来越强,像一种寄生的生命。有时我觉得他好像自己也有所察觉。如果我真的了解他,我认为他会把一切安排妥当,这样当他毅然赴死时,就意味着伏地魔的真正完结。"

邓布利多睁开了眼睛,斯内普神色惊恐。

"你让他活着,只是为了他能在适当的时候赴死?"

"别大惊失色,西弗勒斯。你目睹了多少男男女女的死?"

"最近,死的都是那些我无力相救的人。"斯内普说,然后他站了起来,"你利用了我。"

"什么意思?"

"我为你做密探,为你编造谎言,为你冒着致命的危险。这一切据你说都是为了保证莉莉·波特儿子的安全。现在你却告诉我,你养着他就像养着一头待杀的猪——"

"多么感人哪,西弗勒斯,"邓布利多严肃地说,"难道你真的开始关心那个男孩了?"

CHAPTER THIRTY-THREE The Prince's Tale

'For *him*?' shouted Snape. '*Expecto patronum!*'

From the tip of his wand burst the silver doe: she landed on the office floor, bounded once across the office and soared out of the window. Dumbledore watched her fly away, and as her silvery glow faded he turned back to Snape, and his eyes were full of tears.

'After all this time?'

'Always,' said Snape.

And the scene shifted. Now, Harry saw Snape talking to the portrait of Dumbledore behind his desk.

'You will have to give Voldemort the correct date of Harry's departure from his aunt and uncle's,' said Dumbledore. 'Not to do so will raise suspicion, when Voldemort believes you so well-informed. However, you must plant the idea of decoys – that, I think, ought to ensure Harry's safety. Try Confunding Mundungus Fletcher. And Severus, if you are forced to take part in the chase, be sure to act your part convincingly ... I am counting upon you to remain in Lord Voldemort's good books as long as possible, or Hogwarts will be left to the mercy of the Carrows ...'

Now Snape was head to head with Mundungus in an unfamiliar tavern, Mundungus's face looking curiously blank, Snape frowning in concentration.

'You will suggest to the Order of the Phoenix,' Snape murmured, 'that they use decoys. Polyjuice Potion. Identical Potters. It is the only thing that might work. You will forget that I have suggested this. You will present it as your own idea. You understand?'

'I understand,' murmured Mundungus, his eyes unfocused ...

Now Harry was flying alongside Snape on a broomstick through a clear dark night: he was accompanied by other hooded Death Eaters, and ahead were Lupin and a Harry who was really George ... a Death Eater moved ahead of Snape and raised his wand, pointing it directly at Lupin's back –

'*Sectumsempra!*' shouted Snape.

But the spell, intended for the Death Eater's wand hand, missed and hit George instead –

And next, Snape was kneeling in Sirius's old bedroom. Tears were dripping from the end of his hooked nose as he read the old letter from Lily. The second page carried only a few words:

第33章 "王子"的故事

"关心他?"斯内普叫了起来,"呼神护卫!"

他的杖尖蹦出了那头银色的牝鹿。它落在地板上,轻轻一跃就到了办公室那头,飞出了窗外。邓布利多注视着它远去,注视着它的银光消失,然后转脸望着斯内普,此时他眼里已盈满泪水。

"这么长时间了还是这样?"

"一直是这样。"斯内普说。

场景转换。现在,哈利看见斯内普在跟办公桌后的邓布利多肖像说话。

"你必须把哈利离开他姨妈姨父家的确切日期告诉伏地魔,"邓布利多说,"伏地魔认为你消息非常灵通,你不这么做会引起他的怀疑。不过,你必须把利用替身的主意灌输给别人——我想那样应该能够保证哈利的安全。试着对蒙顿格斯·弗莱奇用混淆咒。还有,西弗勒斯,如果你不得不参加追逐,一定要表现得令人信服……我指望你继续取得伏地魔的信任,时间越长越好,不然,霍格沃茨就会任由卡罗兄妹摆布……"

现在,斯内普正在一家陌生的酒馆里与蒙顿格斯交头接耳,蒙顿格斯满脸的茫然、迷惑,斯内普皱着眉头,全神贯注。

"你要向凤凰社提出建议,"斯内普低声说道,"让他们使用替身。复方汤剂。几个一模一样的波特。只有这个办法才管用。你要忘记这个建议是我提的。要当成你自己的主意提出来。明白吗?"

"明白。"蒙顿格斯喃喃地说,两眼呆滞无神……

现在,哈利伴着骑扫帚的斯内普,在晴朗的黑夜中飞行。身边还有其他戴兜帽的食死徒,前面是卢平,还有一个由乔治扮成的哈利……一个食死徒冲到斯内普前面,举起魔杖对准了卢平的后背——

"神锋无影!"斯内普大喊一声。

魔咒本来瞄准的是食死徒拿魔杖的手,不料却击中了乔治——

接着,斯内普跪在小天狼星的旧卧室里。他读着莉莉写的那封旧信,泪水从鹰钩鼻的鼻尖流淌下来。信的第二页只有几句话:

CHAPTER THIRTY-THREE The Prince's Tale

could ever have been friends with Gellert Grindelwald.
I think her mind's going, personally!
  Lots of love,
  Lily

Snape took the page bearing Lily's signature, and her love, and tucked it inside his robes. Then he ripped in two the photograph he was also holding, so that he kept the part from which Lily laughed, throwing the portion showing James and Harry back on to the floor, under the chest of drawers ...

And now Snape stood again in the Headmaster's study as Phineas Nigellus came hurrying into his portrait.

'Headmaster! They are camping in the Forest of Dean! The Mudblood –'

'Do not use that word!'

'– the Granger girl, then, mentioned the place as she opened her bag and I heard her!'

'Good. Very good!' cried the portrait of Dumbledore behind the Headmaster's chair. 'Now, Severus, the sword! Do not forget that it must be taken under conditions of need and valour – and he must not know that you give it! If Voldemort should read Harry's mind and see you acting for him –'

'I know,' said Snape curtly. He approached the portrait of Dumbledore and pulled at its side. It swung forwards, revealing a hidden cavity behind it, from which he took the sword of Gryffindor.

'And you still aren't going to tell me why it's so important to give Potter the sword?' said Snape, as he swung a travelling cloak over his robes.

'No, I don't think so,' said Dumbledore's portrait. 'He will know what to do with it. And Severus, be very careful, they may not take kindly to your appearance after George Weasley's mishap –'

Snape turned at the door.

'Don't worry, Dumbledore,' he said coolly. 'I have a plan ...'

And Snape left the room. Harry rose up out of the Pensieve, and moments later he lay on the carpeted floor in exactly the same room: Snape might just have closed the door.

第33章 "王子"的故事

会和盖勒特·格林德沃交朋友。

我个人认为,她脑子有点糊涂了!

无限爱意

莉莉

斯内普拿起这页留有莉莉签名和爱意的信纸,塞进了长袍里。然后他把手里的照片一撕两半,留下莉莉欢笑的一半,把詹姆和哈利的一半扔在了五斗橱下……

现在,斯内普又站在校长的书房里,菲尼亚斯·奈杰勒斯匆匆闯进了自己的肖像。

"校长!他们在迪安森林里扎营!那个泥巴种——"

"不许说那个词!"

"——那个姓格兰杰的女孩打开包时说了地名,我听见了!"

"好,很好!"校长座椅后面的邓布利多肖像大声说,"现在,西弗勒斯,拿上宝剑吧!别忘了必须在有需要和有勇气的条件下才能拿它——千万别让他知道是你拿去的!万一伏地魔读取哈利的思想,看到你在帮他——"

"我知道。"斯内普简单地说。他凑近邓布利多的肖像,把它往外一拉。肖像打开了,露出藏在后面的一个洞,斯内普从里面拿出了格兰芬多的宝剑。

"你还是不肯告诉我为什么把宝剑交给波特这么重要,是吗?"斯内普说着,把一件旅行斗篷披在长袍外面。

"是的,确实如此,"邓布利多肖像说,"他会知道拿它派什么用场。西弗勒斯,千万小心,乔治·韦斯莱发生意外之后,他们对你的出现不会表示友好——"

斯内普在门边转过身。

"不用担心,邓布利多,"他冷冷地说,"我自有安排……"

斯内普离开了房间。哈利慢慢地从冥想盆里升了上来。片刻之后,他躺在校长办公室的地毯上,就好像斯内普刚刚把房门关上。

CHAPTER THIRTY-FOUR

The Forest Again

Finally, the truth. Lying with his face pressed into the dusty carpet of the office where he had once thought he was learning the secrets of victory, Harry understood at last that he was not supposed to survive. His job was to walk calmly into Death's welcoming arms. Along the way, he was to dispose of Voldemort's remaining links to life, so that when at last he flung himself across Voldemort's path, and did not raise a wand to defend himself, the end would be clean, and the job that ought to have been done in Godric's Hollow would be finished: neither would live, neither could survive.

He felt his heart pounding fiercely in his chest. How strange that in his dread of death, it pumped all the harder, valiantly keeping him alive. But it would have to stop, and soon. Its beats were numbered. How many would there be time for, as he rose and walked through the castle for the last time, out into the grounds and into the Forest?

Terror washed over him as he lay on the floor, with that funeral drum pounding inside him. Would it hurt to die? All those times he had thought that it was about to happen and escaped, he had never really thought of the thing itself: his will to live had always been so much stronger than his fear of death. Yet it did not occur to him now to try to escape, to outrun Voldemort. It was over, he knew it, and all that was left was the thing itself: dying.

If he could only have died on that summer's night when he had left number four, Privet Drive for the last time, when the noble phoenix feather wand had saved him! If he could only have died like Hedwig, so quickly he would not have known it had happened! Or if he could have launched himself in front of a wand to save someone he loved … he envied even his parents' deaths now. This cold-blooded walk to his own destruction would require a different kind of bravery. He felt his fingers trembling slightly and

第34章

又见禁林

终于，真相大白。哈利躺在办公室的地上，脸贴着脏兮兮的地毯。他曾经以为，他能在这里学习到胜利的秘诀。哈利终于明白他是不能幸存的。他的任务就是平静地走向死神张开的怀抱。在这条路上，他要斩除伏地魔与生命的最后联系。这样，当他最终冲过去直面伏地魔，并且不用魔杖保护自己时，结局才会干净彻底，早在戈德里克山谷就该完成的工作才会真正结束：谁也活不下来，谁也不能幸存。

他感觉到心脏在胸腔里剧烈地跳动。多么奇怪啊，他怀着对死亡的恐惧，然而他的心脏却跳得格外有力，勇敢地维持着他的生命。可是它不得不停止，而且很快就得停止。它跳动的次数不会太多了。当他站起身，最后一次穿越城堡，走过场地，进入禁林，这期间心脏还能跳多少次呢？

他躺在地板上，恐惧潮水般袭来，葬礼的鼓声在他内心咚咚敲响。死会疼吗？多少次他以为死到临头而又侥幸逃脱，却从未真正考虑过死亡本身。他对活的愿望总是比对死的恐惧强烈得多。但现在他没有想到要逃跑，要摆脱伏地魔的魔爪。他知道，一切都结束了，剩下来的只有一件事：死。

如果他在最后一次离开女贞路4号的那个夏夜死去该有多好，但高贵的凤凰羽毛魔杖救了他！如果他能像海德薇那样死去该有多好，在不知不觉间突然毙命！或者，如果他能为了救自己心爱的人，奋不顾身地挡在魔杖前……此刻他甚至嫉妒父母的死了。这样冷静

CHAPTER THIRTY-FOUR The Forest Again

made an effort to control them, although no one could see him; the portraits on the walls were all empty.

Slowly, very slowly, he sat up, and as he did so he felt more alive, and more aware of his own living body than ever before. Why had he never appreciated what a miracle he was, brain and nerve and bounding heart? It would all be gone ... or at least, he would be gone from it. His breath came slow and deep, and his mouth and throat were completely dry, but so were his eyes.

Dumbledore's betrayal was almost nothing. Of course there had been a bigger plan; Harry had simply been too foolish to see it, he realised that now. He had never questioned his own assumption that Dumbledore wanted him alive. Now he saw that his lifespan had always been determined by how long it took to eliminate all the Horcruxes. Dumbledore had passed the job of destroying them to him, and obediently he had continued to chip away at the bonds tying not only Voldemort, but himself, to life! How neat, how elegant, not to waste any more lives, but to give the dangerous task to the boy who had already been marked for slaughter, and whose death would not be a calamity, but another blow against Voldemort.

And Dumbledore had known that Harry would not duck out, that he would keep going to the end, even though it was *his* end, because he had taken trouble to get to know him, hadn't he? Dumbledore knew, as Voldemort knew, that Harry would not let anyone else die for him now that he had discovered it was in his power to stop it. The images of Fred, Lupin and Tonks lying dead in the Great Hall forced their way back into his mind's eye, and for a moment he could hardly breathe: Death was impatient ...

But Dumbledore had overestimated him. He had failed: the snake survived. One Horcrux remained to bind Voldemort to the earth, even after Harry had been killed. True, that would mean an easier job for somebody. He wondered who would do it ... Ron and Hermione would know what needed to be done, of course ... that would have been why Dumbledore wanted him to confide in two others ... so that if he fulfilled his true destiny a little early, they could carry on ...

Like rain on a cold window, these thoughts pattered against the hard surface of the incontrovertible truth, which was that he must die. *I must die.* It must end.

第34章 又见禁林

从容地走向自己的毁灭实在需要一种不同的勇气。他感到手指在微微颤抖，但他努力控制着，虽然并没有人能看见，墙上的肖像都是空的。

慢慢地，很慢很慢地，他坐了起来，这时他比以前任何时候都更真切地感觉到自己活着，更清楚地意识到自己有生命的躯体。他以前怎么从未认识到自己是个多么了不起的奇迹：头脑，神经，还有跳动的心脏？一切都将离去……至少，他将离这一切而去。他的呼吸缓慢、深重，嘴和喉咙都十分干燥，但眼睛也是干的。

邓布利多的欺骗实在不算什么。当然是有一个更大的计划，只是哈利太愚蠢，没有看到。他现在总算明白了。他一直想当然地从不怀疑邓布利多希望他活着。现在他知道了，他生命的长短始终是由消灭所有魂器需要多少时间而决定的。邓布利多把消灭魂器的任务交给了他，他也就顺从地继续削弱那些不仅连接着伏地魔的生命、也连接着他自己生命的纽带！多么简洁，多么干脆，别再浪费更多的生命，把这危险的任务交给一个注定该死的男孩，他的死不会是一种灾难，而是对伏地魔的又一次打击。

邓布利多知道哈利不会逃避，知道他会一直走到最后，尽管那是他的终结，因为邓布利多曾经努力了解过哈利，不是吗？伏地魔知道，邓布利多也知道，哈利一旦发现自己有力量阻止，就不会听任别人为他去死。弗雷德、卢平和唐克斯的遗体躺在礼堂里的情景，又挤进了哈利的脑海，令他一时简直透不过气来：死神迫不及待了……

但是邓布利多把他估计得过高了。他失败了，那条蛇还活着。即使哈利被杀死了，仍有一个魂器把伏地魔绑在尘世间。当然，那意味着别人与之交战会容易一些。谁会做这件事呢，他猜想着……罗恩和赫敏肯定知道需要做什么……因此邓布利多才希望他把秘密透露给他们俩……这样，如果他提早一点实现了他真正的宿命，他们可以继续下去……

像雨点打在冰冷的窗户上，这些思绪纷乱地砸在那个硬邦邦的、不可否认的事实上，事实就是他必须死。我必须死。事情必须结束。

CHAPTER THIRTY-FOUR   The Forest Again

Ron and Hermione seemed a long way away, in a far-off country; he felt as though he had parted from them long ago. There would be no goodbyes and no explanations, he was determined of that. This was a journey they could not take together, and the attempts they would make to stop him would waste valuable time. He looked down at the battered gold watch he had received on his seventeenth birthday. Nearly half of the hour allotted by Voldemort for his surrender had elapsed.

He stood up. His heart was leaping against his ribs like a frantic bird. Perhaps it knew it had little time left, perhaps it was determined to fulfil a lifetime's beats before the end. He did not look back as he closed the office door.

The castle was empty. He felt ghostly striding through it alone, as if he had already died. The portrait people were still missing from their frames; the whole place was eerily still, as if all its remaining lifeblood were concentrated in the Great Hall, where the dead and the mourners were crammed.

Harry pulled the Invisibility Cloak over himself and descended through the floors, at last walking down the marble staircase into the Entrance Hall. Perhaps some tiny part of him hoped to be sensed, to be seen, to be stopped, but the Cloak was, as ever, impenetrable, perfect, and he reached the front doors easily.

Then Neville nearly walked into him. He was one half of a pair that was carrying a body in from the grounds. Harry glanced down, and felt another dull blow to his stomach: Colin Creevey, though under-age, must have sneaked back just as Malfoy, Crabbe and Goyle had done. He was tiny in death.

'You know what? I can manage him alone, Neville,' said Oliver Wood, and he heaved Colin over his shoulder in a fireman's lift and carried him into the Great Hall.

Neville leaned against the doorframe for a moment and wiped his forehead with the back of his hand. He looked like an old man. Then he set off down the steps again into the darkness to recover more bodies.

Harry took one glance back at the entrance of the Great Hall. People were moving around, trying to comfort each other, drinking, kneeling beside the dead, but he could not see any of the people he loved, no hint of Hermione, Ron, Ginny or any of the other Weasleys, no Luna. He felt he would have given all the time remaining to him for just one last look at them; but then, would he ever have had the strength to stop looking? It was better like this.

第34章 又见禁林

罗恩和赫敏似乎在很远很远的地方，在某个遥远的国度。他觉得自己跟他们分开很久了。不要告别，也不要解释，他已经拿定了主意。这是一段他们不能结伴同行的旅途，他们俩会想方设法阻止他，那只会浪费宝贵的时间。他低头看了看十七岁生日得到的那块有些旧了的金表。伏地魔规定他投降的时间已经过去了近半个小时。

哈利站了起来，心像一只疯狂的小鸟，猛烈地撞击着他的胸肋。也许它知道时间已经不多，也许它决定在结束之前完成一生的跳动。哈利没有回头再看一眼，关上了办公室的门。

城堡里空荡荡的。他独自大步行走，感觉像个幽灵，仿佛自己已经死了。那些相框里的肖像仍然空着，整个学校是一片诡异的死寂，似乎所有剩下来的生命都集中在了大礼堂，死者和哀悼者都挤在那里。

哈利把隐形衣披在身上，走下一层层楼，最后顺着大理石楼梯来到门厅。也许，他内心某个小小的角落里希望有人感觉到他，看见他，阻拦他，但是隐形衣一如既往地完美、纹丝不漏，他很轻松地走到了门口。

突然，纳威差点撞在他身上。纳威和另一个人正合力从操场上搬进一具尸体。哈利低头一看，心头又像是挨了一击：科林·克里维。他还不够年龄，肯定是像马尔福、克拉布和高尔那样偷偷溜回来的。死去的他显得那么幼小。

"听我说，纳威，我一个人搬得动他。"奥利弗·伍德说着，像消防队员那样把科林扛在肩膀上走进了礼堂。

纳威在门框上靠了一会儿，用手背擦了擦额头的汗。他看上去就像一个老人。然后他又走下台阶，到黑暗中去寻找别的尸体。

哈利最后看了一眼礼堂的入口。人们走来走去，互相安慰，喝东西，跪在死者身边，但他看不见一个他所爱的人，没有赫敏、罗恩、金妮和韦斯莱家的其他人，也没有卢娜。他觉得愿意用剩下来的所有时间换取看他们最后一眼，可是，如果那样的话，他是不是还有毅力把目光移开呢？还是这样更好。

CHAPTER THIRTY-FOUR   The Forest Again

He moved down the steps and out into the darkness. It was nearly four in the morning and the deathly stillness of the grounds felt as though they were holding their breath, waiting to see whether he could do what he must.

Harry moved towards Neville, who was bending over another body.

'Neville.'

'Blimey, Harry, you nearly gave me heart failure!'

Harry had pulled off the Cloak: the idea had come to him out of nowhere, born out of a desire to make absolutely sure.

'Where are you going, alone?' Neville asked suspiciously.

'It's all part of the plan,' said Harry. 'There's something I've got to do. Listen – Neville –'

'Harry!' Neville looked suddenly scared. 'Harry, you're not thinking of handing yourself over?'

'No,' Harry lied easily. ''Course not ... this is something else. But I might be out of sight for a while. You know Voldemort's snake, Neville? He's got a huge snake ... calls it Nagini ...'

'I've heard, yeah ... what about it?'

'It's got to be killed. Ron and Hermione know that, but just in case they –'

The awfulness of that possibility smothered him for a moment, made it impossible to keep talking. But he pulled himself together again: this was crucial, he must be like Dumbledore, keep a cool head, make sure there were back-ups, others to carry on. Dumbledore had died knowing that three people still knew about the Horcruxes; now Neville would take Harry's place: there would still be three in the secret.

'Just in case they're – busy – and you get the chance –'

'Kill the snake?'

'Kill the snake,' Harry repeated.

'All right, Harry. You're OK, are you?'

'I'm fine. Thanks, Neville.'

But Neville seized his wrist as Harry made to move on.

'We're all going to keep fighting, Harry. You know that?'

'Yeah, I –'

第34章 又见禁林

他走下台阶,来到外面的黑夜里。差不多凌晨四点了,死一般寂静的场地似乎也屏住了呼吸,等着看他是否会做他必须要做的事情。

哈利朝俯身查看另一具尸体的纳威走去。

"纳威。"

"天哪,哈利,你差点把我吓死!"

哈利已经脱掉了隐形衣。这个念头是突然冒出来的,因为他希望确保万无一失。

"你一个人要上哪儿去?"纳威怀疑地问。

"这也是计划的一部分,"哈利说,"我要去做一件事。听我说——纳威——"

"哈利!"纳威突然神色惊恐,说道,"哈利,你该不是想把自己交出去吧?"

"不,"哈利语气随意地说了一个谎,"当然不是……是别的事情。但我可能要失踪一段时间。纳威,你知道伏地魔的蛇吧?他有一条特别大的蛇……叫作纳吉尼……"

"知道,听说过……怎么啦?"

"必须把它杀死。罗恩和赫敏知道,但万一他们——"

这种可能性太可怕了,他一时喘不上气来,无法继续往下说。但他重新振作起来:这是至关重要的,他必须像邓布利多那样保持头脑冷静,确保有人替补,有另外的人把任务执行下去。邓布利多死的时候知道仍有三个人了解魂器的事,现在纳威将取代哈利,这样仍有三个人熟知内情。

"万一他们——很忙——而你又有机会——"

"把蛇杀死?"

"把蛇杀死。"哈利强调了一遍。

"好的,哈利。你没事吧?"

"我很好。谢谢你,纳威。"

哈利刚转身要走,纳威抓住了他的手腕。

"我们都会坚持战斗的,哈利。你知道吗?"

"知道,我——"

CHAPTER THIRTY-FOUR   The Forest Again

The suffocating feeling extinguished the end of the sentence, he could not go on. Neville did not seem to find it strange. He patted Harry on the shoulder, released him, and walked away to look for more bodies.

Harry swung the Cloak back over himself and walked on. Someone else was moving not far away, stooping over another prone figure on the ground. He was feet away from her when he realised it was Ginny.

He stopped in his tracks. She was crouching over a girl who was whispering for her mother.

'It's all right,' Ginny was saying. 'It's OK. We're going to get you inside.'

'But I want to go *home*,' whispered the girl. 'I don't want to fight any more!'

'I know,' said Ginny, and her voice broke. 'It's going to be all right.'

Ripples of cold undulated over Harry's skin. He wanted to shout out to the night, he wanted Ginny to know that he was there, he wanted her to know where he was going. He wanted to be stopped, to be dragged back, to be sent back home …

But he *was* home. Hogwarts was the first and best home he had known. He and Voldemort and Snape, the abandoned boys, had all found home here …

Ginny was kneeling beside the injured girl now, holding her hand. With a huge effort, Harry forced himself on. He thought he saw Ginny look round as he passed and wondered whether she had sensed someone walking nearby, but he did not speak, and he did not look back.

Hagrid's hut loomed out of the darkness. There were no lights, no sound of Fang scrabbling at the door, his bark booming in welcome. All those visits to Hagrid, and the gleam of the copper kettle on the fire, and rock cakes and giant grubs, and his great, bearded face, and Ron vomiting slugs, and Hermione helping him save Norbert …

He moved on, and now he reached the edge of the Forest, and he stopped.

A swarm of Dementors was gliding amongst the trees; he could feel their chill, and he was not sure he would be able to pass safely through it. He had no strength left for a Patronus. He could no longer control his own trembling. It was not, after all, so easy to die. Every second he breathed, the smell of the grass, the cool air on his face, was so precious: to think that people had years and years, time to waste, so much time it dragged, and he was clinging to each second. At the same time he thought that he would not be able to go on, and knew that he must. The long game was ended, the Snitch had been caught, it was time to leave the air …

第34章 又见禁林

窒息的感觉使后半句话哽在喉咙里,他说不下去了。纳威似乎并没有察觉哈利的异样。他拍拍哈利的肩膀,松开他,走去寻找别的尸体了。

哈利把隐形衣重新披在身上,继续往前走。不远处有人在动,在弯腰查看一个趴在地上的人影。相距几步的时候,哈利认出那是金妮。

他猛地停住脚步。金妮俯身安慰一个低声呼喊妈妈的女孩。

"没事了,"金妮说,"不要紧的。我们这就把你抱进去。"

"可是我想回家,"女孩低声说,"我不想再战斗了!"

"我知道,"金妮说着,声音哽咽了,"会过去的。"

一波波寒意掠过哈利的皮肤。他想对着黑夜大喊,他想让金妮知道他在这里,他想让金妮知道他要去哪儿。他想被人阻拦,被拽回去,被送回家……

然而,他现在就在家里。霍格沃茨是他所知道的第一个家,最好的家。他、伏地魔和斯内普这些被遗弃的男孩,都在这里找到了家……

金妮此刻跪在那个受伤的女孩身边,抓住她的手。哈利以极大的毅力强迫自己往前走。他仿佛看见金妮在他经过时四下看了看,不知她是否感觉到有人在旁边走过,但哈利没有说话,也没有回头。

海格的小屋在黑暗中浮现了。没有灯光,也听不见牙牙在门口抓挠、吠叫着表示欢迎的声音。曾经那么多次来看望海格,炉火上闪闪发亮的铜壶,岩皮饼,巨蟒蟥,还有海格那张硕大的、胡子拉碴的脸,罗恩吐出鼻涕虫,赫敏帮助海格拯救诺伯……

哈利继续往前走,现在他已经来到森林边缘。他停下了脚步。

一群摄魂怪在树丛间游荡,他感觉到了它们的寒意,不知道自己能不能安全地通过。他已经没有力量召唤守护神了。他再也控制不住自己颤抖的身体。看来,死亡并非那么容易。他呼吸的每一秒钟,青草的芳香,凉风拂过面颊的感觉,都是那么宝贵。想到别人还有许多许多年的光阴可以挥霍,时间多得简直无以打发,而他,每一秒钟都那么难以割舍。他认为自己无法再往前走了,同时又知道必须往前走。这场漫长的游戏结束了,金色飞贼已经抓住,应该离开空中了……

CHAPTER THIRTY-FOUR   The Forest Again

The Snitch. His nerveless fingers fumbled for a moment with the pouch at his neck and he pulled it out.

I open at the close.

Breathing fast and hard, he stared down at it. Now that he wanted time to move as slowly as possible, it seemed to have sped up, and understanding was coming so fast it seemed to have bypassed thought. This was the close. This was the moment.

He pressed the golden metal to his lips and whispered, 'I am about to die.'

The metal shell broke open. He lowered his shaking hand, raised Draco's wand beneath the Cloak and murmured, '*Lumos.*'

The black stone with its jagged crack running down the centre sat in the two halves of the Snitch. The Resurrection Stone had cracked down the vertical line representing the Elder Wand. The triangle and circle representing the Cloak and the stone were still discernible.

And again, Harry understood, without having to think. It did not matter about bringing them back, for he was about to join them. He was not really fetching them: they were fetching him.

He closed his eyes, and turned the stone over in his hand, three times.

He knew it had happened, because he heard slight movements around him that suggested frail bodies shifting their footing on the earthy, twig-strewn ground that marked the outer edge of the Forest. He opened his eyes and looked around.

They were neither ghost nor truly flesh, he could see that. They resembled most closely the Riddle that had escaped from the diary, so long ago, and he had been memory made nearly solid. Less substantial than living bodies, but much more than ghosts, they moved towards him, and on each face there was the same loving smile.

James was exactly the same height as Harry. He was wearing the clothes in which he had died, and his hair was untidy and ruffled, and his glasses were a little lopsided, like Mr Weasley's.

Sirius was tall and handsome, and younger by far than Harry had seen him in life. He loped with an easy grace, his hands in his pockets and a grin on his face.

Lupin was younger too, and much less shabby, and his hair was thicker and darker. He looked happy to be back in this familiar place, scene of so many adolescent wanderings.

第34章 又见禁林

飞贼。他无力的手指在脖子上挂的皮袋里摸索了一会儿，把它掏了出来。

我在结束时打开。

哈利低头盯着飞贼，呼吸急促而粗重。现在他希望时间过得越慢越好，时间却仿佛加快了速度，他好像是不假思索，便一下子豁然开朗。这就是结束。是时候了。

他把金色的金属表面贴在唇上，轻声说道："我要死了。"

金属壳裂开了。哈利垂下颤抖的手，在隐形衣下举起德拉科的魔杖，轻声说了一句："荧光闪烁。"

裂为两半的飞贼中，正是那块中间有一道锯齿状裂缝的黑石头。复活石上的裂缝沿着代表老魔杖的标志直贯而下，而代表隐形衣和石头的三角和圆形依然清晰可辨。

哈利又一次顿悟了。让死者复活已经不重要了，因为他就要成为他们中间的一员。其实，不是他在把他们叫来，而是他们在把他叫去。

他闭上眼睛，把石头在手里转了三次。

他知道有结果了，因为他听见周围传来了轻微的动静，像是一些柔弱的身体在森林外围树枝散落的泥土上移动脚步。他睁开眼睛，环顾四周。

他看出他们既不是幽灵，也不是有血有肉的活人。他们更像是很久以前从日记里逃出来的那个里德尔，如同几乎变成实体的记忆。他们不像活人的身体那么实在，却比幽灵真实得多。他们朝他走来，每张脸上都带着那样慈爱的笑容。

詹姆和哈利一样高，穿着死去时的那身衣服，头发乱糟糟的，眼镜戴得有点儿歪，就像韦斯莱先生。

小天狼星高大英俊，比哈利当初见到的活着的时候年轻得多。他步履轻松地慢慢走来，手插在口袋里，脸上笑容绽放。

卢平也年轻一些，不像后来那么邋遢，头发也更黑更密。回到这个熟悉的地方，回到青春年少时曾多次游荡的环境里，他显得很高兴。

CHAPTER THIRTY-FOUR   The Forest Again

Lily's smile was widest of all. She pushed her long hair back as she drew close to him, and her green eyes, so like his, searched his face hungrily as though she would never be able to look at him enough.

'You've been so brave.'

He could not speak. His eyes feasted on her, and he thought that he would like to stand and look at her forever, and that would be enough.

'You are nearly there,' said James. 'Very close. We are ... so proud of you.'

'Does it hurt?'

The childish question had fallen from Harry's lips before he could stop it.

'Dying? Not at all,' said Sirius. 'Quicker and easier than falling asleep.'

'And he will want it to be quick. He wants it over,' said Lupin.

'I didn't want you to die,' Harry said. These words came without his volition. 'Any of you. I'm sorry –'

He addressed Lupin more than any of them, beseeching him.

'– right after you'd had your son ... Remus, I'm sorry –'

'I am sorry too,' said Lupin. 'Sorry I will never know him ... but he will know why I died and I hope he will understand. I was trying to make a world in which he could live a happier life.'

A chilly breeze that seemed to emanate from the heart of the Forest lifted the hair at Harry's brow. He knew that they would not tell him to go, that it would have to be his decision.

'You'll stay with me?'

'Until the very end,' said James.

'They won't be able to see you?' asked Harry.

'We are part of you,' said Sirius. 'Invisible to anyone else.'

Harry looked at his mother.

'Stay close to me,' he said quietly.

And he set off. The Dementors' chill did not overcome him; he passed through it with his companions, and they acted like Patronuses to him, and together they marched through the old trees that grew closely together, their branches tangled, their roots gnarled and twisted underfoot. Harry clutched the Cloak tightly around him in the darkness, travelling deeper and deeper into the Forest, with no idea where exactly Voldemort was, but sure that he

第34章 又见禁林

莉莉是他们中间笑得最开心的。她把长长的秀发捋到脑后，走近哈利身边，那双与哈利一模一样的绿眼睛，如饥似渴地端详着哈利的脸，仿佛永远也看不够。

"你真勇敢。"

哈利说不出话来。他尽情地打量母亲，似乎愿意永远站在这里看着她，他觉得这样就够了。

"你还差一点儿，"詹姆说，"已经很接近了。我们……真为你骄傲。"

"疼吗？"

这个孩子气的问题脱口而出，哈利想要止住已来不及了。

"死吗？一点儿不疼，"小天狼星说，"比进入梦乡还要快，还要容易。"

"他会速战速决的，他希望赶紧结束。"卢平说。

"我不希望你们死，"哈利说，话是不由自主冒出来的，"你们每个人。我很难过——"

这话更多是对卢平说的，他恳求他的原谅。

"——你刚刚有了儿子……莱姆斯，我很难过——"

"我也很难过，"卢平说，"很难过我再也不能继续了解他……但是他会知道我为什么而死，我希望他能理解。我是为了创造一个更好的世界，让他生活得更加快乐。"

一阵寒冷的微风似乎从森林中间吹来，撩动了哈利额上的头发。他知道他们不会叫他前进，他必须自己做出决定。

"你们会陪着我？"

"直到最后。"詹姆说。

"他们看不见你们？"哈利问。

"我们是你的一部分，"小天狼星说，"别人都看不见。"

哈利看着母亲。

"待在我身边。"他轻声说。

他动身了。摄魂怪的寒意没有征服他，他和亲人们一起穿越了那股寒意，他们就如同他的守护神。他们一起大步穿过茂密杂乱、盘根错节的古老的树丛。黑暗中，哈利把隐形衣紧紧地裹在身上，一步步

CHAPTER THIRTY-FOUR   The Forest Again

would find him. Beside him, making scarcely a sound, walked James, Sirius, Lupin and Lily, and their presence was his courage, and the reason he was able to keep putting one foot in front of the other.

His body and mind felt oddly disconnected now, his limbs working without conscious instruction, as if he were passenger, not driver, in the body he was about to leave. The dead who walked beside him through the Forest were much more real to him now than the living back at the castle: Ron, Hermione, Ginny and all the others were the ones who felt like ghosts as he stumbled and slipped towards the end of his life, towards Voldemort ...

A thud and a whisper: some other living creature had stirred close by. Harry stopped under the Cloak, peering around, listening, and his mother and father, Lupin and Sirius stopped too.

'Someone there,' came a rough whisper close at hand. 'He's got an Invisibility Cloak. Could it be –?'

Two figures emerged from behind a nearby tree: their wands flared, and Harry saw Yaxley and Dolohov peering into the darkness, directly at the place Harry, his mother and father and Sirius and Lupin stood. Apparently they could not see anything.

'Definitely heard something,' said Yaxley. 'Animal, d'you reckon?'

'That headcase Hagrid kept a whole bunch of stuff in here,' said Dolohov, glancing over his shoulder.

Yaxley looked down at his watch.

'Time's nearly up. Potter's had his hour. He's not coming.'

'And he was sure he'd come! He won't be happy.'

'Better go back,' said Yaxley. 'Find out what the plan is now.'

He and Dolohov turned and walked deeper into the Forest. Harry followed them, knowing that they would lead him exactly where he wanted to go. He glanced sideways, and his mother smiled at him, and his father nodded encouragement.

They had travelled on mere minutes when Harry saw light ahead, and Yaxley and Dolohov stepped out into a clearing that Harry knew had been the place where the monstrous Aragog had once lived. The remnants of his vast web were there still, but the swarm of descendants he had spawned had been driven out by the Death Eaters, to fight for their cause.

第34章 又见禁林

往禁林深处走去。他不知道伏地魔究竟在哪里,但相信一定会找到他。詹姆、小天狼星、卢平和莉莉在他身边悄无声息地走着,他们的陪伴给了他勇气,也是他能够一步接一步往前迈进的动因。

他的身体和思想似乎奇怪地分离了,意识没有发出指令,肢体自动运行,就好像他只是这具他即将离开的身体的乘客,而不是驾驭者。他此刻觉得,比起城堡里那些活着的人,这些陪他一起在禁林里行走的逝者更加真实得多,罗恩、赫敏、金妮和其他所有的人倒如同幽灵,而他正跟跟跄跄、一步一滑地走向生命的终结,走向伏地魔……

砰的一声,接着传来低语声。附近还有别的生命在活动。哈利在隐形衣下停住脚步,左右张望,侧耳倾听,母亲、父亲、卢平和小天狼星也停下了。

"那儿有人,"近旁一个粗哑的嗓子低声说,"他有一件隐形衣,会不会就是——?"

旁边一棵树后闪出两个人影。他们的魔杖在闪光,哈利看见亚克斯利和多洛霍夫瞪眼瞅着黑暗中,正对着哈利、他的父母、小天狼星和卢平所站的地方。显然他们什么也看不见。

"肯定听到动静了,"亚克斯利说,"是动物吧,你说呢?"

"那个蠢货海格在这儿养了一大群废物。"多洛霍夫扭头看看说。

亚克斯利低头看了看表。

"时间差不多了。波特的一小时到了,他不会来了。"

"他还以为他肯定会来呢!他会不高兴的。"

"还是回去吧,"亚克斯利说,"看看下面是什么计划。"

他和多洛霍夫转身朝禁林深处走去,哈利跟了上去,知道他们会把他领到他想去的地方。他朝旁边看了一眼,母亲笑眯眯地看着他,父亲鼓励地点点头。

刚走了几分钟,哈利看见前面有亮光,亚克斯利和多洛霍夫走到了一片空地上,哈利知道可怕的阿拉戈克就曾生活在这里。它那张巨网还残留在那里,但它所繁殖的那群后代已被食死徒赶去为他们战斗了。

CHAPTER THIRTY-FOUR   The Forest Again

A fire burned in the middle of the clearing, and its flickering light fell over a crowd of completely silent, watchful Death Eaters. Some of them were still masked and hooded, others showed their faces. Two giants sat on the outskirts of the group, casting massive shadows over the scene, their faces cruel, rough-hewn like rock. Harry saw Fenrir, skulking, chewing his long nails; the great, blond Rowle was dabbing at his bleeding lip. He saw Lucius Malfoy, who looked defeated and terrified, and Narcissa, whose eyes were sunken and full of apprehension.

Every eye was fixed upon Voldemort, who stood with his head bowed, and his white hands folded over the Elder Wand in front of him. He might have been praying, or else counting silently in his mind, and Harry, standing still on the edge of the scene, thought absurdly of a child counting in a game of hide-and-seek. Behind his head, still swirling and coiling, the great snake Nagini floated in her glittering, charmed cage, like a monstrous halo.

When Dolohov and Yaxley rejoined the circle, Voldemort looked up.

'No sign of him, my Lord,' said Dolohov.

Voldemort's expression did not change. The red eyes seemed to burn in the firelight. Slowly, he drew the Elder Wand between his long fingers.

'My Lord —'

Bellatrix had spoken: she sat closest to Voldemort, dishevelled, her face a little bloody but otherwise unharmed.

Voldemort raised his hand to silence her, and she did not speak another word, but eyed him in worshipful fascination.

'I thought he would come,' said Voldemort in his high, clear voice, his eyes on the leaping flames. 'I expected him to come.'

Nobody spoke. They seemed as scared as Harry, whose heart was now throwing itself against his ribs as though determined to escape the body he was about to cast aside. His hands were sweating as he pulled off the Invisibility Cloak and stuffed it beneath his robes, with his wand. He did not want to be tempted to fight.

'I was, it seems ... mistaken,' said Voldemort.

'You weren't.'

Harry said it as loudly as he could, with all the force he could muster: he did not want to sound afraid. The Resurrection Stone slipped from between

第34章 又见禁林

空地中央燃着一堆篝火，摇曳的火光照着一群沉默不语、神色警觉的食死徒。有的仍然蒙着面、戴着兜帽，有的则露出了面孔。两个巨人坐在外围，给周遭投下巨大的阴影，他们的脸像岩石刻的一样冷酷、粗糙。哈利看见芬里尔鬼鬼祟祟地在啃他的长指甲，金发大块头罗尔轻轻擦着流血的嘴唇。他看见卢修斯·马尔福一副垂头丧气、战战兢兢的样子，纳西莎的两眼深陷，里面满是惊恐。

每一双眼睛都盯着伏地魔。他垂头站在那里，两只苍白的手交握着面前的老魔杖，仿佛是在祈祷，或者在默默地数数。哈利仍然站在空地边缘，荒诞地想到一个在捉迷藏游戏中数数的孩子。在伏地魔的脑袋后面，巨蛇纳吉尼仍然浮在它那闪闪发亮、如同一个巨型光环的魔法笼子里，不停地旋转、盘绕。

多洛霍夫和亚克斯利走到那群人中间，伏地魔抬起头来。

"没有他的影子，主人。"多洛霍夫说。

伏地魔的表情没有变化。火光里，那双红眼睛似乎在燃烧。他把老魔杖放在修长的手指间慢慢地抽动。

"主人——"

是贝拉特里克斯在说话。她坐在离伏地魔最近的地方，头发散乱，脸上有一点血迹，身上并未受伤。

伏地魔举起一只手让她别作声，她便不再说话，一双眼睛狂热而崇拜地盯着伏地魔。

"我原以为他会来，"伏地魔看着跳动的火苗，用他高亢、清楚的声音说，"我原指望他会来。"

没有人说话。他们似乎都像哈利一样害怕，哈利的心脏使劲撞击着他的肋骨，似乎决意要逃脱这具他准备抛弃的身体。他用汗湿的双手脱掉隐形衣，把它和魔杖一起塞进长袍底下。他不希望受到诱惑，出手反击。

"看来……我是错了。"伏地魔说。

"你没有错。"

哈利聚集起全部的力量把声音放到最大，他不想让别人听出他害怕。复活石从麻木的手指间滑落，他迈步走进了火光，眼角的余光看

CHAPTER THIRTY-FOUR   The Forest Again

his numb fingers and out of the corner of his eyes he saw his parents, Sirius and Lupin vanish as he stepped forwards into the firelight. At that moment he felt that nobody mattered but Voldemort. It was just the two of them.

The illusion was gone as soon as it had come. The giants roared as the Death Eaters rose together, and there were many cries, gasps, even laughter. Voldemort had frozen where he stood, but his red eyes had found Harry, and he stared as Harry moved towards him, with nothing but the fire between them.

Then a voice yelled –

'HARRY! NO!'

He turned: Hagrid was bound and trussed, tied to a tree nearby. His massive body shook the branches overhead as he struggled, desperate.

'NO! NO! HARRY, WHAT'RE YEH –?'

'QUIET!' shouted Rowle, and with a flick of his wand Hagrid was silenced.

Bellatrix, who had leapt to her feet, was looking eagerly from Voldemort to Harry, her breast heaving. The only things that moved were the flames and the snake, coiling and uncoiling in the glittering cage behind Voldemort's head.

Harry could feel his wand against his chest, but he made no attempt to draw it. He knew that the snake was too well protected, knew that if he managed to point the wand at Nagini, fifty curses would hit him first. And still, Voldemort and Harry looked at each other, and now Voldemort tilted his head a little to the side, considering the boy standing before him, and a singularly mirthless smile curled the lipless mouth.

'Harry Potter,' he said, very softly. His voice might have been part of the spitting fire. 'The boy who lived.'

None of the Death Eaters moved. They were waiting: everything was waiting. Hagrid was struggling, and Bellatrix was panting, and Harry thought inexplicably of Ginny, and her blazing look, and the feel of her lips on his –

Voldemort had raised his wand. His head was still tilted to one side, like a curious child, wondering what would happen if he proceeded. Harry looked back into the red eyes, and wanted it to happen now, quickly, while he could still stand, before he lost control, before he betrayed fear –

He saw the mouth move and a flash of green light, and everything was gone.

第34章 又见禁林

见他的父母、小天狼星和卢平都消失了。在这一刻，他觉得除了伏地魔，别人都不再重要。只有他们两个。

这幻觉转瞬即逝。食死徒全部站了起来，巨人发出吼叫，四周一片喊叫声和吃惊的喘气声，甚至还有大笑声。伏地魔僵立在那里，但那双红眼睛看见了哈利，注视着哈利一步步朝他走近，他们之间只有那堆篝火。

接着一个声音喊道——

"哈利！不！"

哈利转身一看，海格被五花大绑地捆在近旁的一棵树上，绝望地挣扎着，庞大的身体晃得头顶上的树枝摇摆不停。

"不！不！哈利，你想——？"

"闭嘴！"罗尔大喊一声，挥了一下魔杖，海格不作声了。

贝拉特里克斯早已一跃而起，她急切地看看伏地魔，又看看哈利，胸口剧烈地起伏着。周围还在动的唯有火焰和那条蛇，蛇在伏地魔脑袋后面的闪光笼子里不停地盘绕又松展。

哈利可以感觉到胸口的魔杖，但他没有伸手去取。他知道蛇被保护得太严密了，即使他用魔杖瞄准了纳吉尼，也会先被五十个魔咒击中。伏地魔和哈利仍然互相对视着，然后伏地魔把脑袋微微偏到一边，打量着站在他面前的这个男孩，没有嘴唇的嘴巴扭动着，露出一个古怪而阴郁的笑容。

"哈利·波特，"他说，声音很轻，像是一簇嘶嘶迸溅的火焰，"大难不死的男孩。"

食死徒们谁也没动，他们都在等待，一切都在等待。海格在挣扎，贝拉特里克斯在喘息，哈利却无端地想到了金妮，想到了她光彩照人的模样，还有她的双唇贴在自己唇上的感觉——

伏地魔已经举起魔杖。他的脑袋仍然偏向一边，像一个好奇的孩子，想知道如果他继续的话会发生什么。哈利直视着那双红眼睛，希望那一刻立即到来，越快越好，趁自己还能够站立，还没有失去控制，还没有暴露出恐惧——

哈利看见那张嘴在动，绿光一闪，一切都消失了。

CHAPTER THIRTY-FIVE

King's Cross

He lay face down, listening to the silence. He was perfectly alone. Nobody was watching. Nobody else was there. He was not perfectly sure that he was there himself.

A long time later, or maybe no time at all, it came to him that he must exist, must be more than disembodied thought, because he was lying, definitely lying, on some surface. Therefore, he had a sense of a touch, and the thing against which he lay existed too.

Almost as soon as he had reached this conclusion, Harry became conscious that he was naked. Convinced as he was of his total solitude, this did not concern him, but it did intrigue him slightly. He wondered whether, as he could feel, he would be able to see. In opening them, he discovered that he had eyes.

He lay in a bright mist, though it was not like mist he had ever experienced before. His surroundings were not hidden by cloudy vapour; rather the cloudy vapour had not yet formed into surroundings. The floor on which he lay seemed to be white, neither warm nor cold, but simply there, a flat, blank something on which to be.

He sat up. His body appeared unscathed. He touched his face. He was not wearing glasses any more.

Then a noise reached him through the unformed nothingness that surrounded him: the small, soft thumpings of something that flapped, flailed and struggled. It was a pitiful noise, yet also slightly indecent. He had the uncomfortable feeling that he was eavesdropping on something furtive, shameful.

For the first time, he wished he were clothed.

Barely had the wish formed in his head, than robes appeared a short distance away. He took them and pulled them on: they were soft, clean

第 35 章

国王十字车站

哈利面朝下躺着,聆听着一片寂静。他完全是一个人。没有人在看他。周围没有别人。他不能十分确定自己是不是在这里。

过了很长时间,又也许根本没过一会儿,他意识到自己肯定存在,肯定不只是脱离了肉体的思绪,因为他躺在,绝对是躺在,某个东西的表面。因此他是有触觉的,而他身下的那个东西也是存在的。

刚得出这个结论,哈利几乎立刻意识到自己浑身赤裸。他相信这里只有他一个人,便不觉得难为情,只是有点儿好奇。他有触觉,便想知道是不是还有视觉,他试着睁了睁眼,发现自己还有眼睛。

他躺在明亮的薄雾里,但跟他以前见过的雾不一样。不是周围的景物都笼罩在云雾般的蒸气中,而是这些云雾般的蒸气还没有形成周围的景物。他所躺的地面似乎是白色的,不热也不冷,只是一种存在,一个平坦、空旷的所在。

他坐了起来,身体好像没有受伤。他摸摸脸,眼镜没有了。

一种声音,从周围未成形的虚无中传到了他的耳朵里:某个东西不断拍打、摆动和挣扎发出的细小的撞击声。这声音令人心生怜悯,同时又有些粗鄙猥琐。他有一种很不舒服的感觉,似乎在偷听什么隐秘而可耻的事情。

这个时候,他才希望自己穿着衣服。

这个念头刚在脑海里形成,不远处就出现了一件长袍。他拿过来穿在身上:长袍柔软、干净、暖呼呼的。多么奇特,它就那样出现了,

CHAPTER THIRTY-FIVE   King's Cross

and warm. It was extraordinary how they had appeared, just like that, the moment he had wanted them ...

He stood up, looking around. Was he in some great Room of Requirement? The longer he looked, the more there was to see. A great, domed glass roof glittered high above him in sunlight. Perhaps it was a palace. All was hushed and still, except for those odd thumping and whimpering noises coming from somewhere close by in the mist ...

Harry turned slowly on the spot, and his surroundings seemed to invent themselves before his eyes. A wide open space, bright and clean, a hall larger by far than the Great Hall, with that clear, domed glass ceiling. It was quite empty. He was the only person there, except for –

He recoiled. He had spotted the thing that was making the noises. It had the form of a small, naked child, curled on the ground, its skin raw and rough, flayed-looking, and it lay shuddering under a seat where it had been left, unwanted, stuffed out of sight, struggling for breath.

He was afraid of it. Small and fragile and wounded though it was, he did not want to approach it. Nevertheless, he drew slowly nearer, ready to jump back at any moment. Soon he stood near enough to touch it, yet he could not bring himself to do it. He felt like a coward. He ought to comfort it, but it repulsed him.

'You cannot help.'

He spun round. Albus Dumbledore was walking towards him, sprightly and upright, wearing sweeping robes of midnight blue.

'Harry.' He spread his arms wide, and his hands were both whole and white and undamaged. 'You wonderful boy. You brave, brave man. Let us walk.'

Stunned, Harry followed as Dumbledore strode away from where the flayed child lay whimpering, leading him to two seats that Harry had not previously noticed, set some distance away under that high, sparkling ceiling. Dumbledore sat down in one of them, and Harry fell into the other, staring at his old Headmaster's face. Dumbledore's long, silver hair and beard, the piercingly blue eyes behind half-moon spectacles, the crooked nose: everything was as he had remembered it. And yet ...

'But you're dead,' said Harry.

第35章 国王十字车站

他刚冒出这个念头……

他站了起来,环顾四周。他是在一间很大的有求必应屋里吗?他越看越发现可看的东西很多。一个巨大的圆形玻璃屋顶,在他头顶高处的阳光里闪闪发亮。也许这是个宫殿。四下里一片静谧凝滞,只有那古怪的撞击声和呜咽声,从近旁的薄雾中传来……

哈利在原地慢慢转身,周围的景物似乎在眼前幻化出来。一大片辽阔的空间,明亮、洁净,一个比大礼堂大得多的大厅,上面是那个明净的玻璃圆顶。大厅里空空的,只有他一个人,除了——

他缩了一下。他看见了那个发出声音的东西。那东西的形状是个光身子的小孩,蜷缩在地上,红红的皮肤很粗糙,看着像被剥了一层皮,瑟瑟发抖地躺在一个座位下面,被人丢弃了,被人胡乱地塞在那里,正在挣扎着呼吸。

哈利很害怕。那东西虽然娇小、赢弱,还受了伤,他却不愿意靠近它。不过他还是一点点地挪了过去,随时准备抽身而退。很快,他就近到能碰到它了,但他没有勇气这么做。他觉得自己像个懦夫。他应该去安慰它,可是那东西令他反感。

"你帮不了。"

哈利猛地转过身,阿不思·邓布利多正朝他走来,他腰板挺直,脚步轻快,穿着一件飘逸的深蓝色长袍。

"哈利。"他张开怀抱,两只手都白白的,完好无损,"你这个出色的孩子。你这个勇敢的、勇敢的男子汉。我们走一走吧。"

邓布利多大步离开了躺在那里呜咽的、被剥去一层皮的小孩,哈利晕头晕脑地跟了上去。邓布利多领头走向两把椅子,它们在高高的、闪闪发亮的屋顶下放着,和他们有一段距离,哈利先前没有发现。邓布利多在一把椅子上坐下,哈利坐在了另一把椅子上,呆呆地望着老校长的脸。邓布利多长长的银白色的头发和胡子,半月形眼镜后面那双犀利的蓝眼睛,那个弯鼻子:一切都和他记忆中的一样,然而……

"可是你死了呀。"哈利说。

CHAPTER THIRTY-FIVE King's Cross

'Oh, yes,' said Dumbledore matter-of-factly.

'Then ... I'm dead too?'

'Ah,' said Dumbledore, smiling still more broadly. 'That is the question, isn't it? On the whole, dear boy, I think not.'

They looked at each other, the old man still beaming.

'Not?' repeated Harry.

'Not,' said Dumbledore.

'But ...' Harry raised his hand instinctively towards the lightning scar. It did not seem to be there. 'But I should have died – I didn't defend myself! I meant to let him kill me!'

'And that,' said Dumbledore, 'will, I think, have made all the difference.'

Happiness seemed to radiate from Dumbledore like light, like fire: Harry had never seen the man so utterly, so palpably content.

'Explain,' said Harry.

'But you already know,' said Dumbledore. He twiddled his thumbs together.

'I let him kill me,' said Harry. 'Didn't I?'

'You did,' said Dumbledore, nodding. 'Go on!'

'So the part of his soul that was in me ...'

Dumbledore nodded still more enthusiastically, urging Harry onwards, a broad smile of encouragement on his face.

'... has it gone?'

'Oh, yes!' said Dumbledore. 'Yes, he destroyed it. Your soul is whole, and completely your own, Harry.'

'But then ...'

Harry glanced over his shoulder, to where the small, maimed creature trembled under the chair.

'What is that, Professor?'

'Something that is beyond either of our help,' said Dumbledore.

'But if Voldemort used the Killing Curse,' Harry started again, 'and nobody died for me this time – how can I be alive?'

'I think you know,' said Dumbledore. 'Think back. Remember what he

第35章 国王十字车站

"是啊。"邓布利多淡淡地说。

"那么……我也死了?"

"呵,"邓布利多脸上的笑意更明显了,"这倒是个问题,对吗?总的来说,亲爱的孩子,我认为没有。"

两人对视着,老人仍然笑眯眯的。

"没有?"哈利问。

"没有。"邓布利多说。

"可是……"哈利本能地用手去摸那道闪电形伤疤。伤疤似乎不在了。"可是我应该已经死了——我没有抵抗!我就打算让他杀死我!"

"我想,就因为这个,"邓布利多说,"才使整个事情有了变化。"

快乐像光、像火一样,从邓布利多身上散发出来。哈利从没见过老人这样纯粹、这样明显地快慰。

"说详细些吧。"哈利说。

"其实你已经知道了。"邓布利多说。他旋弄着两个大拇指。

"我让他杀死我,"哈利说,"不是吗?"

"是的,"邓布利多点点头,"接着说!"

"这样,他在我体内的那部分灵魂……"

邓布利多的头点得更起劲了,脸上带着鼓励的笑容,他催哈利继续往下说。

"……它消失了?"

"对!"邓布利多说,"是的,他把它给毁了。你的灵魂完整了,完全属于你自己了,哈利。"

"可是……"

哈利扭头看了看那边椅子下面发抖的受伤的小生命。

"那是什么,教授?"

"是我们都无能为力的一种东西。"邓布利多说。

"可是,如果伏地魔用了杀戮咒,"哈利又问,"这次又没人替我去死——我怎么可能还活着呢?"

"我认为你是知道的,"邓布利多说,"回想一下,想想他因为无知、

CHAPTER THIRTY-FIVE King's Cross

did, in his ignorance, in his greed and his cruelty.'

Harry thought. He let his gaze drift over his surroundings. If it was indeed a palace in which they sat, it was an odd one, with chairs set in little rows and bits of railing here and there, and still, he and Dumbledore and the stunted creature under the chair were the only beings there. Then the answer rose to his lips easily, without effort.

'He took my blood,' said Harry.

'Precisely!' said Dumbledore. 'He took your blood and rebuilt his living body with it! Your blood in his veins, Harry, Lily's protection inside both of you! He tethered you to life while he lives!'

'I live ... while he lives? But I thought ... I thought it was the other way round! I thought we both had to die? Or is it the same thing?'

He was distracted by the whimpering and thumping of the agonised creature behind them and glanced back at it yet again.

'Are you sure we can't do anything?'

'There is no help possible.'

'Then explain ... more,' said Harry, and Dumbledore smiled.

'You were the seventh Horcrux, Harry, the Horcrux he never meant to make. He had rendered his soul so unstable that it broke apart when he committed those acts of unspeakable evil, the murder of your parents, the attempted killing of a child. But what escaped from that room was even less than he knew. He left more than his body behind. He left part of himself latched to you, the would-be victim who had survived.

'And his knowledge remained woefully incomplete, Harry! That which Voldemort does not value, he takes no trouble to comprehend. Of house-elves and children's tales, of love, loyalty and innocence, Voldemort knows and understands nothing. *Nothing*. That they all have a power beyond his own, a power beyond the reach of any magic, is a truth he has never grasped.

'He took your blood believing it would strengthen him. He took into his body a tiny part of the enchantment your mother laid upon you when she died for you. His body keeps her sacrifice alive, and while that enchantment survives, so do you and so does Voldemort's one last hope for himself.'

第35章 国王十字车站

贪婪和残酷所做的事情。"

哈利思索着。他让目光掠过周围的景物。如果他们坐的地方真是一座宫殿，那也是一座奇怪的宫殿，到处摆放着一些成排的椅子，竖着一些栏杆。但除了他、邓布利多和椅子底下那个发育不良的生命外，没有别的生灵。接着，毫不费力地，答案轻松地涌到了他的唇边。

"他取了我的血。"哈利说。

"完全正确！"邓布利多说，"他取了你的血，用它重新塑造他的血肉之躯！你的血在他血管里流淌，哈利，莉莉的咒语存在于你们俩体内！只要他不死，你的生命也不会终止！"

"只要他活着……我就活着？可是我以为……我以为是倒过来的！我以为我们俩都必须死掉，不是吗？或者，这实际上是一码事？"

身后那个痛苦的生命不断呜咽、碰撞，哈利心神不宁，又扭头看了一眼。

"你真的认为我们不能做点什么吗？"

"无济于事。"

"那就再……详细说说。"哈利说，邓布利多笑了。

"哈利，你是第七个魂器，是他无意间制造的。他把自己的灵魂弄得极不稳定，当他犯下那些可怕的罪行——谋杀你的父母并试图杀害一个孩子时，他的灵魂就分裂了。但是，从那屋里逃脱的比他自己知道的还少。他不仅留下了自己的身体，他自己的一部分还附着在你——那个遭毒手却大难不死的孩子身上。

"可悲啊，他始终一知半解，哈利！伏地魔对于他不看重的东西，从不花功夫去理解。关于家养小精灵和童话传说，关于爱、忠诚和纯洁，伏地魔一无所知。一无所知。其实它们都具有一种比他更加强大的力量，一种超越任何魔法的力量，但他始终没有领会这个事实。

"他取了你的血，相信这会使他变得强大。他摄取了一小部分你母亲为你而死时留下的咒语。他的身体使你母亲的牺牲护符不会消亡，只要那个咒语还存在，你就不会死，伏地魔对自己的最后一线希望也就不会消失。"

CHAPTER THIRTY-FIVE King's Cross

Dumbledore smiled at Harry, and Harry stared at him.

'And you knew this? You knew – all along?'

'I guessed. But my guesses have, usually, been good,' said Dumbledore happily, and they sat in silence for what seemed like a long time, while the creature behind them continued to whimper and tremble.

'There's more,' said Harry. 'There's more to it. Why did my wand break the wand he borrowed?'

'As to that, I cannot be sure.'

'Have a guess, then,' said Harry, and Dumbledore laughed.

'What you must understand, Harry, is that you and Lord Voldemort have journeyed together into realms of magic hitherto unknown and untested. But here is what I think happened, and it is unprecedented, and no wandmaker could, I think, ever have predicted it or explained it to Voldemort.

'Without meaning to, as you now know, Lord Voldemort doubled the bond between you when he returned to a human form. A part of his soul was still attached to yours, and, thinking to strengthen himself, he took a part of your mother's sacrifice into himself. If he could only have understood the precise and terrible power of that sacrifice, he would not, perhaps, have dared to touch your blood ... but then, if he had been able to understand, he could not be Lord Voldemort, and might never have murdered at all.

'Having ensured this two-fold connection, having wrapped your destinies together more securely than ever two wizards were joined in history, Voldemort proceeded to attack you with a wand that shared a core with yours. And now something very strange happened, as we know. The cores reacted in a way that Lord Voldemort, who never knew that your wand was twin of his, had never expected.

'He was more afraid than you were that night, Harry. You had accepted, even embraced, the possibility of death, something Lord Voldemort has never been able to do. Your courage won, your wand overpowered his. And in doing so, something happened between those wands, something that echoed the relationship between their masters.

'I believe that your wand imbibed some of the power and qualities of Voldemort's wand that night, which is to say that it contained a little of Voldemort himself. So your wand recognised him when he pursued you,

第35章 国王十字车站

邓布利多笑眯眯地看着哈利，哈利只是呆呆地瞪着他。

"你早就知道？你一直——都知道？"

"我猜的。但我的猜测一般都差不到哪儿去。"邓布利多愉快地说，然后他们默默地坐了似乎许久，身后的那个生命还在呜咽、颤抖。

"还有，"哈利说，"还有呢。为什么我的魔杖击败了他借来的那根魔杖？"

"至于那个，我也不能肯定。"

"那就猜一猜吧。"哈利说，邓布利多朗声笑了起来。

"你必须明白的是，哈利，你和伏地魔共同游历了迄今无人知晓、无人涉足的魔法领域。我认为事情经过是下面这样的，它没有先例，我想也没有一个魔杖制作人能够预知或向伏地魔解释。

"你已经知道了，伏地魔在恢复人形时，无意中使你们之间的联系增加了一倍。当时，他灵魂的一部分仍然附着在你身上，而他为了增强自己的力量，又将你母亲牺牲护符的一部分摄入了他的体内。他如果明白那种牺牲护符的可怕力量，也许就不敢触碰你的鲜血……不过呢，他要能够明白这点，就不可能是伏地魔了，也就不会去杀人了。

"伏地魔加强了这种双重联系，把你们俩的命运紧紧地缠绕在一起，比历史上任何两个巫师间的联系都要紧密，然后他用一根与你的魔杖同芯的魔杖来攻击你。于是，我们都知道，非常奇怪的事情发生了。两根魔杖芯的反应出乎伏地魔的预料，他根本不知道你的杖芯跟他的是孪生的。

"那天夜里，他比你更害怕，哈利。你已经承认，甚至欣然接受了死亡的可能，这是伏地魔怎么也做不到的。你的勇气赢了，你的魔杖打败了他的。在这同时，这两根魔杖之间发生了一些事情，反映出两个主人之间的关系。

"我相信，那天夜里你的魔杖吸收了伏地魔那根魔杖的一些力量和品质，也就是说，它包含了伏地魔本人的一点儿东西。所以，他追你时，你的魔杖认出了他，认出了这个既是同源又是死敌的人，它就把伏地

CHAPTER THIRTY-FIVE King's Cross

recognised a man who was both kin and mortal enemy, and it regurgitated some of his own magic against him, magic much more powerful than anything Lucius's wand had ever performed. Your wand now contained the power of your enormous courage and of Voldemort's own deadly skill: what chance did that poor stick of Lucius Malfoy's stand?'

'But if my wand was so powerful, how come Hermione was able to break it?' asked Harry.

'My dear boy, its remarkable effects were directed only at Voldemort, who had tampered so ill-advisedly with the deepest laws of magic. Only towards him was that wand abnormally powerful. Otherwise it was a wand like any other ... though a good one, I am sure,' Dumbledore finished kindly.

Harry sat in thought for a long time, or perhaps seconds. It was very hard to be sure of things like time, here.

'He killed me with your wand.'

'He *failed* to kill you with my wand,' Dumbledore corrected Harry. 'I think we can agree that you are not dead – though, of course,' he added, as if fearing he had been discourteous, 'I do not minimise your sufferings, which I am sure were severe.'

'I feel great at the moment, though,' said Harry, looking down at his clean, unblemished hands. 'Where are we, exactly?'

'Well, I was going to ask you that,' said Dumbledore, looking around. 'Where would you say that we are?'

Until Dumbledore had asked, Harry had not known. Now, however, he found that he had an answer ready to give.

'It looks,' he said slowly, 'like King's Cross station. Except a lot cleaner, and empty, and there are no trains as far as I can see.'

'King's Cross station!' Dumbledore was chuckling immoderately. 'Good gracious, really?'

'Well, where do you think we are?' asked Harry, a little defensively.

'My dear boy, I have no idea. This is, as they say, *your* party.'

Harry had no idea what this meant; Dumbledore was being infuriating. He glared at him, then remembered a much more pressing question than that of their current location.

'The Deathly Hallows,' he said, and he was glad to see that the words wiped the smile from Dumbledore's face.

第35章 国王十字车站

魔自己的一些魔法回吐到他身上,这些魔法比卢修斯魔杖的力量要强大得多。现在,你那根魔杖的力量中既有你过人的勇气,又有伏地魔本人的致命法力,相比之下,卢修斯·马尔福那根可怜的小木棍还有什么戏呢?"

"既然我的魔杖这么厉害,赫敏又怎么能把它折断呢?"哈利问。

"我亲爱的孩子,它的惊人效果只是针对伏地魔的,因为他极为草率地篡改了最深奥的魔法规则。只有针对他的时候,那根魔杖才表现得异常强势。其他时候,它只是跟别的魔杖一样……不过确实是根好魔杖,这我相信。"邓布利多和蔼地说。

哈利坐在那里想了很长时间,或者只有几秒钟。在这里,对时间这类东西很难有把握。

"他用你的魔杖杀死了我。"

"他用我的魔杖没能杀死你,"邓布利多纠正哈利说,"我想我们可以一致认为你没有死——不过当然啦,"他赶紧补充道,似乎担心自己有些失礼,"我没有低估你的痛苦,我知道肯定很严重。"

"可是我现在感觉好极了,"哈利低头看着自己洁净无瑕的双手,说道,"我们究竟是在哪儿呢?"

"嘿,我正打算问你呢,"邓布利多说着,向四周看了看,"你说我们是在哪儿?"

在邓布利多问这话之前,哈利还不知道,此刻,他却发现自己有了答案。

"看样子,"哈利慢悠悠地说,"像是国王十字车站,可是要干净和空旷许多,而且我看不见火车。"

"国王十字车站!"邓布利多笑出声来,"我的天哪,真的吗?"

"那你认为我们是在哪儿呢?"哈利有点不服气地说。

"我亲爱的孩子,我不知道。就像人们说的,你是当事人哪。"

哈利不明白这是什么意思。邓布利多变得令人恼火了。哈利瞪着他,这才想起一个比他们在什么地方要紧得多的问题。

"死亡圣器。"说完,他很高兴地看到邓布利多脸上的笑容消失了。

CHAPTER THIRTY-FIVE   King's Cross

'Ah, yes,' he said. He even looked a little worried.

'Well?'

For the first time since Harry had met Dumbledore, he looked less than an old man, much less. He looked, fleetingly, like a small boy caught in wrongdoing.

'Can you forgive me?' he said. 'Can you forgive me for not trusting you? For not telling you? Harry, I only feared that you would fail as I had failed. I only dreaded that you would make my mistakes. I crave your pardon, Harry. I have known, for some time now, that you are the better man.'

'What are you talking about?' asked Harry, startled by Dumbledore's tone, by the sudden tears in his eyes.

'The Hallows, the Hallows,' murmured Dumbledore. 'A desperate man's dream!'

'But they're real!'

'Real, and dangerous, and a lure for fools,' said Dumbledore. 'And I was such a fool. But you know, don't you? I have no secrets from you any more. You know.'

'What do I know?'

Dumbledore turned his whole body to face Harry, and tears still sparkled in the brilliantly blue eyes.

'Master of death, Harry, master of Death! Was I better, ultimately, than Voldemort?'

'Of course you were,' said Harry. 'Of course – how can you ask that? You never killed if you could avoid it!'

'True, true,' said Dumbledore, and he was like a child seeking reassurance. 'Yet I, too, sought a way to conquer death, Harry.'

'Not the way he did,' said Harry. After all his anger at Dumbledore, how odd it was to sit here, beneath the high vaulted ceiling, and defend Dumbledore from himself. 'Hallows, not Horcruxes.'

'Hallows,' murmured Dumbledore, 'not Horcruxes. Precisely.'

There was a pause. The creature behind them whimpered, but Harry no longer looked round.

'Grindelwald was looking for them too?' he asked.

Dumbledore closed his eyes for a moment, and nodded.

第35章 国王十字车站

"啊，是的。"他说，甚至显得有点儿苦恼。

"怎么了？"

这是哈利遇见邓布利多后第一次看到他不像个老人，很不像。在那一瞬间，他就像个做坏事被人抓住的小男孩。

"你能原谅我吗？"他说，"你能原谅我不信任你？不告诉你？哈利，我只是担心你会像我一样失败。我只是害怕你会跟我犯同样的错误。我恳求你的原谅，哈利。这段时间以来，我已经知道你比我优秀。"

"你在说些什么呀？"哈利问，邓布利多的语气，还有他眼里突然涌出的泪水都令他吃惊。

"圣器，圣器，"邓布利多喃喃地说，"一个绝望者的梦啊！"

"可它们是真的！"

"真的，而且危险，是愚蠢者的诱饵，"邓布利多说，"我就是这样一个愚蠢者。但你已经知道了，是不是？我不再有秘密瞒着你。你知道了。"

"知道什么？"

邓布利多把整个身体转过来对着哈利，明亮的蓝眼睛里仍然泪光闪烁。

"死亡的征服者，哈利，死神的主人！最终，我是不是比伏地魔好？"

"那当然啦，"哈利说，"当然——你怎么会这么问？你只要能够避免就从不杀生！"

"对，对，"邓布利多说，就像个寻求安慰的孩子，"可是我也曾寻找过征服死亡的办法，哈利。"

"跟他不一样。"哈利说。他曾对邓布利多满怀怨恨，此刻却坐在这里，坐在高高的穹顶下，针对邓布利多的自责替他辩护，多么奇怪的事情啊，"圣器，不是魂器。"

"圣器，"邓布利多喃喃地说，"不是魂器。一点儿不错。"

一阵静默。他们身后的那个生命还在呜咽，但哈利没再扭头去看它。

"格林德沃也曾寻找过它们？"他问。

邓布利多闭了闭眼睛，点点头。

CHAPTER THIRTY-FIVE   King's Cross

'It was the thing, above all, that drew us together,' he said quietly. 'Two clever, arrogant boys with a shared obsession. He wanted to come to Godric's Hollow, as I am sure you have guessed, because of the grave of Ignotus Peverell. He wanted to explore the place the third brother had died.'

'So it's true?' asked Harry. 'All of it? The Peverell brothers –'

'– were the three brothers of the tale,' said Dumbledore, nodding. 'Oh yes, I think so. Whether they met Death on a lonely road ... I think it more likely that the Peverell brothers were simply gifted, dangerous wizards who succeeded in creating those powerful objects. The story of them being Death's own Hallows seems to me the sort of legend that might have sprung up around such creations.

'The Cloak, as you know now, travelled down through the ages, father to son, mother to daughter, right down to Ignotus's last living descendant, who was born, as Ignotus was, in the village of Godric's Hollow.'

Dumbledore smiled at Harry.

'Me?'

'You. You have guessed, I know, why the Cloak was in my possession on the night your parents died. James had showed it to me just a few days previously. It explained much of his undetected wrongdoing at school! I could hardly believe what I was seeing. I asked to borrow it, to examine it. I had long since given up my dream of uniting the Hallows, but I could not resist, could not help taking a closer look ... It was a Cloak the likes of which I had never seen, immensely old, perfect in every respect ... and then your father died, and I had two Hallows at last, all to myself!'

His tone was unbearably bitter.

'The Cloak wouldn't have helped them survive, though,' Harry said quickly. 'Voldemort knew where my mum and dad were. The Cloak couldn't have made them curse-proof.'

'True,' sighed Dumbledore. 'True.'

Harry waited, but Dumbledore did not speak, so he prompted him.

'So you'd given up looking for the Hallows when you saw the Cloak?'

'Oh yes,' said Dumbledore faintly. It seemed that he forced himself to meet Harry's eyes. 'You know what happened. You know. You cannot despise me more than I despise myself.'

第35章 国王十字车站

"首先就是这件事使我们走到一起的，"他轻声说，"两个聪明、狂妄的少年，怀着同样的痴迷。我相信你已经猜到了，他是为了伊格诺图斯·佩弗利尔的坟墓才到戈德里克山谷去的。他想调查第三个兄弟死去的地方。"

"那么，这是真的？"哈利问，"所有这些？佩弗利尔兄弟——？"

"——就是故事里的三兄弟，"邓布利多点点头说，"没错，我想是的。至于他们是不是在偏僻的小路上遭遇了死神……我认为更有可能的是佩弗利尔兄弟都是很强大、很危险的巫师，成功地制造了这些威力无比的器物。在我看来，这些圣器属于死神的故事像是围绕这些发明而出现的某种传说。

"隐形衣，你现在已经知道了，很久以来代代相传，父亲传给儿子，母亲传给女儿，一直传到伊格诺图斯的最后一位活着的后裔，他和伊格诺图斯一样，出生在戈德里克山谷的村庄里。"

邓布利多笑微微地看着哈利。

"我？"

"你。我知道你已经猜到了你父母死去那天夜里隐形衣为什么在我手里。就在当时的几天前，詹姆把它拿给我看。怪不得他在学校里有那些违纪行为却能不被人发现呢！我简直不敢相信自己的眼睛，就提出借回去研究研究。那时，我早已放弃了同时拥有全部圣器的梦想，但我抵挡不住，忍不住要仔细看看……这件隐形衣跟我以前见过的都不一样，非常古老，每一方面都很完美……后来你父亲死了，我终于拥有了两件圣器，完全属于我自己！"

他的语气变得极为痛苦。

"不过，隐形衣不会帮助他们幸存下来。"哈利赶紧说道，"伏地魔知道我爸爸妈妈在哪儿，隐形衣不可能让他们抵御魔咒。"

"不错，"邓布利多叹息道，"不错。"

哈利等待着，可是邓布利多没有说话，于是哈利提示他。

"就是说，在你看到隐形衣时，你已经放弃了寻找圣器？"

"是啊。"邓布利多无力地说，他似乎在强迫自己面对哈利的目光，"你知道发生了什么事。你知道。你不可能比我更轻视我自己。"

CHAPTER THIRTY-FIVE — King's Cross

'But I don't despise you –'

'Then you should,' said Dumbledore. He drew a deep breath. 'You know the secret of my sister's ill-health, what those Muggles did, what she became. You know how my poor father sought revenge, and paid the price, died in Azkaban. You know how my mother gave up her own life to care for Ariana.

'I resented it, Harry.'

Dumbledore stated it baldly, coldly. He was looking, now, over the top of Harry's head, into the distance.

'I was gifted, I was brilliant. I wanted to escape. I wanted to shine. I wanted glory.

'Do not misunderstand me,' he said, and pain crossed the face so that he looked ancient again. 'I loved them. I loved my parents, I loved my brother and my sister, but I was selfish, Harry, more selfish than you, who are a remarkably selfless person, could possibly imagine.

'So that, when my mother died, and I was left the responsibility of a damaged sister and a wayward brother, I returned to my village in anger and bitterness. Trapped and wasted, I thought! And then, of course, he came ...'

Dumbledore looked directly into Harry's eyes again.

'Grindelwald. You cannot imagine how his ideas caught me, Harry, inflamed me. Muggles forced into subservience. We wizards triumphant. Grindelwald and I, the glorious young leaders of the revolution.

'Oh, I had a few scruples. I assuaged my conscience with empty words. It would all be for the greater good, and any harm done would be repaid a hundredfold in benefits for wizards. Did I know, in my heart of hearts, what Gellert Grindelwald was? I think I did, but I closed my eyes. If the plans we were making came to fruition, all my dreams would come true.

'And at the heart of our schemes, the Deathly Hallows! How they fascinated him, how they fascinated both of us! The unbeatable wand, the weapon that would lead us to power! The Resurrection Stone – to him, though I pretended not to know it, it meant an army of Inferi! To me, I confess, it meant the return of my parents, and the lifting of all responsibility from my shoulders.

'And the Cloak ... somehow, we never discussed the Cloak much, Harry.

第35章 国王十字车站

"我没有轻视你——"

"那你应该轻视我。"邓布利多说,他深深吸了口气,"你知道我妹妹身体不好的秘密,知道那些麻瓜做的事情,知道我妹妹变成了什么样子。你知道我可怜的父亲为了给我妹妹报仇,付出了代价,惨死在阿兹卡班。你知道我母亲为了照顾阿利安娜舍弃了自己的生命。

"当时我怨恨这一切,哈利。"

邓布利多的讲述坦率而冷漠。此刻他的目光掠过哈利的头顶,望向远处。

"我有天分,我很优秀。我想逃走。我想出类拔萃。我想光彩夺目。"

"不要误会,"他继续说,痛苦浮现在他的脸上,使他又显得苍老了,"我爱他们,我爱我的父母,我爱我的弟弟妹妹,但我是自私的,哈利,比你这个非常无私的人可以想象的还要自私。

"因此,母亲去世后,我要负责照顾一个残疾的妹妹和一个任性的弟弟,我满怀怨恨和痛苦地返回村庄。我认为自己被困住了,虚度光阴!后来,不用说,他来了……"

邓布利多再次直视着哈利的眼睛。

"格林德沃。你无法想象他的思想是怎样吸引了我,激励了我。麻瓜被迫臣服,我们巫师扬眉吐气。格林德沃和我就是这场革命的光荣的年轻领袖。

"哦,我有过一点儿顾虑,但我用空洞的话语安慰我的良知。一切都是为了更伟大的利益,所造成的任何伤害都能给巫师界带来一百倍的好处。我内心深处是否知道盖勒特·格林德沃是怎样一个人呢?我想我是知道的,但我睁只眼闭只眼。只要我们的计划能够实现,我所有的梦想都会成真。

"而我们计划的核心,就是死亡圣器!它们令他多么痴迷,令我们两个人多么痴迷啊!永不会输的魔杖,能使我们获得权力的武器!复活石——对他来说意味着阴尸大军,尽管我假装并不知道!对我来说,我承认,它意味着我父母起死回生,减轻我肩负的所有责任。

"还有隐形衣……不知怎么,我们始终没怎么谈论隐形衣,哈利。

CHAPTER THIRTY-FIVE   King's Cross

Both of us could conceal ourselves well enough without the Cloak, the true magic of which, of course, is that it can be used to protect and shield others as well as its owner. I thought that if we ever found it, it might be useful in hiding Ariana, but our interest in the Cloak was mainly that it completed the trio, for the legend said that the man who united all three objects would then be truly master of death, which we took to mean, invincible.

'Invincible masters of death, Grindelwald and Dumbledore! Two months of insanity, of cruel dreams, and neglect of the only two members of my family left to me.

'And then ... you know what happened. Reality returned, in the form of my rough, unlettered, and infinitely more admirable brother. I did not want to hear the truths he shouted at me. I did not want to hear that I could not set forth to seek Hallows with a fragile and unstable sister in tow.

'The argument became a fight. Grindelwald lost control. That which I had always sensed in him, though I pretended not to, now sprang into terrible being. And Ariana ... after all my mother's care and caution ... lay dead upon the floor.'

Dumbledore gave a little gasp, and began to cry in earnest. Harry reached out, and was glad to find that he could touch him: he gripped his arm tightly, and Dumbledore gradually regained control.

'Well, Grindelwald fled, as anyone but I could have predicted. He vanished, with his plans for seizing power, and his schemes for Muggle torture, and his dreams of the Deathly Hallows, dreams in which I had encouraged him and helped him. He ran, while I was left to bury my sister and learn to live with my guilt, and my terrible grief, the price of my shame.

'Years passed. There were rumours about him. They said he had procured a wand of immense power. I, meanwhile, was offered the post of Minister for Magic, not once, but several times. Naturally, I refused. I had learned that I was not to be trusted with power.'

'But you'd have been better, much better, than Fudge or Scrimgeour!' burst out Harry.

'Would I?' asked Dumbledore heavily. 'I am not so sure. I had proven, as a very young man, that power was my weakness and my temptation. It is a curious thing, Harry, but perhaps those who are best suited to power are

第35章 国王十字车站

我们俩不用隐形衣就能把自己隐藏得很好。当然啦，隐形衣的真正魔力在于它不仅可以保护和遮蔽主人，还可以用来保护和遮蔽别人。当时我想，如果我们能找到它，或许可以用它来隐藏阿利安娜，不过我们对隐形衣的兴趣主要在于它是三要素之一，根据传说，同时拥有三样东西的人便是死亡的真正征服者，我们理解这意思就是'不可战胜'。

"不可战胜的死亡征服者，格林德沃和邓布利多！两个月如痴如醉，满脑子残酷的梦想，忽视了我仅剩的两个家人。

"后来……你知道发生了什么事。现实以我那位性格粗暴、没有文化，但却优秀得多的弟弟的面貌出现了。还有那些我不愿意听他冲我叫嚷的实话。我不想听说我被一个虚弱的、很不稳定的妹妹拖累着，不能前去寻找圣器。

"争吵上升为决斗。格林德沃失去了控制。他性格里的那种东西——我其实一直有所感觉，却总是假装没发现的那种东西，突然可怕地爆发出来。阿利安娜……在我母亲那么精心呵护和照料之后……倒在地上死了。"

邓布利多轻轻吸了口气，开始动情地哭了起来。哈利伸出手，还好，他发现自己能碰到对方。他紧紧地抓住邓布利多的胳膊，老人慢慢地控制住了自己。

"后来，格林德沃逃跑了，这是除了我谁都能料到的。他消失了，带着他争权夺利的计划，他虐待麻瓜的阴谋，还有他寻找死亡圣器的梦想，而我曾经在这些梦想上鼓励和帮助过他。他逃走了，我留下来埋葬我的妹妹，学着在负罪感和极度悲伤中打发日子，那是我耻辱的代价。

"许多年过去了。我听到了一些关于他的传言。据说他弄到了一根威力无比的魔杖。那个时候，魔法部部长的职位摆在我的面前，不止一次，而是多次。我当然拒绝了。我已经知道不能把权力交给我。"

"可是你会比福吉和斯克林杰要好，好得多！"哈利大声说。

"是吗？"邓布利多语气沉重地说，"我可没有这么肯定。我年轻气盛时候的表现就证明了权力是我的弱点、我的诱惑。说来奇怪，哈利，

those who have never sought it. Those who, like you, have leadership thrust upon them, and take up the mantle because they must, and find to their own surprise that they wear it well.

'I was safer at Hogwarts. I think I was a good teacher —'

'You were the best —'

'You are very kind, Harry. But while I busied myself with the training of young wizards, Grindelwald was raising an army. They say he feared me, and perhaps he did, but less, I think, than I feared him.

'Oh, not death,' said Dumbledore, in answer to Harry's questioning look. 'Not what he could do to me magically. I knew that we were evenly matched, perhaps that I was a shade more skilful. It was the truth I feared. You see, I never knew which of us, in that last, horrific fight, had actually cast the curse that killed my sister. You may call me cowardly: you would be right. Harry, I dreaded beyond all things the knowledge that it had been I who brought about her death, not merely through my arrogance and stupidity, but that I actually struck the blow that snuffed out her life.

'I think he knew it, I think he knew what frightened me. I delayed meeting him until, finally, it would have been too shameful to resist any longer. People were dying and he seemed unstoppable, and I had to do what I could.

'Well, you know what happened next. I won the duel. I won the wand.'

Another silence. Harry did not ask whether Dumbledore had ever found out who struck Ariana dead. He did not want to know, and even less did he want Dumbledore to have to tell him. At last he knew what Dumbledore would have seen when he looked in the Mirror of Erised, and why Dumbledore had been so understanding of the fascination it had exercised over Harry.

They sat in silence for a long time, and the whimperings of the creature behind them barely disturbed Harry any more.

At last he said, 'Grindelwald tried to stop Voldemort going after the wand. He lied, you know, pretended he had never had it.'

Dumbledore nodded, looking down at his lap, tears still glittering on the crooked nose.

'They say he showed remorse in later years, alone in his cell at Nurmengard. I hope that it is true. I would like to think he did feel the horror

第35章 国王十字车站

也许最适合掌握权力的是那些从不钻营权术的人，就像你一样，被迫担任领袖的角色，在情势所逼之下穿上战袍，结果自己很惊讶地发现居然穿得很好。"

"而我待在霍格沃茨更安全些，我认为我是个好教师——"

"你是最好的——"

"——你很善良，哈利。在我忙于培养年轻巫师的时候，格林德沃召集了一支军队。人们说他怕我，也许是吧，但我认为我更怕他。"

"哦，不是怕死，"邓布利多回答哈利询问的目光，"不是怕他用魔法对我的加害。我知道我们势均力敌，或许我还略胜一筹。我害怕的是真相。你明白吗，我一直不知道在那场可怕的混战中，究竟是谁发了那个杀死我妹妹的咒语。你大概会说我是懦夫，你是对的。哈利，我从心底里最害怕的是得知是我造成了她的死亡，不仅由于我的狂傲和愚蠢，而且还是我朝她发出了那致命的一击。

"我想他是知道的，我想他知道我害怕什么。我拖延着不见他，直到最后，我再不露面就太可耻了。人们在惨死，他似乎不可阻挡，我必须尽我的力量。

"唉，后来的事情你都知道了。决斗我胜利了。我赢得了那根魔杖。"

又是沉默。哈利没有问邓布利多有没有弄清是谁击毙了阿利安娜。他不希望知道，更不希望邓布利多不得不告诉他。他终于知道了邓布利多面对厄里斯魔镜时会看见什么，知道了邓布利多为什么那样理解魔镜对哈利的吸引力。

他们默默地坐了很久，身后那个生命的呜咽声几乎不再使哈利分神了。

最后，哈利说："格林德沃试图阻止伏地魔追寻那根魔杖。他撒谎了，你知道，谎称他从没得到过它。"

邓布利多点点头，垂眼望着膝头，泪水仍然在他的弯鼻子上闪闪发亮。

"听说他晚年独自被关在纽蒙迦德牢房里时流露出了悔恨。我希望这是真的。我希望他能感受到他的所作所为是多么恐怖和可耻。也许，

CHAPTER THIRTY-FIVE   King's Cross

and shame of what he had done. Perhaps that lie to Voldemort was his attempt to make amends ... to prevent Voldemort from taking the Hallow ...'

'... or maybe from breaking into your tomb?' suggested Harry, and Dumbledore dabbed his eyes.

After another short pause, Harry said, 'You tried to use the Resurrection Stone.'

Dumbledore nodded.

'When I discovered it, after all those years, buried in the abandoned home of the Gaunts, the Hallow I had craved most of all – though in my youth I had wanted it for very different reasons – I lost my head, Harry. I quite forgot that it was now a Horcrux, that the ring was sure to carry a curse. I picked it up, and I put it on, and for a second I imagined that I was about to see Ariana, and my mother, and my father, and to tell them how very, very sorry I was ...

'I was such a fool, Harry. After all those years, I had learned nothing. I was unworthy to unite the Deathly Hallows, I had proved it time and again, and here was final proof.'

'Why?' said Harry. 'It was natural! You wanted to see them again. What's wrong with that?'

'Maybe a man in a million could unite the Hallows, Harry. I was fit only to possess the meanest of them, the least extraordinary. I was fit to own the Elder Wand, and not to boast of it, and not to kill with it. I was permitted to tame and to use it, because I took it, not for gain, but to save others from it.

'But the Cloak, I took out of vain curiosity, and so it could never have worked for me as it works for you, its true owner. The stone I would have used in an attempt to drag back those who are at peace, rather than to enable my self-sacrifice, as you did. You are the worthy possessor of the Hallows.'

Dumbledore patted Harry's hand, and Harry looked up at the old man and smiled; he could not help himself. How could he remain angry with Dumbledore now?

'Why did you have to make it so difficult?'

Dumbledore's smile was tremulous.

'I am afraid I counted on Miss Granger to slow you up, Harry. I was afraid that your hot head might dominate your good heart. I was scared that, if presented outright with the facts about those tempting objects, you might

第35章　国王十字车站

他对伏地魔撒谎就是想弥补……想阻止伏地魔拿到圣器……"

"……或者不让他闯进你的坟墓？"哈利插言道，邓布利多擦了擦眼睛。

又是短暂的沉默，然后哈利说："你试着用过复活石。"

邓布利多点了点头。

"那么多年之后，我终于发现它埋在冈特家的荒宅里——这是我最渴望得到的圣器，不过年轻时我要它是因为别的原因——我昏了头，哈利。我忘记了它已经是一个魂器，忘记了那戒指上肯定带着魔咒。我把它拿起来，把它戴在了手上，那一瞬间，我以为自己就要见到阿利安娜、我的母亲、我的父亲，告诉他们我心里有多么多么悔恨……

"我真是个傻瓜，哈利。那么多年之后，我竟然毫无长进。我根本不配同时拥有全部的死亡圣器，这已是多次得到证实的，而这是最后一次证明。"

"为什么？"哈利说，"那是很自然的呀！你想再次见到他们，那有什么不对呢？"

"也许一百万人中间有一人可以同时拥有全部圣器，哈利。我只适合拥有其中最微不足道、最没有特色的。我适合拥有老魔杖，而且不能夸耀它，也不能用它杀人。我可以驯服它，使用它，因为我拿它不是为了索取，而是为了拯救别人。

"而隐形衣，我拿它完全出于无聊的好奇心，所以它对我不可能像对你那样管用，你是它真正的主人。对那块石头，我是想把那些长眠者硬拽回来，而不是像你那样，让它帮助自己实现自我牺牲。你才真正有资格拥有圣器。"

邓布利多拍拍哈利的手，哈利抬头看着老人，脸上露出了笑容。他忍不住。现在他还怎么可能生邓布利多的气呢？

"你为什么要把事情搞得这么复杂？"

邓布利多的笑容在颤抖。

"我恐怕是想用格兰杰小姐来牵制你，哈利。我担心你发热的头脑会支配你善良的心。我很害怕，如果你一下子面对关于那些诱惑物的

CHAPTER THIRTY-FIVE King's Cross

seize the Hallows as I did, at the wrong time, for the wrong reasons. If you laid hands on them, I wanted you to possess them safely. You are the true master of death, because the true master does not seek to run away from Death. He accepts that he must die, and understands that there are far, far worse things in the living world than dying.'

'And Voldemort never knew about the Hallows?'

'I do not think so, because he did not recognise the Resurrection Stone he turned into a Horcrux. But even if he had known about them, Harry, I doubt that he would have been interested in any except the first. He would not think that he needed the Cloak, and, as for the stone, whom would he want to bring back from the dead? He fears the dead. He does not love.'

'But you expected him to go after the wand?'

'I have been sure that he would try, ever since your wand beat Voldemort's in the graveyard of Little Hangleton. At first, he was afraid that you had conquered him by superior skill. Once he had kidnapped Ollivander, however, he discovered the existence of the twin cores. He thought that explained everything. Yet the borrowed wand did no better against yours! So Voldemort, instead of asking himself what quality it was in you that had made your wand so strong, what gift you possessed that he did not, naturally set out to find the one wand that, they said, would beat any other. For him, the Elder Wand has become an obsession to rival his obsession with you. He believes that the Elder Wand removes his last weakness and makes him truly invincible. Poor Severus ...'

'If you planned your death with Snape, you meant him to end up with the Elder Wand, didn't you?'

'I admit that was my intention,' said Dumbledore, 'but it did not work as I intended, did it?'

'No,' said Harry. 'That bit didn't work out.'

The creature behind them jerked and moaned, and Harry and Dumbledore sat without talking for the longest time yet. The realisation of what would happen next settled gradually over Harry in the long minutes, like softly falling snow.

'I've got to go back, haven't I?'

'That is up to you.'

'I've got a choice?'

第35章 国王十字车站

真相，你会像我一样在错误的时候、为了错误的理由攫取圣器。在你拿到它们时，我希望你能安全地拥有它们。你才是死亡的真正征服者，因为真正的征服者绝不会试图逃离死神。他会欣然接受必死的命运，并知道活人的世界里有着比死亡更加糟糕得多的事情。"

"伏地魔始终不知道圣器吗？"

"我认为是的，因为他没有认出复活石，而是把它变成了一个魂器。不过，即使他知道圣器，哈利，除了第一件，他恐怕对别的都不感兴趣。他会认为自己不需要隐形衣，至于复活石，他想唤回哪位死者呢？他惧怕死者。他不懂得爱。"

"那你料到他会寻找那根魔杖？"

"自从你的魔杖在小汉格顿的墓地里击败了伏地魔的，我就相信他会这么做。起初，他担心你是凭着出色的技艺征服了他。后来他绑架了奥利凡德，发现了孪生杖芯的存在。他以为这就说明了一切。可是，借来的魔杖依然不是你的对手！伏地魔没有问问自己，你身上有什么素质使你的魔杖变得这么强大，你具备什么他所没有的天赋，而是想当然地去找那根魔杖，那根传说中打遍天下无敌手的魔杖。他对老魔杖有强烈的执念，如同他对你的执念一样。他相信老魔杖会消除他最后的弱点，使他变得真正不可战胜。可怜的西弗勒斯……"

"你安排斯内普把你杀死，那么你是打算让他得到老魔杖的，是吗？"

"我承认我有这样的意图，"邓布利多说，"然而事与愿违啊，是不是？"

"是啊，"哈利说，"在这一点上没有实现。"

他们身后的生命在抽动、呻吟，哈利和邓布利多一言不发地坐了很长时间，比前几次沉默的时间还要长。最后，就像雪花轻轻飘落一样，哈利慢慢意识到接下来会发生什么了。

"我必须回去，是吗？"

"这由你决定。"

"我可以选择？"

'Oh yes.' Dumbledore smiled at him. 'We are in King's Cross, you say? I think that if you decided not to go back, you would be able to ... let's say ... board a train.'

'And where would it take me?'

'On,' said Dumbledore simply.

Silence again.

'Voldemort's got the Elder Wand.'

'True. Voldemort has the Elder Wand.'

'But you want me to go back?'

'I think,' said Dumbledore, 'that if you choose to return, there is a chance that he may be finished for good. I cannot promise it. But I know this, Harry, that you have less to fear from returning here than he does.'

Harry glanced again at the raw-looking thing that trembled and choked in the shadow beneath the distant chair.

'Do not pity the dead, Harry. Pity the living, and, above all, those who live without love. By returning, you may ensure that fewer souls are maimed, fewer families are torn apart. If that seems to you a worthy goal, then we say goodbye for the present.'

Harry nodded and sighed. Leaving this place would not be nearly as hard as walking into the Forest had been, but it was warm and light and peaceful here, and he knew that he was heading back to pain and the fear of more loss. He stood up, and Dumbledore did the same, and they looked for a long moment into each other's faces.

'Tell me one last thing,' said Harry. 'Is this real? Or has this been happening inside my head?'

Dumbledore beamed at him, and his voice sounded loud and strong in Harry's ears even though the bright mist was descending again, obscuring his figure.

'Of course it is happening inside your head, Harry, but why on earth should that mean that it is not real?'

第35章 国王十字车站

"是的。"邓布利多微笑地看着他,"你说我们在国王十字车站,不是吗?我想,如果你决定不再回去,你可以……比如说……登上一列火车。"

"它会把我带到哪儿呢?"

"往前。"邓布利多简单地说。

又是沉默。

"伏地魔拿到了老魔杖。"

"不错。伏地魔拿着老魔杖。"

"但你希望我回去?"

"我想,"邓布利多说,"如果你选择回去,有可能他就永远完蛋了。我不能保证。但我知道,哈利,你没有他那么害怕回到这里。"

哈利又看了一眼远处椅子底下阴影里那个颤抖、抽泣的红兮兮的东西。

"不要怜悯死者,哈利。怜悯活人,最重要的是,怜悯那些生活中没有爱的人。你回去可以保证少一些灵魂遭到残害,少一些家庭妻离子散。如果你觉得这是个很有价值的目标,那我们就暂时告别吧。"

哈利点点头,叹了口气。离开这个地方不会像步入禁林那样艰难,但这里温暖、宁静、明亮,而他知道他要回去面对痛苦,面对丧失更多亲人的恐惧。他站起身,邓布利多也站了起来,他们久久地凝视着对方。

"告诉我最后一点,"哈利说,"这是真事吗?还是发生在我脑子里的事?"

邓布利多笑微微地看着他,虽然明亮的薄雾再次降落,使他的身影变得模糊,但他的声音却那样响亮有力地传到了哈利耳朵里。

"当然是发生在你脑子里的事,哈利,但为什么那就意味着不是真的呢?"

CHAPTER THIRTY-SIX

The Flaw in the Plan

He was lying face down on the ground again. The smell of the Forest filled his nostrils. He could feel the cold hard ground beneath his cheek, and the hinge of his glasses, which had been knocked sideways by the fall, cutting into his temple. Every inch of him ached, and the place where the Killing Curse had hit him felt like the bruise of an iron-clad punch. He did not stir, but remained exactly where he had fallen, with his left arm bent out at an awkward angle and his mouth gaping.

He had expected to hear cheers of triumph and jubilation at his death, but instead hurried footsteps, whispers, and solicitous murmurs filled the air.

'My Lord ... *my Lord* ...'

It was Bellatrix's voice, and she spoke as if to a lover. Harry did not dare open his eyes, but allowed his other senses to explore his predicament. He knew that his wand was still stowed beneath his robes because he could feel it pressed between his chest and the ground. A slight cushioning effect in the area of his stomach told him that the Invisibility Cloak was also there, stuffed out of sight.

'*My Lord* ...'

'That will do,' said Voldemort's voice.

More footsteps: several people were backing away from the same spot. Desperate to see what was happening, and why, Harry opened his eyes by a millimetre.

Voldemort seemed to be getting to his feet. Various Death Eaters were hurrying away from him, returning to the crowd lining the clearing. Bellatrix alone remained behind, kneeling beside Voldemort.

Harry closed his eyes again and considered what he had seen. The Death Eaters had been huddled round Voldemort, who seemed to have fallen to the

第36章

百密一疏

他又面朝下躺在地上,禁林的气味扑鼻而来。他感觉到了面颊下面冰冷、坚硬的土地,感觉到落地时被撞歪的眼镜角扎着他的太阳穴。身上没有一处不疼,杀戮咒击中的地方就像被铁拳打伤了一样。他没有动弹,完全保持落地时的姿势,左臂以很别扭的角度向外拐着,嘴巴张得大大的。

他以为会听见胜利的欢呼,听见他们庆祝他的死,然而空气里满是匆匆的脚步声、交头接耳的说话声和急切的低语声。

"主人……主人……"

是贝拉特里克斯的声音,她就像在对一个恋人说话。哈利不敢睁眼,只让自己的其他感官探究眼下的处境。他知道他的魔杖仍塞在长袍底下,因为他感觉到它梗在胸口和地面之间。肚皮那儿有一种软绵绵的感觉,说明隐形衣还在,藏得好好的。

"主人……"

"没问题。"伏地魔的声音说。

更多的脚步声:几个人从同一个地点往后退去。哈利急于看到是怎么回事,便把眼睛微微睁开了一道细缝。

伏地魔似乎正从地上站起来。好几个食死徒匆匆从他面前逃开,回到空地周围的人群里。只有贝拉特里克斯留在后面,跪倒在伏地魔身边。

哈利又闭上了眼睛,思索着他看到的情景。食死徒刚才聚集在似乎摔倒的伏地魔身边。伏地魔用杀戮咒击中哈利的同时一定发生了什

CHAPTER THIRTY-SIX   The Flaw in the Plan

ground. Something had happened when he had hit Harry with the Killing Curse. Had Voldemort, too, collapsed? It seemed like it. And both of them had fallen briefly unconscious and both of them had now returned ...

'My Lord, let me –'

'I do not require assistance,' said Voldemort coldly, and though he could not see it, Harry pictured Bellatrix withdrawing a helpful hand. 'The boy ... is he dead?'

There was complete silence in the clearing. Nobody approached Harry, but he felt their concentrated gaze, it seemed to press him harder into the ground, and he was terrified a finger or an eyelid might twitch.

'You,' said Voldemort, and there was a bang and a small shriek of pain. 'Examine him. Tell me whether he is dead.'

Harry did not know who had been sent to verify. He could only lie there, with his heart thumping traitorously, and wait to be examined, but at the same time noting, small comfort though it was, that Voldemort was wary of approaching him, that Voldemort suspected that all had not gone to plan ...

Hands, softer than he had been expecting, touched Harry's face, pulled back an eyelid, crept beneath his shirt, down to his chest and felt his heart. He could hear the woman's fast breathing, her long hair tickled his face. He knew that she could feel the steady pounding of life against his ribs.

'*Is Draco alive? Is he in the castle?*'

The whisper was barely audible; her lips were an inch from his ear, her head bent so low that her long hair shielded his face from the onlookers.

'*Yes*,' he breathed back.

He felt the hand on his chest contract; her nails pierced him. Then it was withdrawn. She had sat up.

'He is dead!' Narcissa Malfoy called to the watchers.

And now they shouted, now they yelled in triumph and stamped their feet, and through his eyelids Harry saw bursts of red and silver light shoot into the air in celebration.

Still feigning death on the ground, he understood. Narcissa knew that the only way she would be permitted to enter Hogwarts, and find her son, was as part of the conquering army. She no longer cared whether Voldemort won.

第36章　百密一疏

么。难道伏地魔也晕了过去？看来是这样。他们俩都昏迷了很短的时间，现在又都苏醒过来……

"主人，让我——"

"我不需要帮助。"伏地魔冷冷地说，哈利虽然看不见，却想象得出贝拉特里克斯缩回了要去搀扶的手，"那个男孩……他死了吗？"

空地上一片肃静。没有人走近哈利，但他感觉到所有的目光都集中在他身上。这些目光似乎把他牢牢地钉在了地面，他真害怕他的手指或眼皮会抖动。

"你，"伏地魔说，接着是砰的一响和一声短促的惨叫，"去查看一下。告诉我他死了没有。"

哈利不知道伏地魔派谁来核实。他只能躺在那里等待接受检查，心脏不听话地怦怦狂跳，不过他同时注意到——虽然这并不能给他带来多少安慰——伏地魔不敢贸然接近他，伏地魔怀疑计划出了差错……

一双手，一双哈利没想到会这么柔软的手，摸了摸哈利的脸，翻开他的眼皮，又伸进衬衫下面探摸他的胸口，试了试他的心跳。哈利可以听见女人急促的呼吸声，感到她的长发拂在脸上痒痒的。他知道女人能感觉到他的生命一下下撞击着他的肋骨。

"德拉科还活着吗？他在城堡里吗？"

这耳语声勉强能够听到。女人的嘴唇离他的耳朵只有一寸，她把脑袋埋得很低，长长的头发挡住了他的脸，使周围的人看不见。

"是的。"他用微弱的声音回答。

他感到胸口的那只手抓紧了，指甲掐痛了他。接着手缩了回去。她坐直了身体。

"他死了！"纳西莎·马尔福大声对周围的人说。

他们这才嚷嚷起来，这才开始欢呼、跺脚，哈利隔着眼皮看见一道道红光和银光射入空中欢庆胜利。

他躺在地上继续装死，但心里明白。纳西莎知道只有一个办法能让她进入霍格沃茨，找到儿子，那就是跟着占领军一起进去。她不再关心伏地魔是不是胜利。

CHAPTER THIRTY-SIX   The Flaw in the Plan

'You see?' screeched Voldemort over the tumult. 'Harry Potter is dead by my hand, and no man alive can threaten me now! Watch! *Crucio!*'

Harry had been expecting it: knew his body would not be allowed to remain unsullied upon the Forest floor, it must be subjected to humiliation to prove Voldemort's victory. He was lifted into the air, and it took all his determination to remain limp, yet the pain he expected did not come. He was thrown once, twice, three times into the air: his glasses flew off and he felt his wand slide a little beneath his robes, but he kept himself floppy and lifeless, and when he fell to the ground for the last time the clearing echoed with jeers and shrieks of laughter.

'Now,' said Voldemort, 'we go to the castle, and show them what has become of their hero. Who shall drag the body? No – Wait –'

There was a fresh outbreak of laughter, and after a few moments Harry felt the ground trembling beneath him.

'You carry him,' Voldemort said. 'He will be nice and visible in your arms, will he not? Pick up your little friend, Hagrid. And the glasses – put on the glasses – he must be recognisable.'

Someone slammed Harry's glasses back on to his face with deliberate force, but the enormous hands that lifted him into the air were exceedingly gentle. Harry could feel Hagrid's arms trembling with the force of his heaving sobs, great tears splashed down upon him as Hagrid cradled Harry in his arms, and Harry did not dare, by movement or word, to intimate to Hagrid that all was not, yet, lost.

'Move,' said Voldemort, and Hagrid stumbled forwards, forcing his way through the close-growing trees, back through the Forest. Branches caught at Harry's hair and robes, but he lay quiescent, his mouth lolling open, his eyes shut, and in the darkness, while the Death Eaters crowed all around them, and while Hagrid sobbed blindly, nobody looked to see whether a pulse beat in the exposed neck of Harry Potter ...

The two giants crashed along behind the Death Eaters; Harry could hear trees creaking and falling as they passed; they made so much din that birds rose, shrieking, into the sky and even the jeers of the Death Eaters were drowned. The victorious procession marched on towards the open ground, and after a while Harry could tell, by the lightening of the darkness through his closed eyelids, that the trees were beginning to thin.

'BANE!'

第36章 百密一疏

"看到了吗?"伏地魔在一片喧闹中尖声说道,"哈利·波特死在了我的手里,现在没有一个活人能够威胁我了!看着!钻心剜骨!"

哈利早就知道会有这一着,知道伏地魔不会让他清清爽爽地躺在密林的地上,必要百般羞辱他以证明自己的胜利。哈利的身体被升到了半空,他用全部的毅力让自己保持软弱无力的样子,以为会很痛,然而并没有。他被一次、两次、三次抛向空中,眼镜掉了,他感到长袍底下的魔杖滑到了一边,但他一直让身体显得软绵绵的毫无生气。他最后一次落到地上时,空地上响彻着讥诮声和狂笑声。

"现在,"伏地魔说,"我们到城堡去,让他们看看他们的英雄变成了什么样子。谁来搬尸体?不——等等——"

又是一阵哄笑,过了片刻,哈利感到身下的地面在颤抖。

"你抱着他,"伏地魔说,"他在你怀里比较显眼、好看,是不是?海格,把你的小朋友抱起来。还有眼镜——给他戴上眼镜——必须让人能认出他来——"

有人把哈利的眼镜杵到他的脸上,动作故意很粗暴,可是把他托到空中的那双大手却格外温柔。在海格摇篮一般的怀抱里,哈利可以感觉到海格剧烈啜泣时双臂在颤抖,大颗大颗的泪珠溅在他身上,哈利不敢用动作或语言向海格表示一切并没有结束。

"快走。"伏地魔说,海格跌跌撞撞地往前走,在茂密的树丛间穿行着离开禁林。树枝钩着哈利的头发和长袍,他一动不动地躺着,嘴巴无力地张着,眼睛闭得紧紧的。黑暗中,食死徒们聚集在周围,海格闭着眼睛大声哭泣,谁也没有仔细看看哈利·波特露在外面的脖颈上是否有脉搏在跳动……

两个巨人磕磕碰碰地走在食死徒后面,哈利可以听见他们走过时树木吱吱嘎嘎地断裂和倒地的声音。他们发出的声音太大了,鸟儿尖叫着飞向空中,就连食死徒们的讥笑声也被淹没了。胜利的队伍继续朝空旷的场地前进,过了一会儿,哈利透过紧闭的眼皮感到黑暗逐渐变亮了,知道树木开始变得稀疏。

"**贝恩!**"

CHAPTER THIRTY-SIX   The Flaw in the Plan

Hagrid's unexpected bellow nearly forced Harry's eyes open. 'Happy now, are yeh, that yeh didn' fight, yeh cowardly bunch o' nags? Are yeh happy Harry Potter's – d – dead …?'

Hagrid could not continue, but broke down in fresh tears. Harry wondered how many centaurs were watching their procession pass; he dared not open his eyes to look. Some of the Death Eaters called insults at the centaurs as they left them behind. A little later, Harry sensed, by a freshening of the air, that they had reached the edge of the Forest.

'Stop.'

Harry thought that Hagrid must have been forced to obey Voldemort's command, because he lurched a little. And now a chill settled over them where they stood, and Harry heard the rasping breath of the Dementors that patrolled the outer trees. They would not affect him now. The fact of his own survival burned inside him, a talisman against them, as though his father's stag kept guardian in his heart.

Someone passed close by Harry, and he knew that it was Voldemort himself because he spoke a moment later, his voice magically magnified so that it swelled through the grounds, crashing upon Harry's eardrums.

'Harry Potter is dead. He was killed as he ran away, trying to save himself while you lay down your lives for him. We bring you his body as proof that your hero is gone.

'The battle is won. You have lost half of your fighters. My Death Eaters outnumber you and the Boy Who Lived is finished. There must be no more war. Anyone who continues to resist, man, woman or child, will be slaughtered, as will every member of their family. Come out of the castle, now, kneel before me, and you shall be spared. Your parents and children, your brothers and sisters will live, and be forgiven, and you will join me in the new world we shall build together.'

There was silence in the grounds and from the castle. Voldemort was so close to him that Harry did not dare open his eyes again.

'Come,' said Voldemort, and Harry heard him move ahead, and Hagrid was forced to follow. Now Harry opened his eyes a fraction, and saw Voldemort striding in front of them, wearing the great snake Nagini around his shoulders, who was now free of her enchanted cage. But Harry had no possibility of extracting the wand concealed under his robes without being

第36章 百密一疏

海格突然大吼一声，惊得哈利差点儿睁开了眼睛。"现在满意了吧，嗯，你们不抵抗，你们这群胆小的驽马，嗯？你们高兴了吧？哈利·波特——死—死了……"

海格说不下去了，又伤心地哭了起来。哈利不知道有多少马人在观看他们这支队伍，他不敢睁开眼睛。有几个食死徒在行进时大声辱骂着身后的马人。又过了片刻，哈利感到空气变得新鲜了，知道已经到了禁林边缘。

"停下。"

哈利猜想海格肯定是被迫服从了伏地魔的命令，因为他的身子打了个趔趄。一股寒意把他们笼罩，哈利听见了在森林外围巡逻的摄魂怪们刺耳的呼吸声。它们再也不能拿他怎么样了。他还活着的事实如一团火在他心头燃烧，是一个避邪的法宝，似乎父亲的牡鹿一直在他心中守护着他。

有人从哈利近旁走过，哈利知道正是伏地魔本人，因为他紧接着就说话了，声音被魔法放大了多倍，响彻整个场地，震得哈利的鼓膜生疼。

"哈利·波特死了。他逃跑时被杀死了，在你们为了他舍弃生命的时候，他却只顾自己逃命。我们把他的尸体带给你们，以证明你们的英雄确实死了。

"我们赢了。你们抵抗者的人数折损了一半。我的食死徒现在数量比你们多，大难不死的男孩完蛋了。再也不得有战争。有谁负隅顽抗，不论男人、女人和孩子，格杀勿论，其家人也统统处死。现在，走出城堡，跪在我的面前吧，你们会得到赦免。你们的父母、儿女、兄弟姐妹也会被宽恕，继续活下去，你们和我一起进入我们将要共同建立的新世界。"

场地上、城堡里一片寂静。伏地魔离得太近了，哈利不敢再睁开眼睛。

"过来。"伏地魔说，哈利听见他往前走去，海格被迫跟上。哈利这才把眼睛睁开一条小缝，看见伏地魔大步走在他们前面，大蛇纳吉尼已经离开它的魔法笼子，正缠绕在伏地魔的肩膀上。可是，哈利不

CHAPTER THIRTY-SIX The Flaw in the Plan

noticed by the Death Eaters who marched on either side of them through the slowly lightening darkness ...

'Harry,' sobbed Hagrid. 'Oh, Harry ... Harry ...'

Harry shut his eyes tight again. He knew that they were approaching the castle and strained his ears to distinguish, above the gleeful voices of the Death Eaters and their tramping footsteps, signs of life from those within.

'Stop.'

The Death Eaters came to a halt: Harry heard them spreading out in a line facing the open front doors of the school. He could see, even through his closed lids, the reddish glow that meant light streamed upon him from the Entrance Hall. He waited. Any moment, the people for whom he had tried to die would see him, lying apparently dead, in Hagrid's arms.

'NO!'

The scream was the more terrible because he had never expected or dreamed that Professor McGonagall could make such a sound. He heard another woman laughing nearby, and knew that Bellatrix gloried in McGonagall's despair. He squinted again, for a single second, and saw the open doorway filling with people, as the survivors of the battle came out on to the front steps, to face their vanquishers, and see the truth of Harry's death for themselves. He saw Voldemort standing a little in front of him, stroking Nagini's head with a single white finger. He closed his eyes again.

'No!'

'*No!*'

'Harry! HARRY!'

Ron, Hermione and Ginny's voices were worse than McGonagall's; Harry wanted nothing more than to call back, yet he made himself lie silent, and their cries acted like a trigger, the crowd of survivors took up the cause, screaming and yelling abuse at the Death Eaters, until –

'SILENCE!' cried Voldemort, and there was a bang and a flash of bright light, and silence was forced upon them all. 'It is over! Set him down, Hagrid, at my feet, where he belongs!'

Harry felt himself lowered on to the grass.

'You see?' said Voldemort, and Harry felt him striding backwards and forwards right beside the place where he lay. 'Harry Potter is dead! Do you understand now, deluded ones? He was nothing, ever, but a boy who relied on others to sacrifice themselves for him!'

第36章 百密一疏

可能抽出藏在长袍下的魔杖,那样肯定会被食死徒们发现,他们就在两边,穿行在逐渐明亮起来的黑夜里……

"哈利,"海格抽抽搭搭地说,"哦,哈利……哈利……"

哈利又把眼睛紧紧闭上了。他知道他们正在走近城堡,他竖起耳朵,在食死徒的狂欢声和重重的脚步声中,分辨着城堡里的人传出的动静。

"停下。"

食死徒们都停住了。哈利听见他们面对学校敞开的大门一字散开。他虽然闭着眼睛,也能隐约感觉到红光,那一定是门厅里透出的灯光。他等待着。那些他曾经为之赴死的人,随时都会看见他如同死了一样躺在海格的怀里。

"不!"

这尖叫声太可怕了,因为他从来没想到、做梦也没想到麦格教授能发出这样的声音。他听见近旁另一个女人高声大笑,知道是贝拉特里克斯为麦格的绝望而幸灾乐祸。他又眯着眼睛看了一下,只见敞开的门口挤满了人,战斗中幸存的人都来到门前的台阶上面对征服者,目睹哈利死亡的事实。他看见伏地魔站在他前面一点儿的地方,用一根苍白的手指抚摸着纳吉尼的头。哈利又把眼睛闭上了。

"不!"

"不!"

"哈利!**哈利!**"

罗恩、赫敏和金妮的声音比麦格的更加凄厉。哈利真想冲他们大喊,但他还是强迫自己沉默地躺着。他们的喊声就像引爆器一样,幸存者们应声而起,扯着嗓子大声咒骂那些食死徒,最后——

"**安静!**"伏地魔喊道,只听砰的一声,一道强光一闪,他们都被迫沉默了,"结束了!海格,把他放在我的脚下,他只配待在这儿!"

哈利感觉到自己被放到了草地上。

"看见了吗?"伏地魔说,哈利感到他在自己身边大步地来回走动,"哈利·波特死了!你们这些被蒙蔽的人,现在明白了吧?他根本什么都不是,只是一个依赖别人为他牺牲的小男孩!"

CHAPTER THIRTY-SIX The Flaw in the Plan

'He beat you!' yelled Ron, and the charm broke, and the defenders of Hogwarts were shouting and screaming again until a second, more powerful bang extinguished their voices once more.

'He was killed while trying to sneak out of the castle grounds,' said Voldemort, and there was relish in his voice for the lie, 'killed while trying to save himself –'

But Voldemort broke off: Harry heard a scuffle and a shout, then another bang, a flash of light and a grunt of pain; he opened his eyes an infinitesimal amount. Someone had broken free of the crowd and charged at Voldemort: Harry saw the figure hit the ground, Disarmed, Voldemort throwing the challenger's wand aside and laughing.

'And who is this?' he said, in his soft snake's hiss. 'Who has volunteered to demonstrate what happens to those who continue to fight when the battle is lost?'

Bellatrix gave a delighted laugh.

'It is Neville Longbottom, my Lord! The boy who has been giving the Carrows so much trouble! The son of the Aurors, remember?'

'Ah, yes, I remember,' said Voldemort, looking down at Neville, who was struggling back to his feet, unarmed and unprotected, standing in the no-man's-land between the survivors and the Death Eaters. 'But you are a pure-blood, aren't you, my brave boy?' Voldemort asked Neville, who stood facing him, his empty hands curled in fists.

'So what if I am?' said Neville loudly.

'You show spirit, and bravery, and you come of noble stock. You will make a very valuable Death Eater. We need your kind, Neville Longbottom.'

'I'll join you when hell freezes over,' said Neville. 'Dumbledore's Army!' he shouted, and there was an answering cheer from the crowd, whom Voldemort's silencing charms seemed unable to hold.

'Very well,' said Voldemort, and Harry heard more danger in the silkiness of his voice than in the most powerful curse. 'If that is your choice, Longbottom, we revert to the original plan. On your head,' he said quietly, 'be it.'

Still watching through his lashes, Harry saw Voldemort wave his wand. Seconds later, out of one of the castle's shattered windows, something that looked like a misshapen bird flew through the half-light and landed in Voldemort's hand. He shook the mildewed object by its pointed end and it dangled, empty and ragged: the Sorting Hat.

第36章 百密一疏

"他打败了你!"罗恩喊道,魔咒被打破了,霍格沃茨的保卫者们又咆哮、叫嚷起来。一秒钟后,更加惊天动地的一声巨响,他们又哑然失声。

"他是在试图逃出场地的时候被杀死的,"伏地魔说,似乎因说谎而沾沾自喜,"在试图自己逃命的时候被杀死——"

可是伏地魔没能把话说完,哈利听见了扭打声、喊叫声,接着又是砰的一声,一道闪光,痛苦的呻吟。他把眼睛睁开一点点缝隙。原来有人挣脱人群朝伏地魔冲了过来。哈利看见那个人影被解除了武器,重重地倒在地上,伏地魔哈哈大笑地把挑战者的魔杖扔到一边。

"这是谁呀?"他用轻轻的、蛇一般的嗞嗞声说,"谁主动以身试法,让大家看到战败后继续反抗会有什么下场?"

贝拉特里克斯高兴地笑了起来。

"是纳威·隆巴顿,主人!就是那个给卡罗兄妹制造了很多麻烦的男孩!那对傲罗夫妇的儿子,记得吗?"

"啊,是了,我想起来了。"伏地魔低头看着纳威说。纳威赤手空拳、毫无掩护地挣扎着爬起身,站在幸存者和食死徒之间的空地上。"但你是个纯血统巫师,对吗,我勇敢的孩子?"伏地魔问纳威,纳威面对他站着,两只空手攥成了拳头。

"是又怎么样?"纳威大声说。

"你表现出了勇气和决心,而且出身高贵。你会成为一个难能可贵的食死徒。我们需要你这样的人,纳威·隆巴顿。"

"除非地狱结冰我才会跟你走。"纳威说,"邓布利多军!"他大喊一声,人群里立刻响起激昂的回应,对此伏地魔的无声无息咒似乎也不起作用了。

"很好。"伏地魔说,哈利听出他圆滑的声音里包含着比最残酷的咒语更大的危险,"如果那是你的选择,隆巴顿,我们只好按原计划办了。让它,"他轻声说,"落到你的头上。"

仍然隔着眼睫毛,哈利看见伏地魔挥了一下魔杖。几秒钟后,从城堡被砸烂的一扇窗户里飞出一个怪鸟般的东西。它从昏暗的光线中飞来,落在伏地魔手里。伏地魔抓住这个发霉物件的尖头抖了抖,它便空荡荡、烂糟糟地耷拉下来:是分院帽。

CHAPTER THIRTY-SIX   The Flaw in the Plan

'There will be no more Sorting at Hogwarts School,' said Voldemort. 'There will be no more houses. The emblem, shield and colours of my noble ancestor, Salazar Slytherin, will suffice for everyone, won't they, Neville Longbottom?'

He pointed his wand at Neville, who grew rigid and still, then forced the Hat on to Neville's head, so that it slipped down below his eyes. There were movements from the watching crowd in front of the castle, and as one, the Death Eaters raised their wands, holding the fighters of Hogwarts at bay.

'Neville here is now going to demonstrate what happens to anyone foolish enough to continue to oppose me,' said Voldemort, and with a flick of his wand, he caused the Sorting Hat to burst into flames.

Screams split the dawn, and Neville was aflame, rooted to the spot, unable to move, and Harry could not bear it: he must act –

And then many things happened at the same moment.

They heard uproar from the distant boundary of the school as what sounded like hundreds of people came swarming over the out-of-sight walls and pelted towards the castle, uttering loud war cries. At the same time, Grawp came lumbering round the side of the castle and yelled, 'HAGGER!' His cry was answered by roars from Voldemort's giants: they ran at Grawp like bull elephants, making the earth quake. Then came hooves, and the twangs of bows, and arrows were suddenly falling amongst the Death Eaters, who broke ranks, shouting their surprise. Harry pulled the Invisibility Cloak from inside his robes, swung it over himself and sprang to his feet, as Neville moved too.

In one swift, fluid motion Neville broke free of the Body-Bind Curse upon him; the flaming Hat fell off him and he drew from its depths something silver, with a glittering, rubied handle –

The slash of the silver blade could not be heard over the roar of the oncoming crowd, or the sounds of the clashing giants, or of the stampeding centaurs, and yet it seemed to draw every eye. With a single stroke, Neville sliced off the great snake's head, which spun high into the air, gleaming in the light flooding from the Entrance Hall, and Voldemort's mouth was open in a scream of fury that nobody could hear, and the snake's body thudded to the ground at his feet –

Hidden beneath the Invisibility Cloak, Harry cast a Shield Charm between Neville and Voldemort before the latter could raise his wand. Then, over the screams, and the roars, and the thunderous stamps of the battling

第36章 百密一疏

"霍格沃茨学校再也不需要分院,"伏地魔说,"再也不会分成好几个学院了。我高贵的祖先——萨拉查·斯莱特林的徽章、盾牌和旗帜,对大家来说就已足够,是不是,纳威·隆巴顿?"

他用魔杖指着纳威,纳威立刻变得僵硬,一动不动。然后伏地魔把帽子硬戴在纳威头上,帽檐滑到了纳威的眼睛下面。城堡前注视着这一幕的人群出现了骚动,食死徒齐刷刷地举起魔杖,不让霍格沃茨的反抗者靠近。

"纳威将要向大家演示,那些愚蠢地继续反抗我的人会有什么下场。"伏地魔说着一挥魔杖,分院帽立刻燃起了火焰。

喊叫声划破了拂晓的天空,纳威身上着了火,却被钉在原地,动弹不得。哈利再也不能忍受了,他必须行动——

接着,许多事情在同时发生。

他们听见远处学校界墙那儿传来骚动,似乎千百个人浩浩荡荡地翻过视线外的围墙,高声呐喊着朝城堡冲来。与此同时,格洛普摇摇摆摆地从城堡一侧拐了过来,嘴里喊着:"**海格!**"伏地魔的那些巨人吼叫着发出回应。他们像雄象一样冲向格洛普,震得大地发抖。接着是马蹄声、拉弓声,转眼间,利箭纷纷射向食死徒中间。他们吃惊地大叫,乱了阵脚。哈利从长袍里抽出隐形衣披在身上,腾地从地上跃起,这时纳威也能动了。

纳威身子一挺,一下子挣脱了全身束缚咒,着火的帽子滑落了。他从里面抽出一个银色的东西,柄上闪闪发光,镶着红宝石——

在蜂拥而来的人群的吼叫声中,在巨人们的厮杀声中,在蜂拥的马人的蹄踏声中,银色宝剑砍下的声音没有人能听见,但似乎吸引了每一双眼睛。一剑下去,纳威就把大蛇的头砍掉了,蛇头旋转着高高飞入天空,在门厅洒出的灯光中闪亮。伏地魔张嘴发出愤怒的喊叫,但没有人听得见,接着,轰隆一声,蛇身重重地落在他的脚下——

哈利藏在隐形衣下,没等伏地魔举起魔杖,就在他和纳威之间施了个铁甲咒。然后,在呐喊声、吼叫声和打斗的巨人们沉重的脚步声中,

CHAPTER THIRTY-SIX   The Flaw in the Plan

giants, Hagrid's yell came loudest of all.

'HARRY!' Hagrid shouted, 'HARRY – WHERE'S HARRY?'

Chaos reigned. The charging centaurs were scattering the Death Eaters, everyone was fleeing the giants' stamping feet, and nearer and nearer thundered the reinforcements that had come from who knew where; Harry saw great winged creatures soaring around the heads of Voldemort's giants, Thestrals and Buckbeak the Hippogriff scratching at their eyes while Grawp punched and pummelled them; and now the wizards, defenders of Hogwarts and Voldemort's Death Eaters alike, were being forced back into the castle. Harry was shooting jinxes and curses at any Death Eater he could see, and they crumpled, not knowing what or who had hit them, and their bodies were trampled by the retreating crowd.

Still hidden beneath the Invisibility Cloak, Harry was buffeted into the Entrance Hall: he was searching for Voldemort and saw him across the room, firing spells from his wand as he backed into the Great Hall, still screaming instructions to his followers as he sent curses flying left and right; Harry cast more Shield Charms, and Voldemort's would-be victims, Seamus Finnigan and Hannah Abbott, darted past him into the Great Hall where they joined the fight already flourishing inside it.

And now there were more, even more people storming up the front steps, and Harry saw Charlie Weasley overtaking Horace Slughorn, who was still wearing his emerald pyjamas. They seemed to have returned at the head of what looked like the families and friends of every Hogwarts student who had remained to fight, along with the shopkeepers and homeowners of Hogsmeade. The centaurs Bane, Ronan and Magorian burst into the Hall with a great clatter of hooves, as behind Harry the door that led to the kitchens was blasted off its hinges.

The house-elves of Hogwarts swarmed into the Entrance Hall, screaming and waving carving knives and cleavers, and at their head, the locket of Regulus Black bouncing on his chest, was Kreacher, his bullfrog's voice audible even above this din: 'Fight! Fight! Fight for my master, defender of house-elves! Fight the Dark Lord, in the name of brave Regulus! Fight!'

They were hacking and stabbing at the ankles and shins of Death Eaters, their tiny faces alive with malice, and everywhere Harry looked Death Eaters were folding under sheer weight of numbers, overcome by spells, dragging arrows from wounds, stabbed in the leg by elves, or else simply attempting to

第36章 百密一疏

海格的叫喊声盖过了一切。

"哈利！"海格喊道，"哈利——哈利在哪儿？"

整个场面一片混乱。马人冲锋陷阵，把食死徒追得四散奔逃，每个人都在逃避巨人的践踏，不知从哪里来的增援力量声势浩大，越逼越近。哈利看见带翅膀的庞然大物夜骐和鹰头马身有翼兽巴克比克在伏地魔的巨人头顶盘旋，在抓他们的眼睛，格洛普则对他们饱以老拳。这时所有的巫师，霍格沃茨的保卫者也好，伏地魔的食死徒也好，都被迫退回了城堡。哈利只要看到食死徒就发射恶咒和魔咒，他们瘫倒在地，却不知道是什么人或什么动物袭击了自己，接着他们的身体就被撤退的人群踏在脚下。

哈利仍藏在隐形衣下，被人群推挤着进了门厅。他在寻找伏地魔，接着看见伏地魔在房间那头，仍在大声指挥部下，一边退进大礼堂，一边挥舞着魔杖把魔咒射向四面八方。哈利又施了几个铁甲咒，险些被伏地魔击中的西莫·斐尼甘和汉娜·艾博匆匆从他身边跑进大礼堂，加入那里已经如火如荼的战斗。

这时，又有更多更多的人拥上前门的台阶，哈利看见查理·韦斯莱追上仍穿着鲜绿色睡衣的霍拉斯·斯拉格霍恩。他们身后似乎跟着所有留下来战斗的霍格沃茨学生的亲友，还有霍格莫德村的店老板和房主。随着一阵激烈的马蹄声，马人贝恩、罗南和玛格瑞冲进了礼堂，与此同时，哈利身后通向厨房的门被炸得脱开了铰链。

霍格沃茨的家养小精灵浩浩荡荡地涌进了门厅，尖叫着挥舞餐刀和切肉刀，走在最前面的是胸前挂着雷古勒斯·布莱克的挂坠盒的克利切，即使在这样的喧闹中，他那牛蛙般的声音仍然清晰可闻："战斗！战斗！为我的主人、家养小精灵的捍卫者而战斗！以勇敢的雷古勒斯的名义，抵抗黑魔王！战斗！"

他们对准食死徒的脚脖子和腿肚子又砍又刺，一张张小脸上燃烧着仇恨。哈利不管朝哪里望去，看见的都是食死徒被大批小精灵压得直不起腰，被咒语制得服服帖帖，有的被刺伤了腿，正从伤口里往外

CHAPTER THIRTY-SIX   The Flaw in the Plan

escape, but swallowed by the oncoming horde.

But it was not over yet: Harry sped between duellers, past struggling prisoners, and into the Great Hall.

Voldemort was in the centre of the battle, and he was striking and smiting all within reach. Harry could not get a clear shot, but fought his way nearer, still invisible, and the Great Hall became more and more crowded, as everyone who could walk forced their way inside.

Harry saw Yaxley slammed to the floor by George and Lee Jordan, saw Dolohov fall with a scream at Flitwick's hands, saw Walden Macnair thrown across the room by Hagrid, hit the stone wall opposite and slide unconscious to the ground. He saw Ron and Neville bringing down Fenrir Greyback, Aberforth Stunning Rookwood, Arthur and Percy flooring Thicknesse, and Lucius and Narcissa Malfoy running through the crowd, not even attempting to fight, screaming for their son.

Voldemort was now duelling McGonagall, Slughorn and Kingsley all at once, and there was cold hatred in his face as they wove and ducked around him, unable to finish him –

Bellatrix was still fighting too, fifty yards away from Voldemort, and like her master she duelled three at once: Hermione, Ginny and Luna, all battling their hardest, but Bellatrix was equal to them, and Harry's attention was diverted as a Killing Curse shot so close to Ginny that she missed death by an inch –

He changed course, running at Bellatrix rather than Voldemort, but before he had gone a few steps he was knocked sideways.

'NOT MY DAUGHTER, YOU BITCH!'

Mrs Weasley threw off her cloak as she ran, freeing her arms. Bellatrix spun on the spot, roaring with laughter at the sight of her new challenger.

'OUT OF MY WAY!' shouted Mrs Weasley to the three girls, and with a swipe of her wand she began to duel. Harry watched with terror and elation as Molly Weasley's wand slashed and twirled, and Bellatrix Lestrange's smile faltered, and became a snarl. Jets of light flew from both wands, the floor around the witches' feet became hot and cracked; both women were fighting to kill.

'No!' Mrs Weasley cried, as a few students ran forwards, trying to come to her aid. 'Get back! *Get back!* She is mine!'

第36章 百密一疏

拔箭,还有的在拼命逃跑,却被蜂拥而来的小精灵淹没了。

但战斗还没有结束。哈利从格斗者中间奔过,从那些被制服但还在挣扎的人们中间奔过,冲进了大礼堂。

伏地魔处于战斗的中心,他左右开弓地朝周围的所有人出击。哈利没法瞄准,只能仍在隐形衣的掩护下一点点往前逼近。礼堂里的人越来越多,只要能走得动的,都拼命往里面挤。

哈利看见亚克斯利被乔治和李·乔丹合力击倒在地,看见多洛霍夫在弗立维手里惨叫一声瘫倒,看见沃尔顿·麦克尼尔被海格扔到礼堂那头,砰地撞到石墙,不省人事地滑到了地上。他还看见罗恩和纳威打败了芬里尔·格雷伯克,阿不福思击昏了卢克伍德,亚瑟和珀西把辛克尼斯撂倒了,而卢修斯和纳西莎·马尔福在人群中跑来跑去,根本没有参加战斗,只是大声地呼唤着他们的儿子。

伏地魔正同时与麦格、斯拉格霍恩和金斯莱格斗,他的脸上是残忍的恨意,他们三人在他周围穿梭、躲避,却不能结果他的性命——

距伏地魔五十米开外,贝拉特里克斯也战得正酣,像她的主人一样同时对付着三个人:赫敏、金妮和卢娜。她们都使出了全身解数,但贝拉特里克斯与她们势均力敌。突然,一个杀戮咒差点击中了金妮,真悬,再偏一寸金妮就死了。哈利的注意力被吸引了过去——

他改变方向,暂时放开了伏地魔,直朝贝拉特里克斯冲去,但没跑几步就被撞到了一边。

"不许碰我女儿,你这母狗!"

韦斯莱夫人一边跑一边甩掉斗篷,腾出两只胳膊,贝拉特里克斯原地一个转身,看见这位新的挑战者,粗声大笑起来。

"闪开!"韦斯莱夫人冲三个姑娘喊道,接着魔杖一挥,开始战斗。哈利又惊恐又开心地看着莫丽·韦斯莱的魔杖旋舞劈杀,贝拉特里克斯·莱斯特兰奇脸上的笑容开始消退,变成了咆哮。两根魔杖嗖嗖地射出亮光,女巫们脚边的地板变得滚烫、开裂。两个女人在决一死战。

"不!"韦斯莱夫人看到几个学生冲上前来相助,大声喊道,"回去!回去!她是我的!"

CHAPTER THIRTY-SIX   The Flaw in the Plan

Hundreds of people now lined the walls, watching the two fights, Voldemort and his three opponents, Bellatrix and Molly, and Harry stood, invisible, torn between both, wanting to attack and yet to protect, unable to be sure that he would not hit the innocent.

'What will happen to your children when I've killed you?' taunted Bellatrix, as mad as her master, capering as Molly's curses danced around her. 'When Mummy's gone the same way as Freddie?'

'You – will – never – touch – our – children – again!' screamed Mrs Weasley.

Bellatrix laughed, the same exhilarated laugh her cousin Sirius had given as he toppled backwards through the veil, and suddenly Harry knew what was going to happen before it did.

Molly's curse soared beneath Bellatrix's outstretched arm and hit her squarely in the chest, directly over her heart.

Bellatrix's gloating smile froze, her eyes seemed to bulge: for the tiniest space of time she knew what had happened, and then she toppled, and the watching crowd roared, and Voldemort screamed.

Harry felt as though he turned in slow motion; he saw McGonagall, Kingsley and Slughorn blasted backwards, flailing and writhing through the air, as Voldemort's fury at the fall of his last, best lieutenant exploded with the force of a bomb. Voldemort raised his wand and directed it at Molly Weasley.

'*Protego!*' roared Harry, and the Shield Charm expanded in the middle of the hall, and Voldemort stared around for the source as Harry pulled off the Invisibility Cloak at last.

The yell of shock, the cheers, the screams on every side of 'Harry!' 'HE'S ALIVE!' were stifled at once. The crowd was afraid, and silence fell abruptly and completely as Voldemort and Harry looked at each other, and began, at the same moment, to circle each other.

'I don't want anyone else to try to help,' Harry said loudly, and in the total silence his voice carried like a trumpet call. 'It's got to be like this. It's got to be me.'

Voldemort hissed.

'Potter doesn't mean that,' he said, his red eyes wide. 'That isn't how he works, is it? Who are you going to use as a shield today, Potter?'

第36章 百密一疏

此时,几百个人站在墙边,观看着这两场决斗:伏地魔与他的三个对手,贝拉特里克斯与莫丽。哈利无形地站在那里左右为难,又想出手袭击,又想保护自己人,没有把握是否会伤害无辜。

"我把你杀了,你的孩子们怎么办呢?"贝拉特里克斯奚落道,她像她的主人一样疯狂,跳着脚躲避莫丽嗖嗖发过来的魔咒,"妈咪跟弗雷德同样下场可怎么办呢?"

"再也——不许——你——碰——我们的——孩子!"韦斯莱夫人叫道。

贝拉特里克斯哈哈大笑,那笑声酣畅淋漓,和当年她的堂弟小天狼星后退着穿过帷幔摔下去时她的笑声一模一样。哈利突然就知道接下来会是什么了。

莫丽的魔咒从贝拉特里克斯前伸的手臂下飞过去,击中了她的胸口,正好是心脏的位置。

贝拉特里克斯得意的笑容凝固了,眼珠子似乎突了出来。就在那一瞬间,她知道发生了什么事,接着便倒在地上。周围的人群一片喧哗,伏地魔尖声咆哮。

哈利觉得自己的转身像是慢动作,他看见麦格、金斯莱和斯拉格霍恩都被炸飞了,在空中扑打、翻腾,伏地魔看到他最后的、也是最忠实的助手被打倒,怒气像炸弹一样爆炸了。伏地魔举起魔杖对准了莫丽·韦斯莱。

"盔甲护身!"哈利大吼一声,铁甲咒立刻横贯在礼堂中央,伏地魔环顾四周寻找是谁在发咒。哈利终于脱掉了隐形衣。

惊愕的叫声、欢呼声、"哈利!""**他还活着!**"的喊声在四面响起,紧接着又是一片鸦雀无声。伏地魔和哈利互相对视,同时开始面对面地绕圈子,人们揪起了心,礼堂里突然变得死一般的沉寂。

"我不希望任何人出手相助,"哈利大声说,在绝对的寂静中,他的声音像号声一样传得很远,"必须是这样,必须是我。"

伏地魔嘴里发出嘶嘶的声音。

"波特说的不是真话,"他说,一双红眼睛睁得大大的,"那不是他的做派,对吗?波特,你今天又想把谁当作盾牌呢?"

CHAPTER THIRTY-SIX The Flaw in the Plan

'Nobody,' said Harry simply. 'There are no more Horcruxes. It's just you and me. Neither can live while the other survives, and one of us is about to leave for good ...'

'One of us?' jeered Voldemort, and his whole body was taut and his red eyes stared, a snake that was about to strike. 'You think it will be you, do you, the boy who has survived by accident, and because Dumbledore was pulling the strings?'

'Accident, was it, when my mother died to save me?' asked Harry. They were still moving sideways, both of them, in that perfect circle, maintaining the same distance from each other, and for Harry no face existed but Voldemort's. 'Accident, when I decided to fight in that graveyard? Accident, that I didn't defend myself tonight, and still survived, and returned to fight again?'

'*Accidents!* ' screamed Voldemort, but still he did not strike, and the watching crowd was frozen as if petrified, and of the hundreds in the Hall, nobody seemed to breathe but they two. 'Accident and chance and the fact that you crouched and snivelled behind the skirts of greater men and women, and permitted me to kill them for you!'

'You won't be killing anyone else tonight,' said Harry as they circled, and stared into each other's eyes, green into red. 'You won't be able to kill any of them, ever again. Don't you get it? I was ready to die to stop you hurting these people —'

'But you did not!'

'— I meant to, and that's what did it. I've done what my mother did. They're protected from you. Haven't you noticed how none of the spells you put on them are binding? You can't torture them. You can't touch them. You don't learn from your mistakes, Riddle, do you?'

'*You dare —*'

'Yes, I dare,' said Harry, 'I know things you don't know, Tom Riddle. I know lots of important things that you don't. Want to hear some, before you make another big mistake?'

Voldemort did not speak, but prowled in a circle, and Harry knew that he kept him temporarily mesmerised and at bay, held back by the faintest possibility that Harry might indeed know a final secret ...

'Is it love again?' said Voldemort, his snake's face jeering, 'Dumbledore's favourite solution, *love*, which he claimed conquered death, though love did

第36章 百密一疏

"没有谁,"哈利干脆利落地说,"魂器没有了。只有你和我。两人不能都活着,只有一个生存下来,我们中间的一个人将会永远离开……"

"我们中间的一个人?"伏地魔讥笑道,他整个身体紧绷,一双红眼睛瞪着,像一条准备进攻的蛇,"你认为会是你吗,你这个有邓布利多在后面牵线而偶然幸存的男孩?"

"我母亲为救我而死,这是偶然吗?"哈利问。两个人仍然在侧身移动,绕着圈子,始终保持同样的距离。对哈利来说,除了伏地魔,其他面孔都不存在了。"在那片坟地里我决定反抗,也是偶然?今晚我没有抵抗仍然活了下来,重新回来战斗,也是偶然?"

"偶然!"伏地魔叫道,但仍然没有出击。周围的人群凝固不动,如同被石化了一般,礼堂里有好几百人,似乎只有他们俩在呼吸。"偶然,运气,还有就是你动不动藏到大人身后哭鼻子,听任我为了你而杀死他们!"

"今晚你别想再杀死任何人了,"哈利说,他们绕着圈子,盯着对方的眼睛,绿眼睛对红眼睛,"你再也别想杀死他们任何一个,再也别想。明白吗?为了阻止你伤害这些人,我准备了去死——"

"但是你没有!"

"——我下了决心,这是关键。我做了我母亲做的事情。你再也伤害不了他们。难道你没有发现你射向他们的魔咒都没有了约束力?你折磨不了他们,你伤害不了他们。你从来不会从你的错误里吸取教训,是不是,里德尔?"

"你竟敢——"

"是的,我敢,"哈利说,"我知道的事情你不知道,汤姆·里德尔。我知道许多重要的事情你不知道。你想不想听听,以免再犯一个大错?"

伏地魔没有说话,默默地转着圈子。哈利知道他被暂时迷惑住了,不敢轻易动手,担心哈利万一真的知道某个致命的秘密……

"又是爱?"伏地魔说,那张蛇脸上满是嘲讽,"邓布利多的法宝,爱,他声称能征服死亡,却没能阻止他从塔楼上坠落,像个旧蜡像一样摔得支离破碎!爱,没有阻止我把你那泥巴种母亲像蟑螂一样碾死,

CHAPTER THIRTY-SIX   The Flaw in the Plan

not stop him falling from the Tower and breaking like an old waxwork? *Love*, which did not prevent me stamping out your Mudblood mother like a cockroach, Potter – and nobody seems to love you enough to run forwards this time, and take my curse. So what will stop you dying now when I strike?'

'Just one thing,' said Harry, and still they circled each other, wrapped in each other, held apart by nothing but the last secret.

'If it is not love that will save you this time,' said Voldemort, 'you must believe that you have magic that I do not, or else a weapon more powerful than mine?'

'I believe both,' said Harry, and he saw shock flit across the snake-like face, though it was instantly dispelled; Voldemort began to laugh, and the sound was more frightening than his screams; humourless and insane, it echoed around the silent Hall.

'You think *you* know more magic than I do?' he said. 'Than *I*, than Lord Voldemort, who has performed magic that Dumbledore himself never dreamed of?'

'Oh, he dreamed of it,' said Harry, 'but he knew more than you, knew enough not to do what you've done.'

'You mean he was weak!' screamed Voldemort. 'Too weak to dare, too weak to take what might have been his, what will be mine!'

'No, he was cleverer than you,' said Harry, 'a better wizard, a better man.'

'I brought about the death of Albus Dumbledore!'

'You thought you did,' said Harry, 'but you were wrong.'

For the first time, the watching crowd stirred as the hundreds of people around the walls drew breath as one.

'*Dumbledore is dead!*' Voldemort hurled the words at Harry as though they would cause him unendurable pain. 'His body decays in the marble tomb in the grounds of this castle, I have seen it, Potter, and he will not return!'

'Yes, Dumbledore's dead,' said Harry calmly, 'but you didn't have him killed. He chose his own manner of dying, chose it months before he died, arranged the whole thing with the man you thought was your servant.'

'What childish dream is this?' said Voldemort, but still, he did not strike, and his red eyes did not waver from Harry's.

'Severus Snape wasn't yours,' said Harry. 'Snape was Dumbledore's, Dumbledore's from the moment you started hunting down my mother. And

第36章 百密一疏

波特——这次似乎没有一个人会因为爱你而挺身而出，挡住我的咒语。那么，我一出手，你怎么可能不死呢？"

"只有一点。"哈利说，两人仍然在面对面地转圈、相持，中间隔开他们的只有那最后的秘密。

"如果这次救你的不是爱，"伏地魔说，"那你准是相信自己掌握了我所没有的魔法，或拥有一件比我的更厉害的武器？"

"二者兼而有之。"哈利说。他看见那张蛇脸上闪过一丝惊慌，但转瞬即逝。伏地魔大笑起来，这笑声比他的喊叫声更加可怕：冷酷而疯狂，在寂静的礼堂里回荡。

"你以为你会的魔法比我还多？"他说，"比我——伏地魔大人还多？我施过的魔法，邓布利多连做梦都没有想到过！"

"哦，他想到过，"哈利说，"但他比你知道的更多，没有去干你干的那些事情。"

"你是说他软弱！"伏地魔尖叫着说，"他软弱，没有胆量，他软弱，不敢拿走本该属于他的——现在将属于我了！"

"不，他比你聪明，"哈利说，"是个更优秀的巫师，更优秀的男人。"

"我把阿不思·邓布利多弄死了！"

"你以为是这样，"哈利说，"可是你错了。"

围观的人群里第一次骚动起来，墙边的几百个人同时吸了一口气。

"邓布利多死了！"伏地魔把这句话狠狠地掷向哈利，就好像它能给哈利带来无法忍受的痛苦，"他的尸体正在这座城堡荒地上的大理石坟墓里腐烂，我看见了，波特，他再也不会回来了！"

"是的，邓布利多死了，"哈利平静地说，"但并不是你安排的。他自己选择了死亡的方式，在死前几个月就选择了，他和那个你以为是你仆从的人共同安排好了一切。"

"多么幼稚可笑的梦话！"伏地魔说，但他仍然没有出击，那双红眼睛死死地盯着哈利的眼睛。

"西弗勒斯·斯内普不是你的人，"哈利说，"斯内普是邓布利多的人，早在你开始追捕我母亲那时候起，他就是邓布利多的人。你一直没有

CHAPTER THIRTY-SIX The Flaw in the Plan

you never realised it, because of the thing you can't understand. You never saw Snape cast a Patronus, did you, Riddle?'

Voldemort did not answer. They continued to circle each other like wolves about to tear each other apart.

'Snape's Patronus was a doe,' said Harry, 'the same as my mother's, because he loved her for nearly all of his life, from the time when they were children. You should have realised,' he said, as he saw Voldemort's nostrils flare, 'he asked you to spare her life, didn't he?'

'He desired her, that was all,' sneered Voldemort, 'but when she had gone, he agreed that there were other women, and of purer blood, worthier of him –'

'Of course he told you that,' said Harry, 'but he was Dumbledore's spy from the moment you threatened her, and he's been working against you ever since! Dumbledore was already dying when Snape finished him!'

'It matters not!' shrieked Voldemort, who had followed every word with rapt attention, but now let out a cackle of mad laughter. 'It matters not whether Snape was mine or Dumbledore's, or what petty obstacles they tried to put in my path! I crushed them as I crushed your mother, Snape's supposed great *love*! Oh, but it all makes sense, Potter, and in ways that you do not understand!

'Dumbledore was trying to keep the Elder Wand from me! He intended that Snape should be the true master of the wand! But I got there ahead of you, little boy – I reached the wand before you could get your hands on it, I understood the truth before you caught up. I killed Severus Snape three hours ago, and the Elder Wand, the Deathstick, the Wand of Destiny is truly mine! Dumbledore's last plan went wrong, Harry Potter!'

'Yeah, it did,' said Harry. 'You're right. But before you try to kill me, I'd advise you to think about what you've done ... think, and try for some remorse, Riddle ...'

'What is this?'

Of all the things that Harry had said to him, beyond any revelation or taunt, nothing had shocked Voldemort like this. Harry saw his pupils contract to thin slits, saw the skin around his eyes whiten.

第36章 百密一疏

发现,因为那种事情你不能理解。你从来没见过斯内普召出守护神吧,里德尔?"

伏地魔没有回答。他们继续对峙着转圈,像两匹随时准备把对方撕成碎片的狼。

"斯内普的守护神是一头牝鹿,"哈利说,"和我母亲的一样,因为他几乎爱了我母亲一辈子,从他们孩提时代就开始了。其实你应该发现的,"他看到伏地魔的鼻孔突然张开了,又说道,"他请求你饶我母亲一命,是不是?"

"他渴望得到她,仅此而已,"伏地魔冷笑着说,"但她死后,斯内普也承认世上还有其他女人,血统更纯,更配得上他——"

"他当然会跟你这么说,"哈利说,"但从你威胁到我母亲的那时候起,他就是邓布利多的密探了,后来一直在反对你!邓布利多已经奄奄一息时,斯内普才结束了他的生命。"

"那不重要!"伏地魔尖叫道,他全神贯注地听着哈利说的每一个字,这时突然发出一串疯狂的大笑,"斯内普是我的人还是邓布利多的人,他们想在我的路上设置什么小小的绊脚石,统统都不重要!我摧毁了他们,就像摧毁你的母亲——斯内普所谓的真爱一样!哦,不过这倒说明了问题,波特,但你是不会懂的!

"邓布利多阻挠我得到老魔杖!他想让斯内普成为老魔杖的真正主人!但是我抢在了你的前面,小毛孩儿——没等你下手,我就拿到了魔杖,没等你醒过味来,我就明白了真相。三小时前我杀死了西弗勒斯·斯内普,现在,老魔杖、死亡棒、命运杖真正属于我了!邓布利多的最后一个计划泡汤了,哈利·波特!"

"对,没错,"哈利说,"你说得对。但是在你动手杀我之前,我建议你想一想你的所作所为……好好想一想,试着做一些忏悔,里德尔……"

"这话是什么意思?"

哈利对伏地魔说的所有的话,包括揭露真相的话和冷嘲热讽的话,没有一句让伏地魔这样震惊。哈利看见他的瞳孔缩成了两条窄窄的细缝,看见他眼睛周围的皮肤变白了。

CHAPTER THIRTY-SIX

The Flaw in the Plan

'It's your one last chance,' said Harry, 'it's all you've got left ... I've seen what you'll be otherwise ... be a man ... try ... try for some remorse ...'

'You dare –?' said Voldemort again.

'Yes, I dare,' said Harry, 'because Dumbledore's last plan hasn't backfired on me at all. It's backfired on you, Riddle.'

Voldemort's hand was trembling on the Elder Wand and Harry gripped Draco's very tightly. The moment, he knew, was seconds away.

'That wand still isn't working properly for you, because you murdered the wrong person. Severus Snape was never the true master of the Elder Wand. He never defeated Dumbledore.'

'He killed –'

'Aren't you listening? *Snape never beat Dumbledore!* Dumbledore's death was planned between them! Dumbledore intended to die undefeated, the wand's last true master! If all had gone as planned, the wand's power would have died with him, because it had never been won from him!'

'But then, Potter, Dumbledore as good as gave me the wand!' Voldemort's voice shook with malicious pleasure. 'I stole the wand from its last master's tomb! I removed it against its last master's wishes! Its power is mine!'

'You still don't get it, Riddle, do you? Possessing the wand isn't enough! Holding it, using it, doesn't make it really yours. Didn't you listen to Ollivander? *The wand chooses the wizard* ... the Elder Wand recognised a new master before Dumbledore died, someone who never even laid a hand on it. The new master removed the wand from Dumbledore against his will, never realising exactly what he had done, or that the world's most dangerous wand had given him its allegiance ...'

Voldemort's chest rose and fell rapidly, and Harry could feel the curse coming, feel it building inside the wand pointed at his face.

'The true master of the Elder Wand was Draco Malfoy.'

Blank shock showed in Voldemort's face for a moment, but then it was gone.

'But what does it matter?' he said softly. 'Even if you are right, Potter, it makes no difference to you and me. You no longer have the phoenix wand: we duel on skill alone ... and after I have killed you, I can attend to Draco Malfoy ...'

第36章　百密一疏

"这是你最后的机会,"哈利说,"你仅有的机会……我见过你不忏悔的下场……勇敢点……试一试……试着做些忏悔……"

"你竟敢——?"伏地魔又说。

"是的,我敢,"哈利说,"因为邓布利多最后的计划根本没有误伤到我,却对你造成损害了,里德尔。"

伏地魔握着老魔杖的手在颤抖,哈利紧紧地攥住德拉科的魔杖。他知道那一刻就要来临了。

"那根魔杖仍然不会完全听你的指挥,因为你杀错了人。西弗勒斯·斯内普根本不是老魔杖的真正主人。他根本没有打败邓布利多。"

"他杀死了——"

"你没听我说吗?斯内普根本没有打败邓布利多!邓布利多的死是他们共同策划的!邓布利多计划不败而死,成为魔杖的最后一位真正主人!如果一切都按计划进行,魔杖的力量应该随他消亡,因为没有人从他手里赢得魔杖!"

"可是,波特,邓布利多等于把魔杖给了我!"伏地魔的声音因恶意的快感而颤抖,"我把魔杖从它最后一位主人的坟墓里偷了出来!我违背它最后一位主人的意愿把它拿了出来!它的力量属于我!"

"你还是没听明白吗,里德尔?拥有魔杖是不够的!拿着它,使用它,并不能让它真正成为你的。你没听见奥利凡德的话吗?魔杖选择巫师……邓布利多没死之前,老魔杖就认了一位新主人,而那个人连摸都没有摸过它。新主人违背邓布利多的意愿除去了他手中的魔杖,他根本不知道自己做了什么,不知道世界上最厉害的魔杖已经愿意为他效忠……"

伏地魔的胸脯在激烈地起伏,哈利可以感觉到咒语冲了上来,感觉到咒语在指向他面门的魔杖里聚集力量。

"老魔杖的真正主人是德拉科·马尔福。"

伏地魔的脸上露出茫然的惊愕,但转瞬即逝。

"可那有什么关系呢?"他轻声说,"即使你说得对,波特,对你我来说又有什么关系?你不再拿着那根凤凰羽毛魔杖:我们只凭技艺决斗……等我杀了你,再去对付德拉科·马尔福……"

CHAPTER THIRTY-SIX   The Flaw in the Plan

'But you're too late,' said Harry. 'You've missed your chance. I got there first. I overpowered Draco weeks ago. I took this wand from him.'

Harry twitched the hawthorn wand, and he felt the eyes of everyone in the Hall upon it.

'So it all comes down to this, doesn't it?' whispered Harry. 'Does the wand in your hand know its last master was Disarmed? Because if it does … I am the true master of the Elder Wand.'

A red-gold glow burst suddenly across the enchanted sky above them, as an edge of dazzling sun appeared over the sill of the nearest window. The light hit both of their faces at the same time, so that Voldemort's was suddenly a flaming blur. Harry heard the high voice shriek as he, too, yelled his best hope to the heavens, pointing Draco's wand:

'*Avada Kedavra!*'

'*Expelliarmus!*'

The bang was like a cannon-blast and the golden flames that erupted between them, at the dead centre of the circle they had been treading, marked the point where the spells collided. Harry saw Voldemort's green jet meet his own spell, saw the Elder Wand fly high, dark against the sunrise, spinning across the enchanted ceiling like the head of Nagini, spinning through the air towards the master it would not kill, who had come to take full possession of it at last. And Harry, with the unerring skill of the Seeker, caught the wand in his free hand as Voldemort fell backwards, arms splayed, the slit pupils of the scarlet eyes rolling upwards. Tom Riddle hit the floor with a mundane finality, his body feeble and shrunken, the white hands empty, the snake-like face vacant and unknowing. Voldemort was dead, killed by his own rebounding curse, and Harry stood with two wands in his hand, staring down at his enemy's shell.

One shivering second of silence, the shock of the moment suspended: and then the tumult broke around Harry as the screams and the cheers and the roars of the watchers rent the air. The fierce new sun dazzled the windows as they thundered towards him, and the first to reach him were Ron and Hermione, and it was their arms that were wrapped around him, their incomprehensible shouts that deafened him. Then Ginny, Neville and Luna were there, and then all the Weasleys and Hagrid, and Kingsley and McGonagall and Flitwick and Sprout, and Harry could not hear a word that

第36章 百密一疏

"可是你来不及了，"哈利说，"你错过了机会。我抢先了一步。几个星期前我打败了德拉科，这根魔杖是我从他手里夺来的。"

哈利抖了抖山楂木魔杖，感觉到礼堂里所有的目光都盯在它上面。

"所以，最后的结果是这样，对吗？"哈利小声说，"你手里的魔杖是否知道他最后一位主人已被解除了武器？如果它知道……现在我才是老魔杖的真正主人。"

突然，头顶上的魔法天空爆出一道金红色的光，小半轮耀眼的太阳出现在离他们最近的窗台上。阳光同时照到他们两人脸上，伏地魔的脸顿时火红一片。哈利听见伏地魔高亢的声音在尖叫，而他也同时举起了德拉科的魔杖，朝天空喊出了他最热切的希望：

"阿瓦达索命！"

"除你武器！"

砰的一声，如炮弹炸响，在他们反复踩踏的圆圈正中央，射出了金色的火焰，那便是咒语相撞的地方。哈利看见伏地魔的绿光碰到了他自己的魔咒，看见老魔杖飞到了空中，在初升的太阳里逆着光，像纳吉尼的脑袋一样在魔法天花板下旋转，打着旋儿飞向它不愿杀死的主人——这位主人终于要完全拥有它了。哈利以找球手精湛的技巧，用空着的那只手抓住飞来的魔杖，只见伏地魔跟跄后退，双臂张开，通红的眼睛里细长的瞳孔往上翻。汤姆·里德尔倒在地上，像凡人一样死去，他的尸体瘫软而干枯，苍白的手里空无一物，那张蛇脸空洞而茫然。伏地魔死了，被他自己的咒语反弹回去杀死了。哈利站在那里，手里攥着两根魔杖，低头看着对手的躯壳。

一瞬间令人战栗的寂静，人们惊恐地怔住了。随即，哈利周围爆发出排山倒海般的喧哗，喊叫声、欢呼声、咆哮声震天动地。初升太阳的强烈光芒照在窗户上，人们喊叫着向他扑来，最先赶到的是罗恩和赫敏，他们的胳膊把他紧紧地抱住了，他们不知所云的叫嚷几乎把他的耳朵震聋了。接着，金妮、纳威和卢娜也来了，还有韦斯莱一家和海格、金斯莱、麦格、弗立维和斯普劳特。每个人都在大喊，哈利一个字也听不清，也分不出是谁的手在拽他、拉他，拼命想拥抱到他

CHAPTER THIRTY-SIX   The Flaw in the Plan

anyone was shouting, nor tell whose hands were seizing him, pulling him, trying to hug some part of him, hundreds of them pressing in, all of them determined to touch the Boy Who Lived, the reason it was over at last –

The sun rose steadily over Hogwarts, and the Great Hall blazed with life and light. Harry was an indispensable part of the mingled outpourings of jubilation and mourning, of grief and celebration. They wanted him there with them, their leader and symbol, their saviour and their guide, and that he had not slept, that he craved the company of only a few of them, seemed to occur to no one. He must speak to the bereaved, clasp their hands, witness their tears, receive their thanks, hear the news now creeping in from every quarter, as the morning drew on, that the Imperiused up and down the country had come back to themselves, that Death Eaters were fleeing or else being captured, that the innocent of Azkaban were being released at that very moment, and that Kingsley Shacklebolt had been named temporary Minister for Magic ...

They moved Voldemort's body and laid it in a chamber off the Hall, away from the bodies of Fred, Tonks, Lupin, Colin Creevey and fifty others who had died fighting him. McGonagall had replaced the house tables, but nobody was sitting according to house any more: all were jumbled together, teachers and pupils, ghosts and parents, centaurs and house-elves, and Firenze lay recovering in a corner, and Grawp peered in through a smashed window, and people were throwing food into his laughing mouth. After a while, exhausted and drained, Harry found himself sitting on a bench beside Luna.

'I'd want some peace and quiet, if it were me,' she said.

'I'd love some,' he replied.

'I'll distract them all,' she said. 'Use your Cloak.'

And before he could say a word she had cried, 'Oooh, look, a Blibbering Humdinger!' and pointed out of the window. Everyone who heard looked around, and Harry slid the Cloak up over himself, and got to his feet.

Now he could move through the Hall without interference. He spotted Ginny two tables away; she was sitting with her head on her mother's shoulder: there would be time to talk later, hours and days and maybe years in which to talk. He saw Neville, the sword of Gryffindor lying beside his plate as he ate, surrounded by a knot of fervent admirers. Along the aisle

第36章 百密一疏

身体的一部分。几百个人在往前挤,谁都想摸摸这位大难不死的男孩,正是因为他,噩梦才终于结束了——

太阳在霍格沃茨上空冉冉升起,大礼堂里洋溢着生命和光明。人们尽情表达着哀悼和欢庆、悲伤和喜悦的情感,哈利是其中不可缺少的一部分。人人都希望哈利和他们在一起,他是他们的领袖和象征,是他们的救星和向导,似乎谁也没有想到他一夜没有合眼,没有想到他渴望和其中几个人单独待着。他必须和死难者的家属说说话,抓住他们的手,目睹他们的泪水,接受他们的感谢,聆听早晨四面八方传来的消息:全国被施了夺魂咒的人逐渐恢复了正常,食死徒们有的逃跑有的被抓,与此同时,阿兹卡班的无辜囚犯得到了释放,金斯莱·沙克尔被任命为魔法部临时部长……

他们把伏地魔的尸体搬到礼堂外的一个房间里,远离弗雷德、唐克斯、卢平、科林·克里维和另外五十个为了抵抗他而死去的人。麦格把学院桌放回了原处,可是谁也没按学院入座:大家都乱糟糟地挤在一起,老师和学生,幽灵和家长,马人和家养小精灵。费伦泽躺在墙角养伤,格洛普从一扇被打烂的窗户往里窥视,有人把食物扔进他大笑的嘴里。过了一会儿,精疲力竭的哈利发现自己挨着卢娜坐在一张板凳上。

"如果是我,会希望得到一些清静。"卢娜说。

"我也巴不得呢。"哈利回答。

"我来转移他们的注意力。"她说,"你披上隐形衣。"

没等哈利来得及说话,她就指着窗外叫道:"哟,快看,一只泡泡鼻涕怪!"听见的人都扭过头去看,哈利赶紧把隐形衣披在身上,站了起来。

好了,他可以不受打扰地在礼堂里走动了。他看见金妮和他隔着两张桌子,坐在那里,脑袋靠在她母亲的肩膀上。以后有的是时间跟她说话,说许多个小时、许多天,甚至许多年。他看见纳威在吃东西,盘子旁边放着格兰芬多的宝剑,周围是一群狂热的崇拜者。哈利走在桌子之间的通道里,看见马尔福一家三口搂作一团,似乎不知道自己

CHAPTER THIRTY-SIX The Flaw in the Plan

between the tables he walked, and he spotted the three Malfoys, huddled together as though unsure whether or not they were supposed to be there, but nobody was paying them any attention. Everywhere he looked he saw families reunited, and finally, he saw the two whose company he craved most.

'It's me,' he muttered, crouching down between them. 'Will you come with me?'

They stood up at once, and together he, Ron and Hermione left the Great Hall. Great chunks were missing from the marble staircase, part of the balustrade gone, and rubble and bloodstains occurred every few steps as they climbed.

Somewhere in the distance they could hear Peeves zooming through the corridors singing a victory song of his own composition:

> *We did it, we bashed them, wee Potter's the One,*
> *And Voldy's gone mouldy, so now let's have fun!*

'Really gives a feeling for the scope and tragedy of the thing, doesn't it?' said Ron, pushing open a door to let Harry and Hermione through.

Happiness would come, Harry thought, but at the moment it was muffled by exhaustion, and the pain of losing Fred and Lupin and Tonks pierced him like a physical wound every few steps. Most of all he felt the most stupendous relief, and a longing to sleep. But first he owed an explanation to Ron and Hermione, who had stuck with him for so long, and who deserved the truth. Painstakingly, he recounted what he had seen in the Pensieve and what had happened in the Forest, and they had not even begun to express all their shock and amazement when at last they arrived at the place to which they had been walking, though none of them had mentioned their destination.

Since he had last seen it, the gargoyle guarding the entrance to the Headmaster's study had been knocked aside; it stood lopsided, looking a little punch-drunk, and Harry wondered whether it would be able to distinguish passwords anymore.

'Can we go up?' he asked the gargoyle.

'Feel free,' groaned the statue.

They clambered over him and on to the spiral stone staircase that moved slowly upwards like an escalator. Harry pushed open the door at the top.

He had one, brief glimpse of the stone Pensieve on the desk where he had

第36章 百密一疏

是否应该待在那里，但没有一个人注意他们。哈利看见到处都是家人团聚的场面。终于，他看见了他最渴望在一起的两个人。

"是我，"他在他们俩中间伏下身子，低声说，"你们跟我来好吗？"

他们立刻站了起来，于是，他、罗恩、赫敏一起离开了大礼堂。大理石楼梯缺了好多块，一部分栏杆不见了，每走几步就会碰到碎石和血迹。

在远处什么地方，他们听见皮皮鬼忽地飞过走廊，唱着一首他自己编的欢庆胜利的歌：

   我们获全胜，波特是功臣，
   伏地魔完蛋，大家尽狂欢！

"这场面真使人感到宏大和悲壮，是不是？"罗恩说着推开一扇门，让哈利和赫敏通过。

喜悦会来的，哈利知道，但此刻疲惫抑制了快乐的心情，而且每走几步，失去弗雷德、卢平、唐克斯的痛苦就像肉体的伤口一样锐痛。百感交集之中，他感到如释重负，只渴望好好睡一觉。但他首先需要向罗恩和赫敏解释一下，这么长时间以来，他们一直忠心地陪伴他，现在应该知道真相了。他把在冥想盆里看到的和在禁林里发生的事情原原本本说了一遍，两个同伴还没来得及表达震惊和诧异，他们就到地方了。刚才一路往这里走，但谁也没有提到这个目的地。

自从哈利上次来过之后，看守校长办公室入口的滴水嘴石兽已被撞到一边。它歪在那里，看上去有点被打晕了，哈利不知道它还能不能分辨口令。

"我们可以上去吗？"他问石兽。

"请便。"石兽哼哼着说。

他们从它身上爬过，登上像自动扶梯一样缓慢上升的螺旋形石梯。到了顶上，哈利把门推开了。

他刚瞥见冥想盆还像他上次离开时那样放在桌上，突然一阵震耳

CHAPTER THIRTY-SIX   The Flaw in the Plan

left it, and then an ear-splitting noise made him cry out, thinking of curses and returning Death Eaters and the rebirth of Voldemort —

But it was applause. All around the walls, the headmasters and headmistresses of Hogwarts were giving him a standing ovation; they waved their hats and in some cases their wigs, they reached through their frames to grip each other's hands; they danced up and down on the chairs in which they had been painted; Dilys Derwent sobbed unashamedly, Dexter Fortescue was waving his ear-trumpet; and Phineas Nigellus called, in his high, reedy voice, 'And let it be noted that Slytherin house played its part! Let our contribution not be forgotten!'

But Harry had eyes only for the man who stood in the largest portrait directly behind the Headmaster's chair. Tears were sliding down from behind the half-moon spectacles into the long silver beard, and the pride and the gratitude emanating from him filled Harry with the same balm as phoenix song.

At last, Harry held up his hands, and the portraits fell respectfully silent, beaming and mopping their eyes and waiting eagerly for him to speak. He directed his words at Dumbledore, however, and chose them with enormous care. Exhausted and bleary-eyed though he was, he must make one last effort, seeking one last piece of advice.

'The thing that was hidden in the Snitch,' he began, 'I dropped it in the Forest. I don't know exactly where, but I'm not going to go looking for it again. Do you agree?'

'My dear boy, I do,' said Dumbledore, while his fellow pictures looked confused and curious. 'A wise and courageous decision, but no less than I would have expected of you. Does anyone else know where it fell?'

'No one,' said Harry, and Dumbledore nodded his satisfaction.

'I'm going to keep Ignotus's present, though,' said Harry, and Dumbledore beamed.

'But of course, Harry, it is yours forever, until you pass it on!'

'And then there's this.'

Harry held up the Elder Wand, and Ron and Hermione looked at it with a reverence that, even in his befuddled and sleep-deprived state, Harry did not like to see.

'I don't want it,' said Harry.

'What?' said Ron loudly. 'Are you mental?'

第36章 百密一疏

欲聋的声音惊得他失声大叫,以为遭遇了魔咒,或是食死徒卷土重来了,或是伏地魔死而复生了——

原来是欢呼声。周围的墙上,霍格沃茨历届男女校长全体起立,对着哈利鼓掌,他们有的在挥帽子,有的在挥假发,在相框间冲来冲去,互相紧紧地握手。他们在画里的椅子上又蹦又跳,戴丽丝·德文特毫不掩饰地哭着,德克斯特·福斯科使劲地挥动他的助听筒,菲尼亚斯·奈杰勒斯用他高亢的尖声大喊:"请注意斯莱特林学院也起了作用!别忘记我们的贡献!"

可是,哈利的眼睛只看着校长座椅后面那幅最大的肖像:眼泪从半月形镜片后面流进长长的银白色胡须里,那张脸上流露出的骄傲和感激像凤凰的歌声一样,使哈利的内心充满慰藉。

最后,哈利举起两只手,所有的肖像都恭敬地沉默下来,擦擦眼睛,面带微笑,热切地等着他开口。但他的话是对着邓布利多说的,而且斟词酌句格外仔细。他虽然精疲力竭,两眼模糊,但必须再努一把力,寻求最后一个忠告。

"藏在金色飞贼里的那个东西,"他说道,"我掉在禁林里了。不知道具体掉在哪里,但我不想再去找它了。你同意吗?"

"我亲爱的孩子,我同意。"邓布利多说,其他肖像都显出困惑和好奇的神情,"这是一个很有智慧和勇气的决定,但是你会这样做,我并不觉得意外。有没有别人知道它掉在哪儿?"

"没有。"哈利说,邓布利多满意地点点头。

"不过我想留着伊格诺图斯的礼物。"哈利说,邓布利多笑了。

"当然可以,哈利,它永远是你的,直到你把它再传下去!"

"还有这个。"

哈利举起老魔杖,罗恩和赫敏看着它,眼里满是敬畏,哈利尽管睡眠不足,头重脚轻,但还是意识到并且不喜欢他们的这种神情。

"我不想要它。"哈利说。

"什么?"罗恩大声说,"你脑子有病啊?"

CHAPTER THIRTY-SIX The Flaw in the Plan

'I know it's powerful,' said Harry wearily. 'But I was happier with mine. So ...'

He rummaged in the pouch hung around his neck, and pulled out the two halves of holly still, just, connected by the finest thread of phoenix feather. Hermione had said that they could not be repaired, that the damage was too severe. All he knew was that if this did not work, nothing would.

He laid the broken wand upon the Headmaster's desk, touched it with the very tip of the Elder Wand and said, '*Reparo.*'

As his wand resealed, red sparks flew out of its end. Harry knew that he had succeeded. He picked up the holly and phoenix wand, and felt a sudden warmth in his fingers, as though wand and hand were rejoicing at their reunion.

'I'm putting the Elder Wand,' he told Dumbledore, who was watching him with enormous affection and admiration, 'back where it came from. It can stay there. If I die a natural death like Ignotus, its power will be broken, won't it? The previous master will never have been defeated. That'll be the end of it.'

Dumbledore nodded. They smiled at each other.

'Are you sure?' said Ron. There was the faintest trace of longing in his voice as he looked at the Elder Wand.

'I think Harry's right,' said Hermione quietly.

'That wand's more trouble than it's worth,' said Harry. 'And quite honestly,' he turned away from the painted portraits, thinking now only of the four-poster bed lying waiting for him in Gryffindor Tower, and wondering whether Kreacher might bring him a sandwich there, 'I've had enough trouble for a lifetime.'

第36章 百密一疏

"我知道它很强大,"哈利疲倦地说,"但我拿着自己的魔杖更开心。所以……"

他在脖子上挂的皮袋里摸索,抽出了那根断成两截、仅由细细的凤凰羽毛连接着的冬青木魔杖。赫敏曾说它损害太严重,不可能修复了。他知道如果下面这招还不管用,就彻底没救了。

他把断了的魔杖放在校长办公桌上,用老魔杖的杖尖碰了碰它,说了声:"恢复如初。"

魔杖重新接上时,杖尖迸出红色的火星。哈利知道他成功了。他拿起冬青木和凤凰尾羽魔杖,手指间突然感到一股暖意,似乎魔杖和手正为它们的团聚而欣喜。

"我要把老魔杖放回它原来的地方,"他对邓布利多说,邓布利多带着无限的爱意和赞赏注视着他,"就让它一直留在那里。如果我像伊格诺图斯一样正常死亡,它的力量就毁灭了,是不是?前一位主人永远不会再被打败。老魔杖也就终结了。"

邓布利多点点头。他们相视而笑。

"你真想这样?"罗恩说。他看着老魔杖,声音里还有一丝淡淡的渴望。

"我认为哈利是对的。"赫敏轻声说。

"这根魔杖带来的麻烦超过了它的价值,"哈利说,"而且,说句实话,"他转身离开了那些肖像,心里只想着格兰芬多塔楼上等待着他的那张四柱床,他不知道克利切是不是会给他送一块三明治,"我这辈子的麻烦已经够多了。"

Nineteen Years Later

Autumn seemed to arrive suddenly that year. The morning of the first of September was crisp and golden as an apple, and as the little family bobbed across the rumbling road towards the great, sooty station, the fumes of car exhausts and the breath of pedestrians sparkled like cobwebs in the cold air. Two large cages rattled on top of the laden trolleys the parents were pushing; the owls inside them hooted indignantly, and the red-headed girl trailed tearfully behind her brothers, clutching her father's arm.

'It won't be long, and you'll be going too,' Harry told her.

'Two years,' sniffed Lily. 'I want to go *now*!'

The commuters stared curiously at the owls as the family wove its way towards the barrier between platforms nine and ten. Albus's voice drifted back to Harry over the surrounding clamour; his sons had resumed the argument they had started in the car.

'I *won't*! I *won't* be in Slytherin!'

'James, give it a rest!' said Ginny.

'I only said he *might* be,' said James, grinning at his younger brother. 'There's nothing wrong with that. He *might* be in Slyth—'

But James caught his mother's eye and fell silent. The five Potters approached the barrier. With a slightly cocky look over his shoulder at his younger brother, James took the trolley from his mother and broke into a run. A moment later, he had vanished.

'You'll write to me, won't you?' Albus asked his parents immediately, capitalising on the momentary absence of his brother.

'Every day, if you want us to,' said Ginny.

尾声

十九年后

这一年的秋天似乎一下子就到了。九月一日的早晨像苹果一样脆生生、金灿灿的。小小的一家人在车声中轻快地穿过马路，走向庞大的、被熏黑的火车站，汽车的尾气和行人呼出的水汽像蛛网一样闪闪发光，飘在清凉的空气中。两只大笼子在父母推的行李车顶上格格作响，笼子里的猫头鹰不满地叫着。红头发小女孩抓着爸爸的胳膊，泪汪汪地跟在两个哥哥后面。

"不用多久，你也会去的。"哈利对她说。

"两年呢，"莉莉吸着鼻子，"我现在就想去！"

一家人穿过人流朝第9和第10站台之间的隔墙走去，旅客们好奇地盯着猫头鹰。喧闹声中，阿不思的嗓音从前面飘到了哈利的耳边，两个儿子继续着在车里就开始的争论。

"我不会！我不会进斯莱特林！"

"詹姆，别闹了！"金妮说。

"我只是说他也许会，"詹姆笑嘻嘻地看着弟弟说，"这又没错，他也许会进斯莱特——"

詹姆看到妈妈的目光，不说话了。波特一家五口走近了隔墙。詹姆略带骄傲地回头瞥了弟弟一眼，接过妈妈手里的推车飞跑起来，转眼就消失了。

"你们会给我写信的，是吗？"阿不思趁哥哥不在的这一刻工夫，赶紧问爸爸妈妈。

"每天都写，如果你愿意的话。"金妮答道。

'Not *every* day,' said Albus quickly. 'James says most people only get letters from home about once a month.'

'We wrote to James three times a week last year,' said Ginny.

'And you don't want to believe everything he tells you about Hogwarts,' Harry put in. 'He likes a laugh, your brother.'

Side by side, they pushed the second trolley forwards, gathering speed. As they reached the barrier, Albus winced, but no collision came. Instead, the family emerged on to platform nine and three-quarters, which was obscured by thick, white steam that was pouring from the scarlet Hogwarts Express. Indistinct figures were swarming through the mist, into which James had already disappeared.

'Where are they?' asked Albus anxiously, peering at the hazy forms they passed as they made their way down the platform.

'We'll find them,' said Ginny reassuringly.

But the vapour was dense, and it was difficult to make out anybody's faces. Detached from their owners, voices sounded unnaturally loud. Harry thought he heard Percy discoursing loudly on broomstick regulations, and was quite glad of the excuse not to stop and say hello …

'I think that's them, Al,' said Ginny suddenly.

A group of four people emerged from the mist, standing alongside the very last carriage. Their faces only came into focus when Harry, Ginny, Lily and Albus had drawn right up to them.

'Hi,' said Albus, sounding immensely relieved.

Rose, who was already wearing her brand new Hogwarts robes, beamed at him.

'Parked all right, then?' Ron asked Harry. 'I did. Hermione didn't believe I could pass a Muggle driving test, did you? She thought I'd have to Confund the examiner.'

'No, I didn't,' said Hermione, 'I had complete faith in you.'

'As a matter of fact, I *did* Confund him,' Ron whispered to Harry, as together they lifted Albus's trunk and owl on to the train. 'I only forgot to look in the wing mirror, and let's face it, I can use a Supersensory Charm for that.'

Back on the platform, they found Lily and Hugo, Rose's younger brother, having an animated discussion about which house they would be sorted into when they finally went to Hogwarts.

尾声　十九年后

"不要每天,"阿不思马上说,"詹姆说大多数人差不多一个月才收到一封家信。"

"我们去年一星期给詹姆写三回呢。"金妮说。

"他跟你说的霍格沃茨的事不可全信,"哈利插言,"你哥哥爱开玩笑。"

他们一同推着第二辆小车往前跑,逐渐加速。快到隔墙时,阿不思畏缩了一下,但没有发生碰撞,一家人都来到了 $9\frac{3}{4}$ 站台上。站台被深红色的霍格沃茨特快列车喷出的大量白色雾气笼罩着,模糊的人影在雾气中涌动,詹姆已经看不见了。

"他们在哪儿?"一行人沿着站台一路往前走,阿不思边走边望着雾中从身边经过的人影,焦急地问。

"会找到的。"金妮安慰道。

但蒸汽太浓了,很难看清人们的面孔。看不见人的说话声听起来异常响亮。哈利好像听到珀西在高声谈论飞天扫帚管理问题,他庆幸可以不用停下来打招呼了……

"我想那就是他们,阿尔。"金妮突然说。

雾气里显出了四个人,站在最后一节车厢旁。哈利、金妮、莉莉和阿不思走到近前,才看清了他们的面孔。

"嘿。"阿不思说,似乎大大松了一口气。

罗丝笑盈盈地看着他,已经穿上了崭新的霍格沃茨校袍。

"停车挺顺利吧?"罗恩问哈利,"我也是。赫敏不相信我能通过麻瓜驾驶考试,是不是啊,赫敏?她还以为我不得不对考官使混淆咒呢。"

"我可没有,"赫敏说,"我对你完全放心。"

"其实,我是使了混淆咒。"罗恩帮着把阿不思的箱子和猫头鹰搬上列车时,对哈利耳语道,"我只不过是忘了看后视镜,说实在的,我用超感咒也是一样的。"

回到站台上,只见莉莉和罗丝的弟弟雨果在热烈地讨论将来他们进霍格沃茨后会被分到哪个学院。

'If you're not in Gryffindor, we'll disinherit you,' said Ron, 'but no pressure.'

'*Ron!*'

Lily and Hugo laughed, but Albus and Rose looked solemn.

'He doesn't mean it,' said Hermione and Ginny, but Ron was no longer paying attention. Catching Harry's eye, he nodded covertly to a point some fifty yards away. The steam had thinned for a moment, and three people stood in sharp relief against the shifting mist.

'Look who it is.'

Draco Malfoy was standing there with his wife and son, a dark coat buttoned up to his throat. His hair was receding somewhat, which emphasised the pointed chin. The new boy resembled Draco as much as Albus resembled Harry. Draco caught sight of Harry, Ron, Hermione and Ginny staring at him, nodded curtly and turned away again.

'So that's little Scorpius,' said Ron under his breath. 'Make sure you beat him in every test, Rosie. Thank God you inherited your mother's brains.'

'Ron, for heaven's sake,' said Hermione, half stern, half amused. 'Don't try to turn them against each other before they've even started school!'

'You're right, sorry,' said Ron, but unable to help himself, he added, 'don't get *too* friendly with him, though, Rosie. Granddad Weasley would never forgive you if you married a pure-blood.'

'Hey!'

James had reappeared; he had divested himself of his trunk, owl and trolley, and was evidently bursting with news.

'Teddy's back there,' he said breathlessly, pointing back over his shoulder into the billowing clouds of steam. 'Just seen him! And guess what he's doing? *Snogging Victoire!*'

He gazed up at the adults, evidently disappointed by the lack of reaction.

'*Our* Teddy! *Teddy Lupin!* Snogging *our* Victoire! *Our* cousin! And I asked Teddy what he was doing –'

'You interrupted them?' said Ginny. 'You are *so* like Ron –'

'– and he said he'd come to see her off! And then he told me to go away. He's *snogging* her!' James added, as though worried he had not made himself clear.

尾声　十九年后

"如果你不进格兰芬多,我们就解除你的继承权。"罗恩说,"不过别有压力。"

"罗恩!"

莉莉和雨果笑了,但阿不思和罗丝神情严肃。

"他不是当真的。"赫敏和金妮说,但罗恩的注意力已经转移了。看到哈利的目光,他把头向五十米外微微一点。此刻蒸汽消散了一些,三个轮廓分明的人影站在飘浮的雾气中。

"看那是谁。"

德拉科·马尔福跟他的太太和儿子站在一起,黑上衣一直扣到喉咙口。他的脑门有点秃了,衬得下巴更尖。那男孩是德拉科的翻版,就像阿不思是哈利的翻版一样。德拉科发现哈利、罗恩、赫敏和金妮在看他,冷淡地点了点头就转过身去了。

"那就是小斯科皮。"罗恩悄声说,"每次考试都一定要超过他,罗丝。感谢上帝,你继承了你妈妈的脑子。"

"罗恩,拜托,"赫敏一半严厉、一半想笑地说,"不要让他们还没上学就成了对头!"

"你说得对,对不起。"罗恩说,但又忍不住加了一句,"不过别跟他走得太近,罗丝。你要是嫁给了一个纯血统,爷爷一辈子也不会原谅你。"

"嘿!"

詹姆钻了出来,已经卸下行李、猫头鹰和推车,并显然有一肚子新闻要讲。

"泰迪在那边,"他气喘吁吁地说,指指身后云雾般翻滚的蒸汽中,"刚才碰到了!你猜他在干什么?亲吻维克托娃!"

他抬头望着大人,显然为他们的无动于衷而失望。

"我们的泰迪!泰迪·卢平!在亲吻我们的维克托娃!我们的表姐!我问泰迪他在干什么——"

"你打搅了他们?"金妮说,"你真像罗恩——"

"——泰迪说他是来送维克托娃的!然后就叫我走开。他在亲吻她!"詹姆又说,像担心自己没说明白。

'Oh, it would be lovely if they got married!' whispered Lily ecstatically. 'Teddy would *really* be part of the family then!'

'He already comes round for dinner about four times a week,' said Harry. 'Why don't we just invite him to live with us and have done with it?'

'Yeah!' said James enthusiastically. 'I don't mind sharing with Al – Teddy could have my room!'

'No,' said Harry firmly, 'you and Al will share a room only when I want the house demolished.'

He checked the battered, old watch that had once been Fabian Prewett's.

'It's nearly eleven, you'd better get on board.'

'Don't forget to give Neville our love!' Ginny told James as she hugged him.

'Mum! I can't give a Professor *love*!'

'But you *know* Neville –'

James rolled his eyes.

'Outside, yeah, but at school he's Professor Longbottom, isn't he? I can't walk into Herbology and give him *love* …'

Shaking his head at his mother's foolishness, he vented his feelings by aiming a kick at Albus.

'See you later, Al. Watch out for the Thestrals.'

'I thought they were invisible? *You said they were invisible!*'

But James merely laughed, permitted his mother to kiss him, gave his father a fleeting hug, then leapt on to the rapidly filling train. They saw him wave, then sprint away up the corridor to find his friends.

'Thestrals are nothing to worry about,' Harry told Albus. 'They're gentle things, there's nothing scary about them. Anyway, you won't be going up to school in the carriages, you'll be going in the boats.'

Ginny kissed Albus goodbye.

'See you at Christmas.'

'Bye, Al,' said Harry, as his son hugged him. 'Don't forget Hagrid's invited you to tea next Friday. Don't mess with Peeves. Don't duel anyone 'til you've learned how. And don't let James wind you up.'

尾声 十九年后

"哦,如果他们结婚多好!"莉莉兴奋地说,"这样泰迪就能真正成为咱家的人了!"

"他已经差不多一星期来吃四次饭了,"哈利说,"我们为什么不干脆请他住到我们家来呢?"

"对啊!"詹姆热烈地说,"我不介意跟阿尔合住——泰迪可以住我的房间!"

"不行,"哈利坚决地说,"你和阿尔不能住在一个房间,除非我想让房子被毁掉。"

他看了看那块曾经属于费比安·普威特的破旧手表。

"快十一点了,你们上车吧。"

"别忘了跟纳威说我们爱他!"金妮拥抱詹姆时说。

"妈妈!我不能对教授说爱!"

"可你认识纳威——"

詹姆翻了翻眼睛。

"在校外是认识,可在学校里,他是隆巴顿教授,不是吗?我不能走进草药课堂去跟他说爱……"

他为妈妈的愚蠢而摇头,同时朝阿不思的方向踢了一脚,发泄自己的情绪。

"回头见,阿尔。注意看夜骐。"

"它们不是隐形的吗?你说过它们是隐形的!"

但詹姆只是笑着,允许妈妈吻了他,给了爸爸一个匆匆的拥抱,跳上正在迅速挤满乘客的列车,挥了挥手,就沿着过道跑开找他的朋友去了。

"不用害怕夜骐,"哈利对阿不思说,"它们很温柔,一点儿也不可怕。再说,你们也不会坐马车进学校,要坐船的。"

金妮亲吻着阿不思跟他道别。

"圣诞节见。"

"再见,阿尔,"哈利在儿子拥抱他时说,"别忘了海格请你下星期五去喝茶。别招惹皮皮鬼。别跟人决斗——在你没学会怎么决斗之前。还有,别让詹姆把你逗急了。"

Nineteen Years Later

'What if I'm in Slytherin?'

The whisper was for his father alone, and Harry knew that only the moment of departure could have forced Albus to reveal how great and sincere that fear was.

Harry crouched down so that Albus's face was slightly above his own. Alone of Harry's three children, Albus had inherited Lily's eyes.

'Albus Severus,' Harry said quietly, so that nobody but Ginny could hear, and she was tactful enough to pretend to be waving to Rose, who was now on the train, 'you were named for two headmasters of Hogwarts. One of them was a Slytherin and he was probably the bravest man I ever knew.'

'But *just say* —'

'— then Slytherin house will have gained an excellent student, won't it? It doesn't matter to us, Al. But if it matters to you, you'll be able to choose Gryffindor over Slytherin. The Sorting Hat takes your choice into account.'

'Really?'

'It did for me,' said Harry.

He had never told any of his children that before, and he saw the wonder in Albus's face when he said it. But now the doors were slamming all along the scarlet train, and the blurred outlines of parents were swarming forwards for final kisses, last-minute reminders. Albus jumped into the carriage and Ginny closed the door behind him. Students were hanging from the windows nearest them. A great number of faces, both on the train and off, seemed to be turned towards Harry.

'Why are they all *staring*?' demanded Albus, as he and Rose craned round to look at the other students.

'Don't let it worry you,' said Ron. 'It's me. I'm extremely famous.'

Albus, Rose, Hugo and Lily laughed. The train began to move, and Harry walked alongside it, watching his son's thin face, already ablaze with excitement. Harry kept smiling, and waving, even though it was like a little bereavement, watching his son glide away from him …

The last trace of steam evaporated in the autumn air. The train rounded a corner. Harry's hand was still raised in farewell.

'He'll be all right,' murmured Ginny.

尾声　十九年后

"要是我进了斯莱特林呢？"

这句悄悄话是说给爸爸一个人听的，哈利知道，只有别离时刻才会迫使阿不思泄露这份恐惧有多么强烈与发自内心。

哈利蹲了下来，使阿不思的脸比自己的略高一点儿。在哈利的三个子女中，唯有阿不思继承了莉莉的眼睛。

"阿不思·西弗勒斯，"哈利轻声说，只有父子俩和金妮能听到，此时金妮体贴地假装朝已经上车的罗丝挥手，"你的名字中含有霍格沃茨两位校长的名字。其中一个就是斯莱特林的，而他可能是我见过的最勇敢的人。"

"可是如果——"

"——那么斯莱特林学院就会得到一名优秀的学生，是不是？我们觉得这不重要，阿尔。但如果你很在意的话，你可以选择要格兰芬多不要斯莱特林。分院帽会考虑你的选择的。"

"真的？"

"我就是这样的。"哈利说。

这一点哈利以前从没对孩子们说过，他看到了阿不思脸上现出的惊奇。但深红色列车的车厢开始关闭了，家长们模糊的身影拥上前去，给孩子们最后一刻的亲吻和叮咛。阿不思跳上列车，金妮帮他把门关上。学生们从最近的窗口探出身来，车上车下许多面孔似乎都转向了哈利。

"他们干吗都盯着看啊？"阿不思问，他和罗丝扭头看着其他学生。

"别为这个烦神。"罗恩说，"是我，我特别有名。"

阿不思、罗丝、雨果和莉莉都笑了起来。列车移动了，哈利跟着往前走，望着儿子那瘦小的、已经兴奋得发光的面庞。哈利一直在微笑，挥手，尽管这像一种小小的伤逝，看着儿子渐行渐远……

最后一丝蒸汽消散在秋日的空气中，火车转弯了，哈利挥别的手还举在空中。

"他没事的。"金妮小声说。

As Harry looked at her, he lowered his hand absent-mindedly and touched the lightning scar on his forehead.

'I know he will.'

The scar had not pained Harry for nineteen years. All was well.

尾声　十九年后

哈利看着她,放下手,无意中触到了额头上闪电形的伤疤。

"我知道。"

伤疤已经十九年没有疼过了,一切太平。

WIZARDING WORLD